Annie's Portion

J. FRAN BAIRD

iUniverse, Inc.
New York Bloomington

Copyright © 2010 by J. Fran Baird

All rights reserved. No part of this book may be used or reproduced by any means, graphic, electronic, or mechanical, including photocopying, recording, taping or by any information storage retrieval system without the written permission of the publisher except in the case of brief quotations embodied in critical articles and reviews.

iUniverse books may be ordered through booksellers or by contacting:

iUniverse
1663 Liberty Drive
Bloomington, IN 47403
www.iuniverse.com
1-800-Authors (1-800-288-4677)

Because of the dynamic nature of the Internet, any Web addresses or links contained in this book may have changed since publication and may no longer be valid. The views expressed in this work are solely those of the author and do not necessarily reflect the views of the publisher, and the publisher hereby disclaims any responsibility for them.

ISBN: 978-1-4401-8517-5 (sc)
ISBN: 978-1-4401-8516-8 (ebook)

Printed in the United States of America

iUniverse rev. date: 01/29/10

For my mother – my rock and inspiration

"As the generation of leaves, so is that of humanity"
Homer

My gratitude to my Editor, Dennix Hall, whose help and encouragement made this book possible.

Special thanks to my husband, Jim Baird, my ultimate mentor.

Book One

Sarah

Chapter I

1905 – Galicia

Moishe Tregorvitch was about to embark on the greatest adventure of his life. Soon to enter his middle years my father resolved to leave the land of his birth. To this reticent man the momentous decision had come only after years of persecution and unshared, tortured deliberation.

He was ignorant of the machinations of monarchs, lesser rulers and the Holy Church which established artificial boundaries, carving Galicia out of Poland, Ukrainian Transcarpathia and Bukovina in 1772; annexing it to the Hapsburg Austro-Hungarian Empire. But he suffered because of them. No thought had been given to ethnicity, commonality, religious practices or economic reality and as a consequence of Hapsburg rule, Ukrainians who had never enjoyed a congenial relationship with the Poles found themselves under the boot of Polish aristocrats who retained land ownership, guaranteeing that Polish-Ukrainian rivalry would remain a perpetual feature of Galician life. Thrown into this mix were large numbers of Russian Jews who'd fled the pogroms that followed the accession of Alexander III in 1881. By the end of that year, these raids had hit more than two hundred communities in southern and southwestern Russia leaving twenty thousand Jews homeless.

The *shtetl*, a habitat unique to the Jews of Eastern Europe, was an insular fortress. Here the dispossessed Jew found a haven where he could practice his religion and ply his trade in relative peace and safety. Galicia had become a refuge center for Chasidism, a Jewish movement that opposed rabbinical emphasis on formal learning and Talmudic study. Chasidism provided the indigent Jew a way to commune with his God personally without imposing hours of prayer and study required in traditional religious practice, time which he could little afford.

Moishe Tregorvitch, poor, pious, and unpolished was an inhabitant of such a hamlet. Restricted by a language barrier, he spoke only *Yiddish;* uneducated but for his Hebrew studies, prohibited from land ownership and most professions my father's options were limited. The townsmen made their mean livings as peddlers, tailors, butchers, dairymen or shopkeepers. Despite the humble circumstance, or because of it, these Jews developed a culture, a code of ethics by which they lived and a homespun, self-effacing sense of humor.

My father, better off than most of his neighbors, was employed as a butcher's helper and while his wages were minimal there had always been chicken parts or a bone for the soup pot and his family had never known hunger. Later family accounts of him depicted a frugal man; morose and intractable, his time apportioned between job and prayer and little else.

But by the end of the 1880's, animosity between competing ethnic groups had reached intolerable levels. Lack of land reform, rural overpopulation and an absence of industry worsened conditions for an already destitute Ukrainian peasantry crowded into towns and villages seeking work. This would have been impetus enough for the Jews, impoverished as they were, to leave Galicia. However in 1902, massive strikes against landlords further exacerbated an already explosive situation. Fearing a repetition of Russian style pogroms many Jews joined the great migration to America.

There had been no discussion of Moishe's intended departure, only a declaration and a date. The day my father departed his *shtetl* in Galicia bound for the *goldeneh medina*, we watched him walk down the road; my mother Fanny, my sisters Talia and Chana, and me—Sarah. It should have been a day of celebration, my first birthday. Instead it was a time of sadness and uncertainty. Talia's portrait of his leaving described Moishe as displaying uncharacteristic emotion, promising to send for us as soon as funds allowed.

How this man of limited education and few skills earned a wage sufficient to sustain him in the new country remains a mystery. Yet the newly Americanized Morris Treiger managed to put enough aside to pay for passage of the family he had left behind, and three years later Fanny, Talia and Chana departed Galicia to join father and husband in the golden land.

It was my misfortune during the period of my father's absence I contracted what was, at that time, diagnosed as a rare but insidious form of tuberculosis, one that was ever so slowly consuming my bones. It was common knowledge, even in that Galician *shtetl*; all émigrés were subjected to physical examinations before granted permission to enter America. Those exhibiting any symptoms of illness were immediately isolated and most expeditiously sent back to their ports of call. It was therefore decided to leave me with my *tante* Ruchel until I would, *alevai*, be well enough to travel.

Four long years passed before I was to have an opportunity to rejoin my family. The year was 1912. I was eight and bore visible evidence of the disease that continued to eat away, although more slowly, at my body. During the years since my father's departure the situation had become even more desperate, the result of which was a continuing, expeditious exodus from Galicia. Almost imperceptibly the population of our hamlet diminished, leaving few neighbors and a bare handful of elderly family members.

Ruchel had come to love me unconditionally as though I was her own child, providing for me to the extent she could, creating a bond strong as any between mother and daughter. But her desire to seek the American dream, kept buried for such a long time, engulfed her. As she went about her menial daily tasks her head was filled with thoughts of the new life waiting for her in the Promised Land. Though I slept beside her, Ruchel's nighttime weeping betrayed her loneliness. She knew the time had come for her to leave. There was one evident problem—me. I can only imagine what it must have been like for her to deal with a dilemma of such huge proportions. What were her chances of getting me past the authorities in the new land? She did not want to leave me behind but with no one left in the town to care for me what was she to do? She needed counsel.

In the *shtetl* the aged *Rebbe,* undisputed leader of the small community, was considered the ultimate arbiter on all matters moral, ethical and spiritual. Held in great esteem and thought to possess almost mystical powers he was often asked during crisis or illness to intervene with God on behalf of the believer.

"The *Rebbe* will have the answer," Ruchel said. But since it was unacceptable for a woman to approach him directly, she enlisted the aid of one of the local sages.

"I will take the matter up with the *Rebbe,*" said Yacob Plotkin in answer to Ruchel's plea. "It is a serious matter and will require much deliberation."

It was a week before Yacob returned with the pronouncement, which had come after many hours of argument between the elders and frequent supplications made to the Master of the Universe.

"It is known salt air has curative powers. The voyage to America will be a long one and the child will be exposed to many days at sea. It is very possible such a voyage may restore Sarah to good health."

"But what if it does not? What will I do?"

"You will pray and God will provide an answer."

It was May and leaves had just begun to appear on the trees when Ruchel and I began our pilgrimage. Our excitement at the thought of embarking on such an adventure was unrestrained. Traveling by oxcart along rutted trails we marveled at the vastness of the farmlands, intrigued by the quiet mystery of lush forests, neither of which had we ever seen. When we reached the rural station we boarded a train that would carry us to the port city of Hamburg. The closer we got to our destination the more densely populated the countryside became. Farms and forests disappeared, replaced by large burgs and factory towns. Arriving at last in Hamburg Ruchel, terrified niece in tow, procured papers necessary for our departure and purchased tickets for passage to America.

For fifteen days we remained virtual prisoners in steerage—suffering smells, noise and confinement of limited quarters with little access to the salt air that was to be the panacea. When at last we came within sight of the awe-inspiring lady who guarded New York harbor we joined the many émigrés lining the rails, standing in silent reverence as the ship slipped past her. Until the moment we set foot on the Ellis Island landing the only universe my aunt and I had known were the few dusty streets of a remote, shabby village, a *shtetl* where every face was familiar and a common language spoken. Abruptly we were confronted by a new, more alarming sea—a groundswell of refugees rafted together by a common longing.

I remember clinging desperately to Ruchel's coat, fearing if I let go I would be lost forever in the human tide. I did not release my hold when we were herded through the entrance of an imposing structure of red brick into the main assembly hall where seated on hard wooden benches we waited to be called. Walls of multi-paned glass windows, capped by decorative arches, rose from floor to ceiling of the second floor balcony. Sun poured through windows, filling the cavernous room with dust-flecked filtered light.

Ruchel eyed me nervously. To her untrained eyes, I appeared much improved with no evidence of new lesions—the only obvious remnants of the dreadful disease, small areas of disfigurement on my limbs and fingers. When Ruchel heard her name called she used a corner of her shabby shawl to wipe sweat from beneath her eyes as she mentally rehearsed the story she was about to tell the investigators. With great anxiety she brought her charge before the medical examiners. Communicating by means of Yiddish, a smattering of Polish and animated gesticulation, Ruchel somehow convinced them my condition was the result of a house fire that had consumed all my kin. It appeared as though Ruchel's counselors predicted wisely for having at last grasped her meaning and grown weary of her frenetic recitation, the officials moved us along. Once the necessary documents were completed, stamped with the impressive seal of the U.S. Department of Immigration and filed in the section labeled "Jews," we joined the myriad immigrants who would be swallowed by the New World.

The lighter, over laden with its human cargo deposited us at the cluttered dock strewn with bundles and wicker suitcases. The great metropolis pulsed with unfamiliar energy and vitality; the roar of the city almost suffocating in its intensity; the clamorous union of men and machines electrifying.

The voyagers, united for the moment by the need to fulfill their own desperate dreams soon dispersed, fated to go their disparate ways. Some would leave on great iron horses that would scatter them across the vast continent while others would forever remain captive to the fabled city.

Ruchel and I waited on the pier absorbing the flavors as the vast human flood washed around us. Ruchel scanned the throng hoping to find a familiar face or discern her name amidst shouted voices in countless languages, an American

Babel. It was my father who reclaimed us that day, steering us away from the docks through crowded, noisy, garbage-strewn streets. Third Avenue was alive, bustling—charged with amazing industry. We wended our way between push carts manned by street vendors hawking their wares, past an aromatic bakery and a grocer whose pickle barrel bore a sign that read, "3 for a nickel." Turning the corner of Thirty-Third Street, we came to a halt in front of a grimy old red brick tenement, one among many. Here we were led up a dirty stairwell with groaning steps and sagging handrails, stopping finally on the third floor in front of a door marked with the number twelve. Without ceremony I was reintroduced to my family who by this time had increased by three; two sisters, Becky and Freyda and one brother Emmanuel. Tante Ruchel, with much weeping and many promises to visit, went to live with other family members and the only mother I had ever really known was gone.

Chapter II

1912 – New York

My father presented an imposing figure—tall, thin, ramrod straight, white bearded and handsome, the very image of the Jewish patriarch. He dressed in black garments, a black *yarmulka* crowning his snow-white hair; the only relief the blue and white fringed prayer shawl he wore around his shoulders. His steely blue eyes were piercing and icy reflecting his silent, brooding, ascetic nature. He spoke no English, in fact he barely spoke at all but *davened* three times a day, chanting prayers in front of a window facing east; facing *Eretz Yisrael*, the land of Israel.

Squat and plump, Fanny's round face was creased by the strain of her daily toil. Her brown eyes were small and heavy-lidded, her gray-streaked hair pulled tightly into a bun at the back of her neck. She routinely wore a shapeless cotton dress protected by a clean white apron, which miraculously remained unstained though she carried out her housekeeping chores with zealous dedication. Her culinary ability was legend, her strudel and knishes unmatched. Her daughters were not allowed in the kitchen while she cooked. She had neither the desire nor the patience to pass on her skills and only Talia managed to glean enough information to attempt to duplicate my mother's creations. In addition to her culinary talents Fanny possessed astounding curative skills, which were administered freely to family and neighbor alike and which she likewise refused to share. My mother's animus did not end in the kitchen. I was not welcomed as a long-lost child but regarded as an outsider, an intruder, another mouth to feed, good only as a bed warmer for my father. When I dared question her about my own illness she would tap the bible, the source of all answers in the Treiger household.

"God gives each of us our own portion. It is not for us to question."

Every Friday, while the tantalizing aroma of baking *challah* pervaded the apartment, Fanny cleaned and scrubbed. Only when she was certain no speck of dirt escaped her eye or mop, would she prepare herself for the Sabbath which was strictly observed in the Treiger household; everyone seated, Morris looking every bit like one of the "Ancients" at the head of the table. Fanny, her apron removed and a lace scarf covering her head recited the prayer and lit the Sabbath candles at the exact moment of sundown. Fanny found idle chatter insufferable so there was little conversation at dinner. It was hard to believe she had once been cheerful and filled with hope. Disillusioned, ground down by isolation, childbearing and poverty she'd become dour and laconic, speaking only to criticize or issue instructions to her children.

With few exceptions the Treigers were much like the millions of immigrants who flooded America, impelled by the desire to find a better life. Many would achieve their goals, but for others life in the new country proved to be a struggle only slightly less desperate than the one they left behind, and as filled with hopelessness. During the early 1900's, the lower Eastside of Manhattan was the repository for immigrants from every part of Europe. These were, as Emma Lazarus put so eloquently, "the wretched refuse of the teeming" European shores. Linked tenement buildings rose four and five stories high creating a walled city within a city. Wash lines were strung like so many festoons across alleyways. All through the dog days of summer, fire escapes served as balconies offering a place to escape the intolerable heat generated within the confines of overcrowded apartments. But during the Jewish holiday of *Succoth*, Festival of the Harvest, those same fire escapes provided foundations for small booths, constructed in biblical tradition to shelter the celebrants. Although unadorned with traditional fruit and wine, they remained for the eight days of religious observance. One could always identify Jewish areas on *Succoth*.

A cacophony of discordant sounds from the street below assailed one's ears. Mothers called from windows to their kids playing stickball or potsy or Johnny on the pony.

"Tony, getta some bread." A small packet containing some coins would be thrown out the window to the child waiting on the sidewalk below.

"Sammy, I want you should come up now," followed by a protest, "Aw, ma. I'm in the middle of a game."

"Mickey, go get ya fatha," followed by more protests.

Hallways resounded with loud discourse in native languages. An assortment of pungent aromas permeated the air. The odor of garlic and pork sausage suffused that of sour cabbage. Chicken soup and *challah* mingled with bratwurst and sauerbraten.

Apartments, like the four-room flat we called home, were small but kitchens had many cupboards which were especially convenient for orthodox Jewish families who "kept kosher," providing adequate storage for numerous dishes, pots and silverware required to meet the strict laws of *kashrut*. Washtubs, large enough to accommodate a laundry bundle or a body, replaced the standard kitchen sink. As a result of depositing a coin or two into a slot, a thin stream of hot water trickled through the tub's open tap.

In the Treiger household Sunday night was bath night and once the multi-purpose tub was filled each of us girls took turns in the same bath water. For the sake of fairness the rotation was changed each week. Fannie would hang a sheet from the ceiling in front of the tub to provide a limited amount of privacy. Emmanuel was not included in the rotation process but took his turn at the end of the line. When not in use for washing or bathing, the tub became an excellent receptacle for pickling herring and cucumbers.

The tenement dwellers worked at tedious tasks; bakers, tailors and day laborers not all that far removed from jobs they performed in "the old country." They wheeled pushcarts selling fruit or used clothes or plied their trades by means of horse drawn carts, sharpening knives or delivering ice or seltzer water.

Morris, with his butchering background, found work in a slaughterhouse on the Eastside of lower Manhattan, supplementing his income by selling hot sweet potatoes from a pushcart during off-hours. It was my job to bring his lunch to the plant each day, a chore I came to dread. The horrible stench could be smelled blocks away and in summer heat; to breathe within a mile of the carnage was to become nauseated. When Morris was laid off I secretly celebrated but could never forget the sight of carcasses hanging on large steel hooks or blood-soaked floors that left stains on my shoes. In later years, long after the slaughterhouse was demolished, I swore I could still smell it.

While Talia and Chana attended nearby public school Fanny was not anxious to send me, preferring to keep me at home to help with chores. But somehow local authorities were made aware of my non-attendance and insisted I be registered. Morris was sent to enroll me and whether because of his lack of English, poor communication skills or desire to get me into the work force early, increased my age by three. Here too, the "fire story" came in handy as cover for the lack of birth records.

At first I was shy and self-conscious, attending class reluctantly, welcoming Fanny's oft-invented excuses to keep me at home. But I soon realized that school provided an escape from the suffocating warren, a brief respite from my mother's rancor and sharp tongue, and began to enjoy it. I learned English quickly and devoured books with an insatiable hunger. Although the word "assimilation" would have meant nothing to me at that time, it was exactly what I most wanted.

When I reached the age of thirteen Fanny insisted I leave school to look for a job. Early on she become aware of my unusual skill with a sewing needle and came to the conclusion her daughter was sure to get work in a clothing factory.

"We need the money and it's a good opportunity for you to learn a trade," Fanny said in Yiddish. "You will always be able to make a living."

It was the summer of 1917 and the United States had just entered the Great War that had begun in Europe. As the male population left to fight abroad, demand for workers in all industries increased at home. I had no trouble finding a job in Manhattan's notorious garment center. Drawn to the frenzied activity of "the district," I was captivated by enormous buildings and cavernous lofts; displays of bolts of cloth on shelves and wooden tables; vast colorful arrays of cottons, silks and woolens. I joined thousands of other immigrants eking out livings in the sweatshops of New York and began what was to be a career that would span fifty-two years.

My first assignment was to work with tailors who trained me to be a "cleaner," snipping off loose threads from finished dresses. For this job I was paid the grand sum of two-dollars a week which I dutifully brought home to my mother. The tailors were kind and patiently taught me to use a sewing machine. Enjoying the attention and a natural talent for the task, I was quickly promoted to "pieceworker," sitting in front of my own glossy black Singer sewing machine; one of many in long rows that extended the full length of the building. Immediately my wages improved. The fixed pittance was eliminated, my reward dependent on output.

Annie's Portion

The more skirts, sleeves, waists or collars completed the more money earned. A floorwalker moved between aisles handing out tagged bundles, exchanging them for completed ones that had been tossed into bins stretched between rows of machines. The ticket, with a tear-off section kept by the seamstress, indicated the number of pieces in a particular bundle. Sewing came naturally to me, so did arithmetic. Each Sunday night I laid out my ticket stubs on the kitchen table, each one a valid claim for payment and calculated to the penny what was due. On Monday mornings, when the bookkeeper handed out small yellow envelopes representing a week of toil, I counted the money to make sure it agreed with my own figures. If it did not I was not shy about getting a correction.

The boss considered me an employer's dream; arriving on time, fast and proficient, never absent, never complaining, avoiding gossip and petty quarrels. Hours were long and work grueling. Those of us who celebrated the Sabbath on Saturdays were forced to work on Sundays. Day in and day out, bent over machines in the poorly lighted factory we labored, rapidly moving fingers turning cloth into gold, stopping only once in the long day to eat a meager lunch and use the filthy, foul-smelling toilets. In winter the loft was drafty and cold and operators worked with coats on. Through hot, humid days of summer we sweltered, unable to open windows sealed against winter's chill, fans blowing stale, hot air through unventilated room.

But things had begun to change. In 1900, the fledgling ILGWU (International Ladies Garment Workers Union) embarked on a mission to improve conditions of workers laboring under unfair, unsafe and unsanitary conditions in the many small manufacturing establishments located all over the city. By 1910 several successful strikes had forced manufacturers to begin making some concessions but on March 25th, 1911, a fire which started at the Triangle

Shirtwaist Company near Washington Square resulted in the death of one-hundred and forty-six people. Most of these victims were young immigrant women who were trapped on the eighth floor. With all exit doors locked to prevent theft they leaped from windows to their deaths. There was national outrage that sparked a movement to create health and safety legislation. But it was not until a Polish immigrant and union organizer, David Dubinsky, came on the scene that wages began to increase and hours decrease.

A recipient of these benefits, my self-confidence grew as my income improved. In time I was making complete garments, suffering the sin of pride in my workmanship; rewarded with the opportunity to sew sample dresses for sales and display purposes. For this I received a bonus which I hid from my mother, using it in part to buy fabric. God's "portion" includes blessings he dispenses indiscriminately and so he added to mine by giving me the ability to sketch and copy designs. Fifth Avenue became my haunt; the high-fashion mannequins my instructors, my wardrobe expansive and stylish.

"How do you get this material to make your own dresses?" Fanny questioned suspiciously.

"I get them at the factory. They are remnant pieces, extra from the cutters," I lied.

My carefully conceived dresses were the envy of my younger sisters, who secretly borrowed some of my clothes which, more often than not, they found difficult to fit into. Unlike Freyda and Becky, who evinced our father's height without his lean suppleness, Chana and I were more fortunate, seeming to have inherited the height genes without our mother's undesirable fat ones.

Of my earlier illness, only three vestiges remained; scarred depression on my left calf, shrunken middle finger on the right hand and partial loss of hearing in the right ear. Embarrassed by the disfigurement I attempted, with some success, to mask it. Dark shaded silk stockings hid the calf scar; parting my short, curly hair to one side just above the nape of the neck and styling it in a manner that exposed the left ear and hid the right one, partially resolved the hearing concern. Training myself to use my left hand was most difficult and in the end I became ambidextrous, writing with my right and sewing with my left. The once shy, insecure, non-assertive Sarah was no more, replaced by an attractive, confident young woman. The ugly duckling had become a swan and to celebrate my coming out I changed my name to Sally. This name was used only outside of the home and I smile to think of what my parents would have said had they known.

Inevitably time and events altered the course of all our lives. Talia the eldest of my sisters, short, buxom and apple-faced—a young replica of my mother was being courted by a serious young man. It was a relationship Fanny strongly disapproved of and did her best to discourage.

"I throw him out the door and he comes back through the window," Fanny would say. "When I throw him out the window he comes back through the door."

But Herschel Leiberman was not easily discouraged and in the end won his bride along with a five-hundred-dollar loan from Fanny. His tenacity paid high returns for in a few years the taxi he bought with the money was the means by which he developed a small fleet. He repaid Fanny with enough interest for her to make a down payment on a four-family house; enabling the family, minus the Leibermans, to relocate to the Tremont section of the Bronx where we occupied one of the four apartments.

Withdrawn and not overly bright Chana, the second eldest, married soon afterward and moved into one of the three remaining apartments. Her husband Sidney, a born loser never earned much of a living, never paid rent and died several years later, leaving Chana with three young sons and a serious case of syphilis.

Chapter III

The end of the war brought new prosperity and optimism to America and new freedom for American women. Hemlines rose, hair was bobbed, smoking and drinking were actively indulged in and I, like so many women of the twenties, came into my own. Not the least bit concerned about marriage I remained with my parents, and because I was effectively supporting the family was asked few questions about my lifestyle. Raised in an orthodox Jewish household I was loath to stray too far from my religious indoctrination; dating only Jewish boys, eating only kosher food. Despite earlier incidents with my father I'd managed to preserve my virginity. By 1925, at the age of twenty-one, I was having the time of my life—working hard, playing hard and at long last, dating gentile men. To the outside world I'd become Sally in name and deed.

It was therefore not surprising that my first meaningful relationship was with a gentile man, a *shegitz*, and was carried on in secret. I dared not mention his name to anyone in the household. Even Chana, with whom I shared a bond of parental disfavor and had often taken into my confidence, was excluded from knowledge of the budding romance. Theodore Compton, a successful, handsome businessman was resolute in his pursuit, sending me flowers, buying me gifts and courting me with matrimony his ultimate goal.

On more then one occasion I laughingly related the story of the time Teddy took me to a very elegant restaurant for dinner. While I was well read and could hold up my end of a conversation, I was lost when it came to interpreting the elaborate menu that was big as a book.

"I had no idea of what anything was. The waiter was looking over my shoulder making me so nervous. I decided to try the cherrystone cocktail, thinking it was a fruit salad.

The waiter arrived with our dinners and placed a large platter of raw clams in front of me. Shellfish, like pork, was absolutely verboten. Teddy noticing my discomfort and ever the gentleman said, 'It's okay Sally. I'll eat them'."

Finding myself growing ever fonder of Teddy, knowing I would never be able to marry a Catholic, I sadly ended the relationship, promising myself never to get as involved again with a non-Jewish man.

As Sally, I partied my way through the twenties but even after the crash of '29 Sarah earned enough to maintain the family. By that time my two older sisters were busy raising families of their own. My younger brother had been killed in a tragic street accident and rather than uniting my parents in their shared sorrow over losing their only son, Morris became more reclusive and my mother more bitter.

Rarely was a guest found at the Treiger supper table but on a particular Friday, without explanation, Freyda brought Bradley Kaufmann home to share the Sabbath dinner with the family. If her thoughts had been of a romantic nature, she'd made an irrevocable mistake. When we were introduced the attraction was immediate and mutual. Several months later Bradley and I were married at City Hall by a justice of the peace and at the age of twenty-nine I left the Bronx without regret.

Chapter IV

1933 – Manhattan

Our honeymoon haven was a room above a garage located on the upper Westside. Brad worked as a chauffeur for a wealthy family who provided the room as a condition of employment. Initially, the meagerness of my new home was unimportant. In love with my handsome, debonair new husband, I felt freer and more content than I'd ever been. Sadly this happiness was short- lived for Brad was a scamp, and when he discovered I was pregnant Brad was something less than delighted.

"I didn't plan on being a father," he complained. When presented with his new daughter in March of 1934, his disappointment was undisguised. "If I have to be a father I would certainly have been happier with a son."

But I was thrilled with my little girl and after a heated argument with Brad, who had wanted to name her Julia for his still living mother, something unheard of in Orthodox Jewish circles, insisted on naming her Anne.

For a reasonable stipend, our benefactor's housekeeper allowed her daughter to care for Anne during my working hours, and two weeks after Anne's birth I was back at the machine. Our quarters, which were never roomy, became exceedingly crowded with Anne's arrival. Brad began spending more time away from home, contributing neither money nor explanation for his all-too-frequent absences. I must have been a fool not to have understood his shortcomings sooner. But who was it said, "Love is blind?" And I did love him, it seemed with a desperation that may have been born from my need to escape. Fiercely determined to avoid another pregnancy, too often I discouraged his amorous overtures.

Annie's Portion

When finally confronted about his absences and reliance on me for financial support, he confessed he had a gambling problem. While I was trying desperately to save enough money to rent a larger apartment, time and again Brad had to be rescued from some loan shark. It seemed as though his love for the horses far exceeded his love for me and his little girl. Anne was a charming child, with her father's good looks and blue eyes and a pleasant disposition. But I had so little time to enjoy my baby and missed so much of her firsts. It was the sitter who told me of her first tooth, her first word, her first steps—joys that would never be mine. By the time Anne reached her second birthday my suspicions of Brad included his infidelity. When he was subsequently fired for using his boss's car without permission, I left him and did the inconceivable, went back to live with my mother.

Brad got another job driving for a limousine service in Brooklyn and pleaded with me to come back, promising all the usual things. Living with my family in the Bronx had been a nightmare so I agreed, though halfheartedly, to give it another try.

Moving to Brooklyn was like moving to another foreign country, one that placed me in close proximity to my in-laws whom I'd met only once. Brad's family could not have been more different from mine. As a young man his father Jack, had left Amsterdam for London. His mother's origins were Spanish but she was born in Lisbon, Portugal. Although they were non-practicing Jews, in Portugal as in Spain, life for her family became intolerable and they sought a safer haven in England. Julia Lopez and Jack Kaufmann met and married in London where they started a family. Jack was quite the lothario and Julia, as I would alternately describe my mother-in-law, was either a London fishmonger or a prostitute. Neither proof nor disproof was ever offered to make a case either way.

J. Fran Baird

Julia and Jack had two sons and two daughters before they made the decision to seek their fortune in America and sailed into New York harbor where Lady Liberty opened her arms to welcome them all; Adela, the first born, Albert, Gilbert and Jeanette. They situated themselves in Bath Beach, a district of Brooklyn within walking distance of the Atlantic Ocean, in a predominantly Italian neighborhood.

Unlike the ubiquitous tenements of Manhattan, Brooklyn's vastness allowed for much more diverse housing opportunities. Here small apartment buildings and single-family houses sat side-by-side. Much of New York's Mafia made their homes in the area along the waterfront. Beautiful, large brick houses lined the shore that continued for miles to connect with Fort Hamilton. Well-tended green lawns sloped toward the seaside and offered the passer-by views of flowering shrubs and opulent statuary. Every front lawn displayed a figure of the Virgin Mary, some housed in simple stucco niches while others luxuriated in grand marble altars.

Just two blocks from the beach stood many blackened three-story row houses, perched unsteadily above small shops on the ground floor. The Kaufmann home was one of two "railroad flats" on the second floor of one such building, above a shoe repair shop and a small bakery. The apartment they occupied consisted of six rooms; entry and parlor at one end, kitchen at the other. Each room unveiled another smaller one beyond, thereby giving the apartments their labels. It was there Bradley was conceived and delivered, the first member of his family to be born in America. While Brad was in the blossom of his youth Jack, like my brother-in-law Sydney died of syphilis, a result of his many indiscretions.

By the time Anne and I entered this picture Adela and her husband were in their own house several blocks away. Albert, with his wife and young son, remained in the apartment with Mother Julia. Brother Gilbert, whose wife Kate had recently presented him with a daughter, managed to secure a flat on the same floor as his mother's. There existed a unique means of communication between the two by way of a dumbwaiter shaft used to collect garbage. Each domicile accessed the dumbwaiter by means of a cupboard-like door conveniently located in the kitchen. Three times a week a wizened quasi-caretaker took his position in the basement at the bottom of the shaft. Using an improvised klaxon, the sound of which echoed through the concrete tube, he alerted the tenants to the imminent arrival of a double-tiered, wooden platform making its rickety way up the channel. Propelled by the surprising strength of the gremlin who hauled the lines along which the platform ran, the device would make a brief stop at each floor to allow tenants to deposit brown paper sacks stuffed with household detritus. This convenient arrangement also made it possible for Julia to open the dumbwaiter door, reach across the shaft and knock on the facing door, behind which an obeisant Kate tended little Julie, her three-year-old namesake. Julia was thereby provided the ability to oversee the activities of both daughters-in-law without ever leaving her kitchen.

Having come from a large family I was very accepting of Brad's, hoping the close proximity of his mother and siblings would help keep Brad on the straight and narrow and stabilize our marriage. Unlike my parents, Julia had a very loving relationship with her children, especially her sons. They were dutiful and obedient and she in turn doted on them and overlooked what to others might have seemed unconventional behavior. For the three brothers were proof of the old adage, "the apple does not fall far from the tree." Like their father they believed they should not deprive the women of the world, or at least New York City, of their good looks, charm, wit and very obvious sex drives. Unfortunately for me and my sisters-in-law, Julia found nothing wrong in the behavior of her sons and in fact encouraged them by inviting their girlfriends of the moment to Sunday dinners. These events may well have contributed to my description of my mother-in-law's former trades.

Since Brad needed a home for his family and had limited means for providing one, Adela offered us a room in her house. For a moderate price we could have use of the kitchen and parlor and she would care for Anne. All we had to contribute was a child's bed and some additional bedroom furnishings. Leery at first to accept the offer when I found a job at a dress factory in the same area, it seemed the best option. While the arrangement was far from perfect we thought it would be of short duration and would give us an opportunity to save enough to get our own apartment. Little did we know how short it would be. We'd been at Adela's house for little more than three weeks when I returned from work to find all our belongings out in the street. It seemed Brad had not yet paid any rent and Anne's singing roused Adela at an early hour that did not suit her routine. My hopes of finding friendship and solidarity with my new family were quickly disappearing. Angry and discouraged, I retrieved my daughter and fled the scene. With Anne in my arms I began to wander through the unfamiliar streets aimlessly. A quiet churchyard provided temporary refuge. Sitting disconsolately on a stone bench, pressing Anne close to my breast, tears that for so long had been restrained spilled out, sobs wracked my body. I don't remember how long I'd been indulging in self-pity before there was a light tap on my shoulder. Startled, I looked up to see a priest standing beside me.

"Can I be of assistance?" he asked.

Taught from childhood to distrust the "Church," I'd never before been in close contact with one of its delegates. But close to the breaking point I desperately needed someone. With Anne sleeping in my arms, I poured out my

Annie's Portion

heart to this kind man who listened patiently until the end of my story.

"I think I know someone who may be able to help," he offered.

He took my hand and led me into St. Finbar's chapel. Leaving me to gape at the stained glass windows, the statues and the altar with the figure of Jesus on the cross, he went to use the phone in his office.

Signora D'Antonio arrived within minutes. She was breathless as she bounced into the room with surprising agility. Father Joseph steered us to a pew where she sat down heavily beside Anne and me. I looked at her through red, swollen eyes. What I saw was a large woman with a pleasant smile. What I could not see was the heart within, one that equaled her great size.

"Signora, this is Sarah Kaufmann and her little girl."

"Ah, so young and pretty." Signora D'Antonio smiled as she patted my shoulder.

I think I made a poor effort to smile back.

"Father Joseph told me you need help," the Signora said in heavily accented English. "Maybe you will let me help you, yes?"

The faint, pleasant smells of an Italian kitchen emanated from Signora D'Antonio. "Thank you but I don't know how you can."

"I have a big house and all my bambinos are gone. My husband he's a busy with the grapes all the time and I would love to hava some company. There is a very big room uppa stairs where you and the bambina can stay for as long as you want."

It was useless to protest. The Signora held up her hand. "No, no. Not to answer until you see. We can walk, it is very close." She winked at Father Joseph and helped me to rise. Anne opened her sleepy eyes and looked around the church. She remained quiet, obviously interested in her new surroundings.

"Come, now. It is okay. You not worry. What is the name for the pretty bambina?"

The Signora held my arm gently but firmly and I did not resist.

"Her name is Anne but we call her Annie. Anne sounds too grown up."

"Good. I too call her Annie."

As the Signora promised, a walk of a block brought us to the modest brick house where the D'Antonios had lived for fifty years. The small front garden, with its fig tree and hydrangea bushes was neatly tended. Several stone steps led to the wraparound porch where a well-used rocking chair, two wicker armchairs and a small table formed a semi-circle. Several flower baskets dangled from the overhang.

"What a lovely place you have, Mrs. D'Antonio."

"Thank you. We are very happy here. But please call me Signora."

When the Signora opened the door a hint of mouth-watering garlic greeted me. A central hallway with stairs leading up to the second floor divided the lower level. The parlor, located to the right, was filled with upholstered furniture, several tables decorated with hand-crocheted doilies and small figurines; a window seat invited with plump velvet pillows. A floor lamp dressed in a tasseled shade stood behind an overstuffed armchair. Hardwood floors were covered with several oriental carpets and a canary sang from his perch in a cage near the window. The room, delightfully reminiscent of the Victorian era, looked comfortable and well-used.

To the left of the entry was a dining room dominated by a large, oblong table covered with a fringed lace tablecloth. Eight heavy chairs stood at attention around it while hydrangeas floated in a bowl in its center. An enormous

Annie's Portion

sideboard adorned with glasses and platters hid most of one wall. Lace curtains hung at the window. A door at the further end of the room gave access to the kitchen and the Signora steered us in its direction.

"Please, sit. I will make some coffee for us and some milk and cookies for Annie."

"Please don't bother for us." I was embarrassed by the kind act.

"It is not a bother. When we finish I will show you your new room."

It didn't take long to learn the Signora never took "no" for an answer. I accepted the coffee and hungrily downed several cookies. Annie too seemed to be enjoying the party. When we'd finished the Signora cleared the table and led us upstairs. There was just one bathroom to serve three large bedrooms, one of which was to be ours; a bedroom room furnished in the same homey style as the parlor. Sun spread its glow through several lace-curtained windows.

"This is just wonderful. It's the nicest room I've ever seen."

"I knew you would like it. My two daughters used to share. We will get a crib for the bambina. Papa will bring from the cellar and we will clean for Annie. Okay?"

I put Annie down on a carpet and hugged the Signora. My arms barely reached around her ample middle but I squeezed as hard as I could. She laughed a great belly laugh and hugged me back.

"You will be happy and safe here. Now we will find Papa and give him the good news."

We went downstairs and through the kitchen to the backyard. Sure enough there was Signor D'Antonio pruning grape vines that twined around a trellis he'd built in the fenced yard.

"Papa, come see what I have."

Chapter V

It was the beginning of one of the happiest times I'd known. Signora and Papa became my surrogate parents and wonderful grandparents for Annie. For the first time in my life I felt as though I was home. The Signora loved and cared for Annie with great tenderness and much food. I went to work with peace of mind knowing my daughter was in the best of hands. I was at last able to save most of my earnings because the Signora would take no money from me for room and board. I tried to reciprocate by buying groceries and sewing a dress or apron for her or a shirt for Papa but they did so much more for us than I would ever have been able to repay. Fearing Brad would cause trouble I did not let any of the family know where I was. With no knowledge of my new place of employment he was unable to find us.

Annie and I celebrated our first Christmas with all the D'Antonios seated around the big table, overflowing into the parlor. Annie helped trim the tree and had a great time opening presents and playing with her new "cousins." Soon after her third birthday Brad found me at the factory.

"I've been looking but no one knew where you'd gone," he said. "I checked with your Union to find out where you were working."

"It certainly took you long enough," I remarked and while I had many reservations about a reunion, Brad did not. Though I desperately wanted us to be a family again I was determined not to fall for his spiel. Oh, but he was smooth; knew all the right things to say, all the right promises to make. He wooed me all over again coming to visit, to see Annie, to take me to dinner or a movie.

"I've become a partner at the limo company and I've saved some money."

"But you never hold on to it," I accused.

"I've given up gambling, I promise. I love you and Annie and want to make a home for us."

I so wanted to believe him. It sounded wonderful, real family life with my husband and child while still enjoying the pleasures of our new extended D'Antonio clan. I was beginning to soften but the Signora remained unconvinced of his sincerity. I overheard her tell Papa she could see through Brad like a clean window.

"He is no good, Papa. He will hurt Sarah again. We need to discourage her from seeing him."

"It is not our business. We will try to help them by accepting him here. Annie needs her father."

"He is bad and he is a liar but for Sarah's sake I will try."

With much cajoling Brad was persuaded to move into the D'Antonio household. For a while things went well between us. Papa made him welcome and Signora coolly tolerated him. Brad, on the other hand, hated being there. He knew how the she felt about him and was afraid she'd turn me away from him. When several months had passed Brad confronted me.

"It's time for us to find a place of our own," he said, "one where we can have privacy and live our own lives We've saved some money so there's no better time."

I remained non-committal, holding out for a time when I was convinced my husband had truly reformed. Another week passed with no further discussion about the move. Returning from a long distance trip, Brad arrived with news he'd found a place for us.

"I want to be out of here. I'm tired of smelling like spaghetti and garlic and hearing about the old man's grapes. I want to make love to you without someone hearing me. I've got us a place of our own. It's not perfect but it will give us a new start."

"How can I just leave? These people have been better to me than my own family or yours for that matter. The Signora takes care of Annie and loves her like her own. I love them too."

"I'm not asking you to give them up," Brad coaxed. "The Signora can still watch Annie and you can see them whenever you want. I just want you to myself."

"Where is this place you found and why didn't you wait for me to see it before you rented it?"

"There was someone else who wanted it too, so I had to make a quick decision. You'll like it, I know."

It was with lingering doubts I finally gave in. Brad was part of my life again and I knew I had to trust him if we were to ever make a success of our marriage. To my surprise the place Brad found was quite nice. One of four in an older, large converted single-family home, our apartment consisted of two rooms and bath. The front room was multi-purpose, combining parlor, dining area and kitchenette. The bedroom was small but adequate. It had been freshly painted, the white walls reflecting light from several windows.

"What do you think, Annie?"

Brad was pleased by my reaction. "I like. With our combined savings we'll be able to make this place home."

When I told the Signora of the plan, to her credit she did not protest. She offered to continue watching Annie and told me we could always come back. It was with cautious optimism that we three Kaufmanns began another chapter in our troubled history.

Brad paid the rent on time and gave me extra spending money. He seemed to be working diligently although the nature of his business required him to keep irregular hours and he was seldom home for dinner. But on those nights when he joined Annie and me, he entertained us with animated descriptions of interesting people, places and events. With his dark hair framing the smooth, fair skin of his face and his blue eyes sparkling, with his slightly crooked smile and easy laughter, he charmed us—as he had too often done with other women. Annie giggled and I smiled, seeing the man who had first won my heart, and fell in love anew.

Brad possessed an almost insatiable appetite for sex. Though not openly affectionate, once Annie was asleep he needed no encouragement to guide me to the connubial bed. I resisted his attempts to undress me, insisting on changing into my nightgown in the bathroom—a habit he attributed to my previous living conditions and limited experience but in reality a method I hoped would damp his ardor. In this he humored me, believing with time and gentle persuasion I would succumb to his skilled hands.

There was no way for Brad to know why, when he reached for me in the night, I flinched and moved away from him, or why when he tried to draw me closer, he could feel me stiffen. To me, Brad seemed incapable of considering anything but his own needs, a belief that prevented me from ever disclosing the shame I'd concealed most of my life. Perhaps it would have made a difference if he'd known when he touched me, it was my father's hand I felt. Too humiliated to confide in my husband, I suppressed the bitter memories; memories of Fanny putting eight-year-old Sarah in her father's bed to accommodate him and relieve herself of that burden. Haunted by memories of the five years during which Morris fondled me in the night, I could not admit to Brad that Morris, a man of such religious fervor, a man who sent his prayers to God several times a day, believed so long as he did not penetrate his daughter he was committing no sin.

After a while Brad stopped trying. His evenings at home became fewer. I knew with certainty when Brad's clients "required the limo service for late night business or entertaining," he was seeking his pleasure elsewhere. I did not condemn him but resolved to be prepared for the inevitable and began to squirrel away part of my salary each week. He gave no sign of leaving, continuing to deliver Annie to the Signora each morning while I reclaimed her at the end of the work day, keeping my stop brief.

We lived this way for two years with Brad absent much of the time. When he did come home it was in the wee hours of the morning. He lounged in bed until noon and often did not take Annie to stay with the Signora, leaving instead at the first sound of my returning footsteps. Annie didn't seem to mind. She loved her handsome daddy and was happy just being close to him even if he was sleeping. He often took her with him on trips, some of which were out of town and required overnight stays.

When Annie started school, a neighbor cared for her. For a while I brought Annie to visit the D'Antonios each weekend but was uncomfortable knowing the Signora could sense my growing displeasure with Brad and his frequent absences. Irrationally, my resentment was directed toward the kind woman. When private sewing took up my weekends our visits became fewer and further between.

While garment altering, which I passionately hated, provided a reliable source of extra income, it was earnings from bridal gowns that substantially stuffed the till. I'd never lost the ability to create my own designs and acquired a skill with beadwork that drew rave reviews. Word got out and there was no lack of customers. There was little time for play but my personal savings were growing and I was beginning to feel more secure.

It was Saturday, a day reserved for my necessary sideline. Engrossed in my beading, a relaxing change from the hectic noisy factory routine; enjoying the quiet time, with Annie working diligently on a picture puzzle, I heard loud voices on the stairway, voices that bode ill. Someone began to pound on the door. My stomach knotted. Grabbing Annie I sought safety in the bedroom closet. When she began to protest I cupped one hand over her mouth, placing a finger across my lips with the other to hush her.

There was a cracking sound and we heard the crash of a door as it slammed into the wall. Annie began to wriggle. I tightened my grip on her mouth, much too roughly I'm sure. We were able to hear loud noises and gruff voices shouting in the parlor.

"Son of a bitch. Nothin' here is worth much. Just some crummy furniture."

"Shut up and take it all."

"We gotta carry all this junk down those stairs. It ain't worth the trouble and we're liable to get caught."

"Okay, okay. Just carry the small stuff and get that sewing machine."

I'd remained silent with my hand tightly held over Annie's mouth, but hearing the last remark a small gasp escaped my lips. We burrowed in the closet for what seemed an eternity, listening to the clamor as the two men tromped back and forth, pulling out drawers and overturning furniture. She was terrified and so was I. When a long silence indicated the thugs were gone we crept out of the closet. The parlor was a shamble with lots of broken dishes and pillows on the floor. The rack on which my finished work hung had been thrust onto the sofa. Fabrics, patterns and beads littered the floor. I dropped to my knees and began picking up the pieces. Suddenly aware of the futility of my efforts I stopped, scanning the havoc around me. All the small electric appliances were gone, as was my favorite lamp, a wedding gift—and a treasured shawl I'd hand-embroidered. The greatest loss however, was the sewing machine, the assurance of financial security.

A meager apartment in an aging house seemed a most unlikely target for a lucrative heist. Under usual circumstances it would have been. But these were not ordinary conditions, for once again Brad had bet the house and farm on a horse. The horse ran away with both, leaving him an unpaid bill with the local loan shark. With no other means of collecting Brad's debt, he being out of work, out of cash or out of both most of the time, the shylock had done the next best thing.

Annie and I moved back with the D'Antonios for a short time and despite the Signora's pleas, found and furnished a flat in Bensonhurst. Predictably, Brad was conspicuously absent during our stay with the Signora but turned up at the apartment whenever he was broke, hungry or in want of a warm body. Even those visits became less frequent over time and looking back I realize, in some way, I'd encouraged him. Much as I tried I could not bring myself to shut him out completely. In his own selfish way he loved me and his unannounced appearances continued to kindle my desire for him. He was an addiction. I fed him, financed him and slept with him. Because of the infrequency of our moments of intimacy I grew careless, the result of which was a pregnancy and birth of another daughter. Annie was ten when Hannah was born and once again I found myself dependent on home sewing for a living. Brad flew the coop the moment he heard the news but Annie was delighted with her new sister. For years she'd been begging for a sister or brother to keep her company and while the age difference denied Annie the companionship of a playmate, it provided opportunity for her to play mother. Hannah was a cherub; a plump, rosy-cheeked, blue-eyed, curly-headed, mischievous cherub.

The D'Antonios adored Hannah, bestowing on her the same love and affection they gave Annie but as time passed we saw less of them; exchanging presents at Christmas and celebrating the Signora's birthday with her. Annie was in her first year of high school when I received a call from Angela, Signora's oldest daughter, telling me her mother had suffered a massive heart attack and was not expected to recover. The day after I got the call I went to St. Asthenia

Annie's Portion

Hospital to see her. She'd been heavily sedated and lay unmoving, an oxygen mask covering her face and tubes inserted into both arms. I pulled a chair beside the bed and took her hand.

"Dear, dear Signora," I said softly. "You have been my best friend, my mother, my daughters' grandmother. I'm sorry we did not spend more time with you but please know that we dearly love you." I thought I felt a squeeze of her hand but was never quite sure. On Sunday morning shortly after Father Joseph performed the last rites, the Signora died never having regained consciousness.

The brothers Masconi had a monopoly on Italian funerals in Bath Beach and it was at their mortuary the Signora's remains were held for three days of viewing. On Monday evening, I went to pay my respects to the grieving family, witnessing for the first time an open coffin surrounded by floral wreaths. Loath to look at the body I stayed just long enough to hear the rosary recited by mourners.

The funeral service was held the following Thursday at St. Finbar's church. I'd taken the afternoon off, something I rarely did, to attend. The church was filled with family and friends, all of whom had known and loved the cheerful, selfless woman. Transported to the church, the closed casket covered with a blanket of white flowers, lay on a bier before the altar. Father Joseph officiated at the Mass which included a communion service. I watched transfixed as the line of churchgoers reached the alter-rail where the supplicants received the *matzo*-like wafer and a sip of wine from a silver chalice. The ritual completed, Father Joseph gave a moving eulogy, drawing audible sobs from papa D'Antonio who was seated in the front pew, between Angela and Nicky.

Outside the church, a line of limos and cars waited for the hearse, bearing the Masconi logo, to lead the procession to Holy Cross Cemetery. Angela found a place for me where

I sat silently during the ride remembering the providential day when I met Father Joseph and the Signora at St. Finbar. At the gravesite Father Joseph offered a prayer committing the body back to the earth. The mourners tossed flowers on the casket and departed before it was lowered and the Signora laid to rest.

Wanting to offer my condolences to Papa, I went back to the house where Annie and I had spent so many happy days and where on that day the Ladies Auxiliary of St. Finbar had prepared a bountiful table for the mourners. I walked through the house, committing to memory the sights and smells of it. I visited the room Annie and I shared; the room exactly the same but for the crib, carefully wrapped and stored in the basement to await the next baby. I strolled through the tranquil garden where Papa's vines grew, lovingly tended. After visiting for a little while with an inconsolable Papa, I said my goodbyes and departed. Five months later I found myself at Papa's funeral, knowing he had gone to join his wife of sixty-five years. Angela said the doctor could find no medical reason for his death.

Chapter VI

Occasionally Brad visited us, spending time with Annie and as usual filling her head with grand stories of adventure. He took no interest in Hannah who was only months old. While pressing some money into my hand he doggedly attempted to wrap his arms around me but finding me no longer compliant, soon quit coming.

My sister-in-law Kate was the only member of Brad's family who remained friendly. As working mothers we had much in common; faithless husband, two young children, apathetic in-laws. It was Kate who was the bearer of bad tidings, informing me Brad was planning to marry again. She was surprised by my indifference.

"He is going to try to take Annie."

"He can't do that!"

"Well, if he gets married again he'll have a darn good chance of doing just that. He'll claim that he can provide a better home for her—you know with a step-mother and all. You need a lawyer."

"What about Hannah?"

"He doesn't want Hannah, just Annie."

There'd been no further indication Brad was seeking a divorce and as weeks passed I dismissed the conversation as rumor and put it out of my mind. The next time I spoke with Kate the news was much more disconcerting. She informed me that Brad had gotten married in Florida without benefit of divorce. Once I recovered from the initial shock I filed for divorce. Brad did not contest or respond in any way and the divorce was granted. Months later he attempted, without success, to get custody of Annie.

At last my ties to Brad were completely severed. Annie had gotten used to the idea Brad was no longer an active part of our lives. My daughters were growing up faster than I could sew dresses for them; independent Annie, tall and slim as a reed, rosy-cheeked Hannah with her sunny disposition. Hannah never knew her father but was aware our family was different from others and the question she posed to every man she met, be he delivery person, shopkeeper or neighbor was, "Are you my daddy?" This query caused me many embarrassing moments.

Predictably, another man entered the picture. Dancing was the one extravagance I allowed myself and the renowned Roseland Pavilion, a dance hall providing a safe, friendly environment for singles, presented just such an opportunity. It was at Roseland I met Benjamin Stern. He was an excellent dancer, for which I was grateful, since many of the would-be Fred Astaires were often clumsy and crude. We danced well together and often sought each other out at the Pavilion. It wasn't long before we expanded our exchanges to include dining, theater-going and pleasant drives. Ben lacked Brad's charm and charisma but cherished me unreservedly. He doted on Hannah and when she asked him the ever-constant question, "Are you my daddy," he answered, "No, but I would like to be." Enjoying the attention and companionship, wanting a father figure for Hannah, I accepted Ben's proposal. He was a man of modest income, steady and hardworking and made no sexual demands on me. Ben was, in a word, dull.

It seemed that contentment would forever elude me. There was to be no peace in our home. To my dismay Annie and Ben took an almost instant dislike to one another and the interchanges between them were less than amicable. His obvious lack of business savvy was frustrating and his undisguised bigotry incensed Annie. Their incessant bickering created an atmosphere of armed camp. Whenever they were in the same room there was bound to be a noisy dispute. These bouts would often end only when I was forced to take a side, an untenable position that caused

Annie's Portion

many rifts between us. When Annie's boyfriend offered her marriage as a way out, she accepted the idea as the lesser of two evils. She and Paul Harmon were married a year later and moved into their own apartment and soon blessed us with a grandson whom they named Joshua. Hannah became an aunt at the age of ten. We spent most of our free time with Josh who was the joy of my life and for Ben the child he never had. Ben never failed to bring some plaything for him. Remembering how I'd missed Annie's I reveled in Josh's little accomplishments; first tooth, first step, first word although it wasn't the one we would have had him say. Mimicking his grandpa, who was notorious for his mild oaths, Josh's first distinguishable word was, "goddamnit."

Annie and Paul seemed to be doing fine and before long we had another grandson, Daniel. Hannah was in her second year at Brooklyn College when their third son, Matthew was born. It was the year we celebrated our twelfth wedding anniversary. Ben had been battling emphysema, brought on by years of smoking three packs of Luckys a day. He passed quietly at home. With his last breath he asked for a cigarette.

Chapter VII

Day broke chilly and gray. The rain started just as we reached the cemetery. Annie, Hannah and I sat silently in the back of the limo, Danny and Josh sitting on the small pull-out seats facing us. My daughters and I were dressed in black, each wearing a black band of torn ribbon on one arm. The car stopped and I could see a large mound of dirt under a white tent. A number of chairs were arranged under the canopy and several people were already seated. The driver opened the door and helped me out of the car. Annie put her arm around my shoulder and guided me toward the newly turned earth, Hannah and the boys following awkwardly behind us. It was a small group that came to bid Benjamin goodbye.

A plain pine box sat on a hoist above a gaping hole in the wet ground. A long handled shovel could be seen jutting out of the mounded earth. I stopped at the side of the grave and stood staring at the coffin. Annie led the boys to some seats and returned to my side. We waited for the Rabbi to appear to conduct the service.

Hannah was weeping, I had no tears. The sound of a car door slamming alerted us to the arrival of the "Reb". He hurried toward us bearing prayer shawl, *yarmulka* and prayer book. Jewish tradition required a burial within one or two days of death because Jews do not permit embalming. Just the night before, Annie and I had met with the Rabbi for the first time to discuss the service.

"I'm sorry I'm a little late. The rain and all. Are we ready?"

I confirmed we were. When the short service was concluded the coffin was lowered into the ground. The Rabbi handed the shovel to me. Picking up some earth from the mound I tossed it into the grave. The dirt hit the box

Annie's Portion

with a hollow thud; I shuddered at the sound so inevitable, so permanent, so final. My tears now obvious, I passed the shovel to Annie.

"Do we really cry for the one who's left us or for our own mortality? Am I crying for myself?" I wondered as I watched my daughter shovel dirt onto the coffin.

Josh and Daniel added to the dirt that peppered the pine box. The Rabbi looked around to see if any one else seemed likely to follow suit. Seeing no one he concluded the service. Our contingent turned from the gravesite and walked back to the waiting limo. The last sounds we heard were those of the gravediggers finishing the job.

I'd always remarked that Jewish funerals were so uncivilized, unlike those of the gentile's who threw flowers on a beautiful bronzed coffin and were gone before it went into the ground. My mother told me the bible, always the ultimate authority, instructed Jews they must return to the earth from whence they had come, simply. Thus the burial shroud and closed, unadorned pine box. The purpose of shoveling the dirt was to bring closure to the grieving family. Ashes to ashes, dust to dust.

The mourners moved on to our apartment where several neighbors had prepared a light lunch. We would spend seven days in deep mourning, called "sitting *Shivah*". All the mirrors in the house had been covered, we mourners seated on the several wood boxes the girls brought earlier. The front door was kept open to allow those wishing to pay their condolences to walk in unannounced, many bringing gifts of fruit, candy or food platters. After the seven day mourning period, life would go on as usual or as close to it as possible.

Hannah was in her senior year at Brooklyn College when she joined a very pro-Israel Jewish organization. During the infamous "Six-Day-War" in that beleaguered Jewish state, the Israeli government sent emissaries around the world in an all-out effort to recruit young Jews. Hannah and many of her cohorts signed up, some volunteering to join the army, others to work the land. Annie and I vehemently tried to dissuade her from such a drastic move to a country at war but, with all the passion and optimism of youth, Hannah ignored our pleas and left for Israel. Her first letters arrived often and were long and up-beat. She was living on a kibbutz somewhere in the north near the Syrian border. It was a farming community of about three hundred people and she was teaching English at the communal school. Reading between the lines I could tell that life on a kibbutz was not as glamorous as Hannah had thought it would be. The letters became less frequent and much less positive. Although a truce had been signed with her Arab neighbors, the threat of sniper fire kept the *kibbutzium,* as the members of the commune were called, constantly on alert. It was often necessary to herd her young charges to an underground bunker. Life was hard but Hannah was determined to stay. I feared for her safety but was very proud of her courage and resoluteness.

Life for us, while much less exciting, was eventful. Annie had another son, Matthew and at last gave birth to a girl, a beautiful child with red hair and green eyes. Samantha was born at a time when the Harmons were having severe marital difficulties. There had been several years of break-up and make-up before Annie decided to call it quits and moved out of their house into an apartment. She found a night job and struggled to keep her family housed, fed and cared for—so reminiscent of my travails. Like Brad, Paul rarely made any financial contributions but managed to create havoc whenever he visited the children. On more than one occasion, Annie asked me to move in with her and the children but I hesitated to do so, enjoying my tranquil independence. I remained alone until my retirement at age sixty-five, at which time my boss of thirty-three years hosted a party in my honor, the only time he was known to have done so. Following an emotional speech he presented me with the Singer machine I had slaved over for so long.

A year later I surrender and moved in with Annie and her troop. Her life became my life, leading me to places and adventures I could never have imagined.

Book Two

Annie

Chapter I

1984 – Hawaii

The waning days of autumn signaled an end to the Kona winds which, laden with moist air and flying termites, had subsided for another year. I swiveled the chair, turning to face the floor to ceiling window wall of the 30th floor office. Vaporous clouds drifted by slowly, reflected in the mirrored twin tower of Gothic Center, Honolulu's newest, tallest downtown office complex. The Capitol building, a concrete replication of a dormant volcano encircling the pleated walls of an atrium open to the sky, shimmered in the late afternoon sun; its tall, palm-shaped columns reflected in a shallow aquamarine pool.

Ironically, a grassy green expanse was all that separated the seat of Hawaii's government from Iolani Palace, the only royal residence in the U.S. where Queen Liliuokalani, the last and sole female sovereign to govern the islands had been kept under house arrest in 1895.

In the distance, the lofty spire-topped Century Center building rose like a monolith heralding the entry to Waikiki. I imagined the tourists, smelling of sun tan lotion, lying on white sand or better still, sipping mai tais or blue Hawaiis from glasses decorated with tiny Cymbidium orchids and miniature oriental parasols.

At the far end of Waikiki, Diamond Head's unmistakable crater stood etched against a topaz sky.

Turning back to the desk, barely visible under neat stacks of manila folders, I tried to concentrate on a contract; read a few lines, made a notation on a post-it, stuck it on the page and put the pen down. Heaving a sigh I laid my head against the back of the chair.

J. Fran Baird

"This is not going to work...can't get with it today." In response to my call Karen's voice sounded clearly over the intercom. "Yes, Anne?"

"Karen, anything important happening this afternoon?"

"Hmm, just let me check. No, it's actually a pretty quiet day."

"Good. Try to get hold of Ariana and see if she can fit me in for a massage."

"Will do." Karen buzzed off.

"What a godsend she is, 'my girl Monday thru Friday.' What has it been? Two... no, this is '84. It's been three years. Where did the time go? It seems as though it was yesterday, the call inviting me to that informal luncheon at the Halekulani Hotel."

It had been hosted by Blake, Griffith and Morley, a premier player in both the national and international real estate services business. I dressed carefully for the meeting, knowing mainland executives always wore the usual uniform; suit, white shirt and tie, well aware the casual attire worn by the male Hawaiian contingent would not be acceptable for me; choosing for the occasion a favorite belted beige linen dress, the hem line of which terminated just above the knees and a pair of taupe leather pumps—both intended to exhibit my greatest assets, good legs and a narrow waist. Displaying bogus self-confidence I strode across the courtyard.

Hal Gilmore, Senior Vice President of BGM seemed to have been anticipating my arrival. With unconcealed curiosity he rose to greet me. He glanced briefly at his companion.

"You must be Anne Harmon." He extended his hand and when I took it, remarked about the firmness of my grip. "I'm Hal Gilmore and this is Ellis Grant, our national sales director."

Annie's Portion

Grant stood and reached across the table to shake my hand. He was tall and movie-idol perfect, his well-muscled body the unmistakable consequence of regular, strenuous workouts. He moved around the table to pull out my chair.

"It's a pleasure to meet you." He smiled, exhibiting perfectly capped teeth.

I'd assumed Dick Altman, manager of the local branch of BGM, as well as other local real estate mavens, would be in attendance and was therefore perplexed and more than a little curious when I discovered there were no other guests. We sat on a terrace surrounded by guest cottages and lush tropical foliage. The HouseWithout a Key was one of the oldest hotels in Waikiki and my personal favorite. It still possessed the charm and aloha spirit missing from newer, more extravagant edifices that filled every inch of Waikiki. The air was heavy with the fragrance of pakalana and ginger and the whisper of salt air. Conversation during lunch had been polite but inconsequential. Once dishes were cleared and coffee served there was an uncomfortable lull in the discourse.

"This is a tough place to live." Gilmore's offhanded remark relieved the growing tension.

I liked him immediately. Unlike Grant, he seemed to be a straight talking, sincere guy. It was hard to believe he was the second most important man in a company that spanned two continents.

"Look guys, I don't want to seem rude and I really am enjoying this lunch, but why are we here?"

"Boy," Ellis answered. "Don't pull any punches do you?"

"You're right to ask, Anne." Gilmore eased into the conversation, "We've been having trouble in the Hawaii office of BGM for some time. It's quite apparent that Dick Altman is no longer effective and has become more of a liability than an asset. This office has been losing money and sales people for years. Up until now the only reason we kept it open was to give VIPs an excuse for visiting Hawaii with the ability to charge the trip as a business expense. That's changed. We now see this as a growing market with some good opportunities. We feel our change is long overdue."

Grant put his elbows on the table and leaned closer to me, flashing those beautiful, expensive teeth in a wide grin. "We need something different here in Hawaii. We need to change our focus. We want someone special, with brains, knowledge and street smarts."

"Someone *akamai*." I interjected.

"Yes," Gilmore agreed. "That's what you call it in Hawaiian."

"And you think I can help you locate such a person? How did you happen to find me?"

For a moment Gilmore was silent. He looked at Grant, then back to me. "Adam Rice suggested we contact you."

"Adam Rice." I was surprised. Adam was President of the Australian, Hawaiian and California Divisions of Gothic International Enterprises, developer of Gothic Center. I'd been working as the exclusive leasing agent of the twin towers for more than three years and found Adam to be a stern taskmaster. He was non-communicative and almost reclusive, but rewarded with great generosity those he felt were honest, diligent and tenacious. I'd earned Adam's respect and thanks to my relationship with Gothic improved my financial condition substantially. Still I could not imagine him recommending me to anyone.

Gilmore noted the questioning look on my face. "Adam and I go back a long way. We've been friends since college days. I spent two years in England studying their methods of estimating construction costs, surveying they call it and I met Adam there."

"Well I didn't think he ever gave me a second thought."

Annie's Portion

"Oh, he knows a great deal about you and told me we'd miss a good bet if we didn't offer you the job."

Stunned, I shot back. "You can't be serious. You don't know anything at all about me or my qualifications for such a post."

"We know more than you think," Grant rejoined. "We've done a good deal of research on you. We've seen your résumé and checked with two of your past employers, Manhattan Overseas Bank and Equity Real Estate Investment Trust."

"And," Gilmore added, "Adam's recommendation carries a good deal of weight. He doesn't promote someone often, besides like he said, he'd be losing his best rep if you accept the job."

At that meeting I'd been persuaded to visit the head office of BGM in San Francisco, enjoying the royal treatment for three days. A series of meetings provided opportunity to meet officers, board members and most of the operating chiefs. During dinner with several local Branch Managers it was disclosed my acceptance would establish a precedence; first female veep.

On the last day of my visit, Gilmore met with me privately.

"Anne, you've certainly impressed the people here at BGM. We'd like to make you a formal offer." He handed me a multi-page document. "This is a preliminary agreement. I know you will want some time to review it before making a decision."

"I'll be leaving tomorrow and I'd like to take it with me. I really do appreciate your interest but this is a major decision and I don't want to rush it."

"I understand, Anne. Can you give us an answer in a week?"

Maggie Hamilton, the Comptroller, arranged a meeting at five. We'd connected instantly and over drinks at the Iron

Horse Tavern on Maiden Lane, we discussed terms of the agreement.

"I know I'm revealing trade secrets, Annie, but I think you are entitled to know the whole scoop."

Maggie informed me the proffered compensation package was considerably less than that of my male counterparts with fewer perks.

"Those louses," I retorted angrily. "I'm not sure I want the job anyway but to think they wooed me and now want to shaft me."

"Don't make a hasty decision, Annie. It can be a great opportunity for you and very lucrative if you play it right." Maggie counseled.

Upon my return to Honolulu I consulted with Adam Rice and several other close associates who encouraged me to accept the job providing the terms were more to my liking. Adam had the contract redrawn and armed with the new agreement I returned to San Francisco.

Grant was outraged when presented with the counter offer but once convinced I was willing to walk away from the deal Gilmore upped the ante, agreeing to a new package that included additional remuneration, a percentage of the annual office profits, stock options and life insurance.

"If you do as admirably for the Honolulu office as you did for yourself, we'll all be well satisfied," Gilmore told me as I left his office.

Grant was less enthusiastic, his once radiant smile no longer in evidence. "I'll be keeping my eyes on you."

Maggie provided me with information on all BGM operating and accounting procedures and made arrangements for me to fly to the Phoenix office for some on-the-job training. I took Maggie for a celebration dinner at Julian's Castle where we both got smashingly drunk.

* * *

My thoughts were interrupted by the sound of the intercom buzzer.

"How's four o'clock? I have Ariana on the line."

I checked my watch. "That'll be fine and tell her to have a bloody mary waiting."

"Will do," Karen clicked off.

Ariana Halstrom's main source of income was derived from clientele who benefited from her manipulative ministrations in their places of business. The assured availability of a comfortable chair and twenty minutes of uninterrupted time, procured for oneself the luxury of an upper body massage in the privacy of one's office for the paltry sum of thirty dollars.

We'd first met by way of a collision; me hurrying down the hall to the elevator bank, Ariana just leaving an office where she'd ministered to a client, dressed as was her wont in long filmy skirt, peasant style blouse, beads and sandals. Since that time Ariana came to my office routinely and when especially stressed, I'd visit her inner sanctum. Despite our distinctly different personalities and lifestyles we liked each other immediately and during her aromatic, somewhat spiritual, relaxing massage I found her to be a great listening post and confidante.

By the time I got through afternoon traffic and found a parking place in the narrow street it was four-ten. Ariana's door was open, futon rolled up and massage table extended and dressed in a white sheet. Her residence on the lower level of an atypical Hawaiian-style house was built in the twenties, long before the University of Hawaii established a campus in Manoa. The student influence triggered a metamorphosis of the area transforming it into a downscaled Berkeley and since Ariana had never quite grown out of her early college days this suited her just fine. Serving the dual purpose of home and studio, a large front room was separated from a kitchenette and bath by a curtain of multi-colored strands of beads. The larger room was sparsely furnished with faded futon, tatami mats and large, vibrantly colored pillows strewn along the walls. An oval brass tray nestled in a black lacquered cradle served as repository for a variety of candles. Only Ariana's "special clients" were invited into this sanctuary and only by appointment, amid the incense infused air and dulcet strains of Indian music, did she administer a full body massage replete with scented oil.

Hearing the clatter of beads she called, "Come on in. I'm putting another ice cube in your bloody mary. Pull up a pillow and sit."

Piling a couple of pillows against the wall I plunked down. Ariana came into the room holding two glasses. She handed one to me.

"So what's up Annie girl? Love affair gone sour, kids asking for money, mother complaining?"

I inhaled the incense and took a sip of the drink. "No. Everyone's fine. Sam loves school on the mainland and the boys are doing okay too. Mom is just Mom."

The thought of Samantha, my eighteen-year old daughter attending her first year of college in Colorado, brought a smile. Unexpected as she'd been, the youngest and only girl, she was the delight of my life. An adorable child, Sam with her red hair, green eyes and freckles had grown into an equally affable young woman, never developing the characteristics associated with the stereotypical female teenager. Sensitive, thoughtful and kind she acquired a large and eclectic group of fans; the house always filled with bikini-clad, giggling girls, and tan, horny males wearing the fashion of the times, OPs. She was sorely missed, especially by my mother, Sarah.

The boys, in order of their appearance, were my three sons Joshua, Daniel and Matthew.

"When did they become 'the boys' as if they had lost their identities? It was when they were very young I started

calling them 'the boys,' all lumped together as if they were a unit rather than the distinctly different people they are."

Hard as it was to believe, Josh had just celebrated his thirtieth birthday. By the time we left the mainland he'd already been to two colleges; the first, chosen from a catalog during his senior year at Erasmus Hall High School in Brooklyn. With a paucity of data and uncharacteristic exuberance he departed for Lamar University in Las Vegas, New Mexico, confusing it with Las Vegas, Nevada—thinking it would provide a life style filled with balmy breezes, nearby casinos and a smattering of education. To his great dismay, he discovered that Lamar was in the high desert, where winters were bitter cold and snow could be several feet high. Eighty percent of the student body were Indians, the American variety, and the nearest gambling spot was The Hole, an aptly named dive where pool and punch cards proved to be the only games of chance. He transferred out after his first year, opting for his old New York stomping grounds and Stony Brook College on Long Island.

During that time my ex-husband Paul had taken a fourth bride, a rich Texas widow, and moved to Dallas where she financed a cosmetics manufacturing facility at the behest of her new spouse. Josh, the only one of his offspring to maintain a relationship with Paul, was persuaded to leave school and join his father, with whom he could look forward to an eventual partnership and great wealth. The only good thing that came out of that endeavor was a girl named Wendy O'Doul, whom Josh later married at a wonderful, madcap Hawaiian-Jewish wedding on the north shore of Oahu. They'd occupied the lower level of my North Shore house for several years before moving to Florida where Wendy now programmed computers for a satellite communications company and Josh plied his trade as a manufacturer's rep.

Danny, the middle son—strong, smart, stubborn Danny who'd spent three years with the Coast Guard as a form of rebellion; part of that time based at Sand Island in Honolulu. Following his discharge he moved to Dallas, living with Josh for a year in order to establish a Texas residency. Using his G.I. Bill to help defray the costs of his stint at the University of Texas in Austin, he graduated cum laude with a degree in Electronic Engineering. A year after working for a company specializing in global positioning technology, he and an associate started a company of their own, specializing in GPS equipment eventually used by the Coast Guard. It had been an early struggle but they were now beginning to reap the fruits of their labor. Just three months earlier, on the manicured lawn of the Olympic Hotel in Austin he and Linda Beaumont had taken their vows as a million ominous bats, who dwelt under the Collins Avenue Bridge, filled the sky behind their wedding canopy. Texas born and bred, Linda Beaumont, who believed she was far above Danny's station, was the only child of a daddy who had made his fortune in the plumbing business. She was 6'2" tall, slim, beautiful, smart and spoiled rotten. She married Danny, in her own words, "because he was good-looking and the only decent man I knew who was taller than I am." Predictably, she made Danny's life hell on earth.

Younger than Danny by four years and older than Sam by the same number, Matthew was my pet; pampered, protected, tolerated and otherwise overindulged. Beautiful as a child, he had grown into a strikingly handsome young man with dark hair and eyes framed by long lashes that were the envy of many a *wahine*. His 6'5" frame belied his grandmother's prediction the coffee he'd consumed since early childhood would stunt his growth, and the exercise he got from surfing and sailing kept him tan, slim and well muscled.

Upon our arrival in Hawaii, Matt and Sam entered the school system at a more advanced level scholastically than their classmates. Sam, who was enrolled in a private school adjusted well. But Matt, in an effort to be accepted in a Junior High School of ill repute, fell in with a somewhat less than savory bunch, spending more time surfing and indulging in the local pastime of pot smoking than he did at school. He was an exceptionally quick learner and by sheer good fortune managed to pass the exams necessary to graduate from Kalaheo High School in the allotted time. He was accepted at Klatsop Community College in Astoria, Oregon where he spent two years, hating the weather and the monotony, enlisted in the Navy and was currently stationed at the Great Lakes Naval Training Station on Lake Michigan in Illinois—a locale only slightly less dismal than his previous one.

Then there was Sarah. Ahh...Sarah, my amazing mother, who had attained the ripe young age of eighty and who had been with me, through thick and thin, for the past fifteen years. Never complaining, she had cared for the children and me, moving about the country whenever I had the urge to go, accepting each new home with grace and good humor.

"Hey, wake up. Dream time comes after the massage. Talk to me girl."

"Ariana, Ariana. What would I do without your ear? You should charge me more than fifty dollars for the massage. You should get a psychiatrist's fee as well."

"I might just do that. How's Hank?"

Hank, Henry Clark Forestor, had been my paramour for the past two years. He'd been a business client with whom I'd worked through a long period of negotiations. As the CEO of a major mainland accounting firm, he was in Hawaii to open new offices. Since Gothic Center was the most prestigious office complex in Honolulu and I was the exclusive agent our paths were destined to cross. We were attracted to each other instantly and had cultivated a platonic friendship. Once Hank had been installed in his new office, I occasionally visited him to see how he was doing and to seek business advice from him. He'd been the one whose encouragement most helped me decide to take the job with BGM.

"Just think of the prestige and the opportunities that will open for you," he had advised.

We'd meet for a drink from time to time and have lunch once a month. It wasn't until I'd been with BGM two years before the romance began. Following a lunch date, Hank parked in his assigned stall on the second floor of the Center's garage. He was obsessive about that car and providing a special location for his new Porsche, two adjacent spots on the curve of the helix had been the clincher in getting him into Gothic Center. He turned to face me and finding me admiring him, reached over, pulled me to him and kissed me tenderly. The spontaneity of his action and the response it generated took us both by surprise. There was that proverbial chemistry, the heat spreading to the loins, the hunger for more.

"I knew it would be this way," Hank had uttered hoarsely.

It was one of the few times I was flustered, unable to speak. He was a married man with two young children and was incidentally seven years my junior. I didn't care. I wanted him.

"Oh, he's fine," I responded. "He's really a dear and I do care for him. But he's so…young. It's almost like having another child."

"I'm sure there are compensating factors," Ariana grinned.

"A few. Now he's making plans to get away in February and go to Rio for Mardi Gras."

"Hey, that sounds great."

"I feel so guilty. I just keep thinking of his kids and wife and how I would feel if I was her."

"Well it's really his decision, isn't it?"

"I guess. But I'm aiding and abetting. Anyway I think I'm tiring of the whole thing. The sneaking off, meeting in out-of-the-way places, renting hotel rooms. And this job really sucks. It's just baby sitting on a grand scale. Nursing the male egos, pumping them up, telling them how great they are and getting them to work harder. I used to make twice as much money with responsibility for me only and I had a lot more fun."

"Okay cry-baby. Get out of your clothes and into a sheet while I get the table up."

I took the last gulp of my drink and stood up slowly.

"Oh God, Ariana. I wish you'd get some chairs. It takes me ten minutes to straighten my knees."

"Aha! It's old age catching up with you at last. Besides, do you want to change this great ambiance?"

Beaded curtains provided some privacy for disrobing. I undressed and stood looking in the floor length mirror. I'd turned fifty in March but was often told I looked ten years younger. Maybe it was my genes or due in part to jogging three miles a day. At five foot seven inches and one hundred and thirty five pounds I still had a good figure. I'd started coloring my hair in my twenties, just after Matt was born and with fair skin and blue eyes, people thought I was a natural red-head. Having a red-headed daughter made the deception credible. Wrapped in a sheet I re-entered the front room where I lay down on a massage table. Ariana rubbed some body oil on her hands and began kneading my shoulders.

"My God, you're tight. You're knotted up like a pretzel. Try to relax," she said as she worked on my deltoids and upper back.

"Ouch! That hurts."

"Good. That means I'm doing the job."

I closed my eyes. "Ariana, I'm fifty years old. I'm on the downhill run."

"Oh, here we go again. I've been hearing that since March. Forty was supposed to be the tough one. Get over it."

"Forty was a breeze. The best years of my life were my forties. But this is really it, middle age."

"What are you complaining about? You've got a great job, a beautiful home...no make that two beautiful homes, a boat, a BMW and a young lover. I should be so miserable. What more do you need?"

"Don't know," I thought. "Ariana is right. What do I have to complain about?" Aloud I said, "I'm so bored. I've got to make a change, do something challenging, something worth while."

"What you need is a vacation. Get away from these islands by yourself. What would you like to do?"

Hearing no reply Ariana remained silent as she worked her fingers down my spine. I felt myself begin to relax. She elbowed my hip joints. It felt good. The soft sounds of the tinkling melody and the permeating incense were hypnotic.

"What would I like to do? When did I lose the drive, the joie de vivre?" I drifted back in time, back to my pre-teens, back to Brooklyn.

*   *   *

My parents divorced during an era when it was considered less than fashionable. It didn't take long to discover the stigma attached to divorce or to learn what it was like to be an outsider. The child of a working mother, I had to fend for myself. Independence and self-sufficiency were born of necessity; characteristics that stayed with me and influenced the way I lived. A loner, I compensated for this lack of connection with a determination to excel. In grade school I was an A student. At thirteen I entered high school and remained in the ninety-eight percentile through my senior year graduating with honors, my efforts rewarded with a full scholarship to Syracuse University.

During those years, the mid-forties through early fifties Brooklyn and particularly Bensonhurst, was my world. It was a multi-ethnic community comprised of Irish, some of whom had come during the great potato famine, Italians who lovingly tended miniature vegetable gardens and Eastern European Jews; many first or second generation. For the most part they were blue collar workers; many, like my mother, connected in some way to the garment district. But while it was a place that offered many cultural diversions, my two sources of greatest pleasure were the Brooklyn Dodgers and horses.

A short bus ride past Prospect Park terminated at Ebbet's Field where my best friend Judy Kesler and I would often wait for a chance to snag a ball hit over the ballpark fence. It was the team policy to give free entry to any kid, and friends, who brought one back. During the war years it was also possible to obtain a pass if you brought a piece of scrap metal to donate. Possessing neither, a kid could still garner a freebee by just hanging around long enough for some benevolent soul to take pity and let him in. There we could spend an afternoon in the bleachers watching the boys of summer, a team that would never again be duplicated. Guys named Jackie Robinson, Pewee Reese, Roy Campanella and Gil Hodges took their positions while the crowds yelled and threw an assortment of missiles on the field. Judy went wild at the sight of Duke Snyder, whose pictures continued to decorate her walls long after she became a grandmother.

On the other hand, horseback riding was a luxury afforded only to those with lots of green. To my great good fortune my mother's best friend was married to the owner of the Black and White Stables, where one could board a horse or rent one. Mickey agreed to teach me to ride and allowed me to exercise the horses on the bridle paths through Prospect Park or on the six-mile stretch running along Ocean Parkway from the Park to Brighton Beach. In exchange I shoveled manure, fed and groomed the horses. Lacking a father and spending little time with a mother who worked, my love was transferred to the horses. One, an unusual blue-eyed gaited palomino, became my favorite and I his. It had been years since I'd thought about him.

*   *   *

The daydream evaporated when Ariana applied pressure to my feet. Finished with kneading the soles and manipulating the toes she moved to the opposite end of the table where she repeated the procedure on arms and fingers. Placing her fingers on my temples, she exerted slight pressure as she massaged with a circular motion. This was the signal for the end of the session. Ariana slipped quietly out of the room, allowing me time to relax. With eyes closed, the picture of Blue Eyes returned and I was buoyed by the almost tangible feel of his smooth movements, smelled the steam rising from him, felt his long blonde mane brush my face.

Brought back to the present, I opened my eyes slowly, wrapped the sheet around me and headed for the shower.

"Another drink?" Ariana asked.

"No thanks. I've got to drive home and as it is I feel limp as a dish rag."

"Well gee. I'm glad I not only eased your pain but glamorized you as well."

The most refreshing person I knew, Ariana could always bring a smile to my face. Her philosophy was simple. Just let life take you where it would.

"Want to go sailing this weekend?"

Annie's Portion

"Not this time. I'm already committed to racing practice from Kaneohe." I rarely declined an opportunity to sail; a favorite pastime since my Windjammer adventure in the Caribbean years earlier, a trip that included a visit to my cousins in Antigua and my first taste of island living.

"That's right. Big one to Maui coming up."

"Yes, and besides I haven't been black and blue for a while so I'm due."

"Well, have fun and take care of yourself. I was serious about that vacation thing. Give it some thought."

"Sure will."

A fine drizzle greeted me as I exited through the beaded curtain. I looked up just in time to see the sun shine through a break in the clouds and a beautiful double rainbow arc across the sky; a delightful duo, Hawaiian pineapple juice and rainbow weather. From downtown Honolulu the ride to my house in Kailua took just fifteen-minutes; the Pali Highway rising gently at first, growing perceptibly steeper as it neared the two-thousand foot crest of the spectacular Koolau Range. Once the road left the residential areas it cut through lush tropical forests filled with ironwoods, tree ferns and liana vines. The car window was always open on this drive, even when it rained, allowing me to enjoy the musty fragrance emanating from moist earth and flora. Reaching the crest I pulled into an overlook, captivated by the verdant valley stretching before me. As legend had it, this was the spot from where King Kamehameha flung his most threatening adversary, thereafter uniting all the peoples of the islands.

"God! I love this place...and God must too."

Below the precipice sat Kailua, best-kept secret of Oahu; a small town on the windward side of the island with one of the most beautiful white sand beaches in all Hawaii. The inhabitants were, as the locals would say, "chop suey." There were native Hawaiians, Chinese, Portuguese,

Filipinos and *haoles*—literally translated as foreigners but in practice used to denote Caucasians, as well as a multitude of combinations thereof. The houses ranged from run down shacks to multi-million dollar estates, many of them on the beach or high on the Lanikai hill. The people were accepting and friendly, the lifestyle laid back and the scenery divine. Frequent rains on this side of the island kept everything lush and green, with fragrant flowers of every variety and description dotting the landscape. There were orange birds of paradise, yellow plumeria, magenta bougainvillea, red antherium, white pikake, lavender orchids and myriad others with unknown names.

At the major intersection in downtown Kailua a huge hundred-year-old Banyan tree served as home for dozens of myna birds who convened every day at sunset to argue, complain and fill the air with their raucous sounds. Here, the only traffic light in town was an exceptionally long one; so long in fact the local paper featured an article entitled, "What to do while waiting for the Kailua light." It included such things as, "knitting your grandson a sweater," "doing the Sunday Times crossword puzzle," "giving yourself a manicure" and others. It was also a perfect opportunity to get in on the myna bird discussions. Waiting for the green light provided time to enjoy the flavor of my adopted home and after a short drive I pulled into my carport.

I'd purchased the house seven years earlier and moved in with my mother and two younger children. Sarah adapted to the easy living immediately. We'd discovered a perfect source of transportation for her in a local second-hand shop. It was a bike with three very large wheels, a comfortable seat and a large basket mounted on the front. A neighbor rigged up a lawn mower motor and battery, attaching them to the rear axle, thus providing propulsion that allowed Sarah to ride to the local market—tangerine colored, white flowered muumuu blowing in the wind. The only griping she ever did began when Sam left for Colorado. She had adjusted gradually to the absence of her grandsons but with Samantha, the darling of her life gone, the house was no longer filled with young, half naked people calling her Gram and raiding the refrigerator. No longer was there a need to cook for eight, in the event some hungry kids stayed for dinner, though she still made much more than she or I could possibly eat. Where there used to be dozens of flip-flops outside the door there were now just two pairs. Sarah seemed dispirited and had started to lose interest in the things around her, with all her attention focused on her daughter. It pained me to see her that way.

"Annie, is that you?"

"Yes, Mom. Here I am."

"You're late. Where were you?"

I sighed and kicked off my shoes outside the door, an old Hawaiian custom. "Went to Ariana's for a massage."

"Well you should tell me. Supper's cold."

It didn't seem to matter that I often told my mom not to prepare supper since business, monkey or other, often kept me in town late. Because this was one of the few remaining tasks at which Sarah could feel useful I was resigned to the inevitable.

"Well then I'll have time for a glass of wine while you warm it."

"You and your wine. You're becoming a real *shikker*." That was the Yiddish word for drunk and to Sarah a glass of wine taken on any day other than the Sabbath or a holiday was an indication of the onset of alcoholism.

Amused by the expected comment I went to my room to change. A glass of wine was in my hand when I returned to the dining room where the table was already laden with enough food to feed six. Grimacing, I took a sip of the satisfying elixir and lifted a fork. Tomorrow night would be different. We would enjoy our usual Friday night ritual;

dinner at a fine Honolulu restaurant, Sarah loved good food, a walk through Waikiki and banana daiquiris at the Royal Hawaiian Hotel's beach bar.

As was their custom, the dogs roused me early Saturday morning and after taking them for a run on the beach I headed to Kaneohe for racing practice. The rest of the weekend passed without incident and all too soon it was Monday.

Born in New York City, having spent much of my working life there, I preferred late nights, late mornings and a gradual immersion into the work-a-day world. As in most tropical climates the pace of living in Honolulu slowed down considerably. Because of the five hour time difference between Honolulu and New York, six during daylight savings time, most offices opened by seven a.m. Many adjustments had to be made when I first arrived in Hawaii but rising early was one of the more difficult.

Monday's schedule began with a local developer who insisted on seven a.m. breakfast meetings. I arrived at Jake's Joint about ten minutes late for the appointment—still early for me. Jake's was the local breakfast spot for most of the downtown honchos, including the mayor of Honolulu. As usual it was crowded and noisy, the smells of eggs, Spam and weak coffee filling the air. Rice was a food staple and almost no meal, including breakfast, was complete without "two scoops rice."

Joe Riley was a large, ebullient red headed Irishman who began his career as a construction worker in Boston thirty-five years earlier. With hard work, determination, and a little luck he started his own company. He came to Hawaii with some innovative ideas, successfully developing several industrial parks and shopping centers. Joe purchased a number of contiguous downtown properties and was planning a combination condominium, office and retail complex.

The meeting included a number of real estate mavens, a city planner and several bank representatives. It lasted two hours and accomplished nothing. The planner said it would require zoning changes that wouldn't fly. The bankers wanted eighty-percent guaranteed pre-leasing before they would consider any funding and the real estate people, ever the optimists, thought it was a great idea and all obstacles could be overcome. Frustrated in the end, Riley's famous Irish temper had everyone heading for the door.

By nine, my usual time of arrival at the office, it was business as usual. Unusually quiet for a Monday, there were still calls to return, contracts to review, complaints to resolve; everything one could expect in an active commercial real estate office. At four-thirty Hank called to see if I could meet him for a drink. I was grateful for an opportunity to get out of the office and especially glad it was Hank who provided one. We agreed to meet in Pearl City at the old Monkey Bar.

In its heyday the Monkey Bar had been a popular hangout for locals. Booze flowed freely at a long mahogany bar, behind which were glass windows housing a variety of small monkeys in what passed for native habitat. The music was eclectic and at any given time could be blues, Hawaiian or forties vintage. But as times changed it had become environmentally incorrect to keep the poor monks in such a hostile environment, risky to drive with too many drinks under your belt and hard to find anyone to play the old piano. Slowly but surely the Monkey Bar was heading for obscurity, which is why it was a perfect place for Hank and me to meet.

Hank's Porsche was already in the parking lot when I pulled in. His face lit up when he spotted me. It gave me an instant lift to know how much this, handsome, successful guy adored me. Returning his smile I slid onto the barstool next to him.

"Think I'll have something exotic tonight, probably a mistake with this bartender." I quipped. "Make it a banana daiquiri."

Hank bent over and gave me a quick kiss on the cheek. He took my hands and squeezed them hard.

"God, it's been such a long time. I'd almost forgotten how lovely you are."

My drink came and I took a sip.

"Hey, this isn't half bad." I gave the bartender a thumbs-up. "Hank, if I were the blushing type I would be doing just that right now. You make me feel like a schoolgirl."

"Good. That's the way I see you. Have you got the evening free?"

I knew what he was hinting at. "I'm at your disposal."

"Well slug that down and let's get out of here."

Hank put some bills on the bar and quickly led me to the parking lot where he pulled me into his arms and kissed me. Responding with equal ardor I pressed against his body. He released me and opened the passenger door. Before starting the car he kissed me again and whispered hoarsely.

"I love you. I know this sounds terribly corny but you make my life."

"Please Hank, just go."

We drove to a motel near the airport and Hank went in to register while I waited in the car. The routine was all too familiar. Hank came out of the office and drove the car to the back of the motel. He unlocked the door and we found ourselves in the familiar surroundings of what had become "our" room; modestly furnished but clean and comfortable. In seconds we were undressed and on the bed.

When our affair began I found Hank a very unskilled lover. He claimed this was his first adulterous experience and there was no reason to doubt him. He was ardent but clumsy and had no staying power. Having had a series of lovers since my divorce fifteen years earlier, I'd become

Annie's Portion

fairly proficient at the art and with playfulness and patience taught Hank how to please me and himself. After several awkward attempts at love making we had reached the place where we were comfortable and mutually satisfied. We hadn't been together for three weeks and passions ran high. He pulled me onto him and ran his hands over my body, following every curve. Unable to restrain himself Hank reached a sudden climax. I patiently let him enjoy the moment then bit him gently on the ear.

"Well if you think it's gonna be a 'wham, bam, thank you ma'am' kind of night, you're nuts. My turn."

At one-thirty we left the motel. Our urges satisfied we were famished and stopped at Zippy's all night diner for sandwiches and coffee. Hank drove me back to my car and reluctantly let me out of his.

"It's so late Hank. What will your wife think?" I asked facetiously.

"She doesn't ask. Annie something has to give. We need to make a decision soon. I want you on a much more permanent basis."

"Hank, please let's not talk about it now. But you're right. We do have to think this thing through and decide what's best."

"I know what's best. You are."

"You're just hooked because I taught you how to screw."

Hank laughed, "You're right on that score."

"Good night Hank," I scurried to my car, not wanting further discussion.

"I'll call you next week. Drive safely."

From the rearview mirror I could see he remained parked. I knew he had a premonition I was about to lay something unpleasant on him and he didn't want to face it.

As expected, Joe Riley called Thursday afternoon and we agreed to meet at Michele's, at the Colony Surf.

J. Fran Baird

Michele, a Frenchman, had come to the island years earlier and opened a restaurant in Wahiawa out near Schofield Barracks, the largest military installation on the island. It became a destination spot for locals and tourists alike. The drive from Waikiki was a beautiful one as it followed the shoreline before reaching the center of the island, with its pineapple and sugar plantations. The atmosphere, food and drink at Michele's were exquisitely French. When business dropped off out there Michele moved to the elegant old Colony Surf, a high class, expensive co-op apartment complex on the shore at the Diamond Head end of Waikiki. The restaurant had become an "in" spot. Arriving before Joe at a little past five I ordered a kamikaze on the rocks, a drink made of vodka, Rose's Lime and a dash of Cointreau. It was tastefully served in a fine glass carafe sitting in a silver bowl of crushed ice. I took a sip and savored the drink and the view. There were few people on the beach and the surf was quiet. The sun was still two hours from setting and shone brightly on the blue water, creating the illusion of a sea full of diamonds. Lost in thought I felt a tap on the shoulder.

"Could I hope your thoughts were of me?" There was no mistaking Joe's Irish brogue. He pulled up a chair and sat down heavily.

"Hi, Joe. Sorry but I was just thinking how lucky I am to live Ha-va-ee."

"How right you are." Joe ordered a Tanqueray on the rocks.

We sat silently for a few moments watching as a Hawaiian outrigger canoe came into sight. It was manned by two husky Hawaiian men wearing lava lavas, their bare chests covered by maile leis. They had paddled out about half-a-mile when one of the men stood and emptied the contents of an urn into the sea. He threw several flower leis into the water before the men turned the boat toward shore.

Annie's Portion

"What a poignant tradition that is." Joe raised his glass in deference.

"I wonder who it was." I raised my glass joining Joe in the tribute.

"Well Anne, I guess you know what I want. That Planning Commission meets next week. What can you do to push my project along?"

"Joe, you know I can't do anything. I can't even discuss it at the meeting. I should not be discussing it with you now."

I'd earned my stripes and was well known in the real estate community. My opinions were respected and I'd become a source of industry information for The Star Bulletin. Twice a month I taught a real estate marketing class, on a volunteer basis, at Hawaii Pacific College. Having met the mayor on several occasions, when a seat on the Honolulu Planning Commission became vacant he asked me to fill it. I'd been elected to the Board the year before. In order to win confirmation from the Commission members I agreed to recuse myself from voting on any issues that might be construed as a conflict of interest. What Joe wanted me to do would most certainly fall into that category.

"No one needs to know about our relationship. You would just be recommending they consider the project as an urban renewal benefit to the community. You could still absent yourself from any vote. You know you like the project."

"I do like it Joe. In fact I think it would be great for downtown. But the word is out there that BGM would be directly involved in the leasing and sales."

"You could talk to some of the Commissioners on an unofficial basis. I could make it worth their while, yours too. How would you like a beach house or a horse ranch of your own?"

"Joe, please don't say another word. You're asking me to be party to collusion and bribery. It could land both of us in jail. Forget me and just present your project on its own merits. It is very good you know. And besides I already have a beach house."

"Ah, Annie me girl. You know as well as me there's more damn politics and shenanigans around here than any other place I know, not to mention graft and fighting those Hawaiians. What do they call them?"

"The Hawaii Ohana Council?"

"Yeah...I guess. They're sure a tough bunch. Think the whole world is out to screw 'em."

"Well, they're not all wrong. Joe, I wish you the best of luck but when you see me at the meeting next week don't even give me a nod. Thanks for the drink."

The sun was still an hour off the horizon when I left the Colony.

Early Friday morning I called Mom from the office, letting the phone ring many times. With age her hearing, which had been impaired by some childhood illness, worsened and she reluctantly agreed to wear a hearing aid. But she stubbornly refused to put it on until ready to leave the house. It would take a while before she recognized the ring of the phone.

"Hi, Mom. What you up to?"

"Is that you Annie? Is everything all right?" Mom asked in her usual fashion.

"Yes, Mom. Everything's fine. Just wanted to know if you'd like to go to the North Shore tonight instead of Waikiki."

"Oh, that would be wonderful," she answered enthusiastically.

"Good. I'll try to leave early and be home by four."

"Okay. I'll be ready."

Annie's Portion

And ready she was. Her overnight bag was packed with all her basic necessities; nightgown, underwear, sweater, eyeglasses, false teeth cup, Polident and most importantly hearing aid batteries. Everything I needed for the two-night stay would already be there. By five o'clock we were off.

Chapter II

We left Kailua and climbed to Kalanianiole Highway heading in a northerly direction past Kaneohe and Kahalu'u where the highway began to skirt the shoreline. Here tourists boarded glass-bottom boats that plied the shallow waters of Kanehoe Bay, affording unsurpassed exploration of the vivid underwater coral formations and sea life without ever getting wet. Between the beach-park and Kualoa Point, the twenty-mile shoreline was rimmed with ancient royal fishponds, some still actively farmed. The drive took us past beach houses ranging from million-dollar manors to termite-eaten shanties, past walls of hibiscus, oleander, laurel and bougainvillea. We caught a glimpse of Chinaman's Hat, a small offshore island obviously named for its shape, with its single ironwood tree precariously perched near the peak. Forty-five minutes later we reached Kaaava where the road ran so close to the water's edge the car was covered in salt spray. Passing beneath a grove of fragrant eucalyptus trees Mom pointed out several peacocks strutting under the branches. The raucous birds gave their warning calls, one elegant male spreading his iridescent blue fan in an effort to attract a lady friend. Minutes later a high cliff came into view. Above us could be seen a natural stone figure which bore a strong resemblance to a crouching lion and gave its name to the inn where we would be stopping for an early, leisurely dinner. The food was mediocre, the service slow but the atmosphere magical.

Dinner finished, we continued our trip, passing the impressive Mormon Temple at Laie. The land, which had once been the site of an ancient Hawaiian "City of Refuge," was acquired for a Mormon Mission in 1864. But in 1910 the ethereal white-spired temple had replaced it, its golden messenger rising high above the tropical forest. The Hawaii

Annie's Portion

branch of Brigham Young University was situated at the Mormon compound, as was the educational and profitable Polynesian Cultural Center.

Larger coastal villages were soon replaced by tiny fishing outposts and scant clusters of raised frame houses crowned with corrugated tin roofs. The balance of the drive took us by the abandoned sugar mill at Kahuku and isolated valleys dotted with solitary farms and ranch houses. Those in turn were replaced by an almost unbroken chain of disparate shoreline dwellings.

It was nine o'clock when we arrived at Sunset Beach and the North Shore house, by which time Mother was ready for bed. It would take her at least half-an-hour to complete her bedtime ablutions. I got into my pajamas, poured a glass of red wine and tried to read, but by the time the wine was finished my eyes refused to stay open. I finally gave it up and headed for my bedroom, strangely comforted by the sounds of rhythmic snoring emanating from Mom's room. I crawled into the wonderful king-size bed, lay my head down on the plump goose down pillow and was out in minutes.

Roused from a deep slumber by the enticing aroma of fresh-brewed coffee I left the comfort of my cocoon, poured a cup of coffee and joined Mom on the lanai where she'd been since sun-up; another spectacular day, blue sky clear as topaz, sea calm and sparkling. In old plantation style the house was raised on piers and constructed of planked boards with a slightly sloped shake roof. The lanai, which ran along three sides of the upper level of the two-story house, afforded a one-hundred-eighty-degree view. Portside, white sands of a pristine beach lay just two hundred yards away. Across the narrow lane fronting the garden were several modest frame houses with more sea behind, visible between stands of ironwood trees. To starboard lay the Pohakuloa hills blanketed with scrubby Keawe trees and wild flowers. On the highest ridge the vast white expanse of a military satellite dish stood out in sharp relief against a cloudless sky.

"Sure beats the fire escape in Brooklyn," I offered.

Looking at me with moist eyes Mom responded, "I was just thinking the very same thing."

"We've come a long way, Sarah." I teased.

Mom smiled and nodded. "Remember the first time we came out to the north shore? It will soon be ten years. We drove out with Sam and Matt to see the surf after a big Thanksgiving Day storm."

The waves were twenty-five feet high that day. In several places the road was flooded and I had to do some fancy maneuvering to keep the Volkswagen bus from being swamped. When we reached Sunset Beach we had trouble finding a parking space for dozens of surfers had come to ride the waves. Sunset Beach was a surfing Mecca. Hundreds of enthusiasts invaded the area every November, lingering through the winter to enjoy some of the most challenging waves in the world. But on that day only a few of the hardiest, most daring gave it a try and even they soon gave it up.

"I remember it like it was yesterday," I replied. "Samantha was so young and Matthew was a long, gawky string bean."

I'd made a vow that day that sometime in the not too distant future I would have a home out there, a place for my old age. That day had come sooner than expected. It was just four years later, after I'd started making lots of money in the real estate business, I bought a lot just a mile south of Sunset Beach. The parcel was part of a large private tract that had been divided into several sections. A fortunate find, the land was being sold in fee simple rather than leasehold but had remained vacant for two years before I was able to realize the dream and build my house.

Annie's Portion

Hawaii had a unique system of land ownership. Long before Hawaii became a U.S. Territory, the islands were ruled by a king. He and his family controlled all the land. Ownership, as was commonly understood by haoles, was a concept unknown to Hawaiians who were free to make their homes wherever they liked, provided they did not violate local taboos. During the 1820's, the first missionaries came to Hawaii from New England to "save the pagans" and bring them to the one true God. Several of the King's haole advisors, understanding land ownership better than he, convinced him to divide the land and cede it to his subjects and friends. In the 1860's the King proclaimed the "Great Mahele," literally "give away" and the land was divided with much of it going to haoles for plantations. Several missionaries somehow managed at the same time to wed themselves to members of the royal family, thereby benefiting from ownership of the land. Many natives were convinced to sell their newly acquired parcels in exchange for material goods and whiskey. Much later Federal and State governments acquired additional acreage for public use. In the end a great portion of Hawaiian lands fell into the hands of non-natives. Unlike the natives, they were smart enough to hang on to their holdings and rather than selling made land available for development on long-term leases. The "Hawaiian Ohana Council" of which Joe Riley spoke was protesting this taking and demanding a return of certain lands, development rights or the revenues generated from them. One could often hear a native Hawaiian say, "Those missionaries came here to show us God and while we were looking up to see him they stole our land." It was no wonder they felt great antagonism towards the interlopers.

"I think I'll spend some time in the garden today," Mother proposed.

In just a few short years, with Hawaii's year-round growing season, much of the landscaping had matured.

J. Fran Baird

A profusion of fragrant, flowering plants dwelt within a privacy wall of radiant coral hibiscus. The coconut palms had yet to produce but were a lovely addition to the garden. Three papaya trees were filled with fruit and a not-quite-mature lemon tree flowered out of season. Sarah could keep busy for hours pruning and weeding and trimming, loving every minute of it.

"That sounds like a great plan. I think I'll drive up to Mokuleia and go riding for a couple of hours. Do you mind?"

"Oh not at all, Annie. You go right ahead and have a good ride. I have lots to keep me busy here."

In a few minutes I'd changed into jeans, a denim shirt, a baseball cap and high brown leather boots which had seen a great deal of wear. I waved goodbye to Mom who was still sitting on the lanai having a second cup of coffee and enjoying the view.

"Be careful," her usual parting admonition.

A half-hour drive along the Waimea coast, through a sparsely inhabited region brought me to the Mokuleia Cattle Ranch, owned and operated by Ian and Leilani Cameron. The ranch's claim to fame was their highly-prized prime beef but the cattle's prominence had led to an off-shoot business—catering to tourists who wanted a taste of *paniolo* (cowboy) life. For a few dollars more than the cost of a trip to the Polynesian Cultural Center, a package deal procured half a day of riding and a wonderful chuck wagon barbeque. I'd met the Camerons years before at a social function and we'd become good friends.

Beyond a stone archway, a quarter mile tree-lined drive ended in front of a substantial looking rough-hewn wood building. Hearing the car drive up, Leilani in her usual exuberant fashion bounded through the doorway.

"Annie, Annie! How great to see you," she cried and ran toward my outstretched arms.

Annie's Portion

"It's good to see you too. It's been way too long."

"Ian's out riding with some folks and I'm getting the chuck wagon ready. Come help me and tell me what you've been up to."

We walked hand in hand through the house to the huge kitchen where Leilani had been preparing the food she would later take out to Ian and his riders. There were the usual steaks and ribs, rice and baked beans, salads and a variety of Hawaiian specialties, which would add local color to the outing. We visited while preparing food for transport.

"Well I suppose you really came to see Dolly, not me." Leilani laughed. "Go ahead. She's out in the pasture. Be sure to take some carrots with you."

"Free at last." Pleased to learn Dolly was not with the riding party I grabbed a handful of carrots and dashed out the door. Dolly was exceptionally well-mannered and would respond instantly to a whispered command or a gentle press of thighs against her ribs. She had inherited the grace of her part-Arabian parentage and was my favorite horse. Dolly was grazing in the pasture. The mare spotted me and came at a trot to the fence where without hesitation she accepted the carrots from the bucket I extended.

"That's all you get until I see if you're worth more." Grabbing a hackamore I placed it over Dolly's head, tying the *mecate* to it and adjusting the reins. The braided noseband was preferable because it eliminated the need for a bit and was easier on the horse's mouth. With blanket and saddle in place Dolly was ready to go. A click of the tongue was all that was needed to send us off at a quick clip.

At the further side of the pasture a trail led to the lovely white sand beach where we spent the next few hours cantering along the shore. I never tired of watching the ever-changing sea, from dark blue of distant depths to the blue-green of waves nearer shore, and finally aqua translucence as waves rolled onto white sand. Our energies at last exhausted, we returned at a trot to the ranch house. Once Dolly was unsaddled and hosed down she returned to the pasture where she finished off the rest of the carrots. I went back to the house to clean up and do a little personal repair work. Promising to call soon, I left a long note for Leilani thanking her and explaining that Mother was sure to be champing at the bit, awaiting my return.

By the time I got back to the North Shore Mom had started preparations for dinner. She'd taken steaks out of the freezer, which would be wonderful grilled over a *keawe* wood fire. We ate our meal on the lanai. With dinner finished and dishes cleared, I poured two glasses of wine and we moved to lounge chairs to watch the sunset and listen to the powerful roar of gigantic waves crashing on the beach. We chatted and sipped our wine until the sun was halfway below the horizon. For years I'd been trying to see the "green flash" which many of my sailing friends said happened at the exact moment the last sliver of sun dropped below the horizon. There'd been no "flash" when the sun departed but the air cooled quickly. It was time for a sweater for me and a lap robe for Sarah. Her glass had slipped to the deck; her head drooped on her chest. I picked up the fallen glass and placed it on the table, poured another splash of wine in mine and settled in. As darkness closed in, the sounds of the sea and Sarah's breathing were spellbinding. I felt myself getting drowsy too. I pulled the sweater tighter about me.

Chapter III

1939 – Brooklyn

The sounds of laughter and smell of cigarette smoke woke me. The room was dark but shadows of my father and his lady friend flickered in the glow of their cigarettes. They were in bed at the other side of the room. Not wanting to be scolded as I'd been on other occasions I lay there quietly, thinking about the many secrets I shared with my father. I adored him with intensity akin to hero worship, spending much more time with him than Mother. And time spent with Sarah was never fun. She collected me on her way home from work and after an initial greeting and quick hug we walked the half-mile to our apartment. I'd chatter incessantly about my day but Sarah only responded with an occasional, "That's nice," or "Were you a good girl for the Signora?" Sarah was tired. In addition to her factory job, she sewed at home evenings. Weekends, customers would bring their alteration work or come for fittings of beautiful bridal gowns, her "specialty." She had little time for her daughter.

Daddy always stayed in bed late into the morning. The smell of his cigarette was the signal for me to jump into the big bed and sit on daddy's tummy. Then I'd playfully twist the several small moles that covered his chest. He pretended to be angry, sitting up quickly, tossing me off the bed. I'd giggle and dash off to put his coffee cup on the table. He'd dress and join me in the kitchen to have his usual Kaiser roll dunked in coffee milk. We talked about silly things and when he was done we'd get in the big black car and drive to the Signora's house, where I would spend the day working with Papa D'Antonio in the garden or helping the Signora cook. I was happy there; they were kind to me and showed me love, affection and a sense of family missing from my life. And the Signora certainly kept me well fed.

By the time I started school Brad was away much of the time and Sarah had to find a more reliable system for my care. She settled on a teenage girl who lived in an apartment on the first floor and attended my school. The arrangement seemed to work but resulted in a painful separation from the D'Antonios. Sarah tried to visit them on Sundays but those times got fewer and further between.

One Saturday, while Sarah was sewing and I worked on a picture puzzle, there was a loud banging on our apartment door. Mother looked frightened. She pulled me to my feet, scattering the puzzle pieces on the wood floor.

"What is it Mommy? You've spoiled my puzzle."

Sarah ignored the question and propelled me ahead of her into the bedroom. For a moment she stopped and seemed to be searching for something.

"Come! In here." She shoved me into the small closet and squeezed in after me, quickly pulling the door closed behind us. She placed her hand across my mouth and forced me deeper into the safety of the hanging clothes. The closet was dark. I was frightened.

"Why are we in here Mommy?"

Sarah clasped her hand more tightly over my mouth. I tried to protest but she would not release me.

"Be quiet Annie," she whispered. "Please, please. You must be still."

Tears ran down my cheeks but I no longer struggled. It seemed like a long time before the noise in the next room stopped. Mother tiptoed to the bedroom door and looked through the keyhole. She opened the door slowly, emitted a gasp and turned back to her terrified daughter.

"It's all right Annie. You can come out now."

I'd never seen such a mess. Drawers were pulled out and emptied on the floor. Furniture was overturned and our things scattered everywhere. Sarah sank to her knees and began to cry.

"We're going to leave here, Annie. Help me get some things packed."

With our few personal belongings stuffed into a bag, Sarah took my hand and as we had done many times before, walked the half-mile to the D'Antonio house.

We moved back into our old room but our stay there was short-lived for Sarah was determined to have a place of our own. She'd saved enough to find and furnish an apartment where we were to remain until my high school graduation. When we first moved Brad came to see us often but as time passed those visits became less frequent. On occasion he would take me for a sleep-over at Grandma Julia's house or on a weekend trip with a lady friend to Lakewood or Atlantic City. Sometimes he would stay all night at the apartment.

Then my sister, Hannah was born. I always wanted a sister, but her appearance seemed to put an end to Brad's visits. I missed my daddy and had difficulty adjusting in my new school. Isolated from friends and family I became withdrawn, developing a mature self-reliance that belied my age.

My only real friend during those years was my cousin Julie, named for her illustrious grandmother. Aunt Kate continued to visit us, giving Julie and me, who were close in age, time for girl talk while our mothers shared the latest gossip. During one such visit Aunt Kate told Mother my father was living with a woman whom he was planning to marry. Sarah was terribly upset but when I later questioned her she refused to talk about it.

Much of what happened after that conversation was lost to me but on a certain day I found myself in a large public building Sarah called a courthouse. Ushered into a wood paneled office, the walls lined with shelves filled with thick books bearing titles beyond my understanding, I sat quietly.

Alone in the dim room for several minutes I speculated on the books' contents. The door opened and a giant of a man entered the room and sat heavily in the shabby leather chair behind the large mahogany desk. He appeared too big for the seat and his black robe flowed over the arms like a river of tar.

"So you must be Anne." His voice had the deep raspy quality that acknowledged a lifetime of smoking. His gray beard was cropped short, his dark heavy lidded eyes focused on me with great intensity. He seemed ancient, older even than Papa D'Antonio.

"Do you know why you are here today, Anne?" he asked wearily.

I had trouble finding my voice but finally managed a quiet response. "I think it's because my daddy wants to take me to live with him and Gracie."

Sarah had tried to explain in simple terms, that she and Brad were not going to live together any more and Brad wanted to take me with him.

"You'll be meeting with a Judge of the Court who will ask you what you'd like to do. Then he will make a decision about where you will live. He'll try to find a way that will be best for you." Sarah had told me this hesitantly, fearing that if given the choice I would surely opt for the daddy I adored.

"That's right," the judge agreed. "Would you like to live with your father? You will still be able to visit with your mother often."

"Will he be with Gracie?" I didn't like the woman although she tried many times to ingratiate herself with me, bringing presents little girls were known to love. But I hadn't been the least impressed. Gracie was after Daddy and was just trying to please him.

"Yes, Anne. Now that your parents are divorced..."

Annie's Portion

The word divorce was familiar but I had no understanding of what it actually meant, except that it was real bad. Kids at school talked about divorce in terms that were scary. The one or two schoolmates whose parents were divorced were left out of games and very much alone at recess and lunch. Fingers were pointed at them and it was obvious they were ashamed. Besides, there were no Jewish kids whose parents were divorced.

I interrupted him in mid-sentence. "Are you saying my mommy and daddy are divorced? What does that mean?"

"It means they are not happy together and have agreed to live separate lives. It is my job to decide who you will live with and I need you to help me. Do you think you will be happier living with your mother or father?" The judge pressed gently trying to get some information that would help make his decision a prudent one.

"What about Hannah?"

"She will remain with your mother."

With eyes closed I thought about the fun times we'd had, Daddy and me; the trips in the limo, the breakfasts together, the secrets we shared, remembered the nights in hotel rooms with Daddy and a friend in the next bed, the presents I would get for my silence. What about my mother; sitting at the machine with little time for me, leaving for work each morning and coming home silent and tired. My mother, who helped me with homework, sewed new dresses for me, combed my hair into pretty curls or braids with ribbons.

The judge waited for my response. "Annie..."

Without further hesitation I looked directly at him and said, "I want to stay with my mother."

I had grown up. I was ten.

Chapter IV

1984 – Hawaii

Chilled to the bone, I sat up with a start. Bathed in the dim light of the rising moon, Sarah slept noisily in the chair beside me. I watched my mother with a sense of sadness, suddenly aware of the deepening creases in her tanned face. Slack eyelids concealed the once-bright and devilish brown eyes. The hands that lay folded in her lap were gnarled and spotted, one disfigured finger hidden under a fold in her muumuu, long nails beautifully manicured under glossy red polish.

"We've been together almost all my life yet until now I hadn't noticed how age has crept up on you," I softly murmured. "After all this time there is still so much I don't know about you—your hopes, your fears, your secrets."

Just a month earlier, Sarah decided to put old wrongs to rest while there was still time to do so and after years of estrangement invited the last of her sisters to come for a visit. Becky, who recently lost her husband, seemed genuinely glad to hear from Sarah and accepted the invitation. Two weeks later we were at the Honolulu airport awaiting her arrival.

At six feet tall and two hundred-thirty pounds there was no mistaking Becky. Sarah greeted her with a pikake lei, and the sisters allowed themselves several minutes for tears and remembrances.

With any mainland visitors, I took the longer drive home through the Like Like tunnel, knowing what the reaction would be as mountains, waterfalls and sparkling bay came into view. Never having traveled further than fifty miles in any direction from the Bronx, Becky displayed the usual delight and for the next week all seemed to go well. When

Annie's Portion

Becky asked to see the renowned Ala Moana Shopping Center, Sam offered to be their chauffeur.

I arrived home later that day to find Sam in the role of referee between two angry, shouting women. "What in the world is happening here?"

Sam pulled me aside. "Mom, you won't believe it. We were having lunch at Byron's and out of nowhere Gram started to cry. She grabbed Aunt Becky's arm so hard it left marks. Gram was really sobbing so we could hardly understand her. She said, 'You knew. You all knew and you did nothing to help me.' Aunt Becky was as stunned as I. She jerked her arm away and asked Gram what she was talking about. What did she know? I've never seen Gram so angry. She said, 'You knew Mama made me sleep with him. You knew Papa came into my bed every night. You all knew.' Mom, Aunt Becky was furious. She called Gram a liar and all hell broke loose. I had to get them out of the restaurant. They were making a terrible scene. They've been at it ever since and Aunt Becky is packing to leave."

There was no dissuading her, and the next day I drove my aunt back to the Honolulu airport. There'd been no further discussion and Becky left without fanfare. Sarah made herself unavailable for days and when she eventually came out of hiding pretended the event never happened.

Brushing my thoughts aside I moved to Sarah's chair, unable to resist the sudden urge to cradle my mother in my arms, to comfort her in some way—to try to make up for some of the pain she'd suffered in silence. I knelt beside her and laid my head in her lap.

"Oh, Mom. I wish you had told me. I wish I'd known. It would have explained so much. I would have understood."

A gentle tap on Sarah's arm startled her, she sat up quickly.

"It's okay, Mom. It's just me. We need to go in to bed."

J. Fran Baird

With my help she stood up slowly and with my arm around her we re-entered the house. Sarah dispensed with her usual ritual, slipped into her nightgown and into bed. I followed her example and was soon under the covers and asleep.

We both slept late on Sunday. There was no coffee aroma filling the house. For a second I was afraid something was wrong, a sure sign that a little of my mother's worrying had rubbed off on me. But then I heard the flush of the toilet and was satisfied all was well. We dressed, packed the things Sarah had brought, locked up the house and went out for brunch. From the deck of a charming little restaurant at Hanama Bay we watched some diehard surfers. By the time we ate our eggs and rice and finished our second cups of coffee it was nearly two o'clock and we set off for Kailua.

Monday; the start of another week, the usual routine of problem solving and hand-holding. Tuesday began with a visit to a car dealership accompanied by one of our agents, Bill Darling. When I first started at BGM he'd been one of the most vocal opponents—stirring up a furor among the agents, criticizing the company for the sudden firing of their boss and hiring this "woman." But in time he cooled down and had become one of my strongest advocates. When he heard I was car hunting he offered to accompany me to be sure I picked a good car and did not get fleeced, my being a woman and all. There was a model at the Buick dealership I wanted to try out. The salesman enthusiastically gave the keys to Bill and opened the back door for me. Bill started to correct him but enjoying myself immensely, I encouraged Bill to drive.

On more than one occasion, I'd experienced similar situations. Denied membership in the prestigious Pacific Club by reason of my sex, it took the sponsorship of the Mayor and threat of a lawsuit for the "Club" to endorse my membership. Even so, each time I brought a male client

Annie's Portion

to lunch, it was automatically assumed he was the member and I the guest. The only female member of the Exchange Club, another male dominated milieu, I endured a number of offensive episodes. I well remembered a meeting at which the Lieutenant Governor spoke, delivering several one-liners denigrating women, before he was clued-in to my presence.

We took off with Bill at the wheel as the salesman described all the features and options. Remembering that I was seated in the back he occasionally turned to describe the comfort features such as the utile, lighted mirror on the passenger side sun screen; offering as how convenient it would be for me to fix my makeup. Bill was having a hard time driving because he was choking on his laughter. I went along with the salesman's conversation, leading him on until I too could no longer contain my giggles. The salesman was puzzled by our reactions but when we returned to the lot Bill introduced me as the prospective buyer. The poor salesman turned a bright shade of pink and shrugged sheepishly. Bill and I lunched at a little Korean restaurant on Kapiolani Boulevard where we downed Kal-Bi ribs and had a great time laughing at that salesman's expense.

Wednesday was uneventful and at five Karen and I went to Compadres for margaritas and nachos. I needed to kill some time before the seven p.m. Planning Commission meeting. Karen had just gotten engaged and we reminisced about old times and the fun we'd had at company expense, in San Francisco and Carmel when we attended manager's conferences.

"Annie, you need to find a nice guy and get married," Karen advised.

"Oho, misery wants company."

"That's not true and you know it. This relationship with Hank is a dead end and now with all your kids away doing their own things you'll find yourself very alone."

"Listen, Karen. After all these years surrounded by people, I'm looking forward to being alone." I was all too well aware to a certain extent Karen was right.

"Well, you're not getting any younger."

"Ouch! Now you're hitting below the belt." We laughed and sipped another round of drinks before I checked my watch. "Oops, got to go or I'll be late for all the action." I paid the tab and we drove back to town where I parked and we went our separate ways.

Concerned about the potential for trouble, I'd spoken earlier in the week with Frances Leong, Chairman of the Commission. "Francis, I think we ought to hire some security people. The mood out there is getting pretty ugly."

"That's the last thing we want to do. It will send the wrong message, like we're trying to intimidate the public or isolate ourselves. We cannot appear to be barricaded in an armed fortress."

"What if we use plainclothes people? There's no harm in being prepared."

"They'd be spotted Anne, and that would just invite trouble."

"You have connections, Francis. Surely you could arrange for some inconspicuous muscle."

"I'll give it some thought, Anne. Thanks for calling."

The meeting room at the courthouse was filled to overflowing. I elbowed my way to the platform and took a seat at the end of the table behind one of the other Commissioners. Since I would not be voting on the upcoming issue I hoped to keep as low a profile as possible. I scanned the room to see if Francis had taken my advice but could not see anyone who even remotely resembled security. Joe Riley arrived with some of his cronies and took a seat at the end of the left aisle. I quickly looked away not wanting him to give me any sign of recognition. The meeting was called to order and after numerous attempts to

Annie's Portion

quiet the crowd Francis gave a final bang with the gavel and began to read the proposition under consideration. Many representatives of varying factions gave testimony. They were followed by dozens of interested citizens, for and against and temperatures began to rise. The most heated debate came from lawyers representing the Ohana Council amid cries of support from the Hawaiian delegation. Several of the Commission members were concerned the meeting was getting out of hand and Francis banged the gavel calling for order. Suddenly the exit door behind the area where Joe was seated flew open. A very large, angry *kanaka*, burst into the aisle shouting wildly, waving a forty five. Before anyone realized what was about to happen he pointed the gun at Joe and fired. The bullet struck Joe in the left temple, killing him instantly. A number of men rushed to restrain the shooter and in the melee several other people were shot.

"Anne, quickly. This way." Francis gripped my arm.

The Commissioners were able to leave through an exit behind the platform and did not witness further mayhem. News reports the next day described a scene straight out of Dante's Inferno. Four people received bullet wounds, two of whom were in critical condition. In the mad rush for exits many were injured and a child crushed to death. The courthouse was trashed.

Unbelievable! This was Hawaii, not some third world country. How could something so devastating happen in civilized society?

Sarah had watched the news on TV and was fearful for my safety. "You could be next. You have to get off that Commission. These people are serious and getting more violent every day."

I spent a sleepless night, as well as a troubled Thursday at home. The magnitude of the rage that laid dormant, waiting for a spark that would ignite the unstoppable eruption was astounding. After all, this was Hawaii, a place of beauty and aloha, not violence.

Friday morning I arrived at the office just past eleven, signaling for Karen to follow me and close the door behind her.

"Karen, I've got to get away for a little while. Think I'll go to the mainland for a couple of weeks. See if you can find some kind of guest ranch in the Colorado Rockies that's still operating this late in the season."

"I'll try, although I don't know why you'd pick a place like that for a break. Why not go back to California or on a cruise to someplace warm?"

"No, I want to be by myself for a while, in a quiet place so I can think. Please see what you can do."

The next hour was spent shuffling paper. Karen knocked lightly on the door and entered the room with some faxes in hand.

"Well, you've only got two choices. By October everything closes for the winter."

"What are the choices?"

"There's a really nice sounding place in Golden. It has wonderful amenities, swimming pool, spa, entertainment, good food and trail riding and stays open till November. They faxed me some info and a couple photos. The only other place I could find was in a town called Cutter Lake, at least I think it's a town. But it sounds kind of rough. There are individual cabins and no amenities at all unless you can call fishing in the lake an amenity. It's a working ranch and only has guests from July through the hunting season in early November. You take your meals in the bunkhouse with the hands that are down to a few at this time of year."

"Do they have riding there?"

"Yes. You can ride whenever you like but you need to saddle and care for your own horse."

"Book me there for two weeks."

Annie's Portion

"Anne, you don't want to go to a place like that. You'll go crazy with no one to talk to and nothing to do. Besides, it's up in the mountains and it's going to be freezing. There might even be snow and you could get snowed in."

"Karen, I know it's not your kind of place but right now quiet is just what I want. To quote Garbo, 'I vant to be alone'"

"Ok, but it's your funeral."

"Sure hope not."

The following Sunday a memorial service for Joe Riley was held at Saint Catherine's Catholic Church in Kailua. His body had been flown back to Boston for burial, accompanied by his son. Present at the service were a dozen or so friends and business associates, one of whom gave the eulogy. While I hadn't known Joe for long I liked him and found myself weepy as the priest concluded the service with the Lord's Prayer. With the communion concluded, the congregants and guests were invited to a light luncheon in the church hall. Excusing myself form the festivities I drove home where my consumption of several glasses of wine, gave Sarah an appropriate reason for calling me *shika*.

Chapter V

1984 - Denver

Thursday, Oct.11th

The plane began its descent into Denver's Stapleton Airport. The cabin attendant came around to collect glasses and garbage and to offer little hot wet towels to the passengers. I accepted one gratefully and held it over my face for a moment breathing the moist air. It seemed as though I'd been flying for days and I felt dry as a prune. The redeye flight left Honolulu at eleven-forty-five p.m. and arrived at SFO five hours later, which due to the two-hour time difference made it six-forty-five a.m. in San Francisco.

There'd been an hour-and-forty-minute lay over at SFO before boarding the Denver bound flight of two and a half hours. Another hour's time difference resulted in an ETA of eleven-fifty-five. In fact, the plane landed at Stapleton early by ten minutes allowing me thirty-five minutes to catch a puddle jumper scheduled to leave at twelve-twenty for the big city of Rifle, Colorado.

With minutes to spare and all three booked passengers on board, the pilot had an opportunity to leave early. Climbing swiftly into a cloudless azure sky the plane banked and headed for the Rockies—the grand, snow-capped chain of mountains where the great divide determined the course of rivers, west toward the Pacific or east toward the Mississippi. The pilot dipped lower as we neared the world-renowned ski resorts of Vail and Aspen, as yet snow-free, the hills clinging to the last vestiges of summer's green blanket. The scenery began to change as the plane coursed westward, colors no longer vibrant but muddy. About sixty miles east of Grand

Junction the plane began its descent into Rifle where snarls of tumbleweed blew across the runway as the plane made its way toward the hangar.

The pilot exited first and pulled down the short ladder. I took the hand he offered, alit from the plane and viewed the terrain—a bleak, dusty, sand blown semi-desert. My heart sank. There was no town to speak of, just abandoned shacks, broken-down trucks and rusting pieces of all manner of equipment.

"Good grief. What have I done? Where is the pickup van that was supposed to meet me in this God awful place?" I mused.

Dale Bennett had just finished unloading luggage. Overhearing my mumbled grousing and noting the conspicuous absence of a ride the pilot asked, "Are you expecting someone?"

"Yes I am. There was supposed to be someone from Cutter Lake here to meet me."

"Oh, yeah. The 'Bar L' folks. They're pretty reliable. I'm sure someone will be here soon. Would you like me to wait to be sure you're not stranded here?" His car was parked near the hangar but the other passengers had already gone.

"I hate to impose on you but I sure would appreciate that. What in the world happened here? It looks like a bombed-out area."

"Not quite, but it's certainly a bust area. Back in '73 and '74 when the oil crisis was at its worst, drillers came out here to extract shale oil. The cost was prohibitive but with oil and gas prices going sky high they figured they could still make a lot of money. Unfortunately for them, the shortage was short-lived and prices came down before they could reap the great reward they expected. So they just dumped all this stuff here because it was cheaper than hauling it out and abandoned this place. Pretty isn't it?"

"It's awful. There ought to be a law."

"Hey, here comes your ride." Dale waved to two men in a jeep bouncing down a primitive road.

"Well you'll be in good hands now. Have fun." Not waiting to greet them he disappeared into his car and was gone in a minute.

"Sorry we're a little late. Had a flat tire on the way. I'm Frank and this here's Sanford." A dirty hand was extended and with evident lack of enthusiasm I clasped it. Sanford sat behind the wheel grinning. "Sandy here, rip-rarin ta go."

Frank picked up the bags and put them in the back of the jeep. "We'll put you here in front with us. It's much bumpier in the back. Like, you'll be the rose between two thorns." The men both laughed as they sandwiched me between them. "Do you have a name?"

"I'm Anne Harmon." My response was less than eager.

Sandy put the jeep in gear and with a heavy foot on the accelerator we were off with a jolt. He made a quick U-turn.

"You look kinda disappointed, like. Don't like what ya seen, eh?" Frank opined.

"Well, it's not quite what I expected." I responded with visible irritation. Locked between the two cowpokes I could barely move. To make matters worse every time Sandy shifted gears his hand, intentionally or not, rubbed my leg.

"Waddya expect then?" It was Frank who seemed the more talkative of the two.

"I thought we would be in the mountains with lots of pines and aspens and more greenery."

Sandy guffawed, "Ya just wait a little while missy. Ya ain't seen nothin yet."

"How far do we have to go?"

"Oh, we should be there in about an hour or so."

"An hour!" It seemed impossible to endure that position on that road for an hour.

We began a steeper climb and the road got even bumpier. Sandy became more animated as he explained some of the geological features of the area. He pointed out animal signs, which he called spoor, and described some of the vegetation lining the sides of what was now more of a trail than a road. I noticed the scenery gradually changing. There were more juniper-type shrubs and squat trees began to dot the landscape.

Sandy talked about the flowers that could be found in abundance in late spring and early summer. "Too bad you weren't here then to see them. But you'll get ta see lotsa other great stuff. This is beautiful country."

Then it was Frank's turn to pontificate. "Wait till ya see the critters. There's a zillion deer and beaver and black bears and once in a while ya get ta see a cat."

"You mean a big one, like a mountain lion?"

"Mountain lion, cougar, panther...whatever ya like to call em."

"No wolves?"

"No, they're gone from here, pretty near extinct so I hear."

The obvious pleasure the men took in their surroundings was contagious and I soon found myself enjoying the banter and beginning to relax. Sighting a large silhouette on the trail ahead I asked, "What's that?"

"Oh that there's a coupla does. Bet there's some big buck hangin' around in them woods."

The higher we climbed the more the scenery changed and we were soon in an area covered with pinions and aspens. I inhaled deeply, exhilarated by the almost visible scent of pine. Every so often the trail left the woodlands to pass through meadows where crystalline lakes overflowed with noisy waterfowl. A smile creased my face. In a while the smile changed to a broad grin. I was delighted.

"Look a little better ta ya now?" Frank patted my knee.

I laughed, no longer bothered by the familiarity his touch inferred. Sandy began singing "Home on the Range." Frank and I joined in. We moved on to "Don't Fence Me In" as the jeep climbed upward, the pines growing sparser as the aspens seemed to take over. There were larger open spaces, no longer green, taking on the appearance of amber wheat fields. It was nearly two hours since we had started our trek and I realized how far they had come to get me.

"You guys went all that way just for me?"

"Hey, it's our pleasure. Ain't offin we get such a pretty gal out here. Specially one that ain't attached." Frank patted my knee again. I hardly noticed.

"Well," this time it was Sandy. "There she is."

We passed under a log archway where a weathered wooden sign displayed the ranch logo—a large 'L' underscored by a wide bar. Up ahead were clustered small log buildings and an elongated one standing alone, a bunkhouse. There were several fenced areas with a number of horses grazing in corrals. As we got closer to the compound a modest log ranch house came into view, smoke emanating from the chimney. Sandy came to a stop and both men got out of the jeep. Frank again offered his hand to help me out. This time I willingly accepted his offer.

"We'll leave ya here and take ya bags ta ya cabin. The boss'l show ya where it is after ya sign in."

"Hey now," Sandy called. "We're havin' a barn dance here Satday nite. Gonna be some neighbors comin'. Ya jes make sure ya save a coupla dances fer me 'n Frank here."

"I'll sure do that. And thank you both for the wonderful ride. I had a great time." They waved to me as I climbed the porch steps and used the horseshoe knocker to make my presence known.

Karol Longbranch opened the door. He was impressive to say the least—not in a glamorous way but more in the manner of the "Marlboro Man"—exuding manliness. He was tall and rangy with sandy hair and deep blue eyes, his tan skin leathered by sun and wind. One just knew he was meant to be on a horse. I could envision him riding off into the sunset on ol' paint.

He spoke quietly, "You must be Miss Harmon. Welcome."

"Thanks. And thank you for your two wonderful ranch hands. They turned an initial disappointment into a brilliant experience."

"Glad you had a good trip up. Rifle can discourage anyone. We've been trying to get them to clean up that environmental mess for years. Guess we just don't carry enough votes here. You must be tired after such a long trip—all the way from Hawaii to Cutter Lake. We should have just traded homes." He paused. "By the way, call me Branch. Everybody does." Branch smiled, showing beautifully straight white teeth. I liked him immediately.

"You can fill out the registration form tomorrow. Let me show you to your cabin now. I got the feeling from your secretary you were looking for some privacy so I've got you in one that's a bit away from the others."

He took my elbow and steered me down the stairs toward a row of cabins on the other side of the bunkhouse. "Just about a week from now this place will be as busy as a bee hive. Hunting season starts and all those great white hunters will be out in the hills chasing the deer and each other around."

"Doesn't sound as though you like it very much."

"No, not especially."

"Do you have any other guests now?"

"There's just one young couple here now, newlyweds from Wisconsin. I don't think we'll see too much of them." Branch smiled knowingly.

"Probably not." I agreed. "Where is the lake in Cutter Lake?"

"It's behind the bunkhouse, though it's not a very big lake. Lots of trout in it. We'll have to get you fishing there as long as you remember what you catch, you eat."

"Do I have to clean and cook it too?"

"No, no. We have a cook, sort of. She's my aunt. Came up from Lake Havasu with her boyfriend to help out for a while. They're quite a pair. But I'll let you judge for yourself. You'll meet them at dinner." We had reached the far cabin and Branch opened the door. As promised, my bags were already there and a wood fire was laid in the stone fireplace.

"This is just perfect."

"I hope you'll enjoy your time with us. Dinner is at six-thirty in the bunkhouse so you'll have time to rest up and get comfortable. Are you sure you won't be nervous at night with no one close to you? There are lots of unfamiliar noises out here."

"I'm sure I'll be just fine." I entered the cabin, closing the door behind me and took my first long look around at what would be my home for the next two weeks. It was a neat, uncluttered room about eighteen feet wide and twenty feet long with the fireplace in the center of the longer wall. A queen-size bed covered with a down comforter was at one end of the room and the bathroom and closet at the other end. A small sitting area, with leather love seat and armchair faced the fireplace. A floor lamp was placed next to the chair and an Indian rug pulled the whole together. Several small tables, some holding wrought iron lamps, filled the empty spaces. The walls were adorned with framed pictures of western scenery and an elk's head bearing a huge rack hung above the fireplace.

It was a comfortable place, a perfect hideaway. Clothes and cosmetics retrieved, I peeled and jumped into the steaming hot shower, lingering under the spray for some time. The cabin felt cold after the hot shower and it didn't take long for me to shinny into my jeans and sweater. I started to light the fire but thought better of it, deciding to wait till after dinner. It was past six, time to pull on the boots and head for the bunkhouse.

I discovered "bunkhouse" was really a misnomer. It was actually a general purpose building with what appeared to be sleeping quarters for the ranch hands at one end and a combination dining-recreation room at the other. The pine paneled room obviously served as the latter. One wall was divided by a pair of wooden-louvered swinging doors, next to which a row of picnic tables, placed end to end, formed the dining accommodations—reminding me of a Munich beer hall I'd once patronized. The balance of the room was open and unfurnished except for a ping-pong table and old jukebox. Folding chairs were stacked along two of the walls. Three wagon-wheel light fixtures hung from the ceiling. Branch, his Aunt Claire's friend Howard, several ranch hands and a dog named Star were already there. Claire was notably absent but sounds of banging pots were an indication of her presence in the kitchen. The newlyweds had yet to arrive. Frank and Sandy gave me the high sign and Branch greeted me with a Coors.

"Hope you had a chance to recover from your journey," he said as he offered me the beer.

"Yes, I did. I had a wonderful shower and time enough to unpack and become familiar with my surroundings. The cabin is just perfect, cozy but not cutesy."

A short, stocky woman with carrot-orange hair burst through the swinging doors. She wore an apron that might once have been white but now looked like a painter's pallet. Upon closer examination one could discern mustard, ketchup, barbecue sauce, gravy and other culinary delicacies decorating the apron canvas. Her feet were swathed in something resembling Eskimo mukluks, her hair wrapped in a pink kerchief. All in all she made quite a statement.

"You all about ready to chow down?" Her voice was gravelly as her appearance, probably the result of many years of heavy smoking. I looked questioningly at Branch.

"Your Aunt Claire, I presume."

He chuckled, "Without a doubt."

There was a general murmur of anticipation as people moved to the tables and straddled the benches. Plates, coffee mugs and cutlery lined both sides of the tables. Claire came through the doors carrying a tray filled with steaming biscuits.

"Howard, get off your butt and give me a hand, make that two hands." She laughed heartily and disappeared into the kitchen again, followed by Howard. Seconds later she was back, this time carrying a huge platter of thickly sliced roast beef. For the next five minutes, she and Howard continued to deliver bowls and dishes filled with potatoes, gravy, vegetables and salads.

When Claire made her final appearance the apron had vanished. With great difficulty she managed to get herself seated. Howard squeezed in next to me, joining the group as hands passed plates amid sounds of appreciation. About this time the newlyweds made their entrance to a round of applause. The bride blushed as they approached the table and scooted onto the bench opposite me.

"Miss Harmon, meet Mr. and Mrs. Robert Rieder of Madison, Wisconsin."

"Hi, I'm Annie. Congratulations."

"Thanks so much. I'm Margie and this is Bob."

Annie's Portion

Claire leaned across the table. "You two better dig in before there's nothin' left. Ya gonna need that energy." She laughed her raucous laugh while the rest of us were much less vocal in our responses.

Dinner was a smashing success and everyone lingered over strong, hot cups of coffee and apple pie. It was nine-thirty before anyone made a move to leave. Sandy, Frank and the other hands were the first to say goodnight, followed by Bob and Margie. The crisp air was a waker-upper and so clear the stars looked close enough to touch. The moon was at the half and lent just enough light to create shadows. I was beginning to wonder how I'd find my cabin when Branch came through the door, flashlight in hand.

"Let me walk back with you. Don't want you breaking a leg before you ever get up on a horse."

"Thanks. It was stupid of me not to bring the flashlight. I saw it on a hook by the door."

"Well, you'll remember it next time." We walked in silence not willing to disturb the quiet of the night. When we reached the cabin Branch held the light ahead of me as I climbed the stairs.

"This was a delightful evening. If all dinners are the same as this one I'll need an elephant to carry me, not a horse."

"Claire's an oddball but she is the best cook we've ever had. You can expect more of the same."

"I'll have to run five miles a day to stay in the same place. Will I be able to ride tomorrow?"

"Whenever you like. For the first few days you'll have one of the hands with you but after that, if you feel comfortable about it, you can ride alone. Goodnight, Miss Harmon."

"Goodnight and please do call me Annie."

"Goodnight Annie. See you tomorrow." Branch turned and walked down the path. I followed the light until it was out of sight.

The warmth greeted me as a pleasant surprise. The fire was burning brightly and several small lamps had been turned on. I undressed quickly and slipped into my pj's thinking of how I could just enjoy the fire and read for a while. After all, it was four hours earlier for me.

Chapter VI

1947 – Brooklyn

It was Saturday. Sarah was home and busy with her sewing as usual. "Annie, you've got to go to your father's shop and pick up our money."

The once a month trip to collect child support payments from Brad was a dreaded chore. For about two years after the divorce and his remarriage, he would occasionally put some money in our mailbox without stopping in. The deposits became less frequent and fewer in dollars until they stopped altogether.

Then, having heard nothing at all from him for more than a year, he phoned at a neighbor's; we had no phone of our own. It was summer and all the windows in our court were open. The four attached tenements that made up our complex, in Brooklyn they were called apartment houses, faced the street in an even row. The image of a solid block was deceptive because the buildings were actually U-shaped in the rear, creating a courtyard between them. Laundry lines were strung across the gap between buildings and neighbors frequently chatted, window to window, as they hung out or retrieved the wash. On this occasion Dutchie, who lived one floor higher on the other side of the court, shouted Sarah's name.

"Sarah, hey Sarah!"

My mother went to the window and waved to Dutchie. "I'm here. What's up?"

"Ya got a call."

"I'll be right there."

On her return from Dutchie's apartment she seemed troubled.

"Who was that, Mom? Was it bad news?"

"I don't know if it's good or bad. It was your father. He said he will start making regular payments providing you go to his shop to pick them up. He says that way he'll be able to start seeing you again."

"I don't want to see him again."

"We sure could use the extra money, Annie. Please do it for me."

Knowing how hard my mother worked to make those extra dollars, her request was difficult to refuse. For her it meant much needed income. For me it was the beginning of a three-year nightmare.

My father had improved his lot. He'd become a bookmaker, an illegal but lucrative and almost accepted profession. Using a rented store in Flatbush as a front, he opened a flower shop where he installed a legitimate florist named Harold to complete the subterfuge. The back of the shop became the operations center with a dozen phone lines, an odds board and a card table. A gin rummy game was part of the action and Brad would get the vigorish, a percentage of the ante of each game played.

The first few times my visits to the shop were pleasant. My dad seemed really glad to see me and Harold let me help with bits of trimming while he created lovely flower arrangements or corsages. It became a routine; spend an hour or so at the shop, visit with Harold and leave with thirty-five dollars in my pocket. Mother seemed appreciative of the money and pleased with me for agreeing to be the courier. It was too good to last. I'd intentionally avoided the back room where the clientele was less than reputable. Had she ever met them, my grandmother would have described them as "*prost*"—a Yiddish word which like so many Yiddish words was multi-purpose. The closest one could come to an accurate description was crude, coarse, unclean and unmannered. The conversations were loud, foul and filled with off-color remarks and innuendos, the later made to

Annie's Portion

embarrass me. My father seemed to enjoy the banter which angered me. Instinct told me he was not to be trusted and I avoided the back room like plague. My suspicion was validated when, during one of my visits, Brad offered to treat Harold and me to lunch and sent Harold to pick up the food. Realizing the back room was devoid of the usual mob my anxiety increased.

"Annie, you've grown into a lovely, well formed woman. How old are you now?"

"I'm thirteen."

"Oh yes. March, wasn't it?"

I nodded and started to edge away from Brad. He took my hand and pulled me toward him. "Come give your old dad a big kiss. I promise not to bite."

Not satisfied with a quick peck on the cheek he tightened his grip.

"Annie, you can do better than that. Remember how you used to come into bed with me and I'd tickle you and let you play on my chest? That was good fun wasn't it?"

"Yes, but I was little then."

The more I tried to loosen his grip the tighter it got. Brad was enjoying my discomfort. He put his hand on my small breast and squeezed gently. "Nice, but still a ways to go."

He kissed me hard on the mouth stifling my scream. Grabbing me around the waist with one hand he slid the other under my skirt and up along my thigh. I pushed him away with all the force I could muster shouting, "Stop it! Don't do that."

At that moment the bell on the front door jingled and I heard Harold's welcome voice. "Lunch has arrived. You guys here?"

Brad moved away from me quickly and sat at the card table, placing his finger across his lips. Harold walked into the back room with sandwiches and drinks and put them on the table.

"This okay?"

"Yeah, it's fine, just fine." Brad said irritably.

Taking advantage of the situation I asked Brad for the money. He counted out three tens and a five and put them in my hand.

"See ya soon, honey."

Although I continued to do my mother's bidding because she'd become dependent on the extra money the situation was detestable. Sometimes I would luck out and there would be betters and card players in the back room or people in the shop. My time with Harold, learning to trim flowers and make decorative bows, was pleasant and productive. Brad never paid without my asking for the money and I made sure someone else was nearby when I did. But there were other times, times when he became more insistent, using the payment as an opportunity to fondle me. When I protested he threatened to cut us off without a cent, promising to vilify me and deny any accusation I might make to Sarah.

Sarah dismissed my appeals and persisted in sending me for the ransom. She had to have known but never questioned me about the visits and avoided talking about Brad at all. I felt betrayed. By the time my fifteenth birthday came around I was wiser and a lot tougher, treating Brad with disdain, keeping him at a distance. Harold began to understand the dynamics and used many excuses to stay in the shop when I was there. It was as though a secret pact had been made between us. Brad fired Harold shortly before my sixteenth birthday and I never went back. Sarah no longer pressed me to go. By then I had a part time job and Sarah was making enough money at the factory to give up her weekend work. A few months after Harold was fired we heard from my aunt Kate that someone had squealed and Brad's place was raided. He got off with a large fine and probation.

Annie's Portion

Following my grandfather Morris' death in 1950, Sarah put past grievances behind in an attempt to reconcile with her eighty-year-old mother. To her surprise Fanny welcomed her overture and they developed a friendly relationship as though neither ill will nor time had ever separated them. It may have been Fanny's way of purging the guilt she felt for Sarah's mistreatment and her own failure to put an end to it, but upon hearing of my imminent graduation she had a ring specially designed with my initials and a tiny diamond. Though she'd never been out of the Bronx, Fanny was determined to make the trip to Brooklyn to present it to her granddaughter in person—no small feat.

In the early fifties, trolleys still criss-crossed those two disparate boroughs. It seemed as though every main thoroughfare was scarred by tracks and masonry stanchions marking the numerous trolley stops. Fanny boarded the "Z" car and choosing one of the lesser worn yellowed rattan seats next to the window, gazed at the passers-by until the car reached the East Fremont station. There she climbed several flights of stairs to the elevated line that would take her to Manhattan's 34th Street, an underground hub where trains from three boroughs converged. In order to get from the Inter-borough Rapid Transit to the Brooklyn Manhattan Transit, Fanny had to walk about a quarter of a mile through a series of tunnels, each displaying painted signs indicating the numerous trains that could be accessed through a particular tunnel. Finally reaching the BMT line she waited patiently, examining the reader board each time a train arrived. There were three different routes through Brooklyn. She boarded the "Sea Beach" line, which traveled underground through Manhattan and under the East River, emerging on the Brooklyn side where it continued, through concrete canyons all the way to Coney Island. Fanny however, exited at the Bay Parkway station in Bensonhurst, where I met her and walked with her another half-mile to our apartment. Her trip from start to finish took about three hours.

Fanny toted a canvas shopping bag that had seen better days. Upon arrival she proceeded to pull out all but her undergarments. First to be retrieved was a small brown paper bag which she handed to me. Inside were several strings of rock candy, a confection made mostly of crystallized sugar hardened around long strands of white cord. I'd developed a love of it when Mom and I lived with Fanny years before. There had always been a bag of rock candy in the night table between two great feather beds. Next came two glass plates and a glass bowl, a coffee cup, drinking glass, fork, knife, spoon, kosher soap and dishtowel—all carefully wrapped in newspaper. Fanny, still a strict adherent of *kashruth*, knew Sarah did not keep a kosher home so she came prepared with her own supplies. Once unpacked she visited the local grocery to buy sour cream, cottage cheese and some vegetables that could be eaten raw. This, along with a cup of coffee or glass of tea made up her diet for the three days she spent with us.

The graduation ceremony for the Lafayette High School class of '51 was no different than many others being conducted all over the city, but for Sarah and Fanny it was more than special. When I walked to the podium to accept a full scholarship to Syracuse University, the women were ecstatic. They cried and applauded loudly, calling my name in chorus. I smiled at them and held up the scroll tied with a red ribbon. Fanny was able to present her gift which I placed on my finger and have never taken off. The following day she made the trip back to the Bronx. She died two years later.

At seventeen I was eagerly anticipating the onset of fall when I would depart for Syracuse. But my leave-taking was still months away, and summer a time for celebration. Not to be outdone, the Jewish Community Center of Brooklyn held a big bash for its teenage members in their grand ballroom. The featured entertainment was a live band, performing in a style reminiscent of the "big band" era. Dressed in my finest, I joined some friends and went off to the ball. It was crowded with people; some graduates, some not, many chaperones and lookers-on. An area was reserved for dancers, the floor alive with animated teens. Feeling a tap on my shoulder, I turned to face a tall, gorgeous, guy with a great big grin.

"Hi there beautiful. Shall we dance?"

Not waiting for a reply the hunk steered me through the crowd to the dance floor. He was a great dancer and easy to follow and when the band played a Lindy hop we were a smash hit as he picked me up, tossing me over his knees and through his legs. We had no other dance partners that night. The band gave a signal the event had come to a close by playing "Goodnight Irene," and Paul Harmon asked if he could take me home.

"I mean your home not mine." He laughed.

I accepted, but insisted my friends join us. Paul joked about having his own harem as we boarded a city bus. Reaching my stop he got off with me and walked the few blocks to my house. He kissed me goodnight without encountering any resistance.

"I'm gonna see you tomorrow and the day after that and the day after that and even if we fight I'll be back. You're not gonna get rid of me."

Paul was working at Essner's Furniture Showroom, an all 'round *schleper* and delivery man. He'd dropped out of school midway through his senior year and Irving Essner had made Paul his special project, teaching him the business and training him to be a salesman. It was a perfect marriage; Essner had no sons and Paul's father was at sea most of the time. A part time job at a luggage retailer helped me stash some cash.

Paul was good as his word and we spent every free moment of that summer together. It was a wonderful season of discovery. We went to the beach, to house parties and dances, to the movies and to see our Brooklyn Dodgers. We parked at many a lover's lane and did some heavy necking and petting; in love, each for the first time. As the day of my departure for Syracuse neared Paul pleaded with me not to go.

"You don't need a college degree. You're gonna marry me and I'll take care of you."

Torn, not wanting to leave Paul yet determined to get a law degree; I gave up the scholarship and registered at Brooklyn College. Paul was temporarily appeased but unrelenting in his effort to get me to quit school. My mother was broken-hearted; sure my goals of success and self-sufficiency would never be realized.

As summer drew to a close an opportunity to meet Paul's parents materialized. His father, a merchant seaman, was on shore leave.

"My dad is back. I'd love for him to meet you before he leaves again."

Curious to know more about Paul's family, I accepted the invitation. The building, similar to the one I lived in, was about four miles from my home. But it was planted in the middle of a row of single family houses on an elm-shaded street. The Harmons occupied a four-room apartment on the second floor. Paul opened the door and with me lagging behind shouted to make our presence known.

"Hey, Mom...Dad. I have Annie here with me."

If ever there was an odd couple, Bella and Alfred Harmon were it. Alfred, who for reasons known only to himself and God, had many years earlier changed his name from Goodwin. He claimed to have been born in London but spoke with an affected British accent more suggestive of a person who'd lived in England for a while and mimicked their way of speech. He was five foot six inches tall, somewhat on the stocky side with thinning gray hair and engaging blue eyes. He was a quiet man and the only evidence of his presence was the smell of his stogies, which he smoked continuously. Bella, nee Levitz, was a Russian émigré, although she hated to admit it. She spoke four languages; Russian, Hebrew, Yiddish and a sort of English that was interspersed with one or more of the others—especially when she needed a particular word or expression unavailable to her in her more recently acquired English. She talked incessantly, the subject matter most often being the illness with which she was afflicted at that particular moment. She was four feet ten inches high and was shaped, for lack of a better description, like an inverted pear, with a bosom that extended past the rest of her body by at least six inches. Her fine hair was dyed a most unusual shade of red and her eyebrows, penciled on in matching color, slanted downward, giving her the appearance of perpetual sadness. Just how these two met and married was an enigma and remained so for all the years I knew them. But marry they did, sometime between 1928 and 1930. In 1931 they had a son whom they named Paulie, followed seven years later by a daughter who, through some quirk of fate, they named Joy. Joy was a pretty but mean-spirited child who ridiculed her parents at every opportunity and answered to them not at all. In later years she met and married a rough, tough Italian mason and despite the protestations of mother and brother, converted to Catholicism. Dominic fathered her three children and kept Joy happy by roughing her up several times each week to keep her in line.

Just as Paul said, Alfred spent many months at sea. Upon return from any such sojourn, it was customary for the seamen to be paid in a lump sum for the full length of the trip. Alfred promptly delivered his to any one of the many cashiers at Aqueduct or Belmont raceway who were only too happy to receive it. This habit would of course leave Bella broke and hungry, the remedy for which would be to admit herself to Coney Island Hospital on the pretext of some feigned illness. Paul had confided that on more than one such occasion, he and Joy had been placed in orphanages, there being no other alternative in those years, until the civil authorities could wrest some cash from Alfred's employer.

About the same time Paul and I were enjoying first love, Sarah too, was being romanced. She'd met a gentleman at Roseland, a popular dance spot in Manhattan, and was seeing him often. He loved to take her to fancy restaurants and would drive miles to some special place he'd read about. Sarah enjoyed putting on one of her best dresses and entering a fine restaurant on Ben's arm. She felt like a real lady, following a maitre'd as he led them to a table. At first she was nervous about ordering but with Ben's help she learned to choose dishes to please the palate. It was the first time in Sarah's life a man really cared enough about her to put her needs first. Her pleasure was Ben's joy. The September following my graduation, Sarah and Benjamin Stern were married in a civil ceremony at Brooklyn's City Hall. A quiet reception at our place followed.

Ben's much larger apartment in a fairly well-to-do area of Fort Hamilton became our new home. Hannah and I shared a bedroom but with my own private bath and a fabulous view of New York Bay, I was at first content. From our sixth floor aerie we could watch the ferries that still plied the narrows between Brooklyn and the rural community of Staten Island. In a few years time the view from the apartment would include construction of the Verrazano Narrows Bridge where "spinners" wove huge cables that would hold the longest suspension bridge in the world. With completion of the bridge the Brooklyn/Staten Island ferry run would be discontinued and Staten Island would burgeon into a thriving, bustling bedroom community. The best nickel's value in the city would be gone forever.

In an attempt at congeniality Ben engaged me in small talk, but we had no common interests. He doted on Hannah and she was happy to at last have a daddy of her own. It soon became apparent his limited life experiences had served to turn him into a narrow, bigoted man. After completing high school he'd worked at one retail job after another, finally saving enough to buy a half interest in a minuscule United Cigar store on Fordham Road in the Bronx. The store was open sixteen hours a day, seven days a week. Ben and his partner split the days into eight-hour shifts, alternating weekends off. Between them they managed to each earn a modest income. Paul, who had an uncanny business sense, plus the ability to do complex mathematical problems without aid of adding machine or calculator, was certain Ben's partner was robbing him blind. Ben was incensed when Paul suggested his partner was "cooking the books." It was just one more demonstration of Ben's stubborn, unyielding personality.

But in all fairness to Ben, he was wonderful to Sarah. Certain my mother did not love him; at least not in the way she'd loved Brad, she seemed to be content. From the little Sarah told me about the relationship, Ben made no physical demands of her and was happy just to have her close to him. Though Sarah averted Ben's advances, he never seemed dissatisfied. I remembered Brad saying how cold my mother was, his justification for playing around and for expecting favors from me.

On the other hand the lack of rapport between Ben and me became more evident as the weeks went by. One of the most ignorant people I'd ever known, his biases were obvious and intolerable. He despised blacks and homosexuals, bashing them at every opportunity. A fourth generation American, he did not like "foreigners," believing all immigration should be halted. When he discovered Sarah had never become a U.S. citizen he was appalled. He insisted she take the naturalization class immediately, puffing up like a proud father at her swearing-in ceremony. To Ben those others were all a bunch of "niggers, micks, polocks, wops, spics or krauts," all of whom were "ruining the country." Women were meant to stay home and take care of the kids; never having had any made Ben an expert. He was not a reader, had no interest in current events or the arts, but knew just about all there was to know about everything. I was what he called "a bleeding heart liberal." No two people could have been more ideologically different or more vocal about spouting our diverse views.

Sarah was caught in the middle whenever the two of us were in the same room. If she defended Ben, I would accuse her of desertion or worse—betrayal, such as I'd felt about Brad. When she took my part, it was Ben who would vent his anger at me. One day after an especially heated argument between the two of us, Sarah broke down and started to cry.

"I don't know what to do with you two. You are making me crazy. I can't stand it any more."

Ben, who cherished Sarah, could not abide her tears and blasted out at me.

"You rotten, selfish girl. You're ruining your mother's life. It's time you get a life of your own and leave her and me alone."

When Paul came to visit that night he found me in tears.

"I don't know what to do. I can't stand that man. He is so stupid and narrow-minded. I don't know how my mother can be with him."

"He's her husband, Annie, not yours. You just have to accept him and not respond to everything he says."

Annie's Portion

"I know. I've just got a big mouth. I'm making my mom so unhappy."

"Annie, I've got the perfect solution. Marry me now. You'll be eighteen in March and I'll be twenty-one in April. We won't need anyone's consent."

"You're crazy. How will we live? Where will we go?"

"I'm making some pretty decent money now and maybe if you get a part time job we can afford our own place."

"Maybe that's the best idea," I reasoned.

Paul was a happy-go-lucky guy, a little too carefree and irresponsible sometimes but I did love him and even though he was unpolished I believed he had great potential. Unoriginal and misguided as it was the belief he could change with my help, get some class, maybe go back to school, altered the course of my life. In the way, creating problems for my mother, Paul's offer seemed the best way out.

"Okay, Paul. Let's do it."

"Annie, I love you and I'll always take care of you. You won't be sorry."

The invitations read, "You are invited to join us at the marriage of Anne Kaufmann and Paul Harmon on May 25th, 1952..." With Julie attending as my matron of honor and little Hannah scattering measured handfuls of flower petals on the carpet before us, we were wed in a simple Orthodox Synagogue. As my father led me down the isle to meet my groom he whispered in my ear, "It's not too late, Annie. We can still turn around and walk out."

Oh how I wanted to do just that. The marriage was a mistake...so damn young. My only concern at that moment was what we would tell the guests and how we would give back the gifts. But there we were at the altar, under the *chuppa* and there was nothing else but to go ahead with our vows.

J. Fran Baird

Between the money we'd saved and the many cash gifts we received, a very common Jewish practice, we were able to rent a one-bedroom apartment in a converted single family house and buy a few pieces of used furniture. Sarah gave us dishes, pots and flatware as a wedding present and we moved into what Paul titled, "the love nest." We were happy but inexperienced. While we were courting there had been much playing with breasts and genitals and an occasional ejaculation into a freshly laundered white handkerchief, but I had come to the marriage bed a virgin and Paul just slightly more experienced. We enjoyed making love although I was the more adventurous of the two. He was unwilling to experiment and appeared shocked when I suggested we try something risqué. I began to think I'd inherited my father's traits and lascivious behavior and retreated.

There'd been no problem working full time through the summer but in my sophomore year classes were more difficult and it was necessary for me to spend a good deal of time at the college library. Even part time work; Saturdays and two evenings a week, stretched me to the limit. Paul questioned me constantly about my activities; demanding more of my time, accusing me of seeing someone else on the sly. It was a ridiculous idea.

Wounded by his accusations, I shot back. "I don't even have time to breathe never mind fool around. Besides why would I want to when I have you?"

Shortly after our argument I caught a glimpse of someone resembling Paul on campus. Seeing me look in his direction the man scurried behind a tree, my conclusion; it must have been someone who looked like him. Spotting him a second time, I was convinced it was indeed Paul shadowing me.

"I can't believe you would stoop so low as to follow me at school. What are you thinking?"

Annie's Portion

"I don't want you to go to school any more. You're just gonna get too good for me and find someone better."

We argued back and forth for hours. The arguments went on for days. Realizing how insecure Paul really was I quit school and got a full time job with ITT in Manhattan.

"Now that I'm working full time, why don't you go back to school?" I encouraged.

Paul was smart and I honestly believed he could improve himself and get into some profession. He stubbornly resisted and after a while I gave up that idea too. Once it became clear he needed constant praise and reassurance, our life together improved and soon after our second wedding anniversary I gave birth to a little boy whom we named Joshua. Paul was doing well at the furniture store. He'd been promoted to Assistant Manager and was a natural born salesman. He could charm the ladies, kibitz with the guys, delight the kids and sell the socks off all the other salesmen. With his commissions augmenting his salary we were living well and saving money. We rented a modest house on Ocean Parkway and with Paul's discount were able to furnish it tastefully. With Prospect Park and the stable nearby I succumbed to my riding passion. My old horse, Blue Eyes, was gone but there were one or two other suitable mounts.

Josh's birth brought Sarah and me closer than we'd ever been. As with Hannah, Ben loved Josh as though he were his own, bringing him toys and books from his store whenever he visited. Sarah cherished her first grandchild and Josh returned their affection. We saw little of my in-laws but once-a-month I visited Bella, bringing Josh and bags of groceries to fill her larder.

We'd settled into a comfortable routine. Why wasn't I content? Why so bored and restless? I toyed with the idea of going back to school but pushed it away, knowing what Paul's reaction would be. I'd given up on expecting any improvement in our physical relationship; in fact it had worsened with time. Paul was no lover nor had he any desire to be one. When he had the urge he just attacked. What passed for lovemaking was finished in minutes after which he would turn over and fall asleep instantly, leaving me feeling like so much used meat. A sensual woman, I was dismayed to find Paul would not or could not satisfy my physical needs. However, one did not need to reach orgasm in order to conceive. When Josh was two, I found myself pregnant again. Glad for the diversion, I hoped another child would cure my blues and fill the vacuum left by Paul's indifference. The family added Daniel to the roster in 1957.

Paul's outlet for fun and relaxation was card playing. His weekly night out was spent playing poker. Weekends he played gin rummy or more poker. Because of Paul's working and playing hours the children and I usually had dinner without him. By the time he got home we were asleep. He took no interest in his sons and his sex drive, or what passed for it, diminished further. Which was why, when Paul woke me with a rare burst of excitement following a late night poker game, he got my instant and complete attention. It was not for sex.

"I'm going into business for myself. You know that guy I told you about, Barney Levy, well he's got a great idea and we're gonna do it, go into our own business."

Still half asleep I was puzzled. "What are you talking about? What kind of business can you go into? You don't have enough money to start a furniture store. What kind of plan is that?"

"No! Not a store, a manufacturing business."

"You're crazy or I'm dreaming."

"No, listen Annie. We can really do it. We've been talking about it for weeks and we've got it figured out. Barney's in the cosmetic business. He's got lots of

Annie's Portion

connections and he says we can start our own plant on a small scale and work up."

"Cosmetics! Now I know you're crazy. What in the world do you know about cosmetics, except that they use the lard from the butcher to make them?"

"He's gonna teach me. You know what a fast learner I am. We're gonna start with just one or two items, make 'em ourselves and then add to the line as we start to make money."

"Money...what money? Where will you get it? What are you going to make? You have no idea what you're talking about."

Paul grew angry. "You never give me credit for knowing anything. You always think you're smarter than me. I'm telling you we can do it and I'm goin' for it."

Paul was as determined a man as ever there was and impossible as it seemed at the time he did do it. He borrowed some money from the bank, from Sarah and from Irving Essner. He arranged to work weekends for Mr. Essner and applied his earnings toward his loan payment. He never really planned to pay Sarah back and never did. Barney got his share of the money somehow and between them Paul and Barney leased a suitable warehouse in an industrial area of Flatbush. Barney actually had connections in the cosmetic business and managed to lease some pieces of equipment, enabling them to develop an inexpensive line of beauty products. By creating private labels they were able to sell to discount stores, beauty salons and beauty supply distributors. The product-line broadened and the money started rolling in. The unexpected success required the purchase of additional equipment and employees to operate it. There was no problem getting financing. We were living high.

Paul and Barney ordered new Cadillacs, expensing it to the business. They bought more and more toys, charging them to the company. They were two peas out of the same pod—braggarts who spent hours telling each other, or any one else who'd listen, just how great they were. Paul bought expensive clothing and a diamond pinky ring. Strutting around like a peacock in heat he bought me a two-carat diamond solitaire, topping it with a mink stole. Paul was gambling more often for higher stakes, I saw less of him and missed him not at all. The debts began to pile up, money owed everywhere; the grocer, the pharmacy, the dry cleaner, the butcher.

I had my fill, wanted out. Steeling myself for what was sure to be a cataclysmic scene I asked him for a divorce. He went berserk, totally out of control, screaming all matter of obscenities, shoving me roughly around the kitchen.

"You're never gonna leave me. You're mine and don't you ever forget it." He stormed out of the house.

Where do dreams go? How can love change so quickly to hostility and anger? Did the thought of divorce come so easily because I'd been through it with my mother? Was it really a solution? The question was answered by the attorney I consulted.

"Getting a divorce in New York State is not a simple matter. The only grounds for which you can bring suit is adultery...proven adultery. Either you catch him or he acquiesces."

Paul would never consent and as hateful as he'd become, he was no adulterer. I was inexorably stuck and forced to give up the idea, at least for the time being.

Although Paul could not acknowledge his beastly behavior, he was contrite and tried as best he could to make things right. He brought flowers and a pair of diamond earrings hoping his more amicable performance would make amends for his outburst. "I'm so sorry Annie," he pleaded. "I love you so much I can't stand the thought of losing you. I'll make it up to you, I promise. We can start again."

There were few alternatives. Hoping against hope for the best, I agreed to give it another try and for a while things did get better. Paul continued to gamble but with much less frequency and fewer dollars. He and Barney reined in their extravagant spending and business conditions improved. With the plant running smoothly Paul spent more time with the family. In a moment of jubilation he volunteered to take us on a trip. We vacationed at a resort in the Catskill Mountains enjoying the time so well we bought a cabin in a conviently close, cordial summer community.

On the Thursday before Memorial Day weekend we stuffed the car to capacity with all the gear needed for a summer interlude; linen, dishes, clothing, bedding and pets. The trip was made to the new cabin; the boys gleefully anticipating new adventures away from the city, I looking forward to the sporadic separation from Paul. In a most congenial and optimistic frame of mind, Paul declared the day to be the start of a new and better life for us all. It sounded wonderful in theory but in practice that day resulted in undreamed of consequences.

Paul could no more change his spots than the proverbial leopard. During that very first weekend he ambled over to the clubhouse where he discovered, to his undisguised delight, a group of card players who met regularly and eagerly accepted him into their ranks. Thereafter, Paul arrived early Thursday evenings, had a quick bite to eat and headed for the clubhouse to join his cronies. Friday and Saturday afternoons found him poolside, engaged in his favorite pastime. Friday evenings afforded a slight deviation of sorts, poker cards were exchanged for pinochle ones. Saturday evenings meant reunion with spouses at the clubhouse, which was reserved for a buffet dinner and some form of entertainment or dancing. For Paul Sunday was a time of sleeping late, breakfast of bagels and lox and a poolside game of gin rummy that ended at about four in the afternoon when he would head back to the city.

Josh and Danny attended a community day camp leaving me with too much time on my hands—time for musing and lamenting my fate. A nearby equestrian academy soon became an outlet for my discontent. But that still left many empty hours for which I sought diversion. The problem was resolved when several neighbors, who like me were poker widows, asked me to join them in the cardinal activity of the day, playing canasta while sipping screwdrivers. A stranger to alcohol, I all too quickly welcomed the numbing effect of the innocuous tasting drink, imbibing often. In time the proportions of the brew changed, with the quantity of vodka far surpassing that of OJ, until the destructive behavior became routine. Remaining fairly sober throughout the week, Thursday afternoons signaled a change and a large pitcher of orange juice and vodka was consumed prior to Paul's arrival. Attempting to totter back to the cabin as inconspicuously as possible I deposited myself in bed where my husband greeted me with a peck on the cheek, exchanged trousers for shorts and headed for the pool.

Josh and Danny joined Paul for dinner, sandwiches ordered from the coffee shop, after which they went their separate ways; Paul to the card table, his sons to fend for themselves until bedtime. This course of action was repeated on Friday and Saturday by which time, with a very disagreeable hangover, I began the sobering up process. Without a doubt, had I a predisposition I would have succumbed to alcohol addiction that fateful summer. But if Paul noticed my drunkenness, he never let on and since I was usually asleep by the time he got home, there was seldom any physical contact or social discourse. The few conversations we did have, led me to believe Paul was in financial difficulty again. He was desperately trying to secure additional funds to prop up the over-extended business and was working for the past months with his accountant, Matthew Gold, to find a means of restructuring and refinancing the company. Ever since he acquired their account Matt tried unsuccessfully to curb the exorbitant spending habits of Paul and Barney. During the process he became a good friend, dining with us on weekends or holidays, bringing gifts for Josh and Danny and on occasion acting as mediator. I began to suspect that Matt, a bachelor, was smitten inventing reasons to visit more often than was absolutely necessary.

When we moved to the cabin for the summer, he often made the long trip from New York, knowing his time with Paul would be limited, offering as an excuse the pressing need to obtain certain business details or signatures. But seeing me seemed to be the real impetus for his visits and finding him an intelligent, considerate man, I looked forward to spending time with him, trying my best to remain sober on those occasions.

It was during one of these occasions Matt acknowledged his true feelings. Enfolding me in his arms, overcome with emotion, he whispered tremulously, "Annie, you must know I love you. It pains me to see you like this. Leave him and let me take care of you and the kids. I'll love them like they are my very own."

Moved by his confession, so in need of some one to care for me, I clung to him desperately, responding with unsuppressed desire when he kissed me. It had been so long since I'd felt a tender touch or a gentle kiss. We made love with unrestrained abandon that day, an act that was repeated often that summer. Anticipating the delight that came with Matt's visits I no longer immersed myself in the mind numbing effect of the vodka. For the first time in my life I knew what it was like to be truly loved. Not only was Matt a tender, selfless, patient lover, he represented the kind of companionship I'd been deprived of all my life. He was my friend; sharing stories, laughing with me, crying with me, hoping for better times, refusing to accept the inevitability of our separation. But all too soon, with the arrival of Labor Day, we prepared to make the journey back to Brooklyn.

"You can't go back to him," Matthew pleaded. "I can't bear the thought of you in his bed."

"You know he will not let me go and I have no legal means of getting out." I wept wretchedly. "What can I do?"

"We'll think of something, Annie. You'll be out of there soon, I promise."

Paul brought the family back to Ocean Parkway, oblivious of the relationship that had developed between his wife and his friend, not noticing the palpable changes in my attitude or deportment.

There was an infusion of money and business improved once more. Paul was jubilant, and in a rare amorous mood attempted to engage me in sex. He pulled me close and I recoiled. When he kissed me, he found me cold and unresponsive but he was undaunted and persistent. I was resigned. I closed my eyes, knowing the odious act would be short lived, knowing there would be long periods of abstinence before Paul would approach me again.

I longed for Matthew, needed to be with him, to have him close, comforting me, providing the strength that kept my world together. For months we met infrequently, fearing discovery. There were snatched moments in the park, when we sat holding hands, making plans.

"The laws are changing Anne. You'll soon be free." Matthew encouraged.

"I can't hold out much longer. I can't abide his touch. Few as the times are, when he insists on sex I feel like I'm being raped. I'm afraid of him. He's so erratic, I don't know what to expect. Without you I'd be lost."

Annie's Portion

"I love you more than anything in this world, Anne. I will never let anything or anyone hurt you."

There were other times when contriving some pretext, I managed an escape and we met clandestinely at a seedy motel, losing ourselves in wild, impassioned lovemaking.

"Oh, Matthew, I never believed I could love anyone the way I love you," I confessed. With child-like honesty and openness I shared the fears, emotions, desires I had spent my life concealing behind a stoic façade "You complete me," I said laughing at my own use of the hackneyed expression.

It was becoming ever-more difficult to leave him and separations were unbearable. I was preparing to leave for a long anticipated rendezvous with Matt when the phone rang.

"I'm sorry, Annie, but I've got to cancel our date."

Before I could register my disappointment Matt explained he had to leave for Chicago and would be out of town for at least a week putting final touches on some merger. He signed off, promising to stay in touch often, but several days passed without a word from him. Having received no call by the end of the week I was frantic.

Distraught, my head aching and filled with all manner of absurd images, I questioned, "Why hasn't he called? Something's wrong. He wouldn't leave me hanging this way."

Looking haggard Paul surprised me by coming home from work earlier than usual. The expression on his face told me the bad news was not about business.

"What's wrong? What's happened?" I shook him violently.

"Oh, Annie…"

"What?" I shrieked.

"It's Matthew."

"Don't tell me, don't tell me," I screamed silently.

"He was on the way to O'Hare. He was in a car accident. He's dead."

An umber mist blurred Paul's face as he knelt beside me, rubbing my wrist;

"Annie, you scared the hell out of me. Are you okay?"

Our long time family doctor, Manny Thayer, took my hand. "Annie, you've had quite a shock but you're all right now. I've given you something to calm you."

The mist was evaporating. "It's not true. It can't be true. There's been some mistake." My voice trembled.

"Paul, would you please get Annie some water." Dr. Thayer sent Paul from the room. "What's wrong Annie? Talk to me."

Dr. Thayer had been Sarah's family doctor for years. He'd delivered Hannah and me, given us all our shots, taken care of me through measles, mumps, whooping cough and all the other childhood illnesses I'd suffered. He was there for Sarah through good times and bad and was as close a friend as we ever had. He sensed my reaction to the news of Matthew's death was extreme. His knowledge of human nature led him to believe there was more to the relationship than just business or platonic friendship.

I was sobbing bitterly. "I can't...Oh, dear God, let it not be true."

"It's all right Annie. I understand." My response confirmed his diagnosis. Dr. Thayer shook his head sadly as Paul re-entered the room.

"Is she going to be okay, Doc?"

"Yes, Paul. I guess he was a very good friend." He took Paul aside. "Paul, I think Anne should come into my office for a check-up. She's gotten so thin. She may be a little anemic and I'd like to run some tests. Will you see that she comes to see me?"

"Sure, Doc. I'll make the appointment myself."

Annie's Portion

Paul was good as his word and despite my protests, made sure I went for the exam. The result was indisputable. I was not anemic nor did I have any serious disorder. I was pregnant. Seven months later, my obstetrician delivered another boy into my arms.

Dr. Thayer came to visit me at the hospital. "Well, Annie. You have another boy. He's fine and healthy. There was no jaundice and no problem indicated by the blood test. He's a perfectly normal, type O positive."

To someone unfamiliar with the term "Rh blood factor," his remark would have been puzzling but its significance was not lost on me. As with my two prior pregnancies, the words "RH NEGATIVE" were stamped prominently in red on my medical records to alert the attending physicians to the potential for a life-threatening event. Rh disease, a condition known in layman's terms as "blue baby", was spawned by an incompatible genetic union affecting the baby's blood. For me, carrying an Rh-positive child meant there was a fifty-percent probability that during the delivery my antibodies would attack the baby's red blood cells with dire consequences. There was no way for the doctor to know Paul was Rh-negative too, so a sample was immediately drawn from the infant to determine if there was a need to transfuse his blood.

Up until that moment I believed the baby was Paul's. "Are you sure?" I was shaking uncontrollably.

Manny Thayer watched me helplessly. "I'm sure, Annie."

"He's not Paul's. The baby can't be positive. It can't be right. Paul's Rh-negative too."

It was Dr. Thayer's turn to be shocked. "How do you know that?"

"I remember when he went for his army induction exam. When he came home he was wearing dog tags. I asked what the letters H and ON meant. He said the H was for 'Hebrew' and the ON indicated 'O-negative' blood type. He'd served only three months because of medical issues and we never thought of it after his discharge. "Oh God, oh God! What can I do? It's not his."

"Anne, there is no reason for Paul to know. As far as he's concerned, this baby is his and it will do no good if, in order to absolve yourself, you cause great harm to the rest of your family."

"He'll find out and it will be so much worse later." I was on the verge of hysterics.

"Annie, you've been through some bad times, but you're tough. This will be our secret. No one need ever know."

My words were barely audible through my sobs, "I won't be able to do it. Every time I look at that baby, I'll be reminded of his father."

"Annie, I'm your doctor but I'm also your friend. Believe me when I tell you with time that will pass. Please pull yourself together. Don't let Paul see you this way."

"Please stay a while longer," I pleaded.

"I'll be here as long as you need me, Annie, any time you need me."

When Paul made the decision to name the new baby after our dear friend, I offered no objections.

Dr. Emanuel Thayer died one year after Matthew's birth, taking my secret with him to the grave.

Chapter VII

Friday, October 12th – Cutter Lake

I'd been dreaming and woke with a start, realizing I was crying. The cabin had grown cold, the fire extinguished; glowing embers the only evidence of the warmth it had earlier imparted. Burrowing under the warm down comforter, I drifted into a deeper, restless slumber.

The sun was well above the horizon by the time I roused myself from the warm bed. "Goodness, I've really slept late." The thought produced a smile. Back east it was always "slept late" while on the west coast it was "slept in." Hearing the phrase for the first time I remarked, "That's a really dumb expression. Where else would you sleep unless you were camping out?"

Well this day I had slept in and late and had probably missed breakfast and the morning ride. Dressing at a leisurely pace, I donned a pair of jeans, a turtleneck sweater and my well-worn boots; bought shortly after Josh was born, at a Macy's department store on Flatbush Avenue. They attracted me because of their unusual color and design. Made in true western style they sported a pointed toe, angled wooden heel and a buckle-trimmed strap across the instep. What made them so unique was the use of pink suede for the boot itself. They were on sale for twelve dollars and even though they were totally impractical they were irresistible. I'd worn them for almost thirty years; on the sands of the Middle East, the towns of Europe and Ireland and the rugged hills of New Zealand. They'd been in many a stirrup on many a horse and had been re-stitched and repaired many times. In an effort to get them clean the shoe repairman had tried to polish them resulting in their transformation to a pair of light brown leather boots, different but still as well loved. I grabbed a denim jacket and a grand five-X Stetson that Paul had given me years ago during one of his many unsuccessful attempts to win me back.

The short distance to the bunkhouse was covered quickly; to see, in western vernacular, if I could rustle up a cup of coffee. The air was crisp and heavily scented by the many pine trees lining the path. Inhaling deeply the cold mountain air fill my lungs, so different from the warm moistness of Hawaii. It was wonderfully invigorating. "I'm going to love it here."

The bunkhouse appeared deserted but hearing the noise of clattering dishes I followed the sounds into the kitchen where Claire and Howard were discovered, doing the cleanup chores from breakfast.

"You're late, Annie," Claire spouted in her gravely voice. "Well," she laughed, "Pull up a chair and we'll see how we can fix ya up."

"Oh, please don't fuss Claire. A cup of coffee will do fine."

"It's gonna be a long time till lunch. Better have a bite of somethin'." With that she put a plate of biscuits and a mug of steaming coffee on the table in front of me. "Sure ya don't want some bacon and eggs? Won't take but a minute."

"No thanks Claire, this is just fine. Good morning, Howard."

"Good morning to you Miss Annie. Guess ya slept ok."

"Sure did. That bed was so comfortable and toasty warm...just couldn't pull myself out."

"Well ya missed the ridin' group. Those newlyweds actually got outa bed and went fer a ride with Frank. But if ya like ya kin come with me to check the salt lick."

"What is it you do with a salt lick?"

Annie's Portion

"We have a place out in the woods in a little clearing where we put a salt lick for the deer. Then the folks kin hide behind a log till some deer come fer the lick and they kin get some real up close pictures."

"Oh, that sounds like a great idea." I took a last sip of coffee. "I'll just go grab my camera and be right back."

Claire gave Howard a dirty look and grunted. "Always somethin' ta keep ya from workin'."

"Now Claire. I'll only be a short while and it'll give Star a chance for a walk."

"Well ya ain't gonna see no deer with that dern dog there."

"She's quiet as a lamb. Knows exactly what ta do."

"Don't ya be too long." But Howard was already out the door.

When I caught up with Howard he was by the corral. We walked toward the lake, Star following on my heels.

"Seems she likes ya and she's pretty fussy bout the people she takes ta."

Star sat at my feet, waiting for a pat. It was obvious why she got the name. She was black and white and looked like she had a good deal of Australian sheep dog in her. Right above her nose was a white star, so perfect it looked as though it had been painted on. Walking in silence we entered the woods, stepping over fallen trees, crushing leaves beneath our feet. The salt lick sat in the middle of a clearing. Howard signaled for me to drop behind a large rotting log. He knelt down beside me and Star pushed her muzzle between us. We'd been in that position for about twenty minutes; my camera at the ready, when two does entered the clearing and headed for the salt lick. Positioning the camera quietly I managed to snap one shot when suddenly, Howard moved behind me. He reached under my arms with both hands and grabbed my breasts while kissing me on the neck and muttering incoherently. The first reaction was shock, but suddenly realizing how ridiculous the situation was, I began to giggle. The chuckles morphed into raucous laughter, tears rolled down my cheeks. Star began barking and nipping at Howard's feet. The deer did not stick around to watch the show but went dashing back into the woods. Poor Howard, who'd backed away from me at Star's insistence, stood looking embarrassed and insulted.

Poor Howard was in need of consolation. "It's okay, Howard. I know you didn't mean any harm. This will just be our little secret...so long as it doesn't happen again."

He just nodded in agreement and made a beeline for the path with Star still barking behind him. By the time Star and I returned to the corral the riders had returned and were unsaddling their horses. Still smirking I went to greet them.

"Hi, cowboys! Have a good ride?"

"Hi, Annie. Yes it was great but I'm sure we will feel it tomorrow." Margie winced as she pulled the blanket off Casey.

"Don't know how ya kin tell." Frank muttered.

The *sotto-voce* remark revived my grin. "How about you Bob? You good?"

"Yeah Annie, it was a great ride. Sorry you didn't join us. Lots of beautiful country. We got some terrific pictures."

The mention of pictures brought on another fit of giggles. "I'm going to see if I can ride after lunch. Want to do it again?"

"No thanks!" Margie and Bob said in chorus. "Maybe tomorrow. We'll try some fishing this afternoon," Bob added.

Claire was on the porch, rattling a big spoon around in the steel triangle hanging from a beam above her head.

"Come and git it. No time like the present and him who's last loses."

Annie's Portion

In great good humor, like a bunch of juveniles, we lined up at a water trough where we splashed water on ourselves and at each other. Lunch was a more simple meal than dinner had been but just as satisfying. There was a hearty homemade soup and stacks of sandwiches lined up on the sideboard. Salads, relishes, drinks, cookies and lemon bars rounded out the menu.

"Good grief we're going to roll home."

"No one's gonna accuse me of starvin' em," echoed Claire's response from the kitchen.

"I've got to start getting some exercise to burn some of this food off. Frank, do you think I can get in some riding this afternoon?"

"I'm sorry I can't go with ya pretty lady but one of the other boys will be happy to have that chance. Two o'clock be okay?"

Hoping my afternoon would be more productive than my morning and somewhat more predictable, I replied, "That'll be just fine."

Branch was noticeably absent as I strolled to the corral where several mounts waited at the hitching rail. Star appeared and sat beside me as I scanned the fenced pastures where clusters of horses grazed untethered. In one of the smaller, more isolated pastures a lone horse stood attentively, inviting my interest; a golden palomino stallion with a long, white tail and mane and white boots on the forelegs. It was uncanny. He was a mirror image of Blue Eyes.

"Impressive, isn't he?" It was Branch.

"Oh, hello. You startled me. I was just thinking how much he resembled a horse I used to ride years ago. Yes he is grand."

"Difficult too. He's got a mind of his own. He's a *mesteno*."

"You mean he's a wild mustang?" My excitement was all too evident.

"Yep, he sure is. About as wild as they come."

"How did you get him?"

"The BLM. rounds up a number of these wild mustangs every so often to thin out the herds. They keep the young pretty ones who are more adoptable and auction them off. I go down to Canon about twice a year to see if there are one or two that look interesting."

"I didn't know there were wild mustangs in this part of the country. From the little I've read about them I understood them to be a bit squatty. He seems fairly tall."

"There are quite a few here in western Colorado. There's a refuge area just north of Grand Junction. A fair sized herd makes it their home. As a matter of fact, they've brought in some wild pintos and palominos from other places to add to the stock, makes their colors more interesting. Sandwash Basin, over near the Dinosaur Monument, shelters a couple hundred real colorful animals. They're bigger than most too. It might have been where Beau here was raised."

"So that's his name, Beau."

"Well that's what we call him but he sure doesn't respond." Branch grinned. "Got a mind of his own, that one does."

"How old is he? Will you geld him?"

"Not sure of his age...three maybe four. No, no gelding for him, at least not yet. They would have done the job at the Canon facility if I'd wanted but he has so much spirit, didn't have the heart to take that away from him. It's kind of an interesting place. The animals are trained by inmates from a minimum security prison. They sort of take to each other, I hear."

"Really? That's neat. But won't Beau be difficult to manage and train the way he is?"

"Uncut you mean." Branch laughed. "Probably, but I'm hoping we can gentle him just enough to make him useful without breaking his spirit. If he doesn't respond after a few months, we'll have to geld him but I'm sure hoping that won't become necessary."

"Why Branch, you're just a sentimental softy."

"Guess so. But don't go telling anyone and ruining my reputation. You going to ride today?"

"Hoping to but I seem to have gotten a late start."

"I'll get one of the hands to go with you. You can still get a couple of good hours in."

Branch walked toward the stable area, from the rear the slight bow of his long legs obvious. To be honest, my thoughts were less than modest. The man was born to ride.

Minutes after Branch's departure Pete appeared, leading two saddled horses from the stable. Somewhat disappointed I thought, "Too bad." But since I hadn't mentioned my preference to saddle my own mount there was no one to blame but me.

"Hi, miss Anne. Ready to ride?"

"Just the two of us?"

"Yup. Looks like you get the special treatment. Me." He laughed and handed me the reins of a pretty Appaloosa mare.

Mounted and waiting for Pete to lead off, I noticed Beau trotting my way. He was no more than ten feet from the fence before he came to a halt and stood directly in front of me, pawing the ground and bending his head as if in greeting.

"Why hello Beau, you wondrous thing. I wish it was you I was riding."

Pete heard me. "You don't want to be on that fella's back. He's a wild one. Won't even let Branch near him and Branch is the best horseman around."

"He can't be all that bad. Look how he came to greet me."

"Just came to greet this pretty mare, is all." He gave a couple of clicks and both horses trotted off. Ginger took off without a signal from me giving rise to concerns the equines were already conditioned to trail riding and would afford little opportunity for a good ride. I made a mental note to question Branch about it and to ask for a more spirited animal for future rides.

Star ran in front of us as we ambled across a green meadow. Several times she circled back to position herself on my right flank before dashing ahead of us again.

"Looks like you made a real friend there."

Howard came to mind. "I think she wants to protect me from myself."

A copse of golden aspens appeared before us, shimmering in the late afternoon sun like a desert mirage and we intruded on its stillness for a brief moment. Then a wide expanse of yellow grass opened before us.

"Care to canter a while? This is a real good place for it."

"Love to." The slight increase in Ginger's pace was hardly noticeable when I pressed my heels against her flank. More forceful the second time, the mare took off at a quick canter; further insistence produced a gallop. For a few exhilarating moments we sped across the open field, Star barking behind me.

"Come on Star. We'll wait for you."

Pete caught up with us too. "You ride real well, Miss Anne. Next time we'll get you a horse with a little more spunk."

"Hoping you'd say that."

We rode on at a gentler pace through open meadows dotted with pinion pines and families of aspens. About half a mile into a piney wood Pete pointed to a beaver dam on a rapidly flowing stream, the water frothy white as it reached the diversion. Many of the trees in the surrounding area bore signs of the diligent critters. I reined in my horse and waited for a few minutes hoping to catch sight of one. The

Annie's Portion

only sounds were those of the horse's hooves. Pete had slowed his horse to a walk but was almost out of sight.

"Well Ginger, the birds must have all left for southern climes. A sure sign that winter's on its way. Let's go catch Pete."

With a few clicking sounds and a gentle prod Ginger moved off at a trot. Suddenly, a large fully-antlered stag ran across the trail in front of us. Unprepared for the reaction of my startled mount who came to a sudden stop and reared, I was thrown from the saddle and made a hard landing, rolling quickly out of the way of Ginger's dancing hooves. Up ahead Pete heard the commotion and raced back in time to see the tail end of Ginger who'd made a beeline for home.

"You all right, Anne?"

"Yes, embarrassed but unhurt."

Pete took off at a gallop to retrieve Ginger. Salvaging my expensive 5X Stetson, brushing the leaves from my jeans, I walked back towards the dam site. A small tree fell with a crash on the path in front of me. Seconds later a large brown ball trailing a furry paddle, shuffled hurriedly to the leafy end of the tree, from where his rat-a-tat gnawing could be heard. Transfixed by the beaver's seemingly endless industry I hadn't noticed how late it was. By the time Pete returned with my horse the sun was beginning its descent.

"Sorry it took so long to get this ornery so and so. She just got to goin' home. Are you ready to mount up again?"

"Yes. I feel like a damn fool, letting her get away from me like that."

Pete laughed. "It happens to the best of us. We'd better get a move on. Don't want to be riding around in the dark."

We urged our horses on, this time with me sticking close to Pete. It was dusk as we entered the corral and dismounted.

I tied Ginger and unbuckled the cinch, removed the saddle and blanket and laid them over the rail.

"You go on and get ready for dinner Miss Anne. I'll finish with these fellas."

"Thanks Pete. It really was a great ride, fall and all."

"I think you're gonna be a little sore tomorrow."

"You're probably right. But it'll be a good reminder to keep a better seat."

By way of the fenced pasture where Beau had been sighted earlier, I made for the cabin; pausing at the rail, hoping to catch sight of the golden palomino. It wasn't long before his shadowy silhouette was detected, no more than thirty feet away, watching me.

Not wanting to scare him off I whispered. "Why don't you come closer? I won't hurt you. Ah, there you are, you beautiful creature." He flicked his ears and took several measured steps in my direction. "Come on Beau. Aren't you lonely out there? Come and visit with me for a while."

At this hour the only glow came from the bunkhouse windows. He stopped and for a brief moment I glimpsed reflected light in his eyes. Coaxing, tempting him to get closer, his scent was palpable; his warm breath touched me as he gave a contracted snort.

"Ah, you did want to visit. You're as curious about me as I am about you."

He backed away, the movement of his ears an indication of uncertainty. The bunkhouse door opened suddenly and just as suddenly Beau was gone.

"Where is everybody?" Claire's dulcet tones rang through meadow, corral and barnyard. "My good dinner is waitin' fer ya."

The feel of Beau's breath on my face lingered and I hadn't realized how cold the night had become. The trough provided the means for a quick cold wash and the warmth of the dining room was welcome.

Annie's Portion

As usual dinner was good and the animated conversation turned to my escapade as embellished by Pete. He made me sound more like a heroine than a careless rider.

It was my turn to praise him. "Don't believe Pete. He's the real hero."

There was applause all around and Pete blushed, initiating a bout of laughter. Once the coffee and desert vanished the group began to depart.

"I see you forgot your flashlight again." It was Branch who had edged up beside me.

My pulse quickened. "Oops. Guess I did. Came straight from my ride without stopping at my cabin."

"But you found time to make another stop."

We were outside, walking toward the row of cabins. Saddened by the thought my private moment of intimacy with Beau had been observed I turned to face Branch. "You were watching me." It was more of a statement than a question.

Sensing my displeasure Branch tried to reassure me. "I had no intention of prying Annie...just happened to be on my way to the bunkhouse and saw you standing at the fence. I knew any movement would startle Beau so I waited and watched. You certainly worked your magic on him."

"I'm sorry. I didn't mean to sound offended. I was just kind of surprised to find out someone else was there."

We'd reached my cabin. "Good night, Branch. Thank you for seeing me home again. I'll try to make a point of having my light with me next time."

Not waiting for his response I opened the door quickly and entered the room where once again, a fire was burning brightly in the grate.

Saturday dawned misty and chill, a forewarning of the early onset of winter in the Colorado Rockies. A thin coat of rime had transformed the aspen leaves into sparkling gold coins. I pulled my jacket tightly around me as I headed for the bunkhouse, the ground crackling beneath my boots. Gray smoke wafted lazily from the bunkhouse chimney, dissolving into the low-lying clouds. The myriad aromas emanating from the kitchen caused an immediate olfactory response, propelling me to the breakfast table where Margie and Bob were already seated.

Without hesitation I filled a plate with eggs, hash browns and a thick slice of sugar cured ham.

"The anticipation of Claire's outstanding cooking makes vultures of us all," Margie mumbled through a mouth full of pancakes.

Pushing a plate of steaming biscuits toward me Bob commented, "It's sure nippy out there this morning."

"Well, if we keep eating like this, we'll put on enough fat to keep us insulated through the winter," Margie added.

There was a curious absence of our chef and her assistant. "Where is everyone this morning?"

"Been and gone, I guess. Busy getting ready for the big hoe-down," Bob answered.

"Oh, that's right. I'd forgotten the dance tonight. Guess I'll have to get out my best bib and tucker. By the way. What is a bib and tucker?"

Margie grinned. "I think the bib is that thing on the top of coveralls. You know, the part with the straps and buckles."

"And the tucker?" I pressed.

"That's what yer plumb out of after ya danced a few." Claire had come through the swinging doors with a thermos of hot coffee.

"Good morning, Claire. As usual breakfast is onolicious. By way of explanation, that's a Hawaiian word—ono, meaning good and licious is the back end of dee. But really Claire, what is a bib and tucker?"

"Well, like Margie said. The gents wear those overalls with them buckle things on top. Them's the bibs. The

Annie's Portion

tucker is a lace scarf the gals wear 'round their necks and tucks in."

"Guess you've got to get a pair of those things, Bob. And we ladies will have to figure out how to tuck." Margie was enjoying herself immensely.

"Never you mind. You all better get yerselves outta here now so us workin' folks kin git to it. Gonna be a skinny lunch and a late dinner. If you're goin ridin', I kin pack ya a lunch 'stead of ya commin' back here fer it."

"What do you say guys? Sounds like a good idea."

Margie and Bob agreed.

"Ya jest gimme a few minutes and by the time ya saddle up, I'll have it ready."

I'd left strict instructions Karen was not to contact me unless there was a dire emergency. My friend Rose had come from Kaneohe to stay with Sarah for the duration of my trip but well aware Mom would fret and fuss until she heard from me, I needed to call home.

"You jest come into this here kitchen and do your callin', Annie."

Rose answered the phone on the fourth ring. Sarah had gone on her bike to the grocery and all was well. We spoke for a few minutes and I assured her I was enjoying myself immensely. Duty dispensed with, I thanked Claire and rejoined Margie and Bob who were headed for the corral.

"Fabian," Bob called to one of the hands.

"Buenos dias, señor. How can I help you?" Fabian was three parts Mexican, one part Anglo and spoke with a distinct accent. He was one of the *mestizos* who worked at the ranch year round.

"We'd like to ride this morning, if it's all right," Bob said. "We know you're kind of busy with the party and all but we can probably go by ourselves."

"I will get the horses ready but I will check with señor Branch as soon as he comes back to see if he will let you go alone."

We thanked him and walked to one of the pens where Sandy and a couple of other ranch hands stood watching some activity in Beau's pasture.

"Hi, Sandy."

"Hi, Miss Annie. Good mornin' ta ya all. A little cool today."

"Brr, yes," I said with a mock shudder. "What's happening?"

"Beau's gonna have his first lesson. Branch and a couple of the boys are out there. Gonna herd him inta this here pen. Least wise, that's what they're hopin'."

"Looks like he has other ideas," Bob said.

The unmistakable sound of horse's hooves could be heard. Several riders appeared to be driving Beau across the pasture toward an open gate in the pen. Instinctively, he employed every innate or learned technique to elude his pursuers. He sped across the pasture, halting suddenly and rearing, charging his would-be captors—agitating their mounts before dashing away and spinning on his rear legs in order to execute a spectacular change of direction. I watched the persistent struggle for ten minutes, recognizing Branch as one of the horsemen. Beau was tiring. He was stopping more frequently to fill his lungs. At one point he stumbled and I emitted a loud gasp.

Using their lariats to spur him on Branch and Pete had Beau headed for the enclosure. A sturdy, wooden slide-bolt secured a high, ten-foot wide, mesh-covered gate, providing access from the large pasture. Frank was waiting at the gap and seconds later Beau was penned, head down, breathing heavily, pawing the ground. My eyes welled with tears. Branch and the other hands dismounted near the stables and unsaddled their exhausted horses. Branch strode to the

Annie's Portion

corral, which I estimated to be roughly fifty feet square and about eight feet high. A woven wire screen stretched around the perimeter of the split rail fence. Though open to the sun and weather, tall trees provided patches of shade and it was in one such spot Beau had sought refuge.

At some moment during those few minutes of struggle, Branch slipped off the pedestal I'd built for him. After taking a large swig of water my fallen hero was headed my way.

"Oh Beau, I'm so sorry." The horse lifted his head and flicked his ears. His sides were still heaving and white foam covered his flanks. I was angry. "Did you have to treat him so harshly?"

"If we're ever going to control him Annie, we have to break him. This pen is designed to make the job as easy as possible."

Pointing to a post about six feet high protruding from the ground at one end of the pen, I asked what it was used for.

"It's a snubbing post. We use it to teach the bronc to stand tied...that is if we can ever rope him. Using the post gives the horse a three-hundred-sixty-degree area to move around in so he can't injure himself if he tries to pull away. If you look closely, you can see a deep notch cut into the post about four feet up from the ground. That will keep the rope from sliding down."

Afraid to speak lest I reveal my highly emotional state, I nodded. Beau seemed to have gotten his second wind but was standing quietly observing the two of us.

"Guess I've put this off as long as possible." Branch picked up a long, straight pole, slightly thicker than a broomstick. It had been leaning against the fence. He made a loop in his lariat placing it in a notch at one end of the pole. Then he stretched the rope along the length of pole, holding it tightly near the other end. He lifted the U-shaped latch protruding from a narrow, double-hung man-gate close to where he and I were standing. With measured steps he entered the pen, securing the latch on its pin behind him.

"It's okay, big boy," Branch said softly. "No one's going to hurt you. You just stand quiet and with a little cooperation, we can make this easy on both of us."

Beau took a step back. His ears were straight up, not a good sign. Branch stopped to give him a chance to calm down. Then, ever so slowly, he tipped the pole, allowing the loop to hang free at the far end. Branch circled the horse cautiously while Beau followed him with his eyes. Branch moved closer to Beau's flank, all the while talking softly. I could not hear what he was saying but the *mestino* seemed calmer.

"Oh, Beau, do behave," I thought. "It will be so much better for you...and Branch."

Branch was edging closer to Beau by inches. When he was within the pole's length of Beau's neck, with one swift motion he dropped the noose over Beau's head and grabbed the rope letting the pole fall to the dirt. The angry animal reared, momentarily lifting Branch's feet off the ground. Branch pulled hard on the rope and dug his heels in. Beau tried to pull away but each time he did, a strong, sharp pull on the rope jerked him to a stop. Branch stood his ground and within minutes Beau was once again quiet. Branch loosed the rope. Beau, feeling the slack, tried to back away but Branch yanked the line. This act was repeated several more times until Beau finally seemed to settle down. Branch approached the horse from the side, still keeping firm hold of the lariat. Then, talking softly, he reached his hand out and gently patted the mustang's neck. The horse flinched but Branch kept a tight grip on the lariat and after a few seconds had passed, ran his hand down Beau's neck once more. This time Beau remained quiet, letting Branch stay close, getting his scent. Deftly removing the lariat Branch turned and walked slowly back to the gate. Once outside he

Annie's Portion

took my arm and led me away from the pen. Disinclined to leave, Branch's firm grip gave me little choice.

When we were out of earshot he said, "That wasn't too bad, was it?"

"No. It was easier than I thought it would be."

"Sure, easy for you. But I tell you Annie, he's smart. He got the message real quick."

"What's next?"

"We'll keep him in the pen for a bit and try the routine again. It's a slow process. But each visit will be a little longer with more physical contact until he realizes that we aren't going to hurt him."

I told him of my planned ride and hurried back to the bunkhouse to pick up the lunch basket.

"I'm so sorry we didn't get right back, Claire."

"That's okay, Annie. I figured you was watchin' that bronc. Kinda got a love affair goin'."

For a brief moment I thought she meant Branch.

"I put a couple apples in there," Claire said pointing to the basket. "He might like one or two."

Claire was referring to Beau although she had a funny smirk on her face.

"Thanks again, Claire. I'm sure he'd love a bite from the apple."

Branch had insisted Fabian go with the eager trio and he led us in a new direction; tracing the road to Rifle for about half a mile before turning off through some pines and across an open meadow. My replacement mount was Samson, a spirited gelding who having been unexercised for several days was raring to go. I'd been keeping a tight rein on him in order to stay alongside Margie and Bob.

"Do you mind if I let Samson out for a run? He's really of a mind to let off some steam."

"No Annie, not at all. You go ahead. We'll just plod along behind," Margie replied.

"Keep your horses reined or they're likely to follow Samson," I cautioned.

Fabian moved between Margie and Bob taking hold of both their reins. "It's okay, Miss Annie. You go now."

Samson needed little encouragement. As soon as the reins were eased, a clicked of the tongue sent him off at a gallop. With thighs gripping his ribs tightly we raced across the amber meadow, the full force of the wind in my face. Reaching the base of a rise I turned him and headed back toward my companions. Samson was breathing hard, his flanks gleaming with sweat. He was satisfied to trot quietly beside Margie's horse, Casey.

"That looked so exciting, Annie. I wish I could ride like that, but I'm really just a coward."

"It just takes time, Margie. Time and practice."

We'd reached the hill and Fabian guided us to a narrow but well traveled switchback trail leading to a ridgeline that seemed to run in an east-west direction for many miles. Opting for the easterly route we snaked our way for several minutes, before passing through a small copse of aspens. Below us lay a vast expanse of golden meadow, framed by the snow-capped mountains. Low-lying clouds had melted away, leaving a topaz sky dotted with puffs of white cotton.

There was a mutual murmur of appreciation. Fabian dismounted and we three followed suit. Silently, he pointed below where a heard of elk grazed contentedly on the autumn grass. There were at least a dozen of them, the bull elk standing regally aloof and apart from his harem and calves. Fabian laid out a blanket and we sat down to enjoy the exquisite panorama, the good food and pleasant camaraderie of new friends.

We'd been out riding when Branch made his second visit to the pen that day, trying unsuccessfully to get a halter on Beau. I returned unaware of Beau's lack of progress

Annie's Portion

but before going back to my cabin to change, Star and I went to say hello to him; me with an apple which he at first ignored then cautiously took from my outstretched hand. Delighted with the outcome of my first approach, I returned to the cabin where the fire burned brightly in the hearth. The air outside had cooled rapidly with the setting sun and the warmth was a welcome luxury.

Sore muscles begged for relief. I'd forgotten how many places could hurt after a strenuous workout. Allowing myself a mere ten minutes in the steamy shower, I rubbed my mollified body dry and doused myself in moisturizing lotion. A blow drier put some curl back into my hair and the daubed on war paint completed the restoration project. The roar of motors and unmistakable sounds of a spirited group of revelers reminded me company was coming. I slipped into a fresh pair of jeans, denim shirt embroidered with my initials and a navy blue, fringed suede vest. My dusty boots got a quick wipe and after a satisfied look at the finished product, I grabbed my jacket and made for the door. The flashlight was not in its usual spot. Its disappearance was puzzling but with a shrug thought no more of it, braved the cold and made for the party.

During the absence of the three guests the bunkhouse had been transformed. Strings of colored lights hung from the ceiling and framed the windows. The long table had been disassembled leaving two near the kitchen to serve as a buffet with others placed strategically around the room. All were covered with colorful cloths and adorned with small, brightly lit lanterns. Chairs that had been stacked along the wall were unfolded, providing adequate seating for all the newly arrived party-goers. A dozen or so wooden pallets were laid flat next to the wall facing the door, forming a bandstand on which stood two speakers, a couple of drums, and a bass. Four musicians dressed in their best bibs, neckerchiefs and well-worn cowboy hats were in conference in front of the platform. One very large, bearded fellow had a guitar hanging from his neck and another, much slimmer but also bearded was obviously the fiddler.

Excusing himself, Branch abandoned a group of people he was visiting with to greet me.

"What do you think of the transformation?" he asked.

"Oh, Branch. It's wonderful. Where did all these people come from?" There had to be at least two dozen.

"They're folks from other ranches close by. We have this hoe-down every year just before hunting season opens."

"When you say 'close by', what does that mean? Your ranch stretches for miles in every direction."

Branch laughed. "Out here it can mean twenty, thirty miles."

"Do they all come up that road from Rifle?" I asked in disbelief.

"Some do but there are other trails big enough for jeeps or four wheel drive vehicles. They'll spend the night here, in the bunkhouse and cabins."

Just then the band, having agreed finally on the tune they would play, sounded off. What they may have lacked in talent they made up for in noisy enthusiasm. The fiddler began calling out the steps of a square dance and folks were forming up. Frank approached me.

"Remember your promise, Miss Annie?" He extended his arm and I graciously took it as he led me to the dance floor where we do-si-doed until I was out of wind.

"Please, please. I need to catch my breath."

"I'll let you go but I'll be back."

No sooner had he left when Sandy grabbed me for the next dance. He swung his partner, circled left, circled right and skipped to the center after which I collapsed into a chair.

"Now Miss Annie. Don't tell me you're all tuckered out already. The night is young," Sandy teased.

Annie's Portion

"The night may be, but right now I'm feeling like an old nag," I smiled and wiped my brow in mock distress.

"Hey, you guys. Give Annie a break," Branch came to my rescue. "How about a drink Anne? There's an ice cold keg over there just waiting for us."

"Sounds wonderful." With his arm about my shoulders we skirted the dancers. Spotting Margie and Bob, who were right in the middle of things, I gave them a thumbs up.

"They sure are having a good time."

"And you? Are you having a good time?" Branch was more serious.

Before I could think of a response the fiddler stepped to the microphone. "This one's for all you sissies. We'll give ya'll a break and play somethin' slow so's ya kin cool down."

"May I?" Branch slipped his arm around my waist as he steered me through the other dancers.

Warmth spread over me and I wondered if he could sense it. He put his face closer to mine.

"You sure do smell good, Annie."

I smiled at him, feeling like a deb at a first dance. We didn't speak again until the band quieted.

"Now for that drink." Branch made his way to the beer cask with me following behind him, my hand in his. "Are you hungry? There's lots of good stuff on the buffet."

I shook my head. With a lump in my throat and a thumping heart, I was not hungry. The band took a break giving Branch an opportunity to introduce me to some of the other guests.

"You sure this gal ain't teched in the head? Leavin' that warm Hawaii to spend cold nights here in the mountains." Lou Marsten chided.

"Now Lou. Don't you go pestering this lady. She knows this is the best place in the world. Right Annie?"

"It sure is. Besides Lou, it must be good. You're here too."

They all chuckled. I felt like a fool.

"Gonna be here long?" Lou asked.

"Another ten days."

"Then you're gonna get to see those huntin' fools before ya leave. Best wear a bright red shirt and watch out some jackass don't mistake ya for a nice little doe."

"I'll be sure to stay out of the way," I shouted as the band struck up another reel.

The evening passed swiftly, with me dancing often, although to my mind not often enough with Branch. I'd downed several beers but no food and was slightly tipsy by the time the band played the old standard, "Goodnight, Irene." I was in his arms again, leaning heavily against him.

"Are you tired, Annie? Shall we head for home?"

"Uh huh, I think that's a good idea."

We said our goodnights as we made for the door where Branch helped me into my jacket.

"Did you bring your flashlight?" he asked.

"Couldn't find it. It wasn't on the hook. I don't remember..." Branch took the flashlight from his pocket.

"Snitched it. Wanted a sure excuse to take you home."

The night was cold but with Branch's arm around me I felt warm all over. We walked in silence, the air no longer as fragrant with pine as it had been before the frost. He walked up the steps with me and opened the door to the cabin.

"Will you come in Branch?"

"Don't think it would be a good idea tonight." He stepped just inside the doorjamb and took me in his arms. I was trembling as he kissed me long and hard.

His voice was husky. "I'd better go Annie. It was a lovely evening."

"For me too."

He kissed me again, this time less ardently. "Goodnight."

Through the closed door I listened to his footsteps on the stair, realizing he'd taken the flashlight with him.

The chatter at the Sunday breakfast table was noisy and animated, each one trying to be heard between bites, over the din of clattering dishes. Several of last night's guests had joined us. Branch banged a spoon against his coffee cup in an attempt to get the attention of the boisterous group.

"You've got a couple of hours to play or fish or lounge but remember, today being Margie and Bob's last one with us, will be special. We'll meet at the corral at eleven to saddle up. Bring some warm gear because we'll not be getting back till dusk and no complaining about the long ride."

Margie and I were like a pair of curious cats. We bombarded Branch with questions and when he refused to cooperate we attacked Frank and Pete.

"Where are we going? What will we be doing? What's the big secret?"

The hands just smiled. "You jest hang on ta yer britches ladies," was Frank's parting admonition.

Anxious to see Beau again I'd taken two apples from the kitchen and was hoping he would come close enough for me to make him an offering. Branch told me Beau had been released from the pen so I hurried to the pasture fence with Star in her usual spot beside me.

"Now Star, don't you go scaring that boy off. If you want to come along, you've got to be absolutely quiet."

The only response from Star was a frenzied wagging of tail.

Beau was grazing near the rear fence of the pasture. A low whistle resulted in a turn in my direction. I waited unmoving, with Star sitting beside me. For a few minutes

Beau stood motionless, watching us. He walked several feet in my direction stopping after every few steps, repeating this slow, deliberate pace a number of times before breaking into a trot. When he was about thirty feet from me he came to an abrupt halt, his front right hoof pawing the ground, ears pricked, emitting audible snorts.

Imitating Branch, I spoke softly, "Come on, Beau, just a little closer this time. We can be good friends. Star, you stay...and do be quiet."

Star lay down near my feet. Beau moved forward guardedly until he was within five feet of the fence. I palmed an apple and holding my breath, reached toward him. With a sudden whinny, he spun around and raced back across the pasture.

"Oh damn! We were so close this time." My disappointment was undisguised. I watched him for a few minutes more before heading to the cabin to prepare for the upcoming ride.

Unbeknownst to the three dudes, Claire and Howard, with Sandy driving the chuck wagon and Frank riding beside them had left earlier to prepare a western style picnic at a pre-arranged site. Branch and Pete stayed behind to guide the neophytes and some of the visitors to the rendezvous, a trip of about two hours. It was a beautiful day, a warm sun shining in a cloudless blue Colorado sky. Samson was in fine spirits and it was with great pleasure I found myself riding beside Branch. We started out along a familiar trail but once past the beaver dam Branch took a right. In a few moments we came out of the woods into a broad meadow. On a distant hill a profusion of aspens assumed the guise of a golden cloud.

"Oh, how extraordinary. It takes one's breath away."

"Yes. It's a great time of the year. Shall we stop here for a short break?"

Annie's Portion

Branch's suggestion was received with unanimous agreement. The riders dismounted and Pete handed out some drinks and fresh baked muffins.

"It'll be a while before we feed you again," he said.

Finished with our snacks and respite, we walked for a while leading the horses and stretching our legs. Once remounted, we made our way toward the cloud of aspens.

A wisp of smoke floated above the distant hill. "Are those Indians?" I asked Branch playfully.

He laughed. "I believe it may be a war party led by an orange headed woman in a pink bandana."

"Oh, you are the sneaky one. Sent out a scouting party, did you?"

"The 'Great Meadow' barbecue is always the grand finale, but I guess we'll have to plan something else for you."

A large baron of beef was roasting over a campfire and the delicious aroma greeted the riders as we pulled up near a line of hitching posts fronting a pine-board hut.

"You see before you a combination comfort station and supply depot. One is at your disposal and the other is strictly Claire's domain." Branch dismounted and tied his horse to a post. The others followed suit.

Before long the simmering traces of corn bread, beans and bacon, chili and coffee began to fill the air. One of the *mestizos* pulled out a guitar and began playing some lively Mexican tunes and with a good deal of noisy encouragement sang some familiar old favorites. There was much feasting and friendly palaver and a contented contingent made for the corral.

With Claire and the chuck wagon following behind the riders the trip back to the ranch was pleasant and noisy. It was dusk by the time our happy but exhausted troop unsaddled the horses and took our aching bodies to bed.

The cold night air permeated my cabin. It would be a good idea to light the fire before taking my shower but since it would take a few minutes to warm the room a visit to Beau was in order. Grabbing the recently replaced flashlight and two apples I'd kept for Beau, I made my way back to his corral. Turning off the torch, I waited at the fence for what seemed an interminable time, hoping he would sense my presence. About to return to the cabin, a slight sound caught my ear. I smelled him before I saw him, standing not more than four or five feet away.

"Hi Beau. Have you decided to make friends? I'm really not very dangerous and if you're good, I have a treat for you."

Talking softly I held out one of the apples, putting my arm between the fence rails. Cautiously, the stallion stretched his neck out toward my open hand and moved closer. His nostrils flared as he sniffed the apple and again I could feel his warm breath. Lowering his head ever so slowly, he lifted the apple from my hand—this time with much less reticence than he'd last exhibited. He stepped back but I could hear his crunching. Done with his treat, Beau moved stealthily, inching closer to the fence. He did not stir when I placed my palm against his neck but I traced a series of ripples as they traveled along his body. Too soon it was over. Beau backed off, turned and made his way to his retreat at the other side of the pasture.

"I've done it!" With the flashlight pointing the way to my warm and welcoming room there were no mishaps. Without removing my sweats I fell into bed and a contented sleep.

Monday, Oct. 15th

We three tenderfoots were noticeably sore as we struggled to seat ourselves comfortably on the benches. The mood at the breakfast table had taken a somber turn knowing it was to be the last meal we would share with Margie and

Annie's Portion

Bob. Branch tried to make light of their imminent departure but found an unreceptive audience.

"Hey you guys. Snap out of it. Someone would think we were sending them to the gallows. They're just going home to…what was the name of that place?"

There were a few smiles.

"Oh, Branch. You know it's…it's… What is the name of that place, Bob?" Margie teased.

"Well if it ain't Colorado, it don't matter no how." Sandy got his licks in.

"I don't want ta break up this happy party, but I think we need to get a move on if we're gonna catch that plane in Rifle." Frank slid off the bench.

Margie and Bob left to put the last of their baggage into the jeep, with the rest of the breakfast group, including Claire and Howard, close behind. There were hugs all around, Margie squeezing me a little longer than she did the others.

"Thanks for making this so much fun. I'll write and send some of the pictures," she said. Then, as an afterthought, added, "And maybe visit you sometime in Hawaii."

"The best of everything to you both. Safe travels." I waved as the jeep started its dusty trek.

Bob turned for a last wave. "Good luck with your Beau, Annie." They were soon out of sight; a dust cloud and Star's barking the last evidence of their progress down the road.

"It isn't going to be the same without them," I remarked to Branch.

"No, I guess not. They sure are a nice couple. I hope the fates will be kind to them."

"Why Branch, not only are you a softie but a philosopher as well."

"Add audacious to the list. How would you like to go see some of those *mestanos* in their haunting grounds?"

"Are you serious? I'd love to."

"It will mean a long day with lots of riding. Cold too. Think you're up to it?" Before I could reply he added, "On second thought, we could make an overnight trip of it." He watched me, trying to gauge my response.

"I've brought my long johns for just such an occasion. When do we go?"

"I'll double-check the weather and if it looks good, we can go tomorrow. There are several small cabins...well really emergency shelters, located on the preserve and we could bunk at one where I've seen a herd several times."

"That's great. What do I need to do?"

"Take essentials only, things that will fit into a saddlebag. Be sure to wear a warm sweater over a tee shirt...windbreaker too, and gloves. If you need anything we can fix you up. Since we'll stay the night, we won't have to leave at six like I originally planned."

"Six!" I was appalled. "Do you mean A.M.?"

Branch laughed. "I did but we'll go at eight instead. It will be at least a four-hour drive, trailering the horses. Do you want Ginger?"

"You are a stinker. You know darn well I don't. Actually, since you asked, I'll have Beau."

"Like hell you will. We haven't even been able to keep a halter on that devil yet. You'll take Samson, the gelding you rode yesterday." He threw the last word over his shoulder as he headed for the corral.

Strolling casually to the tack shed, not wishing to be noticed, I was glad Star was off on a jaunt of her own. All manner of gear was stashed there; blankets, saddles, bridles, reins. Spotting a hackamore and twenty foot long *mecate* I snatched them from the hook

"These should do."

With the hackamore under one arm I rolled the *mecate*, a rope woven of horse hair, and shoved it under my denim jacket.

Annie's Portion

"I feel like a criminal." I grinned, thinking of the carrots swiped that morning from right under Claire's eyes, the carrots now buried in the pocket of my jeans. Reaching my customary spot at the fence, I scanned the meadow.

"Damn! Branch must have him in the pen." Just to be sure I sent out an imperfect whistle and Beau stepped out from under the trees.

"Oh, you irresistible equine. Come to mama."

Crouching down it was possible to slide between the rails of the fence, entering Beau's private domain. I managed to squat on the lower rail, albeit awkwardly and placed the hackamore and *mecate* on the ground next to me, then waited. Ever so slowly he made his way across the pasture, stopping every now and again to sniff the air and look around. The *mecate* was now attached to the hackamore and the brace coiled over my arm. My backside and spine were beginning to complain due to my pretzel-like position but I dared not change it lest I scare Beau off. He stopped about thirty feet from me, pawing the ground and throwing his head up.

"Thirty feet seems to be the standard distance between us."

When Beau seemed at ease, I cautiously raised myself until fully upright with my back pressed against the fence. Beau stiffened his ears and backed away. I waited a few minutes longer before inching my way toward him, trying to approach from the left side. Within arms reach I placed my hand on his powerful neck, feeling his muscles ripple. He remained still as a statue as I gently stroked his neck and flank—all the while talking softly to him, saying nothing in particular. With slow movements I let the loose end of the *mecate* drop to the ground. His ears flicked but he seemed to accept the touch of my hand. Remaining at his side, holding my breath, I slipped the noseband and headstall on him. He jerked his head several times then was still, the rope dangling at his side. I was jubilant, my heart pounding in my chest as my hold on the rope tightened. Beau pulled back at the first tug and I eased the line out, reaching in my pocket for a carrot which I offered him. "This is an absolute no-no. Branch would be furious if he saw me hand feed you." The thought brought a smile to my face.

Beau lifted the carrot and made short work of it. Tightening my grip on the me*c*ate, leaving several feet between us, I began to walk slowly in the direction of his hideaway. As soon as the line became taut he jerked his head and pulled back. Each time he stiffened I stopped and waited for him to relax before trying again. In this manner we made our way across the pasture until, nearing the trees, I halted our progress. Approaching as before from his left side, leaving the line slack I moved closer to Beau, stroking his flank while whispering sweet nothings to him. He remained quiet when the *hackamore* was removed and took a second carrot.

"Oh, Beau. I think I am going to burst. I want to jump and scream, but I promise not to scare the hell out of you."

There were slight movements of his ears and he muttered as though he was apprising me of his discontent.

"Branch is right. You are smart but speaking of him, I'd better go while I'm still ahead. Now this is the tricky part. I've got to turn my back on you. Please don't pull any shenanigans on me."

Alert to any sound of hoof beats or whisper of breath on the back of my neck, I slowly made my way across the pasture. It seemed a lifetime before the fence would be within reach. To my chagrin I slipped through the rails and came face to face with a deadpan Branch and a nervous Fabian.

In measured tones Branch asked, "What the hell do you think you were doing? That is a very wild animal. He could have killed you."

Annie's Portion

"But he didn't," I answered sheepishly. "He was quiet as a lamb and stayed right where I left him when I crossed the field."

Fabian stifled some sort of noise. Branch grabbed my arms roughly and turned me toward the pasture. Beau was not more than ten feet from me. He'd followed me all the way back to the fence.

Branch took the hackamore and *mecate* from me, coiling them as he spoke. "I'm not finished with you. But I've got work to do first." He turned and strode quickly away with Fabian following a few paces behind.

There being no other guests, I sought refuge in the kitchen with Claire and Howard.

"Ya sure stirred up a hornet's nest, young lady. I ain't seen Branch so mad since his son ran away." Claire offered no sympathy. "You'd best steer clear of him for a while, till he vents some steam."

"I didn't know he had a child. Is he married?"

"Was. But that's for him to say. Now eat your lunch and go find somethin' safe ta do, like go fishin' for a while. Howard can help ya with the gear."

"Sure can, Miss Annie. Be glad to."

Star, who was lying under the table, gave a low growl.

Howard was a perfect gentleman as he showed me how to bait the hook and throw the line into the wee lake that gave the place its name. He left me to my own devices, with Star as guardian. Dangling the rod absentmindedly, I watched Branch working with Beau in the pen. After an hour without a nibble, I went back to the cabin for a shower and nap.

Chapter VIII

1965 – Brooklyn

The dining table was strewn with papers. Paul was standing above me, trying to force a pen into my closed fist. Barney and Phyllis Levy were at my side pressing against me. The room seemed to be getting smaller and I was suddenly overcome by a feeling of claustrophobia. When Barney bent down to insure he had my ear, the lingering foul smell of his last cigar nauseated me.

Paul was shouting, "You red-headed bitch. You'll do what I tell you or I'll break your rotten neck." He struck the side of my head with his open hand. The force of the blow caused me to wince and I struggled to hold back my tears. Stunned by the intensity of his scorn I could only shake my head.

Phyllis drew in her breath as Barney put his arm out to shield me from another blow. "Cool it, Paul. That won't help. Annie you really have to sign these papers. You're the treasurer. We can't get the loan without your signature."

Refusing to be subjugated by their bullying I shook my head vehemently. "I'm not going to do it Barney. Phyllis, I'm sorry but I've done what Paul wanted for way too long. We are over our heads in debt now."

"Annie, if we don't get this money we're going to have to shut down. We'll go bankrupt." Paul was shouting again.

Phyllis interjected, "Annie, please. We have children to think of. We need to keep the business going. Things will get better but you have to sign for the loan. I have."

"My answer is no for the final time." I made an attempt to stand but Paul forced me back into the chair.

"You're not going anywhere till you sign."

Annie's Portion

Grabbing the pen from Paul's hand I threw it to the other side of the room with all the strength I could muster. Paul turned to retrieve it giving me an opportunity to escape. He started after me but Barney stopped him.

"Paul, don't. It's no use. We'll figure out some other way. Leave Annie alone."

Paul stormed out of the room with Phyllis and Barney in hot pursuit. I did not see him again for several days by which time I'd moved into Matt's room. Upon his ominous return Paul said little, ignoring the implied significance of my action. Fearing a reoccurrence of his outburst, I avoided any conversation about the loan or his absence. But he apparently was able to obtain either additional financing or a loan extension, allowing him to keep the operation going. In the ensuing days an undeclared truce brought calm to the Harmon household. Paul seemed more relaxed and as time passed we treated each other more affably, though I was still sleeping in Matt's room. He and his brothers could sense something was very wrong, whispering among themselves but never questioning either Paul or me. In an attempt to resume a more normal relationship Paul put his arm around me or gave me a kiss on the cheek. The attempt invoked a shudder; unable to abide his touch I recoiled.

"Annie, remember when you wanted to get some counseling? I wouldn't go. But Barney said he knows a good psychiatric marriage counselor. Maybe we can go see him."

By this time I'd lost all hope for reconciliation, had come far beyond that point and was just biding my time. After years of debate, the state of New York was going to enter the twentieth century by taking the first steps needed to change the divorce laws. But while the legislature was debating the extent of those changes, the exact terms, conditions and language of the bill were still a long way from final. At last I could see the light at the end of the tunnel. It would be best to try to appease him and delay the inevitable.

"All right, Paul. You make an appointment and we'll give it a try. But you have to promise me you'll be honest and willing to follow his advice whatever it is."

"I promise, but that goes for you too Annie." Paul was satisfied with my answer and was able to secure an appointment for the following week

"Dr. Brightman will see us but he has his own screwy system. Seems he wants to see me alone first. Then he'll see you alone. Then he'll see us together to work out a plan. Is that okay, Annie?"

"Sure Paul. That's fine."

The following week Paul visited Dr. Brightman.

"How did it go, Paul? Do you like him?"

"I don't know. He sure doesn't say much. Just nods or mumbles and asks a few questions. At this rate we'll be going to him forever." Paul was not well impressed.

"Did you tell him much? Were you able to get some idea of his program for us?"

"Yeah, I talked a lot. Had a lot bottled up I guess. No mention of any plan...just that he wants to see you next week."

"Well, I'll go and then we'll see what happens." I was not the least bit optimistic. My mind was already made up. Divorce was the only solution.

A week later I found myself in front of a brownstone building in Brooklyn Heights. The area had once been home to an upper middle class society but had long since fallen into disrepair. Recently, many buildings were purchased by young professionals who were restoring them to their former elegance.

There'd been a time I tried to get Paul interested in buying one of those very same brownstones, paying down our own mortgage instead of leasing the house on Ocean

Parkway. The handsome structures with their dark paneled walls, curved staircases and lovely marble fireplaces were irreplaceable. It would have been wonderful to restore such an historic part of the city but Paul could only see dilapidated, old buildings with no redeeming qualities. For some peculiar reason he'd always had an aversion to buying any house. The brownstones certainly did not change his mind so we remained renters.

In response to my signal with a brass knocker on the mahogany door, Dr. Brightman emerged. A tall handsome man, he had a quick disarming smile. Extending his hand he took mine with a firm grip. I liked him instantly.

"You must be Annie Harmon."

"Yes, I am Dr. Brightman."

"It's nice to meet you. Please come in."

He led the way through a long narrow hallway to a wood paneled room where a small fire burned in the grate. Indicating one of the leather chairs in front of a large mahogany desk, he planted himself in a well worn, high backed swivel chair. Lifting a briar pipe from an ashtray on the desk he proceeded to relight it. When the tobacco caught he took a few puffs, blowing small, aromatic clouds into the air.

"Oh, I'm sorry Annie. Do you mind if I smoke?"

"No, not at all. It's very pleasant." As a matter of fact the whole experience was very pleasant. Completely at ease, I wondered why Paul had seemed so ambiguous.

"Annie, I'm going to be quite brief but painfully honest with you. I just want to ask you one question. Please be as open with me as you can."

"I'll try, doctor."

"Annie," he leaned forward on the desk, his dark eyes searching mine intently. "Are you in love with Paul?"

My answer came without hesitation. "No doctor, I'm not. I was once but that love is long gone."

He made no comment, expecting me to continue. When I did not he probed further. "Do you think we can make this marriage work? Do you want it to work?"

Vowing not to cry proved useless. Tears spilled from my eyes so easily, a handkerchief was always at the ready. Once open the floodgates refused to close and I began to sob, my shoulders shaking. Dr. Brightman made no move to console me. After several minutes, sorrow seemingly spent, I regained my composure, blew my nose and wiped away the last few tears. Finding my voice, hoping my thoughts were expressed with conviction I confessed, "I don't want to stay married to Paul. I'm afraid of him. I can't bear to have him touch me. I've been trying for years to get a divorce. I've even thought of ways to kill him." Tears began to resurface and run down my cheeks.

"Do you sleep with Paul?"

"No. We haven't shared the same bed in months. I sleep in my little boy's room."

"Anne, what I'm going to say will probably surprise you but based on what I've learned from Paul I do not think your marriage can be saved. As a matter of fact I believe you should separate as soon as is practicable."

"Did Paul tell you he wants out?"

"No, on the contrary, he will make it very difficult. He loves you deeply but his is an obsessive and very destructive kind of love. He is jealous and suspicious of your every move. He thinks you are unfaithful. He is very capable of harming you."

"What can I do?"

"This is the way I'd like to proceed. Since Paul has agreed to this counseling, we should plan several more visits for him. I will see you one more time. I'll recommend we schedule an appointment at which time you'll come here together. At that meeting I will suggest a separation as the first step toward restoring this marriage. I'll add that living

Annie's Portion

apart will provide a chance for healing as we continue the counseling sessions."

"He won't agree to that."

"That's very possible. But it's worth a try. Have you ever heard of manic depression?"

"Yes, I've read a little about it in my psychology classes. Do you think that's Paul's problem?"

"It may be. But in order to confirm that diagnosis he needs to undergo a series of tests, some of them chemical. I don't think he's ready to accept that yet. And that's why I hope for an opportunity to work with him a while longer. There's really no reason for you to continue unless you feel it would help you."

"I don't know what to do."

"Does Paul have family you can consult with or close friends?"

"Not really. His mother is a kind of screwball. His father is a merchant seaman and is gone for long periods of time. His closest friend is his business partner Barney, but he can't be of much help."

"Well, we'll just have to do this together Anne. Do you feel comfortable working with me? Do you trust me?"

"Yes, I do doctor. We'll give it a try."

"I want you to start thinking about how the separation, if Paul agrees to it, will work. Will he leave? Will you? Do you have a place to go, any funds? What will you tell the children? There will be many decisions for you to make. Can you do this?"

"There are no other options."

"Take heart Anne. With some time and patience things will sort themselves out."

The plan was put into action. Paul met with Dr. Brightman several times in the ensuing weeks. We consulted once more before the confrontation was to take place. The day of that final visit found Paul somewhat anxious but subdued. Inwardly terrified, I tried to project an unconcerned demeanor. Dr. Brightman answered the door in response to Paul's knock and ushered us into his office. He patted me on the back as I sat down. He did not sit in his chair as usual but perched on the edge of his desk in front of Paul.

"Paul. During the past weeks I think we've come to know each other quite well. You've come to me for help and I have listened carefully to you both. What I see is a couple, once very much in love who have over the past few years, encountered many difficulties. These problems have created great stress for you and Annie, causing you to move away from each other."

"I never pushed Annie away from me." Paul shouted as he stood up. "It's her. She pushed me. I love her." He did not like the turn this conversation was taking. He was already suspicious.

Dr. Brightman tried to calm him. "Paul, it will not help if you lose control. Please let me finish and we can discuss your concerns when I'm done."

"Please, Paul. You promised me you would listen. Please calm down," I added.

Paul returned to his chair where he slumped down, arms folded.

"Very often, couples who experience problems, whether they are financial, familial, emotional or sexual…"

"What have you told him?" Paul was out of his seat again, standing menacingly above me. "Did you tell him I'm a lousy lover? Did you tell him you won't even sleep with me anymore?"

Dr. Brightman moved to put himself between Paul and me. "Paul, you must sit down. You haven't even heard my conclusions before jumping to your own. Be sensible man. I know you want this to work. But you're not helping. Please sit down." He forcefully pressured Paul back in

Annie's Portion

the chair but remained standing. "Paul!" He quickly added, "And Anne. You've had your share of trouble and I find you are blaming one another. This is very common. Unfortunately, your situation has been allowed to go on far too long. Outwardly you put on a good front so your friends and family don't know you're having these problems. That's unfortunate because often these people can help by acting as intermediaries. You both have tried to bear this load alone and with no outlet for your anger or frustrations, have begun to take them out on each other."

Dr. Brightman tried to calm Paul, to reason with him before he struck the last blow. "Do you see that Paul, Anne?"

"Yes I can see how that happens. I know money has been a big problem for us. And Paul not taking much interest in the boys has really made me angry." I too, was trying to reassure Paul by taking some of the blame.

"Paul, do you see how that can happen?"

"Yeah, I guess so. So how do we get out of that rut?"

This was the opening Dr. Brightman was looking for. He watched Paul intently trying to anticipate his reaction. "Paul, in my professional opinion, if you and Anne are ever going to make this marriage work you first need a cooling off period."

There was no sound in the room. I held my breath. Paul glowered.

"I think it would be best for both of you and for your children if you and Anne separate for a brief while."

Paul bolted from the chair, knocking it over as he stood. He grabbed the nearest thing he could reach which happened to be the ashtray and threw it, smashing a window. He turned over a lamp and pulled several books from the bookcase, all the while shouting obscenities. Dr. Brightman and I tried to restrain him but he pushed us away.

"Paul, please stop, please. We don't have to decide this now. We can talk about it. Please, please stop."

"We're not going to separate, right?"

"No, no. We have to talk it over. It was just a suggestion."

Paul grew calmer. Dr. Brightman had reached for the phone.

"It's all right, doctor. Paul and I will consider your recommendation but for now I think it's best if we just go home. We can call you later and let you know what we plan to do."

"We're not going to split, not even for a little while." Paul was adamant.

We drove home in silence. Paul seemed calmer but his temper could flare in a moment. At a loss, with no idea of what to do I refrained from speaking. He let me out at the house without saying a word and drove off. I was relieved when he left. Sarah, who'd been caring for the children, saw my distress at a glance.

"Annie, dear. What's wrong?" Sarah knew of our counseling sessions.

"It did not go well today, mom. We've just got a lot to work out."

"Do you need me for anything? Can I help?"

"No thanks Mom. We just have to work things out for ourselves. Thanks for staying with the boys. Were they good?"

"Well, you know how they are when they're together. But I just got out my wooden spoon and stopped them in their tracks."

That brought a smile to my face. The wooden spoon was Sarah's ultimate weapon. When she had it in her hand the kids knew she meant business and even though she couldn't do much harm with it, they pretended to be scared to death of that spoon.

"If you're sure I'll leave now. I feel like Chinese."

"You and your Chinese food. Have a nice dinner and thanks again." Sarah's way of leaving us to our own devices.

Boys being boys they had no trouble devouring their dinner, but the food stuck in my gullet. Restless, anxiously anticipating Paul's return, not knowing what to expect, sleep eluded me. Finally about two a.m., the door slammed proclaiming Paul's return. A silent prayer he'd go to bed without a fuss went unanswered. Paul made a heck of a rumpus, bumping into things and swearing. Knowing he never imbibed, I dismissed my first thought; he was drunk. He started up the staircase and must have fallen because there was a loud thud then some more swearing. He was drunk. Slipping out of Matt's room into the hallway, I paused momentarily on the landing. Through the darkness, Paul's shadow seemed larger than life. I had to quiet him and get him to bed before he roused the household.

"Paul, be still. You're going to wake the boys," I said in hushed tones.

"I don't give a shit for the boys."

The smell of liquor on his breath and his clothes was easy to detect. "Where have you been? I can't believe you're drunk. Be quiet."

"I am drunk, very drunk. And I will not be quiet. You are not going to leave me, not ever."

"Paul, stop it. You're going to terrify the children."

"I don't give a God damn about those damn brats. And you're coming to bed with me, right now. You're not gonna go into that brat's bed tonight or any other night. You're my wife and you're comin' to bed with me, right now. Ya hear?"

His behavior was frightening. The children were certainly awake by now, cowering in their beds.

"If I come with you will you be quiet?"

"Quiet as a mouse." He whispered.

Placing his arm around my shoulder I half-carried him to our bedroom and dumped him onto the bed. There was no chance for me to leave. He grabbed my arm and yanked me down on top of him. He reeked from booze, his grip on my arm like that of a pit-bull.

"Let me go Paul. You stink. Sleep it off."

"You always thought I was a lousy lover," he shouted. "Well tonight I'm gonna show you a thing or two." He started pulling on my nightgown.

"Stop it Paul and for God's sake be quiet."

"God's gonna learn a thing or two now." He ripped the front of my nightgown and it fell to the floor. He pulled me back on the bed rolling me onto my stomach. He straddled me and drunk as he was managed to penetrate me from the rear.

"Want something different do you? Well now you got it."

In his usual form he ejaculated immediately, slid off me and passed out. Debased by the obscene act, wanting only to feel clean again, I ran a steaming hot bath. Scrubbing my body with an unyielding brush, I remained in the tub until the water grew cold and numbness blunted my humiliation. Once again Matt's room became my refuge and Paul made no further attempt to get me back in his bed.

Chapter IX

About this same time the legislature was putting the final touches to the act that would, at long last, change the New York State divorce law. It was encouraging to read of the unanimous approval of the bill even though many compromises had to be made, and it was not as liberal as expected. I immediately called the attorney.

The complex new law, as he explained it, allowed a husband or wife to obtain a two-year legal separation without cause. Once a separation suit was brought to the court, the terms of an agreement would be established. These terms covered such things as alimony, child support, visitation rights, property disposition or any other items that would normally be included in a divorce decree. But there was one small hitch. At the end of the two-year period, the parties would have to appear before a tribunal of judges who would review the case, interview the combatants, examine any related documents, and make a determination as to whether or not they believed the couple could be reconciled. If the court decided the adversaries were irreconcilable, a divorce would be granted and the terms of the separation agreement could either be made permanent or adjusted to the satisfaction of the participants. If, in their great wisdom, the black-robed trio of Solomons, concluded the applicants had a shot at reconciliation they would not grant a divorce, the idea being cooler heads might prevail after the two-year separation. No one explained what would happen if, when two years expired, the tribunal did not grant a divorce to the plaintiff who had been anxiously awaiting the moment of freedom. Fortunately for all concerned it was the rare case.

My attorney was instructed to prepare the necessary paper work. There were many things for me to do; preparing the children and making plans for our departure. When I missed my period I assumed it was because of my great excitement but when morning sickness struck it was time to visit my gynecologist. I was pregnant.

My reaction was predictable, disbelief followed by rage and utter despair. "Oh God. Why did you make me so fertile?"

"Give me something to abort the baby." My pleading; begging, weeping and suicide threats were dismissed. My doctor said no. I asked friends and friends of friends, old women and even a few prostitutes how to get rid of a pregnancy. Boiling hot Epsom salt baths, ingested pills that would choke a horse, concoctions that included everything from cod liver oil to strange Chinese herbs; nothing worked. In an unplanned accident I fell down a flight of wooden stairs. But that baby was determined to be born. Overcome with self-pity, I notified my attorney of the change in circumstances and put an end to the separation proceedings, of which Paul was still unaware.

One month prematurely, I gave birth to a baby girl, weighing in at four pounds eleven ounces. When the nurse brought her to me for the first time I stripped the baby naked, examining every part of the tiny body, counting fingers and toes to insure I'd done no harm to that precious innocent. My little girl, Samantha was perfect. The family teased me. "You finally delivered a daughter who everyone will call Sam."

In June, we once again packed up and moved to the cabin for the summer. Resigned to the fact there was no way out for me, the idea of divorce slipped into the shadows. My darling little girl so filled me with joy it was possible to endure Paul's increasingly erratic behavior. With a mother's helper caring for the baby two afternoons each week and the boys attending day camp, riding lessons recommenced. Happier than I'd been in a very long time my exuberance spilled over, infecting the entire family.

Samantha was a delightful, happy child, adored by me and spoiled by the neighbors. With auburn hair, green eyes and the hint of freckles she provided me, whose red hair came from a bottle, with a certain authenticity. If a boy can be described as beautiful, Matt was just that. He had dark hair and large, expressive brown eyes enhanced by long dark lashes. His small, well-shaped nose and engaging smile made him the darling of the counselors. Danny developed a love of fishing, one that would stay with him the rest of his life. Josh was a natural athlete, specializing in baseball, swimming and girls.

All but Paul were enjoying a wonderful summer. The few conversations we had convinced me Paul's company was on the rocks once again. He'd been able to stave off bankruptcy twice before, once with a large infusion of cash I'd suspected had been borrowed from Matthew Gold. It was only after Matthew's death, when his estate was settled, my suspicions were confirmed. Matt had used most of his assets as collateral so Paul could save the business. In his own, selfless way, he had tried to spare me and my two boys from financial calamity.

Fearing the worst, Paul was desperately trying to squirrel away some funds to carry us over until he could earn a living again. We moved back to the city after Labor Day with Paul, engulfed by bankruptcy proceedings, becoming more and more irrational. His mood swings were extreme. One moment he was happily blabbering about his new plans and how glad he was to be getting out of that "damn partnership". Then, just as suddenly, he would cry bitterly, wondering how he would be able to earn a living again. He talked incessantly, repeating phrases over and over, then suddenly fell silent staring into space; he dropped off to sleep, only to wake and begin the whole routine again. Remembering what Dr. Brightman had said about Paul's manic depressive symptoms, convinced he'd been right I tried to get Paul to see a doctor, but he now mistrusted all doctors and refused to go. He became argumentative and verbally abusive. Ignoring his mad behavior enraged him and he'd shake me, screaming obscenities as he'd done in the doctor's office. Conditions continued to deteriorate. Failing to provoke a reaction following an especially raucous tirade, Paul threw me along with the chair I was sitting in, across the dining room, slamming me into a wall. It was imperative I get out.

My father and I had spoken rarely since my wedding but desperation overcame pride forcing me to ask for a small loan. He gave me a long speech about how he warned me not to marry Paul, asking why I had so damn many kids with him. It was his opportunity to play savant and he milked it. In the end he gave me three-hundred dollars.

Locating an affordable apartment was no easy task but eventually one was found in the Midwood section of Brooklyn. The building was another walk-up tenement but the neighborhood was respectable and close to a good school. The flat, on the third floor consisted of bedroom, bathroom, dining room, living room, kitchen and large foyer. The rent was a hundred dollars a month. With assistance from a couple of goons my father sent to help, we moved a few pieces of furniture, some pots, dishes and clothing, from the ten room house on Ocean Parkway to the four room flat on Dorchester Road. I'd come full circle.

Sitting on the floor in the middle of the living room I took inventory of our assets and mentally dissected the living quarters. The boy's dorm would be adequately furnished with a set of bunk beds, trundle included; desk, chair and small chest of drawers. The dining room, fitted with twin-size bed and crib, would be somewhat less lavish. A dilapidated couch taken from the porch, generally accepted as our pet dog Brandy's bed, would remain in the living room; complemented by a pine desk and hutch of recent vintage I'd refused to leave behind. It would be a tight fit but the card table and two chairs would go in the kitchen. There'd be space enough to hide the few remaining items; baby carriage, linens, blankets, towels, shopping cart. It did not take long to get our meager possessions organized and within a few days we had made the place home.

"Well," I thought aloud, "It could be worse."

Overhearing my remark Josh responded, "Yeah, but not much."

But I was satisfied. The items of greatest value; my three sons and my baby girl were with me, shielded from the unpredictable behavior of their father. It had been unthinkable for us to leave the pets behind so Brandy, a beagle terrier mix, whom we had rescued from the pound three years earlier, one hamster named BW Hammy (BW for black and white), and one white rabbit named Murgatroyd made the passage with us.

An SOS went out to my attorney. "Resurrect the separation documents without informing my husband; do it quickly."

"He'll have to be told where the children are."

"Stall as long as possible. Maybe Dr. Brightman can help with documentation that will enable you to get a restraining order for Paul."

Mother was next on the list of obligatory calls. Fearing she'd try to dissuade me from making such a drastic move, I hadn't told her of my plans. After the initial tongue lashing she agreed not to disclose my new address to Paul. Sadly for Sarah, it was a replay of her own separation from Brad.

Julie was having marital problems of her own but when I gave her the glad tidings she had a suggestion regarding job hunting. She'd been a waitress for years and made a good living from non-taxable tips.

"Annie, you're crazy if you look for some cheap-paying office job. Find a good waitressing spot. With your looks you can make big buck tips and work just weekends. You'll earn three times what you can in an office."

"Julie, what do I know about waitressing? I'd be a disaster."

"What are you talking about? You've been a waitress without pay for the last fifteen years. Try it. What have you got to lose?"

"What do I do?"

"You read the want ads, find a place that's easy to get to. Go check it out and see how they serve. If they use trays you say you're experienced with arm service. If they use arm service you're experienced with trays. That way if you screw up the first few days they won't get suspicious."

"Okay, Julie. That may be just what I should do."

Shortly after we moved in our new neighbors, Randy and Maria Carlotti came by to introduce themselves. With their two teen-age daughters they became our surrogate family, a circumstance that proved to be most fortunate. We had built in baby-sitters. Once the children were registered at their new school I began scouring the want ads looking for restaurants within easy traveling distance. One ad seemed promising, a steak house in Flatbush. Observing they used trays for serving I decided right then to apply for the job.

George Pappas had been in the restaurant business most of his sixty-two years. When he questioned me about my previous experience he instinctively knew I had none. But he liked me, pretending to believe my tale.

"I've worked in Manhattan but I'm looking for a job closer to home because of my kids. I've never worked using a tray but can certainly learn quickly."

He hired me, instructing me to show up at five p.m. on Thursday wearing a black skirt and white blouse. He emphasized "short black skirt."

An arrangement was made for Laurie Carlotti to baby sit every Thursday through Saturday with Sarah taking over the job on Sundays. My new career began at the Premier Steak House on Thursday at four-fifty p.m. with me in my black skirt, white blouse and comfortable black flats. I was apprehensive as George introduced me to some of the wait staff and left it to them to teach me the ropes. The Steak House was an upscale restaurant with a distinct method of service. Each station employed a waiter, waitress and busboy. Waitresses took dinner and drink orders and served the drinks and salads. "Salad" was really a misnomer for all it consisted of was a large chunk of iceberg lettuce in a small wood bowl. Assortments of dressings were presented on a lazy-Susan tray so each patron could choose one to his liking. Along with the salads, the waitresses brought individual loaves of bread on cutting boards. Busboys cleared the first course dishes after which the waiters served the entrees and deserts. It seemed pretty straight forward and not very difficult and the first night passed without mishap. The short skirt seemed to be an invitation to several customers, permitting them a pinch here and there, but the best way to deal with the infractions was to ignore them. George seemed pleased and was very complimentary. He noticed the pinches and approved the way I handled myself. Forty dollars in tips made it worthwhile.

Julie was first to hear the good news. "That's terrific Annie. I knew you could do it."

The Premier Steak House was always busy. It catered to businessmen, which was great because they tipped well. My tips were averaging fifty dollars a night. The drawback of course, was the continued abuse by rude patrons; use of off-color innuendos along with varied pats and squeezes.

J. Fran Baird

My tolerance level was dropping and on more than one occasion the customer knew it. My response adversely affected my reward. On one particularly busy Saturday night I'd taken dinner orders for a party of six men. Returning with the salad tray, I placed the lettuce bowls on the table. A hand slid under my skirt, making its unchecked way along my thigh. Startled, I tipped the tray sending the dressings flying, some falling on the men at the table, some spilling on me. I rushed out of the dining room into the kitchen where George stood laughing.

"George, I quit!"

"Now, now Anne. Don't let it bother you. It'll be fine. Go clean yourself off and get back to work. You smell like an Italian salad."

"No, George. I've had enough of this crap. I'm just not cut out to be subservient to anyone, especially not these crumbs."

George could not change my mind so he paid me off and once again I found myself among the unemployed, searching through the want ads. Worried about running out of funds, not wanting to borrow any more I sold my two-carat diamond ring to Randy Carlotti for five-hundred dollars.

The fates finally seemed to smile on me. Manhattan Overseas Bank was looking for trainees to work the night shift in their telecommunications center. The Wall Street district was foreign to me but I applied for the job, giving as reference a friend who agreed to provide me with backup, concocting a history of my prior business experience and performance. Notice of my acceptance came by mail. My salary would be ninety-eight dollars a week, half that of my tips. But as a condition of employment I was provided with health benefits, employee savings program and the possibility of overtime. Initially scheduled to work from four p.m. to midnight I'd been able to negotiate a time

Annie's Portion

change by starting my workday at six, giving up a "lunch" hour and extending my shift to one a.m. The time change made it possible for me to spend the full day with the kids.

I'd led what might reasonable be called a sheltered life and was totally unprepared for the environs in which I found myself. My new world was inhabited by several blacks from Harlem and the island of Jamaica, two tough young Irish women from Queens, a delightful older, German gent and an equally delightful elderly Danish lady, both from the Bronx. My supervisor was a giant of a man with a loud booming voice and a heart of mush. A more diverse collection of people could not be found. There was not a Jew among them nor was there any Jew I ever knew of, in that entire division of thirty-five-hundred people. It was a congenial society, each member doing a specific job but able to fill in at any of the other positions.

Assigned to a restricted area, I'd been fingerprinted and bonded. Literally locked in a cage, it was my job to code incoming and outgoing transfers of funds that were wired to associate banks all over the world; released from my pen to cut tapes that ran through the teletype machines, finishing the transfer process. I loved the job, people and immediate acceptance. My mentor, a short black man named Billy Simpson, who was never seen without his red beret covering his mass of dark kinky hair, taught me the ropes, teased me incessantly about my being "lily white" and covered my ears with his hands whenever a raunchy story was being told. And many such stories were always being told. When allowed to be privy to these tales they sounded like some writers' wild plots, often leaving me open mouthed.

There were times some of the group would go out after work. On one such occasion Billy invited me to join them for a trip to a Harlem club. We were seated in a large booth with other customers who passed around a joint which I declined, and where I had my introduction to the homosexual community. Another time we went to a porn movie, my first and only one. The screen of the grubby theater was behind us as we entered the aisle. Looking back at the screen I was greeted by the vision of a naked man with an exaggerated lower member about to enter a very accepting woman. Thereafter, I declined the invitations.

But at least once a month two Irish lassies, Eileen and Molly insisted on my company as they bar-hopped from Greenwich Village to Central Park. Bars had never been my habitat and my only drinking had been one summer in the mountains. The colleens could drink any man under the table and often did while I nursed one or two watered down hi-balls. Some nights I did not get home until five a.m. When Billy asked how I explained my return at such a late hour, my response was, "I walk in backwards. My neighbors think I'm leaving for work."

Going home alone on the subway in the wee hours was unpleasant but it came with the job. The worst part of my travels was the walk through the tunnels under the Canal Street station where I had to change trains. Several vagrants could always be counted on to make an appearance but that didn't bother me as much as did the many rats that had the run of the place. My earnings were decent and by putting in overtime the paycheck increased substantially. There was money enough to begin improving our living conditions. The old couch was recovered and louvered doors installed between the living and dining-turned-bedroom. Brad gave us a TV set on his first visit and life was getting better.

Paul had been frantic when he found his family gone and was served with the separation papers. He questioned Sarah incessantly and accused our mutual friends of hiding me, but no one gave us away and there seemed to be no way for him to locate his family. He finally tracked us down through the Hebrew school Josh and Danny were attending.

Annie's Portion

Resorting to old tricks, Paul followed them home making a very loud and unwelcome appearance at the apartment building. Unable to gain access through the security door he raised a furor in the street, forcing me to meet him there in an attempt to quiet him. For weeks thereafter he appeared each weekend demanding his visitation rights, making our lives an endless nightmare. My refusal to allow him in the apartment forced him to conducted his visits with the boys in his new Cadillac, which he parked conspicuously in front of the building. There he held them captive, questioning and badgering until I retrieved them. My appearance would catapult Paul into a screaming rage during which he accused me of all sorts of vile acts, terrifying his sons and providing a wonderful street show for the neighbors. With surprising ferocity Matt would strike out at Paul, kicking and biting him, eventually refusing to see him at all. Dr. Brightman made an unsuccessful attempt to procure a temporary restraining order.

Samantha developed Bell's palsy as a result of a serious ear infection and Matt was seeing a child psychologist. The IRS sent me a bill for eight hundred dollars in back taxes because my separation agreement did not stipulate my payments from Paul as child support. Arguing that he never paid me anything at all was an effort in futility. Since Paul had claimed alimony payments on his tax return I was forced to pay the bill.

Months went by; good days and bad. The family settled into a routine. The boys, at first unhappy and complaining, began to adjust to their new environment, relieved there was no more fighting. They were doing well in school but my insistence that Josh and Danny continue with their Jewish education and Bar Mitzvah preparations created an unforeseen problem. Wearing their *yarmulkas,* the required skullcaps, with blatant reluctance they made the trek from public school to Hebrew school each Monday through

Thursday, returning at dusk. Sunday morning attendance was also required. Their route took them past a large frame house occupied by a family of ten. The head of the household, a Captain with the New York City police department, had proudly fathered six sons and a pair of daughters of little significance to him. The mother of this illustrious group manifested her authority by denying Josh and Danny access to the sidewalk fronting her house, whacking them with her broom each time they passed, insisting that no Jew would defile her sidewalk. The situation was avoided only on Sundays while the pious O'Malley family attended church services.

When I finally decided to put an end to the harassment of my sons, Mrs. O'Malley took the broom to me shouting obscenities and oft repeated phrases that included the words, "Jew bastards, prostitute and whore." A brouhaha ensued with the Harmon boys coming to their mother's defense and the O'Malley boys taking full advantage of the opportunity to gang up on Josh and Danny who were years younger. The dust cleared revealing several black eyes, bloodied noses and a pair of Juvenile Delinquent Cards issued to Josh and Danny.

There were times I locked myself in the bathroom, the only place that allowed for some privacy; sobbing uncontrollably until my tear ducts were empty.

"Why is it?" I asked my mother. "For some people life seems to go just as they plan it. They get married, have a son and a daughter, buy a house and move to the suburbs. Everything falls exactly into place. But for others everything they do is wrong. I never catch a break."

"If your grandmother was here she would tell us, 'God gives each of us a portion.' We have to make the best of it, Annie." But Sarah decided it was time to intervene, and while it had been years since she'd spoken to Brad concluded he was the only one who could help, both with Paul and the

Annie's Portion

O'Malleys. He was understandably surprised to hear from her but when Sarah explained the intolerable situation he assured her he would take care of it. Sarah did not question him further but familiar with his modus operandi, she was reassured. Her assurance was confirmed shortly after the call. Paul's visits became infrequent, I received the child support payments on time and Mrs. O'Malley no longer troubled us.

As the 1967 holiday season approached my spirits seem to lift. The brightly lit streets of the city and decorated trees in the stores and office buildings dispelled the gloom for a while. It was the first time since I'd left Paul I had enough money to surprise my children with presents. But with the disappearance of lights and trees, and spring still months away, my depression returned. Sensing my distress Maria Carlotti, in an effort to cheer me, took me on a shopping spree.

"I know a great little shop on Kings Highway where they have really cute stuff at reasonable prices." Maria offered to drive.

Enticed by the novelty of shopping for myself I was easily persuaded. "Some new dresses for work would be nice...and a new coat. Let's do it."

Maria had not exaggerated. The shop was perfect and after trying on several items, I selected a simple but stylish black wool coat. It was eighty dollars, more than contemplated but very practical.

"This will last a long time and never go out of style," I voiced to Maria and the sales clerk.

With the purchases paid for and wrapped we made our way to the exit door. Suddenly I stopped. Hanging on a display hook was the most beautiful coat I'd ever seen. It was made of fine wool, gray blue in color and trimmed with a gray fox collar that extended down the front to the hem.

J. Fran Baird

A wide belt of the same material served as the finishing touch.

"Oh, Maria. Don't you just love this coat?"

"Yes. It is truly exquisite, Annie. Do try it on, just for fun."

The clerk took the coat from the display and helped me into it. It looked fabulous. Both Maria and the clerk oohed an aahed.

"Annie, that coat was made for you. It sets off your blue eyes and the fur looks great with your red hair." Maria smiled.

The sales clerk nodded her agreement.

"But it's so impractical. When would I ever wear it?"

"Whenever you want to. Annie, it's time you did something foolish, something just to please yourself. You work so hard for your money you deserve to enjoy it."

"You convinced me." I exchanged the black coat for the blue one and paid the additional hundred and twenty dollars. "I may be lighter in the pocketbook but I sure do feel good about it."

Maria and I celebrated with milkshakes at Jerry's Ice Cream Parlor. Once home the dresses were stowed in the closet but as an afterthought the coat was hung on the outside of the closet door where I could enjoy it each time I passed by. Later that same evening I experienced severe intestinal pains. By morning the pain was gone

"Must have been Jerry's milkshake."

Days later the pain was back. Always hungry, it seemed eating increased the intensity of the pain. My new dresses were too big, evidence of weight loss.

At Maria's insistence I went to see a doctor who diagnosed my condition as an ulcer syndrome. "It's not a surprise considering the stress you're under." He put me on a special diet, gave me some medication and said I'd be feeling better in no time. The pain worsened and the weight loss continued. Maria made an appointment for me with an internal specialist who spent a good deal of time questioning me about my symptoms. He pointed to a screen and asked me to disrobe and don one of those fashionable hospital gowns with the opening in the back. His nurse was preparing a barium concoction and I could hear her remarks.

"I don't know what all the fuss is about. She's probably just pregnant."

I responded loudly from the other side of the screen, "If I'm pregnant the Jews are finally going to get their Messiah."

An exhaustive series of tests confirmed that neither ulcers nor pregnancy were the problem. The cause of my discomfort was a gall stone the size of a quarter. Immediate surgery was advised. The operation was no simple procedure. I woke from the anesthesia with numerous tubes, drains and IV's attached to my thin body. The surgeon came to consult with me advising, "All's well. We gave you a twofer. We made a detour and took out your appendix while we were in there. It looked a little inflamed. Bad news is you won't be able to wear a bikini again."

Due to the tube installed in my gullet, the only response he got was a moan. The hospital stay lasted a week after which I spent two weeks recuperating at home. Fortunately, Manhattan Bank had provided a good medical plan and time off with pay.

About a week into the recovery period, the intermittent but unmistakable acrid smell of smoke began to fill the apartment. My first thought, someone had burned dinner but as the odor became stronger I put down my book and waddled to the window. The darkness prevented me from distinguishing what seemed to be fleeting gray clouds were actually puffs of smoke. When flashes of orange pierced the clouds it became apparent a fire was raging in the apartment below mine. Black smoke rolled into our apartment from under the entry door, the door hot to the touch. Sleeping the sleep only children enjoy it was difficult to rouse them. It took several desperate minutes for me to get them up and into their coats. With Samantha in one arm and Brandy in the other I herded the boys toward the fire escape. Noticing my blue coat hanging on the closet door I put my burdens down and quickly slipped the coat on over my nightgown.

"There's no way I'm leaving this coat here."

Retrieving my two dead-weights I made for the window. Josh opened it and Danny helped Matt out onto the snow-covered fire escape where the below freezing temperature had rendered the steps icy and slick. An unsuccessful attempt was made to maneuver myself, Sam and Brandy out the window. Through the thick billows the dim outline of a man materialized.

"Put the damn dog down and give me the baby."

Assuming it was a fireman I obeyed instantly and followed down the fire escape to the street where a large crowd had gathered. Fire trucks blocked the road, their hoses turning the street into an icy obstacle course. Where was my baby...and the boys? They were nowhere to be seen. Panic was about to set in when, amidst the throng, I heard a voice calling my name.

"Mrs. Harmon! Over here."

The voice was familiar...a male voice. The second time he called I recognized the voice as the same one I'd heard on the fire escape. We made our way towards each other.

"We have your family at our house."

He led me across the road to a large single family house where an open door framed a woman holding a baby. Clutching my mid-section which was throbbing painfully, I hurried across the road and up the front steps.

"Please come in, Mrs. Harmon. Everyone is fine."

The large living room was vaguely reminiscent of Signora's; the smell of tomato sauce and garlic permeated the air. The boys were huddled under blankets and jumped up to greet me; laughing and crying, suddenly realizing what a ridiculous picture we made; boys in cocoons, me in a fur-trimmed coat, nightgown hanging out the bottom and bare footed. Karl and Rosemarie Schultz laughed with us before introducing themselves and their children, Karl Jr. and Theresa but made no mention of my outlandish costume.

"Thank you so much for helping my children. I was terrified when I couldn't find Samantha."

"I guess we didn't have time for a proper introduction," Karl senior smiled.

"Please have something warm to drink and put these socks on your feet, they're blue." Rosemary handed me some coffee and helped me into the socks.

"Does anyone know what happened there?"

It was Karl who answered. "Seems like someone left two young kids alone in the apartment below yours. They found some paint cans in a closet and set them on fire with matches."

"Was anyone hurt?"

"No. By some miracle, you know God watches children and fools, they all got out okay."

"Why don't you all stay here tonight? We have lots of room and you can figure out what to do tomorrow." Rosemarie suggested.

By this time Karl Junior had taken the boys upstairs to his room. They could be heard playing some game seemingly without a care. Sam was fast asleep in a love seat where Rosemary had placed a high back chair to keep her from falling.

"I guess that's a good idea, although I hate to put you folks out. You've done so much already."

"It's no problem at all." Rosemary replied.

J. Fran Baird

That was the beginning of a warm relationship between Rosemary and me. Karl Schultz Senior was another story; a believer that the intelligence gathered after the war concerning the death of six million Jews was a myth. Nonetheless he formed a strong bond with Danny whose mechanical ability and capacity to learn quickly, impressed the usually stoic automaton. With his tutelage and encouragement Danny applied and was accepted at the highly regarded Poly-Tech High School where he excelled in the engineering program. Danny and Karl Junior, a disappointment to his rigid father, formed a friendship that would last all their lives. In later years Josh and Theresa dated but nothing serious ever came of it. We were soon able to move back into our apartment, which had sustained only smoke damage, my wounds healed and life went on.

A year passed during which time numerous men flowed in and out of my life. Losers who could spot an easy mark and provided temporary affirmation I was still an attractive and desirable woman. I dated and bedded several men at the same time. A wealthy insurance broker whose wife had an "incurable illness" could call at the last minute and find me an eager participant in a late night tryst. A call at the office and I'd be off for a late dinner and a romp in bed at a nearby hotel. He was several years my senior; a great lover, fun to be with and oddly enough made me feel good about myself.

My romantic liaison with a cop who also worked crazy hours, took an entirely different form. We drank, made love and consoled each other. Mike took me to Riker's Island, to "the Tombs" in order for me to absorb the flavor of his work environment. It was the most horrible place I'd ever seen. The scum of the earth were housed there. It was supposed to be temporary quarters for suspected criminals awaiting trial but most of the inmates had been there for many months. Mike said things happened there, too terrible

Annie's Portion

to describe. He said a young guy didn't stand a chance with hardened criminals and often a kid would be raped in the paddy wagon bringing him to the Tombs.

"It's no wonder you cops are all warped," was my only comment.

On another occasion, after visiting several bars, Mike insisted on taking me to Jersey—to the Empire Burlesque Theater on Washington Street in the lovely locale called Newark. Somehow we managed to get on the Pulaski Skyway on the wrong side of the road and were forced to travel against oncoming traffic, glaring headlights and angry horns for a mile before we were able to exit. Miraculously, we survived the trip without incident but I was reminded of Karl Schultz's remark regarding God protecting fools and children. We certainly fit into the former category.

Never considering the risks or consequences I lost count of my one-night stands. But the routine was losing its initial appeal. It was no longer fun; jumping into bed with guys whose names I couldn't even remember. It was time for me to put an end to that shameful period of my life.

Molly and Eileen continued to invite me to join them after work but I did so with much less frequency. At the end of a particularly busy Friday night, when the work crew was shorthanded and the volume of cables excessive, we three opted for a well earned, relaxing night on the town. By two in the morning, having made several stops along our route, the colleens had long lost all semblance of sobriety. With me only slightly more coherent we reached what should have been our final oasis, a seedy place on West 86th street. Molly immediately hooked up with an opportunist of the male gender and disappeared. Two nondescript, apparent regulars ordered drinks for the ladies who were sitting at the bar. Drink in hand, Eileen staggered to their table to say thanks and joined them. There was much slobbering and giggling at the table. Not wishing to encourage them, I remained at the bar.

"Hey Anne. This bar is gonna close and these guys know an after hours place we can go to," Eileen slurred.

"I really need to get home Eileen, and so do you."

"We have lots of time, Annie girl. Let's go."

"Eileen, let's go to the ladies room first." Steering Eileen toward the restroom I attempted to convince her it would be a bad idea to go with those guys to a place we knew nothing about.

"Well if you're too scared to go, I'll go myself. I really like this guy."

Knowing there was no stopping her and fearing to leave her alone with two strangers, I went along with the plan. We piled into a car parked nearby and set off for the after hours spot supposedly owned by a friend. The trip took us across one of the bridges into Brooklyn but I, whose magnetic compass had long been the butt of many a family joke, had no idea where we were. At last the car stopped in front of a waterfront dive. Staggering across the smoky, malodorous, nearly empty barroom, we found seats at a burn-scarred, wooden table. Eileen and her new friend—no way to determine whether he was named Guy or Eileen was referring to him as "my guy"—went to the bar for drinks. My eyes were fixed on the unsavory patrons scattered about the smoke-filled den, several of whom were slumped across the tables.

"Oh, my God. Where the hell are we?" I thought, eyeing the fourth member of our little group with suspicion. He'd been the driver but said little since we left the city.

Eileen was so drunk she was sure to pass out at any minute. Her guy, or Guy, was all over her. The situation was bound to end badly...for both of us.

"Eileen, we really need to go, now! Maybe we can get a cab."

"I don' wanna go. I'm havin' fun. Leave me alone."

Her guy put his two cents in. "What are you, her fuckin' mother? She can take care of herself. She's a big girl."

Eileen was forcefully dragged from the chair by me. Her guy made a move to grab her but the quiet man pulled him back.

"Let them go," he said. "You're too drunk to do anything anyway."

Eileen was yanking on my arm, trying to pull me away from the exit.

"I don' wanna go."

"You are going whether you like it or not." Once outside the extent of our predicament became clear. "Now, where the hell are we?"

There seemed to be a better lighted area about a quarter-mile away. Maybe we could find a cab there or at the very least a bus stop or train station. Pulling and pushing Eileen, hoping she would not pass out before we could get to some transportation; I glanced at a slow moving car behind us. It became evident the driver was following us. With my arm around Eileen's waist I tried to increase our pace. The car pulled up along side us and the window rolled down.

"Get in. You're gonna get raped or killed out here."

It was the quiet man at the wheel. Without a moment's hesitation I pulled the rear door open and shoved Eileen in.

"Where do you need to go?"

"To Brooklyn, the Midwood section."

"Fuck. This is Brooklyn. Where the fuck is Midwood?"

"It's kind of between Flatbush and Bensonhurst. But you don't have to take us there. Just find us a cab."

"Like hell. This is Red Hook. There are no cabs. Do you have any idea how to get where you live?"

I'd heard of Red Hook. It was where the movie "On the Waterfront," starring Marlon Brando, was supposed to have taken place—not somewhere a nice girl would want to be. "Well if you can get to Prospect Park, I can give you directions from there."

"How the hell did a nice girl like you get into this fix?"

Eileen had passed out and was snoring loudly.

"I didn't want to leave her alone. She's got a little girl waiting for her at home."

"You should be more careful about the friends you pick."

We didn't speak after that and when we reached Prospect Park I was able to direct him to my building.

"Thanks. I don't know what we would have done if you hadn't picked us up."

He got out of the door and helped me with Eileen who was dead to the world. We dragged her up the three flights of stairs. I unlocked the door and pushed Eileen into the apartment.

"Thanks again."

"Yeah."

"Never again. I didn't even get his name."

Eileen woke with a terrible hangover and an even worse disposition. She washed her face, combed her hair and left without so much as a thank you. Neither of us ever mentioned the incident again and I declined all future invitations to go for a drink. Several weeks after the incident, Eileen cornered me in the office restroom.

"Annie, I'm in terrible trouble. I'm pregnant."

"Oh dear, Eileen. What are you going to do?"

"I've got to get rid of it."

Her remark reminded me of my own experience trying to abort a pregnancy.

"It's almost impossible, Eileen. I know. I've tried it."

"I want to get an abortion."

"Where are you going to get an abortion? It's illegal."

Annie's Portion

"I found out about this doctor in Jersey. He'll do it for five-hundred dollars."

"You can't take such a chance. What do you know about this person? It can be really dangerous."

"I have to do it. What are my choices? Annie I don't have the money. Can you help me?"

"If you're determined to do it I can give you some money but not that much."

Between Molly, Eileen and me we managed to come up with the necessary dollars. Molly and I both tried to dissuade Eileen but she was adamant.

"Annie, will you come with me?"

Even though the idea was repugnant I understood Eileen's desperation and agreed to accompany her. With Brad's borrowed car we made for Newark. Eileen had explicit directions and amazingly, we found the place without incident. The man who answered the rap on the door of the run down foreboding shack did nothing to allay my growing apprehension. He'd been squeezed into a wrinkled suit that partially covered a dingy, tieless shirt. His graying hair, hanging down over his left eye, was stringy and greasy looking. He ushered us into one of the shack's two rooms, a dimly lit kitchen in the center of which sat a bare wooden table. The only other furnishings in the room were a filthy sink, hot plate and small refrigerator.

"You got the money?"

On the verge of tears, Eileen was unable to reply. She nodded and pulled out a wad of bills. Growing more suspicious by the minute, I stopped her from giving him the money.

"Eileen, please don't do this. Look at this place."

"I have no choice." She pulled away from me and handed the cash to the "doctor."

He counted it. Satisfied it was all there he began to get his operating arena ready. From his medical bag he pulled out a sheet and tossed it over the table then extracted some surgical instruments placing them at one corner.

"Take off you pants and get on the table."

He went to the dirty sink and washed his hands, returning to the table where Eileen was now lying. He picked up one of the instruments and inserted it roughly into Eileen's vagina. She screamed.

"Aren't you going to give her an anesthetic?" I was appalled.

"It'll be over in a minute. She won't need one."

He was as good as his word. Several minutes later he was back at the sink with his few instruments, washing them and his hands, wiping all on the sheet.

"You can get up and go in the other room. There's a cot there and you'd better rest for a while to be sure there's no excessive bleeding. I'll be back in an hour to check."

With that he left. Eileen was in great pain but with my help made it into the other room and onto the bare cot.

"Eileen, are you going to be all right? Maybe I should get an ambulance or some other help."

"No, no. Don't do that, please. I'll be okay. I don't think I'm bleeding too much and the pain's not so bad."

For more than an hour we waited in silence, me holding Eileen's hand. The sadistic butcher returned to review his handiwork.

"You're gonna be fine. You can leave any time."

I'd brought a box of sanitary pads and helped Eileen pack several of them between her legs. We walked slowly out to the car and I drove her back to her home in Queens. Two days later she returned to work.

Chapter X

Discussion of the awful event was intentionally avoided, though it hung in the air like an ominous cloud. Eileen was finding it difficult to face me and our working relationship took a downward spiral. As a way to assure her there was no ill-will between us, a belief she surely harbored, I invited her to accompany me on a previously planned weekend trip to the Catskills. The Concord was a well known, high-end hotel noted for its good food, great comedians and a fun crowd. We caught an early bus from the Port Authority Terminal and arrived at the hotel a little late for lunch on Saturday. After checking in and sending our bags to our room, we popped into the coffee shop for sandwiches and coffee. Eileen had never been to a hotel like this and was awestruck at the size and scope of the place. A quick tour revealed a large swimming pool complete with lotion covered bodies draped over lounge chairs, while waiters in white jackets walked around taking drink orders. There were tennis courts where white clad participants banged balls over nets strung above clay courts and a riding stable where several people were heading out for a trail ride. Indoors we found a large ballroom, an equally large dining room dressed in white linen for the dinner crowd and several intimate lounges where drinks were offered around the clock. Finding a couple of unoccupied large plump chairs we sank down in pleasant comfort. A waiter was there in less than a minute and we ordered bloody marys for two.

"This is the life," Eileen remarked. "A person can get used to this real fast. Thanks for bringing me here, Annie. You're a good friend."

"My pleasure. We can't do this often but it sure is nice."

One we'd drained the last drops from our glasses I suggested we go to the room to shower and get ready for dinner. Eileen would not get drunk on my watch. We left the lounge area and headed for the elevator, which was run manually by a uniformed operator. A tall, handsome blonde man in his early forties managed to squeeze into the elevator just before the doors closed.

He smiled, "Good afternoon ladies."

Eileen said, "Hi," about the same time we arrived at the fifth floor and took our exit, leaving him to go on to his higher destination. Eileen with a beer and I with a coke spent the next hour sitting on the balcony telling stories, comparing notes on the men we'd known and talking about the office. Once showered, made up with great care and dressed in our best duds we threw bouquets at one another.

"You look terrific, Eileen."

"You're pretty hot stuff yourself. We are a very attractive pair."

Eileen with her blonde hair and hint of freckles, I with my red hair and blue eyes; both of us tall and shapely, we knew we looked good. Heads turned as we followed the maitre'd across the dining room to our table. He held a chair for each of us and waited while we were seated. We both felt pretty good, Eileen grinning like the Cheshire Cat. There were four other diners at our table, two couples, which seemed to reflect the general makeup of the guests. Introductions were made and supper was served. I'd told Eileen to expect good food and lots of it but nothing could have prepared her for the abundance of the repast, as one dish followed another ending with a sumptuous dessert of crepes l'orange. Wine had also flowed freely at the table but I managed to keep the bottles out of Eileen's reach.

"I'm so stuffed I don't think I can get out of the chair." Eileen groaned.

Annie's Portion

"Me too. Let's walk around the garden and see if we can work some of this off before show time."

We excused ourselves and aimed for the French doors leading to the terrace. There was still another hour of daylight so we took advantage of the warm evening and joined a number of other guests strolling through the gardens. At eight-forty-five a gong sounded the signal for the assemblage to head for the theater. It was almost show time. Eileen and I scurried with the crowd and managed to get a table close to the stage. We each ordered a drink, I a screwdriver and she a gin and tonic. The curtains opened and the audience quieted somewhat. On stage were a four-piece band and a female vocalist. There was polite applause and the group began to play a popular Simon and Garfunkel tune, "Bridge Over Troubled Water." The singer was very good and the crowd started to warm up, which was just what the act was intended for. By the time our drinks were finished, the third number had the crowd applauding and yelling with great fervor, due in part to the liquor consumption as well as to the good music. The vocalist made the introduction for the main attraction, a young Jewish comedian named Jackie Mason who was totally irreverent and vulgar and had his audience roaring. He did a one man, one-hour act, receiving a standing ovation amidst hoots and howls. By then the crowd was quite mellow since booze flowed throughout the presentation. Limiting myself to one drink I allowed Eileen two, not without complaint. Strains of music, reminiscent of the "big band" era, drifted across the lawn from the main ballroom where a band of significant size was already playing. Eileen was asked to dance immediately. It took a little longer for me to be invited.

There was a light tap on my shoulder. It was the good-looking guy from the elevator.

"Remember me?"

"Oh, hi. Sure I do."

We made some small talk, commenting on the food, the show, the good weather and he asked me to dance. He was a wonderful dancer, steering me deftly through a fox trot, a cha cha, a rumba and another fox trot. When the band got into some rock and roll numbers he maneuvered me outside.

"Would you like something to drink?"

"No thanks, I think I've had enough."

"By the way, I'm Mark Gladding."

"Anne Harmon." He seemed like a nice guy.

We had lots to talk about. He was a stockbroker who coincidentally worked just a few blocks from my office. We returned to the ballroom for the last dance, had a nightcap at one of the cafe bars and said our goodnights at my door.

"I haven't seen your friend all night."

"No, me neither. She has a way of just wandering off." I'd noted Eileen's absence and was a bit concerned but was certainly not going to discuss it with Mark.

"Well, goodnight Anne. It's been a lovely evening. I hope we can spend some time together tomorrow." He bent down and kissed me lightly on the lips. The kiss was pleasant, a bit of a teaser. "I'd like to do that Mark. I really enjoyed your company."

He kissed me again, this time with more resolve. I pushed him away gently.

"I'll see you tomorrow, Mark. Sometime after breakfast."

"Tomorrow then." He turned and walked back toward the elevator.

Hoping to find Eileen there before me, it came as no surprise to discover her missing. The bed was exceedingly comfortable and I was soon asleep.

Eileen had still not made an appearance by the time breakfast was served. Mark spotted me and came to sit in Eileen's empty chair. He made no mention of her absence nor did I. He suggested a boat ride and picnic lunch, which we could pick up from the kitchen. It sounded like a wonderful idea. The hotel kitchen staff was very accommodating and had a lunch ready for us in short order. There was a fair assortment of boats tied to the dock. Mark selected a sturdy looking rowboat, helped me in and pushed off.

It was a lovely day and the scenery was spectacular, the lake reflecting an unclouded sky and tall trees, air heavy with the smell of pine. A loon was calling for his mate and Mark drew a little closer to watch as she responded to his call. We were both silent, taking in the special beauty of the moment. Mark skimmed the water with the oars so as not to break the spell and for a while we just drifted. Finally, he dipped the oars in more aggressively and headed for a beach where he poled the boat onto the sand and jumped out. Reaching for my hand he helped me out, conveniently forgetting the picnic basket. We sat for a while on the warm sand making quiet, small talk then Mark took me in his arms and gently kissed me. Not since my affair with Matthew had I responded with such fervor. During all those years, my rutting years, there'd been no such craving. I felt hot yet I was trembling. Mark sensed my tremors. He stopped kissing me and for a few moments just held me close, close enough for me to inhale his manliness.

"Anne, am I being too forward? Shall we stop now?"

Suddenly mute, I shook my head and put my arms about him. He kissed me again, more ardently, his mouth brushing my neck and the exposed parts of my breasts. My heart was pounding. He began to explore my body with gentle hands, opening my blouse and unzipping my shorts. My breathing was spasmodic but it did not faze him. He caressed my breasts with his lips. I heard a moan and realized it had to have come from me. Warm hands slid down my body, across my stomach then between my thighs. Mark knew all the right moves; slow and measured and when he finally entered me I was ready. We climaxed together and lay silent and spent for a long while.

"We've completely forgotten our lunch." Mark smiled. "But my hunger's been completely satisfied."

During the return trip Mark asked, "When are you planning to leave for the city?" He had decided to start back early that evening.

"Oh my gosh. I completely forgot about Eileen. She must think I died or something. We're not going back till later tomorrow. We have to be at work by six."

"Did you drive up?"

"No. We took the bus from the Port Authority and we'll go from there right downtown. Gee, I've got to find her."

"I'm sure she's keeping herself entertained. I can stay tonight and give you a ride back to the city tomorrow if you like."

"There's really no need for you to put yourself out." I secretly hoped he would.

Once the boat was docked we made for the main building, catching sight of an irate Eileen heading our way.

"Where the hell have you been? I've looked everywhere for you." She was furious.

"We've been rowing. More to the point, where the hell have you been? You didn't come to the room at all last night or this morning. I didn't plan to baby sit you."

"Well you dragged me to this shit house and you should have stayed with me instead of going off to fuck pretty boy here."

Mark started to walk away. Appalled, embarrassed he was privy to Eileen's foul behavior, I called after him. "I'm sorry Mark. Thanks for the nice day and the offer."

He turned and threw back a terse response. "I'll see you for a drink before dinner."

Eileen felt the full blast of my anger. "You are a first class bitch. You're an embarrassment to be with. You drink

Annie's Portion

too much and have no regard for other people. I'm sorry I tried to show you what it's like to be with decent people."

"Oh, so that's it. You think I'm not good enough for you. You're no damn better than I am just quieter about it."

"Maybe you're right. Come on. Let's go back to the room."

We walked through the lobby in silence. The operator made some small talk as we rode to the fifth floor.

"I'm sorry, Annie. I was just mad at myself I guess. As usual I ended up with what was probably the lousiest guy in the place. I was drunk, he was drunk, we ended up passed out in his room and he threw me out as soon as he came to this morning. I wanted your shoulder to cry on and you were nowhere to be found. I thought maybe you had gone home without me."

"Eileen, why are you so bad to yourself? You know I wouldn't leave without you. Mark has offered to drive us back to the city tomorrow. Do you want to do that?"

"Yeah. That sounds good. I think I'll take a shower and get fixed up for dinner."

"That's a good idea. I'll phone Mark and tell him we've accepted his offer."

Our trio had a quiet dinner together. It was Sunday night and most of the guests had left for the city. Eileen excused herself right after dessert saying she was really tired and wanted to do some packing. Mark had not been thrilled with the idea of taking her back with us but I would not hear of letting her go home alone by bus. I too, excused myself early and Mark offered no objections.

On Monday we drove back to the city in Mark's Jaguar. Conversation was limited and very strained. He pulled up in front of the bank building, said a dour-faced good bye and drove off. Our shift had not yet begun so we walked the few blocks to Fraunce's Tavern. Located across the street from the New York Stock Exchange, the Tavern was an historic landmark. It was there George Washington said goodbye to his troops and a museum on the second floor held many mementos from that critical time in U.S. history. Additionally, the bartender was known to make the best bloody marys in the city.

We killed some time there, each having one drink and walked back to the bank. My mind was made up; my relationship with Eileen would end. I would be cordial but cool and would no longer spend time with her outside the office.

Billy met me at my wire enclosure with a grin. "Oh ho. The bird flew the cage and had some fun with a young cock."

"What are you talking about, Billy Simpson?"

"Some dude's been callin' you for the past hour. Sure sounds hot to trot. You must have made quite an impression."

"Did he leave a name or number?"

"Nope. Said he'd call again after six. Hot time in them there Jewish Alps?"

A blush spread from neck to forehead. "You mind your own business you horny bastard."

"Ooh, what you said Miss Lily White. You must surely be hangin' with some ba-a-a-d folks."

At six Mark called. "I miss you already. I'm sorry for my bad exit but I really wanted to get away from that leech."

"Oh Mark. Don't be too hard on her. She's a sorry case. But I'm so glad you called. I can't talk now, too busy. Can you try later?"

"Just wanted to arrange to meet you tomorrow. How about four at Fraunce's?"

"I'll see you then." I looked up to see Billy watching me.

Annie's Portion

"I think Miss Lily's in love."

It was true. I'd hook up with Mark two or three times a week at Fraunce's. We spent many late nights together. On those nights we did not eat or drink. We spent hours making love getting out of bed only to go to the bathroom. We both lost weight. My happiness was evident and Mark seemed to be just as pleased. It was some months later, while waiting for Mark at Fraunce's the bartender spilled the beans.

"Annie, I know this is probably none of my business and you can tell me to butt out, but I think an awful lot of you and I think someone should clue you in."

My heart dropped to my feet.

"Annie," he watched my face and knew I was expecting the worst. "Mark is a very married man with three kids on Long Island. I'm really sorry but I thought you deserved to know."

"How do you know that? He can't be. We spend too much time together for him to have a wife."

"I don't know what he tells her but I know for certain he's got one...and kids."

It couldn't be true, Mark loved me. In a daze, I made my way to the office. Billy saw it in my face. There was trouble.

"What's up Annie? Somebody do you bad?"

I broke down and cried while Billy patted my shoulder and tried to comfort me. He was a man of the world and knew I'd been had. Mark tried to reach me but his calls went unanswered. Heartsick, sleep wouldn't come; there were dark circles under my eyes. Physically ill, food wouldn't stay down. My menstrual cycle was irregular. Grief can do that but I should have known better. Two months passed—the prognosis irrefutable. I was pregnant.

The message left on Mark's answering machine was brief. "Meet me at Battery Park. Same place, four o'clock." When he heard I needed five-hundred dollars for an abortion, he didn't know what to do or say. He apologized for not having told me about his wife, told me he really loved me and didn't want to lose me. He told me he was afraid for my safety, gave me the five-hundred dollars.

Eileen provided the doctor's number and offered to go with me. The offer was declined. Brad's car was called up once more for the trip to Newark. I knew what to expect and was not disappointed. He was the same scrubby man, in the same run down shack. The wood table was still in the middle of the room, instruments on the sheet. The five-hundred dollars changed hands. This time it was me who received the benefit of his empirical ministrations. When it was over I helped myself into the back room where I wept and waited for him to come back and tell me to leave. Then I drove myself home.

Chapter XI

1968 – Antigua, BWI

It was to be my first real vacation. An advertisement featuring a photo of a sleek, twin-masted sailboat on a turquoise sea, white sails billowing, scantily clad bodies lying on the deck underscored by the words, "Come join us for a Windjammer cruise," caught my eye. I read on, "Sail the beautiful Caribbean to uninhabited islands while you work as crew or just lay back and enjoy good company, great food and excitement of exploring new places." The ad went on to hype the congenial groups, the snorkeling, white sand beaches and sunshine. Fishing was not listed as part of the itinerary but I was hooked. I sent for information and when it arrived was delighted to discover the boat, a one-hundred-ten-foot clipper, set sail from the port of St. Johns on the island of Antigua, where my cousin Noreen had been living with her second husband, Lou Turner, since 1964. They'd moved to an old plantation house Lou had been restoring for the past several years.

Noreen responded quickly to my letter of inquiry, encouraging me not only to take the cruise but to plan on spending some time on the island with my cousins. Once Sarah agreed to stay with the brood I accepted the invitation, and booked the trip for the end of September.

The Eastern flight landed in Miami where a British West Indies Air puddle jumper would carry me to the idyllic Caribbean. Beewee, as it was called by the natives, delivered me safely to the isle of Antigua where Noreen waited to greet me at the airport.

Noreen, the middle daughter of Sarah's sister Talia, had always been a beautiful girl. Now in her fifties, she was still a strikingly attractive woman.

"You are still as pretty as ever," I remarked sincerely.

"Flatterer. Look at you. You're a knockout. Wait till Lou sees you. He will positively drool." Noreen gave me a bear hug and led me to a dusty, tan Vauxhall, a British made car with the steering wheel on the right and the trunk in front. We loaded the bags in the boot and departed.

"I'd forgotten this is still a British possession," I remarked as Noreen steered through the narrow streets of the tiny Capital on the wrong side of the road.

"Yes but they just can't make up their minds. One day they want independence and the next day they want the Queen Mother to take care of them. We're in the middle of an anemic revolt now. See?" Noreen pointed to a British frigate in the harbor. "That's here to scare the rabble."

We left the town behind traveling between cane fields bordering the sole dusty road traversing the fifteen mile long island. A short drive brought us to a private lane lined with palm trees. About half a mile from the turn I spotted the white house with its wraparound veranda and sloping roof line.

"Oh Noreen! This is just beautiful."

"You should have seen it when we bought it. It had no roof and Lou said the only thing keeping it together were the termites holding hands."

"Is that man playing golf?" I asked in disbelief, pointing to an elderly black man in the field.

Noreen laughed. "No, that's Franklin, our gardener. He's lickin' the grass."

"Licking the grass?"

"Lickin' not licking. He's using a double edged blade to cut the grass."

"Seems like by the time he'd finished one part he'd have to go back to the other and start again."

"That's right," Noreen agreed. "This way we can keep him busy all the time."

Noreen pulled up in front of the house where a well tanned, dark-haired man, looking every inch the football player, bounded down the steps, taking two at a time, followed not quite as exuberantly, by a young black woman.

"What have we here? Is this my cousin Annie?" He wrapped his muscular arms around me in a bear hug as he kissed my cheek. "Welcome to our humble abode."

"It doesn't look very humble to me. It's grand, just like Tara." It was truly impressive.

Noreen called to the black woman, "Come, Essie. Meet my cousin Annie. Annie this is the best cook on the island."

"Welcome, Miss Annie. Here, let me take your bags." She spoke with that wonderful, sing-song, island cadence.

Lou hefted the bags effortlessly and carried them up the steps. "I've got these, Essie. Why don't you go make us a couple of those special rum drinks of yours?"

"Let me show you to your room. You must be exhausted after that trip," Noreen said as she hurriedly led the way to one of several louvered doors bordering an expansive central room. There was time for just the briefest glimpse of the heart of the house before a door was thrown open revealing an attractive bedroom.

"This will be your home away from home. Please make yourself comfortable then come join us for a drink on the veranda."

Examining my surroundings with interest, I noted the simplicity with which the room was furnished; the same quiet elegance I would later discover marked my cousin's style. White wicker furniture provided an airy tropical feeling, augmented by lime green and peach bed covers and floral paintings that added color to the otherwise antiseptic impression. To my great delight, the bathroom was my very own.

Quickly slipping into shorts and a tee shirt I washed my face, ran a comb through my hair and exited by way of a pair of louvered doors that opened onto the veranda. Noreen and Lou were comfortably seated in lounge chairs, sipping drinks and munching hors d'ouvres from a colorful ceramic platter.

"Come, sit and sip with us," Lou invited as he handed me a frothy drink. "Essie makes the best daiquiris around."

"Umm...this is wonderful." I reached for a slice of shrimp topped avocado. "A person could get used to this real fast."

"Well, you have a few days to enjoy it."

Noreen loved the good life. She was used to it. Daddy provided well and money had never been a problem for her or her sisters. All they had to do was ask. Hershel had started poor but with the help of Grandma Fanny, he turned one taxi into the second largest fleet in New York City. He and Talia were simple, unassuming people but their daughters grew up in the grand style; private schools, expensive clothes, cars of their own, and all the luxuries money could buy. Daddy even bought their husbands although Noreen could not manage to keep her first one.

She'd been divorced about five years when she met Lou. There was no way, on a truck-driver's salary; he could afford to give Noreen the life she was accustomed to. They visited a friend in Antigua and Noreen decided she would not need to maintain that life style if they moved to a simple place like this speck in the Caribbean. Lou's hobby had always been furniture making. Noreen had been trained as a commercial artist and was quite good. They combined their talents and opened a shop in St. Johns where they designed and built custom home furnishings for the well-to-do islanders. Business was flourishing and they currently decorated many of the new hotels sprouting up like weeds on the beaches. They'd bought the plantation with Hershel's help and were almost finished with its restoration.

It had grown dark but the air was still warm. Essie called us in for dinner and we obliged by devouring the sumptuous meal she placed before us. Lou gave me a brief tour of the house, proudly pointing out all his meticulous handiwork. The floors were mahogany polished to mirror sheen. The cabinets and nearly all the furniture was made by Lou, much of it hand painted by Noreen. He designed and fitted the doors and windows with special antique hardware.

"You both have done a magnificent job restoring this place."

"It was a complete wreck when we found it. And of course Daddy came to the rescue with a bunch of bucks. But it's really been Lou who transformed it. He's put in every spare moment working on it, with very little help." Noreen smiled proudly at her husband.

"Before my head gets too big ladies, I think I shall retire. Tomorrow morning will be here right soon. Goodnight Annie. So glad you're here." He bent and kissed Noreen on her forehead.

"Goodnight, sweetheart."

"He seems like a really neat guy."

"Yes he is. You can tell by looking at me how fat and happy I am. Would you like a nightcap?

"No thanks, Noreen. I'm kinda beat. I think I'll call it a day."

"Yes, do get some rest. I've got a busy day planned for us tomorrow. Have a good night."

I started across the large central room then stopped, somewhat confused.

"Lost already?" Noreen laughed. "All the bedrooms are accessible either through these louvered doors," she made a semi circle with her arm, "or from the veranda. Let me show you yours." She led me to my door. "This is it, but don't worry if you make a mistake. There's just us. Goodnight Annie. It's so good to see you." She gave me another hug and a peck on the cheek.

By nine the sun shone brightly through the open windows and a gentle breeze moved the sheer curtains of my canopy bed.

"What a lovely fragrance," I said to no one in particular. The scent was familiar but the name eluded me. A large tree wound its branches around a support post on the veranda. Picking a leaf I inhaled deeply. "This is where the scent is coming from."

Just then Essie made her appearance from the other end of the house. "Good morning, Miss Annie," she said in her Caribbean lilt. "You just in time for breakfast on da veranda."

"Thank you, Essie. I'll be right there." Hair and teeth brushed, it was shorts and tee once again.

Noreen was sipping coffee at an outside table. "It's about time you got up, Miss Lazy Bones. Lou is long gone and we have things to do and people to see. Come sit."

Essie had disappeared into the large kitchen and returned with a tray of breakfast goodies. She poured my coffee and I helped myself to a freshly baked biscuit and a slice of thick cut ham.

"That all you gwanna eat, Miss Annie? They's lotsa good stuff heya."

"That's all for now, Essie. I've a feeling I'll get more than enough to eat while I'm here." The view from the veranda was exceptional. "What is that wonderful tree in front of my door? It has the most delicious smell."

"Delicious is right," Noreen responded. "It's a bay tree."

"You mean bay as in bay leaf?"

"The very same. We use it in much of our cooking."

Annie's Portion

"No wonder it smelled so familiar. How nice to just go pick some leaves anytime you need them."

"We pick lots of our own food. We grow pumpkins, avocados, papayas, coconuts, lemons, limes and some other stuff."

"Is that Franklin out there in the field? He's still lickin' the grass. Wouldn't it be more productive to get him a power mower?"

"Oh, sure it would. But then how would we keep him busy? He needs to be doing something to earn his keep." Noreen snickered. "Now, hurry and get ready to go to the big city."

I was just beginning to learn about island living.

We drove into St. Johns making our first stop a modest factory where we found Lou, covered in wood chips, giving instructions to his crew of three. He was noticeably frustrated.

"Hi, ladies. Don't mind us. We're just having a lovers quarrel." Lou greeted us. "Where are you off to?"

"We have some shopping to do for tonight's party. Oh, I forgot to tell you, Annie. We've invited a few friends to the house to meet you. Any excuse for a party." Noreen was happy for an opportunity to play hostess.

"I don't know if it's safe to let you two beauties out on your own. I wish I could go with you but duty calls."

"See you later. But don't you dare get home late." Noreen waved goodbye and we were off again.

The next stop was a quaint boutique in St. Johns where a young, pretty black woman greeted us.

"Annie, this is my right arm, Josephina. I don't know what I would do without her." The woman smiled, a lovely, white-toothed smile, at the compliment from her boss. Noreen showed me around the shop, proudly pointing to the custom jewelry, paintings and varied artifacts she had created. I expressed sincere admiration.

"Enough of this mutual admiration society. We've loads to accomplish before we head home."

And off we went again, I dutifully following my dynamo of a cousin. We busied ourselves dashing from one stand to another in the open market, stopping only long enough to pile the many and varied provisions in the back seat of the Vauxhall. We rewarded ourselves with delicious lobster salads at an outdoor bistro before making the dash back to the plantation, Noreen honking at several walkers on the dusty road. Essie and Franklin came to help unload the packages while Noreen and I sat wearily on the veranda.

"Daiquiris, Essie. Daiquiris please," Noreen pleaded. "I'm pooped."

"Noreen, you are an absolute whirlwind. Quite honestly, I never saw you work so hard."

"That's what island living does for one. But we have to make this a special event, just for you."

We finished our drinks and went off to our respective rooms to prepare for the soiree. By seven that evening, I counted fourteen guests lounging about, enjoying drinks and the delectable assortment of foods Essie prepared. Lou, looking striking in navy slacks and a white sport coat, stood at the bar creating exotic drinks. He waved to me.

"Come, Annie. Catch up with the rest of us." He made a frothy banana daiquiri and handed it to me.

"Without a doubt, this is the best drink I've ever had."

Noreen took me in tow. "Come and meet everyone. They have been anxiously awaiting the arrival of the guest of honor."

In a few minutes I'd been introduced to the most interesting and eclectic group of people I'd ever seen in one place, only one of whom was born in Antigua.

Thirty-five year old Peter Sheffield was born to English parents who had emigrated fifty years earlier. He'd attended prep school and university in England but decided to return

Annie's Portion

to Antigua where he felt most at home. He'd been elected to the newly formed parliament with the altruistic idea of helping bring independence to the island.

In addition to Peter, there was an amusingly colorful retired couple who had "left foggy London to wait for the undertaker in a warm place," representatives of Germany, Spain, Belgium and of course the U.S.A.

An American named Bill, owner and captain of a sixty-foot schooner on which he took tourists for scuba diving adventures, was especially interested in my Windjammer cruise. His daughter Rowena, somewhat dour and standoffish served as his first mate and cook. He invited me to sail with them on the following day to as he put it, "to kinda get your feet wet." Rowena's displeasure registered on her face.

In an aside, Noreen informed me that they lived in a geodesic dome Bill had built.

"Thanks, Bill. But I don't want to be a bother or interfere with your charter."

"It's no problem. Just a group of four. I won't take no for an answer. You be on the dock, in your bathing suit, at eight."

Muttering to myself, "The hell with Rowena, I want to go." My response to her father, "You're on Bill. See you at eight."

When the guests had all left, we sat on the veranda discussing the unusual group. I told them of Bill's invitation and Rowena's noticeable reaction.

"He's an interesting guy. He's in his early sixties but you'd never know it. He built that odd house of his almost entirely by himself. Took him a couple of years. It's really quite a marvel. He lived alone until Rowena fell in on him, didn't have a good relationship with her mother or her husband. Bill was not delighted with the idea of suddenly having a daughter around but he seems to have made the best of it." Lou was just getting started. "He's lived quite the adventurous life. Do you know what this guy did?"

"How would I?"

"Well you're going to know now," Noreen snickered.

"He took that boat out by himself all the time. He was sailing somewhere south of here when he got caught in a dreadful storm. His radio went out, he lost his jib and the mainsail was torn to shreds. He managed to beach on an atoll where he spent two weeks while search parties went looking for him. You know how they found him?"

"Uh uh."

"A sailor on a search vessel spotted the boat. They anchored offshore and rowed a dinghy onto the beach. There he was, Bill Conahan calm as you please, sewing his sail. Unperturbed, unconcerned, just sewing his sail."

"Reee-markable," an expression picked up from the Little Rascals.

"You should really feel flattered. I've never known him to show much interest in women," Noreen sounded just the slightest bit jealous.

"I'm sure looking forward to the day although I know Rowena is not too pleased."

"Don't let her bother you," was Lou's last remark as he toddled off to bed.

Arriving at the dock before eight I found Bill and his daughter loading provisions aboard the Grenadier.

"Can I help with anything?"

"No!" was Rowena's curt reply. "We've got it handled."

"Just climb aboard, Annie. Make yourself comfortable. The others should be here any minute now."

The others were two couples in their thirties who were just then pulling up at the wharf. Twenty minutes later we were heading out to sea under a typical cloudless sky with a stiff breeze filling the sails. It was the first sailing

Annie's Portion

experience for all but the Captain and his daughter and we neophytes were enjoying ourselves immensely. Rowena served coffee and cinnamon buns as the boat slid gracefully through the waves at about eight knots. Secluded bays, shoals and headlands fringed with reefs appeared along the diverse coastline. There were long stretches of flat, lowlands relieved by a volcanic formation rising to a substantial height on the western side of the island. Noreen had remarked about frequent droughts that required an infusion of fresh water brought to the island by boat.

Just before eleven o'clock Bill changed his heading and sailed into a calm, aqua bay where he lowered the sails while Rowena dropped the anchor.

"This is it, folks. One of the greatest scuba spots you'll ever find."

He and Rowena began pulling out gear. There were tanks, fins and masks for all. As Rowena helped us into the gear, Bill explained what we were about to see.

"Many years ago, a ship bearing a hold filled with tar caught fire just outside this bay. The Captain tried to get his ship close to shore but it exploded just out there." Bill pointed to a spot close to the entrance of the bay. "When the boat sank the hot tar began to cool as it hit the water. It drifted down forming an undersea canyon of weird, unusual shapes as it cooled. Over the years it's become home to limitless varieties of fish and anemones. It's truly a wonderland."

Unfamiliar with the gear we novices listened attentively to Bill's directives for using the fins and breathing apparatus. "Stay in pairs and remember, no matter what you see, don't panic. There are often barracuda down there. Some can be pretty big but don't let them scare you. If you see one remember he's just as curious about you as you are about him. Swim for the boat ladder but don't hurry."

Sure he'd given that same speech many times, the pair thing puzzled me. The puzzle was solved when Bill slipped into a scuba tank harness and we went over the side on a rope ladder. Dropping from the ladder into the surprisingly warm water I drifted slowly downward, the pastel shade of the sea's surface mutating to blue green at the ocean floor. At the lower depths the sun radiated weakly, its rays barely piercing the subterranean world into which I'd descended. The other swimmers appeared surreal as they glided between stark black columns and grotesquely unnatural figures, made stranger still by the rippling effect of the water. At first it was frightening but soon adjusting to the dark labyrinth I was captivated by the bizarre world.

Fish of varying sizes and colors darted through the maze. Sea anemones of every hue beckoned eerily as the underwater plant life swayed with the motion of the waves. Mesmerized, lost in a dream, I glimpsed a slow moving shadow from the corner of my eye. With a slight turn of my head I came face to face with an evil-grinning barracuda, as long as I was tall. Instinctively I impelled myself forward, my scream muffled by the scuba regulator, unheard. Bill and the other swimmers were no longer in sight but seeing the outline of the boat reflected ahead of me kept moving in that direction, the barracuda swimming slowly beside me. The ghostly white rope ladder beckoned. Keeping one eye on the macabre fish I propelled myself ever so slowly toward the ladder then upward until my feet were on the lowest rung. The barracuda circled the boat and having satisfied his curiosity and grown bored with the whole episode, turned tail and disappeared.

Once aboard I confronted my mentor. "Where were you? I had a companion who scared the bejeebers out of me. Weren't you supposed to be my partner?"

Bill laughed, "I was right near you all the time. You did just fine."

Annie's Portion

The statement served to pacify me somewhat.

"Here, look what I brought up for you." He held an ugly, brown blob in his hand.

"What in the world is that horrible thing?"

"It's a sea cucumber. See what it can do?" Bill took a telephone receiver, kept on board for just this purpose, and laid the sea cucumber on it. Within seconds, the creature had taken on the shape of the phone, ear perforations and all. Bill further impressed the party with the cucumber's ability to impersonate a series of assorted items, a routine obviously performed many times before.

"Lunch is on," Rowena called from the galley where a bountiful lunch had been set on the gimbaled table.

The hungry group attacked the food with zeal. Once our appetites were satisfied we lazed on the deck, letting the sun bathe us in its warm embrace until the return to the dock. As the others disembarked I remember thinking, "If only my cruise could be as good as this…"

Bill interrupted my musing with a whispered question, "Can I see you later?"

"I'll only be here for a few days and I really should spend some time with Noreen and Lou."

"I'll call this evening. Maybe you'll find some free time."

At dinner that night I related the events of the day, amplifying my experience with Baron Barracuda. Noreen, who never went near the water, was appalled but Lou thought it was great fun. "Bill asked me out for the evening but I put him off."

"Why'd you do that, Annie? He's no playboy." Lou said.

"I don't know, Lou. I really admire him but he seems so…intense, almost unbending. It's just a feeling…hard to explain."

J. Fran Baird

"Well, you're here to enjoy yourself, so you just do whatever pleases you," Noreen added.

Just then the phone rang.

"Answer it," Lou ordered. "It's for you anyway."

I picked up the receiver expecting to hear Bill on the line.

"Hi. Is this Anne?" The voice was not Bill's.

"Yes it is. Who's calling?"

"This is Peter Sheffield. Do you remember me?"

The British accent was instantly recognizable. "Yes I do. How are you Peter?"

"I'm just fine. Are you enjoying your stay?"

"Yes. I'm having a wonderful time. Went sailing and scuba diving today."

"You're not wasting any time, are you? Anne, I'd like to see you again and wondered if you might enjoy attending a dinner party with me tomorrow evening. Give you a chance to meet some of the politicos here and see who makes the island function."

"I'd be delighted to, Peter. It sounds like it would be very interesting. Is it a dressy affair? I don't have much in the way of formal clothes."

"You just dress in whatever makes you comfortable. I'm sure you will look lovely. I'll pick you up at about seven-thirty."

"I'll be ready and thanks for the invite." I no sooner put the phone down when it rang again. "Hello, Turner residence."

"Annie, is that you?" This time it was Bill.

"Oh hi, Bill."

"Are you recovered from your trying experience?" He asked with a smile in his voice.

"Fully recovered?"

"Are you ready for something less exciting this evening?"

Annie's Portion

"I'm sorry, Bill. I'm afraid my hosts have already made other plans. Maybe when I return from my windjammer trip.

"I'll try again before you leave our tropic isle."

Noreen and Lou were sipping Irish Cream on the rocks. Lou fixed one for me and waited for me to fill them in.

"The first call was Peter Sheffield. I'm going to some fancy dig with him tomorrow night. The second call was from Bill. I'm sorry to have used you for an excuse but I told him you'd already made plans for us."

Lou laughed. "These men are starved for the affection of a beautiful girl. You fit the bill Annie. You should just enjoy your popularity."

"Ah," Noreen sighed. "It used to be me they fussed over. Now I'm just a fat old married house frau." She said it jokingly but I had the feeling that underneath it all she was mourning for her lost youth.

Noreen had to go into St. Johns on business the next morning but her absence gave me the opportunity to help Essie make "goat water," a stew made with pumpkin, goat meat and fragrant spices.

"Essie, one could learn to love this island living."

"Bet your family would love for you to stay Miss Annie," was Essie's simple solution.

When the kitchen chores were done a luxurious hot bubble bath waited for me in my very own tub. There were no interruptions, no kids fighting, no one banging on the door—just absolute serenity. With eyes closed I breathed in the lovely fragrance of the bay tree, unwilling to stir until the bubbles had completely dissipated.

The only dress I'd packed was a long, slightly fitted muumuu that Sarah brought back from a Hawaiian trip. Planning to press out the creases I returned to the kitchen where Essie insisted on doing the job.

"Oh, Miss Annie. This dress is some brilliant. These flowers be plumeria, yes?"

"Yes they are. It is a pretty dress isn't it?" I retrieved the now wrinkle free dress from Essie and held it against my body. "What do you think, Essie? Will this do?"

"Miss Annie. You gonna be da star."

Once in my room I dropped the muumuu over my head and adjusted the spaghetti straps. Slipping my feet into a pair of white sandals I glanced at my reflection in the floor length mirror. The pink flowers of the dress set off my red hair and blue eyes. "Not bad."

Lou gave a long whistle when he spotted me making my way along the veranda. I curtsied as he handed me a vodka gimlet.

"Anne you are just lovely," Noreen praised. "You're going to break another heart tonight. We're dining out here, on Essie's goat water. Want some?"

"Since I helped make it I have to at least taste it." It was delicious. "I'll have to make that for the kids when I get home, though getting the goat might be difficult." The stew was washed down with a second vodka. By the time Peter arrived I was already quite mellow or as one would say in sailor's nomenclature, "three sheets to the wind."

He waved from his red convertible MG. "No time to visit."

With a shrug of my shoulders I hurried down the stairs. Peter held the car door open, bending to give me a peck on the cheek as soon as I was comfortably seated.

"Anne, you look smashing. I'll be the envy of every male for miles around."

We took off in a cloud of dust and raced to the main road where Peter turned toward town.

"Is the party in St. Johns?"

"Yes it is. All political gatherings are held in what we lovingly call the 'State Building'."

"Isn't this actually a British possession?"

"The answer is yes and no. It is the epitome of empire. Rumor has it that old Chris Columbus gave the island its name when he visited it sometime in the late 1400's. Named it for some Spanish church in Seville. It wasn't until 1632 that the Brits colonized it."

"And have they been here ever since?"

"That is the 'no' part. The French made an attempt to grab it. Those terrible cannibals, the Caribs, raided the island several times, yet it remained British. But enough of my lecture. You're sure to hear much more about the subject at dinner."

We'd pulled up in front of a colonnaded brightly lit white building where a liveried valet greeted us. Lou's prognostication was borne out for many heads turned in our direction as we made our entry into an ornate, baroque ballroom. In a visibly suggestive declaration of ownership, Peter placed my arm on his and held it there as he guided me down several steps leading to the main level.

"Peter, you old son-of-a-gun. Where did you find this treasure?"

Peter smiled politely at the tuxedo-clad man but continued to make his way through the assemblage. Crisscrossing the crowded room he introduced me to a select few, several of whom I recognized as Noreen's dinner guests. Fashionably dressed dancers, inspired by an orchestra situated on a balcony perched above the ballroom, twirled across a raised platform. Sparkling chandeliers filled the room with dazzling light amplified by the exquisite jewels worn by many of the ladies.

"What is your pleasure?" Peter inquired. "Would you like to dance or do you prefer a libation?"

"A dance sounds lovely."

He proved to be an accomplished dancer, steering me expertly through the high spirited crowd, interrupted only once by the man who had earlier greeted us. Peter ignored his request for my company.

"Brash chap, that one." Peter said.

"Why Peter, I do believe you were jealous."

He was prevented from responding by an announcement that dinner was being served and the elegant company moved into the dining room where as in the ballroom, crystal chandeliers radiated a profusion of light. Wine glasses and sterling flatware shone with reflected brilliance on the elongated table. Ornate, high backed chairs stood at attention at either side of the table. Each china dinner plate bore a gilded place card indicating the name of the intended seat occupant.

Looking at Peter for direction I marveled at the opulent display. "What next?"

"Ah, my sweet. I will be deprived of your company for too long a while."

He pulled out a chair in front of a table setting displaying a neatly embossed card with my name on it.

"You will have the Hammonds on either side of you and I will be relegated to the seat opposite your lovely face."

"Aren't they the couple who came to Antigua to wait in the sun for the undertaker?"

"That they are and here they are."

Walter and Eleanor Hammond took their seats beside me.

"How delightful to see you again." Eleanor exclaimed.

Walter concurred and for the next two hours they entertained me with stories of their travels, experiences and mishaps. His many years with the Foreign Service had provided them the opportunity to live in India, Africa and Egypt.

"I just went along for the ride." Eleanor explained.

The dinner, consisting of typically English fare was accompanied by an overabundance of alcohol, the drink of choice for most gin and tonic which I declined, preferring wine. Explaining to the Hammonds I was about to embark on a sailing adventure I asked Walter to tell me more about the history of Antigua and the Windward Islands. He was only too happy to oblige.

"You know, my dear, Americans were not the only ones to exploit the blacks. Barbuda was planned as a breeding place for slaves who could provide the labor for the tobacco and cane fields. Fortunately the plan failed and the blacks were eventually given their freedom." Walter ordered another drink for himself and me.

"That's fascinating, Walter. Do go on, please."

"Oh, Anne, don't encourage the bloke or he'll bend your ear all night." Eleanor was beginning to feel the effects of her fourth drink.

"Antigua has had a troubled history. It was part of the West Indies Federation, which was dissolved in 1962. Last year, Antigua assumed the status of an associate state of the UK who maintains the responsibility for its defense; although what they would defend it from I really don't know. Antigua has recently attained the right of self-government and your young Mr. Sheffield is one of our newly elected representatives. I wouldn't be the least bit surprised if he becomes Governor in the not too distant future."

"Walter, you are an absolute fount of information." I took a sip of a fourth glass of wine.

"Did you notice the frigate in the harbor, Anne?" Eleanor was developing a slight slur.

"Yes, I did. I wondered about it."

"Well, there is a movement afoot to gain complete independence from Britain, which of course the Brits are not happy about. There have been several uprisings here on the island and as a matter of fact there is an expectation of trouble even as we speak."

"Now, Eleanor. Don't frighten the girl. Don't pay attention to her Anne. She's become a flibbertigibbet in her old age."

We finished dessert and the gentlemen were invited to the smoking room while the ladies retired to the lounge. Peter approached me, silently indicating the doors leading to the veranda. I got the message and eased my way to the exit where Peter was waiting.

"Have you had enough? Shall we cut out, as they say?"

"Brilliant idea, Mr. Sheffield."

Peter signaled for the car and in a few minutes we were off again. An unusually large, agitated crowd filled the main street of St. Johns requiring Peter to make a detour through an alley to avoid contact with the angry mob.

"What's going on, Peter?"

"Oh, it's this independence thing. Not to worry."

After making several turns down the narrow back streets we reached a well lit area and parked near a flashing neon sign.

"Welcome to the Pink Banana." A bouncer greeted us at the door and recognized Peter immediately. "Good evening, Mr. Sheffield." He acknowledged me with a broad smile. "I'll keep a watch on your car."

"Thanks, Germane." Peter slipped him a five-pound note.

The disco was packed with writhing bodies, looking like so many other-worldly creatures in the unnatural strobe lights. The air was thick with the smoke and smell of marijuana. Peter ordered drinks at the bar and elbowed his way to the dance floor with my hand in his. We joined the madly gyrating throng, dancing till we were out of breath. Alternating between bar and dance floor until exhausted and overcome by the fumes, we fled into the clean night air. I could still hear the strains of "Rollin" as Peter lit out on the road toward the plantation. Completely relaxed, with my head resting on the seat back, I was enjoying another pleasant night, warm and moonlit. With a quick twist of the wrist Peter made a sharp turn on two wheels and pulled to a jolting stop. The scent of citrus, lemons or oranges perhaps, suggested we were in an orchard. Peter cut the engine and reached for me. His kiss was politely reserved and I responded in like manner, both of us conspicuously inebriated.

From the dashboard Peter retrieved a small packet containing a substance resembling tobacco. He rolled some of the ground leaves into a cigarette paper, twisted the ends and handed it to me. I watched with interest as he repeated the process, put the butt in his mouth and lit it. He inhaled deeply then slowly exhaled, observing the smoke as it floated in the air.

"Let me light you up Anne." Peter struck another match and reached toward me.

"I don't smoke, Peter."

"Ah, but you'll love this. Best you can get anywhere." He raised my hand, still holding the joint, and lifted it to my mouth which I opened just enough to keep the butt steady as he lit it. "Just draw on it real slow. Don't swallow the smoke. Inhale slowly and take it into your lungs." Peter took another pull to teach me by example.

I did as instructed but with the first puff experienced a burning sensation in my throat and thought I was about to choke.

Peter encouraged me to try again. "It takes a little practice." He was beginning to feel the effects of the marijuana and leaned back against the headrest.

Taking small puffs, watching the end of the paper flicker with a red glow, I experienced a sense of detachment, lightheadedness and utter tranquility.

"This is nice." I wasn't sure if I'd spoken aloud and looked to see if Peter gave any indication of having heard me. The spark from his cigarette was no longer visible.

"Have you finished?" My voice sounded distant and strange to my ears.

"Ah, Anne. I have corrupted you." He opened the door and got out of the car.

Feeling exceedingly playful I asked, "Are you leaving?"

"Not on your life." He walked around to my side of the car, opened the door and pulled me out. Then folding the passenger seat down, he gently coaxed me onto the back seat. He unzipped his pants, removed mine and, in what seemed like slow motion, attempted to enter me. The effects of the drug were beginning to wear off. There I was, in the back seat of a red sport car, my panties around my ankles, my would-be lothario struggling to pull his pants up. I was swamped by a wave of hysterical laughter. Humiliated by my reaction and his failure to perform, Peter hiked up his trousers, got behind the wheel and sped off leaving me giggling in the back seat. We returned to the plantation where the house was ablaze with lights and a number of cars were parked on the drive.

"Something must have happened, Peter."

He'd recovered his composure and as he braked the car asked if I wanted him to come in with me.

"Yes, please do." I scrambled in my purse for a comb and ran it through my hair, then wiped my smeared eye makeup with a handkerchief as we hurried up the steps.

"Oh, Annie," Noreen ran to meet us. "We were so worried about you."

"What's happened?" Peter asked looking around the room. At least a dozen people, including the Hammonds, were engaged in animated discussions. Eleanor seemed exceptionally distressed as did Noreen.

Annie's Portion

"There was a riot in St. Johns. A bunch of drunken rabble-rousers ransacked the town, breaking windows and setting some trivial fires. They tried to break into the State House but by then a platoon of marines from the British frigate were ashore and were attempting to put down the uprising." Lou explained.

"Didn't you hear the cannons?" Eleanor joined the conversation.

"We were at the disco. The music is so loud there we probably didn't notice." Peter looked at me and I sucked in my breath in an attempt to stifle another spate of giggles.

"What are all these people doing here?"

"Well Anne, this being the center of the island, we all thought it would be the safest place to spend the night and wait for the crisis to end." Walter was not going to be left out of the conversation.

"Now that we know you are both safe, I think its time to arrange some sleeping accommodations." With Essie's help, Lou and Noreen gathered pillows and blankets and arranged them on the sofa and floor.

"Walter, you and Eleanor can have the spare bedroom." Lou offered. "Peter, you can figure out your own sleeping quarters." He winked slyly.

"No thanks, Lou. I'd best be getting back to the State House. Anne, I'll call you later."

"I'm supposed to be sailing at four tomorrow afternoon. I wonder if that will still be on."

"I'll find out for you." Peter kissed me lightly on the cheek. "Thank you for a lovely evening."

"Thank you, Peter. It was a real adventure. And do be careful."

With Peter's departure, the group retired to their various sleeping quarters. I slipped away before Noreen had a chance to ask too many questions.

Peter rang up about ten the next morning, by which time the assemblage had eaten a hearty breakfast prepared by Essie and served by Franklin who had finally been called out of the field.

"Good morning, Anne. Are you well?" he asked.

"Yes, thank you Peter. How about you? Did you have any problems last night?"

"There was quite a ruckus but things have quieted a bit. Town is in a mess, however. It will take a while to clean it up and repair the damage. May I come by this morning?"

"I think that would be fine. Most of the guests have left and we are just picking up."

"See you in a bit then." He rang off.

The Hammonds were the last to leave.

"Goodbye dear. Have a lovely trip if you go, and do be careful." Eleanor admonished me.

"Cheerio, my girl. See you on your return." Walter waved as they climbed into their Rolls.

"Peter is coming by in a little while. I hope you don't mind Noreen."

"It will be good to get all the news from him." Noreen was anxious to hear the outcome of the disquieting events.

Just then Lou made an appearance. I was glad for the distraction knowing Noreen was ready to question me about the previous night's adventure.

"I think we've got everything set here. I'll drive into town and see how the factory and your shop fared."

"Please wait until Peter gets here. He'll be able to tell us if it's safe yet."

"I'm sure it will be fine. You know how quickly these blow-ups end."

At that moment, Peter's red car was spotted on the drive.

"Here's the man now. He certainly made a quick turn-around."

Annie's Portion

We walked out on the veranda to greet him, anxious for the news. Noreen was the first to ply him with questions. Lou went to get some coffee.

"What have you found out? Is the town quiet? Was there much damage?"

"Whoa, Noreen. Give the man a chance." Lou handed Peter a steaming mug.

"There are troops off the frigate patrolling the town so it's fairly quiet now. There was a bit of gunfire and several injuries, some serious. The State Building was vandalized and many of the shops looted. All in all, not a good night."

"That's terrible." I was appalled. "It sounds so uncivilized, so third world."

"This is the third world, Annie. Haven't you noticed?" Noreen pointed to the field where Franklin had retrieved his scythe and was once again pursuing his never-ending task.

"As for you, Anne," Peter took my hands in his. "Your trip is delayed, indefinitely I fear. I spoke with Captain Wilde, whose demeanor matched his name. It seems the Southern Star was damaged by a misdirected volley from the frigate."

"You mean the British one in the harbor? How could that happen?"

"Annie, these seamen are sent here for training. They're quite inexperienced. I imagine all the rioting in town sent them into a tizzy and in their haste to fire a warning shot, damaged several yachts in the harbor. The Star lost her mizzen-mast. I am sorry."

"Thanks for getting that info for me. I'm so... disappointed. I love you all but I was so ready to become a sailor."

Peter could not stay long. "There's a lot to do to get things in order again. Anne, will you walk back to the car with me?" He said his good-byes to Noreen and Lou and took my hand as we walked back to his car.

"I'm not completely sure about what transpired last night, but I do believe I behaved rather badly. I hope you can find it in your heart to forgive me. The last thing I wanted to do was cause you any distress or dampen our relationship."

"We had way too much to drink, Peter. And that pot business was just a bad idea for both of us. I did have a lovely evening and we can forget the last part of it."

"I hope you will see me again." He kissed me, exhibiting more emotion than I expected.

Returning to the patio, I dropped dejectedly into a deeply pillowed chair.

"Say, Annie. You may not have to give up your sailing experience after all. I'm sure Captain Bill will be happy to substitute for Captain Wilde." Lou attempted to cushion my disappointment.

"And," Noreen added. "We will be delighted to entertain you till you leave. You've only seen a small bit of our island paradise."

I was inconsolable. Essie handed me an extra potent daiquiri. "Miss Annie. It gonna be so good to have you here. We be no sailors but sure do know how to have fun."

"Maybe they'll be able to repair the mast sooner than we think and there'll be just a short delay." Lou put his arm around me.

"You're right Lou. I just have to be more positive."

Bill called as soon as he'd heard the news. "Jack Wilde's misfortune is my good fortune. Do you have time for me now?"

"Oh, Bill...that's cruel."

"Maybe, but it's honest. After all, I've suffered misfortunes of my own. Will you see me tomorrow?"

"Are you taking out a group?"

"No, Annie. Several of my charters have cancelled because of the teapot tempest. I will spend as much time

Annie's Portion

with you as you'll allow. I'll make a sailor of you if that's what you want."

"That's an offer just too good to refuse."

"See you at the wharf at eight."

"This is supposed to be my vacation. Can you make that ten?"

The laugh was hearty and sincere. "Okay, six bells it is."

"What does that mean in English?"

"Ten, but you'll start your lessons tomorrow."

Bill wasted no time. The moment we were out of the harbor my tutorial began.

"Today, you're going to learn the basics of sailing, starting with the nomenclature. We'll start with locations on the boat. There is no downstairs, no front or back, no left or right. There's no floor and no bathroom aboard this vessel."

"No bathroom? Easy for you. You can just hang it over the side."

Bill grimaced. "You will, however, find a head available." He went on to describe the meanings of foredeck, aft, below, starboard, port, on and on ad infinitum.

I learned ropes were halyards or lines or sheets, there were mainsails, jibs, Genoas, staysails and square sails. Then there were instruction in knot tying, which Bill insisted was of primary importance. By half-past-one I was saturated with language of the sailor, my fingers sore from knot tying.

"Have you had enough for today? Are you hungry?"

He received an unqualified "yes" as his answer.

"Come below and I'll show you the head and the galley. You can help with lunch."

The head was the size of a postage stamp; a toilet and sink on one wall, a showerhead protruding from the wall opposite with a drain below. I used the toilet, stepped on the foot pedal and released a gush of water that was quickly sucked out into a holding tank somewhere.

"Feeling better?" Bill asked as he handed me a bloody Mary.

"Yes much, although this boat living certainly takes some getting used to.

The ships clock struck four.

"I know times passes quickly when you're having fun but it can't be four o'clock, can it?"

"No, it's only two."

"What do the bells mean?"

"They designate changes of the watch. Not the ones you wear the ones you're on duty for. At twelve midnight the bell chimes eight. Every four hours, eight bells chime to indicate a change of the watch. In between the bell sounds in twos with an additional quick chime on the half hour. Does that help?"

"Not likely."

"You'll get used to it after a while. Of course, during daylight hours, you can judge time by the position of the sun. When it's over the yardarm, it's time to party. I know you'll learn that in a hurry." He smirked as he placed some sandwiches on the gimbal table.

"I guess we should think about getting back...so I'm in time for happy hour at the plantation."

It had been a wonderful day and my earlier opinion of Bill had been greatly upgraded. The sun was near the horizon when we pulled up to the dock.

"I've got some things to attend to tomorrow but shall we try another lesson the day after? Maybe a beach and some snorkeling if you like."

"That sounds wonderful. I'll have Essie pack us a picnic lunch. Thank you for turning an awful disappointment into a pleasant surprise."

Bill kissed me just as Peter pulled up in his red sport car. He waved and shouted, "We were concerned about you." As he neared he added, "Never know what can happen when you're out with this fellow."

Bill acknowledged him with a grunt. "See you later, Anne."

"Is that bloke going to take up all your time?"

"Don't fret, Peter. I'll save some for you."

The days passed all too quickly. Bill continued his instructions, allowing me to take the helm while he stood behind me, guiding my arms from time to time until I got the feel of the Grenadier. When he told me to take a northerly heading and left me at the wheel alone I was uncertain, trying to remember everything he told me. With frequent glances at the compass, I tried to keep the arrow on the point indicating north. When the sail began to flap I turned the wheel to port. If the flapping increased, I turned the wheel to starboard. After a while I was able to judge the wind direction by the feel of it on my neck and face. I realized the Grenadier interacted with the waves as well as the wind. By anticipating her reaction and keeping a light hand on the wheel, the lady made her own adjustments. But she seemed to heave a sigh of relief when he took the helm.

"You're going to be a sailor before long."

"I want to be able to sail like you."

"No problem. Do you have thirty years?"

We sailed to a beautiful black sand beach where we dropped our towels and dashed into the warm surf, returning to the boat in the dinghy along a moonlit path reflected in the glassy water of the cove. Sailing back to St. John a pod of porpoises swam alongside, racing the Grenadier with apparent glee. They swam ahead and under the bowsprit then appeared abaft, leaping and diving through her wake, disappearing suddenly. One by one stars became visible as we moved silently up the west side of the island and into the harbor.

There were evenings with Peter, dining and dancing to the Calypso music of a steel band and days of exploring the island with Noreen and Lou.

Three days before my departure Jack Wilde called to say the Southern Star had been repaired and would I like to spend a day or two aboard her. The sleek hundred-fifty-foot clipper was heavenly and I spent two days and one night with the angels. Favorable winds gave the Star a welcome boost north. Several times along the way, porpoises accompanied us. At night the boat lights reflected off hundreds of flying fishes. I spent some of the time at the wheel with Captain Jack, honing my sailing skills.

On my last day aboard I asked Jack how far we had to go."

"As the seagull flies, about twenty miles. Are you tiring of the adventure?"

I was quick to assure him. "Oh no, I don't want it to be over."

A short time later we sighted an atoll, waves crashing in wild profusion across the coral outcrop. Jack skillfully steered the boat through a narrow opening in the reef and the Star glided into an enchanted opalescent lagoon. An arc of gently waving palm trees hugged an ivory white sand beach. It was the most beautiful spot I'd ever seen. There was a hushed atmosphere on board as the anchor was lowered, no one wanting to spoil the pleasure of the moment.

It was Jack who broke the silence. "Well, what are you waiting for? Get your suits on and grab the snorkels. This is the *piece de resistance*."

The group disbanded only to return moments later in swimsuits. Spence handed us snorkeling gear and encouraged us to dive off the boat. Most of the guys did just that but the ladies were more timid, using the ladder

Annie's Portion

to lower our fragile bodies into the crystal clear lagoon. Jack joined and with his charges in tow, swam to a calm area on the inner curve of the reef. The abundance of fish and sea creatures was unimaginable. I saw a cuttlefish, a small octopus and several sea horses. The coral was a living tapestry of marine life and water plants. I snorkeled, utterly entranced for an hour, before Jack gave the signal to return to the boat. Sadly we climbed the ladder, leaving the magic water world behind us.

"Don't look so glum. We have just the thing to ease your pain." Jack pointed to the table where a delectable brunch replaced the muffins.

"Maryanne, you have outdone yourself." Gordy was head hog at the trough.

The hungry horde made short work of the delectable morsels set before them. I found it hard to decide whether to have eggs Benedict or crepes. I nibbled on cream cheese and caviar and sipped a mimosa. I thought, "Life is good." The table was cleared, my merry companions went below to dress and the Captain took the Southern Star out to sea for the sail back to her home port. Once through the reef, the sails were raised, the engine cut and the Southern Star seemed impatient to take us home. The wind had taken an unusual turn, filling the sails from behind. Jack issued some additional commands sending the crew to man the sheets. The result was a glorious spreading of wings, sails to each side of the graceful lady, sending her skimming through the water on a run. The boat suddenly seemed to be motionless, the only evidence of its swift movement the wake it left in its path. For me it was an exhilarating experience and one of the more memorable moments of the trip.

The Southern Star motored up to the dock at English Harbor just as the bell sounded eight. I did a quick calculation in my head and came up with four o'clock just as I caught sight of a red flash between two sheds on the wharf as the boat slipped into her mooring. Captain Jack had radioed the estimated time of arrival and I was certain Peter had come for me. Passengers and crew said their emotional goodbyes, with lots of hugs and a few tears. We promised to keep in touch, knowing full well we would not. Jack took my bag and carried it down the gangplank. He waved to Peter who wasted no time in his effort to disengage me from Jack's arm.

"Anne, you look marvelous, brown as a nut. No need to ask if you had a good trip."

"It was unimaginably grand, Peter. And today was the most special of all."

"This lady has turned out to be a great sailor. Better hang on to her or I'll hire her myself." Jack told Peter.

"No chance," Peter smiled. "But thanks for taking care of Anne for me."

He urged me towards the car and helped me in. I turned to wave to Jack and the others and took a last look at the graceful lady who had given me unforgettable, precious memories to take with me—and a desire to sail I would never lose.

Peter zipped through the crowded town and onto the main road. He pulled into the spot I recognized as the orchard where we had behaved like fools.

"Oh, Peter. We're too sober to do this again."

Peter smiled. "No, this will not be a repeat performance." He grew more serious. "Anne, don't leave tomorrow. Stay a while longer."

"I'd love to stay. But you know as well as I, there's a family and job waiting for me."

"Forget the job. Send for the family. You can all stay with me. I have a house big enough for a small army."

"I can't do that Peter." I tried to sound as convincing as possible.

Annie's Portion

"Do you have any feelings for me? Any at all?" Embracing me, he attempted to kiss me.

I pushed him away gently. "Peter, we hardly know each other. I have a life back in New York."

"I know all I need to know about you. You can learn more about me by staying. This is not a difficult place to live."

"I know that all too well." I recalled the last two weeks. "Please, Peter. Let's not talk about this now. Noreen and Lou are expecting me."

The tires squealed as Peter turned into the main road and raced the two miles to the plantation. Noreen and Lou were all ears. I had to relive the trip with them, beginning with a description of the Star and Captain Jack, ending with the lovely morning in the lagoon. The phone rang just as I put the last flourish on my saga.

"You might as well answer it. We've never been quite so popular. If it's Bill, say yes."

"Hello, Turner residence."

"Annie, is that you?"

"Oh, hi Bill."

"Are you recovered from your sail? Learn anything more?" he asked with a smile in his voice.

"Fully recovered."

"Are you available for something less exciting this evening?"

"Yes. I've already gotten parental permission."

"I knew Lou would be all for it. Had some doubts about Noreen. She probably thinks I'm a bounder."

"Not true. She adores you."

"I hope I will have the same effect on you. Is half-an-hour too soon?"

"That will be just fine. See you then."

I returned to the veranda where my cousins were sipping Irish Cream on the rocks. Lou fixed one for me.

"I'm being picked up in half-an-hour."

"My goodness. You're going to need a dance program to keep your suitors straight."

By the time I'd finished my drink Bill had arrived.

"Good evening, all you lovely people."

"Hey Bill," Lou was feeling good. "What's the idea of stealing this lovely lady away from us?"

"Would you like a drink, Bill?" Noreen asked, hoping to delay his departure.

"Thanks but no thanks. You've had her long enough. Are you ready Annie?"

The main road was now familiar and I recognized several moonlit landmarks. The rutted dirt road into which we turned required our passing under the cover of tall trees which for a brief time obscured the moon. The Rover bounced heavily through a series of potholes, the silence broken by the steady grumbling of the old Land Rover. The warm night breeze was strangely scented by the cane grasses. Through the inky darkness I discerned the lights of a house about half-a-mile ahead.

"Sorry I can't smooth this out for you, Annie."

"Every life needs a little bump now and then."

Bill braked in front of the geodesic dome looming like an ancient cairn, oddly out of place amid the tropical surroundings.

"Welcome," he said as he led me up several steps to the large deck. He paused dramatically by the front door before throwing it open.

I was suitably impressed. The cavernous room, in the shape of a pentagon, was faced with smooth timber, the domed ceiling constructed of hexagonal sections of the same wood fitted together seamlessly.

"This is awesome," I exclaimed. "It's nothing like I thought it would be."

Annie's Portion

Bill beamed with pride of ownership as he guided me through the open sphere of the lower floor. The kitchen, dining and living areas were unencumbered by walls. A waist high counter delineated the kitchen area while the rest of the room was partitioned by articles of furniture, a couch here a table there, plants and floor lamps everywhere. Taking my arm he led me to a circular stairway leading to a balcony ringing the upper floor. Three large bedrooms and two bathrooms completed the sleeping level, from where four skylights, one facing each of the cardinal points of the compass revealed the moonlit sky, and would in daytime provide a good deal of natural light.

"Bill, this place is too good to be true. It is absolutely perfect in every way."

"Do you really like it Annie?" His arms were around me and I could feel the great strength of his muscular body. His kiss was a true representation of the man; firm, honest and determined, no sissy this one. When he released me he was unapologetic although he did offer a frank explanation.

"I guess I got carried away, Annie. It's been a very long time since I felt this way about a woman. You seem to bring out the animal in me."

He had me off-guard. I was flustered and didn't know how to respond. When I started down the staircase Bill caught my arm.

"You're not angry with me, are you?"

"No, Bill. Just a little taken aback."

"I'm not one to pull punches. I know I'm a lot older than you but I'm fit, and ready and able to take care of all your needs."

I reached the first level and waited for him to catch up. "Bill, that sounds like a proposition." I laughed trying to make light of an awkward situation. "We hardly know each other. I'm very attracted to you but this is a little too soon for any kind of commitment."

He reached for me again and held me firmly in his embrace. "It's a proposal. I'm too old to waste a lot of time on formalities. You would not find it hard to live here, would you?"

At that moment my thoughts were about Rowena, realizing she was conspicuously absent. "Rowena would not like another woman in her kitchen."

"The hell with her. It's time she got a life of her own," he answered irritably.

I could well imagine how he'd react when crossed. Without relinquishing his hold on me he placed his hand on the back of my head and effortlessly lifted my face to his. When our lips met a second time I returned his embrace, knowing what was about to happen, and did not resist when he steered me to a large sofa and pulled me toward him. He undressed me with rough hands but gentle movements. We made love with feeling, he whispering words of endearment, I accepting him lovingly. Satisfied, we broke from each other's embrace.

"Isn't this when he lights up a cigarette and offers her one?" He said it with a touch of irony. Then more seriously he added, "Annie, pack your skivvies in a bag and come away with me."

"Just like that?"

"Just like that."

"You can't be serious."

"I've never been more serious."

"We're strangers. What do you know about me...or for that matter, I about you?"

"Enough. Enough to know I could be content spending the rest of what's left of my life with you by my side."

"Bill, I have four children waiting for me."

"Leave them to their father. You're entitled to your life and I can make it better."

Annie's Portion

"Bill, I can't do that. I've never run from responsibilities in my life. I certainly am not going to do it now." I dressed quickly. "Please take me home."

He pulled on his jeans and sweatshirt without further comment. We drove to the plantation in silence and Bill parked a short way from the steps of the house.

"If you ever change your mind, I'm here."

With those few parting words I left him and ran up the stairs, walking quietly to my veranda door so as not to wake my cousins. My lovely four poster bed welcomed me. Fully clothed, I cried myself to sleep.

As usual, Lou had left for work and Noreen was having breakfast by the time I coaxed myself to leave the comfy bed.

Noreen could not contain her curiosity. "Well, tell me. What was it like?"

Careful not to disclose too much I asked innocently, "What was what like?"

"Oh don't be coy. What was the house like? What was he like? What happened?"

"He asked me to run away with him."

"Very funny. Now really. Give with the dope."

"He asked me to leave my kids and sail away with him."

"Annie, he didn't." Noreen could now see that I was telling the truth. "What in the world did you tell him?"

"I told him no. For a moment I was so tempted. Just think how nice it would be, Noreen. Just leave the kids, the job, the problems. Run off with this strong, passionate man who wanted to do everything to make me happy."

Noreen, for once in her life, knew when to be silent. She let me go on, understanding from her own past experience, all the emotions I must have been feeling. When I finally ran out of steam and ended my tearful tirade I smiled weakly at my cousin. "Thanks for listening. I'm just a fool."

"You're no fool. But isn't it nice to know that you brought out the best in that confirmed bachelor?"

Peter came to say goodbye. He sat sullenly, sipping a gin and tonic.

Lou managed to take me aside and ask, "What's with him? He's behaving like a spurned suitor."

"That's about the size of it."

"Annie, that makes two offers you've turned down in two weeks. You're going to set a world record."

"I think the men down here are starved for mainland women." I was about to say, "Young white women," but thought better of it.

Essie called us all in for my last island brunch. Peter made his apologies and I accompanied him to his car.

"You can change your mind any time. I'm not going anywhere."

Taking the initiative I kissed him, and waved a farewell as he disappeared in that now familiar cloud of dust.

During breakfast, Noreen and Lou filled me in on all the details of the night of the riots. It seemed as though Peter was an island hero. He had single-handedly disarmed several thugs who'd broken into the State House taking a woman hostage. He'd interrupted an attempted rape and prevented a conflagration, all in the space of thirty minutes.

"And you turned him down?" Noreen teased.

"Maybe he's just too much man for me."

We moved to the veranda for coffee and liqueur. The sun was warm on my face. Franklin was in the field lickin' the grass. I tried to absorb all the sounds, smells and sights of the tropical morning, wanting to keep them always with me. I excused myself and went to my room by way of the veranda. The fragrance of the bay tree lingered long.

Chapter XII

1984 – Cutter Lake

Shaken from my nap by the sound of Claire's dinner bell, not wanting to see Branch and face his disapproving posture once again, I argued with myself for a good ten minutes before finally deciding to skip supper. Plunking down on the rug in front of the hearth, I lit the fire and had just started pulling off my boots when there was a knock on the door.

"Annie, are you there?" It was Branch. Not waiting for a response he opened the door and spied me sitting on the floor. "Are you okay?" He came closer and knelt beside me. "We were concerned...I was concerned...when you didn't come in to dinner."

Choking down the lump in my throat I answered, "I'm fine. Just not very hungry tonight." Staring into the flames allowed me to avoid his eyes.

"I'm sorry if I sounded so abrupt today but you scared the hell out of me. I know you're fond of that animal but he's wild and unpredictable. One kick from those hooves would have seriously injured you."

"I don't know how to explain it, Branch. But Beau and I have made a connection. Somehow we really have connected. I know he would not hurt me."

"I won't argue the point now, only promise you won't do anything that foolish again."

"I promise."

"Let's go into supper. I bet your appetite will return when you get a load of Claire's eats."

"Actually I'm starving."

He pulled me up from my seated position and helped me slip my arms into the sleeves of my jacket. Wrapping his arms around me, he clasped them together under my breast and kissed me lightly on the nape. My knees turned to jelly. He released me and gave me a gentle push out the door.

At supper, which was delicious as usual, the conversation turned to the Beau and Annie love affair. Frank and Sandy teased me about my choice of men.

Pete was much impressed with my competency saying, "You did such a great job, Annie. You softened him up for Branch."

There was general agreement and much joking.

Fabian shyly offered an apology for squealing to Branch. "Miss Annie. How did you know to use a *falda* and *mecate*?"

"A *falda*? Oh, you mean the hackamore. Learned it from a Hawaiian cowboy. Were you able to get a halter on him, Branch?" I was feeling quite smug.

Branch was not amused. "I almost had a halter on him yesterday, without carrots or apples. Which reminds me…" he was stopped in mid-sentence by the jibes of his crew and laughed with the rest of them.

Branch walked back to the cabin with me, my flashlight in hand. "Well, you had the last laugh on me tonight."

"You just take yourself too seriously." In a most coquettish manner I blinked my eyes several times. "You're not still mad at me, are you? Is our trip still on?"

We'd reached the door. "The answers respectively are no and yes. We leave at eight sharp. Be ready." He kissed me lightly on the forehead, quickly turned away and took the steps two at a time.

Tuesday – Oct. 16th

The first light of dawn found me sleepily stumbling through the frigid cabin searching for the clothes I'd laid out the night before. A flick of the switch on the nearest lamp bathed the room in a pale yellow glow.

Annie's Portion

"Ah, there you are," a comment made upon rediscovering the neat bundle on the chair beside the fireplace. Skirting the cold floor, trying to keep bare feet on the rug, I hurried to retrieve it. Thinking the clothes would retain some heat from the fire, I'd placed them with meticulous care in the order in which I planned to wear them; wool sweater at the bottom of the pile, jeans, denim shirt, tee shirt and lastly, thermal underwear. Unfortunately, the few remaining embers on the hearth neither warmed the clothing nor dispelled the chill in the room. Shivering, I removed my pajamas and systematically dressed. Once my feet had been stuffed into some thick woolen socks I began to warm up. Dropping the sweater next to the Stetson and leather gloves already on a side table, I proceeded to the bathroom to begin my morning ablutions; brushing teeth, washing face, combing hair. Suddenly reminded of how the kids referred to my makeup bag as, "Mom's bag of tricks" a smile creased my face. My response had always been, "It's one way to turn a sow's ear into a silk purse."

Knowing time was of the essence, realizing a make-up job was an unnecessary embellishment and risking the possibility of looking more like a gunny sack than a silk purse, I limited myself to moisture cream, blush, lipstick and the merest hint of waterproof mascara.

"This will have to do for two days," a remark made to the face in the mirror. Adding comb, toothbrush and packet of Kleenex to the four items, I stuffed the renovation combination into a fanny pack and rolled it, along with my jacket and gloves into a tight bundle cinched with a leather belt. At seven-ten the sweater and boots went on. Grabbing my hat I made for the kitchen where there was sure to be a hot pot of coffee waiting.

"Good mornin', Annie. I see ya made the early reveille." Claire, in her usual getup, was standing at the stove tending

J. Fran Baird

several sizzling pans. The aroma of baking biscuits made my mouth water.

"Certainly didn't want to keep the boss waiting. Can I snatch a cup of coffee?"

"Yul hafta do better than that. Branch says yer ta have a good breakfast before ya take off. How about some oatmeal and biscuits?"

"Sounds great but will there be time?"

"Ya jest sit yerself down. It's all ready fer ya." Claire placed a steaming bowl of freshly cooked oatmeal and two biscuits in front of me. The brown sugar, cinnamon and cream were already on the table as were some butter and honey.

"You certainly know how to treat a girl," I said appreciatively.

"Got my orders. Now you finish that and git yerself out to that barn."

After downing several spoons of oatmeal, a biscuit and some coffee, too excited to eat more I dashed out. "I'm off. See you tomorrow."

Claire's parting words, so very reminiscent of Sarah's, were "Ya have a good time and take care".

Nearing the stable Branch's voice was easily recognizable. "Let's get the lady in first. Then maybe Samson will follow." He and Pete were attempting to load the horses into a trailer. Samson was being particularly uncooperative. Pete held Samson back while Branch led his horse, Jessie to the trailer ramp. She was an imposing animal, a dark brown bay with jet-black mane, tail and stockings. She hesitated briefly but with Branch's coaxing finally moved into the trailer. Pete led Samson to the ramp but could not get him to step up.

"You are one dang stubborn s.o.b.," he scolded. "Say, Annie. Seein' as how you got such a way with the boys, maybe you kin get this one in the trailer."

Annie's Portion

"You've got a much better chance than me." Joining the assemblage I patted Samson on the neck. "Are you going to be trouble even before we start? Come on now. Let's just move on in and keep that pretty lady company."

Taking hold of the halter I walked beside Samson and with gentle persuasion edged him toward the trailer. He halted a moment at the foot of the ramp. Seeing Jessie he found his courage and cautiously moved the last few feet to stand beside her.

"You sure do know how to charm your men," Pete teased as he lifted the ramp and locked it in place.

Ignoring Pete's intimation, Branch took the bundle from my hand. "All set? Got everything you'll need?"

"Think so. It's not much but I'm sure I'll be plenty warm."

"The rest of the gear is already stowed in the truck so I guess we're set to go." He opened the passenger door of the Ford diesel and helped me climb into the cab. "No second thoughts?" he asked as he shut the door.

"Nary a one."

Branch switched on the ignition and the diesel engine responded with an explosive surge of power, disrupting the quiet of the morning.

"Sure is noisy."

"But dependable. You'll get used to it after a while."

We pulled away from the stable, trailer in tow, and passed through a wide gate at the northwest end of the large corral.

The fast fading sound of the diesel was barely audible when Beau began his rampage. He reared and expelled an ear-splitting bellow. The first act was followed by an unthwarted attempt to kick down the fence. Pete and Fabian went running post-haste from the barn and stood watching the unsettling performance. Beau charged the snubbing post then raced around the pen at frightening speed.

J. Fran Baird

"He's gonna kill himself." In his agitated state Fabian's Spanish accent became more pronounced.

"Sure looks like it." Pete scratched his head. "Whaddya think we oughta do amigo?"

Hearing the ruckus, Frank approached at a gallop, jumping off his mount before it had come to a full-stop. Holding on to the reins he said, "That stallion has gone just plumb loco."

Fabian, who'd spent his entire life around horses, was nervous. "He does not want to be penned up. We should turn him loose...into the pasture."

"Branch left orders for us to keep him penned till he gets back."

"He's gonna be crippled or dead in two days," Frank added.

The three conferenced for several minutes while watching Beau's performance.

"I knew he was not gonna like it, especially when Miss Annie left."

"He's pretty damn smart. If we let him loose, we may never get him back...now that he knows where we'd be takin' him."

"Well," Pete said thoughtfully. "Branch would be madder n' hell if we let him out. I don't think it'd hurt him to stay in there. Maybe if he sees we're not watchin', he'll stop."

Fabian shook his head. "I don' think so."

"He'll tire himself out afta a while, if he don't break his neck first." Frank mounted and rode back to the corral.

About a mile down the road I asked Branch about our destination. "Where are we going?"

"Originally I thought we'd go back to Rifle, take route 70 west past Grand Junction to Palisade. Little Bookcliff wild horse range is fairly accessible from there. But since we're taking an extra day for the trip, I figured you might like to see what was most likely Beau's former home."

"Oh, I'd love that. Where is it?" My eagerness was quite apparent.

"In all probability he was rounded up at Sandwash Basin. It's the largest HMA in Colorado."

We turned onto a dirt road running parallel to the split rail fence marking the ranch boundary. "This is the road some of our neighbors used to come to our party."

"It's seems considerably better than the one from Rifle." I smiled thinking of the trip with Frank and Sandy. "Please tell me more about Sandwash Basin. What is an HMA?"

"It's a horse management area. Sandwash encompasses over a hundred-and-sixty-thousand acres. It's very interesting geologically speaking, lying between two buttes and not far from Dinosaur National Monument."

"And you think Beau was raised there?"

"I'd put my money on it. There are about two hundred horses on the range. Like Beau they tend to be larger than those from other areas. There are also quite a few palominos in the herd and they're a rarity in most other places. We kind of talked briefly about it the other day."

We crossed a cattle guard where a posted sign indicated we were entering a forest service area. Branch had been quiet, focused on avoiding the bumps and potholes, trying as much as was possible to spare the horses and his passenger.

"Where are we now?"

"We're traveling through the White River National Forest. Nice of the forest service to maintain this road for us."

Lodgepole pines and Douglas firs stretched toward the cerulean sky. For the most part the area was not densely forested but occasional groves of huddled trees created dark tunnels where intermittent rays of dim sunlight managed to break through the thick canopy. We'd been driving about forty-five minutes when the road veered east becoming less bumpy. Approaching a junction Branch slowed and turned north onto a two-lane gravel road. More relaxed, he resumed the conversation.

"We still have a long way to go. This truck offers few amenities. Are you comfortable, Annie?"

"Yes, I am...and enjoying every minute of the ride."

"You seemed to have heard about *mestanos*. How much do you really know?"

"Not an awful lot. I've seen mention of them being sold to make fertilizer or dog food. Think I saw a documentary on PBS and an animated movie about a captured mustang who was put to work on a railroad and saved by an Indian. That's about it."

Branch laughed. "There's some truth to the first part but I'm afraid the rest is a fairy tale."

"Go on, please."

"Do you want a complete history lesson or just the most recent stuff?"

"Nothing less than all will do for me."

"I can be very long-winded, Annie. Be sure to stop me when I start to bore you."

While my answer was positive, it was a certainty he could never bore me.

"Although they were commonly used in Europe and Asia, the ancestors of the horses we see today were long gone from North America by the time the Spanish conquistadors arrived. The Spaniards brought many horses with them and eventually established breeding ranches throughout the Southwest. There's still a great dispute over the mustang's origin. The more accepted opinion is that some animals escaped, while others were intentionally released, forming the first wild herds which the Spaniards called *mestanos*. With so much open grassland for them

Annie's Portion

to feed on and so few natural enemies, they continued to expand and improve so that by the late 1800's there were a couple million of them competing with ranchers for graze. The ranchers began building fences, keeping the wild herds from reaching sources of food and water. It also kept them more confined and victim to winter storms. Not satisfied with the rate of decline in the herds, Texas ranchers declared war on the wild horses. They initiated mass roundups and sold the animals to slaughterhouses as you said, to be turned into fertilizer or pet food."

We'd reached a multilane highway and Branch made a left turn heading west.

"We're on a scenic highway now, Flat Tops Trail. This road winds for about sixty miles through some of the most beautiful scenery you'll ever see, all the way east to Yampa. Too bad we're going west to Meeker—less impressive but still pretty. We'll be on it for only a short time. Do I still have your ear, Annie? You're so quiet."

I'd closed my eyes and assumed he thought I was asleep. "I've been listening with rapt attention. To Meeker, our next port of call." I raised my arm in a mock toast then added more seriously, "Just thinking about those poor animals. It seems to me you've given this oration more than once."

Branch smiled. "I guess I do sound like a preacher. Yeah, I'm pretty avid about the subject. I've spoken at some hearings with the Bureau and ranchers. Sometimes I do an informal presentation at a school. It's good to make kids aware of their natural environment and how easy it is to destroy it."

"Sounds like the *mestanos* have a real friend in you."

"They need all the friends they can get. They've sure had some bad times. Slowly but surely, the herds were being decimated. But then, low and behold, their defender came along. Any idea who it was?"

"None. A cowboy I suppose."

"Wrong. It was another Annie."

"Really! Oh, you're just pulling my leg."

"Lovely as that idea is, I am not. A woman living somewhere in Nevada, nicknamed 'Wild Horse Annie,' spearheaded a movement to save the American mustang, their name having been Anglicized. Through the persistence of Annie and the influence of a few of her well-heeled friends, Congress was persuaded to pass the 'Wild Free-Roaming Horse and Burro Act of 1959.'"

By this time we had reached the small community of Meeker where Branch pulled into the parking lot of "Jodi's Diner – home cooking and apple pie our specialty."

"It's time for a break. Need to tend to our other passengers too."

"That was a delightful drive Branch, and a very informative one. Is there more?"

"Just a little. We'll complete the saga after some lunch. But don't expect gourmet food. The words 'home cooking' or 'Mom's place' are generally a warning sign." He walked to the back of the trailer, opened the tailgate and pulled out two buckets. Filling them at a tap outside the building, he carried them back to Jessie and Samson. They drank thirstily. Branch tossed an oat and alfalfa mixture into a narrow trough located at the head of the trailer before closing the gate. Taking my arm, he conducted me to the small restaurant where we made use of the washroom facilities before ordering sandwiches and coffee. The sandwiches, thin on filling and thick on pasty white bread, were left mostly uneaten. We had a few sips of the stale, muddy coffee and took leave of "Moms."

"It'll be smooth going from here to the park entrance. We should be there in less than two hours." Branch went back to the trailer to retrieve the two buckets and comfort Jessie and Samson with a couple of pats. "It won't be long now and then you two will have enough exercise to satisfy you for the next week."

Leaving Meeker, Branch turned north on Route 13. We'd left the forest behind and were traveling through vast open stretches of rolling grassland—thickly matted buffalo grass deceptively appearing to be cultivated. The landscape was dotted with grazing cattle. In some places the land wrinkled into a series of gullies covered with scrub oak and pinon pines.

"Now finish the story. What happened once the law was enacted?"

"The law didn't have any teeth. Annie continued to collect evidence of abuses, which was made public and resulted in national support for the wild herds. A more comprehensive bill was passed in 1971.

"The protection of the wild mustang herds became the responsibility of the Bureau of Land Management. Over the years, their protected status led to a resurgence of their population. And once again they are competing with cattle ranchers and sportsmen who want easy access to hunting areas. There's also a greater demand to set aside large tracts of protected land for recreational use. With so much competition for finite resources something has to give. Unfortunately but inevitably, it's the mustangs."

"Why unfortunately? What happens to them?" Branch's narration was riveting.

"The BLM. is now in the unenviable position of controlling the population growth. Each year scouts are sent out to locate the herds, count heads and determine whether there is sufficient forage to support their numbers. They use helicopters to cover large tracts of land known to be mustang habitat. If it's determined that a particular herd is in danger of starving for lack of graze or freezing on unprotected range, they'll initiate a roundup."

"Like they do with cattle?"

"No, not like that. It's done in a much more sophisticated way. We are living in a modern, progressive society."

"Do I hear a bit of sarcasm in that remark?"

"Probably."

Lost in his private thoughts Branch drove in silence until, having passed the little town of Hamilton, he resumed his dialogue.

"The specialists have devised their own humane way of capturing the herds. Before the winter cold sets in—when the foals are big enough to run with the herd—portable corrals are put in place, usually in a narrow canyon or other confining location. Then spotters, again using helicopters, locate the herd and drive it toward the corral. Often they'll employ the talents of a well trained mare, acting as a decoy to lure the mustangs into the corral."

"That's terrible. The horses must be terrified," I was appalled. "What happens then?"

"The herd is separated—foals into one pen, mares into another and stallions into a third."

"They take the foals away from their mothers?" It was hard to believe.

"That they do, Annie my girl."

"And what other humane methods do they use?"

"They're taken to one of the management areas where they're branded and sorted for disposition. Depending on age and physical condition, they are either put up for adoption or destroyed. Some few lucky ones are returned to the wild."

"So they are still being turned into dog food or fertilizer." I was saddened by the thought. "But you saved Beau. I'm so glad you did."

"I am too. He's very special, as you well know." Arriving at a highway interchange near Craig, Branch turned west on Route 318. "We'll be there in half-an-hour."

I sighed then gave Branch a grateful smile.

Annie's Portion

Branch was as good as his word and thirty minutes later we turned into the southern entrance of the Sandwash Basin management area. Enclosed by horizontal barriers made from split logs, the wide dirt parking lot was deserted. There were a number of small, gated pens abutting the lot. He parked the truck and walked around the trailer.

"Common, Annie. Let's release our next means of transportation."

Branch lowered the ramp and backed Jessie out of the trailer. He walked her into the nearest pen where he hitched her to a rail then repeated the procedure with Samson. I'd started to unload some of the gear and Branch joined me at the truck. Lifting out one of the saddles he carried it to the pen placing it over a rail. Following his lead I did the same with the second saddle. Between the two of us we unloaded the balance of the gear, stacking it beside the pen. Branch threw a saddle blanket over Jessie and placed the saddle on it. I did likewise with Samson, cinching the belt tightly and adjusting the stirrups—I liked them long. Branch tied a blanket roll on the back of each saddle and filled the saddlebags with provisions. Concentrating on our preparations we'd remained silent but with everything seemingly in order, Branch helped me mount up.

"Are you warm enough? Stirrups comfortable?" he asked.

"I'm fine and rarin' to go. So is Samson." I was keeping a tight rein on him.

Branch walked back to the truck for a last minute check, locked it and mounted Jessie. We started out on a dirt road wide enough to accommodate a standard size vehicle. The course became increasingly narrow and rougher until it merged with a trail that would have been inaccessible to anything wider than a four-legged animal. Branch led Jessie onto the path with me right behind, urging Samson to follow.

About this same time, back at the ranch, the trio of troubled cowpokes was reconsidering a course of action regarding the mustang. For four hours he had stormed around the pen, stopping only briefly to catch his breath. He'd kicked the water bucket clean over the man-gate and had made several attempts to kick down the larger one. Just in the last minute he'd come close to achieving that goal when the lower rail had been split by a pair of flying hooves. There were blood flecks on his rear pasterns and forehead and he was well lathered.

"Pete, we have to let him loose." Fabian was distraught.

Pete nodded. "Yeah, I guess you're right. Best to spare the animal and take the tongue lashing from Branch."

"How ya gonna do that?" Frank asked.

"Me!" Pete exclaimed. "Who decided it was gonna be me?"

"Well, you're the boss when Branch is away. Seems only right for you. Besides, you n' Fabian are the best horsemen here. Don't seem right for him ta do it."

"I guess. Shit! How the hell am I gonna get in there with that loco bronc?" Pete was not the least bit inclined to tackle the mustang.

When Beau split the rail, part of it had been jammed between the gatepost and the swinging side of the gate. Now it would be necessary for one of the men to remove the broken rail from inside the enclosure.

"I'll get to the other side of the gate and remove the slide. Frank, you can try to distract him so Fabian can have time to get the rail out of the way."

"How the hell am I gonna distract that devil? You want I should dance for him?"

"Sounds like a plan," Pete smiled for the first time.

Smiling too, Fabian suggested, "You get somethin' to wave at him—somethin' colorful."

"Sure. I'll get Claire's pink kerchief." Frank laughed at his own absurdity.

After a brief hiatus, Beau had recommenced his wild performance.

"We'd better do whatever it is we're gonna do. Go get a blanket, Frank."

Frank dashed off to the tack shed and returned pronto with a colorful saddle blanket. He moved to the far corner of the pen and waited for Fabian who had ridden Frank's horse to the pasture and was nearing the gate. As soon as Fabian had dismounted, Frank began waving the blanket frantically. Beau saw it and shied, backing away from the movement. Pete moved quickly through the man-gate and edging along the fence made his way to the broken fence rail. Frank was hooting and howling. Fabian released the slide bar and Pete worked furiously to free the swinging gate. Beau had seen him and with bent head and ears laid flat back, was eying him tentatively.

"Don't you go doin' nothing foolish now," Pete muttered under his breath.

With a last desperate yank, Pete had the gate free and moved aside. Fabian pulled the gate open wide. Frank quit his waving and hollering and after a slight hesitation, Beau dashed off into the pasture at a breathtaking pace. The three caballeros walked slowly to the bunkhouse where they collapsed into chairs and relieved their stress with several shots of hard liquor and an unknown quantity of beer.

Out at the basin Branch and I had been on the narrow trail for about twenty minutes.

"I'll stay in front for a while, Annie. That will help keep Samson in line. The trail will widen out ahead of us and we'll be able to give the horses more breathing space." He'd turned to look over Jessie's back.

Nodding an assent I held Samson back to give Jessie some lead-time. The terrain, flat and sparsely covered by sagebrush and creosote, afforded an unobstructed view of distant, purple mesas. Enjoying the cloudless sky and warm sun on my back, I encouraged Samson to draw abreast of Jessie. Knowing how directionally challenged I was, my question was asked tentatively.

"Are we going east?"

"You're almost right, Annie. We're going north, but it's hard to tell with no moss on the trees." Branch laughed, remembering what I'd told him of my terrible sense of direction.

"Very funny. This looks like pretty rugged country but it sure is majestic."

"Yes it is and fortunately it's fairly difficult to get to, which keeps it unspoiled."

"What are those beautiful reddish hills to our left?"

"That range is called 'Vermillion Bluff.' The cliffs get their color from a high content of mercuric oxide."

"I prefer to think it was Mother Nature's paintbrush that did it."

The breadth and beauty of the land through which we rode was awe-inspiring. Behind us the white-capped southern Rockies floated above the hills while to the west, multihued mountain ranges, cleaved by narrow canyons provided a backdrop for the desert flora; sage brush, twisted junipers and creosote bushes.

"How far will we go today?"

"We'll go at a fairly steady pace so we can make the line shack before dark. That's about six miles...three hours or so."

"Will we see any *mestanos* today?"

"You never can tell but more than likely we'll find them near the junction of Sand Wash Creek and Dugout Draw. The cabin's at the head of the wash. We've already had a good deal of rain so there should be plenty of water."

Annie's Portion

"I feel like I've time warped into a John Wayne movie. Are places really called washes and draws or are you …" I almost said "pulling my leg", but thought better of it and instead finished with, "kidding me?"

"We knew you were coming and changed the names for your benefit."

Branch urged Jessie forward, again taking the lead as the topography changed once more, sloping gently downward. Samson had settled into a comfortable walk, content to stay behind Jessie as we moved onto a sandy trail cut into the wall of a constricted gully, the stillness broken only by the sound of a sinuous stream of clear water flowing unhurriedly southward below us. We'd been riding for about two hours, the sides of the draw growing steeper; the sun lower in the western sky providing less warmth.

"Are you getting cold Annie? Want to stretch your legs?" Branch asked over his shoulder.

There didn't appear to be anyplace where we could safely dismount. "I'd like to stop for a few minutes, but where?"

Branch pointed ahead to a rift in the wall of the ravine obviously created by heavy rains. He turned Jessie into the break, leaning back slightly to help her keep her balance on the steep incline. I waited until he was at the stream bed before following his lead. By the time I'd reined Samson beside Jessie, Branch had dismounted and was untying his blanket roll to retrieve his jacket. I jumped down and looped the reins around the pommel. Shaking fingers were so cold I was having difficulty untying my pack.

"It gets cold in a hurry once that sun drops below the horizon." Branch helped me into my jacket. "You might want to put some gloves on too." He rubbed my hands to warm them and placed them in his jacket pockets, pulling me close to him. Lifting my chin he kissed me affectionately.

"I've wanted to do that all day." He kissed me a second time with greater zeal.

The wide brims of our Stetsons collided sending both hats tumbling to the ground. I laughed nervously, invoking a similar but louder response from Branch who bent to retrieve our hats, bringing an end to the magic of the moment.

"We'd better get a move on," he said handing me the topper.

We remounted and headed out, keeping to the relative comfort of the wider, less irregular wash.

"We can make better time now," Branch said as he spurred Jessie into a trot.

A slight prod from me sent Samson following easily. Twilight was fast approaching by the time the outline of the cabin came into view. We climbed out of the ravine on a stony path that ended at a small frame building where we dismounted. Branch led Jessie to the rear of the cabin where a split rail enclosure, with the added feature of a lean-to, would comfortably accommodate the horses. Samson and I followed close behind. Once the saddles and tack were removed the horses were turned loose. I helped Branch carry the gear to the unlocked cabin. He quickly lit a lantern and got a fire started in the wood stove.

"You make yourself comfortable while I feed and water our traveling companions."

The cabin was rather confined but much less primitive than I'd expected. In fact it was quite homey. There was a cot sporting two army surplus blankets, a table, two chairs, several shelves containing canned goods, lamp oil, a couple of pans, a coffee pot and some tin plates. A ledge next to the stove displayed a tin of coffee, a box of sugar and several cups, one of which held some forks and knives. A stack of wood had been neatly piled beneath the ledge

Opened saddlebags confirmed Claire had made sure we were well provisioned. There was fried chicken, potato

Annie's Portion

pancakes, a can of applesauce, biscuits, a container of gravy, oatmeal, canned milk, several slices of whole grain bread, sliced ham, coffee and brownies. Placing the chicken and pancakes on a tin plate I laid it on top of the stove. Removing the coffeepot from the shelf, intending to fill it with water, I discovered there was no sink in the cabin.

"Whoops. Forgot about that. No water, that means no toilet either."

Night had descended quickly, the open door providing just enough light for me to locate the pump. It took a number of pulls on the handle before the pump was primed and the icy water spilled out. Once the coffeepot was filled I hurried back inside where the wood stove had already warmed the room and the food. A few moments later Branch came through the door.

"Oh boy. Smells like Claire's kitchen." He threw his jacket on the cot.

"Did the best I could to emulate her." I placed the chicken, pancakes and applesauce on the table then installed the coffeepot, biscuits and a tin cup filled with gravy on the stove to heat. "I discovered washing up is an outside job. Where's the outhouse?"

"I'm afraid the outhouse is just out," Branch grinned.

"Easy for you." I feigned dismay. "I'll tackle that problem later. Right now I'm going to tackle that chicken."

The wee house had grown comfortably warm. Removing my jacket I tossed it on the cot where it landed beside Branch's. He spooned some coffee into the pot then brought the biscuits and gravy to the table. We sat across from one another but hardly said a word as we made short work of the delectable dinner.

"This is a neat place. Do you reserve it in advance?"

"No. It's not a tourist stop, Annie. There are several of these line shacks spread out across the basin. They're used as emergency shelters, in the event of sudden storms. It can snow here with little or no warning and last for days. You're expected to replace the provisions you use to insure the next occupant can survive. That includes chopping and stacking wood for the stove. We're kind of cheating tonight."

After dinner it was Branch's turn to fetch water for the wash-up. I heated it on the stove and washed the few plates and pans, retuning them to the shelves. Branch tossed out the dirty water and refilled the basin placing it on the stove.

"It will not only put a bit of moisture in the air, but will provide us with hot water for washing. Would you like me to walk outside with you?"

"No, no thanks. I'm not afraid of the dark. Where do you suggest I go?"

"Take your choice." He held out an army surplus folding shovel and a roll of toilet paper.

"Wipe that grin off your face, soldier." I took the proffered items and headed for the door.

"I don't know what I'm going to do with you Annie. You always forget your flashlight." Branch shoved the torch under my arm. "If you need any help, just holler."

He opened the door and I stepped into the frigid night air. The sky was filled with pulsating stars and try as it might the rising quarter-moon could not obscure them. I stood gazing into the flawless night sky for a few moments, literally star struck, before the chill reached into my bones and reminded me of why I was out there. Skirting the cabin I made my way to the lean-to.

"Guess this will be as good a spot as any," I said aloud, grasping the rail for balance.

I'd pulled my jeans down and was in an awkward squatting position when I found myself looking into two pairs of very large brown eyes. Jessie and Samson had come to see the performance.

Annie's Portion

"You devils. You wipe those grins off your faces too."

By the time I returned to the cabin Branch had made up the cot and placed his bedroll near the stove. I sat on the bunk and removed my boots.

"Will you be comfortable there?" I asked pointing to the bedroll.

"I'll be fine, don't worry about me," Branch replied with a martyred expression.

"I'm not very sleepy. Come sit beside me and tell me some more stories."

There was no hesitation in Branch's response. He moved to the cot where he placed his arm around me and cradled my head on his shoulder.

"I've been doing all the talking. Tell me something about Anne Harmon."

Branch listened to a less than in-depth synopsis of my history, from the time of the divorce to the moment I landed in Rifle. He heard about my children and Sarah, the move to Rhode Island sans the "why" and the journey to Hawaii; the story ending with Joe Riley's shooting and my decision to come to the ranch.

"You've had quite an adventure, Annie. And you still have the best part of your life ahead of you. What do you suppose you'll do with it?"

"I don't know Branch. I've learned not to plan too far in advance. Just take one day at a time."

"And one night," he said starting to unbutton my shirt.

There was no protest. My heart was pounding so loudly I was sure he could hear it. "Oh my God! Now he gets to the thermal underwear." I smiled broadly just thinking about that.

"Are you laughing at my clumsiness?" Branch asked.

"No, my glamorous underwear." At the mention of which, we both laughed.

"This cot won't do," Branch said, tossing the blankets to the floor.

He lifted me and placed me gently down on the yielding heap then turned out the lantern and undressed in the soft glow of the fire. I pulled my thermal tee over my head and Branch did the rest. We made love for hours—caressing, exploring, unhurried, until contentedly weary we fell asleep.

Chapter XIII

Wednesday – Oct. 17th

The sound and smell of percolating coffee woke me from a dreamless sleep. I stretched lazily, emitting a low whimper.

"Good morning. A little sore this morning?" Branch rummaged through his saddlebag and came up with a bottle of liniment. "This doesn't smell great but it will help ease those aches."

He sat on the floor next to me and lifted a bare leg out from under the blankets. Pouring a small amount of liquid into his palm he began to massage the calf and lower thigh of my left leg

A grateful sigh escaped my lips. "Oh, that feels sooooo good, it's a *mechiah."* I had a penchant for grabbing on to words in Hawaiian or Yiddish that would more colorfully express my intent than English words could. The Brooklynese came naturally and was often apparent when I said dawg and cawfee or dropped the "er" at the end of a word so for example, water came out sounding like watah and drawer became draw.

"What does that mean?"

"It's a Yiddish term for a kind of pleasurable gift...a blessing."

"I've got to learn three languages in order to understand you." He lowered my leg to the blanket and lifted the right one, repeating the process. I sighed contentedly.

"Turn over," Branch ordered, giving me a pat on the buttocks.

I obeyed without objection and was rewarded with a gentle kneading of my shoulders and neck. Totally relaxed and feeling the heat rising in my groins, I was ready to make love again.

"That's it, sweetheart," Branch said in a dreadful imitation of Humphrey Bogart. He stood quickly and replaced the liniment in the bag. "Up and at 'em. We've got lots more ground to cover today."

"Can't we stay in our cozy lair just a little longer?" I pleaded.

"Not if you want to meet Beau's family," he reminded me. "There's some hot water here for your morning wash and some oatmeal and biscuits for your breakfast, my lady. I've already had mine. I'll go and get the horses ready."

"Oh, you're so cruel." I pouted as he closed the door behind him. Still naked, I eased out from under the covers slowly, grimacing as I made my way to the table where a basin of hot water waited. I washed hurriedly, brushed my teeth, combed my hair and using the mirror from the blush, re-applied lipstick and mascara. Back on went the thermals, jeans, shirts and sweater. I'd just finished clearing the dishes when Branch came through the door. Together we folded the blankets and stowed our gear, then made a last minute check to insure we'd left the cabin the way we found it.

"Will we be coming back here?" I asked hopefully.

"It depends on where we go to find our quarry. We'll bring all our stuff with us in the event we take a different route out." Branch had tied the saddled horses at the front of the cabin making short work of the loading process. "Are you ready?" he asked as he helped me mount Samson.

The initial stiffness in my limbs dissipated and I answered truthfully and with obvious enthusiasm, "I most certainly am. Lead on."

The cabin sat at the confluence of two creeks, one narrower and shallower than the other. The left fork of the trail followed the course of the broader stream. Branch pressed Jessie into a trot. As usual, Samson needed no urging. We rode side by side in the flat basin, following the creek for about half a mile. Branch slowed the horses to a walk as we approached the base of a low-rising butte. We climbed steadily. The creek, now constricted and closer to the headwaters, flowed more swiftly.

"We'll ride toward the head of Sand Wash Creek. There's a bend not far from here that seems to be a favorite watering hole for the herds."

The land flattened out again, giving us all a chance to take a breather. "Want to stretch your legs, Annie?"

"No, I'm too excited. I know those horses are close... and so does Samson."

With nostrils flared he'd been flicking his ears and tugging at the reins.

"I think you're right. Let's head up to that rise where we can overlook the basin."

Branch turned Jessie to the left and began a steep climb to the ridge top. It was with considerable trepidation I followed his lead. Several times Samson faltered then regain his footing. Bending forward, I placed my head and shoulders closer to his neck, hoping it would help him maintain his balance. Ahead of us, Jessie seemed to be more sure-footed and had reached the ridgeline, the mare's head and shoulders disappearing over the top. Then as she pushed with her hind legs for the final assault, Jessie dislodged some sand and rocks, sending them plummeting down on me and Samson. Samson balked and for a moment I thought we were both about to tumble into oblivion. Samson slid backwards for several feet before he managed to dig in and stop the freefall. Branch was moving down the slope toward us on foot.

"Don't move, Annie. Hold Samson till I get to you."

He had tied Jessie to a juniper on the plateau and was making his way down the slope. With a tight rein on Samson I talked quietly to him, rubbing his neck to calm him. To my great relief, Branch was soon beside me. He took the reins from my clenched fist and led Samson upward to the crest without further incident. After tying Samson to the juniper, he helped me dismount.

There are few times in people's lives when they are fortunate enough to know absolute contentment, utter security. Looking back I realize up till then, my past relationships had all been born out of need; the need for adventure or change, the need for safety, the need to feel loved and wanted. Even my relationship with Matthew Gold was spawned by desperation. But when Branch wrapped his arms around me I experienced a profound sense of well-being. Standing there, on the edge of the high desert, I knew without the slightest doubt, I was home at last.

"You scared the hell out of me."

"How do you think I felt?" I was sure he could hear the quiver in my voice.

"I should have stayed closer to you...led Samson. I was stupid. You could have been hurt or worse." He castigated himself.

"It's okay, Branch. I'm fine, really." I had regained some composure.

"I know this sounds crazy, but when I thought I might lose you, I realized how much I...care for you."

Branch, his blue eyes reflecting his concern, took my face in his hands and touched it lightly with his. He held me close for several moments then embarrassed by the unbridled and to his way of thinking, unmanly display of emotion, released me.

"Are you ready to go on?"

"I'm fine, really I am." I watched him turn away and untie the horses. "And Branch, thank you for caring."

We walked for a while, leading the horses, stopping every so often to scan the landscape below. The semi-arid butte on which we found ourselves supported the growth of scrub oak, junipers and pinon pine; the seeds of which, as Branch advised, were edible. The sun, had reached its apex in the clear azure sky and burned hotly, creating heat waves that deceived the eye, pretending to be inviting pools in the distance. Nearing the headwaters of the creek we heard them, muted at first then growing louder, their hooves sending shock waves along the desert floor. The dust cloud became visible to the west as horses thundered across the tableland, manes flying in the wind. The herd passed within a quarter mile of where we stood and slowing slightly made its way down an easy grade to the stream below.

Branch handed me the binoculars. I peered through them, enthralled by the sheer majesty of the sight—thirty or more untamed, fearless, free-spirited *mestanos*. They spread out along the creek; mares and foals together, stallions guarding their harems. There were grays and browns, dappled and blond. I sat down slowly, barely moving lest I startle them and send them away. I spied two palominos in the herd. They could well have been Beau's family members.

Branch sat beside me and in a whisper I asked if he had spotted the palominos.

He nodded in agreement, as charged by the experience as I was, his pleasure intensified by watching my reaction. Once the herd had taken its fill of water the horses ranged alongside the creek bed, bending every so often to nibble on some tender young green shoots. Inquiring about the unusual plants growing along the low bank, their tiny leaves barely hiding the few remaining flower clusters, I was informed by my guide that they were "pesky Tamarisks", a non-native, water consuming plant that had been accidentally introduced along the Colorado River and rapidly spread.

The foals, under the protective eyes of their mothers, acted like normal youngsters, kicking up their heels from time to time. The stallions moved farther afield with the older colts, who challenged one another playfully. We'd been watching the mesmerizing scene for almost an hour when a handsome war scarred palomino stallion, who had remained quite apart from the others, gave a loud whinny. A moment later he turned from the stream and raced across the flats with the herd in hot pursuit. In a flash all that remained of them was the dust storm they'd created. We spectators continued to watch in silence until the dust settled, leaving no further evidence of the herd's ever having been there.

"We've got to get started, Annie." Branch stood and reached for my hand.

I was unwilling to leave, hoping for another glimpse of the herd. Hopefully I asked, "Will we see any others?"

"It's hard to tell. We're going back by a different route and we may stumble on another herd somewhere along the way. In the meantime we'd better eat something. It's going to be another long ride." He handed me a hastily constructed sandwich of wheat bread and ham and poured some coffee from a thermos into a cup which we shared.

Mounting the steeds contentedly nibbling on the plentiful forage, we turned southward. We rode about a half-mile on the plateau, the sun providing barely enough warmth to offset a breeze that had suddenly turned cool.

"We'll be climbing a bit here. Do you feel comfortable about riding up?"

"Yes. Samson and I will be fine. That incident was just a fluke." I made a stab at sounding cheerful but was more than a little uncertain.

The ridgeline was reached in short order, free of mishap. We crossed the narrow strand of plane without sighting any herds and began a descent on the opposite side of the ridge. The grade was not steep and I regained some confidence. Reaching the floor of a valley we turned eastward. It was much colder riding in the shadow of the yellow ridges so we stopped to put on jackets and gloves and snacked on brownies. The valley fanned out, allowing us to quickly cover the short distance to another cliff, rising as though forced through the earth in one monumental heave. The sound coming from behind us, reverberating through the valley, was unmistakable.

"Annie," Branch shouted. "This way!"

He pulled Jessie sharply to the left with Samson hard on her tail. The horses were able to reach a narrow ledge a few feet above the valley floor, just in time to watch another, much larger herd of mustangs race dangerously close and up the slope ahead of us.

Branch removed his hat and used it to brush off some of the dust. "That was a little too close for comfort." He laughed, seeing me covered from boots to hat in the yellow powder. "Have you seen enough of your *mestanos* yet?"

"No," I shot back. "They're wonderful. I want more! I want more!" I chanted.

"You may very well see this bunch again. They may be headed for Sand Wash Creek on the other side of that ridge and that is exactly the direction we're taking."

"Are there any Indian reservations in this area?"

"There were never large tribes here. The few in the area were gatherers and stayed in small family groups. The Utes, who by the way gave their name to Utah, were possibly a branch of the larger Paiute nation. They speak the same language. It wasn't until the early 1800's that they began to use horses."

"Did they capture wild ones?"

"Maybe. More than likely they borrowed them on a permanent basis and made good use of them...to hunt and rustle. When the Indian wars ended in 1870, most of the Colorado Utes were placed on the Ute Mountain reservation, in the southwest corner near Mesa Verde. The others are on the Uinta and Ouray reservations in Utah just northwest of Grand Junction."

"Do they capture any of the wild horses now?"

"They could. Remember we talked about the Little Book Cliffs Wild Horse Range?"

"Yes, I do. That was the one we almost went to near Grand Junction."

"Well, the Book Cliffs are just north of I70 near the border on the Utah side. And I'm sure the mestanos don't respect borders. In any event, there's no longer a need. At last count, there were fewer than a thousand Utes on any of the reservations."

"It's very tragic...what we did to the Indians. It's a real stain on our history."

"And still do."

"Yes, sadly. Isn't Mesa Verde a cliff dwelling site?"

"Yes. It's quite amazing. It's been designated a world heritage site. On your next trip, we'll have to see it."

Branch urged Jessie forward followed by a very impatient Samson with his equally eager rider. At the top of a steep incline a broad ridge afforded a panoramic vista of craggy yellow pinnacles, purple and red escarpments and serrated domes. From its easternmost side a creek could be seen sparkling below. The wild horses, looking every bit as grand as the herd we saw earlier, ambled lazily through the scattered sage and creosote and drank from the clear stream. I watched entranced, unwilling to leave. Branch spared me a few minutes before prodding me into motion.

"I know you don't want to leave but if we don't get going now, we'll never make it back to the truck by nightfall. How'd you like to be up here, freezing your tail off, waiting for the big cats?"

"Oh, you don't scare me."

But indeed he did. We followed the ridgeline south, tracing the creek and caught a brief glimpse of Rt.318 before descending. At a shallow spot, we crossed the creek picking up a trail paralleling the highway. Turning east toward the park entrance the mini-cavalcade reached the truck just as the sun touched the crest of the hill behind us. The horses were quickly watered, unsaddled and loaded into the trailer. Knowing he was on his way home, Samson cooperated fully. Branch poured out the last of the coffee and handed me a brownie.

"This is going to be all the supper you'll have tonight. No stopping until we pull up in front of our cabin door."

"Hmm, sounds fine to me." With a mouth full of brownie my answer was muffled.

The journey back along Highway 318 was fast and uneventful, each of us silently recalling the day's incredible events. The turn south brought us into Hamilton, where the streets had been rolled away and put to bed for the night, leaving a few dim overhead lamps to indicate its existence. Driving back through the grasslands, the inky darkness was relieved by an occasional light seen glowing in some distant farmhouse.

"Those places look so cozy. You can imagine a family sitting around a fire or dinner table, tired but gratified by the thought of a day's work well done. Farmers, and ranchers," I quickly added, "are a special breed unto themselves. It must give you a wonderful feeling of satisfaction, seeing the results of your labors each day. Not like leasing a building or working in one."

"I guess that's true, but sometimes it gets discouraging. And it can be a lonely existence."

"Branch," I mused. "That's an odd name. Are you the family scion?"

The play on words was not lost on Branch. "Well you might say that. I am my father's only son and heir."

"No, really. How did you come by that name?"

"Our family name is actually Langerast, which my father Anglicized when he came to America—langer meaning long and ast meaning branch. How'd you like to have a handle like Karol in cowboy territory?"

I just snickered. "Karol Langerast. That is a mouthful."

"Well the ranch hands just called me 'Little Branch' until I developed a complex and the 'Little' part of it got dropped off."

Like Hamilton, Meeker was shut tight. The only signs of life were at Jodi's Diner where several semis and a number of pick-ups waited in the parking lot for those with cast iron stomachs who found 'home cooking and apple pie' irresistible. Several of the drivers stood leaning against the fenders of their rigs, the smoke from their cigarettes wafting in the pale glow of the street lamps. Branch veered east at the scenic highway, switching on the high beams and moderating his speed, on the lookout for deer. I tried to stay awake but the shadows, cast across the road by the now risen moon, were hypnotic and I soon dropped off, my head resting on Branch's shoulder. He too, was finding it difficult to keep his eyes open and nearly missed the turnoff onto the gravel forest service road. It was even darker there with trees blocking out what little moonlight there was. It seemed an interminably long time before the truck crossed the cattle guard and Branch turned onto the road paralleling the ranch. He drove through the open gate and parked near the barn. The only light showing came from the kitchen where Claire and Pete had been awaiting our return.

Branch lifted my head from his shoulder. "Wake up sleeping beauty. We have arrived."

Pete came to greet us carrying a Coleman lantern. Branch helped his complaining passenger out of the truck, took the lantern from Pete and escorted me to my cabin door. He kissed me on the forehead, opened the door and gave me a gentle prod.

"Goodnight, Annie. Sweet dreams."

The room was cold. I stumbled around in the dark, pulling off boots; jeans and sweater, then dropped onto the bed and wrapping myself in the down comforter, fell into a deep sleep.

Chapter XIV

Thursday – Oct. 18th

The morning was half over by the time I stole into the kitchen for some coffee. Claire was scolding Howard for some untoward behavior. Cup in hand, I removed myself from the premises before I could be discovered sticking one-half of an apple in each of my back pockets. Star was waiting just outside the door, tail wagging relentlessly.

"One of these days, you're going to screw that tail right off."

We spent a few minutes engaging in some roughhouse before going to find Beau. He was not in the pasture so I strolled to the bronc pen hoping to find my two favorite boys.

Branch had been angry when he discovered Beau was back in the pasture. Pete explained the danger Beau's confinement had presented and Branch was now anxious to get him back in the pen to examine him for possible injuries. They'd been grappling with Beau for nearly two hours; a third of that time Branch, Pete and Fabian had been riding herd on him in the pasture. He was wise to them now and maintained a safe distance between himself and his would-be captors. His years in the wild had conditioned him; he was powerful, fast and wily. Still he'd been trapped twice before, in the canyon land and in this very same pasture. He did his utmost to avoid a third capture, seeming to anticipate their every move and eluding them easily. Finally, as a last desperate resort, they called in the reserves. Frank and Sandy were recruited and with their help, Beau found himself lassoed and unceremoniously hauled, bucking and kicking all the way, to the bronc pen. He was turned loose and abandoned, leaving him to vent his anger, which he did with much gusto. Finally spent, he backed into a corner from where he watched defiantly, awaiting the next round. Branch let him stew for half-an-hour before he and Pete tackled him again.

I found them locked in an untenable embrace. Branch and Pete were each holding a rope, the opposite ends of which encircled Beau's powerful neck. He was using that power to resist all attempts to harness him. He bucked and snorted, they jerked on the ropes. He dug in his hind legs, refusing to give an inch. Sweating profusely Pete swore, emitting a string of expletives.

"Let's ease up for a bit, Pete," Branch said. His denim shirt clung to his back in wet patches. The men loosened their holds on the ropes. Beau remained cautiously quiet, alert to their every move.

"Come on, Beau. You've behaved better than this. What's bothering you?" Branch tried to sooth him.

"He's madder 'n a whore who jest found out she ain't getting paid," Pete suggested.

Beau snorted and moved back.

"Let's give it another try, Pete."

The men tightened their grips on the ropes. Branch walked toward Beau, the halter hanging over his left shoulder. He shortened the line as he closed in on Beau while continuing to talk to him. The palomino was wary, unmoving. Branch was within three feet of him when he reared, throwing both men off balance. Pete was on the ground, his grip still tight on the rope. Branch had regained his equilibrium and was trying to rein in Beau who had started to jog around the pen dragging Pete behind him, managing to get both lassos entangled around the snubbing post. Fabian was racing toward the pen. I reached the fence just as Beau began his sprint and called to him as he passed. He slowed, stopped and turned, looking directly at me. Pete

Annie's Portion

was on his feet but both he and Branch remained still, the ropes slack. Fabian too, had stopped in his tracks.

"Beau," I chastised softly. "You are behaving like a big bully."

The stallion lifted his head then dropped it slowly as if in greeting and made his way cautiously to the fence, stopping directly in front of me. He pushed his nose against the wire netting between the rails, trying to get to my pocket.

"Oh, you devil you," I chided. "You want the apple. Well you can't have it when you behave so badly."

He pushed again. I took a piece of apple from my pocket and walked to the narrow gate. Beau moved along the rail, following me. Placing my hand through a small opening I offered him the tidbit. Without the slightest hesitation he laid claim to it. Once it disappeared down his gullet he snorted and gave me a nod.

"You have gotten to be a spoiled brat. You win. You can have the other half, but next time you won't get it until your manners improve."

He took the second half from my hand. Knowing I had all eyes on me, I turned from the pen, sipped my coffee, and slowly walked away.

Branch and Pete had been observing the remarkable scene from inside the pen.

"Let's give ourselves a break," Branch said as he headed for the gate.

Pete picked up his hat and lasso and followed Branch out, watching over his shoulder to see what the devil horse was doing. He slipped the U-shaped hasp over the pin fastened to the post. Fabian joined the two men and shook his head.

"I never see such a thing, boss. That horse, he sure likes Miss Annie."

Pete poked Branch in the side with his elbow. "Look."

Branch and Fabian followed Pete's finger with their eyes. Beau had managed to lift the hasp and unlock the gate. He'd pushed through the narrow opening. I'd almost reached the bunkhouse where the ever present Star gave a short bark then backed up onto the porch steps. I turned just as Beau reached me. Astonished, I dropped the cup and moved to his side.

Rubbing his neck I said, "Well, you are a one. What do we do now? I have no apples, no halter, no lasso."

I grabbed a handful of mane and continuing my dialogue led him back to the pasture. He did not object when I urged him through the open gate. He seemed happy to be back in his familiar environment and after stopping briefly for a last look in my direction, raced off to his shelter near the trees.

Now that I was the only guest mealtimes were unannounced and unceremonious. Claire still prepared three copious spreads each day serving them buffet style. The food remained on the table, some in warming dishes, for an hour; seven to eight a.m., eleven-thirty to twelve-thirty and five-thirty to six-thirty p.m. This day all the cowpokes appeared for lunch by noon and as might have been expected, the focus of the conversation was Beau.

"Hey, Pete. Whadya think about that mustang? Ever seen the likes?" Frank asked.

"Well, I been around a lot of horses, most broken, some wild. But I never seen anythin' quite like that one."

"He's too dang smart ta be a horse. He thinks like a human," Sandy added.

Frank pressed, "What about you, Fabian? You're practically a horse yourself. Ever see any like this one?"

"No, I haven't. That Beau, he sure likes Miss Annie. Very smart too. You see how he opens the gate?"

Using an old horseshoe, Fabian had made a unique lock on the double-hinged man-gate. By drilling holes in the open ends of the shoe and in the top of the gatepost, then running stainless steel wire through both he'd created a novel latch which dropped over a steel pin imbedded in the adjoining fence post. Beau had used his nose to lift the hasp then pushed through the gate without any difficulty.

"What's more amazing is the way he let Annie lead him to the pasture, just holding onto his mane. Hell, we can't move him with two ropes 'round his neck." Pete shook his head incredulously.

Branch had seen me and waited for me on the bunkhouse steps. We walked in together, putting an end to all further discourse.

"Seems mighty suspicious, Annie. It suddenly got awful quiet in here. Could it be they were talking about us?"

"Why Branch. What do you suppose they could say about either of us that would be of interest?"

Pete broke the tension. "Ya know very well what we were gabbin' about. It's the devil horse, is what."

"Don't you go calling my Beau a devil, Pete. Why he's just a lamb." I said with mock indignation.

"You keep feedin' him apples and carrots and we'll be able to make a fruit salad out of him." Claire came from the kitchen to start clearing the tables. "If ya all want any more grub you better git it now. I got lotsa things ta do, what with the mob comin' in two days."

"Is Claire referring to the hunters?" I was curious as to why there would be hunters at the ranch.

"Yes. The first ones will arrive Saturday morning."

"Do they come up from Rifle?"

"No. We have a small air strip a couple miles from here. Most of the *machismos* will arrive on charter flights."

"What is a *machismo*?"

"Ask Fabian."

"Fabian." I pleaded in characteristic female fashion. "Will you tell me what that means?"

"An hombre who needs to do somethin' to prove he's a tough guy. You know, make an act to show he is a real man."

"Oh, I see. A macho type. Just put a gun in his hand and he's all man."

"You got it, Annie. They's just shootin' fools. 'Cause, most of the time they don't shoot nothin' but the trees." Frank laughed.

"Yeah," Pete added. "But they shore are pretty, all decked out in them camouflage suits and red hats."

His comment and the vision it invoked set off a round of guffaws.

Trying to restore a semblance of seriousness to the conversation, Branch asked, "Don't you guys have work to do?"

Frank responded with a snicker. "Yep, we're gonna board up the windows and hide the stock." The result of the comment was a further explosion of laughter that could be heard long after the men shuffled off the benches and headed for the door.

"Come on, Annie. Let's take a walk." Branch waited as I slid my legs over the bench.

Intermittent clouds obscured the sun chilling the autumn air. I turned up the collar of my jacket and pushed my hands deep inside the pockets.

"Cold?" Branch asked.

"Just a little. I bet winters are pretty grim up here. What happens to the animals?"

"The ones we keep grow fur coats and we feed them on hay. They're quite hardy."

"Do you stay here through the winter?"

"I take a vacation once in a while, go someplace warm. Pete and Frank stay on. Sandy works at one of the ski lodges in Aspen. From time to time Fabian goes down to Durango

Annie's Portion

where he has family and some of the other *meztinos* go back to Mexico for the winter."

"What about your Aunt Claire?"

Branch smiled. "She takes her pink kerchief and Howard back to Lake Havasu to enjoy the social events of the season."

We walked in silence for a while, enjoying the sights and smells.

"Annie," Branch took my arm. "I missed you last night."

I stopped to face him and hesitantly murmured, "Me too."

"There is an option available to us. Are you concerned about your reputation?"

"Not likely. What do you have in mind?"

"There are going to be lots of jerks running around here. They're bound to put the make on a pretty lady like you. You can spare yourself the ordeal and make my life brighter at the same time if you move into my place."

"Did I hear you right? You want me to move to your house?"

"There's nothing wrong with your hearing. I want you with me."

"What about your reputation?"

"It can only be enhanced."

We continued our walk with Branch still holding my arm.

"Besides, I could really use the extra cabin," he prodded. We'd reached the cabin. "What do you say? It will only take a few minutes and we can have your stuff moved. I think you'll like the house even better than you do the cabin."

"I don't know what to say." I was of two minds Wanting to accept but concerned about the ramifications. It certainly wouldn't look good but that wasn't my foremost concern.

What would I do if I changed my mind? How would I get out of the situation? What if I liked it too much?

Branch interrupted my trend of thought. "Try me." He embraced me and kissed me hard and long.

I was a goner and made no attempt to stop him when he began gathering my belongings, stuffing them into my suitcase. We made the move to the ranch-house in one trip. Branch put the bags down just inside the doorway. Awkwardly I peered over his shoulder into the spacious, wood paneled retreat. Branch took my hand, encouraging me silently to take the plunge.

Once inside he said, "Gotta get to work. I'll leave you to explore. Mi casa es su casa."

With that he turned and taking two steps at a time bounded off the porch. I watched him for a minute thinking of how confident he looked striding purposefully in the direction of the barn; lean, strong, muscled, and though he made the mark just under six feet appearing taller, his boots adding another inch or so. He was a man of great presence, conveying an image of independence and moral and physical strength, a man to be relied upon and trusted. I closed the door and leaned heavily against it.

I was standing on the black slate floor of an anteroom about five-feet square, one wall of which held wooden pegs where several articles of outdoor clothing were hanging. Under the coats a boot stand, displaying three pairs of boots of varying heights, stood alongside a shoe scraper. On the opposing wall a beautifully carved, dark wood bench showed evidence of long use, the center section more polished and lighter in color than the rest. An archway, framed in the same wood as the bench, offered a view of a sizeable, heavily timbered room. Two large skylights set in the vaulted ceiling admitted the sun's soft rays and bathed the room in a golden glow.

Annie's Portion

"What have I done?" I mused as I looked about, noticing immediately the unpretentious quality of the large room I'd entered.

To my right, a river-stone fireplace, large enough to roast a steer, was framed by bookshelves; some of which held what appeared to be Native American artifacts, the balance crammed with books. A flintlock rifle, powder horn and ramrod were hung above the bare mantel. A seven-foot long, brown leather sofa and two matching armchairs formed a "U" in front of the hearth. There were dark wood end tables with tall parchment shaded lamps, between the sofa and the armchairs. On the opposite wall an area had been carved out to function as an office. A substantial oak desk and tan leather swivel chair partially obscured a computer set-up, the presence of which came as a surprise. The walls were hung with a number of paintings depicting western scenes, among which I noted some Frederick Remington prints. Dark stained wood floors were offset by rugs woven in muted shades of blue and tan. Facing the entry a wide stairway made of split logs led to an upper level. It was graced by a highly polished carved handrail and further enhanced by a beautifully patterned Indian rug hanging on the wall midway between the foot of the stairs and the landing. Beneath the stairway an étagère, the only elaborate piece of furniture in the room, held a number of castings; bronze cowboys on bucking horses, Indians on pinto ponies.

From outside the house had appeared much smaller, single storied. My eyes followed the steps to a balcony fronting several solid wood doors, probably bedrooms. Turning left under another archway I located the dining room. Here too the furnishings were tastefully simple. Six high-backed chairs sat around an oval pine table. An old brass lantern, now electrified, hung above the table. A pine sideboard and hutch displaying pewter and enamelware completed the décor. Swinging doors opened into an oversized kitchen, the walls and floor of which were faced with red brick. With the exception of the old cast-iron, wood-burning stove, the accoutrements were all up-to-date. The window above the double, stainless steel sink and another by the breakfast nook provided light and a view of the trees beyond. Pulling out a chair I sat gazing at the scene outside where several small birds flitted from branch to branch.

"This must be a dream. It can't possibly be real." I reprimanded myself. "I don't believe I'm doing this. He just says jump, and without another thought," I snapped my fingers, "I jump. Well, guess I'd better find the bedroom and put my stuff away."

Returning to the main room I'd placed my foot on the first step before noticing a door missed earlier. It was located inconspicuously just to the right of the stairs, between them and the fireplace wall, and opened into the master's domain, which was dominated by a wood frame bed of massive proportions. There was no doubt as to the gender of the occupant for it was every inch a man's room. The furniture was heavy, the colors muted, the fixtures masculine. The Remington over the bed was an original. I would have described the whole as somber if not for the relief of colorful, hand woven scatter rugs. The bathroom too, was manly, housing a large Jacuzzi tub, an equally large shower stall and a sink set into a custom built, higher than average cabinet; all in shades of tan and brown. I walked back into the bedroom and plopped on the bed, bouncing a couple of times.

"Hmm...not bad. I can just hear my father saying, 'Whatta ya gotta do for this?'" The thought generated a smile.

The new quarters provided ample space for my gear; clothing in the walk-in closet, toilet articles in the bathroom.

I wondered how the man was going to deal with lipstick and perfume on his counter and underwear drying on towel racks.

That thought brought more than a smile to my face. Grinning ear to ear, I sought out my host. I'd devised a plan and was hoping to get him to cooperate by using my feminine wiles. He was at the stables, giving orders to his crew in preparation for the hunting parties.

"Hi, Annie. Did you find everything you need...settled in?"

"Yes, I am." I moved closer to him and said in a whisper, "That's a real big, comfy bed in there. Somebody could get lost in it."

A slight tinge of pink colored Branch's cheeks. He turned to see if he was being watched. He was but his men quickly turned away. He took my arm and steered me away from the crowd.

"All right, you hussy. What are you really after?"

"Why Branch. What makes you think a thing like that?" I practically cooed at him.

"It's that dang horse again. Now what?" he questioned trying but unable to sound harsh.

"Seein's as you're so busy with other things, maybe I can work with him a little bit." I waited for the eruption.

"You're not going to give me any peace about that mustang, are you?"

"Uh uh. But if you cooperate, I can be very appreciative."

"Trying to play the femme fatale doesn't suit you. What is it you want to do?"

"Well, I thought..."

Branch interrupted me. "Now I know I'm in trouble... with you thinking."

"You remember how I got a halter on him, don't you?" Not waiting for his answer I continued. "If you get him in the pen and I'm ever so careful, can I try again?" I waited for the explosion, there was none. "I'll use the hackamore. He didn't seem to mind it."

"If you can get close to him. He's wary now. He doesn't like the pen."

"I'll try in the pasture if you think it's better." My hopes were beginning to rise.

"Annie, it's too dangerous. He's wild. There's no telling what he'll do at any time. Besides, I really can't spare anyone to work with you. Why don't you go take Samson out for a ride? He misses you too."

"I don't want Samson. I want Beau. I don't need anyone. He's better when it's just me. Let me just try. I promise if he gets the least bit out of hand I'll give it up."

"I surrender. He's in the pen. But I'm going to have Fabian standing by."

I reached up and hugged him. "Oh, you're wonderful. Thank you so much."

He blushed again. "But remember. The first sign of trouble, I want you out of there."

"I promise." The words tossed over my shoulder as I raced toward the tack room.

Branch walked back to his crew. "Fabian, I want you to watch that horse…and that woman. First sign of trouble, you get her out."

There were some obvious smirks as Fabian took off after Annie.

"And not one of you had better say a single word...or else."

The tack was the same used during my prior successful attempt with Beau. I'd already equipped myself with a couple of apples although I was planning to leave those outside the pen until he'd fully cooperated. Beau was not happy. Once again he'd been chased around the pasture, lassoed and brought kicking all the way. He stood snorting and pawing the ground. My approach was deliberately slow.

"Hi, Beau, you beautiful creature. It's gonna be just the two of us." Fabian got my signal to move further away. "Won't you come closer to see me?"

The stallion did not move but looked directly at me. His ears were back and he pawed the ground with his right hoof. Cautiously, I entered the pen locking the gate behind me, noticing the latch had been fixed making it impossible for Beau to undo. With my back against the fence I stood and waited, the hackamore and *mecate* coiled around my arm. Beau stopped pawing and expelled a muffled snort.

Back at the stable, Branch was giving orders to the men with one eye on the pen. "We're going to be really busy with this group. Frank, you and Sandy will be in charge of transportation. Get on the horn with Dave to find out the flight schedules."

"Will do, boss," Frank answered, his eyes darting to the pen.

"Pete, make sure we know what the weather will be like. They'll want to get out first thing Sunday morning. Same routine as usual. We'll pack a couple of burros and get them on the tamest horses. We'll break into a couple of parties once we pass the beaver dam. Fabian spotted a large herd of elk over the north ridge of Yellow Butte. Maybe take a ride out there to see if they're still around."

"Got it," Pete replied looking over Branch's shoulder towards the pen.

I inched closer to the guarded mestano, progress intentionally slow; for every two steps I took forward, he moved back slightly until he was stopped by the pasture gate. Speaking quietly I approached from his left side as I'd seen Branch do. Within arm's length I reached out and touched his flank, feeling the nervous rippling as he tightened then relaxed his muscles. He lowered his head, turning it to touch my hip, sniffing and pushing his nose next to my pocket.

"Why you are a devil. You're looking for the apples. Well, you're not going to get them yet. Let's just see how well you behave."

Fabian had been recruited to act as keeper of the apples until I requested them but unaware of the ploy, Beau circled around me in an attempt to get to his treat.

"Oh, no you don't. There's no apple in the other pocket either."

Moving closer to the stallion, I leaned against him lightly, my hand gently sliding along his neck. He backed away and winnied, startling me as he pawed the ground once more. He seemed to become more anxious, his ears stiffening as he began to pace slowly around the pen. Fabian was in a quandary, not wanting to interrupt but afraid for my welfare. Once again I motioned him to stay put.

"Come on, Beau. Come back to me."

The one-sided inconsequential conversation continued as I tried to keep his attention. Beau moved back and forth across the pen's expanse, until at last he approached me one more time. His nose was just inches from my face when he came to a halt.

"This is not a good position for us my friend."

Having heard many a story of how a horse had butted a would-be rider causing serious injury, I was a bit uneasy. Palominos were also known to be very adept at using their front hooves to attack. My attempt to move to the side had the desired effect. He lowered his head to my hip, pressing it against my pocket, looking for his treat. Beau seemed unfazed by the feel of my hand as I stroked his neck and withers. Encouraged, I bent to rub his leg and touch his hoof. He made no move as I ran my hand from his poll down alongside his mane to his haunch. His breathing was regular, he seemed calm as I pressed against his ribs and placed my arms across his flank. I loosed the *mecate* from my arm and taking the hackamore in my hands slid it over his nose and head. Beau shook his head, not liking the feel of the horsehair noseband, but remained unmoving. I coiled the *mecate*, all the while continuing my whispered conversation. Using the reins I led him close to the pasture gate. From his position outside the pen, Fabian sensed what I was about to attempt but did not know how to stop me. By the time Branch, who was still near the stable, realized what I had in mind it was too late to do anything about it. He mounted Jessie and headed for the pasture.

With the *mecate* tightly clenched in my left hand, I eased the slide bar through the gate retainers then guiding Beau close to the fence lifted my left foot and placed it on the lower rail. Positioned between Beau and the fence, holding tightly to the *mecate* and upper rail with my left hand, I was able to swing my right leg over his back. Keeping my full weight on the rail I allowed my leg to touch him ever so lightly, feeling his muscles contract. He exhaled noiselessly and pawed the ground with his right hoof, but seemed unperturbed. Ever so slowly I lowered myself onto his back and bending my head over his neck stroked him with my free right hand. He bucked slightly but I had no difficulty in restoring his composure. A gentle pull on the reins turned his head toward the gate. He knew instinctively where we were going and moved forward just enough for me to reach down and give the gate a push. It opened grudgingly. Seeing his way to freedom, Beau needed no further urging.

We were through the gate and out in the pasture long before Fabian could get into the pen. I gripped Beau's ribs tightly with my thighs and grabbed a handful of mane with my right hand. Bending low on his neck I tightened the reins with my left hand, making sure to keep them low to discourage him from pulling his head up and rearing. Beau headed for the trees at the opposite end of the pasture. He slowed slightly allowing me to release his mane and get hold of the reins with both hands, turning him twenty feet short of the trees. When he slowed to a walk I loosed the *mecate* and keeping it in my hand, slid off his back. I'd been frightened but thrilled when Beau took off across the pasture. Relieved the initial ordeal was behind me I led him slowly back to the pen.

Intending to enter from an alternate gate Branch had raced to the far end of the pasture. There he hoped to subdue the untamed animal before he brought both himself and me to harm. Branch had just reached the opening when he saw me rein Beau in and slide to the ground apparently unharmed. He brought Jessie to a halt and watched me lead my conquest back to the pen. Fabian held the gate open and as I passed him put out my hand for the apples. Beau, sensing he was about to get his treat, nudged my back with his nose as if to hurry me along. Once inside the pen he received his reward and downed it immediately. Removing the hackamore presented no problem.

"Thank you, Beau...for behaving so well and for such a great ride."

The second apple was accepted with equal enthusiasm. Branch was headed my way. Hoping to avoid the inevitable clash until we were out of the public eye, I made a hasty retreat. He made no move to intercept me but instead directed Jessie toward the stable.

Dinner at the bunkhouse was something to be avoided. After turning on the lamps and lighting the fire already laid in the grate, I browsed through the books lining the shelves and selected "The Virginian", an old Owen Wister classic. The sun had long since set by the time I reached the last chapter of the tale about a proper eastern schoolmarm who goes west and falls in love with a tough ranch hand. The gun duel at the end of the story was considered to be the first "show down" in the western novel. Hearing Branch's

Annie's Portion

footfall on the porch, I steeled myself for what I knew would be a present day show down. Without raising my head from the book I measured his progress by the intermittent steps; on wood, on carpet, on wood again.

"I've brought you some dinner," Branch said placing a covered dish on the table next to me. "I'm sure you must be hungry after the strenuous day you've had."

"Go ahead. Lay it on and get it over with." I was resigned to the inevitable.

He sat beside me and took my somewhat roughened hands in his. "I've been trying all day to think of what to say to you. Without success, I may add. Isn't there anything I can do to discourage you from being so foolhardy...other than throw you off the place?"

"You wouldn't do that, would you? I'll sign a disclaimer saying anything that happens to me is my own fault."

"I don't want anything to happen to you, especially now that I have you in my clutches."

I responded with what I hoped was a most captivating smile. "So you do." We never had dinner that night but did discover the bed accommodated two comfortably, with no prospect of either party getting lost in it.

Friday – Oct.19th

We were awake at first light, made love with renewed energy, showered, dressed and walked to breakfast in the crisp autumn air. I attacked the buffet table, filling my plate to overflowing. Branch and I chose to ignore the murmured comments tossed out by the wranglers who remained at the breakfast table. Branch ate quickly and departed the bunkhouse followed shortly thereafter by his entourage, leaving me to devour the substantial repast in solitude. At Branch's behest I'd agreed to limit my time with Beau. Feeling at loose ends I saddled Samson as Star looked on and headed up the trail to the beaver dam with the canine running alongside. Once at the dam I dismounted and sat on a fallen tree to wait for the industrious critters. The woods were strangely silent; the only sound that of the clear stream coursing over the polished stones. Star lay quietly at my feet while Samson nibbled the succulent young growth at the end of tree branches. My thoughts were of Branch and the tenuous situation I'd gotten myself into.

"I've done some dumb things in my life, but this has to be one of the dumbest."

Star flicked her ears and wagged her tailed expectantly.

"He's got me at his disposal and it sure didn't take much persuasion on his part. What's worse, I'm falling for the guy."

Star tilted her head and looked at me with evident interest.

"And that darn horse too." A breeze had come up, rustling the leaves of the golden aspens. I shivered. "It looks like we're out of luck today. There's nary a critter about. Awfully quiet too, like everybody senses the impending onslaught. Guess we'll head back."

It was well after the designated lunch hour when I returned to the ranch but my appeal to Claire's better side produced the desired result, a sandwich and a large carrot. Beau came to greet me at the pasture fence. He bobbed his head, gave a low whinny and took the carrot he was offered. Reluctantly, I took my departure and went back to the ranch house where the last chapter of "The Virginian" waited for me.

At four-thirty I stirred, freshened up, changed into a clean shirt and made my way back to Claire's bailiwick. She was a whirlwind of activity, slicing, chopping and tending several pots on the stove.

"Hi, Claire. Can I be of any help?"

Annie's Portion

"Naw, honey. I got everythin' under control. But I shore do welcome your company. Set ya self down with a cuppa java."

I poured a cup of coffee and pulled a chair up to the table.

"How will you manage when the horde arrives? Seems a lot for you to do, even with Howard's help."

"You're just joshin' me. You know he ain't no help. I keep him around cause he warms the bed." Claire gave a cackle. "Seems you're doin' a bit of bed warmin' yerself."

"I guess I am. You must think I'm a real hussy." I could feel my face redden.

"No such thing. You're jest doin' what's natural. You bein' a healthy, warm-blooded female attracted to a mighty attractin' fella. And he has sure takin' ta you. It's real good for him." Claire continued her puttering as she talked.

"I'm wondering what happens next."

"No use to wonderin'. What'll be 'll be, like they say."

Hoping Claire would be more forthcoming with information about her nephew but not having much success in drawing her out, I tried another tack.

"Who changes the beds and cleans the cabins?"

"Oh, we get some help. Fabian's sister'll be here tomorrow. She'll come up on the charter from Junction and stay till the end of the season. Then the twins, that's the Marsten girls, they'll come on the weekends to take care of the cabins and the washin'."

"And when the season is finished, what does Branch do?"

"He stays here most of the winter with a couple of the boys to tend the stock and see to the ranch. But he'll take some time off to go someplace warm. Never comes to see me. I think he gets enough of me."

"He adores you."

"Nah. He tolerates me," Claire laughed. "He adores you."

"Oh, Claire. How do you know? Has he said anything to you?"

"Doesn't need to. I can tell just the way he looks at you. He don't fall easy."

"Will you tell me about his wife and son? You mentioned he had one who left."

"Well, Annie. I ain't gonna tell ya much. He was married in sixty-one to a real beautiful gal. Brought her up here but she didn't take to ranchin'. Liked the ranch hands though. She'd come and go. Take off, be gone a couple months then come back, mostly in the summer. Then one day she just disappeared. I thought she musta been pregnant. A few years later some guy calls Branch and says he's got Abby's son, Thad. Says she's dead and he don't want to be burdened with the kid. Branch met them in Chicago and brought Thaddeus back here. It was hard for him. I don't think he really believed Thad was his. But ya looked at that boy and there was no doubt 'cept in Branch's eyes. He musta been about six, meybe seven...tough and cagey. Didn't trust nobody. Probably been through a lot in his young life. Mother a substance abuser, lived with a lotta bums. But Branch was hard on him too. Wanted to straighten him out overnight. The kid tried but couldn't seem to please Branch no how. He grew up tall and very handsome, jest like his pop, smart too. He was gettin' close to his eighteenth birthday when they got into a real rhubarb over school. Branch wanted him to go to Fort Collins. He wanted to stay on the ranch. Lotsa mean things got said. You know how that is. No takin' it back once it's out. Anyway, Thad took off sometime in the night."

"That's what you meant when you said Branch was so mad. Did he find Thad?"

Annie's Portion

"Oh, Branch was mad alright, but not at Thad. Mad at himself. Didn't hear from Thad for a real long time...more 'n a year. He'd enlisted in the Navy but got tossed out after a year, when he got caught usin' marijuana. That was about the time they were crackin' down real hard in the military and with nary a by-your-leave, he had to pee in a cup and that was that. He came back to the ranch, tail between his legs. But time heals and they're okay now. He's at Colorado State, in the agricultural program."

"Really?" I was excited. "My daughter, Samantha is there too."

"Now ain't that a coincidence! She's not plannin' ta be a farmer, by any chance?" Claire thought that was hilariously funny.

"Don't you laugh, you old battleaxe you. She'd wanted to get into the veterinary program but sadly, her grades were not good enough for it. So she settled on the next best thing, journalism."

"Well, that's sure a far cry from bein' an animal doc. Maybe she'll report on em, cover the rodeos and such." That statement brought on laughter from both of us.

"But all joshing aside, Claire. What a sad story. Makes me want to make it up to him...for all the grief I mean."

"Kinda like him, I think."

"Yes, kind of."

"You two'll work it out. Now ya can get the biscuits out of the oven and we'll get supper on."

The men straggled in, one or two at a time, with clean hands and faces and dusty clothes.

"Let me at that chow," Sandy said. "Today I'm even hungrier than Annie."

There were several chuckles from the men standing at the buffet table. Branch sat next to me, waiting for the crowd at the buffet to disperse.

"Annie, it's about time these fellas earned their keep. They're grumbling because they're not used to doing any work and today I put the whip to 'em," he said in a voice loud enough to insure they all could hear him.

"Well then. I guess I'll just let them have first dibs." On second thought I added, "But you all make sure you leave something for me."

Claire kept the platters full and when it seemed all were sated, she joined us at the table.

"You loafers got all ya gear oiled and polished? Got ya trackin' shoes out? Ya know how them huntin' fellas are. They'll be chompin ' at the bit once they get here. Ya better have them deer lined up for em, just like in a shootin' gallery. Cause that's the only way they can hit em." She cackled at her own joke.

Frank motioned toward Fabian. "Fabian's got a whole bunch of elk hobbled out there near Yella Ridge. Don't ya Fabian?"

"Si. I will keep moovin' them around, one day here and one day there. So they will think it is a different bunch each day."

"Do they ever really get any game?"

"Oh sure they do, Annie. Some are pretty good shots. But most of them just come to get drunk and sit around bull...that is...shootin' the bull." Branch caught himself.

"How long does hunting season last?"

"It varies according to the estimated animal count. When the numbers are high, the season can be as long as six weeks. Cruel as it sounds, it's really a good idea to thin the herds. If there's over-population, the deer would starve instead of getting shot. We keep the camp open until mid-November or first heavy snow fall, whichever comes first."

Claire started clearing the plates and the men headed off to the showers. Before leaving the bunkhouse with Branch I thanked Claire for the coffee and earlier conversation.

"Did you two palaver today?"

"Yes, we did. Since you forbade me to ride Beau, I had lots of time on my hands."

"Learn much?"

"Not much. Just women's talk. I did ride out on Samson, up to the dam. It was so quiet, like everyone had gone into hiding."

The motivation for my subject change was not lost on Branch. We walked in the brisk air to the house and sat in silence for a while on the steps, looking at the night sky. Branch stood and reached for my hand to help me up. The blaze in the grand fireplace had gone out and the house was cold. Branch stoked the embers and added more logs. I plunked down on the leather sofa, tucking my legs beneath me, watching the embers flare and fire come to life. Branch sat down beside me, pulling me close.

"It's so nice to have you here with me. The house feels different—like it's been waiting for you."

I snuggled closer but said nothing.

"My father built this house...forty years ago. It was his dream and now it's mine."

"Has he passed on?"

"Yes. Been dead," he thought for a moment, "guess it's been more than ten years now. He's buried here on the ranch. It was what he wanted."

"And your mother?"

"She died in childbirth when I was eight, in the old country."

"Oh, I'm so sorry."

"I barely remember her. What I do remember was probably reinforced by pictures and the stories my father repeated many times."

"Where was 'the old country'?"

"Austria...Koflach to be exact, just west of Graz...in the southern part of the country. It was a town of some significance owing its existence to the lignite mines and the railroad terminus."

"That's really interesting. My mother was born in Austria. At least that's the country recorded as her place of birth, the one she called her home. She was actually from a shtetl in Galicia when it was still part of the Austro-Hungary Empire."

"That part of the world changed hands so many times; it's really difficult to track down one's ancestry. But ours can be traced as far back as the sixteen hundreds. The churches kept very detailed records. Have you ever heard of a breed of horse called the Lipizzaner?"

"Oh yes. As a matter of fact I've seen them perform in New York. They're those wonderful white dancing horses."

"Our family was involved with the breeding and training of Lipizzaners ever since the breed was first developed. Austria's Archduke Charles had a passion for horses and maintained a stud farm in Lipizza near the Italian border. They crossed Andalusian stallions, a Spanish-Arabian mix with local mares and voila...the Lipizzaner. When the stud farm was moved to Piber, a little berg a couple of miles from Koplach, my family moved with it."

"How did your family first get caught up in such an enterprise?"

"Who knows? Love of horses, skill, innate kinship..."

"It certainly seems to run in the family. But why did your father leave Austria?"

"The horses were trained at a very famous school in Vienna, oddly enough called 'The Spanish Riding School.' My mother had been dead for four years. My sister who'd never been a well child, died in 1937—about the same time the Germans were preparing to take over Austria. My father was terribly depressed. He envisioned the end of the school and consequently the end of the breeding program. War was imminent and he felt there was nothing left for him in Austria. We were lucky we got out in time and here we are."

"How did you end up here, in Colorado?"

"Horses. His life was all about horses. Don't get me wrong. He was a wonderful father and very devoted to me. But for him there was no life without horses. We didn't come directly to Colorado but he'd decided early on this would be our final destination. It must have been the western movies or books, he knew he wanted to come west and start a horse ranch. He managed to get out of Austria with most of his assets, some of which he'd inherited from his father. Knowing what it costs to breed horses and not wanting to fail for lack of funds, he decided to add a few more gold coins to the till while adjusting to the new world and learning the language. We lived in Kentucky for a while—he worked on a thoroughbred farm. He got a better offer from a breeder in Virginia, so we moved there. That was about the same time he heard about Quarter Horses. They have a real interesting history."

Not wanting him to stop, I prompted, "Tell me about it."

"It's the first breed of horse native to the U.S., and there's an ongoing debate about its origin. Some breed historians contend that it's also the oldest, having its true beginnings in 17th century Virginia."

"Why is it called a Quarter Horse? Seems like such an odd name."

"Story is their bloodlines can be traced back to Arabians, African Barbs and Turk breeds. Colonists bred the animals that resulted from a blending of these bloodlines, with stock brought from England. Have I lost you yet?"

"No, it's quite interesting. Though I don't understand why the farmers would want anything but sturdy animals to do the hard work."

"Ah, but that's where you're wrong. Those colonists loved to race their horses for sport. They discovered the combination resulted in compact, heavily muscled horses good for work but also exhibiting an ability to run short distances with amazing speed."

"A quarter-mile!"

"Smart girl. In Virginia, it's believed that the first Quarter Horse races were held at Enrico County in the late 17th century. At the farm where my father worked, they had started to crossbreed the Quarter Horse with thoroughbreds from England. That was right up my father's alley. It was the kind of thing he most loved to do."

"And you ended up here."

"Yep! Us, and eventually Claire. She was married to one of the trainers and sort of adopted me."

"I wondered how she was related to you."

"She's no blood relative but she might as well be. She was heartbroken when my dad figured he'd squirreled away enough to move west and start his search."

"And you found this place?"

"Yes. We used a land broker and looked for a while without much success. We were living in Junction and my dad got to talking with a local cowboy, Ernie Carson—claimed to be related to Kit—who told him about this ranch. He took us up here and my father decided, Johnny-on-the-spot, this was the place. Ernie had to clamp down on dad to keep him from letting his enthusiasm show. Told him in America you have to bargain. With Ernie's help, dad did make a good bargain.

"But the place was pretty run down. The ranch house was almost unlivable. Ernie moved up here with us and we lived in the bunkhouse for a couple of years before this one was completed."

Branch's brief recitation in no way revealed the years of toil, deprivation and disappointment the men and the boy had endured; the times they froze or went hungry; the loss of animals unused to the harsh environment. How could he describe the strength and determination of two men—a hardened cowpoke and a European aristocrat as unlike as any two people could be, who joined forces to tame the wilderness and establish one of the best Quarter Horse ranches in the country? Branch was lost in thought for several minutes. I remained quiet, recognizing this now familiar pattern.

He turned to me suddenly. "And now that I've bored you to tears with another longwinded historic recitation, can I interest you in the bedroom?"

"You haven't been the least bit boring. It's a fascinating story and I want to hear more of it. But tomorrow is another day."

I got to my feet first and offered Branch my hand.

Chapter XV

Saturday Oct. 20th

Branch was showered and dressed before I was out of bed. "I've got to leave you, lovely lady. Better get some breakfast 'cause lunch will be late today...waiting for the hunting party." He bent to kiss me giving me the opportunity to latch on to him and pull him back to bed.

"Oh no you don't, you sinful siren. I've got to git." He pulled away from my outstretched arms.

"Can I spend time with Beau today? After all I am a guest here and your ad says guests can ride or fish or whatever, at their own pleasure."

"Annie, you are a pesky thorn. Is there no convincing you of the risk involved when you mess with him?"

"No. He won't harm me and I'll be careful. I'm not a fool you know. I don't want to go home on a stretcher."

"Okay. I give up. I'll trust your good judgment." He reached the bedroom door and turned back to look at me. "You sure do look good in the morning."

He muttered under his breath as he pulled his boots on in the anteroom, "This is one smart, competent, fearless creature of action, more than capable of holding her own in a man's world." To me he said, "And don't go feeding that bronc any more apples or carrots."

I dressed quickly, excited at the prospect of working with Beau, this time with Branch's consent. Hurrying to the kitchen I quickly downed some biscuits with honey and a cup of strong black coffee.

"Where ya off ta in such a hurry?" Claire asked.

"Got a date with my Beau." I dashed out leaving Claire to wonder which one I was referring to.

Beau spotted me before I reached the pasture and came at a gallop. This time I'd picked up all the more conventional tack; halter, reins and leather strap and was ready and eager to get started with his training. Once again, I slipped through the rails into the field. This time Beau did not run from me. He nuzzled my hip but sensing there was no treat for him, backed up and pawed the ground.

"You're going to have to take me without dessert you big baby. Come over here and let me dress you."

The halter went on with surprisingly little protest. Pressure against Beau's flank prompted a repositioning at the fence where I used the rail to mount him. The muscles on his neck rippled responsively when I patted him.

"That's a good boy. You don't mind me at all, do you?"

He took a little side step then quieted.

"All right, Beau. Now we're going to head for the pen." I clicked my tongue and pressed my knees against his sides. He moved ahead about a foot. "You've got to do better than this." Once more I grabbed a handful of mane and used my boots to exert pressure on his ribs.

He got the message and started off at a trot, heading for his hide-away. "Oh no you don't. We're not going that way today." A jerk on the reins served to turn him. When we neared the pen he came to an abrupt stop, all but throwing me from his back. "You are going to cooperate, aren't you?" It was a rhetorical question. "Let's try this again."

My heels gave him the message. He tried to turn but another yank dissuaded him from taking that route. He threw his head back and snorted, ears back—delivering a warning as he firmed his stance.

"I see this is not going to work. Let's try another tack."

Keeping tight hold of the strap attached to the halter, I slid from his back and used the lead to head him toward the open gate. We covered the distance slowly but just when I thought I had him, he reared, lifting me off my feet for a second before we both returned to terra firma.

The miscreant received a scolding. "Now that was a nasty thing to do. We are going through that gate whether you like it or not." The struggle continued for ten minutes. "Damn I'm sorry I don't have that apple to tempt you with." I chuckled at the thought. Suddenly, with no prodding at all, Beau stepped through the gate into the pen. "You son of a gun." I followed his lead. "I'm going to leave the gate open to make you feel more comfortable, but don't you go anywhere."

The next step was to get him tied to the snubbing post. No problem there, but finding himself tethered he began to circle the post.

"You're going to get yourself all tangled up that way." Taking hold of the noseband I steered him back around the post. "I'm going to leave you for a few minutes and if you're real good I'll come back with a treat."

I walked through the man-gate, turning to observe the mustang-in-training. He was still, watching my every move until my disappearance into the bunkhouse, whereupon he began his pacing around the post. Speeding to the pantry I grabbed a couple of carrots and stuck them into my pockets. The tack room was the next stop. I'd earlier identified a saddle that should fit Beau well. Hefting it from the wooden horse, and grabbing a blanket, I carried the unwieldy burden back to the pen. Beau, having taken several turns around the post, was now a disconcerting two feet from it. Spying me, he raised his head and whinnied.

"I'm coming, you baby. Hang on to your britches."

Unlocking the gate with saddle in hand proved difficult but once inside the pen I dropped it on the ground. Hoping to sooth the nervous horse, I stroked him. "Not to worry, Beau. This is a nice soft blanket for your hide. See."

Annie's Portion

I held the blanket under his nose. He sniffed at it for a second then lost interest. With his nose down he began to nibble my pocket.

"You stinker. You smell the carrots. Well, you have been a good boy." I pulled one out and offered it to him. He downed it quickly and went back for more. "No sir. No more until we finish this operation."

The blanket was presented to Beau once more before it was placed over his back. He backed up and began to prance. I settled him down and walked the perimeter of the pen with him, ultimately steering him to the spot where I'd laid the saddle. This time the lead was tied to a fence post, causing a bit of head tossing and snorting before he calmed again. Hoisting the saddle ever so slowly, I lowered it across his back. He did not like it one bit and tried to pull away, kicking out with his hind legs. I kept to his side holding the saddle in place, talking to him until he quieted. It was time to reach under his belly to grab the cinch. He turned his head to watch and pawed the ground with his right hoof. I pulled the cinch and secured it, leaving it fairly loose. He squirmed under the weight of the saddle. His chest expanded as he tried to free himself from the strange constricting belt. After walking him another few minutes, he exhaled and the cinch was tightened.

"Just one more ordeal for you and we're finished. You really have been so good." Beau seemed to understand every word. He nodded and flicked his ears.

"I could swear you're actually smiling at me."

Grabbing the saddle with both hands I slipped my left foot into the stirrup and eased myself up. Holding tightly to the saddle I stood and with my right foot dangling put my full weight on the stirrup. Beau did a little dance and snorted but did not attempt to throw me. We remained in that position for about two or three minutes before I dropped back to the ground.

"Done." My exuberance startled the mustang. "And here's your other treat."

As usual, he took the carrot with evident pleasure. After removing the saddle, blanket and halter I gave him a slap on the rear. He headed straight for the gate and flew across the pasture. Saddle and tack replaced in the shed, I returned to the house to shower and change clothes before lunchtime.

Chapter XVI

Seated on the bunkhouse porch I had a bird's eye view when the pack arrived; some in trucks and jeep, some on horses. I counted eleven boisterous, eager, renegades as they were disgorged from their various transports. A strikingly beautiful young woman jumped lithely from the jeep, driven as usual by Sandy. She received numerous offers of assistance from the randy men, some of whom were already well on their way to inebriation. Sandy moved quickly. Wresting Magdalena from the madding swarm he snatched up her duffle bag and maneuvered a course up the bunkhouse steps.

"Hey, Annie. This here's Fabian's sister, Magdalena. Ain't she a pip?"

I had to agree with Sandy. "Yes, she is lovely. Hi, Magdalena. It's nice to meet you."

The girl blushed and lowered her eyes. "Buenos tardes, Señorita." Magdalena was obviously a *mestiza*, although she was lighter skinned than her brother. Her features were finely carved, her brown doe eyes framed by long dark lashes. Her slim figure and perfect posture deceived the eye, giving her the appearance of greater height than her five feet four inches.

"If you'll excuse us, I've gotta get this pretty lady settled." Sandy hurried her up the steps.

"I'll see you later, Magdalena."

With the departure of the girl, I found myself the new target of their admiration.

"This is too much to have hoped for," one of the men shouted. "Two beautiful women for us to enjoy."

"You can enjoy them all you want. Just make sure it's from a distance." Branch dismounted in front of the steps.

"Aw, why'd you have to spoil our fun," said Tom Haggert, a frequent guest. "Branch, you're still the same stiff, kill-joy."

"Hey, Branch," Murray Blackman called. "How ya gonna bunk the odd man out? I'd sure be willin' to shack up with one of these pretty young things."

At that moment Claire, wearing a clean white apron and green kerchief, appeared at the door. She clanged the triangle with her big stainless steel spoon.

"Hey there ya pesky hombres. Git yourselves washed and come in for the best dang vittles ya ever ate."

"If you like, Murray, you can bed down between Claire and Howard. Otherwise it's the bunkhouse for you."

"I'd rather wrestle a mountain lion than bed that loco female. I'll take the boys at the bunkhouse."

"Better be careful how you treat Claire or there'll be no chow on your plate for a week."

There was much jostling for position around the water trough. The bar of soap was tossed from hand to hand, falling more often than not, into the trough. Retrieval required a search in the water, which in turn led to a splashing free-for-all. By the time they made it to the lunch buffet, they were dripping wet, tracking water clear across the bunkhouse floor. This resulted in a tongue lashing from Claire, who used a long string of expletives that would have made a sailor blush.

"Hey fellas," one of the newcomers blurted. "Looks like we miscounted. There's a third beautiful lady here."

Even Branch chuckled at that and Claire threw a biscuit, which was dead on target. I managed to grab a seat next to Branch and was relating my recent success with Beau. "It was wonderful. He not only let me saddle him, but I stood for a few minutes in the stirrups."

"You certainly have him eating out of your hand," Branch said with a mouthful of chili.

"If you're referring to the carrots…," I stopped in mid sentence and grinned sheepishly. "I did give him a couple, but only after he'd done all I asked of him."

"I'm just teasing. You have done a great job with him. How did you get him into the pen?"

I gave a brief narration of the episode, the telling of which elicited a hearty round of applause from the ranch hands. The puzzled guests joined in although they did so with no understanding of why. Howard and one of the stable boys had witnessed the exploit, and Howard took advantage of the opportunity to reinforce the story with great flourishes.

Magdalena cleared the dishes with Claire holding the swinging door open.

"I'm givin' you louts fair warnin'. This here gal's Fabian's sister. Ya keep yer dirty paws off her or ya'll answer ta me." She waived her spoon in the air threateningly. "Now git and don't come back without a coupla big bucks."

She re-entered the kitchen, from where her familiar cackle could be heard. The men shuffled out of the dining area leaving Branch alone with me for the moment.

"I'll see you at supper. I'm going to take a few of the sober ones out for a couple hours. See what's out there and show them the lay of the land, so to speak." He smiled and turned to see if there were any witnesses. Seeing none he took me in his arms and kissed me roughly.

"Promises." His unexpected grasp left me struggling for breath. "All I get are promises." I watched him walk away then went into the kitchen where Claire and Magdalena were busy washing up.

"Claire, you ain't nothin' but an ole fake."

"Why, honey. Whatcha mean by that?" Claire fretted.

"Branch told me about you being from the east. You're just putting on an act for us poor dudes."

"Ya got me," she laughed. "It's just part of the atmosphere...gives the greenhorns a little taste of the old west."

"What you know of the old west probably comes from Louis L'Amour or Zane Grey."

"Whatever works."

Magdalena was giggling as she worked.

"So, you're in on it too."

"Si, Señorita," she laughed. "I've been coming here since I was fifteen. But next year Claire will have to find another stooge. I've decide to go back to Camargo. I will be working at Ojo Caliente, the hot springs."

"Camargo? Where is that Magdalena?"

"It is in the state of Chihuahua. Very famous for touristas. My English will be very useful there. It is also where my family lives.

"Say, mebbe I'll get Miss Annie here ta come 'n help out."

"Claire, tell me. How long have you been working at the ranch?"

"I was heart sore when Emil left with Karol. I had no kids of my own so he kinda took that place in my heart. I tried to talk Willie—that was my husband, into goin' with them but he loved his thoroughbreds and wanted no part of the west and raising Quarter Horses. But he died. That was about '52 and Emil asked me to come out here to take over the housekeeping chores. I was overjoyed when I got his call. And here I am."

"But you spend the winters in Lake Havasu?"

"I'm getting too old for the winters here. My bones ache. I saved a lot of money, getting paid well and havin' no place to spend much. So I bought the house and met Howard and am havin' a good life."

I hugged Claire and gave her a kiss on the cheek.

Annie's Portion

Claire cackled. "Now, that's fer real. Where ya off to now? Not that horse again."

"No. Think I'll try my hand at fishing."

With Star at my side I sat by the lake for a while, dangling an unbaited hook in the water. The air was cool and fresh, light gusts brushed the aspens and sent ripples across the lake. The sun was beginning to slip behind the trees as I walked back to the house. The raucous noise of the men returning from their hunting expedition could be heard as the door closed. Not long after, I perceived Branch's now familiar footsteps on the porch. My heart beat a little faster.

"Hi there," he called from the anteroom where he had stopped to hang up his hat and pull off his boots. I went to meet him.

"Sorry I'm such a mess." A thin film of dust covered his jeans and shirt.

"Kiss me anyway."

We showered together and had a wonderful romp in the huge bed. By the time we came up for air, no light showed through the windows.

"I think we've missed supper," Branch said as I lay comfortably nestled in his arms.

"There you go starving me again."

"I don't know how you manage to keep so slim with the way you eat." He kissed my forehead. "I can sneak into the kitchen and bring something back for us. Would you like that you ...what's that Yiddish word you use, the one that means 'eater'?"

"Fresser, to fress...meaning to eat a lot." I chuckled. "And the answer is yes and why are you still here."

He jumped from the bed, threw on a shirt and pants and scurried out of the room. As soon as the door shut, I got up and took another quick shower, donned my pj's and waited for my dinner to arrive.

We had a wonderful meal of steak and baked potatoes with all the trimmings. Branch opened a bottle of aged Burgundy and we sat in front of fire savoring its lusty quality.

"Are you tired?" he asked.

"No, just content."

"Would you like to visit your other love for a few minutes?"

"Oh, Branch. I'd love to."

We slipped our coats on over our night garb, pulled on our boots and stepped into the cold night air. It was black as pitch. Branch went back for a flashlight and we made our way to the pasture where reaching the fence, he turned off the light.

"Have you ever seen horses sleep?"

"Sure. Not necessarily at night."

"Do they lay down? Someone once told me that it's not good for a horse to lay down for too long. Something about their weight crushing their lungs."

"I think that's an old wives tale," he laughed. "They're smart enough to get up when it hurts."

"Now you are laughing at me."

"Not true," he responding, laughing all the more.

We were standing at the fence near the spot where I always waited for Beau. "I don't whistle very well, but he always seems to hear it."

"What will you do if he comes and you don't have a carrot or apple to give him?"

"I'll just give him a big hug and kiss. That seems to satisfy most men." Branch moved closer.

"He's here."

Branch searched the darkness but did not see Beau. "How do you know?"

"I smell him."

Branch shook his head. I wondered what he was thinking.

"Come, Beau. It's just me, Annie...and my friend Branch. You remember him. He was very kind to you... sort of."

Branch poked me in the rib. Out of the darkness we heard a snort. I bent to slide through the fence rails. Branch grabbed my arm and tried to stop me.

"It's okay. I'm fine."

Once on the other side of the fence I stood and put my arm out. Branch still did not see him but the sound of his hoof pawing the ground was quite discernible. Beau moved close enough for me to touch him. I rubbed his nose and put my face close to him. "There you are you big scaredy-cat." I stroked his flank, then put my arms around his neck and hugged him, his head resting on my shoulder.

Branch's eyes had become accustomed to the dark and he watched this display of affection in awe, telling me later he felt like an interloper witnessing an intimate act of love. "Uncanny," he repeated several times.

"Beau, you must come and say hello to Branch." I'd taken hold of his mane and was gently pulling him toward the fence where Branch waited. Cautiously, he inched forward until the fence halted any further progress. "Branch, give me your hand."

Obediently he put his hand across the top rail. I took it and placed it on Beau's neck. Beau whinnied and stamped but I held tight to his mane, pulling him closer to Branch. He bobbed his head, his nostrils flared.

"Talk to him. Say something sweet and tender. Make believe you're talking to me." I prompted.

Branch complied with my suggestion. "Hey, Beau. I hear you've been taking care of this lady." He ran his hand along the mustangs flank. He too, could feel the muscles ripple under the silky hide. Beau was uneasy. He flicked his ears and bucked his head. I held him close to the fence

"See, I told you there was no need to be afraid of him. He's a friend."

Branch extended his arm and put his hand under the horse's nose. Beau sniffed it cautiously.

"No carrot, Annie. I've disappointed him."

"You can bring one next time. I'm out of here."

Letting go of his mane I bent to work my way through the fence. Beau nosed my rear looking for his treat. I laughed and pretended to scold him.

"You cannot have a treat every time you see me. You just need to love me for myself."

He raised his head over the rail and allowed me to nuzzle him one more time. In an instant he was gone.

"Are you satisfied now? Do you believe me when I tell you he won't harm me?"

"From now on I'll believe the sun is purple and the moon is pink, if you tell me so. I felt like a voyeur watching two lovers. It was almost obscene."

"We are two lovers. Are you jealous?"

"I am. I just hope he isn't."

Sunday dawned cold and gray with a sky filled with heavy, ominous clouds. I woke, took one look at the foreboding firmament and pulled the comforter tightly around me. Branch had already gone.

I thought, "No need to get up early today. The guys are long gone. I'll just sleep a little longer and have a relaxing bath before I go out and see my Beau."

It was ten o'clock when I finally roused myself, made my way to the bathroom and turned on the tap, filling the tub with steaming water. I allowed myself half an hour of luxurious soaking before pulling the stopper and jumping into the shower to wash my hair. There was plenty of time for primping and I made good use of it. I fussed with my hair, was extra careful with my makeup application and picked out a white shirt to wear with my denims and hand knit Danish, wool sweater. I examined the finished product in the floor length.

"Not too bad for an old broad but then a lover puts a glow in one's cheeks and I have two of them right here. Ariana was right. This is exactly what I needed."

The sun was just beginning to appear between the scudding clouds as I made my way to the bunkhouse. Claire and Magdalena were busy in the kitchen when I barged in on them begging for some scraps.

"You're lookin' mighty spiffy this morning," Claire remarked giving me the once over. "But you're wastin' your time on us. Ain't that right, Maggie?"

"You look wonderful, Miss Anne. You're sure to be a hit with the boys, especially…"she stopped in mid sentence.

"Claire's been filling your ears, I bet."

"Sure I have. No big secret is it, you sleepin' in his bed and all."

"Well it sure wouldn't stay a secret long, around here. How about filling my innards. I'm as hungry as a bear."

"Maggie, you've gotta get used to this one eatin' us out of house and home—always hungry. See what you can find to fill 'er up."

A hearty brunch was on the table in no time and I quickly devoured it.

"Thanks ladies." I grabbed two apples. "Guess where I'm going." I was gone before there was any response.

The day went by quickly. As on Saturday, I rode Beau bareback to the pen and re-introduced him to the snubbing post and saddle. All the movements were the same excepting for the finale, when I used my right foot and the left stirrup to accustom him to being handled from his right side. Before removing the saddle I ran my hands along his golden flank, then his legs and hooves—first on the right side, then on the left. He remained quiet, seeming to enjoy the rubdown. I gave him his apple and slapped his rear to send him back to the pasture. The mustang took a few steps in the direction of the gate but returned to me and nuzzled my shoulder with his head. He pressed his nose against my hip, trying to free the other apple. I laughingly withdrew it from my pocket, put it in his open maw and headed out the man-gate. Beau munched contentedly then sidled out through the wide gate and pranced across the pasture.

I saddled Samson, who was eager to go, and having been given explicit instructions on where I could or could not ride followed the path toward Rifle. That route would keep me out of the line of fire and out of some over-zealous hunter's range. I missed my customary riding companion since Star had gone with the hunting group. But the ride proved invigorating, affording me an opportunity to gallop Samson across some open meadowland.

The hunting party returned to the ranch before I did. They'd had a successful trip and were in a celebratory mood. The table groaned under the weight of the provisions Claire had stacked on it. Beer streamed from the tap like the continuous flow of white water from a swollen river. Several of the men were singing to the accompaniment of the musical wrangler and a guest who had brought his guitar along.

I decided to skip mess and returned to the seclusion of the house. Branch soon appeared bearing gifts; rack of lamb, roast potatoes, creamed spinach and strawberry rhubarb pie. He opened another bottle of wine, this time an Oregon pinot noir and we dined as before, in front of the blazing fire.

"How in the world does Claire manage to put out such a spread? Strawberries in October?"

"Big freezer," Branch replied as he wiped the juice from his chin.

"Did you guys have a good day?"

Annie's Portion

"Yes. It was a pretty good start. There seem to be lots of deer. Two of the guys each nailed a buck. The others experienced acute pleasure while in pursuit of their prey."

"I hear that hint of bitterness in your voice again. You don't like this scene very much, do you?"

"No, Annie. I hate it. Now you'll ask, 'why do you do it?' Because it brings in a lot of money. Raising cattle is risky business. Some years you make money, some years you break even and some years you lose your shirt. Raising horses is even worse. You almost never come out ahead. But like my father, I do it for the love of it."

"Your father didn't run cattle, did he?"

"Not at first. He had no interest in punching steers. He wanted to breed horses, fine Quarter Horses, horses he could train. It's an effort in futility. Do you know that horses have the lowest reproductive efficiency of all species of domestic livestock?"

"I had no idea. Why?"

"It's a complex science. Only fifty, at most sixty percent of mares bred, actually foal. But don't get me started or you'll be listening to another Karol Langerast diatribe. Besides, I'm hungry."

"Hungry," I exclaimed. "You just finished a huge dinner."

"I'm hungry for you. I haven't made love to you in a dog's age."

"The average age of a dog is twelve years. Larger dogs live only…" I had no chance to finish the sentence.

Monday – Oct. 22nd

The room was dark when Branch kissed me lightly on the cheek. I opened my eyes briefly, mewled contentedly, rolled over and went back to sleep. Branch closed the door silently and quickly covered the distance to the bunkhouse, the tempting aromas from the kitchen spurring him on. His boots crunched as they struck the ground, now coated with the first real frost of the season. Four of the tyros were noticeably absent from the breakfast table.

"Looks like we lost a few this morning."

Branch moved to the table carrying a plate of ham and eggs and a mug of coffee. Tom Haggert was already up to his elbows in pancakes and sausages.

"It must have been something they ate." He laughed, dribbling maple syrup down his chin.

"Aw, they're just hung over and 'fraid of the cold." Murray Blackman chimed in.

"How many die-hards we got today, Frank?"

"Well boss, looks like we're only gonna have seven... hey that's a lucky number."

"Besides," Sandy added. "With less shootin' fools out there, we got a better chance to nab some deer."

"Finish your chow and let's get to it. We'll split into two groups today. Frank, you and Fabian take Tom, Murray and Walter out to Devil's Gulch. Walter can learn lots from those two guys."

Walter was on his first hunting trip and a little nervous. "Sounds like a plan," he said willingly.

"Sandy and I will go with the other four up to Yellow Ridge. That way we'll be sure to avoid shooting each other."

That brought on a round of laughter but Branch thought, "With three out of these seven, rookies in training, it's going to be easier said than done."

The hills had just begun to lighten, the deep purples fading to pink, as the hunters rode out on their divergent paths. The sun was high and the frost gone by the time I reached the corral. Fully equipped with apples, saddle, blanket and harness I entered the pen through the small gate, dropped the gear alongside the fence and moved to the pasture gate. Giving my faint whistle, I waited expectantly. Beau came from the opposite side of the meadow, heading in the direction of the place where he'd become accustomed to finding me. I whistled a second time, watching him turn in my direction. There was just the briefest sign of indecision. With long, powerful strides he sped toward me, his long white mane flowing above his golden shoulders and over his back like an intricately woven banner.

"You are a magnificent creature." He came to a sliding stop in front of me. "Today you're going to have the real test. Come on. Step lively now." I backed into the pen with Beau following irresolutely. "Come on in you handsome hunk of horseflesh." Lifting the blanket, I extended it in his direction. His nostrils flared as he came closer to take a sniff. Satisfied with the now familiar scent, he remained in front of me and in his typical manner, pawed the ground with his right hoof. I laid the blanket across his back with no adverse response.

"Now let's put your headdress on." With the harness in place over his nose and forehead I clipped the reins to the bitless bridle. Beau shook his head and flicked his ears but offered no further resistance. I nudged him close to the fence and tied the harness strap leaving about three feet of slack. "Now for the acid test." Lifting the saddle I lowered it slowly into place at the curve of his back. He threw out his rear hooves and snorted but I preventing him from throwing it off by keeping a good hold on the saddle. When he settled down I reached under his belly and grabbed hold of the cinch and secured it loosely. Once he released the air in his lungs I tightened the cinch and secured it. Taking hold of the reins I latched on to the saddle with both hands, slipped my left foot into the stirrup and swung my right leg over his back. Remaining astride I placed my foot in the right stirrup, holding the position just long enough for Beau to finish his sidestepping dance, then inched myself into the saddle. The stirrups cushioned most of my weight; still he balked at the unfamiliar load on his back. The routine never varied much. I talked to him in soft tones and stroked his neck until he stood quietly; releasing short breaths of warm air with muffled sounds then lowered my butt onto the saddle, allowing him to feel my full weight for the first time. He kicked out with his hind legs and bellowed angrily as he tried to shake the load off. I'd been prepared and was holding tightly to the saddle horn with my right hand while I tried to rein him in with my left.

"Easy Beau. Ease up now." My words sounded disjointed as his movements jounced me unceremoniously.

I clung firmly to the saddle, my thighs in a scissor grip about his flanks. He jumped—all four legs leaving the earth—before striking the ground with a thud that rattled my bones and nearly unseated me. The apple, still stashed in my pocket, was thrust into the air by my hard landing. It fell to the ground a few feet in front of the angry mustang. He watched its descent and eyeballed it as it came to rest within easy reach of his outstretched jaws. His tantrum came to a sudden end as he bent his head to salvage his favorite tidbit.

By this time we had attracted an avid audience. Several stay-behind members of the hunting party, a couple of ranch hands, as well as Claire, had come to watch the show. There was much whooping and hollering as I guided Beau through the gate and into the open meadow. I spent the next half-hour putting him through the traces before relieving him of saddle and halter and making my weary way back to the house.

I downed two Tylenol tablets and eased my bruised limbs into a steamy tub, grateful for the soothing, therapeutic effect it had on my throbbing muscles. The cumulative power of painkillers and hydrotherapy brought enough temporary relief to allow me to dress and shamble to the bunkhouse.

Claire was holding forth in her green kerchief and apron, no longer white, but rather reminiscent of the one I'd first seen her wearing.

"Well, come on in and set yourself down. You've sure enough earned yer vittles this day."

I eased myself onto a bench with just the slightest hint of a groan.

"I'll bet you're more than a little sore right now." Lincoln Gould, facing me across the table, was an atypical sportsman. Nothing about him seemed to fit the mold. He could only be described as rotund; round face accentuated by a bulbous rose tinted nose, round bald head ringed by downy white fuzz. His stubby arms ended in stubby, baby-like fingers. Having suffered a severe wound during the Korean "peace keeping mission", he wore an aluminum brace on his stunted leg. Yet he moved with amazing agility and grace.

"I am that. How about you guys?" I posed the question accusingly. "Too hung over to get out of bed?"

Harley Mason laughed a contagious belly laugh. "You got that right pretty lady, that and the blasted cold. It's no fun rutting through those washes before the sun is up. Ain't that right fellas?"

There was general consensus among the three men at the table.

"I thought that was what hunting was all about. Ferreting out your quarry, getting a bead on it and getting off a shot at some dangerous wild animal, like a deer." I was teasing but I was sure they got my message.

Magdalena placed a heaping bowl of beef stew and some fresh baked bread in front of me, the aromas of which propelled my salivary glands into overdrive. I had devoured half the toothsome repast before the sounds of stamping horses and shouting men signaled the return of at least one of the hunting parties.

"They're back awful early," Claire said. "They either shot their quota or each other," she cackled.

The men laughed along with her but the thought of Branch being hurt by one of the three tyros in his party did not amuse me. I hurried to the door, reaching it just as Kenny Mankiewicz, his pants and shirt bloodstained, came bounding up the steps.

"You guys gotta see this," he said excitedly.

There was a mad shuffle as the diners evacuated the bunkhouse with astounding alacrity. Jack was keeping pace with me, dogging Kenny's footsteps across the yard. "Don't you worry, Annie. He's much too cheerful to be the bearer of bad news."

Frank and two of his group were near the barn entrance, engaged in unloading what appeared to be a large buck from one of the pack animals. Kenny sped past them, coming to a halt next to the other mule where Branch and Brigham Ames were wrestling with an exceptionally large deer.

"Wow! I never knew deer could get so big."

"That, my dear girl," Jack informed me, "is half of a trophy size beast."

There was much shouting and backslapping as the slugabeds congratulated the huntsmen. I watched the gruesome scene with growing dejection. The animal had already been slit and gutted; about to be dressed.

"This is a little too much for me. Why do they call it 'dressing' when they skin it and hack it into pieces?" I sought solace from the golden *mestano*.

Knowing exactly where he'd find me, Branch sauntered to the pasture. I was standing in the usual place, just inside the fence rails, fondly stroking and murmuring to a contented Beau.

"Hey lady! Any room for me in that huddle?"

"Oh Branch. Come say hello to this most wonderful of all horses," I called exultantly.

Not wishing to startle Beau, Branch moved unhurriedly. At his approach the *mestano* took his customary posture; ears back, rear legs extended, right hoof tearing up tufts of grass.

Holding on to a handful of mane, I scolded him. "You must not be jealous of Branch. There's enough love for both of you. Come on in Branch. The water's fine."

Branch climbed over the rail. Laying a hand on Beau's neck he spoke softly. "You and I have got to become friends. After all, this lady is going to abandon both of us in a few days, leaving us to console one another."

My heart sank at the thought. "Oh, don't be cruel." There were those damn tears again.

"I'm sorry, Annie. I'm just a fool, hoping he can convince you to stay a little longer."

"I don't want to talk about it...or even think about it. Besides, you didn't give me a chance to tell you what happened today."

"No, I didn't. Talk away."

"I saddled him and rode him...across this very same meadow."

"You didn't!" Branch said unbelievingly.

"I did. He put up a little fuss in the pen, but once he got used to the idea he was just fine."

Branch had stopped scratching Beau who gave him a nudge with his nose.

"You have spoiled this animal absolutely rotten. How am I ever going to get him back on the straight and narrow?" He pulled an apple out of his pocket and offered it to the always-accepting mustang.

"Aha!" I cried accusingly. "You've succumbed to his charm."

"Not true. I've succumbed to your charms." He gave me a peck on the cheek. "Can I take you home now?"

"Only if you promise to come back later and try the saddle."

"I don't know if I have your courage but I will promise to try."

We returned to the house and the grand bed that had become so comfortably familiar. Branch enclosed me tightly in his arms his loins on fire, hard as rock, my tremors fueling his fervor. I pressed my lips against his neck, my gentle biting sending perceptible shudders through his groin. He kissed my breasts, able to feel the rapid pulsing of my heart. Our lovemaking that day took on unrestrained burning urgency, spawned by the knowledge that our time together was coming to an end. At last, physically and emotionally drained we lay breathing heavily, our bodies glistening—each distracted by unshared thoughts.

Branch confided he was surprised and disconcerted by the intensity of his feelings. He'd never known unconditional love, never allowed a woman to get close to him. Mother love was a concept foreign to him. His father provided for him and was a competent instructor but he was undemonstrative and cool, leaving Branch to feel he was merely an essential element of his father's plan for empire.

He'd inherited the love of horses from his father and at Emil's insistence had gotten his degree in equine sciences at Colorado State in Fort Collins. He met Abby while at Texas A&M, acquiring an advanced degree in cattle management, and married her because he was lonely and she was a lovely spirited girl who for a short while brought gaiety and light into his otherwise somber existence. Sadly, Abby had no capacity for love and deserted him, leaving him disillusioned, determined not to let himself become ensnared ever again. The guests at the ranch had provided many such opportunities and he'd had several affairs, some lasting months—more often they were short lived. He was well traveled and on more than one occasion had tasted a delectable exotic tidbit. "But," he confessed, "Nothing in my past prepared me for the unbound affection I feel for you." And for the first time in his life he wanted to care for and protect a woman who needed no protector. And for the first time he had to admit to himself that he needed someone. I'd become his obsession, a weakness that frightened him. Throughout this disclosure there had been no mention of his son, Thad.

Pondering the implications of our unrestrained ardor, no stranger to love affairs, I was at a loss to explain my communion with this man I'd known for such a short time. He made me feel safe, wanted, loved. His feelings for me were no longer secret and I was finding it more difficult to face the reality of my leaving. There were too many consequences to consider. Like Scarlett, I would think about it tomorrow.

Sated and impatient to have Branch witness the taming of the beast, I wheedled. "Now that you've had your way with me you have to keep your promise."

He was disinclined to leave the warmth of the bed. With one quick pull the comforter lay on the floor. "Hurry," I urged. "It will soon be dark."

The house had grown cold, the light showing through the windows sunless and shadowy. Stimulated by the chill air we dressed quickly. Once outside, I raced ahead of him like a puppy dog, turning every few steps to make sure he was there, making a beeline to the tack room where Beau's saddle sat in its cradle.

"I won't dare say this is man's work, but would you like me to carry that for you?" Branch said jovially.

"Yes. I'll get the blanket and harness. Let's hurry while we still have some daylight."

We carried the gear to the pen and I sprinted to the pasture gate to summon my other love; whistling and waiting.

"Hey, Annie. No apples. I'll run back and get some." Branch made a dash to the pantry and returned with two apples in his pockets. "I can't believe I'm doing this," he mumbled. "And it ain't over. I can hear Claire now," he chuckled.

Beau had come at my bidding and was poised on the pasture side of the gate, nervously stamping. Seeing Branch he whinnied and set his ears back.

"Let's not do this again Beau." I settled the halter on his head, throwing the reins over his back and marched him to the fence. He followed me hesitantly, tugging at the restraint. He nosed the blanket disdainfully then threw his head back, snorting with flared nostrils. When he settled down I lifted the saddle and settled it on his back. Bobbing his head as was his modus operandi, he pawed the earth with his right hoof.

Branch watched me bend beneath the mustang to retrieve the girth and fasten it. A quiet observer, he said nothing when he saw me give the stallion a cursory nudge to the belly with my knee and retie the cinch. Easing myself onto the saddle, I hugged Beau's sides tightly with my thighs. He threw his head up, kicked out with his hind legs before making a quick exit through the gate. A firm press of my heels drove him forward. "Come on, Beau, let's ride." He needed no further urging.

Branch watched heart in mouth as we raced across the pasture, my shoulders just above Beau's neck his mane billowing around my head. I was deliriously happy, my joy seemingly contagious as he galloped in a wide circle over the meadowland. We took several laps before I reined him in and brought him at a trot back to the gate where Branch was anxiously waiting. Beau was barely sweating but I was out of breath, my hair an unruly tangle.

"What do you think of your wild *mestano* now?"

"I'm dumbstruck," was all he could say.

Dismounted, I passed the reins to Branch. "Now it's your turn."

Branch believed the stallion would give him a lot more trouble than he'd given me but not to be outdone, took the reins from my hand. Standing well away, wary of Beau's front hooves, he could smell the rich musk emanating from the horse's steamy flanks. He ran his hand along the mustang's neck and side, feeling the reflexive shiver of his muscles.

"You are a noble animal," he whispered. "We were so right to save you." To me he said, "He's never let me get this close to him before. It must be your sweet, calming influence."

"Well fella, this is the moment of truth. Dare we try it?"

Branch coiled the strap and placed it over the saddle horn. Taking the reins in his left hand he grabbed onto the saddle waiting briefly for Beau's reaction. The mustang remained quiet. Branch slid his foot into the stirrup then lifted himself off the ground. Beau shook his flanks and snorted. Branch brought his right foot over the saddle and placed it in the other stirrup. He stood, knees bent, above the saddle waiting for Beau to adjust to his weight.

"I'm a little heavier than your last passenger," he said speaking softly.

Taking hold of the horn, Branch lowered himself into the saddle. The stallion reared, letting out a loud bellow. I made a move to calm him but Branch shouted at me.

"Get out of the way!"

Standing near the gate I watched the two males in a contest of wills. Beau bucked in an attempt to get Branch off his back. He kicked out with hind legs, reared again and threw his huge body from side to side. Branch left the saddle several times but managed to keep from being thrown. He was talking to Beau, bits of halting speech reaching me.

"It's…o...kay…fell...a. Calm …do...wn now."

I added my voice to the jumbled mix. "Beau, calm down. Behave yourself or there'll be no apples today."

Beau's less frenzied movements allowed Branch to regain his seat but he was determined to shake the rider off. Branch leaned forward; bending over the stallion's arched neck. He gentled the agitated mount, feeling the muscles ripple beneath his flattened palm, speaking into his laid back ear. In another moment Beau was still, breathing heavily through flared nostrils. Branch aimed for the gate. Reaching the pasture he dug his boot heels into the horse's flanks. Beau leaped ahead, galloping across the meadow once again, his white mane and tail catching the wind. Branch heard the thud of the hooves, felt the intricate synchronization of head, heart, sinew and muscle power. The wind rushed at him, filling his lungs, blowing through his hair.

Now it was he, who threw back his head in sheer delight, a rip roaring "ya hoo" resounding across the field.

He returned to the pen at a slow pace, cooling down the now sweating stallion. I waited for them, a wide grin spreading across my flushed face. Branch dismounted and led Beau through the man-gate. Together the three of us walked to the barn where Branch unsaddled the golden mustang and cooled him with a quick hosing. I rubbed him dry, planting kisses on his neck as I did. He tolerated the ministrations but eagerly took the apples Branch offered. Branch walked him back to the pen and opened the gate, allowing Beau to make his way back to his pasture. In the meantime I'd sneaked into the kitchen and was busily gathering up the makings for our dinner. Claire went through the swinging doors pretending not to see me.

Dinner things put away, Branch and I sat in front of the slowly dying fire drinking the last of the wine.

"You know, Annie. I've been doing some thinking too."

"Oh no, not again."

He smiled, "Yes, but this time I think you're going to like it."

"I'm all ears." I turned to face him with feigned anticipation.

"You have really mellowed that *mestano*," he paused briefly. "To the point where I think it's time to socialize him."

"Socialize him how?" I was puzzled.

"It's not good for him to live a life of solitude. We need to get him used to being around other horses. And I think with your help it can be done. Mind you, we don't have much time—with your leaving. But we can make a start."

The mention of my imminent departure was a downer. "What will we do?"

"I think I'll let the boys handle the hunters for the next couple of days. You and I will attempt to introduce Beau to a couple of non-threatening companions."

"Who do you have in mind?"

"I'm kind of working that out in my head."

Watching him, I visualized the wheels turning as he devised a plan.

"Mmm...Maybe Samson," he mused. "Or another younger gelding."

Curious yet disinclined to interrupt Branch's thought process, I began to fidget. My restlessness was transmitted by way of the leather cushion on which we both sat. Branch turned to me.

Placing his index finger across his lips, he whispered, "Shh."

A few minutes were as long as it took for me to blurt out, "Why them? Why not Ginger? She's too old to give him any trouble. If I were Beau, the lady might be more acceptable. After all, he took to me first." I smiled coquettishly.

"Ginger doesn't have your charms. Besides that, there's a real danger of our mustang trying to mount her and she'll kick the hell out of him," Branch laughed. "You women are all alike."

"Seems they'd get to figure things out in a hurry."

"A stallion won't take no for an answer. So, do you have any other thoughts on the matter?" He pulled me close to him, kissing me on the forehead, then with much more vehemence on my yielding lips.

"We'll think about it and make a decision in the morning. Right now my head is filled with other images."

Tuesday - Oct. 23rd

Long before dawn Branch woke and lay unmoving in the comfort of the great bed that had taken on new meaning for us. No longer an obliging berth for tired bodies, it had become a place of shared discovery and unimagined delight, a sanctuary of immeasurable comfort. He believed me to be asleep as I lay beside him with my arm resting lightly on his shoulder. In my languid state I could sense rather than see his eyes on me. He seemed to be transfixed by the even rise and fall of my breast with each quiet breath I took, unwilling to part from me. Branch sighed and carefully dislodged his shoulder from under my arm. I opened my eyes in time to see him move to the edge of the bed. There was barely a ripple when he stood. He dressed quickly and moved silently to the front door. A blast of cold air greeted him, felt even in the bedroom. It must have roused him from his lethargy for I heard his rapid footfalls, certain he was running posthaste to the bunkhouse.

The breakfast hour had been changed to afford ample time for the avid hunters to fortify themselves before heading out at first light to their appointed hunting grounds. Branch joined them for coffee, reviewed his previous directives then assisted in getting the gear loaded and the men mounted. He wished them good fortune, taking pleasure in the sight of the steaming breath of horses and men, watching until they disappeared from view.

Branch returned to the house. Finding me in the shower he sat on the bed gazing at my shadowy form through the clouded glass door. Seeing me reach for the tap he hurriedly snatched a bath towel and held it open as I stepped from the tub.

"What a nice surprise. These are the best bed and breakfast accommodations I've ever had."

"Pleased to please. What shall it be...bed or breakfast?"

It was after ten when we stole into the kitchen, hoping to grab some grub unnoticed.

"Aha! Caught ya. No need to ask what you two have been up to. What do ya think this is, anyway? A twenty-four hour diner?"

"No need for you to bother. We can fix something for ourselves," Branch gave Claire a peck on the cheek.

"You ain't gonna mess up my kitchen, you sly fox. Set yourselves down and I'll rustle ya up some grub."

"Now Claire," I chided. "Cut out that phony jargon. You're not fooling anyone here."

"Oh, that big boy's been shootin' off his mouth, I reckon." Claire was busily banging pots and pans and before long had bacon, eggs and toast on the table. "What you folks got planned for the rest of the day? That is if you can …"

Branch cut her short. "We can and we are planning to have a coming out party for Annie's Beau."

"Well then. You just hurry up there so I can come to that party before I have to start gittin' your next meal ready."

Branch and I washed down the food with some good strong coffee and beat a fast retreat. The early morning frost dissipated with the first hint of sunlight and the air warmed corral in closer proximity to the other horses but he's a loner and a loner he'll stay."

"So you'll just move him to a smaller prison."

"I'll ride him from time to time; take him out on the trail with one or two of the hands on other horses—that is if he'll cooperate with you not around."

"What about Jessie? Won't she be jealous?"

"Horses are much more sensible than women. Besides, she'll be delighted when I introduce her to her intended."

"Intended! Are you going to try to mate them?"

"That's the plan."

Our horses were eager to go and once we left the enclosure we gave them free rein. Heading in the direction of the forest we forded a small stream and climbed a steep embankment before reaching a vast expanse of rangeland dotted with grazing cattle.

Astonished, I asked, "Is this part of your ranch?"

"It shore is. Them's my critters too."

"How many are there?"

"Oh, probably only three hundred or so now. The others went off to market just before you arrived. Too bad you missed the roundup."

"How many did you round up?"

"About ten, mebbe twelve hundred head."

"Karol Langerast! How big is this ranch?"

"Well, I reckon we got nigh on to fourteen-thousand acres, give or take a few. Then of course there's lots of open range too—leased from Uncle Sam."

I was dumbstruck.

"Say lady. Yer mouth's open. Better shut it before ya swaller some flies." Branch could no longer contain the laughter that had been welling up in him.

"But I thought you raised horses," I said in disbelief.

"That too. Got more'n a hundred mares and a couple dozen stallions, not counting Beau." He was still grinning.

"But you told me…I had no idea, I thought…"

"See what happens when you start thinking." Branch was having a wonderful time.

It was after three by the time we returned to the corral and unsaddled the horses. Fabian greeted us flushed with excitement.

"I cannot believe what I saw. El Diablo is no more. He was like a lamb making baa baa with that *mariposa*."

"Now Fabian," I chided. "Haven't I told you not to call my Beau a devil? You boys just didn't understand him. What's a *mariposa*?"

"You hear that Fabian?" Branch was in great good humor. "This lady thinks she's going to teach us all about horses now."

"Ha! Maybe she can, boss."

"How did it go with you guys?"

"Very, very good, boss. We got two bucks today, one a six pointer. The men are cleaning up by the barn."

"Deer or elk?"

"Oh, señor, you make a joke. Only deer, but they are happy." He took the reins from us. "I will take care of them for you."

"Thanks Fabian," Branch placed his arm on my shoulder.

"Yes, Fabian. Thank you for everything." Turning to Branch I commented on the fact that neither of them had answered my question. "What is a *mariposa*?"

"If you must know, it's a butterfly…gay. Happy now?"

"Bah, humbug!" I pointed in the direction of the barn. "Think I'll skip the slaughter house scene and go back for a shower, some clean clothes and some time to digest what I've learned today."

Bedlam was the word that best described the scene at the dinner table. All eleven men had gone on the hunt and two had been successful at nailing a deer. They had split into three parties, two of which had made hits. Lincoln had gotten the largest deer, weighing in at just under two-hundred pounds. There was much toasting, with everyone receiving an accolade or two. Frank, Pete and Fabian were lauded loudly for their great scouting skills and Sandy thanked profusely for the mule handling. Branch was teased about his very noticeable absence and I was congratulated for my taming of two mustangs. The party was in full swing when Branch and I made our getaway.

"I don't think they'll be up for the hunt tomorrow."

"Probably not. But they've already had an unusually successful trip."

"Don't they all get at least one?"

"Rarely. They're only allowed one buck each. But if they don't get them in the first day or two chances are they won't get one at all. With all that shooting, the deer disappear very quickly. The rest of the time they'll spend boozing it up, male bonding—that sort of thing."

"But no one got an elk."

Branch laughed. "We don't shoot elk, Annie. The joke's on those clowns. But Claire will keep them well fed and maybe a couple of them will go on a ride. It's getting cold and they'll be glad to stay inside. They'll go home happy."

"Will I go home happy?" I reflected. "I think not."

The house was cold and we wasted no time in wrapping up in the down comforter and each other's arms.

Wednesday – Oct. 24th

Branch was awake early, but sure there would be no hunting party that day he indulged himself. Coiled contentedly around my body he went back to sleep. It was after nine—the sun streaming from the skylights pouring warm amber light throughout the house when he finally stirred. Believing I was still asleep he was reluctant to disturb my slumber.

"You might be in the middle of a lovely dream," he reflected softly. "How fast the time has gone. How can I let you walk out of my life? Tomorrow it will be all over. In a few weeks it will be as if this never happened." His chest seemed to constrict at the thought.

I stirred and cuddled closer in his arms. He held me tightly.

"I won't let you go," he whispered. "I'll keep you here, locked in my arms, in my bed—in this house that was so empty until you filled it and will be even emptier when you leave." He breathed a sigh. "Some he-man I turned out to be. The guys were right. You broke me just like you broke that stallion."

"Good morning." I pretended not to have heard and brushing my eyes as if to get the sleep out said lazily, "Did you say something?"

"No, just complaining because you're snoring interferes with my sleep patterns."

"You rat!" I was on him in a second, bouncing on his chest, knocking the wind out of him.

"Easy pardner," he gasped. I bounced again. "How... uh...do you...find...so much...en...uh...gy...so," I stopped bouncing, "early in the morning?"

"It's not hard," I laughed rolling off him. "But maybe I can work on it."

We made it to the bunkhouse in time for a light lunch and Claire's usual commentary. Branch had been correct in his assumption there would be no hunting party that day. The stragglers made it in to lunch with small appetites and large headaches. While Branch talked with Pete about Thursday's plans, Claire had a few moments alone with me.

"Annie, are you really gonna leave us tomorrow?"

"I have no choice, Claire."

"Sure ya do. We all have choices. It's just a matter of trying to make the right one."

"I have a job, a mother, a family and lots of responsibilities."

"I guess ya do. But what about your responsibility to yourself? You're a lovely young woman, but youth is fleeting and opportunities don't come around all that often. He loves you, you know. I've known Branch most of his life and I've never seen him like this. He was like a strong oak wine cask that was empty, with no purpose. You've filled him, brought him joy and a renewed love of life and living. You can't just take it away. And what about you? I'm not so dumb that I can't see what you feel for him. Annie, please think about this. Don't be rash. You may regret it the rest of your life."

"Claire, do you think I'm not torn? I've made two terrible mistakes and I'm not about to make a third. I've been single for twenty years. I'm tough, independent, self-sufficient, bossy— all the things he hasn't seen. This has been wonderful and yes, I do have strong feelings for Branch. But I won't be pushed into anything. I have to be sure."

"You two are a pair, both afraid to admit what you feel, neither one willing to say it, 'I love you'. There, how hard was that?"

I was crying. I could not face Branch and slipped out through the kitchen door.

When Branch discovered my absence he confronted Claire. "Well, bigmouth. What have you done now?"

Claire was sniffling, "I ain't done nothin' and I ain't gonna say no more." She turned from him and scurried to the sanctuary of her kitchen.

He found me at the house, locked in the bathroom. "Annie," he shouted. "Are you all right?"

Annie's Portion

There was no immediate response so he called again. "Annie, what's wrong?"

"I'm fine, Branch. Something didn't agree with me. A little stomach problem. I'll be out in a few minutes."

Branch paced nervously outside the door. On the other side, I was trying to cover up the evidence of my crying bout. I put some drops in my eyes and dabbed at them gently. I ran a cover stick under my eyes and around my red nose then applied makeup over it. Finally, I reapplied mascara and lipstick.

"This will have to do. Now if I can keep my damn emotions under control, we can get through this day." I unlocked the door.

"Annie, are you okay?"

"Yes, I'm much better. I've just been eating and drinking more than I'm used to. But I'm fine now."

Not willing to press the issue or ask what Claire had said to upset me so, he accepted the explanation. "Are you feeling well enough to try another introduction?"

"Without a doubt." Glad for the diversion I put on a sweater and made for the front door. "Come on slow poke," I called over my shoulder.

With one exception, we repeated the system that had worked so well the day before. It was now Rocky's turn to meet the golden palomino. I waited with Beau in the pasture, holding tightly to the reins as Branch rode up on Rocky. Beau seemed much more agitated when they neared the fence. He snorted and attempted to break my hold on him.

"Easy, Beau. It's just Rocky and he's really harmless. Come and meet him."

Beau resisted. I put my arms around his neck, laying my head against him. I could feel his warm breath as I stroked him.

"Oh God. How can I leave you both?" I gripped his sides with my thighs and legs and turning him away from Branch and Rocky, urged the mustang to a water-trough at the far end of the pasture. Regaining my composure I took him for several turns around the pasture before setting off at a good but manageable pace, heading for the encounter. Branch had been viewing the scene with increasing trepidation as we moved away from him. He seemed of a mind to move Rocky off, afraid of Beau's reaction if I brought him too close to the gelding.

"I'm acting like a fool," he voiced. "He's under control and there'd be hell to pay if I left."

I called to him. "Don't leave. I'll bring him on." Beau tensed as we closed in on Rocky. Bending over his neck I spoke into his ear. "I expect you to be a gentleman. If you're good today there'll be two apples for you."

On the other side of the fence, Rocky was also getting restless, pulling at the reins tied to the fence.

"Here we go, take it easy now," Branch soothed.

I slid off the mustang's back when we were ten feet from the fence. Holding tightly to the halter I urged him forward. He nudged my pocket with his nose. "It's apples, always apples." I took one out of my pocket and tempted him with it. "Come on now. If you want the apple you have to be good." He lifted his head pulling my arm to its farthest reach. "Come down here you brat."

We were within a nose of the fence. Rocky whinnied and Beau returned the call. Both horses sniffed the air, nostrils flared. Rocky ceded, lowering his head. Beau acknowledged him with several quick snorts.

"Why don't I ride Rocky into the pasture. You can climb back onto that wonder horse and we'll see if we can take a few turns together," Branch offered.

"Deal," I responded. "Be sure to lock the gate behind you," I added as an afterthought.

Tension released, Branch gave a hearty laugh. "Yes sir, boss sir."

I gave Beau the last of the apples and remounted. He accepted Rocky's presence without incident and we spent half an hour in pleasant accord.

"I think I'll take Rocky back to the corral and let Beau have the pasture to himself. We'll take them out for longer periods, Samson too. Thanks for your help, Annie. I don't think we could have done it without your calming influence. Just think. You may have saved his manhood." Branch was trying to sound lighthearted. "Come on. Slide off your friend and release him. You can ride double with me. And you might as well give him that other apple."

There was no other apple but I did as I was told and Branch pulled me up behind him on Rocky. Beau walked alongside us until we reached the gate. Once we passed through he gave a triumphant bellow and sped away.

"Shall we ride out to see if any of the elk are still around? Fabian promised to hobble them to keep them in place."

"Yes. That would be nice."

Branch saddled Jessie and we rode to the spot where Fabian had taken the newlyweds and me to watch the elk herd.

"Was that only ten days ago," I thought. "It seems like ages since we were here."

Reaching a high spot on the ridge we dismounted and gazed out over the wheaten rangeland, neither of us with any real expectation of seeing the herd.

"I guess they figured a way out of those hobbles," Branch said.

I just nodded.

There were so many things we wanted to say, so much we wanted to tell each other, but this time words would not come. The sun had begun its descent, transforming the scattered cirrus clouds into ribbons of turquoise, pink, violet and amber.

"It is so beautiful, it makes me want to cry," I whispered.

"Me too," Branch could say no more. He embraced me and kissed me softly at first, then with uncontrolled emotion. "Anne, I…" He let go of me. "It's getting late. We'll have to hurry if we want to get back before dark."

Claire had pulled out all the stops and with help from Magdalena and Howard had outdone herself. Dinner was an extraordinary affair; venison stew, sizzling steaks and barbequed ribs done on the outdoor grill. Heaps of creamy mashed potatoes and bubbling baked beans seasoned with bacon and molasses vied for equal billing with baskets of hot biscuits and bowls of rich, dark gravy. A separate table groaned under the weight of platters piled high with cheddar cheese and apples, rhubarb pies, lemon squares and chocolate nut brownies. One had a choice of beer, cider, cranberry punch and freshly brewed coffee.

"My God," I exclaimed. "Claire you are a wonder…and you too Magdalena."

"What about me," Howard complained.

"You too Howard," I cajoled.

"We sure are gonna miss you, Annie," Frank mumbled. "Seems like you always been here and," he teased, "The food's never been this good before."

"You sure taught us a thing or two," Pete said. "You better come back next year so you can finish the lessons."

Fabian and Sandy were in full agreement. "Miss Annie, you make this place very happy. Me also." Fabian, unused to long speeches, blushed.

"Yeah. And next time I expect to git more 'n one dance or you'll have to walk from Rifle," Sandy added.

"Me and Star would sure like for you to stay a while longer," Howard said.

Star, lying across my feet under the table, whined in soulful accord.

"Hey you guys. This ain't no memorial service. Fill your craws and your glasses." Claire winked in my direction.

Bellies full, minds clouded by drink we made our way in the frigid night air to the sweet seclusion of our hideaway. Branch lit the kindling earlier laid in the grate, added some small logs and the fire leaped to life.

"Can I get you something? A glass of wine...some brandy?"

Curling my legs under me as I dropped onto the sofa, I inhaled the leathery maleness of it. "No, nothing. Come sit here with me." I patted the place next to me.

Branch complied, reaching out to touch my fingers. He flinched as though he'd been hit in the gut. Warmed by the hypnotic flickering flames, we sat in silent reverie. In the end, it was Branch who broke the spell.

He sighed, "It's going to be an early start tomorrow... and a very long day. Better get some rest."

Wanting to delay the inevitable I protested, "It's so pleasant here, I hate to leave." Inwardly I implored him to give me some encouragement, some incontrovertible justification that would convince me to remain. Failing to generate the desired response I conceded, "But I suppose you're right." A sigh, then "Will Sandy be driving me to Rifle?"

"No. I will." He was already on his feet.

We both averted our eyes as we passed my bags, which were already packed and waiting at the foot of the stairs. Visible through the open door, the seductive bed beckoned us. We undressed without speaking and eased under the down comforter feeling its instant warmth. Branch drew me close to him, holding me with an implied sense of deep sorrow, until my even breathing deceived him into believing

I'd fallen asleep. He lay awake for a long time before sleep overcame him.

Thursday – Oct. 25th

Branch slipped from the bed quietly and made for the shower. I'd been awake for hours. "Good morning. I slept like a log," I lied. "All that beer. How about you?"

"Yeah, me too, but no hangover. You'd better get a move on." He was resolute—there would be no further displays of unrestrained fervor. As far as he was concerned, he'd anguished long enough over the dozen reasons for bringing an end to the relationship. I could tell from some of his remarks he thought he'd be just one more name on my list of conquests, displaying no desire to remain in the wilds of Colorado with a cowboy lacking charm and sophistication. He'd already insinuated I was beguiled by the thrill of the chase, the challenge of the horse. "You'll go back to the islands and talk of what a great experience it has all been... of the rancher who provided entertainment for a while." Then he was overcome by remorse. "I'm sorry. You're not like that at all."

"No, I'm not," I responded in anger. "I came hoping for a chance to unwind, to renew my spirit in a place far removed from family, friends and responsibilities that were weighing me down. I did not seek you out and when you pressed me I accepted your offer but I never made any promises, expecting nothing more than a brief interlude."

My last remark hurt him and wanting to avert further friction he disappeared into the relative safety of a cold shower. He soon reappeared, wrapped in a towel, much more in control.

"I'm thinking like an immature, lovesick fool. It's over, done. In a few hours you'll be on a plane, I'll feel sorry for myself for a while but life will go on. You get ready. I'll take your bags and see you at the bunkhouse."

I tried to conceal my feelings. I should have apologized but never one to admit I could be wrong, I answered, "That's fine. I'll just shower and dress. I won't be long."

Branch was in the kitchen, seated at the small table with a cup of coffee in his hand. His mood had not improved with Claire's ministrations and he stared at the eggs and ham congealing on the plate in front of him. As soon as Magdalena left the room Claire lit into him.

"You can't just let her walk out. If you don't stop her, you're a bigger fool than Howard."

"Claire, please. There's no use talking about this. People do what they have to do."

"If you won't try to stop her, at least tell her what you feel. Tell her you want her to come back. For God's sake tell her you love her."

"Do I? I don't know what I feel, so how do you?"

"You know darn well. Just scared is all. Once burned, twice shy."

"She hasn't once mentioned the word 'love'. Why should I?"

"Because that's the way women are. You gotta be the one to make the first move."

"I did. I moved her into my house, my bed. Shouldn't that have told her anything?"

"Sure. You wanted a warm body. That's what it told her." Claire was angry, her voice rising as she chastised this man she loved like her own son. "I've watched you man and boy...do great things, overcome hardships, make foolish mistakes. But I tell you now, if you give up Annie, you'll regret it the rest of your life. Now! That's all I'm gonna say." She strutted out of the kitchen, the swinging doors banging loudly behind her.

There was no way Claire's outburst failed to reach the ears of those of us seated just outside the swinging doors. Conversation resumed once Branch joined the group at the breakfast table where, with eyes averted, I pushed my food around on the plate.

"You better eat that missy," Claire ordered. "You won't get another good meal for a long time."

"She ain't never gonna get a meal like she gits here," Sandy added.

"I'm not very hungry this morning."

"What!" was the surprised retort from Fabian, Pete and Frank.

"You're not sick, are you?" Pete asked jokingly.

"No, just a bit sad." Looking at Branch I asked, "Do I have time to say goodbye to Beau?"

"Sure. I'll wait for you in the jeep."

I made the rounds, saying my farewells to the guests and ranch hands, with special hugs for ones I'd gotten to know best. "Thanks to all of you for making this such a wonderful trip. I will never forget you or this place." I hugged Claire. "Take care of things here, you big faker. And be sure to write to me at the address I gave you."

Claire wiped her eyes with her soiled apron. "I sure will. You travel safe now."

I hurried from the big room, glad for the chill air that greeted me as I made my way to the pasture, apple in hand. Beau came at the first call and I climbed through the fence to hug him. I made some whispered comments in his ear as I lovingly caressed the magnificent animal, then gave him his treat and blinded by tears hurried back to the waiting jeep. His bellow resonated across the meadow as Branch pulled out and we passed under the arch where the wooden sign proclaimed "Bar L."

Our last ride to Rifle had been made in strained silence. The passing weeks wrought considerable change on the landscape. No longer green, the meadows looked sterile and uninviting, the barrenness broken briefly by scraggly pinon pines and naked scrub brush, the golden leaves of the aspens now withered and brown. There were no signs of the waterfowl or of any animal life as we passed lakes and woods. It was with a fair degree of relief we reached the rutted road to Rifle and the deserted airstrip.

"We're a little early," Branch said. His words after such a long stillness startled me. "Looks like you may be the only passenger."

"I guess there aren't many people here when it gets this cold." I shivered and pulled my jacket more tightly about me.

"I should have brought a blanket for you. I forgot how much colder it must seem to you. Well you'll soon be back in the warmth of your tropical island."

I thought I detected a note of hostility in his voice. "Yes. But I will miss Cutter Lake and the wonderful people at the ranch."

"And Beau...don't forget Beau."

"I will never forget Beau." I was struggling to keep my emotions in check.

"And me, Annie? Will you forget me?"

Unable to suppress my tears any longer I groped in my purse for a handkerchief. The roar of the Twin Otter drowned out my muted reply as it taxied to a stop. Branch clutched me tightly, smothering me with his kisses, our tears mingling.

"Annie," he gasped. "I can't bear to lose you. Come back to me."

*   *   *

The flight out of SFO departed on time, climbing into a dismal, gray, drizzly sky— obscuring the fabled city and the Golden Gate Bridge. My mood matched the weather and as soon as the plane leveled out I ordered a bloody Mary. Halfway through the drink the plane broke out of the clouds into a dazzlingly blue, sunlit sky—the gray blanket now far below. When I'd finished the drink I leaned back in the seat, reflecting on the strangeness of the last few hours I'd spent in Cutter Lake and its environs.

The stewardess startled me, shaking me from my daydream. Can I get you another drink?" she asked.

"Yes, thank you. Only this time make it vodka and tonic." I glanced out the window. All signs of the clouds were gone revealing the vast expanse of blue-green ocean below. The stewardess returned with the drink and I sipped it slowly, staring out the small pockmarked oval.

"I feel so empty." Thoughts tangled. "What a joke on me. *'Take a vacation to clear your head, get away from the sameness, the confinement, the boredom.'* And look what I got...a double whammy, a horse and a man. And God help me, I love them both. So now what do I do? Haven't I been here before?" I answered my own question. "Maybe not the horse, but surely the man." Beginning to feel the effects of the two drinks I placed the small pillow against the window and rested my head against it, dropping instantly into an inebriated slumber.

Chapter XVII

1969 – Las Vegas

Paul was dating, seeing less of his children, child support payments sporadic. The two-year separation period had drawn to an end and he and I were ordered to appear before the all-powerful Tribunal. The hearing was convened at the County Court House. It lasted twenty-minutes and I departed a free woman. Sarah planned a party at the apartment and even Brad joined in the festivities, offering his congratulations. It seemed an odd thing to celebrate but after all the years of bad times and bitterness we were happy to put the past behind us at last.

The phone rang and as usual Josh and Danny dashed to answer it.

"Don't pick it up," Josh shouted from the bedroom. "It's for me."

Too late, Danny already had his hand on the receiver. He kept it there without answering just to aggravate his brother. The moment Josh was within grasp of the phone, Danny lifted the receiver to his ear.

"Oh, hi Brad," he said as his brother punched him in the arm.

"Give me that phone," I demanded, wrenching it from Danny's hand. My action freed the brothers, ages fifteen and twelve, to engage in one of their infamous wrestling matches.

"Is anyone going to talk to me?" came a disembodied voice.

"Hey Dad, is that you?"

"Why don't you do something about those two brats?"

"Can't...they're so much bigger than me. What's up?"

"Got a proposition you can't refuse. Have you got supper for me?"

My father hadn't made an appearance in nearly a year, since my divorce festivities. We'd come to a kind of tacit truce. He called occasionally and visited once in a while, like Santa, bringing gifts; TV set, radio, electronic gadgets—things he felt we could not live without but actually allowed him to check on sporting events. He stayed for diner, always the same at his request; roast beef no garlic or onions, mashed potatoes and rye bread with unsalted butter.

"Guess so, but it won't be roast beast."

"Was that Brad?" Sarah asked.

"Yes it was. He's coming for dinner...and to make us a proposition."

"I don't like the sound of that"

It had taken me a year to convince my mother to move in with us after she retired. She said, "You don't have the room and I'm not ready to give up my serene security. But now she was with us and with us she would stay.

Brad arrived thirty minutes later with bags full of Chinese take-out. His proposition was interesting. He'd managed to get back in the good graces of his Mafia friends and was again operating a bookmaking establishment out of his and Gracie's house. Often he would arrange to take groups on junkets to Las Vegas. In exchange for bringing the suckers down he would get all his expenses paid.

"Hey, Annie. How'd ya like to really celebrate? Come on, I'll take you to Vegas with me. You haven't had a vacation in a while. The treat's on me."

It was a tempting offer. I'd never been to Las Vegas but had often heard about how exciting it was. Julie had been there on junkets with Brad several times and had told me about the great connections he had, how he'd gotten them in to see all the great shows, including Frank Sinatra. I'd been extremely miffed upon hearing of my father's great generosity while I was struggling to pay rent and put food on the table. Never once, since giving me the small move-in loan, did Brad offer any financial assistance.

"Come on Annie. Give yourself a break."

The offer was accepted and while Sarah wasn't pleased with the arrangement, agreed to take charge of the household for the few days we'd be gone. I'd flown only twice before, to Florida on my honeymoon, Antigua for an ill-fated cruise, and was eagerly anticipating the trip. On this occasion the take-off signaled the commencement of party time. As soon as the chartered plane leveled out the booze began to flow. And it kept on flowing all the way from Newark to Nevada. We landed at LAV in varying states of insobriety and were met by a tour bus that carted us off to Caesar's Palace in the heart of the Vegas Strip.

Knowing neither day nor night Vegas provided breakfast at midnight, dinner at five a.m. or vice versa. Maine lobster, Nova Scotia salmon, Nebraska beef, Virginia ham or Chinese spare ribs; Vegas could provide it at any time in any quantities; twenty-year old Scotch, vintage wines, exotic liqueurs, no problem. Want a massage at two a.m.? Just ring. Casinos operated twenty-four hours a day with croupiers literally raking in the green, slot machines singing, coins jingling and people winning and losing fortunes at a throw of the dice.

Brad secured a suite consisting of two bedrooms, sitting room and bath. It was elegant and provided sweeping views of the neon-lit city. I loved it. As soon as we arrived Brad abandoned me for the craps table and I headed for the room to shower and change into an evening dress; famished and looking forward to dining at one of the fabulous restaurants in the hotel. Returning to the casino floor I found Brad still at the table.

He called to me, "Come on, Annie. Change my luck. Toss for me." He handed me the dice.

"I haven't got a clue what to do."

"You just throw numbers. Just take these little babies in your sweet hand and throw numbers." He pressed the dice into my hand. "Shake em and roll."

I rolled the dice across the table.

"Seven." It was the croupier.

"Throw again, Annie." This time it was Brad.

Obediently, I threw the dice again.

"Seven."

"Atta girl, Annie. Roll 'em again."

"Four."

"Oh, did I get a bad number?"

"No, no Annie. Just roll numbers." Brad was excited now.

"Six."

I looked at Brad questioningly.

"Roll," he persisted.

"Four."

A number of people were attracted by the commotion at the table. They cheered me on. Exhilarated by their obvious enthusiasm, I rolled again.

"Seven."

The crowd was yelling, "Come on, Annie."

"Five." Brad called.

"Five, it is."

The excitement level increased audibly with each throw of the dice. I rolled them for nearly half an hour before finally "crapping out," a term I learned was not a good thing, resulting in a collective sigh from the audience. The croupier raked in the dice and handed them to another player.

"Was that bad?" I asked Brad.

"Yeah, Annie. It sure ain't good."

"I'm sorry."

Standing elbow to elbow with a fellow player who'd overheard the brief dialogue I heard him remark, "Lady, you got nothin' in the world to be sorry for. You can roll for me anytime."

Only later, during dinner, did I discover that Brad had won close to twenty-thousand dollars.

Waiting to be seated at "The Mermaid," an exclusive seafood house located in the hotel, Brad spotted some former junket clients and invited them to join us at our table. He introduced me as his daughter eliciting evil grins and snickers. Brad's womanizing reputation was well known.

"No, really guys. Annie is my little girl. Doesn't she look like me?"

Much as I disliked the comparison we really did look related, blue eyes and all.

"Well, she does kinda but she sure ain't no little girl."

The men accepted Brad's dinner invitation and the maitre'd led our foursome through the imposing surroundings to a booth configured in the shape of a large seashell. In the center of the domed room a waterfall cascaded into a large pond upon which a piscine mermaid floated in a mock scallop shell playing a harp. Colorfully tinted water sprays surrounded her as she drifted on the pond. It was magical.

Tony Minetti and John Spirtos were from Providence, Rhode Island and had come to Vegas for a business conference. No one discussed the kind of business at dinner and I assumed they were plying the same trade as Brad. Conversation was lighthearted, enhanced by the assorted wines the sommelier brought for us to taste. Each scrumptious course was preceded by a wine sampling, accompanied by recommendations and followed by a unanimously agreed upon selection. With salad came a fruity rosé. The fish course demanded a wonderful dry white while the rare beef required a hearty but elegant French Bordeaux. Too full for dessert we finished off our extravagant repast with snifters of brandy, slightly warmed over a candle.

John was the more outgoing of the two and kept the group entertained with stories of his trips to the Orient.

"Returning from Hong Kong," he remarked, "I landed at LAX as did a large group of Japanese tourists. Seems it was customary for their tour guide to carry a small flag, the color of which matched the armbands worn by the tourists in his party. This enabled them to spot their guide in a crowd by looking for the colored flag, and him to find them by searching for their armbands. While waiting for my luggage I noticed a flag left behind by one of the guides. I picked it up and hurried to catch up with him to return it. When I turned around I had an entire group behind me wearing the same color armbands as the flag I was carrying. Took me quite a while to make them understand I was not their guide."

As often happened, when a bit tipsy I began to giggle and found it impossible to stop. John seemed pleased to find such an appreciative audience and added a few one-liners. I was enjoying myself immensely.

Tony, possessed of Latin good looks and quiet manner, intrigued me and I rather hoped he would stick around. He did not, however and shortly after thanking Brad for the wonderful dinner, left for the casino. Brad, playing the big sport, signed the tab and excused himself leaving John and me alone at the table.

"Well, Annie. It looks as though we are left to our own devices. Would you like to go to the casino?"

"Thank you, John but I've had my taste of it already. Besides, I work too damn hard for my money to throw it away."

John laughed. He had a contagious laugh and I found myself giggling again.

"Too much wine, I'm afraid. Please excuse my silliness."

"I find you delightful. Look, here's a couple-hundred bucks. Go play blackjack. That's a pretty simple game and if you lose, well, it's my dough." He pressed two hundred-dollar bills into my hand.

"Thanks, but I can't accept it, John." I tried unsuccessfully to give it back.

"Please keep it and go have some fun. I'm going to give the poker tables a try and I'll look for you in an hour or so. We can take a drive down the Strip and see some of the new construction going on, maybe have a nightcap."

"If you're that determined to give money away, I'll take it."

John gave a quick salute and hurried away. Back at the casino I ambled for a while scanning the activity, stopping at a blackjack table, watching several players until one of them gave me a dirty look. I moved on, pausing at each of several tables before deciding to take a seat at a two-dollar game. I placed a two-dollar bet, drew my cards and lost the money. The transaction took all of three minutes.

"The hell with this," I thought. "It's just plain stupid to throw good money after bad." Leaving the casino thrills behind I strolled through the outdoor promenade, lined with exclusive and expensive shops. Eyeing a striking pink wool suit in one of the boutiques, I decided to try it on.

"Oh, that suit was just made for you with your coloring and figure. You just have to have it." The salesgirl bubbled with praise.

"It really is nice. How much?"

"With tax, one-hundred-ninety six dollars."

"I'll take it."

I found John searching for me in one of the black jack table areas.

"Hi there," he smiled obviously glad to see me. "Where have you been? I thought you must have made a big hit and run out on me."

"Not quite. I lost two dollars and decided not to be a fool. So I let you buy this lovely suit." I opened the package to show John the prize. "I even have two bucks left over."

"Annie, you are a kick. You can wear it tomorrow night when I take you out on the town. Are you up for that ride?"

"John, I hate to poop out on you but I'm really beat and still a little tipsy. Do you mind if I opt out?"

"No, Annie. That's fine. I'll see you tomorrow."

"Good night, John and thanks for the lovely present."

I took the elevator to the fifteenth floor and wasn't surprised to find that Brad had not returned. I was asleep before my head hit the pillow. The phone woke me at ten-thirty, John inviting me to breakfast.

"I accept, providing it's just coffee and toast."

"Hung over?"

"No, just stuffed."

We met at the coffee shop where we had several cups of black coffee and shared a bagel.

"Since you don't want to play what would you like to do?"

"I don't want to keep you from doing what you came to Vegas to do."

"Annie, I'm glad for an excuse to get out of the hotel for a while. Besides, your company beats the tables anytime. So what shall it be?"

"Hmm. Isn't Hoover Dam near here?"

"Hoover Dam?" John exclaimed. "It's way over at the Arizona border. Is that where you want to go?" He sounded unbelieving.

"I've read about it. I think it's the highest dam in the country and it would be nice to see it since I will probably not get the chance again."

"Guess I asked for it. Okay! Hoover Dam it is."

Taking a blanket, some oranges and several bottles of water we headed out in John's rental car, a funny little Pinto the same color as the oranges. We drove the thirty-odd miles to the Dam during which time John astounded me by mentioning he had his degree in structural engineering from Northeastern University. He'd worked for a time with the Army Corps of Engineers disenchanted with the bureaucracy, left to go into his own construction business. He'd been very successful until a one, two blow broke him; high interest rates and a divorce. He was currently in an export-import business, which was the reason he spent a good deal of time in the Orient.

After a leisurely forty-minute drive we spied Lake Mead shimmering in the distance. Then the high span separating Nevada from Arizona came into view. As we neared it I realized the road actually ran across the top of the Dam. Pulling into a parking spot, we walked to the edge where a low art deco wall served as a safety barrier. It was an awesome sight. There, seven hundred feet below us, the great roaring Colorado River was captured and tamed, forming the vast expanse of Lake Mead and providing enough electricity to power large metropolitan cities like Los Angeles and Phoenix.

"What an amazing feat this was. The lake is huge."

"This lake is one-hundred and fifteen miles long and as deep as five-hundred feet." John was a font of information. "One-hundred and twelve men died during the construction."

We walked to a plaque that was dedicated to the men who were killed during the construction and read the inscription. "Death Is Permanent." Among the listed names, two Tierneys drew my attention.

"Do you think these two were related?"

"Sadly, yes. They were father and son. The father was the first man killed working here and strange as it may seem, the son was the last."

"That's incredible. How do you know all this stuff?" There was a lot more to the man than I had previously surmised; my curiosity was sparked.

"Told you...was with the Army Corp of Engineers for a time. They work closely with the Bureau of Land Management who was in charge of the project. Learning about the Dam was part of our training program."

"I've heard this called Hoover Dam and Boulder Dam. Which is right?"

"The Dam is built in an area called Black Canyon. When the project was started in 1930, it was called "The Boulder Canyon Project. Hoover, then President, had the name changed to honor himself. In 1934, the head of the Dept. of the Interior, Harold Ickes, who hated Hoover, had it changed again to Boulder Dam. When he became president, Truman renamed it once again and it is now officially Hoover Dam."

We took an elevator down to the generating plant on the Nevada side of the Colorado River, where eight massive turbos spun ceaselessly imparting a soft, monotonous hum. The sterile stillness was disorienting. Surprisingly, we were alone in the cavernous expanse.

"I would have thought these things would make a lot more noise."

John disturbed the silence with his cheerful laugh. "This is not a cathedral, Annie. You don't have to whisper."

"It demands the same reverence. This whole thing is awesome."

"There are nine more of these monsters on the Arizona side. Together they generate two billion watts of electricity."

"Amazing." I examined the beautiful inlaid balcony floor. "This looks like an Indian pattern."

"It is. There are several others. Supposed to be representative of the tribes who lived in these parts."

Suitably impressed I began to examine John more closely, and although I'd not been attracted to him initially was beginning to find him intriguing. He was not tall, maybe five ten or eleven and a little bit on the stocky side, but impeccably dressed in obviously expensive clothes. He was intelligent, articulate and had a terrific sense of humor. He was good company and I was having a wonderful time.

The elevator returned us to the surface where the bright sunlight was startling.

"Kind of forgot where we were. Want some more info?"

"By all means, do go on Professor."

"It was too expensive for any one company to commit to, so six construction companies joined together to secure the contract for building the dam. Bet you know the name of at least two of them."

"I can't even imagine one," I smiled with exaggerated interest. "But if you're trying to impress me, you're doing a good job."

"Ever heard of Kaiser or Bechtel?"

"Really?"

"Yep! Made their fortunes here. Know how much rock was hauled out?"

"You know I don't, showoff."

"Ten-million tons."

"Now I am really impressed."

"Lesson over, Annie. What's your pleasure?"

"Let's look at the map and see if there's a different way back."

We opened the map and I spotted a thin, wiggly line that seemed to run from the lake to Death Valley. I pointed it out to John.

"How about this road. Can we take it and come back by way of Death Valley?"

"It looks like we could but that would be a very long trip. Look at the small print near that road. It says, 'One way only'."

"The arrow shows it going in the direction we want to go. Can we try it? It might be fun and I'm sure we'll get to see some spectacular scenery. I love adventure." I had my camera and was eager to bring some interesting photos home.

"It will certainly be an adventure. But if you're game, I am. Let's do it."

With the map as a guide we did indeed find the little squiggly road with the sign that indicated one way. John turned into the narrow road and we were committed.

"There's no turning back now, Annie. You're stuck with me."

I nodded in his direction and turned to watch the road ahead as it seemed to get narrower and more precipitous. We were in a canyon with steep, vertical walls of colorful sandstone

"It's a long way down there. I sure hope this trail doesn't get any narrower."

Just as the last word was out of his mouth we noticed a small boulder in the road ahead of us. There was no way around it. John stopped the car in front of the impasse, as close to the canyon wall as possible.

"What are you going to do, John?"

"I've got to get that pebble out of the way so we can continue our adventure."

With that he opened his door and looked at the void below him then back at me.

Annie's Portion

"Like I said, Annie girl. It's a long way down."

There was no way for him to get out on that side. My door was too close to the cliff face to open. He climbed into the back seat and managed to release the rear hatch door. He squeezed out onto the road behind the car and climbed up over the roof, down onto the hood and finally landed on the ground between the car and the boulder. Placing his back against the wall he pushed at it with his feet. It did not budge. I could see him straining to get a better purchase on both the wall and the giant stone. Try as he might he couldn't move it. He looked at me through the windshield and shrugged.

"I guess we'll just have to walk back to the main road." I shouted out the window. Turning to look out the rear hatch I was startled to see what appeared to be a wild apparition. There, coming up the incline was a tall, heavily bearded man in army fatigues and boots. He had a large pack on his back and a thick walking stick in hand. His head was bent and he nearly bumped into the car before pulling up with a start.

"What in blazes..." He scratched his beard and stared at me.

"Hi there!" I tried to act nonplused.

"What in the Sam hill are you doin' here, young lady?"

"We're stuck. There's a large fallen rock in our path. My friend is up in front trying to move it."

The hiker peered through the car and could see John and the boulder ahead.

"Sure looks like you can use a bit of help. Mind if I crawl on in?"

He slipped out of the pack harness and laid it on the ground next to his walking stick. Without so much as a "by your leave" climbed up and over the roof the same way John had, dropping on the ground in front of the car. John, who was deeply engrossed in devising some engineering miracle to move the boulder, looked up with a startled expression.

"I'll be damned. Where did you come from?"

"Say, young fella, I was just gonna ask you the same thing. Looks like you're in a bit of a fix."

"Yeah, we sure are. I can't budge this thing."

"Maybe if we work together we can get that bugger off the edge. I've got a real heavy cane that might work to pry it just a little bit loose. Then maybe we can kick that son-of-a-gun to Hades."

With that he crawled back over the car, got his staff, crawled back again and proceeded to poke the stick under the rock. He managed to force his lever under the boulder, just enough to free it.

"Looks like we loosened the son-of-a-bitch. Now if we work together we should get her to go."

He and John positioned themselves side-by-side against the canyon wall. They placed their feet against the boulder.

"Ok, together now."

I thought I saw some slight movement as the men pushed and strained against the rock. "It's moving a little. Keep it up."

They both turned to look at me, grimaced and pushed some more. The rock was indeed moving.

"Gotta be careful now son. Don't want to push ourselves over with that s.o.b."

The boulder had been nudged just enough.

"One more push should do it." John offered.

They strained one last time; the boulder teetered at the edge for a moment then went over the side crashing finally into the gully below. The men shook hands.

"Thanks seems like an inadequate word. I don't know what we'd have done without your help." John held onto the hiker's hand.

Annie's Portion

"Just call it providence. So now that we've got the road clear do you suppose I could hitch a way with you?"

"You sure can, though I don't really know where we're going."

"Oh, there's but one way to go and eventually we'll get to the end."

Both men climbed back over the car and got into it through the rear hatch. John slid into the driver's seat and started the car. He turned to me.

"Some navigator you turned out to be."

"I should have warned you about my sense of direction. My family calls me 'Wrong way Corrigan'."

We enjoyed a hearty communal laugh recalling the story of the pilot who, in the late thirties filed a flight plan in New York indicating San Francisco or L.A. as his final destination. Somehow he managed, either because of a storm or fog, to end up in Ireland or some such.

Ainsley Winston was a retired British officer who had come to the states after his retirement to hike the West. He'd been on the road for six years. He regaled us with stories of his many adventures during that time. After what seemed like hours, we began to descend. The sun too, began to inch closer to the horizon. We breathed a collective sigh of relief when we finally departed the canyon and found ourselves in the great expanse of Death Valley.

"Sure am glad we got off that hill before dark." Ainsley expressed aloud what we'd all been thinking.

"What do you think Annie? Enough excitement for one day?"

"John, this has been enough excitement for a year. Where are we now?"

"Well, young lady. You are now at the edge of the Mojave Desert in California." Ainsley was consulting his map. "But I don't think we're going to get much farther today."

John pulled up next to an outcrop and turned off the engine. "I think Ainsley is right Annie. It would be best if we just spent the night here and made our way out in daylight."

Ainsley climbed out the hatch and hauled his pack to the ground. He opened his bedroll and wrapped it around his body.

"Hope you two are prepared for a cold night. This is the desert you know."

"We are well prepared travelers, old man." John smiled. "We have a blanket, some oranges and lots of water."

He passed the oranges and water bottles around. As soon as the meager meal was finished Ainsley slipped into his bag, pulled it over his head and went to sleep.

"How are we going to manage this, John? I'm so sorry I got us into this mess. Me and my great ideas."

"We'll be just fine, a little cold and uncomfortable but a.o.k." He opened the blanket and laid it in the back of the car. "We'll have to bend ourselves around the spare tire but it won't be too bad."

John pulled me close to him. "For warmth," he said as he rested my head on his arm.

He tucked the blanket around our contorted bodies and after a brief attempt at idle conversation we dozed off. We woke at first light, cold and cramped. The temperature had dropped substantially. Ainsley was still snuggled deep in his bag. John woke him to tell him it was time to get going.

"This is as far as I'll travel with you. I enjoyed our visit but I'm used to being alone and I'll just make my way when I'm ready."

"You're more than welcome to travel with us to a town." John didn't like the idea of leaving him out in the desert alone.

"Please do stay with us Ainsley. We may need your help again."

He chuckled. "No thanks, pretty lady. You'll do fine." With that last comment he pulled his head back into his bag.

John looked at me and shrugged. "Suit yourself. But a million thanks for your help."

There being no response he held the door open and with complaining limbs I slid into the front seat. We arrived at Caesar's Palace in late afternoon and after agreeing to meet at eight for dinner we parted company. I found my room unoccupied, took a shower, placed a wake-up call for seven p.m. and went to bed.

The phone rang exactly at seven, waking me with a jolt. I'd slept all day, the room dark. Disoriented, I switched the lamp on and stretched in the luxurious bed, disinclined to leave its comfort. The effects of the previous night's sleeping arrangement had yet to improve. Finally able to extract myself from my bunting, I dressed in my new pink suit, put on a fresh coat of war-paint, fixed a few curls and checked the finished product in the full-length mirror. Satisfied with the result I said aloud, "Vanity thy name is woman." With no idea of Brad's whereabouts, yet fairly certain he'd either be in the casino or some female's bed, I placed a note on his bed assuring him of my well-being.

John was waiting for me near the concierge's desk and brightened discernibly when he saw me. "Annie, you're a knockout. I'd be honored to have you on my arm." He took my hand and placed it on his arm.

"Where are we going?"

"Do you like steak?"

"I most certainly do and I'm starving."

We dined at "El Gaucho," a well-known Argentine steak house where I gorged on a one-pound T-bone steak but limited my drinking to one gimlet before dinner and a glass of wine with the main course.

"How about that drive now, Annie?"

"That would be nice. I'm so full I can't even move."

"I can't seem to satisfy you."

John drove along the Strip, pointing out places of interest. Las Vegas was the neon capital of the world as well as a storybook wonderland. We passed The Dunes, Circus Circus, The Flamingo, The Riviera, The Sahara; names I'd heard my father speak of many times. Nearing the far end of town I could see a distant ring of lights that appeared to be suspended in the air.

"Whatever that is, it looks like it's hanging from a sky hook."

John laughed. "No sirree. That's just Howard Hughes' newest monument."

He pulled into a parking space at the base of the needle and hurried to open the car door for me.

"Let's go to the top of the world, Annie."

It was difficult to keep my smile hidden as I was reminded of New York City's skyscrapers and the fact that I worked on the sixtieth floor of Manhattan Overseas Bank Plaza. Here was John trying to impress me with a tower that was probably twenty stories high. An elevator, running on a track attached to an outer wall of the circular structure, delivered us to the uppermost level. The doors opened, revealing a quite impressive picture. We stepped out of the lift and onto a balcony that ringed the tower. The thin string of tiny white lights we'd seen from below clung to the rail encircling the gallery. We stood transfixed, suspended in air with the twinkling city spread out like a luminous carpet beneath us, competing for attention with the star-studded umbrella above our heads. As we made our way slowly around the circle, the scene below morphed before our eyes; growing slightly dimmer with each step we took until reaching the side furthest from the city, there was nothing but a black void. John embraced me and I pressed closer to him, sharing the wonder of the moment.

Annie's Portion

"Annie," John whispered huskily in my ear. "You've got me tied up in knots. I've never known anyone quite like you."

Afraid to speak and break the spell, afraid to say the wrong thing, I moved out of his reach and kept silent, gazing into the distance.

"Annie, look at me. Do you think we can be more than just friends?"

My response was one of caution. "I don't understand what I feel. I am attracted to you but it's much too soon to know what that means."

"Sure Annie, I understand. I'm not trying to rush you."

He started to walk toward the elevator but I held him back and when he kissed me, I did not resist. The moon had disappeared, the darkness below seeming to engulf a great plane inhabited by shadowy figures. The city lights had dimmed and lost their magic luster. There was no dialogue during the ride down to the desert floor nor was there any on the return drive. At Caesar's the valet took the car and we strode through the lobby at a leisurely pace, John's arm about my waist.

"Would you like a brandy?"

"No thanks. I think I'll hit the hay. We'll be taking an afternoon plane home tomorrow so I'd best try to get some rest."

"I'll take you to your room. It will give me an excuse to stay with you a little longer."

We'd reached the door to my room and I was rummaging in my purse for the key.

"Take a look at this." John was grinning.

I looked down and there, hanging from the doorknob, was a sign in bold letters that read, "Do Not Disturb."

"Oh no! How could he do this?" I was certainly disturbed as well as humiliated to have John witness my father's unseemly behavior. "What must you think? John, I'm so embarrassed."

"You needn't be, Annie. It just proves you really are his daughter." His laugh was contagious.

"What do I do now?"

"Why don't we go back down and have that drink. Then we'll phone him to tell him we're on the way up."

And that was what we did. Brad's door was closed when I got back to the room and not wanting to confront him, I too went to bed. The sunlight streaming through the window woke me at nine. I showered and dressed before going into the sitting room, where I found Brad watching TV.

"I thought you were kidnapped. I haven't seen you for days."

"I'm surprised you noticed. You seem to have been very busy yourself. Didn't anyone tell you you're getting too old for this kind of stuff?"

"Well, the ladies sure don't think I'm too old." Brad answered.

"Once a scoundrel always a scoundrel."

Just then there was a knock on the door and Brad went to open it. It was a bellhop holding a bouquet of two dozen red roses.

"For Miss Annie," he said.

Brad tipped the bellhop, took the flowers and placed them on the table in front of me.

"Whad'ja have to do for those?" Brad snickered.

"Not a damn thing!"

John found us having breakfast in the coffee shop.

"Been keeping busy, Brad?" He gave Brad a knowing look.

"I should have kept busier and I wouldn't have lost all the money Miss Annie here won for me." He put particular emphasis on the "Miss Annie."

John sat down next to me. "Before you disappear out of my life I need to get your phone number. You will see me when I get into the Big Apple, won't you?"

I wrote my number on the back of his card but had little hope I'd hear from him again. Brad and I departed for the airport where we found our flight had been delayed. I passed the time away throwing change into the ever-present slot machines. Just as our departure was announced I inserted my last quarter and hit a jackpot. Refusing to leave without my winnings I continued to scoop coins into my purse till I heard the final call. By the time we boarded my purse weighed at least ten pounds.

Chapter XVIII

It was three weeks before I heard from John again. The phone rang and Danny and Josh raced to answer it. Josh beat Danny out by tripping him in a most unsportsmanlike way and picked up the receiver.

"Hello, Joe's Pool Hall. Who in the hall do you want?"

There was a brief silence on the other end of the line then a male voice answered. "Is this the home of Anne Harmon?"

Danny and Josh were still battling over the receiver. Finally wresting it from Danny, Josh answered, "Yeah, it is. One minute." Then holding the phone away from his mouth he yelled, "Hey, Miss Harmon! It's for you."

I pushed my way between the two, still struggling boys.

"Hello, this is Anne."

"Hi, Miss Annie. This is your desert companion. In case you've forgotten, it's John."

"Oh, hi John. How've you been?" I'd given up the idea he'd ever call so was surprised but pleased to hear from him.

"I've been fine, very busy with an overseas trip but back home now and anxious to see you."

"Thought you'd forgotten all about me by now."

"Impossible. How could I ever forget the great adventure? Say Annie, who was the kid who answered the phone? Sounded like more than one."

Believing there was little likelihood of ever seeing John once I'd departed Las Vegas, I'd limited any discussion of my personal life. When asked where I worked I did some quick thinking giving John a less than honest reply; telling him I worked for a children's shelter, offering no further

Annie's Portion

explanation. I was in the untenable position of having to embellish the lie. "Oh, you remember I told you I worked for a children's shelter. Well some times I take one or two of the kids home for the weekend to give them a taste of the good life."

My sons, listening attentively in the cramped kitchen, began hooting and shaking their fingers at me intimating "shame on you."

"Well they sure need to learn some manners. You'd better rein them in Annie, give 'em the back of your hand." John laughed.

"I try. God knows I try. But boys will be boys."

"Say, Annie. All kidding aside, no pun intended, I'll be in the city tomorrow and would love to take you to dinner. Are you free?"

Still playing the game, I replied, "Yes. I'll have the boys back at the shelter by then and I can meet you any time after five."

"That's great. Where would you like to go? What is my lady's pleasure?"

"Would you think I was a bore if I suggested steak again?"

"Not at all. I'm just a meat and potatoes man myself. Where shall I meet you?"

"Where are you staying?"

"I'm at the Sheraton, midtown at fifth-third."

"There's a great steak house not far from there."

"I know the one," was John's enthusiastic reply. "Gallagher's. I've been there many times. That's a good idea. Shall I pick you up?"

Not wanting him to come downtown to the Plaza for fear he might discover my little ruse, I suggested meeting him at the Sheraton.

"I can take the Broadway Line and meet you at six."

"Good. We can have a drink and then walk down to the restaurant. I'll make a reservation for seven. And please wear that pink suit for me."

We met for a drink, had a wonderful dinner, which I finished off with a bowl of fresh strawberries accompanied by a side of real whipped cream, then had a brandy at the bar. The crowd was friendly. Seated between John and a woman who seemed unattended, I struck up a conversation with her. We'd been chatting for a bit, with John adding an occasional comment, when I excused myself. Returning from the restroom I noted the absence of the woman. John appeared flushed and had a smirk on his face.

"You remember that nice lady you were visiting with?"

I nodded. "Uh-huh. Did she leave?"

"Not before opening her coat and offering me her naked body."

"She didn't! What did you do?"

"I told her I'd already been booked."

"You rat. Maybe you should have taken her up on her offer. It might be the best and only one you'll get."

John took the hint and phoned for a cab. "Are you sure you don't want me to take you home?"

"No, John. That would be crazy. You'd have to come all the way to Brooklyn and back. I'll be fine."

"It would give me all the more time to be with you." Holding both my hands in his, John kissed me lightly. "I'll let you go this time. But next time will be different."

Two weeks later I received an overnight letter containing a round-trip airline ticket to Providence along with a brief note.

"Annie, please come. I want to show you my part of the world. No demands, no obligations. I will arrange for you to stay at a hotel near my place."

Annie's Portion

The following Friday, I landed in Rhode Island at seventen p.m. John as usual, looked glad to see me, running to greet me with a dozen red roses.

"You can't imagine how pleased I am that you came." He kissed me on the cheek and handed me the roses.

My blush betrayed my excitement. "You're going to spoil me."

"That's just what I want to do." John took my bag and steered me to the parking lot. Nearing his car, he dropped the bag and reached for me.

"Cynic that you are I know you won't believe me when I say I've counted the hours waiting for this moment."

"I'm glad to be here too." Until that moment I hadn't realized just how much I'd been looking forward to seeing John.

"I hope you brought your appetite with you. Tonight you will have the best New England has to offer."

Wrapped in paper bibs, we dined at an unpretentious waterfront restaurant where clams steamed in a seaweed-infused bath, and lobsters were dropped into boiling cauldrons on order. John instructed me in the art of lobster eating, showing me how to excavate every last morsel with the aid of a smaller claw torn from one of the large pincers. Once we'd stuffed ourselves to the limits of our capacity we walked along the sea wall, enjoying the salty, cold night air.

"I'm sure you're ready to get to your hotel," John said. "I hope you like your room as well as you did your dinner."

The historic inn situated on the shore of Narraganset Bay was just minutes from the restaurant.

"I'll say goodnight here, Anne," John said as he extended his hand to help me from the car. He embraced me gently, planting a polite kiss on my receptive mouth. "I'm sure you're tired and tomorrow will be a long day. I'll see you at nine."

I was disconcerted by John's abrupt departure, thinking "It's his turn to play hard to get. But that's fine. I'm not in a hurry to get involved with another man."

John arrived at the inn promptly at nine. Seated in the intimate breakfast room overlooking the bay, we enjoyed cranberry scones topped with Devonshire cream and strong coffee.

"Now for the grand tour," John said with his usual effervescence.

We spent the rest of the day sightseeing. I'd never been to New England and found Rhode Island absolutely charming. John drove through little historic villages, past beautifully maintained old homes with manicured lawns and English gardens. We saw fertile farmland enhanced by gambrel-roofed red barns and numerous white steepled churches. We drove along the shore passing neat little Cape Cod cottages, to quaint Bristol, then to Jamestown and across the Newport Bridge to the town of Newport with its mansions and restored historic houses.

"Want to have some oysters and the best New England chowder you'll ever eat?" John asked.

"I've never eaten an oyster but I'm willing to give it a try."

John parked near the wharf. The air was filled with the salt smell of the sea and a hint of garlic. An unremarkable gray clapboard building appeared to be the source of the tempting aroma. The "Black Pearl" seemed on the verge of falling into the water lapping against the piers on which it stood. We sat on the outside deck of the restaurant, watching the sun sink below the horizon, slurping oysters and enjoying the wonderful chowder.

"A perfect ending to a perfect day." John sighed.

"Yes, it has been an absolutely wonderful day."

In a repeat performance of the previous night, John departed the inn without seeing me to my room, discharging me with an impassive embrace and abbreviated kiss. Church bells had struck ten by the time he returned the next morning to take me to brunch.

"Are you upset with me, John?"

"Not one bit Anne. I'm captivated by you. But I promised to behave and I've tried my damndest, difficult as that's been, to keep my word. The last thing I want to do is scare you off. Have you enjoyed your time with me?"

"I've loved every minute. And I do appreciate your honesty. It's not often a man gives so much without expecting a lot in return."

"Don't make a martyr of me. I'm only human and it took all I had to keep my hands off you. But so be it. I will await your pleasure."

Before surrendering me at the airport, John took me in his arms. "I love you, Annie Harmon."

With no reply in the offing he asked, "Does that surprise you? Sorry, guess I should have waited longer."

"Please don't apologize, John. I'm not sorry."

We saw each other often in the next few months. The first few times the routine was the same. John flew into the city, either from Providence or some foreign port. He called me at the office and we'd meet for dinner and drinks. A time came when John suggested we have a drink in his room. It was a night when we did not dine at all, spending the time in discovery, he slowly undressing me, seeming to delight in every line and curve of my body.

"Don't make a move. Don't do anything. Just let me love you."

He kissed my eyes, the tip of my nose, my lips. He moved his hands down my body with a touch light as a feather. He kissed my throat, my breasts, my stomach, my thighs. He parted my thighs and moved his head close, his hair brushing my body. I gasped and tried to close my legs. John gently restrained me and brought me to climax. It was the most exquisite sensation I'd ever experienced. He moved his body onto mine and entered me. He moved slowly, deliberately, thrusting deeply inside me. His pace quickened and at last he uttered a loud groan and lay spent. After a few moments he rolled off and lay beside me, placing his arm under my head. I nestled there contentedly, my thoughts unspoken. We dozed off and woke an hour later, only to begin our lovemaking again. We showered together, taking turns washing each other's bodies, leaving no parts untouched.

There were other nights when we spent hours in bed, ordered an extravagant meal from room service and ate it while telling each other stories about our past lives, neither of us ever telling the whole story.

"I'm going to get as fat as a pig at this rate," I said as I soaked up the last bit of egg yolk with a piece of toast.

"Not to worry. They say you burn off two hundred and fifty calories every time you screw." John bent across the table and whispered the last words then led me back to the bed.

It was often dawn when John placed me in a cab for the ride back to Brooklyn but shortly after Thanksgiving in '71 things changed. I realized our relationship was growing more intense and knew we were heading for something more than clandestine meetings.

"John, why don't you come into Brooklyn this time and pick me up at my apartment," I suggested.

"That would be fine, Annie," he replied cautiously. "Is there some special reason?"

"Oh, I'd like you to see where and how I live. Besides, you'll love Brooklyn." I gave him the address and directions that he could relay to the cab driver. "By the way, I'm on the third floor, apartment C3. Just ring downstairs and I'll buzz you in."

At seven-fifteen there was a knock at the door. Josh and Danny, both close to six feet tall, answered the knock and opened the door. John stood, mouth agape, staring at them as I walked up behind my young men.

"Please come in, John, and meet the children from the shelter. This is Josh."

Josh took John's hand giving it a mighty shake. "Hey man, how's it all hangin'?"

John looked dazed.

"And this is Danny."

Danny, the quieter of the two, mimicked his mentor Karl Shultz, and in his best "Rocky" voice said, "How's it?"

John finally found his own voice and replied, "Nice to meet you."

"Say hello to the rest of my family. The two peeking around the corner are Matt and Samantha." I nudged him into the living room where Sarah sat watching her favorite TV show, "The 'A' Team."

"John, may I present the matriarch of the family, my mother Sarah."

"How do you do? So nice to meet the mother of this charming lady." John pointed to me.

"Well, it's high time she brought you home." Sarah responded.

Brandy came out from under the couch, her usual spot since the time of its reincarnation, and growled a warning.

"This is Brandy, our guard dog." Sarah laughed. "Best not to get her mad at you. She's been known to try tearing a man's throat out when he came too close to Samantha."

"I'll keep my distance."

"Brandy won't have a chance because I'm taking John out for dinner." I latched on to his hand and led him toward the door.

"Really nice to have met all of you. A bit of a surprise but nice."

He received a general, "Good night."

We were silent as we descended the stairs and exited into the quiet street.

I spoke first. "So, what do you think of my entourage?"

"Why did you keep it from me all this time?"

"I wanted to be sure I had you hooked first. Come on. There's a pretty good Chinese restaurant around the corner."

We ordered some soup, pot stickers and the house special chowmein. John was unusually quiet.

"I'm sorry I didn't tell you sooner. I meant to but at first thought our romance would be a short one and there was no need to tell you my business. Then events seemed to get away from me. But I knew I had to come clean, so here we are."

"You certainly played me along."

"I don't blame you for being upset. I'd certainly feel betrayed if you hid something this important from me. I'll understand if you want to end this right now. I'll miss you but I certainly…"

John did not let me finish the sentence. "Stop right now. Don't say another word."

The waiter came by with the check and two fortune cookies. I took one and broke it open.

"Ha! I hope yours is better than mine. It says, 'Your good humor will serve you well.'"

John opened the other cookie. "Mine says, 'Good fortune is about to overtake you.'"

He paid the bill and we walked out into the cold night air. I shivered and pulled my collar up around my neck. John put his arm around me and held me close to his side.

"Cold?" He could feel me shiver and held me even more tightly. "Annie, I do love you. Your family will be my family. Did you think I was so shallow I couldn't accept them?"

"Four kids, a mother and a dog might be too much for anyone to accept."

"I have to admit it was quite a shock when those two giants greeted me." We both laughed at the thought. When we reached the lobby doorway, John kissed me affectionately. "I won't come up now. The kids are probably asleep and I don't want Brandy barking at me. I'll get a cab on the avenue."

"Are you sure? I can phone for one." I did not want him to leave.

"No, don't bother. I really need to walk a while. I'll call you during the week."

I unlocked the door with an aching heart, sure I would never see John again. He embraced me once more.

"I will call, Annie, I promise. You can't get rid of me easily."

John appeared at Christmas, carrying a small artificial tree trimmed with white balls, blue ribbons and a Star of David at its top. Sarah was not particularly pleased to see his "Chanukah bush" but everyone else thought it was great. It was the first Christmas tree we'd ever had and we were all especially excited by the many gift-wrapped packages John placed under it. Eventually even Sarah joined in the festivity. He surprised us again in late spring with the news he'd rented a beach house in Charlestown, insisting the family oblige him by vacationing there for the summer.

"Sarah will love the seashore and if you take vacation time in days, you can have long weekends at the beach." John continued before I could respond. "I'm just an hour away and can bop in every so often to check on everyone. Of course my motivation, while well intentioned, is also the bike in John's truck, to Woods Hole where we parked and rode the bike onto the ferry taking us to Nantucket. The day turned stormy and cold and by the time we reached the island the wind and sleet were fierce. We crossed a narrow spit bringing us to the little town and were wet and freezing by the time we reached the Eagle Cove Inn where we were to spend the night. Barely able to walk we stumbled into the tavern and raised many an eyebrow, looking like an apparition. Warmed and fed we spent a long night in one of our favorite pursuits.

John taught Josh and Danny to ride and spent lots of time with Matt showing him how to bait a hook, or whittle or fly a kite. He adored Samantha calling her, "my little love," bringing her gifts each week. He was the father they never had and they grew to love him. Sarah too, warmed to him.

"You know, John. You're not too bad for a *shaygitz*," she would often say.

The summer passed all too quickly. I came to hate the trip back and forth from Manhattan to Charlestown, which took about four speeding hours, but loved the short weekends I spent there. On what was to be our last weekend at Charlestown, John took me aside while the others were noisily packing.

"Honey, you know how much you've all loved being here. Why not make it permanent?"

"John, I've told you I'm not ready to get married again."

"I'm not talking marriage. But I want you to be closer to me. I can't leave my business but you certainly can leave your job. Please think about it."

It was a subdued group that departed Charlestown and made the long trip back to Brooklyn in our very own Ford.

The apartment felt strange and small after living at the beach house. For the first few weeks following our return we seemed to always be in each other's way. The fight over the bathroom became so intolerable I threatened to throw both Josh and Danny out of the house. Danny beat me to it by running away, only to be found a day later at Sheepshead Bay looking for a fishing boat to sail away on. Josh had just entered his senior year and was researching out-of-state colleges to which he might apply. He was not in the least threatened by faux menacing statements. John was away more often on business and for a long period our only communication was by mail. He was a prolific writer and I would receive three or four long, impassioned letters each week. I missed his gaiety, his unbridled optimism, the fun and laughter he brought into all of our lives. I missed him.

Meanwhile, my life had taken on the comfort of predictability. With Sarah's retirement I'd been able to switch to the day shift, no longer restricted to an exhausting routine. I'd been with the bank for three years, learning more about the numerous functions of my specialized department. I'd suggested a cross-training program that allowed for more efficient use of current employees and had been promoted to the newly created position of Training Coordinator. The training manual I developed had been well received and was being used in several departments. The success of the manual earned me kudos from my co-workers and attention from upper management.

"Annie, you have done really well in the short time you have been with us." It was my boss, Joe Hildebrand, Vice President of the International Transfer Division. "There is great opportunity for you to grow with Manhattan Overseas Bank. We're looking for talented women to move into management positions and you have all the qualifications to enable you to be in the forefront. I'd like to see you the first female officer in our division."

Just prior to the New Year holiday, Joe called me into the conference room where several of the bank's bigwigs and a few of my closest co-workers were meeting.

"Ms. Harmon," Joe began. I knew this must be something serious because Joe always addressed me as Annie.

"It's a real pleasure for me to be able to tell you you're about to become the first female officer in this division of Manhattan Overseas Bank."

There was polite applause and the Senior Vice President, Jared Henderson cleared his throat. "Mrs. Harmon, you have been an outstanding employee and an example of excellence and fortitude for your department and all members of Manhattan's family. It is our understanding that you will soon receive your Associate Degree in Business Administration from Pace. It has been our great pleasure to have afforded you this opportunity, one which you took advantage of and brought to such a successful outcome. As a way of acknowledging your achievements and encouraging you to continue your endeavors, we are pleased to promote you to Assistant Treasurer."

The second round of applause was much more enthusiastic and was accompanied by congratulations from my friends and co-workers.

"Thank you so much for the opportunity and encouragement you have all given me. Thanks, especially to you Joe, for giving me a push and much-needed support these last few years."

My salary was increased substantially and I was given a promise of better things to come. I enrolled for additional classes which, I hoped, would lead to my BA degree. Josh opted for Lamar University in New Mexico and although he'd gotten a school loan and had a part time job, Josh would need help with his expenses. I was doubly grateful for the additional income because not only did my paycheck grow but my employee benefits grew with every dollar I saved.

The bank matched my savings dollar for dollar and invested it. I had close to ten thousand dollars in my account.

John was gone for months at a time. The letters kept coming but when he returned in June he made no reference to Charlestown. We continued seeing each other whenever he came to the city and he persisted in asking me to move to Rhode Island. We were in love, I wanting him as much as he wanted me. I could envision a better future for my children away from New York. Danny was at an age when he needed a man to confide in. He respected John and had enjoyed the times they'd spent together. Samantha and Matt had also benefited greatly from John's attention.

I discussed my dilemma with Sarah. "Mom, what do you think I should do? Is it right for us to leave New York? Will you be happy in Rhode Island?"

"You have to make that decision for yourself. I will be happy wherever you and my grandchildren are."

"Am I just a glutton for punishment? I've worked so hard to get where I am. You and I have never been lucky with men. Dare I give this up and take a chance with another one?"

"John seems sincere and he likes the children and they like him. You can't judge all men by your father and Paul."

I thought, "And Mark and the other cheaters I've known".

Finally, after much soul searching, I came up with a proposition and informed John I would agree to move to Rhode Island providing I was able to do two things.

John was ecstatic, "I'll do anything you want, Annie, anything."

"No, you don't have to do it, I do."

"What? What do you have to do?"

"I have to buy my own house and find a good job. Then I can feel secure and be willing to leave New York."

John protested, "I can take care of you. There's no need for you to work and I'll find a place for us."

"No. You have to keep your apartment. We have really known each other long distance. I want to be close to you, with you in your surroundings; know your friends, really know you before I commit to anything further."

John was not pleased with the agreement but accepted my terms. Over the next weeks I made several trips to Rhode Island to explore housing and job opportunities. Seven miles from Providence, in Cranston, a small town near the entrance to Narragansett Bay, I found what I was looking for. Located on a cul-de-sac two miles from the bay, surrounded on two sides by forest, the Dutch colonial was perfect. The four bedroom, two bath house planted on a large lot with a detached garage, would easily accommodate our tribe. It had a large family style kitchen with a pantry and bay window opening onto the rear garden. A formal dining room adjoined the kitchen. The living room was large with a red brick fireplace capped by a carved mahogany mantel. Off the living room was a sunroom, completely encircled by windows. The upstairs bedrooms were spacious, the bathroom of ample size and updated. There was a full attic and full partially-finished basement with bath. The asking price was thirty-five thousand dollars. I loved it.

"Oh John, I want this house. But I think it's just more than I can afford."

"Annie, I told you I'd help."

"I know you did but I told you I have to do this myself."

"Well then. Let's just make them an offer. The agent told us the owners had already moved into another home and were anxious to get rid of an extra mortgage. We'll make a firm offer of twenty-six thousand. That's our best offer."

Annie's Portion

I held my breath fearing the agent would be insulted by such a low offer.

"Let's write it up," he said.

We did, and thirty days later I became a homeowner for the first time with a down payment of six-thousand-dollars and monthly payments of one-hundred and ninety. Talk about buyer's remorse—I was terrified.

For the next several months, I continued the old schedule of working in Manhattan and going to Rhode Island on long weekends. John and I were doing some remodeling and painting and wanted to wait until it was all finished before moving the family up. I took some Mondays off as vacation time using my extended stay to job hunt. My perseverance was rewarded when I landed a position with a real estate investment firm located in downtown Providence, just ten minutes from home. The salary was to be two hundred dollars a week. I would be in clover. Two weeks prior to our departure date, I gave Joe Hildebrand notice.

"Annie, you can't do this. Think about your career. You're on your way up. You can buy a house on Long Island or Staten Island if you're so hell bent on an island."

"I have thought about it, Joe. But we need to be a family, a real family. Besides, I made the dumb mistake of falling in love with the guy."

"I guess that takes all the steam out of my argument. There's no need to tell you how much you'll be missed. But if you ever change your mind, there will always be a place here for you."

We moved into the new house in time to celebrate the holiday season. The move however, was not without incident. Sarah, the children and I drove up to R.I. followed by the moving van. We arrived at the house to find the wood floors, which were to have been sanded and varnished, were not yet dry. The mover agreed to keep the furniture in the truck overnight but insisted on unloading the next morning.

We all went to stay in a motel and returned to the house at eight a.m., finding the floors still tacky. John met us at the house and determined we could not place any furniture on the wet varnish. He directed the mover to put as much as possible on the carpet in the living room and the remaining stuff out on the newly built rear deck. John went for a couple of pizzas, which we ate halfheartedly.

Exhausted by the day's effort the weary clan arranged itself around the living room, in sleeping bags, on the sofa and on chairs pulled together. During the night Brandy, who was out in the yard, began barking. I got up to see what the problem was and reached the sliding glass doors in time to see a skunk climb the back stairs. Brandy, lacking any prior knowledge of a white striped civet, continued her harangue. Calling her, I started to open the door. Suddenly, the animal made an about-turn and lifted its tail. I shut the door just in time to have the spray spatter against the glass and leave a distinct aroma on Brandy and the goods stashed on the deck. The upstairs windows open to encourage quicker drying of the floors, allowed the perfumed air to waft through the upper level. It took days to clear the air and gallons of chemicals to disperse the stink. Poor Brandy was scrubbed and hosed and scrubbed again, to no avail. At last, a good-hearted neighbor suggested washing her in tomato juice which, strange as it sounded, did the job.

Steven Kudrow and Rob Forsythe were both young, upwardly mobile, Harvard men who'd offered me a management position during a lunch meeting at their club. While Steven, President of Equity Real Estate Investment Trust, was an Iowa man who made good, Rob, Executive VP and Legal Counsel, was "born to the purple." His family dated back to the arrival in America of the Mayflower and he never missed an opportunity to remind those around him of that fact. Steven, while technically of higher rank, looked to Rob for direction and tried to emulate his very persona.

Annie's Portion

They were both snobs, one inherently, the other imitatively. My new career was launched the week following New Year's Eve. Although somewhat apprehensive I was looking forward to the new challenges I would face. I'd been given the label of Administrative Assistant to the President, and while it was long on title I soon discovered it was short on substance. My duties were to include management of the company's real estate portfolio, inputting computer data and developing an improved filing system. I'd made it very clear I possessed no secretarial skills nor was I interested in that kind of position but the first morning on the job I was greeted by Steven via the intercom.

"Anne, would you come into my office. I would like to dictate some letters."

Grabbing a note pad and pen I did as I was bid. "Good morning, Mr. Kudrow."

"Please call me Steve. We don't stand on formalities here."

I sat on the edge of a chair, facing him across a huge desk. "You're going to have to talk real slow, Steve."

"Why's that?"

"I explained to you I don't take dictation so if you want me to get your message, you will have to talk very slowly." I said it hoping it would be he who got the message.

He did not look happy. "I see. Then we'll have to figure something else out. You may go."

Returning to my office I busied myself with housekeeping chores. Three other employees made up the workforce and one by one, each came to welcome me. The Public Relations officer was of the same ilk as Rob but the Accountant and his assistant were commoners, like me. Five o'clock finally arrived. Dejected and most decidedly disappointed I made my way home. The fifteen-minute bus trip provided time to assume a more positive outlook before greeting my kinfolk. John was first to inquire about my day.

As I usually did when not truly pleased I replied, "Oh, it was all right." Familiar with that kind of response my tribe asked no additional questions and further discussion was discouraged. The following morning I discovered a dictating machine on my desk. Alongside it was a disc and a set of earphones. I tried the earpieces on and placed the disc in the machine. Pressing the "play" button I recognized Steve's voice, "This letter is going to Joe #!:&*^@#$%. That's spelled J...O...E." He continued with a brief, inane message and ended with, "This tape will self destruct in two minutes."

During the following months there were more tapes, of greater substance however, which I typed. I did learn to input computer files, some of which had to be installed at a mainframe housed at Brown University. I familiarized myself with the many real estate properties in the portfolio and managed their day-to-day operations. I also became much more cognizant of the way business was done at "EREIT."

The company was founded on two premises. The first, you could lend money for mortgages to high-risk clients at exorbitant interest rates. The second means of increasing the bottom line was by way of purchasing commercial properties and acquiring mortgages based on values exceeding their actual worth. The excess proceeds were then skimmed off the top. The interest rates on these mortgages were variable and tied to the prime rate.

Steve and Rob took great pleasure from calling in their markers. They wasted no time in foreclosing on some poor sap who'd missed a couple of payments. To add insult to injury, they required a personal appearance by the borrower; anxious to comply with their demands, hoping to get a reprieve. But alas, pleas were of no avail because the decision had already been made. The only reason for arranging a face-to-face meeting was to provide the duplicitous duo some demeaning entertainment. Upon his departure the two merciless adversaries would be heard gleefully mocking the deposed victim.

Each morning found me in front of the office building, dreading the day ahead, delaying the inevitable as long as possible. I despised the job but I was locked in, making good money by Providence standards. Rhode Island was the costume jewelry capital of the nation and unless they were housewives or secretaries, most working women were on the production lines. I loved my house, mortgage and all; the kids were doing well in school and Sarah had joined a nearby synagogue where she'd made many friends her own age. My relationship with John flourished and after several months of separate living Sarah suggested, in her inimitable way, it was time for us to put an end to the farce.

"If you're doing this separate thing on my account, don't. I'm no fool. John, you might just as well move in here and save the rent money."

John wasted no time. Some neighbor's eyebrows were raised but after all I was just a New Yorker, so what could you expect.

Our family celebrated our second Christmas in grand style. John took the boys to a tree farm where they selected and cut a lovely blue spruce, which was set up in the living room. It was decorated with silver and gold balls and artificial candles which, when lit looked like the real thing. John draped evergreen garlands on the stair rails and mantel. The children hung stockings, embroidered with their names, over the fireplace. Presents spilled out from under the tree including some for John's three children and though I'd never met them, gave their wrappings special attention. Both Sarah and I insisted the family also observe the eight days of Chanukah which coincided with Christmas, by lighting the eight-branched Menorah. *Goyish* or not, Sarah was delighted with all the festivities.

Summer arrived on schedule and the children were set free to gambol and otherwise engage in the myriad activities commonly devised by kids enjoying warm days and time on their hands. Danny secured a job busing at a hotel dining room and had saved enough money to buy a fourteen-foot wooden boat complete with a twenty-five-horsepower engine. He spent every free moment fishing in Narragansett Bay. I indulged myself by buying an eighteen-foot Herreshoff, an historic sailboat built in the twenties. In an attempt to relive my wonderful Caribbean adventure, hired a sailing instructor at the nearby yacht club and learned, by trial and many errors, to be a passable seaman. I harbored no illusions of ever acquiring the expertise of Captains Jack or Bill.

Life was good but as is often the case, there was a wolf in the henhouse. John and I had begun talking marriage but I was more than a bit uneasy. There was still so much I didn't know about him. He'd kept his son and two daughters out of our lives, which I deemed somewhat suspicious. Though he moved in with us and spent a good deal of money on gifts or things for the house, John never again offered to make a financial contribution to meet our living expenses. I really knew very little about his business enterprise. In gambler's vernacular, he "played his cards close to the vest." He no longer wore suits and ties to work and had even become sloppy about his appearance. When I pressed him for answers he sidestepped and never responded directly. Having been through it before, I had the uncomfortable feeling that he was in financial difficulty. Apprehensive and frustrated by John's determined evasion I approached one of his long-time employees. "Tommy, what's happing with John? Is business bad, is something wrong?"

Tommy was at first hesitant to offer any information but I persisted. "I thought we had become friends. I really need to know. Maybe there's something I can do."

"He's out of business."

"What do you mean?" I was unwilling to believe his brief statement.

"It's been going down the tubes for a while and some outside pressures forced him to shut down."

"What kind of outside pressures?"

"His wife."

I was too stunned to say another word. Tommy turned slowly and with his head down walked away from me.

When John arrived at the house later that night, I ushered him to our bedroom where I confronted him. "Why didn't you ever tell me about the business going bust?"

"I knew how you felt about security and was afraid to lose you if you found out I was broke."

"We've known each other for five years. We've lived together almost three. Why didn't you tell me you were still married?"

John paled, dumbfounded by the fact I was on to him. "How did you find out? Was it Tommy?"

"What does it matter how I found out? You've lied to me all this time."

"I was planning to get a divorce. You have to separate for six years here in Rhode Island."

Because of my own familiarity with the circumstances I was able to feel empathy for him but not enough to dispel my anger. "You should have told me. I would have understood. Now I know why you would never let me see your children. Why did you keep lying?"

"She's a Catholic. I didn't want to give her additional ammunition. I didn't want to lose you."

"Stop saying that! I can't abide liars. I could have taken just about anything else but to lie and lie and lie." I was sobbing.

"Annie, nothing has changed. We still love each other. We can work things out."

"How can I ever trust you again? How can things ever be the same again?"

"Annie, don't be rash. Please, let's try to make it right."

"Just go. I can't even look at you right now."

John moved out of the house. He came often to see the kids and Sarah, trying to convince Sarah to plead his case.

"There's nothing I can do, John. This is between the two of you," she told him repeatedly.

"No it's not. It concerns all of us...you, the boys, Sam."

But Sarah would not interfere and once I cooled down I agreed to see John again. We had dinner, made small talk, held hands but both knew the magic was gone. He'd called our relationship "Camelot", but like Camelot, the ending was not to be a happy one.

The job was becoming intolerable. Interest rates were soaring and EREIT was about to go bust. Rob and Steve were in a frenzy and while Rob had family resources to draw upon, Steve was about to lose everything. They were so highly leveraged there was no way to save the company. Steve was angry, unbelieving; this couldn't be happening to him.

"Why do you think it can't happen to you?" I remarked. "You were delighted to see others in this bind."

"Well, you just wise-cracked your way out of a job. You're fired."

"Oh, God!" was my surprising reaction. "Thank you. Thank you." I knew I was free. I knew what I had to do.

The following week I drove back to New York to keep an appointment I'd made with Joe Hildebrand.

"It's great to see you again. You're looking well. Anne."

"It's nice to see old friends again, Joe." Explaining my predicament, excluding the part about John, I asked if there was any possibility of joining the bank again.

"I told you you'd be welcome here as long as I had any pull and that still goes. I'm not sure about reinstating the pension and saving plans but I'll do my best. When do you plan to return?"

"I've got to find a place to live and get moved back to the city. I'd like to start as soon as possible."

"You just let me know when and we'll have a desk waiting for you. I'm really sorry things did not work out but Rhode Island's loss is our gain."

We shook hands and I made my way out, greeting co-workers as I passed their cubicles, thinking how nice it was to see their friendly faces again.

I picked up a newspaper on the way to the parking garage and retrieved the Ford. Pulling out the classified section I searched for apartment rentals, hoping to find something in the old neighborhood. The sale of the house would put me in a position to rent a classier place with lots of room. There were three listings for units in the Prospect Park area that appeared promising. I highlighted them as well as a few in Bensonhurst. Exiting the garage I inched my way through the heavy traffic to the stately Brooklyn Bridge and crossed over the East River to the Brooklyn side. I was home! So why did it feel so dreary, so dirty, so alien? It had been my home all my life yet suddenly I felt like a stranger. I eased through the Flatbush Avenue interchange and entered the cool, green refuge that was Prospect Park. Exiting at Ocean Parkway I located one of the apartment buildings listed in the ad. It was grim. I drew a black line through it and drove to the next address; and the next and the next, until I'd seen all the listings I'd underscored. Staring at the paper I saw a confused jumble of lines, a latticework, a maze leading nowhere. I remained parked for a while in front of the last building on the list. It was all to no avail. Whoever said, "You can't go home again," was right.

"How can I possibly bring the kids back here, or Sarah for that matter? I'm screwed."

It was getting dark and I decided it was too late to drive back to Cranston. I drove to a gas station where I used the public phone to call Julie.

"Hey cuz. Got an extra bed for a night?"

"Where the devil are you?"

"I'm about twenty minutes from your house."

"Well come on over and you'd better have a good story."

"I don't know how good it will be but it will be a story. Do me a solid will you? Call Sarah and tell her I'll be with you tonight and back home tomorrow."

"Will do. See you soon."

Julie had a couple of kamikazes on ice waiting for my arrival. "What are you up to now?"

In between drinks I recited all the gory details, "So that's all there is."

"What are you going to do now?"

"I don't know. That's why I came to hear your expert advice."

"Some advice I can give you." Julie had been divorced for a number of years and she and I had done much playing in the streets together. "I've had one lover who was a gambler, one who's a drunk and one who dropped dead on me." Julie was on her second drink and was growing mellow. It was sad; the man who died was the one Julie was in love with. What was even sadder, he was also very much married. "Annie, we are a pair."

We talked about old times, fun times, not so fun times and finally fell silent, each lost in our own thoughts.

"Hey, Annie! Remember that trip to the Pocono's?"

"I've tried to forget that chapter of my life."

It had been the summer following my traumatic abortion. Julie asked me to join her and two friends, Frances and Rose for a weekend trip to the *"Italian Alps."* Desperately in need of consolation, I agreed to meet them, looking forward to seeing the Poconos for the first time.

To our dismay the hotel had been booked for a weekend convention with three-hundred attendees. The convention part would have been okay if it were not for the fact it was a gathering of seniors, none of whom appeared to be younger than seventy, most accompanied by walkers or wheelchairs willingly manipulated by the most agile of the group. We young ladies however, were greeted with much enthusiasm by the hotel staff, many of whom were of the male gender working their way through college.

Julie, who had made the reservations, was all apologies. "I'm so sorry. But maybe we can go to some other hotel for the entertainment."

Our waiter arrived carrying the soup course, minestrone. He greeted the youngsters with a wide grin.

"Where's the matzo ball soup?" I joked.

"Well, well, well. What have we here? Did you girls make a wrong turn?"

The old folks thought that very funny but we "girls" were less appreciative of Buddy's humor. When he whispered into Julie's ear she smiled and nodded in agreement. The "other entertainment" turned out to be at an exclusive country club where with Buddy's help, dressed to the nines we gained illicit entry through the kitchen. Following his instructions, anticipating an intercept at any moment, we made our way to the lobby whence Buddy, with a girl on each arm, crossed the concourse leading to the brightly lit grand ballroom. Once there, to Buddy's great surprise, his girls exhibited unabashed disregard for their gallant escort and dumped him. We'd all had a good laugh at poor Buddy's expense.

"Annie, I've got an idea. You remember Rose?"

"Sure." I nodded.

"She moved to Hawaii a couple of years ago. She has a pretty big house there and knows her way around. Let me call her and see if she has any suggestions.

"Hawaii? Are you nuts?"

"No, I'm very serious. Why not? You're the adventurer. You said you wanted to get as far away from John as possible, right?"

"What I said was I was afraid I wouldn't be able to resist John's pleas if I was close to him. I wanted a place as far away as possible, as long as they spoke English."

"Well they speak English in Hawaii. I'm gonna call her right now. It's five hours earlier there." With that she grabbed the phone and dialed a ten-digit number. "Hi Rose, it's Julie. Yes, I know I just spoke to you but I need to talk to you again." Julie related my story stopping every once in a while for Rose's comments. "Ok, I'll tell her and we'll get back to you. Thanks." She turned to me with a smile. "She says if you have to starve, you might as well do it in a warm place."

I was reminded of the couple in Antigua who were waiting for the undertaker in a warm place. "Why not?" I agreed.

In two weeks Matt would be celebrating his Bar Mitzvah at Temple B'nai Torah. He'd been a fair-to-middling student and was extremely apprehensive, opting out of an appearance on the *Bimah* at the Saturday morning service with the entire congregation in attendance, the traditional practice. Hearing of his plight, eighty year old Isaac Meyerson convened some of the old timers for a *minion*, a group of ten men needed to conduct any ritual. The private service was performed in an anteroom at the synagogue. They were wonderful to Matt, easing him through his reading of the Torah portion before presenting him with a prayer shawl and bible. The formalities concluded there

Annie's Portion

was much hand shaking and many effusive congratulatory remarks as the celebrants gathered to share the wine and cakes at the *oneg* I provided.

Josh had already departed from Lamar University because as he explained with well-delivered, although suspect inventiveness, Lamar catered to the Indian population and he felt unwelcome there. I never quite bought that excuse believing he'd been disappointed to find instead of basking in the warm sun of the New Mexico desert, he'd been subjected to the snow and cold of high mountains. He transferred to Stony Brook College on Long Island where he seemed, at least for the moment, to be content.

At thirteen Brandy was ailing and partially blind and had been relocated to a farm belonging to a friend of John's. She had the company of several dogs, one of whom, a border collie named Fetch, adopted her and kept her out of harm's way. That parting had been especially emotional for us all, prompting Danny who was headed for the Coast Guard following his graduation in May, to attempt to lighten the situation by remarking, "I bet you don't cry as much for me."

I decided the time for our departure would not get any better. Against John's protestations, I put the house up for sale. The ad I placed in the Sunday paper drew an immediate response and by the following Wednesday, I had a full price offer in hand. The sale closed thirty days later, leaving me with a net profit of five-thousand dollars. All the furniture and most of our other possessions were delivered to a storage facility. John moved in with Tommy temporarily and the family moved into John's apartment to wait for Danny's graduation and enlistment ceremony. I traded the Ford LTD and a thousand dollars for a Volkswagen van. The day before we were to leave, I drove Danny to the Coast Guard Induction Station. John and I spent our last night together drinking champagne, making love and weeping while we listened to the strains of "For the Good Times." John promised to write.

The following morning we loaded bedding, books, summer clothing and camping gear into the van. Sarah and Samantha piled into the back seat, with Matt taking the navigator position next to me. It was a beautiful spring day and I drove off, headed for California, certain I'd made the right decision.

Chapter XIX

1976 - Hawaii

From thirty thousand feet the white flecked, undulating Pacific seemed endless, offering no clue as to the imminence of the beautiful islands of Hawaii. Yet there they were little specks that grew larger and greener as the plane descended. I watched from the small pitted window as the plane tipped its wings preparing for the landing after five hours of flight through a cloudless sky, catching a brief glimpse of Diamond Head shortly before the wheels touched down on the reef runway at the Honolulu airport. The passengers applauded as the plane rolled to a stop at the terminal, recognizing the feat of the Captain who brought them safely to these tiny atolls floating on an infinite blue green sea.

It seemed like an interminably long time before the cabin door was opened and a slow stream of eager vacationers snaked its way to the main terminal. I rounded up my family and headed for the baggage claim area. We'd had to check our bags and boxes at the San Francisco Airport two days ahead of our flight in order to get the VW to the dock in Oakland for its voyage to Oahu. I was somewhat dubious about the prospect of actually finding our luggage. Signs pointed the way up an escalator to a platform where a mini-bus waited to take us to the main terminal. At the claim area, crowds milled about the rotating carousels, hauling pieces off as they were identified. The tedious process continued for some while, until the shinning metal surfaces of the revolving carriers were devoid of all signs of further activity.

"Where is our stuff, mom?"

"I don't know Matt, but I sure hope it's not back in San Francisco." I intercepted a Skycap as he hurried by with a loaded cart. "Do you know of any other place to find luggage? It may have come in on an earlier flight?" I thought, "Like days earlier."

He suggested we look in a nearby impound where unclaimed baggage was stored for a day or so. Taking his advice we traipsed down a narrow hall that ended at a wire enclosure where stacks of suitcases and boxes stood in varying degrees of tilt.

"How in the world will we ever find our things?" Sarah asked with obvious concern.

"Why don't you guys make yourselves comfortable in the lounge while I try to find some help? Keep your eyes open for Rose who'll be looking for us."

I returned about forty minutes later, Skycap, cart and luggage in tow, to find Rose and her retinue engaged in animated conversation. Seeing me they rushed like a team of linemen heading for the receiver.

Fearing the onslaught, I put my arms up protectively. "Whoa, whoa guys!"

"Anne, you look marvelous." Rose greeted me with unrestrained enthusiasm. "Come let's get all this stuff out to the van."

Rose had somehow managed to borrow a VW van, exactly like the one that had dependably conveyed the nomads from Rhode Island, seven-thousand miles across the continental U.S., to California and was at that very moment on the high seas headed for Honolulu. Within minutes the substitute vehicle was loaded, bags and passengers neatly stowed for the trip to Rose's house on the windward side of the island.

The airport ramp connected with Nimitz Highway, which ran through a disappointing industrial district. The ocean to our right was not visible from the road but on the left side, small houses clustered in great profusion on green carpeted hills.

Passing a sprawling warehouse complex, Sam called out excitedly. "Look, there's a pineapple on top of that building."

"That's the Dole plant," Rose explained. "That pineapple is really just symbolic. The plant has been closed for quite a while."

Turning left at Middle Street she made for the town of Kaneohe by way of Like Like Highway.

"What a strange name for a road," Sarah commented.

"It's not pronounced the way it's spelled," Rose laughed. "It's Leeky Leeky. You're going to have to get used to the language."

The highway took us through residential sections, a mix of high-rise projects and old plantation style houses. Lush gardens, filled with a multitude of colorful, fragrant flora surrounded each house. Climbing steadily higher, the houses became less evident, the foliage growing more abundant, until we reached the first of two tunnels cut through the mountains called the Koolaus. Exiting the second tunnel, a unified gasp of delight escaped the mouths of Rose's passengers. We were within the remaining walls of a crater formed eons ago by a now extinct volcano. Behind and to either side, stood craggy, forested mountains etched by waterfalls which, encouraged by spring rains cascaded with glorious abandon. Ahead, where there had been a breach of the crater wall lay an exquisite turquoise bay, surrounded by wide stretches of green hills. Descending rapidly, we passed a herd of grazing cows and wide ranging banana plantations on both sides of the main highway.

At the base of the foothills Rose turned onto a dirt road passing through a stand of banana trees. The road ended at the junction of a narrow paved street, lined with a hodgepodge of dwellings, fruit trees, flowering shrubs and old cars in various stages of repair. Rose turned again, this time into a short lane where she pulled up in front of a white painted wood structure built on piers, encircled by a skewed lanai under the limited protection of sloping eaves projecting from a shingled roof.

"Welcome home," Rose bubbled. "Leave the stuff for now." She hurried ahead of us throwing open the unlocked door.

Her guests followed, albeit with less enthusiasm, to find ourselves in a bright, comfortably furnished parlor. While pleasant enough, it was certainly not the "big" house Julie had talked about. Rose, with increasing exuberance showed us through the homestead; kitchen open to living area, three rather small bedrooms and one and a-half baths, the half consisting of toilet and sink. The back door led to the lanai and a large garden filled with flowering plants and numerous fruit trees.

"The house may seem small," Rose anticipated our concern, "but we do much of our living outdoors. It will work out fine." She seemed truly happy to have us there, especially considering she and I had only met several times by way of the Julie connection.

"Just pile the stuff you don't need in the storage shed. Bring the rest in here and we'll find a place for it." Rose shouted. "It's been ages Annie. How the hell are you?"

Chapter XX

Matt, tall, dark, well-muscled, feisty and outgoing was registered at Samuel King Intermediate School, the notoriously anti-haole public elementary school. It was not an option for shy, freckle faced, red-haired Samantha. I met with Father O'Donnell, Principal of St. Anne's Catholic School in Kaneohe, explaining my dilemma and convincing him to accept Sam as a student while exempting her from religious instruction.

With the children safely installed in their respective academic institutions I was single-minded in my determination to get a job as soon as possible. Not wanting to impose any longer than was absolutely necessary, for the third time in my career I scanned the newspaper want ads. Rose cautioned me about the job situation for *haoles* the Hawaiian term for Caucasian newcomers, while at the same time assuring me I and my family were welcome for as long as it took.

Believing my prior experience would make me a desirable commodity I hadn't expected the open bias displayed to haoles. At interview after interview I was told, more or less, the same thing. "Your background and experience are exemplary but we have found too much of a turnover with newcomers seeking paradise but finding it difficult to live here."

With the arrival of the VW van I was able to expand my search. I fell in love with the island and grew ever more determined in my desire to succeed and make Hawaii my permanent home. Several weeks passed without a nibble and I became more discouraged with every turndown while Rose encouraged me to persevere.

"You will find something, Annie. I told you it would take time. I love having you all here and you have a home for as long as you want."

I'd arrived on the island with the grand sum of three thousand dollars in my pocket and while Rose would not accept payment of any kind, I insisted on buying food and other household necessities. My small cache was diminishing at a frightening rate. I feared if I didn't find something soon, I'd be out of money with no way to get back to the mainland. Much as I hated it, I decided to try the old waitress ploy, but even there I was denied any offers. Leaving after another rebuff at a plant in the industrial area near the airport, I spotted a help wanted sign in the window of a small warehouse.

"What the hell. All they can do is say no."

Entering the building I found myself in an unoccupied office. It was sparsely furnished but from several signs posted on the walls I determined it to be the sales room for an aluminum siding company

"Hello! Is anyone here?"

"Who's it?" came a response. A small, pleasant looking, dark skinned man walked into the office. "Oh, hello. Can I help you?"

"I saw your sign in the window and thought I might find a job." I was sure this was the wrong place for me but asked, "What kind of help are you looking for?"

"I look por secretary. What you can do?"

"I can answer phones, type, write letters or invoices, do the books."

"You have experience?"

"Yes, lots." I thought I'd best keep the answers simple.

"Where you prom?" He sat in a chair behind a metal desk. "Sit, sit." He pointed to a chair in front of him.

Annie's Portion

Taking the seat he indicated I replied, "I'm from the mainland, New York."

"I neber been to New York. Por how long you here?"

I wasn't sure if he was asking how long I'd been in Hawaii or for how long I planned to be there. "I plan to live here. I've been on Oahu for five weeks."

"What your name?"

"It's Annie."

"Annie. Why you like work here?"

"I've been looking for a job for weeks. I have two children and a mother to take care of. I need to work."

"I don't pay much. Pibe hundred dollars one month."

I drew in my breath. "Well maybe if you like my work you will give me a raise. When can I start?" I was not about to give him a chance to turn me down.

He smiled a broad, white-toothed grin. "I think I like you. You wait here." He disappeared into the warehouse returning in a few minutes with another man who looked like his clone. "This my accountant, Jaime. He show you what to do. You start now?"

So began my career in Hawaii, with a Filipino boss, a Filipino accountant, a Filipino foreman and a Filipino work crew in a less than reputable business. It was more fun than I'd had in years.

Benny Rizal, my boss, had been in the business for several years, starting as a laborer and saving enough to open his own business. He dressed impeccably in a three-piece white suit, white shirt, tie and shoes, all of which remained spotless. Jaime Sindiong, appearing and disappearing like a wraith, provided some basic instructions and gave me a prepared script to be used on prospective phone-in customers. He told me Benny had hired me to give the company some class.

"Also because he think the men not plirt with you because you not too pretty." Jaime whispered conspiratorially.

On the third day of my employment, Benny had a new communication system installed.

"Annie," he called. "You come."

I hurried into his office, note pad in hand. He loved to dictate although most of his letters were of a personal rather than business nature.

"Come see my new pone." He pointed to a new white telephone on his desk. "Here," he said, handing me its twin. "This one for you. Go fix it and I call you."

I did as I was told, disconnecting the old phone and replacing it with the new white one.

"Annie!"

I jumped as his voice echoed from the intercom.

"You hear me?"

"Yes, Benny. Loud and clear." I could hear him stereophonically, from his office located just behind me as well as from the new intercom on my desk.

Days later, Benny raised me on the squawk box. "Annie. You call important meeting at one o'clock. Get Jaime, get Chris and you come with note pad."

Making the necessary calls, I informed Jaime and Chris Malapan, the foreman, of the one o'clock meeting. At the appointed hour, all three of us sat in Benny's office, I with note pad and pencil in hand. Benny in his white suit, leaned back in his swivel chair, slapped his knees and with his usual grin said, "Okay, now what we gonna talk about?"

The job was easy and on several occasions, I'd made sales on the phone, using the prepared script Jaime had given me. Benny generously gave me a bonus for each sale. Contrary to the opinions of both Benny and Jaime, Chris and I started dating within a month of my employ. He was tall, good looking and a fabulous dancer, introducing me to many local nightspots and local food. Plate lunches were purchased from a street cart and always included "two scoops rice." I was having a good time.

Three months from the time we landed at Honolulu International Airport, the three Harmons and their chaperone were happily ensconced in our own place. I'd found a small house owned by an affable elderly Chinese couple, just a short distance from Rose. The rent was three hundred dollars a month. I bought some used furniture and Matt created tables and bookcases from "crack seed" crates. He also perfected a stratagem to induce his mother to adopt an, "I couldn't help it, he followed me home" dog.

Returning from work one day I found a note on the kitchen table. It was in Matt's scrawl and read, "I went to baseball practice and there's a puppy on the back lanai."

"Puppy! What puppy?" I opened the door to find a wriggling cardboard carton on the concrete slab. Cautiously opening the lid I beheld a scraggly yellow dog growling at me. Remembering the unhappy parting from Brandy I'd been adamantly against any further adoptions of pets. To further reinforce my resolve, I'd read about heartworm, ticks and myriad other afflictions suffered by the animal population in the tropical isles. I was therefore quite angry with my son but by the time Matt came home I'd already fed the puppy, which as anyone knows, made it ours.

"You know," Samantha observed. "That puppy has awfully big feet."

After due inspection, it was unanimously agreed that he, for it was indeed a he, did in fact have extremely large feet for such a small dog.

"I think he's going to grow up to be a Golden Retriever," Matt said hopefully.

Sadly, Tigger never proved to be a Golden Retriever. He was just a small, crazy, yellow dog with extraordinarily big feet. He was a whirlwind who was never still for more time than it took to inhale his food and drove us all nuts. Happily, he was re-adopted by an elderly couple who loved him, improved his manners, traveled with him and enjoyed his company at their dining room table.

Sarah loved to take "Da Bus" to the Ala Moana shopping mall in Honolulu or for a ride out to the north shore. She occasionally visited the senior center, making friends with several local ladies who adopted her and made her feel very much at home. On one occasion, a neighbor invited Sarah to her home for some "grass". Sarah declined gracefully but was extremely puzzled by the offer, which brought peals of laughter from all as she related the incident. The younguns, after some initial trials and tribulations, were adapting well and had made friends at school. Matt joined a baseball team where he, being one of the star players, enjoyed the accolades of his teammates. Somewhat less coordinated than her brother, Sam did not fare as well in the Bobby Sox League—hit in the head by a high pop fly, stung on the neck by an irate wasp and reamed out by a very unsporting, unforgiving coach. The experience, while doing nothing for her self-esteem, provided Sam the continued friendship of two of her fellow teammates.

Jeannine, who became Sam's everlasting best friend, was invited to join Sarah, Sam and me on a trip to Sea Life Park, a Mormon-managed aquarium and water-park that featured an exhibition of trained orcas. The day was spent visiting the many and varied sea creatures on display and delighting in the antics of the four orcas. It was a happy but exhausted troop that shuffled out to the dirt lot which by that time was crowded with parked vehicles. The girls ran ahead looking for the van and after several cases of mistaken identity found it sandwiched between two smaller cars. Once Sarah and I caught up with them, I opened the side panel door to let them climb in. Suddenly, a dark, stocky, bearded man appeared from nowhere. He pushed the girls further inside as he jumped into the van, blocking the door with his arms.

"Dis my car," he yelled in heavily accented pidgin.

I was horrified and frightened for the girls who had become hysterical. "You've made a mistake." I tried reason. "This is my van. Please get out."

He became more animated. "Dis mine," he shouted as he tried to slide the door shut.

I tried to calm him. "Please come out. This is not your car."

Still standing spread-eagle in the doorway, he pushed one hand under his shirt and pointed through the fabric. "I have a gun. You go."

I realized he was loco and was using his finger in an attempt to make me think he had a gun. It was crucial that I protect my charges, huddled in fear on the backseat of the van.

"Get out. You don't have any gun." I reached up with both arms and grabbed his shirt. With a determined pull I yanked him out of the van into the narrow space between cars. He was trapped between Sarah behind him, me in front of him and two vehicles blocking any escape route. He hauled off and socked me in the jaw, pushing my teeth into my cheek which began to bleed profusely. I staggered against the small car, dazed by the punch. Sarah, seeing her daughter injured by the ape, kicked him with all her strength. He turned away from me and socked Sarah in the eye, giving me just enough time to recover. I leaped on his back, wrapping my legs around his waist and one arm around his neck. With my free hand I began pummeling him on the head and face. He realized he was in a no win situation and succeeded in shaking me loose as he squeezed past Sarah. With one last act of bravado he grabbed the shoulder strap of my purse, taking the top half of my muumuu with it and managed to get free. He ran across the lot with me in hot pursuit wearing a bra and the bottom half of my dress. I'd kicked off my sandals and was determined to get my purse back. Despite my screams no one in the lot came to our aid. I spotted a pipe lying on the ground and, still at a run, stooped to pick it up, not realizing it was attached to a loose chain hanging across the entrance. When I reached the end of the length of chain I was pulled unceremoniously to the ground. By then a young marine had intercepted the goon and retrieved my purse although he allowed the villain to escape. The police were called and took a report, telling us there was not much they could do.

"Aren't you even going to dust for his fingerprints?" I asked in amazement. "His hands were all over the van."

"Wat you tink? Dis Hawaii Five 0?" was the response.

Later that day, two detectives arrived at the house with some photo albums. Sam was able to identify one of the pictures.

"We picked this guy up further down the highway attempting another robbery. There'll be a grand jury hearing. You guys look terrible."

"Thanks," I said through my bruised and swollen face while Sarah held an ice pack to her black eye.

The hearing was held at the downtown courthouse where we were each questioned separately. At the end of the hearing, one of the officers approached us.

"Hey! You should see 'im. He look worse den you. You lucky he no sue you for assault and battry."

We never did hear any more about a trial or his probable conviction.

Life in Hawaii went on as usual. All would have been perfect if only my income was greater. After five months with the Rizal Siding Company, I started looking for another job. Discovering from the few telephone sales I'd made that I seemed to have a natural ability to connect with potential buyers. Arriving at the conclusion the only way to make some real money was to go into sales; the sensible thing to do was explore the possibilities.

Unlike previous job searches, this one took me directly to the "Sales Positions Offered" column where one ad in particular caught my eye. It read: "Seeking ambitious, hard working salesperson to join Institutional Sales Division of International Company. No prior experience necessary, training provided. Salary plus commissions."

As luck would have it, the address given in the ad indicated the firm was located in the same industrial area as Rizal's Siding Company, making it easy for me to investigate during my lunch break. I parked in one of the spaces in front of a large impressive brick building, bearing a tasteful sign indicating the occupant to be "Abbott International Laboratories." Entering a well-appointed reception area I obtained an application from a pleasant although somewhat hesitant young woman.

"You're the first woman who applied for the job." She smiled quizzically.

"The ad said salesperson, not salesman, so here I am."

"Well, it will be interesting to see the reaction from our sales manager."

Within minutes Joe Polanski appeared, dressed in jeans and aloha shirt. Walking briskly towards me he extended his hand. "Hello there. You're kind of a surprise. Let's go into the conference room."

Following him into a paneled room, I took the seat he offered.

"I don't imagine you know anything about our company or what the job entails." Joe opened a folder he'd brought with him. "I read your résumé and noted you don't have much sales experience."

"That's true, however your ad specified no experience was necessary and training was provided." I gave him my most conciliatory smiled. "I'm a really fast learner. What is the product I'd be selling?"

Joe spouted a quick rundown on the company, ending his spiel by handing me what appeared to be a test paper. I scanned it quickly but was puzzled by its contents.

"Before we go any further with this interview, I need to know whether or not you have a mechanical aptitude. This test is designed for that purpose. I'll leave it with you. Please take as long as you need to finish it." With that last remark he gave me a wide, somewhat Machiavellian grin, under a rather large handlebar mustache and left me to my own devices.

Closer examination of the test paper revealed it was made up of a series of pictures and multiple choice questions. After careful scrutiny I determined it was a study in logics. Looking at a particular picture one would have to decide the end result of a series of actions. For example; looking at a sketch of a large, heavily loaded truck on a curved road, one would make a determination as to which way the truck would lean as it came around the turn, marking the correct answer. There were twenty-five similar type questions, getting progressively more difficult, requiring the better part of an hour to complete. I left the completed exam with the receptionist, explaining I'd been on my lunch break and would call back.

"Good luck," the young woman called as I hurried out the exit.

As was her wont, Sarah greeted me at the door when I arrived home that evening. "You had a call from a Joe Polanski about your test. What test?"

Over dinner I described the brief interview and the unusual exam I'd taken. "I don't know very much about the job but it's a mega company with branches around the world. They make and sell cleaning compounds and chemicals for use in industrial plants, hotels, hospitals, restaurants and even for home use. I'll call Mr. Joe tomorrow and see if I

Annie's Portion

passed muster. I still have no idea what the job would entail but I don't think they hire women."

The enigma was solved the following day when Joe asked me to come in and meet with the President of the Hawaii office. Larry Fillmore was as unlike Joe as was possible. He was well-dressed, well-educated and well-mannered.

"We are looking for a sales representative for our Institutional Division. That person will be given a number of existing accounts to service and will be expected to acquire new accounts as well. When we say 'service' we mean, do an inventory of on hand supplies, introduce new product lines, instruct in their uses and actually service some of the dispensing equipment used with our products. Your test result was extraordinary. You are the first person in the Hawaii district to achieve a score of one-hundred."

Sarah would be delighted.

Larry continued, "You are also the first woman to be considered for this job, not just in Hawaii. With your aptitude you would make the ideal trial candidate. If you are still interested the salary is seven hundred a month plus commissions on product sales. You would also be provided with a company car. Do you want to give it a trial?"

Despite some initial misgivings I accepted. My timing couldn't have been better, for within a few short weeks Benny was forced to close his business.

"Joe will take you under his wing and provide you with the training and information you'll need." He stood and shook my hand. "Remember Anne, you are the test case. If you succeed it will open the door for many women. Good luck."

To say Joe was less than delighted or a lousy trainer would be a gross understatement. He was abrupt, uncommunicative and obviously anxious to see me fail. My first day of work proved to be a rude awakening and just the briefest hint of what was to come. Joe greeted me with a grunt, strode past me indicating with a wave of his hand for me to follow him and led me to an auxiliary building which served as work shop and supply facility. Once there he tossed a sizeable, leather tool bag at me and pulled out what appeared to be an inventory sheet. One by one, Joe handed me the tools of the trade, ticking each one off on his sheet.

"Ball peen hammer," tick; "large monkey wrench," tick; "set of Philips screwdrivers," tick; "two pairs of pliers," tick; "set of flat head screwdrivers," tick; "set of lug wrenches," tick; "two crescent wrenches," tick; "Greeley punch," tick; "three solenoid repair kits," tick.

With each addition the bag grew heavier and I more apprehensive. I waited for Joe to give some indication of what I was supposed to do with the tools but he remained sullenly silent as he gathered up product brochures.

At last handing me a massive tome Joe, grinning his wide, red mustached grin stated with evident malice, "That's your training manual. Learn it!"

For the next week my day was spent following Joe as he visited numerous hotels and restaurants that were to become my "territory," introduced me to managers, chefs, housekeepers and engineers. I peered over his shoulder as he tested the chemical contents of dish washers, some of which were twenty feet long and utilized conveyor belts to transport dish racks through several water tanks into which one of the Abbott Lab products was dispensed. I observed Joe as he made adjustments, disassembled and reassembled various parts that needed cleaning; watched as he checked for water spots on glasses and silverware, looked on as he inspected sheets and towels removed from four-hundred-pound-capacity clothes washing machines; watched him take inventory. I studied the process as Joe and another salesman installed dispensing equipment at a new account and learned what the Greeley punch was used for as I scrutinized a hole being punched through a stainless steel tank. And all the while, I glanced at Joe's grin from under that damn mustache as he observed my reactions.

At home, I poured over the manual, ingesting the information in great gulps, until I was saturated. Matt tested me on what I'd read; a neighbor explained the workings of a solenoid by examining the one on my car; practiced testing chemical content by adding products to my own laundry or dishwasher. In two weeks, with several denim jumpsuits added to my wardrobe, I was ready to go out on my own.

At first I found the experience intimidating but within a short time grew more comfortable, developing a routine whereby two or three days a week I'd don the denims and do the service work. The other days would find me dressed for business, visiting with managers, making friends with hotel engineers or drumming up new accounts. I was an attractive novelty and took advantage of that fact, using my feminine wiles to garner help in making difficult repairs, introducing new products and obtaining introductions to buyers. At one of Waikiki's most upscale hotels, I encouraged the friendship of the Chief Engineer, a good looking, hot blooded *Portagee,* who not only helped me with any mechanical problems but became my inamorato. I was often invited to sail on the hotel's yacht, a most satisfying perk.

My sales exceeded all expectations and I became the highest producer in my division, earning an additional five to six-hundred dollars a month in commissions. Larry was so delighted with me he leased a sporty new Camero for my use. At a party held at the Sheraton for the Abbott staff and some preferred business clients, Larry presented me with a national award. It was there I met a Japanese restaurant owner with whom I became good friends.

Kazu Tanaka was a head shorter than me and the dearest, kindest gentlest man I'd ever known. He asked nothing of me but delighted in taking me to the finest restaurants and bringing presents for Sarah, Matt and Sam. He'd arrive at our house in his yellow Cadillac convertible, jump out, open the trunk and look on with pleasure as we examined all the goodies he had brought. Many of the offerings would be promotional items picked up through business. There was a radio shaped like the Green Giant, Charlie the Tuna tee shirts, Tony the Tiger back packs and food; lots and lots of food.

Rose teased me, saying "You've got it all now. Good kids, good job and three beaus, one for dining, once for dancing and one for love."

Thanks to Matt, I once again became the owner of, not one but two dogs. The divorced father of his best friend Andy was in the Marine Corps, stationed at the Kaneohe base. At one time the boys conspired to make a match between their parents but the blind date they arranged had proved to be a disaster. We two never dated again but maintained a cordial relationship. Andy's dog Tita, had just given birth to seven puppies when his dad received notice of a re-deployment to Germany. Matt and I went to say goodbye to Andy and found him loading Tita and four of her puppies into their truck.

"Where are you taking them?" Matt asked innocently.

"We haven't been able to find anyone to take them so I guess we'll have to bring them to the pound." Andy responded.

Matt, who loved Tita, often told me about the dog, citing her intelligence and love of the water. "You can't do that. They'll kill her."

"We have no choice, Mrs. Harmon." Andy said dejectedly.

"Mom, can't we take them...just until we can find homes for them?"

Annie's Portion

Tita, her brown eyes nearly on a level with mine as she sat on the tailgate, wagged her tail furiously.

"You never told me she was part Collie, Matt. She's beautiful. It shouldn't be too difficult to find a home for her or the pups."

I'd been conned but pretended not to know I was. We were successful in placing three of the dogs but decided to keep Tita and a little white puppy we named Bandit because of his black mask. We also discovered that incest was not verboten in the dog world and soon found ourselves the owners of seven more dogs. I placed an ad in the paper and fortunately was able to find homes for all the pups. Sarah made it her business to interrogate all prospective takers to insure they would have good homes and turned down more than one would-be adopter. By the time the puppies were disposed of, the house was infested with ticks and had to be tented and fumigated.

Word also seemed to have gotten out to every stray dog in the area, "If you want a free meal or shelter from the rain, just stop at Anne's house." I would find some stray following me when I went jogging; or would come home to find a dog on the doorstep. In one instance, the doorstep dog was the size of a small pony. It took all the strength of Matt and me to squeeze the brute into the car in order to get him to the police station, where the cops placed him in a cell until they could find the owner. In desperation I tried an old Hawaiian custom of placing large plastic bottles filled with water on the lawn to keep the dogs away. Strange as it sounded, it worked.

But all was not honey and roses. The job, while great fun at times also presented great difficulties and hazards. All too often, I found myself standing in puddles fixing electrical gadgets I knew little or nothing about. I'd been scalded several times by water heated to the sanitizing temperature of one-hundred-eighty degrees; called out in the middle of the night on more than one occasion to make some emergency repair; stood waist deep in suds when some idiot put floor soap in the dishwasher; bombarded by roaches; ridden down a conveyor belt and lain inside a tank to make a repair.

When I came home hurt or discouraged and ready to quit, Matt and Sam prodded me. "You can't give up. Just think how happy Joe would be," Matt teased. "Just think, if you quit he'll prove a woman can't do the job," Sam persuaded. And I would stay.

I'd been at Abbott Labs for two years, winning accolades and prizes, making good money. Kazu was still in the picture and we were dining at the renowned "Third Floor" restaurant on the top floor of the Hyatt Regency. The waiter had just placed a huge platter of iced shellfish on the table.

"Kazu," I exclaimed in horror. "Are you going to eat those black spiders?"

Kazu laughed. "Annie, those are crabs, just small black crabs. Very good. Try one."

"No thanks." I reached out to take some oysters.

"What in the world is that on your arm?"

Just the day before I'd received a scalding on my right arm that produced an angry red burn. "It's just a burn Kazu. It's nothing, really."

"Annie, it's time you gave up this terrible job. Have you ever thought about going into real estate sales? I think you would be very good at it."

That suggestion, innocent as it appeared at the time, redirected my life and launched me on a new career path.

Chapter XXI

The test results had just been posted outside the large conference room at the Honolulu Municipal Building, triggering an immediate surge of excited hopefuls. I waited for the crowd to begin dissipating before making my way to the bulletin board, which while seemingly innocuous, would determine many a future. Behind me the buzz of disappointment or approval muted the usual din of the busy civic environment. I scanned the alphabetical list, finally locating the section headed "H". There it was, Harmon, Anne…96%. I allowed a smile to crease my face, thinking of Sarah who was sure to ask me what happened to the other four points.

As expected, my announcement of imminent departure from Abbott Labs prompted mixed responses. Larry was surprised and dismayed, trying unsuccessfully to get me to reconsider the decision. Joe found it difficult to contain his elation, pumping my hand with great enthusiasm, wishing me the best of luck. The other salesmen exhibited contradictory responses, relieved to be rid of the highly competitive paragon, yet sorry to lose a good-spirited, team player who had elevated the job description from serviceman to District Representative. At the farewell party, thrown by "spare no expense Larry", held at the Royal Hawaiian Hotel, there were many laughs, some tears and more than a few stories, related with drunken exaggeration and embellishments.

Joe, now certain of my departure gave a slurred toast. "Here's to Annie, who learned how to use a Greeley punch and repair a solenoid as good as any of us."

Charlie, an old-timer who had survived the A-bomb attack at Hiroshima and had been my friend and mentor, raised his cup of warm sake, leading the traditional Japanese toast. "To Annie, the best of us. Banzai, banzai, banzai!"

Unaccustomed as I was to hard liquor, by the time the party broke up I was pickled and teary-eyed. Much less sober than I, Larry offered to walk me to my car. We leaned on each other, staggering to the parking garage, discovering that neither of us could remember where we parked. Singing, "Show me the way to go home," we circled our way up the ramps.

"There's my car." I pointed to my snazzy Camero, which I would soon be relinquishing. "Get in and I'll drive you around till you find your car."

"Thas a great idea." Larry melted into the passenger seat.

Managing at some length to get the key in the ignition, I started the car, backed up and slowly made my way around the double helix.

"There! There she is."

I pulled up next to Larry's Porsche. "Are you sure you can drive?"

"Sure, sure. I'm fine. Hey Annie, want to fool around?" Larry, a happily married man, reached across the seat in an unsuccessful attempt to grope me.

"Larry, don't be an idiot," was my immediate response. "You couldn't manage to do anything even if you really wanted to."

"Hmm...guess you're right." Larry oozed out of the car and made his way unsteadily to his.

I drove down the ramp and out into the darkened streets of Waikiki along Kalakaua Avenue toward Diamond Head. Making a left turn on Kapahulu I headed *mauka*, then *Ewa* on Beretania. Since the islands did not lie in a true North-South position, directions were not described in terms of east, west, north or south but rather *mauka*, meaning toward the mountain, *makai*, toward the water. East or west was indicated by a particular town, in this case the town of Ewa, pronounced Eva, on the western coast. Diamond Head referred to an easterly direction. It could be quite confusing for visitors who could be told, "Go mauka", across the Koolau mountains, from the windward side of Oahu to Honolulu and still be told to "Go mauka" from the leeward side of the island, across the Koolaus to Kailua or Kaneohe. It had taken "wrong way Corrigan" quite some time to get the hang of it.

Turning mauka, onto Likelike Highway, I passed the unlit, sleeping district of Kalihi. It was a moonless night; murky shadows the only indication of trees and houses. "It's so dark here," I said to no one in particular. "I'd better put the brights on." I pressed the button on the floor with my left foot. "No lights. Now what?" I continued stepping on the floorboard to no avail. "It's darker than the inside of a cat's stomach." Climbing higher into the mountains I looked in the rear view mirror to see the flashing blue lights of a police car. Unable to see the speedometer on the dark console I muttered, "I hope I'm not speeding. I guess if he wants me he'll let me know." I drove through the first tunnel with his lights still flashing behind me. As I exited the second tunnel the police car sped past me and blocked the lane up ahead. I stopped just short of hitting it. A uniformed officer, flashlight in hand, approached the car.

"Do you know you're driving without lights?" he asked politely.

"I know. I've been trying to get them on but the floor button isn't working."

He reached through the open window and pulled out the light switch illuminating the highway ahead of us. He stood back and watched me silently.

"Can I see your license and registration?"

I searched for my purse. "It must have slipped off the seat." Bending to feel under the seat, I bumped my head on the steering wheel. Covering my mouth with my hand, hoping to conceal the evidence of alcohol, I stated the obvious. "I can't seem to find it."

"Why didn't you stop when you saw me behind you?"

I grinned stupidly. "I saw those blue lights and thought it was a flying saucer. I was afraid to stop." I let out a giddy giggle.

The cop tried to restrain his own laugh. "Where do you live?"

"Just down the road, through the banana trees."

"Go home. Drive real slow and go home. And if you get stopped again, you never saw me."

That was exactly what I did.

Still hung-over the next afternoon I went to the office to pick up my last check and some personal belongings. Larry crossed my path but barely lifted his head when he said, "Good luck Anne." I could see and would long remember the embarrassed blush on his face.

The commercial heart of Oahu was an area covering not more than ten square miles. Bishop Street, the lineal center of the business district, ran from Nimitz Highway at the shore to Beretania, a distance of about a mile. A couple of blocks east of Bishop laid Chinatown, a hodgepodge of small office buildings, markets and restaurants. During daylight hours, Chinatown's Hotel Street bustled with pedestrians carrying baskets or mesh bags bursting with local produce and delicacies. Here it was possible to buy fish, dried or fresh, of every color and description; papayas, mangoes, passion fruit, lilikoi or kumquats; crack seed—a Chinese snack made from fruit seeds which were dried and heavily salted; aku or tako poki—raw tuna or squid marinated with seaweed; poi—a Hawaiian staple made from the root of the taro plant, mashed and fermented for a day or more, with a consistency dependent on the ageing process and eaten with fingers. One could order one-finger or two-finger poi, which in either case took a great deal of getting used to.

Annie's Portion

Hotel Street at night was a different animal. It was the red light district, a magnet for the military contingent stationed at numerous bases scattered around the island as well as many visiting Asian businessmen.

The Star Bulletin and The Advertiser had for weeks been filling their front pages with the story of two Marines who'd spent the good part of a night in the dens of Hotel Street, drinking and shooting up with a lady of dubious repute. The three, having reached the saturation point, drove to a pineapple field in Wahiawa, not far from Schoffield Barracks, fully intending to enjoy a sexual escapade. The guys tossed a coin to decide the order of attack, the loser waiting in the field while the lucky winner crawled into the back seat with the lady. One can only imagine the surprise and anger resulting from the young lad's discovery; the object of his affections was a guy in drag. In a drug induced rage the marine reacted instinctively by wrapping his arm around the transvestite's neck and snapping it. He was sentenced to life without parole while his buddy got twenty years for aiding and abetting.

Hotel Street at night was a place into which no respectable lady would dare venture.

On the Diamond Head side of Bishop Street, older office buildings housed banking operations facilities, collection agencies, insurance and title companies. Built in the fifties the low rises evidenced their age. They were hidden behind concrete latticework or pock marked in an effort to give them a touch of originality in an otherwise dull conglomeration. One particularly ugly edifice, the color of algae on a stagnant pool, was nicknamed the "Punchcard Building", its pock-marked concrete facade the obvious reason for the cognomen.

Bishop Street alone projected an appearance of a vibrant financial community. The First Hawaiian Bank and Bank of Hawaii buildings sat diagonally across from each other at the intersection with King Street. The Pacific Trade Center, Theo Davies Building and white towers of Amfac Center had relinquished their positions as premier downtown office complexes to the new, twin glass towers of Gothic Center. Low-rise buildings, exhibiting Hawaii's missionary influence, bore the names of Dillingham, C. Brewer, Castle and Cooke, Alexander and Baldwin. Here lawyers, bankers, stock brokers, developers and real estate moguls sauntered from one building to another; easily identifiable by the suits, white shirts and ties they wore.

I'd designated this nucleus of business activity the starting point for the pursuit of my new career. Often, on the way from Mapunapuna to the Waikiki hotels I would drive through the downtown area and Kakaako, a compact, more diverse replica of the out-of-town industrial parks. I'd noticed the proliferation of signs publicizing the "Commerce Real Estate Company."

"They seem to have a lock on the market here," I thought. "I'm going to start with them."

My first call to Edward Wright was less than productive. Given a not-too-polite brush-off by his secretary each time I called, it had been impossible to set up an appointment. Undeterred, I called several more times before reaching him directly.

"I know you've been calling but I don't bring on any inexperienced people. You'd be better off working for a residential company."

After several more unsuccessful attempts to convince Wright to give me a try, I changed tack and signed on with a highly regarded residential brokerage house. Marie Henderson was a tough taskmaster, demanding excellence, honesty, hard work and a thorough knowledge of the market. She was an excellent trainer, requiring her staff attend weekly meetings during which she would review listing strategies, good sales practices and contract writing.

She was adamant about the importance of producing sales agreements that were concise, accurate and indisputable. Her last words at the end of each session were, "Remember! A signed copy of everything to everybody." That training was to stand me in good stead.

I worked for Marie for four months, during which time I made a number of sales, enduring the weekend open houses, the chauffeuring of families from one house to another, listening to gripes about carpet colors or musty smells. I did not lose my determination to work for Ed Wright, calling him every week to tell him about my progress. During one such recitation he cut me off in mid-sentence.

"All right already. Come on in. I'll probably hear less from you if you work here than I do now."

There were only two successful women in the commercial end of the business, one of whom worked for Wright. Several women had tried unsuccessfully to enter the market but Honolulu being a traditional "old boy" domain, quickly discouraged their enterprises. Ed spent about half an hour with me, giving me some trivial pointers and sharing his pearls of wisdom, most of which were self-aggrandizing.

"Ellen has offered to work with you for a while. She's the best damn broker in Honolulu, except for me," Ed smirked.

Ellen Tillman and I hit it off immediately. Though I'd come from the Big Apple and Ellen from a small town in Kansas, we'd experienced many of the same tribulations. Ellen had been in an abusive marriage, provoked and exacerbated by a zealous relationship with the bottle. The birth of a daughter motivated her to seek treatment and eventually a divorce. Like most haoles who ventured to the magical isles, Ellen came seeking a new life. She'd been a remedial reading instructor at an elementary school; exactly what the Hawaii Department of Education was looking for, and was offered a job with decent pay, free housing for a year as well as transportation and moving costs. After several years of growing dissatisfaction with the system, Ellen quit and found a job as property manager with an old established office buildings developer. It was there she met Ed Wright, Director of Honolulu operations, who introduced her to many of the wheeler-dealers on the Hawaiian scene, including politicos, financial big-wigs and real estate magnates, and partied with the best of them. She fell off the wagon and in a drink-and-drug induced depression, attempted suicide. Ellen credited Ed with saving her life, her sanity and her career. She remained his most trusted and loyal friend through his many unsavory escapades and when he left to open his own office she went with him. It was through her efforts and reputation that Ed became the exclusive agent for Gothic's properties.

Ellen was honest and generous, not only in business dealings but in her personal life as well. Her only hang-up, if one could call it that, was her obsessive devotion to her newly found "born again" Christian church. When her religious fervor began to intrude into her business dealings, Ed cautioned her. When she began to hold bible studies in the office he forbade them. The other office agents urged Ed to put a stop to her continued proselytizing but he was reluctant to press her since in actuality, she ran the office. Ed, who had a reputation for being a hard drinking womanizer, concluded Ellen finally stepped over the line when she began preaching to him. In the end she left to go out on her own.

Ellen's leaving, while disheartening at first, turned out to be a boon for me for it was then Adam Rice asked me to be the exclusive leasing agent for the new Gothic Towers. At last I was in my element. I identified every potential tenant who could occupy more than three thousand square feet of space and contacted each. I used every convenient pretext to get a foot in the door and rather than seeing my femaleness as a hindrance, used it to gain access to the top honchos. I roped them in a little at a time; first taking them to the construction site and placing helmets on, encouraging them to ride the worker's cage to the unfinished thirty-second floor where, with the wind howling around them, they could see all of Honolulu. It didn't hurt when my skirt flew up, exposing my legs.

"Now," I would say with a smile. "If you want to get back down you have to sign."

Thanks to Marie's training I'd become a stickler for detail and was good at preparing contracts. Adam trusted my judgment and eventually encouraged me to expand my territory and solicit large mainland firms. He financed my trips allowing me to seek tenants from San Francisco and L.A., which I did with much enthusiasm and equal success. It was not all work and no play. I especially loved San Francisco, staying at the St. Francis Hotel, dining at Vanessi's, the Tadich Grill or the Iron Horse. Standing at the bar drinking Irish coffee at the Buena Vista on Fisherman's Wharf I met all sorts of interesting people from all over the world and bedded a few of them.

Provided with a generous commission structure, I was getting rich. My second year with Gothic saw my earnings move into the six-figure range. I purchased a house in Kailua bought a sailboat and became a member of two yacht clubs. I'd succeeded beyond my wildest expectations and the day I bought a leather handbag for two hundred dollars, without giving it a second thought, I knew I'd arrived. As an afterthought I bought a hand tooled, leather wallet for Sarah and put a one-hundred-dollar bill in it before presenting it to my mother.

Chapter XXII

1980 - Seattle

I needed a break. I'd been driving myself hard and asked Adam for some time off. A small group of Ellen's friends, some of whom I'd met previously, were planning a trip to Israel and I accepted their invitation to join them. There were six Hawaii residents in the party that left the Honolulu airport for Seattle; a Chinese-American couple, Carrie Crawford and two bachelors in their sixties, Tom Farrell, a Protestant Minister, and Bruce Stone, a retired military officer. Six hours later we were on a bus headed for a small hotel in downtown Seattle where we were to meet a couple from Indiana. For the purpose of economy I was paired with Carrie, a young woman whom I'd met several times at Ellen's office bible studies. Carrie was a thirty-something, very overweight, very sweet, never-been-married Southern belle, and while we were to be room mates for the three weeks of the trip, I decided early on to discourage a more-than-casual relationship.

Determined not to be saddled with a permanent tagalong, the moment we agreed on who got what bed, I left Carrie counting out her assorted vitamin and herbal supplements and headed for the waterfront. It was a balmy, sunny day, unusual by Seattle standards. I discovered a stairway descending from First Avenue to Alaskan Way, a boulevard skirting Elliot Bay. The street was home to antique shops, stalls where hawkers promised the cheapest tee shirts in town, fancy waterside restaurants and quick food stops claiming award winning clam chowder. Joining a group of people waiting to sample Ivar's "world renown" seafood I ordered a cup of chowder, served in a Styrofoam bowl accompanied by oyster crackers. Tables and benches were

Annie's Portion

scattered along the wharf and I savored the, "not as good as Rhode Island", chowder while watching the boat traffic in the bay. A number of ferries, carrying cars and walk-on passengers, made their way across the sound. Finished with the snack, I decided to take the shortest run to Bainbridge Island, a trip of about thirty minutes, to the quaint town of Winslow where I toured the shops before boarding the boat back to Seattle. People were very friendly and on the return trip I struck up a conversation with a well dressed, attractive man who offered to show me some more of the city and buy my dinner.

Dan, a native Seattleite took me first to the "Pike Place Market"; a farmers market spanning four or five blocks running parallel to the waterfront and accessed from the dock via a series of stairways. The market displayed an amazing array of foods to delight the eye and the palate. There were fruits and vegetables of every description grown by local farmers, fresh-cut meats and homemade sausages, honey from every flower, cheeses, baked good, myriad flowers and, of course, fish. The highlight of any trip to the Market was the show put on by the fishmongers. There were tiers of Dungeness crab, barrels of oysters, clams, mussels and beds of ice displaying halibut, salmon, ling cod and snapper.

"What would you like today? Salmon? Here it is." A fish would fly through the air, over the counter to a clerk waiting to clean and package it. "How about you lady? Nice fresh Alaskan halibut?" Another fish would follow its mate to the chopping block.

"This place is incredible." I was delighted with the sights, the sounds and the endless enthusiasm of the shoppers and tourists. "It makes me want to sample everything in sight."

"Well, it would be difficult for you to take a salmon back to your room." Dan cautioned. "And if you eat anything here you'll spoil your dinner."

The lights of the city were beginning to come on as we made our way to First Avenue where we caught a cab. Ahead of us I could see the lighted outline of a high tower, the top of which supported a slowly rotating disc.

"That's our destination. The Space Needle was built for the 1962 Worlds Fair and has become a Seattle landmark."

An illuminated glass elevator moved along an external track to the top of the tower.

"We're going for a ride Anne. I hope you are not afraid of heights."

I laughed, "No I'm not the least bit afraid. Lead me to it."

We boarded the elevator and began an ascent that afforded a magnificent view of the city, the harbor and the mountain ranges to the east and west.

"The sun is setting behind the Olympics. On the east are the Cascades and if you strain your eyes you can just make out Mount Rainier to the south of us."

The elevator came to a stop more than five-hundred feet above the city. A maitre'd greeted us and led us to the dining room.

"Please watch your step. The room is turning." He took my arm as I made the small step from the stationary floor to the moving one.

"This is quite extraordinary. I thought I'd seen all there was to see back in New York." I followed the maitre'd to a window table where he pulled a chair out for me. I gave him my most beguiling smile and thanked him. He bowed. "Enjoy your dinner."

We ordered drinks and sipped them as the city appeared to circle around us.

Annie's Portion

"We'll make one complete rotation in an hour so you'll have a chance to see it all."

"Dan, this has been such a surprisingly wonderful day. Thank you so much."

"It's been my pleasure, Anne. It's always nice to see familiar things through someone else's eyes. It's as though I'm seeing them for the first time too." We ordered the salmon, the specialty of the house, and finished with Brandy at the bar. In the cab, on the way back to my hotel, Dan kissed me.

"I'm sorry we didn't have more time to spend together. Maybe on your way back."

I was sure Dan was a married man although he'd not said so. "Dan, you've made this trip really special but I think it's a good thing I'm leaving tomorrow." I kissed him again as we pulled up in front of the hotel. "Thanks for everything."

Carrie was pacing the floor when I unlocked the door.

"Where have you been? I've been so worried about you."

The last thing I needed was another mother. "Carrie, I've told you not to be concerned when I take off. I just like doing things on my own." To mitigate the unintended harshness of my response I related the events of my day; the ferry ride, the market and dinner at the Space Needle, omitting the meeting with Dan.

The flight next day via SAS was to be a long one. It was nine hours from Seattle, by way of the North Pole, to Copenhagen. I slept through most of the trip, waking once to see the spectacular show put on by the Aurora Borealis. Copenhagen was cold, gray and exceedingly expensive. I had my own wee room in the equally diminutive Kong Royale Hotel where I luxuriated in a hot bath and feather bed. The buffet breakfast was scrumptious, offering herring, smoked meats, Danish cheeses, fresh baked rolls and authentic

Danish pastries so light and flaky the group cleared the table of them. Hot chocolate, served in individual pots, was so thick it poured like molasses.

"Oh," I groaned holding my stomach. "If I keep eating like this I'll soon look like Carrie." I confided to Tom during a walk through the shopping malls. Tom had traveled to Israel several times. He was an interesting, informative companion. We ate a late lunch before heading back to the hotel to join the group for the last leg of the journey on El Al to Tel Aviv.

The relationship between Jews of every nation and the land of Israel is an enigma that defies explanation or reason. When Israel gained statehood, Jews around the world rejoiced. When Israel was at war, Jews from countries as far away as South America, Africa and the U.S. went to fight alongside the Israelis. When Israel needed funds, millions of dollars were collected by the combined efforts of American Jewish organizations. Every Passover Seder, a Jewish celebration of the miraculous delivery from Egyptian enslavement, concludes with the prayer, "Next year in Jerusalem."

For me this journey fulfilled a desire inspired by my grandparents who had spoken often and longingly of returning to "*Eretz Yisroel.*" The talk of unimaginable tribulations overcome and goals miraculously achieved by my kinsmen had inspired in me a sense of pride, as if in some way I'd been part of the success story. Now I would have the opportunity to see with my own eyes the birthplace of my people. I found myself teary-eyed as I stepped for the first time on the soil of Israel. A mini-bus was waiting for us as we exited the airport. Sensing my emotion, Tom put his arm around my shoulder as he guided me towards the vehicle.

The trip along the uncrowded road was a short one providing the merest glimpse of the progress that had been made in the thirty-odd years since Israel's statehood was confirmed. Forests grew on the once barren rock face and new communities of rose-colored stone, hugged the hillsides. We climbed higher into the sun lit hills under a clear blue sky and having reached the pinnacle began a descent into Jerusalem, passing the old walled city on the way to our final destination near Ben Yahuda Square. The passengers were awed by the historical and religious implications of the trip on which we had embarked.

The driver pulled up in front of a three-story stone building, vaguely suggestive of a monastery. Tom, who'd stayed there before, commented, "This was formerly a Christian Mission. It was a residence for missionaries en route to other locales in Palestine; a stopping off place where they were provided with tools and information they would need before departing for their ultimate destinations."

"Proselytizing," I thought cynically.

The first floor of the Mission contained offices, a reading room and several tiny cells. The upper two floors consisted of larger, sparsely furnished sleeping/sitting rooms. Each floor had a shared kitchen and bath. The price was a modest seventeen dollars a week and the building, which was to be our headquarters for the next few weeks, was ideally located within walking distance of the main open market and the Old City.

I enjoyed my first evening in Jerusalem with Tom and Bruce, eating a light supper of Mediterranean specialties; falafels, humus and salad with the freshest, reddest tomatoes, seedless cucumbers, olives and feta cheese.

In an unusually pensive mood I remarked casually, "Have you ever considered the number of hours we spend devoted to food? I bet we spend a third of our lifetimes concerned with matters relating to food. What do you talk about when you tell people about your vacation?" With no reply forthcoming, I continued. "Food. It's the great restaurants you've eaten in or the food markets you've visited or the hours spent around a dinner table with new friends. It seems I never describe a place or event without mentioning food."

"Besides sex, what else is there worth talking about?" Bruce responded, displaying complete disregard for the presence of our minister companion.

With his mouth filled with falafel, all Tom could do was blush and nod.

We strolled through brightly lit, lively Ben Yahuda Square with our arms linked, stopping to enjoy strong coffee and delicious desserts at an outdoor cafe. Sated and weary we made our way back to the Mission. Carrie had not yet returned from vespers or some such and thankful for the privacy I showered in the community bathroom and slid into bed and a contented sleep.

By the time I awoke she was already busy in the kitchen. "I shopped at the wonderful market so we can have breakfast in," she said in her usual cheerful way.

I had a fresh roll and the best yogurt I'd ever eaten. "The coffee takes some getting used to but the food is the best," I commented aloud while thinking, "And it's food once again."

Tom called from the hallway to inform us of our guide's arrival. Carrie hurried back to our room to swallow a handful of her daily vitamins.

"Carrie," I said good-naturedly. "You're going to rattle when you walk if you keep taking all that stuff."

"You'll always be able to find me." She rejoined.

Geoffrey Howard was a most unlikely representative of his profession. He'd probably seen his sixtieth birthday, was somewhat shy of six feet tall, slim, mustached and very British, dressed in starched khakis, the crease in his pants a study in perfection. He herded us into the van where our driver of the previous day awaited his orders.

Annie's Portion

"I know you are anxious to see the Old City and the historical religious sights but today we will see the new Jerusalem. It will make it easier for you to get your bearings if we work from the outside in. I know Tom will be the color man. He probably knows more about this city than I do. Eh Tom?" The English accent was undeniable.

Tom nodded in agreement and made the introductions. "Don't let Jeff fool you. He's been here longer than Israel's been a state. There isn't anything he doesn't know."

The first two days were spent getting familiar with the bustling city; visiting the Knesset, several museums, many monuments and commemorative sites and a miniature replica of Jerusalem, circa 70 CE. We enjoyed a sinfully sumptuous lunch at the world-famous King David Hotel.

The next three days were spent with Geoffrey guiding his charges through many Christian holy sites located within the walls of the Old City. We were collected at ten, toured, had delicious, inexpensive meals at insignificant restaurants, toured some more and were deposited by four. We walked the "Via Dolorosa;" following the trail that Jesus was supposed to have taken carrying a cross to the outskirts of the city, stopping at each of the fourteen "Stations of the Cross;" saw many beautiful, historically-significant churches, including the Church of the Holy Sepulcher and visited the room where Jesus was said to have had his "last supper" with his disciples, a scene made eternally famous by Leonardo Da Vinci's painting. The tour was expanded to include Golgotha, the site of Jesus' crucifixion, and the Mount of Olives where thousand-year-old olive trees still grew overlooking the Jewish cemetery. For Gentile or Jew, no trip to Jerusalem would have been complete without a visit to the Western Wall of the second Temple. Constructed under the auspices of Herod on Mt. Mariah, it had been the site of the first Temple built by Solomon to house the sacred "Ark of the Covenant." Herod's Temple was destroyed by the Romans in 70 CE. Ironically, the Temple Mount now served as the foundation for the beautiful gilded Dome of the Rock and the al-Aqsa Mosque, where according to Muslim tradition, Muhammad, founder of the faith, left his earthly bonds on a white stallion and ascended to heaven.

For decades, Jews had been denied access to their most holy site but with the advent and ultimate success of the Six-Day-War in 1967, the Israeli army regained control of Jerusalem. With great rejoicing and many tears, soldiers were first to celebrate a great victory in prayer, touching at last the historic symbol of the new Israel.

It was Friday, the eve of the Jewish Sabbath and the large courtyard below the Mount teemed with men and women, separated by a low barrier, facing the Western Wall. A steady, low hum pervaded the air as prayers were chanted by bearded men wearing blue striped *talaysim*, prayer shawls. Soldiers too, prayed at the wall, with rifles slung over their shoulders and *yarmulkas* covering their heads, and many slipped pieces of paper bearing messages for God into the minute crevices between the stones. Once again I wept.

Geoffrey approached me quietly. Either intuitively or from Tom, he determined I was Jewish. "What the hell are you doing here with all these *goys*?"

"They're my friends and very good people," I responded defensively.

"I have nothing against Gentiles personally. Tom is a great guy and has more of a love for Israel than many Jews. It just surprised me to discover you were traveling with such a devout, born-again group and seemed so interested in Christianity. But tonight you will be the guests of a local family for a *Shabbat* dinner. Tomorrow the city shuts down. Stores and restaurants close and public transportation stops so we will have a hiatus. May I take you to see the real Israel?"

Annie's Portion

Without hesitation I accepted.

"I will pick you up at ten." He seemed to be devising some plan as he spoke. "No, make that nine. Are you old enough to stay out all night?" He dared me with a devilish grin. "I promise there will be no hanky panky, everything on the up-and-up as you Americans say."

"I don't need permission but the real question is, 'Can I trust you?'"

"The real question is, 'Can you trust yourself?'" He did not wait for a response. "Bring a change of clothes and a toothbrush and ask no questions. See you tomorrow. Good *shabbes*."

At five-thirty, the driver appeared with the van to transport the group, now dressed in our finest, to our dinner destination. We were taken to a newer part of the city, near the Montessori district. The setting sun cast a glow on the pink stone of which most new buildings were constructed. The effect was startling, giving the entire city a golden cast.

"Now I know why they call this 'the City of Gold'," Carrie remarked.

The driver deposited us at our destination in short order and we passed through a low stone wall into a small courtyard surrounded by flowering shrubs. The building was three stories tall with four entry doors on each floor. A woman appeared on our left, in a ground floor doorway.

"Come, come. Welcome to our home." Taking Tom's arm she introduced herself as Ruth Kaplan. We followed them into a pleasant parlor. "Joseph, come meet our guests."

Introductions were made all 'round as Joseph offered glasses of sweet red wine.

"We are so happy to meet you all," Joseph said with a distinct eastern European accent. "We want to hear all about America and your trip."

"Later Joseph," Ruth interjected. "It is almost sundown. Please, everyone into the dining room."

The table was covered with a lace cloth and set for ten. A pair of brass candlestick sat near one end of the long table and I caught a glimpse of a *challa*, traditional braided Sabbath egg bread, under a white linen napkin.

"Oh, Ruth," I exclaimed. "The table looks beautiful."

"It's nothing. But please sit. It is almost sunset."

Joseph sat at the head of the table while Ruth at the other end prepared to light the Sabbath candles. She placed a white scarf on her head and made a small circle with her hands over the candles as she said the *broche*, the prayer for the lighting of the candles.

"Broche a ta Adonai, Elohenu Melech ha'a olom…"

I closed my eyes as I listened to the familiar words I'd heard so often at my grandmother's table.

"…l'hav licht ner. Amen!" Ruth translated for her guests. "Blessed art thou o' Lord our God, King of the universe who commandeth us to kindle the Sabbath lights."

A chorus of "Amen" was heard as Ruth hurried to the kitchen to bring on the feast. The traditional Jewish Friday night spread began with light-as-air matzo balls floating on a sea of aromatic chicken soup. This was followed by roasted chicken, a peppery potato *kugel*, and *tsimmes* filled with cooked carrots and prunes. Dinner finished we returned to the parlor for coffee and conversation. At eight-thirty, the ever prompt Herschel re-appeared; ready to drive us back to the Mission. Ruth would have none of it. She and Joseph were having a wonderful time exchanging stories with their guests. She insisted Herschel join us for more coffee and applesauce cake. It was after ten when we finally said our thanks and good-byes.

For me, morning could not arrive soon enough. I showered, dressed quickly and threw some things in a bag. Carrie was already in the kitchen brewing coffee.

Annie's Portion

"Morning, Carrie. Did you sleep well after all that food?"

"I did. Wasn't that a delicious dinner and what nice people."

I agreed and sipped the weak cup of coffee Carrie had put before me.

"Ready for your outing?" Carrie asked cautiously.

"Ready and eager. Do you have plans for the day?"

"Yes, Tom and I are going to a Messianic service in the Christian Quarter. Then we'll wander around for a while and wait for sundown to have dinner in Ben Yahuda Square."

"Well you guys have fun. See you tomorrow." I dashed out before Carrie's curiosity got the better of her.

Geoffrey arrived in his car promptly at ten to find his charge waiting in the courtyard. Glad to see you don't have that irritating woman's tendency toward tardiness," he smiled.

"Actually, I do. But today is different."

"Oh! How is that?" Geoffrey held the car door open for me.

"I'm just so excited to have the day and you all to myself," I flirted. I could see he was pleased by my response although he tried to look nonchalant.

"I hope you haven't had breakfast yet."

"No, just some very bad coffee."

"I've heard your friends call you Annie. May I call you Annie? It's such a charming name."

"Yes and thanks. What do your friends call you?"

"I haven't any friends but you may call me Jeff."

He drove quickly, his small car darting past streets crowded with pedestrians. We passed through the Jaffa Gate into the Armenian Quarter of the Old City where Jeff maneuvered the car deftly through narrow streets, parking at the side of a stone archway. Taking my arm, he led me through the arch into a courtyard lush with fragrant fruit trees and flowering shrubs. A small fountain, decorated with blue and white mosaic tiles, sprayed a fine mist into the air. Tile-topped tables, some with umbrellas bearing the name of a local beer, and stools sporting colorfully decorated leather cushions was the first indication that we'd entered a restaurant. At the far end of the courtyard a rose colored limestone building housed a cooking area. A long table spread with a copious bounty of fruits, cheeses, yogurt, hard cooked eggs and freshly baked, aromatic breads still warm from the oven was positioned close by.

"What a delightful surprise," I exclaimed

Jeff, obviously pleased by my reaction, pointed to a table under a large broad-leafed tree. As soon as we were seated a waiter brought us a pot of steaming coffee and two small cups.

"Good morning, Aram. This is my friend Annie from America."

"Good morning Mr. Jeff." Aram bowed. "Welcome to you Miss Annie. Can I get anything special for you?"

"I think coffee will be just fine." Jeff looked to see me nodding my head in agreement as I sipped the first good coffee I'd had in days.

"Then help yourselves." Aram pointed to the heavily laden table.

"Thank you Aram. Shall we?" Jeff pulled my chair back from the table.

I thought, "How gallant. He's a real toff." I couldn't help smiling.

"What put that grin on your face, Annie?"

"Just the pleasure of this place."

We filled our plates and returned to the table.

"You're going to have a hard time besting this," I said with a bite of crusty bread in my mouth.

"This is just the appetizer."

I hoped it was.

Annie's Portion

"Breakfast was great. What's next?" I asked as the car moved slowly through arches, alleyways and ever narrowing streets.

"An adventure, Annie." Jeff pulled into a depression between two shuttered stalls and got out of the car. I was puzzled. There didn't seem to be anything worth seeing in the immediate vicinity.

"Come, come Annie. Hop to it." Jeff opened the trunk and pulled out two pairs of waders and a couple of waterproof windbreakers. Tossing one of each in my direction he said, "Take these, you'll need them."

I did as I was told. Jeff grabbed two large battery-operated torches. I followed him to the basement entrance of one of the stalls, where he opened a low door and turned on one of the torches.

"Down we go." He moved down a narrow stairway to a wide landing about fifteen feet below street level.

"Put your waders on. They'll fit over your shoes." Jeff's voice echoed in the cavernous darkness.

He helped me adjust the straps of the waders, which were about two sizes too large for me. We slipped into the jackets and he handed me one of the flashlights. "You hang on to this one. We won't use it unless the other torch runs out of battery."

We descended another ten feet, the light now reflected in a shallow pool.

"Hold on to my arm Annie. I'm about to take you on a journey back in time."

I was quiet and uneasy. I never liked close spaces and was beginning to feel claustrophobic. The water rose higher as we made our way in the dark tunnel and I could feel the cold through the waders. Then we were climbing and soon on dry stone again. Jeff shone his light around the enormous chamber carved out of the rock bed. To his right the torch revealed a gaping crater at least twenty feet in diameter. He moved closer to the edge, with me clinging tightly to his arm. He stooped to pick up several small stones, dropping them into the black hole. It was seconds before I heard the splash.

"What is this place? Do you always take your girls here to scare the hell out of them?" I said lightly, trying to hide my nervousness.

"This my dear lady is a cistern; part of an aqueduct system built in the eight century BCE by King Hezekiah, thirteenth successor to King David's throne, a feat so great it is still in use today."

We started off again, re-entering the channel where the water reached clear to my waist.

"This ancient pipeline runs for six miles under the city."

I gasped. "Are we going to walk six miles in the bowels of the earth....in the wet and dark?"

Jeff laughed, the sounds bouncing eerily off the walls of the tunnel.

"No, we will exit long before that. Look, Annie." He pointed to a series of large niches along the wall. "Burial chambers."

I shuddered. We waded through the water with Jeff stopping every so often to relate more of the tunnel's history. At one spot he pointed out ancient markings carved into the wall indicating the water levels. He continued his historic narration.

"Hezekiah was the leader of a rebellion in Palestine against the Assyrians. In order to strengthen the defenses of Jerusalem, he had this tunnel dug. The Siloam tunnel brought water from the spring at Gihon to be stored in the cistern we just passed. The rebellion however was crushed and Hezekiah paid a King's ransom...get that...a King's ransom."

"British humor," I laughed. "I got it."

Annie's Portion

"The Assyrian King demanded the city's surrender. But, as in many Jewish folktales, just when all hope was lost…"

"The Calvary arrived. Get that? Calvary," I interrupted. Now it was Jeff's turn to laugh.

"Nope. A miraculous plague struck and decimated the Assyrian army. This astounding event fostered the belief that Jerusalem was unconquerable and under the protection of the Jewish God. It wasn't until one-hundred years later that the Babylonians finally conquered Jerusalem."

"God must really love us," I giggled through chattering teeth.

"I'm sorry, Annie. You're really chilled. I guess my hot air was not enough to keep you warm. We're coming out now." Jeff pointed to a beam of light ahead. We reached a metal ladder leading up to a grating in the street just eight feet above us. Jeff went first, lifting the grate and helping me out through the small opening.

"Made it. Something to tell your great grandchildren about."

We pulled off our wet jackets and coveralls, which Jeff rolled into a neat bundle and placed under his arm. We'd come to the surface outside the Old City walls. Jeff hailed a taxi and warmed my hands as we rode back to his car, stopping at a street side cart where he snagged two steaming hot Arabic coffees.

"I promise the rest of the day will be much easier and much warmer."

"Oh, I loved the adventure and the stories. Jeff, you're a real spellbinder."

There was little traffic on Saturday and we made good time as we left the Old City behind, headed in what I thought might be a southerly direction. Stopping on a high crest above the city Jeff led me to an overlook. He brought out a pair of binoculars and handing them to me said, "Look at our country Annie," emphasizing the word, "our." "Look across to the east. You are looking at the Dead Sea and the Jordan River. Beyond lie the mountains of Moab. Somewhere above the Jordan on Mt. Nebo Moses stood and watched his people, our forebears enter the Promised Land. High on a mountain pinnacle rests the tomb of Aaron to this day. Can you feel it? Can't you just feel it?"

I could feel his passion and my own. I put the glasses down to wipe my eyes, my inherent tendency to cry easily exhibited once again. "Yes," I whispered. "I do feel it."

"Those *goys* will never know this feeling. This is our land, our home."

My chest constricted. Jeff brushed a tear with his thumb and gently kissed me on the cheek.

"He makes me feel like a foolish child."

"Come, we have more to see."

The highway took us past signs pointing to Bethlehem, Efrata and Hebron.

"On Monday we will take the others to Bethlehem and Hebron where you will visit the tombs of our fathers, Abraham, Isaac and Jacob. But today and tomorrow are ours."

We continued south at a leisurely pace passing fewer cars the further we got from Jerusalem.

"The Dead Sea is on our left but we'll not stop there today."

Jeff pulled off the road at a fenced grove of palm trees. "Do you notice anything unusual about those palms?"

"Not really, except maybe they're young."

"Not young, short. This is an experimental grove. These are date palms which have been engineered to grow no higher than seven feet to make it easy to gather the fruit."

"May I ask you some personal questions?" My curiosity could no longer be contained.

"Ask away, Annie. But remember, turn about is fair play."

"You are obviously a Brit, but how did you get here?" Interested in Jeff's marital status I hoped he would offer the information without being asked directly.

"I was a British citizen—raised in London by German-Jewish though not orthodox parents. Anti-Semitism had been a way of life for my family even though almost half the Jews in Germany had intermarried. My father hoped after the War, the first one Annie, things would be better for Jews. He couldn't have been more wrong. Germany's defeat only made things worse for them. The economy had been devastated, the people humiliated, the Jews as usual the scapegoats. My father owned a small clothing factory and prospered during the war by making uniforms. We lived well and that made us a prime target for the almost manic hatred of all Jews. My sister and I were attacked at school, my mother embarrassed in the shops and finally my father's factory burned to the ground. They got out of Germany in 1920, when I was five. England provided a safe haven and with the meager funds he'd managed to take out of Germany, my father opened a dry goods business. He changed his name from Horwitz to Howard and tried, as much as was possible, to assimilate."

"Like so many other stories. I guess we are just meant to survive."

"Ah, Annie. But are we?" Jeff was quiet, lost in thought for the next few miles. "But I didn't answer your question, did I?"

"You don't have to say more if it bothers you."

"Not any more. But if I'm boring you please stop me."

"No, do go on."

"Well I grew up in a loving family, had a limited Jewish education, celebrated the holidays and was a disappointment to my father. My sister had the brains and excelled at everything she did. I was not a good student and it was evident college was out of the question. Following my father's example I changed my name, from Joshua to Geoffrey, very British and all that, joined the army and was sent to Suez with a small contingent to secure the canal. There were not many Jews in the British army back then, in fact the army was spread quite thin. In 1936 we were sent to Jerusalem to put down an Arab uprising. As a Jew I was welcomed into many homes, getting to understand the people and there love of country.

"By that time Hitler had become the new German Chancellor and Jews were excluded from public office, civil service, teaching and all branches of the media. Anti-Semitism was national policy and it was just a matter of time before there would be more serious consequences. War was imminent and Jews were trying to get out of Europe with no place to go. Palestine seemed their only hope. Britain reneged on its promises to help Jews establish an Israeli state. The Arabs were in revolt, forming alliances with Mussolini and Hitler, and the Brits were impotent. In 1939 the Brits issued another of its many 'White Papers,' the 'Passive White Paper,' prohibiting a Jewish state and restricting further immigration. No longer objective, angry at the betrayal of what I'd begun to think of as 'my people,' I was having thoughts of leaving the army. But it wasn't until 1942 that I jumped ship, after the Struma sank."

"I'm sorry to sound so stupid but what was the Struma?"

"Forgot how young you are. The Struma was a boat that sailed from Constanza in the Black Sea with about eight-hundred Jewish refugees. The boat was an unseaworthy cattle scow but managed to get to Istanbul where the refugees applied for entry visas from the Colonial Office. The illustrious Lord Moyne rejected the applications and the Turks forced the Struma to leave with no known destination.

Annie's Portion

It finally sank taking all but two passengers down to the bottom of the Black Sea. In a great act of 'clemency', the Brits allowed the two survivors to enter Israel. That summer of '42 some of us were sent to a kibbutz to train Israelis to fight in the event of a German incursion into Palestine, Kibbutz Mishmar Haemek. When the training was complete I left with the new army and went underground with the Hagana and spent the rest of the war years getting Jews out of Europe." His mouth twisted in a sardonic grin.

"What put that odd smile on your face?" I asked.

"Life does have its little ironies. Had to change my name back to Horwitz."

The road took us along the west bank of the Dead Sea, through an uncharacteristic area of tropical vegetation. We were nearing a green expanse broken intermittently by groves of date palms and banana trees. Jeff pulled off at the entrance to Ein Gedi.

"We have arrived. Ein Gedi, a beautiful oasis in the desert."

"Is this a kibbutz?" I thought of my baby sister Hannah who had died many years before on a kibbutz in the north but said nothing.

"My favorite one."

The half mile drive leading to the compound situated on a low plateau was a bumpy uphill climb. A stiff breeze sent up whirling dust devils behind the car. To either side of the road the verdant fields displayed neat rows of the season's first crops. Once past an opening in a chain link fence, the road forked. Jeff took the right fork heading for what appeared to be a residential section where shade trees and green, well manicured lawns veiled the more ominous aspects of kibbutz living. Neat bungalows formed a three quarter circle, their communal backyard demarcated by a high chain link fence topped with barbed wire.

"If you noticed, they took a page from John Wayne's book and put the wagons in a circle." Jeff pulled into a parking area.

"For safety reasons?" I queried as he opened my door.

"An ounce of prevention. We are very close to the Jordanian border here. Every day brings a new challenge; the sniper, the shelling, the sudden infiltration and here," he made a circle with his arms extended, "the *Khamsin*."

"What is a Khamsin?" I asked.

"It is a hot, fierce desert wind that usually comes in late spring."

The door of a nearby bungalow opened and a young, thin towhead came running across the yard.

"Uncle Jeff! Uncle Jeff!"

As soon as he reached us, Jeff picked the boy up and laughingly swung him around several times.

"Ah, my little *kibbutznik*. How big you have gotten."

"I'm seven and you missed my birthday. Did you bring me a present?"

"I brought you this lovely lady. Micah, this is my friend Annie."

"Hello, Annie." Not waiting for a reply Micah said, "But she's not a present. She's just a girl."

"Ah, but what a girl." Jeff reached into the car and pulled out two packages. "Well, if you don't want the girl you'll have to settle for these."

A taller version of Micah came through the doorway. "So there you are. We thought you forgot about us."

"You couldn't be so lucky. Neil this is Annie."

"I'm so happy to meet you...and Micah."

He'd already dashed into the house to open his presents.

"Come inside and have something cool to drink."

Annie's Portion

The bungalow was surprisingly bright and breezy; two bedrooms, bath, kitchen and sitting room open to the kitchen.

"Helen. Meet Jeff's friend, Annie."

Helen was a stunning woman in her early thirties. She had short-cropped dark hair and eyes so blue they were riveting. Like Neil, she was tall and willowy. She walked toward us with unstudied grace, carrying a tray of lemonade-filled glasses.

"Hi, Annie. Hi, Geoffrey." She placed the tray on a table in front of the sofa and gave Jeff a hug as he planted a kiss on her cheek. We sipped lemonades while catching up on news and gossip.

"Enough jabber. Come Annie. Let me show off my Garden of Eden."

"If you don't mind, Neil," Helen quipped, " I've already seen it and have some things to take care of."

Neil's rusting pickup looked as though it had been made of scavenged parts. "Don't judge this heap by its looks. It actually works," he said as he helped me surmount the high running board.

After a couple of unsuccessful tries the engine turned over with a burp, exhaled a large plume of black smoke and bumped its way down the rutted road towards a grove of date palms.

"This was just a small oasis when the kibbutz was first established. Many of the palms were already here. Now we raise dates for export."

"How many years ago was that?"

"The kibbutz was started in 1953. I've been here for ten years."

"You two have something in common," Jeff interjected. "You're both from Brooklyn."

"Really? What brought you to Israel?"

"I came as a volunteer consultant. My specialty is botany but now I'm a ditch digger, tractor driver, delivery man, soldier and ...botanist," Neil smiled.

"But you stayed. You must like it."

"I met Helen. She's a *Sabra*, native born Israeli."

"Just after the Six-Day-War my younger sister Hannah joined a kibbutz in the north... somewhere near Lebanon. She was killed in'73. I've always regretted not having visited her."

Jeff raised an eyebrow but did not comment.

Leaving a telltale trail of dust Neil played guide, identifying the varied crops that were the specialty of Ein Gedi, while I marveled at the transformation of the once barren desert.

"Our fruits and vegetables are in great demand," he said proudly. "You know it was the Israelis who first developed the drip irrigation system...also fish farming, although we don't do that here."

Stopping at a large excavation, Neil informed me it was an on-going archeological dig. Because of the spring in otherwise totally arid country, the site had been inhabited for an indeterminable number of years. Excavations in the 60's and 70's at an adjoining tel, had revealed remnants of a sanctuary of the Chalcolithic period, fourth millennium BC as well as evidence of habitation from the seventh Century BC through Byzantine times.

The subject was fascinating. All the people I'd met in Israel had such a craving to know their history and a pride in the knowledge.

"I'm sure you noticed the tropical forest."

I nodded in agreement.

"That is really an oddity in nature. But the particular climate generated by the spring encouraged its formation. Now it is a National Nature Reserve." Neil looked at the sun

Annie's Portion

beginning its descent. "We'd best get back. We don't want to be late for dinner."

Dinner was a communal affair in a large hall filled with chairs and round tables dressed in white linen. Several tables displayed candles and spice boxes.

Giving Jeff a gentle poke with my elbow I asked quizzically "Are we celebrating my birthday or are we going to have a *Havdalah* service?"

"Yes, it's a Saturday evening ritual. You should...Is it really your birthday?"

"Yup...born on Saturday forty five years ago."

"This really is a special occasion. We must have two glasses of wine. Happy birthday, Annie."

I'd not seen such a service since my grandmother died. "Oh, how wonderful," I said sincerely, looking forward to the sweet-sad ritual that signaled the end of the Sabbath.

The buffet style dinner was as delicious and varied as any I'd ever eaten. Once the dishes were cleared the room quieted and several male voices were heard reciting the solemn benediction. The lovely, braided candles were lit and the spice boxes gently moved through the air, their sweet aroma scenting the room. Somewhere a chord was played on a piano and many voices were lifted in jubilation. A quartet; two fiddles, a bass and piano began to play. My spirit soared.

"No wonder you stayed, Neil."

"Be careful," Jeff whispered in my ear. "It's contagious."

There was more singing and exuberant dancing. I joined hands with Helen and Micah in the circle required to dance the Hora. The circle opened and the line of dancers passed between the tables, grabbing less willing participants as we moved around the room. All too soon the party ended.

"Tomorrow is a work day for us," Neil reminded us.

"And a school day for Micah. It has been so nice to have you with us, Annie. Please try to come again before you leave for the states."

"Thank you Helen. Goodnight Micah...Neil."

Walking to the guest quarters later that evening, I held Jeff's arm. The night was cool and clear, lit by an incredibly bright half-moon. Above the shadows of the Judean hills, the stars shimmered, emitting an ethereal radiance.

"This has been one of the most enjoyable times of my life. These people are so special. I know I must sound corny as hell, but my heart is truly bursting with the joy of it all. Thank you for a most perfect day."

We'd reached the female guesthouse. Jeff kissed me goodnight.

We were on the road early Sunday morning, having first breakfasted on oranges, yogurt, warm rolls and strong coffee. Leaving Ein Gedi we turned south, still driving along the west bank of the Dead Sea. Soon, a flat-topped mountain appeared on the horizon.

"Masada," I cried as Jeff pulled off the main road.

"Come on Annie. First I froze you, now I'm going to fry you." Jeff grabbed a couple of canteens and two wide brimmed hats from the car. "If you remember your history you will recognize this road."

"Not the old Roman road!" I replied with disbelief.

By the time a Jewish child was five or six, he was sure to have heard the story of Masada. During Herod's reign he built a royal citadel on the plateau atop the fifteen-hundred-foot mountain, believing it to be an impregnable haven. It was a grand affair that included two palaces; one of which was on three levels, defensive walls and towers as well as an aqueduct that brought water to cisterns with a capacity of two-hundred-thousand-gallons. After Herod's death the Romans took the citadel and held it for a period of time until a surprise attack in 66 CE, by a sect called Zealots under the leadership of Ellazar Ben Jair, put Masada in Jewish hands once more. Following the destruction of the second Temple by the Romans, the band of about nine-hundred refused to surrender. The Roman Legion, fifteen thousand strong, besieged Masada for two years before they finally built a ramp of stones and earth which brought their army within reach of the stronghold. When they breached the wall, the Zealots, preferring death to enslavement took their own lives. The Romans found two women and five children still alive and it was they who bore witness to the desperate events. Masada had since become a symbol of resistance against tyranny for all Jews.

Jeff and I made the climb to the top, traveling along the original road built by the Romans. It took us about an hour to reach the mesa where to my surprise, a troop of men and women in uniform were forming up.

"Good," Jeff said. "We're just in time. These are new recruits who are going to be sworn in."

The commander called the troop to attention and a color guard of two men and two women presented the Israeli flag with its Mogen David , Star of David, fluttering in the wind. An officer recited the oath, which was echoed by the recruits then followed with the singing of *Hatikvah*, the Israeli National Anthem. The new soldiers were then dismissed.

For the umpteenth time since my arrival in Israel I found myself teary-eyed and tried to clear the lump in my throat. "Does this happen with all new recruits?"

"Yes it does. Makes quite an impression on those kids."

"On me too."

The soldiers made tracks but a few tourists remained to explore the ruins. Much of the old site had been excavated and the remains of the palaces, storehouses, defense works and a Synagogue containing a *mikva*, a ritual bath for women, were in evidence.

J. Fran Baird

"This is amazing. So much is uncovered. You can actually see the citadel as it must have existed back then."

"Yes. During 1963 through 1965, thousands of volunteers arrived from all over the world to help with the excavation. They even uncovered a number of potsherds inscribed with Hebrew personal names. Theory has it that they may have been used instead of straws to determine the order of the suicides."

The wind had picked up and Jeff suggested we get a move on before we were engulfed in sand. We were relieved to reach the shelter of the car and head back to Jerusalem where Jeff parked at the Mission and we walked to Ben Yahuda Square for an early supper.

"What a weekend this has been. My head is swimming with all I've seen and learned. Thank you, Jeff. You really went beyond the call of duty."

"This was pleasure, Annie. We'll have to do more of it. But tomorrow I will have to share you with your friends."

Our parting at the door of the Mission was casual out of necessity, but a fire had been kindled and we both knew it.

The next two days were spent visiting the Israel Museum and the Shrine of the Book in west Jerusalem. The Shrine had been built to house a scroll discovered in a cave at Qumran near the Dead Sea, containing the passages from the biblical book of Isaiah.

At Yad Vashem, the Holocaust Memorial covering a forty-five acre area on Mt. Herzle, the group split up. I walked along Avenue of the Righteous, where names of those who during World War II had facilitated the escape of condemned Jews, were displayed. The path led to Warsaw Ghetto Square where a sculpture in black depicted with stark realism, the horror, pain and struggle of the Jews in their doomed ghetto.

On the third day the group headed for Galilee and an overnight stay on a kibbutz. There were many stops along

Annie's Portion

the way as Jeff described the area and Tom embellished with the biblical tales of Jesus' journeys throughout that area. When the entourage was happily established at the kibbutz, Jeff and I left them for some private time. Jeff drove the van to an unpretentious restaurant on the shore of the Sea of Galilee where we watched the sunset while feasting on Peter's fish.

"Are you enjoying yourself Annie?"

"So much so, I'm dreading the time when I have to leave."

"Come back, Annie. Bring your children. Bring your mother and come back to stay. We need you."

"I would in a heartbeat, but I don't know about them. It would be so hard to uproot the kids at this age."

"You can make *Alliya*. You will be given all the help you need to start a new life here. You will have a place to live, go to school to learn Hebrew, be given a stipend and helped to find a job...or you can go to a kibbutz."

"Like Ein Gedi?"

"Yes, that one or any other of your choosing."

"I won't make a decision like that now. I'm too emotional about this place, these people and..." I stopped short of saying, "and you."

"Perhaps you are right. But let me try to convince you. Come with me this weekend to Eilat. We will swim in the beautiful warm waters of the Red Sea. We will lie on the warm sand and let the sun bath us in its golden rays. We will feast and we will make love."

On Friday, as soon as the others had been returned to the Mission, Herschel drove Jeff and me to pick up Jeff's car. It was to be a four-hour drive to Eilat with no travel stops once we reached the Negev. As soon as we were out of the city, Jeff took my hand in his.

"And so now it's your turn."

"My turn for what?"

"Your turn to answer my personal questions."

"You have a memory like an elephant."

"So begin, we have a long drive. Tell me about your life."

And so I did, telling him about my father, my husband, my children, my lovers and my Hawaii career. I'd never revealed so much about myself to anyone and it felt good. Jeff listened, interrupting occasionally to ask a question. The last few miles were spent in silence. It was almost nine when Jeff pulled up in front of the hotel. He went in to register, returning in a few minutes with a key to a private bungalow.

"Are you hungry? We can have some supper here or have it sent to us."

"Let's call from the room."

Jeff parked the car in front of a white bungalow surrounded by palms and flowering trees. He picked up our two bags, unlocked the door and let me enter first. In no more than a second I was in his arms. Jeff kissed me fiercely, his fingers pressing into my buttocks. I tried to pull away but he was strong and refused to loosen his hold. Finally, when it seemed I was about to smother he released me. I drew in a lungful of air and sank into a nearby chair.

"Whew," I gasped. "You literally take a girl's breath away."

"I'm sorry, Annie. But I've wanted to do that since the first time I met you." Jeff knelt in front of me and began undoing the buttons on my blouse. I was trembling but did not make a move to stop him, nor did I stop him as he unzipped my shorts and slid them down my legs. He kissed my stomach, my groin. I felt his warm breath as he caressed my body with his lips. Jeff stood suddenly. Lifting me in his arms he carried me to the bed where he dropped me unceremoniously. Quickly, he pulled his own clothes off and moved on top of me. He wasted no time, moving

Annie's Portion

slowly at first, then ever faster until with a cry so loud it frightened me, he pulled out and ejaculated on my thigh. He rolled off me and lay heaving at my side.

"Again I must apologize. I didn't mean for that to happen Annie. You bring out the beast in me." He kissed me more gently and began to slowly caress me, his hands and his mouth exploring. Lovemaking a second time was most satisfactory. Dawn broke before it ended.

I awoke first, glancing at the clock which read ten-ten. Slipping out of bed quietly I jumped into the shower. With eyes closed I let the steaming water engulf me. Minutes later, the glass door opened and Jeff was beside me. We made love under the pulsating shower and took turns soaping each other until contented and cleansed, we toweled each other dry.

"Are you hungry, Annie?"

"Hungry? I'm famished. You've starved me and used me. You got me here on false pretenses."

"Well, lest I completely ruin my impeccable reputation, I shall feast you till you are happily sated."

Finishing a delicious, American style breakfast, without the bacon, we lounged by the pool soaking up some rays and sipping fresh lemonade.

"Do you like to swim?" Jeff asked.

"Well, I much prefer to be on the water rather than in it, but I do enjoy snorkeling."

"Then you've come to the right place." He rose quickly from his lounge chair and taking my hand pulled me up.

"What now?"

"Snorkeling. Eilat is one of the best places on earth for it."

Jeff hired a boat to take us to a reef, well known for its vast array of fish and sea life. We spent the afternoon playing in the warm waters of the Red Sea then returned to the hotel were once again we indulged ourselves in exploratory research. Emerging at eight, we betook ourselves to a posh restaurant where we feasted on racks of perfectly cooked lamb with all the accoutrements. We danced to the big band sounds of the forties, provided by a quartet enhanced with the electronic wizardry of the eighties.

That night sleep came quickly, lovers spent and utterly content. Sunday morning was a repeat with slight variations of Saturday's performance. All too soon it was time for the trip back to Jerusalem and our last week together.

That week was a whirlwind as Jeff tried to cover the more important historical and biblical sights. We visited Mt. Zion and King David's tomb; Hebron and the tombs of Abraham, Isaac and Jacob; the Qumran caves; Tel Aviv where we attended a Saturday evening performance of the Israel Philharmonic Orchestra. No visit to Tel Aviv would have been complete without an evening walk on Disengoff Street. Although not as religiously observed as in Jerusalem, Saturday night signaled the end of the Sabbath. The tree-lined boulevard was alive with friendly people filling the many outdoor cafes, drinking tea or coffee and noshing on delicate pastries. The group joined the revelers at a large table filled with soldiers and shared in the animated conversation and great strudel before making our way back to Jerusalem.

All too soon it was over. Jeff and I had spent little time alone together since Eilat. On the night before my departure, we strolled down to Ben Yahuda Square. Though not quite Disengoff Street, it too was a hub of neon-lit activity.

"Will you come back, Annie?" Jeff asked somberly.

"I don't know. Right now I want to come back. I'm captivated by this land. I'm so proud of the people, my people. I think I could make a contribution, be part of it all. But I have my family to think of. Matt is eighteen, just old enough to have to serve in the Israeli army. Samantha is fourteen, an age when transitions are difficult."

We sipped strong, dark coffee and picked at pastries, each lost in his own thoughts. At last Jeff stood and held his hand out to me. In silence, we walked back to the Mission.

"I shall miss you, Annie."

"Me, too," was all I could manage to say. We kissed farewell and I lingered in Jeff's arms, unable or unwilling to make the final cut. At last I pushed him away, turned and walked to the doorway without looking back, knowing as he did, we would not see each other again.

*   *   *

It was business as usual when I arrived back in the islands. Before long I was caught up in the hectic routine of leasing the second tower of Gothic Center. The memories of Jeff and Israel no longer pained me.

The Christmas following the trip, I successfully negotiated a ten-year lease for two floors of Gothic Tower with one of the big-eight mainland accounting firms. The terms had been extremely favorable for Gothic and earned for me a fifty-thousand dollar commission. Adam invited Ed and me to celebrate at the Colony Surf where we three had gotten slightly tipsy. Upon our return to the tower plaza, Adam gave me the keys to a BMW parked there, wrapped in cellophane with a huge red ribbon affixed to the roof.

Plans completed, permits issued—on Monday, January 28, 1981, construction began on the north shore house. Life was good.

Chapter XXIII

1984 - Hawaii

"We are beginning our descent into Honolulu airport. Those of you seated on the left may be able to see Maui and Haleakala." The metallic voice of the captain shook me from the fitful slumber I'd succumbed to an hour out of SFO. The pressure in my ears increased as the plane descended from thirty-three thousand feet.

I caught a passing glimpse of the flat-topped cone of Haleakala, House of the Sun, a volcano whose dormant crater was the world's largest and the place where legend had it the demigod Maui confined the sun in an attempt to prolong the day. I'd retraced my steps, from Rifle to Denver to San Francisco and finally Honolulu where Rose and Sarah greeted me with beautiful fragrant leis of tea roses and white ginger.

"Oh, Annie. It's so good to have you home," Sarah threw her arms around me. "Rose has been wonderful but I really missed you."

"It's good to be home, Mom. I missed you too," I said not quite truthfully.

"Let's get your bags. We can catch up on the way home." Rose hurried us along.

The utilitarian Wiki Wiki bus conveyed us unhurriedly via a meandering route, to the baggage claim area where bags and parcels had already been disgorged onto the carousel. Passengers dressed in shorts and flowered shirts or cut off jeans waited, with their newly acquired leis of welcome, to catch a glimpse of the familiar pompoms, ribbons or other ornaments that would identify their possessions. I watched for my bags thinking of the first time I stood in front of this very same carousel. Then as now, I'd filled my lungs with perfumed, moist Hawaiian air so reminiscent of Antigua. Then I knew I was home, now I was plagued by doubts.

Filled with the chatter of three women, Rose's four-cylinder Datsun struggled to gain the summit of the incredibly majestic Koolaus, and having miraculously done so rapidly descended into Kailua town. Detached and apathetic I listened with feigned interest as Rose related in great detail the events of the past two weeks.

"Shall we stop for dinner?" She asked. "We can go to Byron's or The Steak House."

"Thanks, Rose, but I'm beat. All I want is a shower and bed."

"Sarah, how about you? We can drop Annie off and you and I can go out on the town."

"No thanks, I'll just go on home."

Her passenger delivered, Rose made a hasty retreat. "I'll give you a call tomorrow." Sarah brewed a pot of coffee while I showered. Mother and daughter had a long chat with me relating my tale of man and horse—long on horse, short on man.

"You know Mom, when I landed today it was so reminiscent of our first arrival, everything; the smells, sounds, the beauty...the same. I've been off the island many times but never had this response. It was eerie, like I went back in time."

Sarah shrugged. "I remember that trip often and with great fondness." She removed the cups and gave me a hug. "But I'm glad you're home. Now get some sleep."

"How strange," I thought. "The older she gets the more affectionate...and the more dependent."

I dropped heavily onto the bed and pulled the sheet up to my neck. The bed felt small and oh so empty.

Wearied by the tedious flight and mental anguish I skipped work on Friday but knowing how Sarah looked forward to her Friday night out in Waikiki I'd compromised, taking her to Buzz's Steak House in Lanikai. Rose made it a threesome, returning with mother and daughter for a nightcap. For Sarah it had been just that but for Rose and me the nightcap became a wine-assisted gabfest. I was thankful for the opportunity to share the events of the past two weeks with a simpatico friend.

"Seems like you're always around to hear my sad stories regarding the male gender. If it isn't Hank it's John or Jeff and now Branch." I was on my fourth glass of wine, my words slurred as my tongue sloshed about in the red nectar. "What kind of a name is that anyway? Branch, Branch Longass, formerly Karol." I poured another glass for Rose. "How come you stayed married to the same guy for so long?"

"I didn't. The first one died. He was a no good bum, a real loser. But Tony...aah Tony. Now that was a man but another hard luck Charlie," Rose sighed. "Hey, you forgot Mark the shark. Well at least you didn't come home pregnant this time."

"Talk about losers," I hiccupped.

"Remember that Pocono fiasco? We thought we'd lost you but Julie found you at the piano bar at the Holiday Inn." Rose had a fit of giggles. "We went to see the male strippers but you stuck your nose up at that and went off on your own."

"Ah yes, I remember it well."

"Do you remember Buddy?"

"He was sure young," I sighed.

"Weren't we all?"

Except for the appalling hangover I suffered Saturday, the rest of the weekend was uneventful. Monday morning found me heading over the Koolaus for Honolulu, indifferent but resigned.

Karen greeted me warmly as I walked through the reception area. "Great to have you home."

Annie's Portion

"Thanks, Karen. Give me a few minutes to have my coffee and scan the 'urgent' pile. Then come in and we'll visit."

I glanced through the neatly organized stacks of files. There were the usual new contracts to review, listing agreements to sign, checks to approve and one potentially serious legal matter to consider. Karen and I had no more than ten minutes alone before the parade began. Under the best circumstances Monday was always the busiest day but after a two-week absence the lineup outside my door was intimidating, each of the salespeople needing to have my ear or advice on some "imperative" matter. By noon I needed a break and took Karen to lunch where we had an opportunity to catch up without interruption.

"Gosh, Anne," Karen said when I concluded my tale of love and adventure. "Sounds like you got more than you bargained for. What now?"

"I don't know. But one thing I am sure of...and that is to end this affair with Hank."

"Oh boy! I don't envy you that job."

I heaved a sigh. "What's your story?"

"It's been fairly exciting here. Not business wise but regarding Joe Riley's murder. There's been a public outcry for an investigation into the Ohana. There are some who think they were responsible. Your friend the Mayor, tried to ignore the whole thing but the Governor, under pressure himself, put the heat on."

"Everyone's so damned afraid to make waves. Maybe this will be the impetus for cleaning house."

"And another blockbuster. The trustees of the Honaunau Trust are being sued for misappropriation of funds."

"Let the good times roll." I was delighted to hear t some action was finally being taken to oust the pompous, self-serving trustees. "They've been given free rein far too long. That fund was established for the benefit of the natives, not their pockets. Enough of my pontificating. Let's go deal with our own muddle."

Disappointed there was no message from Colorado on my desk, I listened to several from Hank but it was two days before I accepted his call and arranged to meet him in Pearl City. From the start the encounter was strained. He'd primed himself for what he believed would be a termination notice but was unprepared for the abrupt ending I'd insisted upon.

Unwilling to let go, he persisted, "Annie, you can't just toss me out like an old shoe. Did I mean nothing to you?"

"You know that's not true."

"Then, why? What have I done...or not done? No, don't answer." Hank pressed.

"Hank," I said with quivering voice. "You know how much you mean to me...how wonderful our time together has been. You are my dear friend. But it's time to put an end to a relationship that has nowhere to go."

Trying to control his emotions Hank said thickly, "I'd better leave while I still have some dignity left."

Cruel as it might have been, it was with a great sense of relief I watched him walk away.

The weather matched my mood; a week of gray overcast skies followed by a week of intermittent showers. Despondent, I watched water dripping from eaves and wondered why I'd heard nothing from the man whose last words had been, "I can't bear to lose you. Come back to me."

I thought, "Turnabout is fair play. I dumped Hank and Branch dumped me."

Sarah tried unsuccessfully to pull me out of a persistent slump. "Just think, Annie," she cajoled. "You've got the big Maui race this weekend. Hopefully the weather will improve by then."

Annie's Portion

Sarah was none too pleased by my sailing escapades. Racing practice or day sails always left me a little the worse for wear. Just the past year a July 4th evening sail ended with our boat on a reef within view of the Honolulu city lights. Fortunately, the Coast Guard responded to the SOS by sending a helicopter to lift the revelers from the bounding main.

Sarah would often lament, "Look at you. You're black and blue, battered and bruised and half-drowned. You call that fun?"

Loving it I continued to hone my racing skills by volunteering to crew on the "Belle Dama," the vessel soon departing for Maui.

I nodded without enthusiasm still Sarah persevered. "And we'll soon have Samantha home for Thanksgiving. Won't it be grand to see her?"

"Yes, it will be nice having her home for a while. The house is so quiet without her...and neat too." The factual comment brought a grin to both our faces and lightened the somber mood.

That same day a letter arrived bearing a postmark from Lake Havasu. Eager for any news of the Bar L I tore open the envelope, exposing a short letter and several photos. There was Claire in a hooded parka standing on the bunkhouse steps with Star at her side. Star's tail was blurred and I smiled remembering the ever-wagging appendage. A second photo showed Howard, shovel in hand, standing beside a huge mound of white snow. There were two other pictures, one of the house surrounded by snow-laden trees and lastly a snapshot of Beau at the fence rail against a backdrop of his snow blanketed pasture.

The letter was bright and newsy. A week following my departure there'd been a dusting of snow but the sunlit days of late autumn soon melted the last remnants. Less than a week later, the evening sky turned an ominous slate gray. Snow began falling the next day, lasting thirty-six hours, dropping two feet of dry white powder. The Bar L was officially closed for the season with all hands busy buttoning up the place. Claire decided to stay on through Thanksgiving. Howard made his escape before the second storm by way of the forest road to Meeker where he'd caught a flight to Denver. He was now enjoying the warmth in Lake Havasu and seeing old friends. He had the pictures developed and sent them along with her letter from there. She hoped I had a good trip home and was looking forward to hearing from me. There was no mention of Branch. It was signed, "Your good friend, Claire."

By the time the day of the great race arrived, my enthusiasm had re-emerged and I sped off to meet my mates at the Kaneohe Yacht Club. While still a novice, I'd been introduced to Harrison Manning, a semi-retired surgeon and owner of a sleek racing yacht aptly named the "Belle Dama." Harry, an odd but sociable bachelor, found me interesting and uncommonly competitive—for a woman. He invited me to join his crew. I'd since spent many months polishing my skills on the graceful sloop, participating in practice sessions and competing in a number of inter-island races.

The Captain and crew spent weeks preparing for the pre-Thanksgiving race to Maui, confident of our chances of garnering one of the top three prizes. We convened at the Kaneohe Yacht Club to provision the boat and tend to last minute details. Motoring out through the channel leading to Kaneohe Bay we skirted Coconut Island, home to the Hawaii Institute of Marine Biology. Once past the Marine base and Pyramid Rock sails were hoisted, motor cut and the Belle made way smoothly through a calm sea. The sun dropped behind the Koolaus, turning them pink with its last rays; evening became night, stars appearing at first singly then in recognizable constellations, Orion directly above, the Dippers, the Pleiades, and of course the planet

Annie's Portion

Venus in a sparkling display of reds, greens and blues. We sailed throughout the night, watching the glimmering lights of Kailua, Waimanalo and Sea Life Park. As soon as we made Makapu'u Point our heading changed, the glow from Hawaii Kai signaling a turn westward around Koko Head and Kawanihoa Point.

The crew took turns at the helm, standing watch and catnapping. At first light unmistakable Diamond Head crater appeared. The Belle skirted Waikiki heading north and made port ahead of schedule. The waterway was crowded with dozens of sailing vessels, every one a study in elegant symmetry. They'd come from far-flung homeports and now circled the harbor awaiting a signal from the race officials. Each would be checked in, weighed and handicapped.

I recalled the first time I raced, an untutored novice with no idea of how complex the rules and regulations could be. "How does one weigh a boat?" I'd asked.

Captain Harry had been very patient in explaining the methodology. "The weight of a boat is measured by the water displacement. Because of the different classes of boats entered in the race, a formula is used to level the playing field. The handicap is based on a number of factors including the boat length, the height of the mast, the size of the sails, the keel weight, which is recorded on the boat registry and of course the actual displacement weight. For example, a smaller or lighter boat may be given a time allowance to make up the difference in size. We may get a fifteen minute advantage over Ed Gailey's 'Irish Rover' because we are two feet shorter. It's quite an exact science."

The complex formula was extraordinary. I'd done some racing in Rhode Island but all the boats had been in the same class, eliminating the need for handicapping.

"If you are forced to replace a sail, you must report the change to the stewards and your handicap will be reevaluated. Of course, this is a gentlemen's sport and we rely on the honesty of the competitors."

At times, Harry could be a real pompous snob. "Are the women excused from good-sportsmanship?" I'd teased.

"Now, Annie," he blushed.

We used our waiting time to good advantage, practicing jibes, changing sails, raising and hauling in the spinnaker; a massive, cumbersome sail used only when the wind was astern of the boat. By eleven a.m. we'd been checked in and given our handicap. The Captain moored the Belle at a guest slip in the Marina and took the crew to the Yacht Club for lunch. The Club was packed with racing crews, a very male-dominated society—as well as their ever-present entourages, ladies included. The conversation got louder in direct proportion to the inordinate consumption of the free flowing booze. By three p.m. I'd extricated myself from the tumult and made my way back to the Belle for a well-needed nap.

The five members of our crew spent the night on the boat but Captain Harry went home to his luxury condo on the Ala Wai Canal, just minutes away.

Dawn broke and with it a came a chaotic scramble for position along an imaginary starting line between two steward's tenders. The wind-filled sails of thirty-odd boats, like scudding clouds, obscured the ascending sun and the Honolulu skyline. The shouted orders of Captains were carried on the wind. Crews rushed to comply, hauling in sheets, winching them tighter. Boats crisscrossed one another, narrowly avoiding disastrous collisions while sailors used the vernacular they were so famous for.

At eight the starting gun fired, and one by one the boats were timed as they crossed the nebulous boundary. The Belle was well positioned. Captain Harry, well known for his "give no quarter" mindset had pulled ahead of his toughest competitor, Ed Gailey on the Irish Rover.

"Watch that son of a bitch Gailey," the Captain roared. "He'll try to cover us." Harry was referring to the untenable practice of moving along the windward side of another vessel to block the prevailing wind.

"So much for good sportsmanship," I thought as I tended the starboard jib sheet.

The course was plotted so as to keep the boats on an east southeast heading which would take us close to Molokai. No longer clustered, the armada was spread in a wide arc, each Captain trying to pick up the best wind. The Kaiwi Channel, which we were about to traverse, was one of the roughest bodies of water to navigate. Coursing between the islands of Oahu and Molokai the channel, wide at both ends constricted in the middle, provided the perfect conformation for a venturi effect. The northeasterly trades barreled through, churning the sea into wild, spasmodic waves that attacked the boats from every direction. Only the best seamen or damn fools made that crossing in a sailboat. By the time we sighted the coastline of Molokai, the sun was well over the yardarm and the Irish Rover was out sight.

For most of the trip we'd been on a broad reach, a fairly easy point of sail. Once we passed Laau Point we were in the slot between Molokai and Lanai. There the trade winds became erratic, deflected by the rising slopes of the islands. I had to earn my keep on the run to Lahaina, working the jib sheet as we changed tack a number of times.

Catching sight of several boats, behind and ahead of us, Harry yelled at his crew, "Get the lead out, we're in the home stretch. Move your bloody asses."

We changed course as soon as we passed the little town with the big name, Kaunakakai, bearing south southeast on the last leg of the race. The setting sun sent elongated shadows ahead of the Belle. It would be dark long before we reached the harbor. One by one the running lights of the flotilla were turned on. As the darkness deepened it became more difficult, almost impossible to identify any of the dozen or so boats that accompanied us through the Auau Channel. But at last the finish line—two converging beams of light emanating from two official lighters, one on each side of the channel—was crossed and the time marked by the stewards. For the Belle it had been a twelve-hour, twenty-minute ride. The results of the race would not be confirmed until the last boat crossed the line. Captain Harry order the sails lowered and we motored up to anchor in the Lahaina Roadstead, once a favorite mooring site for the whaling fleets. Here the vessels rafted up, three or four together and the animated sailors hopped from boat to boat —drinking, talking story, drinking, entertaining the visiting wahines and drinking. While the merriment in the Road continued unabated, the crew of the Belle opted for grub and grog and rowed ashore in the dinghy.

The Pioneer Inn was an historic landmark in old town Lahaina, as much an institution as was the more than century-old Banyan tree said to be the largest on any of the islands. Once a gathering and watering spot for whalers, it served the same purpose for modern day voyagers. The honky-tonk piano player could be counted on to give his bawdy rendition of salty ballads while sailor and tourist feasted on burgers big enough to satisfy Paul Bunyan and sucked up beer so cold ice crystals formed on the outside of the glass.

Early, if not quite bright, on Sunday morning the Lahaina Yacht Club was packed tighter than Bobby McGee's disco on a Saturday night. A row of bloody maries stood on the long mahogany bar, disappearing as quickly as the bar tender could replace them. Once again the discordant sounds of shouting, laughing and clinking glasses assailed the ears.

The Commodore, Mack McKenzie took his place behind the small stand that usually served as a menu board. With no way to be heard above the din, he resorted to a loud pull on an air horn. Unbelievably, the mad horde was silenced.

"First I want to thank all the volunteers who served as race officials," he began.

There was loud applause and several off-side comments. Mack attempted to continue with a long-winded explanation of how the results of the race were tallied, as if the seasoned racers knew not.

"Get on with it," came a disembodied voice, answered by a chorus of approval.

"Just the facts, man," more shouting.

Not famous for brevity, Mack finally conceded. "Okay, okay! You want the results?"

A roaring "Yes" provided his answer.

"Here they are," he said dramatically. "In fourth place, with a time of thirteen hours, three minutes...the "Phoenix," followed by loud whooping. "In third place, with a time of twelve hours, forty eight minutes...the "Irish Rover."

Captain Harry looked at his crewmembers with glazed eyes. "No wonder we didn't catch sight of him."

"In second place, with a time of twelve hours, twenty one minutes...the "Belle Dama".

"Oh," I cried with obvious disappointment.

"And the winner with a time of twelve hours, seventeen minutes...the "Calliope".

"Well," said Harry. "At least we beat out that jackass Gailey," he laughed. "Good show men. Good show."

"I can't believe we lost by four lousy minutes." I was brokenhearted.

"Now, Annie. Don't you go playing the 'what if' game. We did exceptionally well. That Calliope is made to race and only beat us by four minutes." He lifted his glass. "Here's to the best damn crew in the islands. What say we spend today and tomorrow here on Maui? The treat's on me."

J. Fran Baird

Our Captain's frugality was well known so his proposal to treat the crew to a stay in Lahaina came as a pleasant surprise. I, like the rest of the crew jumped at the offer.

We watched from the Yacht Club as high-spirited groups of threes and fours departed for their respective crafts to prepare for the return trip. The original fleet, somewhat reduced in number, scattered as boats weighed anchor, slipped their moorings and one by one raised the sails.

"They'll be at the point soon." I commented.

"Yes. Amazing how close Molokai and Maui are once they hit the Pailolo Channel...not more than fifteen miles. Unusual wind too..." Captain Harry agreed.

"I love to watch those great rainbow spinnakers pop open one at a time. It's an awesome sight, never disappoints...nor does Maui."

"Maui no ka oe," Harry sighed.

"Yes," I thought. "Maui is the best. If only Branch could see this paradise he'd know why I find it so hard to leave."

I'd spent many days exploring the island's treasures; visiting the remote town of Hana on the east coast by way of a three-hour drive along a narrow, switch-back route, then beyond the village to Wailua falls and the seven sacred pools carved by wind and water for millennia. Just past the falls a small churchyard had become the final resting place of Charles Lindbergh.

I'd hiked and camped for three days in Haleakala's vast crater; seeing the rare silver swords, the *nene*, Hawaii's protected state bird, bumping heads with a herd of goats in a cloud bank, watching a sky so bright with stars the night was lit by them. I traveled up country to the only vineyards on the islands and dined at the notorious Makawao Steak House where a small steak weighed two pounds and the mud-pie desert could feed six. I never tired of my trips to

Annie's Portion

the Valley Isle. The two extra days would give me a chance to visit some of my favorite spots again.

We set sail early Wednesday morning. Benefiting from brisk trade winds we reached the Kaneohe harbor before sunset.

The moment she heard the car door slam, Sarah pounced on me. "It's a good thing you're finally back. Samantha will be here tomorrow and there are things to be done."

"Yes, I know. We'll get on it right away," I sighed.

"Oh! I almost forgot. You had a call from someone at that ranch. I couldn't make out his name...just ranch I think."

In answer to Branch's inquiry concerning my return, Sarah told him I was long overdue. He had called several times. The phone rang often on Wednesday, every ring resulting in uncertain expectancy. Hoping to hear the slight twang of a Colorado cowboy, I was unable to disguise my disappointment when a caller turned out to be someone other than Branch. I was disinclined to leave the house lest I miss his call but Sarah's persistent reminders about holiday preparations left me no choice. Choosing the turkey and the various accompaniments associated with a Thanksgiving Day feast occupied more than an hour of my time at the market. I hurried home to retrieve my phone messages, which for the most part were from well-meaning, concerned friends. The chimes of the hall clock reminded me of the need to get to the airport in time for Samantha's arrival.

"Mom," I cautioned. "If there's another call from the guy at the ranch, tell him I'll call back as soon as I return. Can you do that for me?"

"Certainly I can," Sarah retorted. "I'm deaf, not stupid."

I gave my mother a hug. "I know that. I'm just anxious to talk to him, and by the way...it's confusing because his name is Branch."

The plane arrived on time depositing its cargo of lively passengers in the bustling terminal. Samantha's five-feet-eight inch frame, crowned by a wreath of red curls was easily discernible in the crowd. I watched my daughter thinking, "My baby is no longer a baby. She's become a lovely young woman."

"Hey, mom," Sam said, grasping me tightly.

"You look wonderful." I placed a fragrant ginger lei over Sam's head.

"Oh, it smells so good. It's so nice to be home."

Thanksgiving usually heralded the onset of the rainy season and the Koolaus were blanketed by heavy, dark clouds. The rain splashed against the windshield as we headed up Like Like. Sam chattered away, describing life at school, the classes and professors and her apartment. This being her second semester, she'd moved out of the dorm and rented an apartment off campus with three other girls.

"Sounds like life is good. But I didn't hear any mention of your social life. No boys?"

"Oh Mom. I don't have time for boys. Most of them are just jerks anyway."

A slight flush appeared on Sammy's cheeks, belying her brusque response.

"Aha," I thought. "Must be a fella in this scenario."

"Look," Sam pointed as we exited the tunnel.

A double rainbow arced across the sky, painting the clouds with its vivid hues.

"Was there ever a place as beautiful as this," Sam said not really expecting an answer.

"No, but Colorado's not bad either."

"Aha," Samantha answered.

I had an inkling she suspected something more than riding in my response but decided to avoid any further discussion by changing the subject. "Your grandmother can't wait to get her hands on you…and her food into you."

"Well, I can't wait to get my chocolate cream pie, but I don't relish, you should pardon the pun, her standing there force feeding me."

"Hey kiddo. I've had my share now it'll be your turn for a few days."

While I was away completing my errands I had no doubt Sarah had been busy in the kitchen with one ear, her good one, alert for the sound of the car. At last her vigilance was rewarded and she dashed out to greet her little *bubeleh*. There was much hugging and kissing accompanied by some joyful tears and the omnipresent, "Are you hungry? I'll fix you something to eat. Look how skinny you're getting."

"Mom," I finally interjected. "Did I get any calls?"

Sarah stopped in mid-sentence. "Oh yes. That ranch fella called again. I told him you went to pick up your daughter and would get back to him when you had time."

"Aha, I was right," was Sam's expected comment.

I heaved a deep sigh of resignation. "Thank you. If you two girls will excuse me, I have a call to make."

Branch answered on the second ring. "Hello. You've reached the Bar L."

"Branch? This is Anne."

"I was hoping you'd call. I've been sitting at this desk for two hours, making an unsuccessful stab at reconciling the accounts."

"Sorry I wasn't able to get back sooner." We made polite conversation for a while, skirting the subject that was most on our minds.

It was Branch who took the initiative. "Annie, I've missed you. The house echoes, the ranch feels sterile, monotonous. When you packed your bag you filled it with all the best this place had to offer. Won't you bring it back?"

"Branch, I've missed you too. Not a day goes by I don't think of you and wish I was with you. But I love this place too. I've made a life for myself here. I'm so torn; I don't know what to do."

"I know you'll be busy with family during the holidays but once they're behind us would you mind if I came to spend some time in your world?"

"Oh, Branch. That would be wonderful. Yes, yes, please come."

"Annie, there's so much I haven't told you. Perhaps we can be more open with one another next time."

"I'd like that."

"You haven't asked about your *mestano*. Forgotten him so soon?"

"You know better than that. I just didn't want you to think my only interest in the Bar L was the horse."

"He misses you as much as I do. The first week you were gone he mooned around that pasture railing for hours. Then he got mad and tried to wreck a few fences. He won't have anything to do with the ranch hands and the only horse he'll allow near him is Samson."

"That's awful. What about you? Will he let you near him or ride him?"

"No riding but he will take an apple from me. Some things don't change."

"I'm sorry, I've got to go. My daughter is here and Mom is sending all kinds of nasty signals my way."

"Yes, I know. I won't keep you. I'll make some reservations and call as soon as I've got them confirmed."

"It's so good to hear your voice. Call soon."

"I will and Annie…"

"Yes?"

"Stay safe."

For four days the housed buzzed with the gay exuberance of youth. Perpetually in motion, half-clad bodies moved

Annie's Portion

about, in the front door and out the back, picking fruit and flowers for leis, playing with the dogs. To Sarah's great pleasure the flip-flops and sandals piled up on the step. Thanksgiving dinner was a smashing success with a dozen guests seated at the large bountiful table. While some lay groaning in mock distress, ukes were pulled out and the strains of Hawaiian music entertained us. Sam's friend Shelly Hanakea, a lithe, stunningly beautiful *hapa-haole* performed the lovely hula for us; her graceful movements of hips, arms and fingers providing a picture of the story the lyrics conveyed. It was well into the evening when the last sated guest said goodnight.

But for the young wahines the night was just beginning. Dressed in colorful blouses and skirts that barely skirted much, they were off to the local Kailua nightspot, a disco of questionable repute. When we finished the clean-up chores, Sarah and I sat on the back deck, Sarah with iced coffee and me with Kalua on the rocks.

"It's really shameful, the way those girls dress. Why my underwear covers more than their clothing does."

Sarah had never quite gotten used to the local style of undress. Bare chests and OP briefs for boys, bikinis for girls were considered appropriate daytime wear. The much improved, more modest evening attire included floral shirts and cut-off jeans for the boys while the girls covered up in halter tops and mini-skirts that revealed very skimpy panties as they writhed and gyrated to the incessant pulsating, earsplitting sounds of the music of the '80s.

"We're in the tropics, Sarah. No need for cover up." I teased in the local vernacular. "But you must admit. They sure look good; slim, long legged, tan. Ah, to be young again."

"I suppose it's a sign of the times. My mother was shocked by the flapper outfits I wore in the twenties."

"Yes, I'm sure. And I remember how you hated the rolled-up jeans and men's shirts I wore."

Sarah nodded. "I hate to admit it but Samantha is growing away from us. Remember what a shy, scrawny, klutzy tomboy she was when we first got here? The waitress showed her the way to the men's room in that place in Texas." Sarah laughed.

"It seems like only yesterday. We got here just a month shy of her tenth birthday."

Chapter XXIV

Claire was a prolific writer. Her detailed letters—more aptly they were like diary pages—kept me informed of all that happened at the ranch during the weeks following my departure. The weather remained clear and cold providing excellent conditions for the hunting parties that continued to occupy the cabins and the help. The Bar L crew had been busy, with little time for reminiscing or idle chatter and the talk of my visit soon abated. Claire was determined to remain silent as she watched Branch become more and more disinterested in daily activities. Unless there was an absolute need for his participation in the hunting expeditions, he remained at the homestead occupying himself with the care and training of his equine companions. Once the last of the hunters departed with their prized trophies and coolers of frozen venison, the hands went about the various tasks required to put the Bar L to sleep for the winter. The stock was relocated, sufficient quantities of feed hauled in, and cabins buttoned up. Shortly thereafter the part-time crew made an exit, leaving Pete, Frank and Branch to enjoy the gratifying quiet that descended on the ranch. It was Claire's usual custom to depart with Howard and the others when they took their leave, but she had decided to stay on to await Thad's arrival. Branch seemed somewhat less than pleased at the change of plans and soon grew weary of Claire's incessant third-degrees, admitting he'd been resisting the temptation to call me. She told him to stuff his pride in his hat and make the call to Hawaii. But it was a particular visit with Beau that provided the impetus which in the end sent him to the phone. With undisguised disappointment he heard I'd gone on a sailing trip and his conversation with Sarah did nothing to improve his disposition.

J. Fran Baird

My call had come the day before Thad returned to the ranch for the Thanksgiving break where, to his surprise, he was welcomed warmly by his usually reticent father. They shared a simple holiday dinner with Claire, Frank and Pete in the main house during which time Frank provided the entertainment with stories of hunting escapades. Thad was especially interested in the striking blonde mustang and Pete described Beau's progress without mention of me. Thad thoroughly enjoyed the evening listening to Frank's effusive commentary and Pete's much more subdued story telling. To her credit, Claire boasted, she kept her mouth buttoned up and when their two guests left she retired leaving Thad and Branch relaxing in front of the grand fireplace, drinks in hand, enjoying the warm glow produced by both. That's not to say she didn't keep an ear on the ensuing conversation between father and son which, in her most recent letter, she went so far as to put in quotes.

She wrote that it was Branch who broke a long silence. "How are things going at school? Are you enjoying classes?"

"Yeh, I sure am. But it's very different learning about stock in a classroom. I kinda miss the action out here."

Branch agreed. "I remember how I felt when Emil insisted I get an education. Seemed so unnecessary at the time."

"Well I've gotta admit, there is a ton of new stuff going on. The lab has become as important to the success of a ranch as the cowboys."

Branch grinned, "Seems to me…"

Thad cut him short. "I know, I know. You told me so. Well Branch, you can't always be wrong." Thad could never quite bring himself to call his father, "Dad." "So what are your plans for vacation this winter?"

"I guess there's no better time. Things have sorta changed."

"Changed how?"

"You know that story Pete was telling...about that mustang?"

"Sure, striking animal. His devil horse."

"Well, there's much more to that story."

Thad later provided Claire with a detailed rendition of "that story."

In a manner much more open than was his wont Branch filled in the blanks, omitting only the most personal stuff, ending with the phone call from me. Thad had never known Branch to express his feelings so unreservedly and was momentarily dumb struck. Instinctively, responding to Branch's emotional disclosure, Thad reached for his father.

With his hands grasping Branch's shoulders he said, "That's great. It's time you had a woman in your life." Then embarrassed by his own display of affection added, "Maybe she'll improve your disposition."

A curtain had been removed from between them and they talked long into the night; about the past and their respective hopes for the future. Thad was full of ideas about improving the stock through artificial insemination and improving the grazing areas with new varieties of grain. His animation and excitement were contagious. Branch seemed better than he had in weeks. In the past there was a sense of relief when the obligatory visits were ended. For the very first time the men were reluctant to say goodbye and when the time came for Thad to leave they parted, both sincerely looking forward to his return.

As before, Claire signed the letter, "Your friend."

Branch finished the story when we finally had a chance to talk to each other instead of to the answering machines. On the first day of Chanukah, the same day Claire returned to Lake Havasu, he was in Aransas, Texas. He'd gone to Austin to see about a horse he was interested in.

I interrupted his narrative. "Went to see a man about a horse, did you? That's sure a very old, lame excuse."

"I'll ignore that," he said. "...but I but detoured, made a brief stop to do some fishing before I returned to the ranch."

He'd been doing a good deal of thinking since Thad's visit. When he called on Saturday, the background noise discouraged conversation but now, hearing my voice he knew the decision to call me was the right one. He told me he missed me and would stay in touch. In the meantime I was to watch for a package.

As usual, the house was full all through the Christmas break. Matt was home on leave, Sarah spent her days at the stove, Sam was getting sunburned, the dogs were adding to the clamor and I was hoping for a break in the noise level. The blessed lull finally came the day after Christmas and the house returned to some semblance of normalcy. In mid-afternoon a package arrived via Express Mail. Excitedly I tore open the envelope not knowing what to expect. But I could never have dreamed of what would be inside; a small box containing a diamond ring, and round trip tickets to Denver. The date of departure was December 27th, the next day. The enclosed note read, "Don't call, be there. I love you. Karol Langerast."

On the 28th of December, after spending a sleepless night of mutual confessions at the Stockmen's Hotel in Denver, Anne Harmon and Karol Longbranch were married by a justice of the peace. Branch told me about his son Thaddeus and Branch learned of my love affair with John. Neither of us revealed nor seemed to care about any additional indiscretions. We spent the two days of our honeymoon seeing Denver, eating in Larimer Square and making love. On Monday morning I flew back to Honolulu, arriving in time to celebrate the traditional Hawaii New Year's eve, replete with the lighting of hundreds of thousands of strings of noisy, smoking firecrackers. The family gathered for a late brunch on New Year's Day.

"Before you all take off today, I have something to tell you." I was about to drop my own bombshell. I left the table and disappeared down the hallway. Sam and Matt exchanged knowing smiles while Sarah just shook her head. I quickly returned and in an exaggerated attempt at dramatics raised my left hand to my head. "Dahlings, I have this dreadful headache."

The light bounced off the beautiful, multifaceted diamond. Sam was the first to acknowledge the shocking revelation. "Oh, what a gorgeous ring! You got engaged?"

"Hey mom. That's cool. Do we know the lucky guy?"

All eyes moved to Sarah. "Another shegitz I suppose."

"Yes, Mom. Another shegitz. But there's more." Defensively, I faced my family. "We were married in Denver."

I was greeted by stony silence. Teary-eyed, Sam ran from the room.

"Wasn't that kinda quick, Mom?" Matt did not wait for a response. "You could have at least clued us in before you left."

"It wasn't planned Matt. It just happened." I was not about to apologize. "I know you will like Branch."

Sarah had seemed not to be listening. "That ranch fella again. You couldn't bring him here to meet us? You're ashamed of us?" She began clearing the table.

Matt kissed my forehead. "Nice ring. Congratulations Mom." He picked up some dishes and walked into the kitchen.

"Mom, I'm sorry I didn't say anything sooner but I really didn't know this was going to happen."

"*Mittnen derrinen*, you take off. A man sends you a ticket and you go. Just like some *kurveh*."

I drew in my breath. "That was a terrible thing to say. I'm no whore, I'm his wife."

"Some wife. He's there and you're here."

I left the room and went to seek solace from my daughter. Sam's door was closed so I tapped lightly. "Samantha. Can I come in?"

"Yes?" came a less than enthusiastic reply.

I entered and sat on the bed next to my baby. "Are you really angry with me? I thought you would understand better than anyone."

"Why would you do such a stupid thing? You have the world by the balls. You have everything you want...career, money, friends. You can have a man anytime you want."

"Honey, listen to me. You're right. I do have all those things but it's not enough. When all of you were home my life was full. I had no time and no reason to commit to one man. But things have changed. You're all out and making lives for yourselves. You know how depressed Grandma has been since you've gone away to school. Well, I feel the emptiness too. I'm fifty years old and the clock won't stand still. I found someone to love, someone wonderful. He's smart and kind and shares so many of my interests. And," I added lightly, "It doesn't hurt one bit that he's got money and looks great on a horse."

Sam sniffled and allowed a grin to crease her face. "I'm sorry. It just came as such a shock."

"To me too. But I'm sure going to need your help with Sarah."

A week went by. Being far removed Josh and Danny though surprised, seemed really happy for their mom. Sarah was relentless in her condemnation of her daughter.

"So now what? You're going to fly back and forth every time 'he' gets an urge?" or "What kind of marriage was it... common law? Very common, I bet." Or again, "Were you so ashamed to show this *trayf,* that you have to hide it?"

Annie's Portion

At the end of my rope, I enlisted Rose's help. "What am I going to do, Rose? I haven't even told her the worst of it... that we're going to leave Hawaii and move to Colorado."

"Well Sarah doesn't have to leave. She can stay with me. I'd love to have her here."

"Oh, Rose. Thanks so much. You have been such a good friend. But that's out of the question. Sarah and I have been together for all our lives. There's no way I would go without her."

"Let's put our brains to work. What is her biggest objection?"

"Everything."

"That's no answer. Let's try to sort it out, one problem at a time."

"He's a *goy...trayf.*"

"English, please."

"A Gentile, not Kosher."

"We sure can't change that. What else?"

"She doesn't believe we are married."

"What about showing her the marriage certificate?"

"A phony, says she."

"You gotta admit, your mother is one tough broad." Rose laughed and poured another glass of wine for each of us. "Next."

"He's a redneck cowboy."

"Where does she get this stuff? Is he?"

"TV. And no, he's not. He's sure a cowboy but not the way she means. He's educated, cultured, sensitive and good fun."

"Good looking? That would certainly be in his favor."

I smiled thinking of Sarah's flirtatious ways, even at eighty. "Yes. He has very rugged good looks. But then they say love is blind."

"Hmm. There sure is plenty to work on."

J. Fran Baird

We sat in quiet contemplation for a long while. From time to time, Rose would mumble something unintelligible. With eyes closed I rested my head on the back of the couch.

"By George, I've got it! Tom. Annie, it's Tom."

"Rose, I think you've gone off the deep end. What's Tom?"

"Tom Farrell is what. He's the answer."

I'd learned during the Israel trip that Tom, who officiated at Sunday services at a Waikiki hotel, had a great love for everything Jewish. He'd spent several years at seminary in St. Louis studying the Hebraic language, lore and traditions. He went on to obtain a doctorate in Hebrew bible studies and spent many years in Israel learning everything about the country and the people. Every vacation he took was spent in Israel and he hoped some day to retire there.

I bolted upright. "Oh, Rose, you're a wonder. Of course Tom's the answer."

"Ha Ha! He can't make Sarah like Branch but he sure can do the rest."

"Uh oh. Forgot about Branch. How do I convince him?"

"The way women have been convincing men ever since Eve tempted Adam."

We were delighted with the solution and spent the rest of the night celebrating our brilliance until deliriously drunk, we passed out.

It had taken all my copious selling techniques, much cajoling and many seductive promises to finally secure Branch's reluctant acquiescence.

"The things I do for you, Annie my girl. I'm really much too old to start living with a Jewish mother-in-law."

"You will love her. And just wait till you taste her matzo ball soup and *ruglach*. So when?"

"I've got to stay here through the end of the stock show. That's on Saturday the twelfth. If I can get a flight out of Stapleton that afternoon, will that work?"

"Perfect, just perfect. Then we'll make our plans for Sunday."

"You're not going to make me wear one of those funny little hats. I draw the line there."

I was absolutely giddy with happiness. "No not that. But you will have to practice breaking the glass."

"What glass?" Branch responded with mock terror.

"I'll send you all the info. I love you, you marvelous phony. Stay safe."

"You too."

"One down, the hardest one to go."

Rose and I had already met with Tom who'd been only too delighted to join forces with us in convincing Sarah. Tom had been a guest at our home on many occasions and had frequently given the blessing before the meal. Sarah was very fond of him and often spoke about his thoughtfulness in leaving "all that 'Jesus' stuff out".

And so we three conspirators plotted and planned and presented the finished product after an amicable dinner at the Kailua Steak House. Upon our return to the house Tom took Sarah's arm and led her to the rear deck while Rose and I secreted ourselves at the most advantageous eavesdropping location.

"Sarah, we have a serious matter to discuss with you," Tom said quietly. "Please be patient and hear me out before you reply."

I could imagine my mother's thoughts at that moment. "Oh these three are up to something. I'm not going to like it one bit." But she just nodded and said nothing.

It was a lovely evening and for a few moments they sat quietly enjoying the clear starlit night and fragrant scents of the garden.

"Anne and Sarah will miss this more than they know," Tom muttered. "Sarah, you're much too smart not to know what we're about tonight."

Getting no response, he continued, "Things have changed and you will have to make some concessions too... as you have done so many times. Annie is in love and is entitled to her happiness but she can't be happy if you are not. We have come up with a way that is a compromise to be sure, but one I believe you can live with."

He spent the next hour describing the program and answering Sarah's many questions. In the end she agreed, albeit grudgingly.

Karen had been informed of the marriage my first day back in the office. She typed up my notice and resignation and assured me she'd keep things confidential until I was ready for the rest of the staff and agents to get the news. Karen was stunned but happy for her boss. Many calls were exchanged between the head office and the Honolulu office. I agreed to stay through the end of March. That would give Hal Gilmore time to find another manager and me time to provide some training. It would also give me time to sell the Kailua house and my boat. I was unwilling to sell the north shore place and not the least bit anxious to move to Cutter Lake while snow was still on the ground. The thought of all I still had to do was almost overwhelming but Branch would soon arrive and that expectation buoyed me.

As promised, he arrived on the twelfth and to my surprise and delight, Thad was with him. Fortunately, I'd stopped in Chinatown on my way to the airport to pick up several leis, which I draped over the heads of the two men.

"This is a wonderful tradition, but where are the hula dancers?" Thad grinned.

"Thad, I'm so happy to have you here."

"Branch brought me along to provide moral support. Are you sure you want this grumpy old man?"

Annie's Portion

"Too late, Thad. It's already a done deal." I steered them to the Wiki Wiki bus and the baggage claim area.

"Do you realize its winter in Colorado?" Thad was embraced by the warm, moist air and the ever-present fragrance of tropical forests.

"For the next week I don't want to hear about Colorado winters. And you two will have the chance to bask in the Hawaii sun."

I chose the route home through the Like Like tunnel knowing the effect the drive would have on my visitors. Always a treat for the eyes, the view of the Koolau waterfalls, verdant slopes and sparkling bay elicited the expected reactions. Once in Kailua town, I drove to the unpretentious Kahili Palms Motel where Branch and Thad were registered. Though not on the beach the motel, which had seen better days did provide a certain amount of tropical ambiance. It flaunted a mini-man-made lagoon bedecked by flowering plants and waving palm trees.

"Sorry this is not the Moanakea Beach Resort but it's Kailua's best," I said. "If you two are prepared to face the matriarch and her entourage, we should get going." I drove back through town, stopping at the notorious Kailua light in time to hear the culmination of the myna bird chatter. The last vestige of daylight disappeared as we turned into the driveway.

Josh and Wendy arrived with Danny and Linda on Wednesday. Matt managed a three-day pass and arrived in the wee hours on Sunday. The telltale sandals and flip-flops decorated the front step. Branch and Thad had only a second to take note of them before encountering what could only have been described as pandemonium. Food was in various stages of preparation with the boys out back grillin' and chillin'. Wendy and Sam were on the floor, stringing leis amid baskets of flowers and Sarah was in the kitchen putting last minute touches to salads and side dishes, while

Linda offered much unwanted advice as she prepared drinks. As usual the dogs provided the chorus that accompanied "the Eagles" in their attempt to destroy any remains of one's eardrums.

I turned to my guests and bowing low before them said, "Welcome to my humble home."

Introductions were made all around but all eyes were on Sarah as she reluctantly took the hand Branch offered her.

"It's good to meet you, Sarah. I hope we will become friends." Branch turned on all his rugged charm as he placed his other hand over hers. His voice was strong, his smile warm as he continued. "After all, we both love Annie."

Sarah was not about to be smooth-talked but was obviously less inclined to dislike this "cowboy" than she'd previously been.

The Harmon household rose early on Sunday and final preparations were made for the big event. The living room was cleared to provide a large open space, at the end of which stood a narrow table covered with a white cloth. White tapers sat in two brass candlesticks at one side of the table. A tall glass vase filled with ginger, anthuriums and orchids graced the opposite end. A wine flask, glass and linen napkin sat dramatically in the center. The rest of the room had been decorated with strings of maile and pikake, scenting the air with their perfume. Having breakfasted with Branch and Thad at the motel, Tom arrived to make his own preparations. He laid a white prayer book on the table and reviewed his notes before sitting down to chat with me and Sarah. By one-thirty several guests had arrived. Karen and Ariana made the trip from Honolulu, picking Rose up on the way. Following Tom's instructions Ariana had created a work of art, which she proudly presented to him. At two o'clock Branch and Thad arrived and Tom called the group to order. At his signal, Matt turned on the tape deck and the lovely strains of the Hawaiian wedding song filled the room. Samantha entered from the hallway. Dressed in pale yellow, carrying a lighted candle, she walked slowly to the table where Tom now stood, wearing a prayer shawl and white skullcap. Samantha lit the two candles from hers as Tom recited the Hebrew blessing. She stood to the side, allowing Branch to approach the altar where she placed a traditional groom's maile lei around his neck. Nervously, he turned to watch his bride enter the room. I wore a simple white embroidered dress and a wreath of flowers, a haiku lei, on my head. When I reached him, Branch took my hand and we turned to face Tom.

Tom was in his element. He had been rehearsing for days and now performed the traditional Jewish wedding ceremony flawlessly. Branch and I exchanged rings. Tom poured the wine into the glass, which he presented first to the bride and then the groom. Each in turn took a sip. He wrapped the glass in the linen and laid it on the floor in front of Branch. There was an audible intake of breath before Branch's foot came down heavily on the glass. The sound of the shattering glass gave rise to a communal, "*Mazeltov*". Branch looked questioningly at me.

"It means 'good luck'"

Tom unrolled the scroll Ariana had brought with her. "This is your marriage contract, a *Katuba*", he said. "Once you both sign it and I endorse it, you're stuck with each other."

Branch signed first, I followed suit and finally Tom confirmed our signatures with his own.

"I now pronounce you man and wife."

There were cheers and congratulations all around. Of course, Tom had no more authority to perform that ceremony than the man in the moon, but it satisfied Sarah who now indicated her acceptance by dispensing with the term "him" or "he" whenever she referred to Branch.

J. Fran Baird

A wedding luncheon was held at Byron's Two in downtown Kailua, after which the bride went home with her mother and the groom went back to the Kahili Palms with his son.

The next two days were spent days touring the island with my husband. My stepson spent the time sightseeing with Samantha and all four of us enjoyed a two-day trip to Maui, after which husband and stepson returned to Colorado, followed shortly thereafter by my daughter.

The first week in April, Sarah and I bid tearful farewells to our many friends and departed the beautiful islands we had called home for nearly ten years. Smothered in leis, we caught a last glimpse of Oahu as the plane lifted into the blue sky and turned eastward. We spent that night at an airport hotel in San Francisco and had dinner in a somewhat less than elegant restaurant offering mediocre food at exorbitant prices.

"I guess this will be our last mother-daughter night out for a long time," I said sadly.

"It's not the Royal Hawaiian," Sarah agreed.

Conversation was strained and it was with tacit relief we returned to our room and the silent comfort of our beds. Morning was to bring with it one more in the series of uncertainties mother and daughter had yet to confront.

Knowing it would be late spring ere winter would loosen its grip on the Colorado foothills, Branch suggested it might be better if Sarah waited for warm weather before being introduced to her new home. Josh and Wendy invited her to visit them in Florida and stay as long as she liked.

"You'll love it here, Gram. It's warm, there's lots to do and we have great Jewish delis," Josh coaxed.

"I'll come," Sarah conceded. "But only because Wendy is my *yidisha* daughter."

Of all the children, Wendy was the only one to observe the Jewish holidays; cook special foods just as Sarah had taught and insist Josh attend High Holy Day services. Now, overcome by feelings of guilt, I would see Sarah boarded on the flight to West Palm Beach before I headed for Denver.

Chapter XXV

Branch came to collect his bride at the modest Meeker airstrip, returning to the ranch by way of the more traversable Forest Service road. April at Cutter Lake was cold, with snow still blanketing the hills and meadows. Wisps of gray smoke rose from the chimneys of the two main buildings. Branch followed the rutted track that ran from the gate to the bunkhouse and brought the truck to a stop. A young mestizo hurried to greet us.

He lifted his hat, exposing a head covered by an unruly mass of black curls. "Bienvenida, Señora Branch." His broad smile revealed his gleaming white teeth. "I am Ernesto."

"Annie, please meet the aptly named Ernesto. He is one of our new hands." Branch offered a further explanation as he helped me from the car. "He is somehow related to Fabian."

I extended my hand. "Hello, Ernesto. It's so nice to meet you." As an aside I whispered to Branch, "Fabian certainly has a lot of relatives."

Ernesto was already pulling bags out of the truck. "We chave already muchos paquetes en la estancia."

For the past few months, I'd been shipping cartons of clothing, books and mementos that I absolutely could not part with. "Muchas gracias, Ernesto."

He smiled once more and hurried with his load to the house.

"I guess, I have to carry you over the threshold." My feet had been slowly sinking into the muck. With feigned groans Branch lifted me and carried me up the steps, depositing me, mud and all, in the entry hall. Through the archway I could see the golden sunlight as it reached into the living room through the skylights, transforming minute

Annie's Portion

particles of dust into shimmering specks. A fire blazed in the hearth.

"I'd almost forgotten how wonderful this place is."

"You're home now, Annie."

Beau had been set out in one of the sheltered pastures with several young stallions. It was to be two more days before I would see my other love. It had taken Pete and Frank that long to catch him and bring him back to the pen.

"It's been so long. Maybe he won't remember me," I confided to Branch.

"Just remember to bring him an apple."

Dubiously, I approached the pen. Beau was restlessly making his way around the perimeter. He came to a sudden stop and sniffed the air through flared nostrils. My whistle was answered by a whinny as Beau reared and tossed his flowing mane. I hurried to the fence.

"You do remember me." My elation was undisguised as I entered the pen. Beau hesitated not a minute, quickly moving to the gate where I stood waiting. He lowered his head, placing it on my shoulder, nuzzling me. Tears streaming down my cheeks, I hugged him and stroked his neck. In another minute I'd grabbed a handful of mane, and using a fence rail hoisted myself onto his back, allowing him to take me where he would. His choice was the high pasture, where the snow was sent flying by his dancing feet. Branch and Jessie caught up with us just as I was about to turn Beau in the direction of the house.

"Still think he wouldn't remember you?"

"I didn't even have to bribe him." We laughed thinking of the apples and carrots.

Those times brought me greater happiness than I'd ever thought possible. There was no aspect of my new life that disappointed. Each day brought Branch and me closer together as we revealed more of ourselves, discovering in the process a passion and intensity of feeling neither of us had ever known.

Our pleasure was greatly enhanced by the friendship that was developing between our children. Samantha and Thad spent a week of their Easter break at the ranch. Our quartet rode every day, shared cooking chores and spent evenings in front of the huge fireplace, sipping wine and talking story." By the time the young pair left, spring had come to mountains. The snowcaps were retreating, buds had appeared on the aspens and green shoots forced their way through the thawing ground. The cowhands were returning to the ranch and were kept busy checking and making repairs to equipment, which needed constant looking after. Nearly a thousand acres were planted in alfalfa and oats. Long past were the days when the herds roamed the unfettered range. Now the land was sectioned into summer and winter feeding grounds and cattle often attempted to jump the fences to get to greener pastures. Work parties went out early each morning to inspect and mend fences and scout the herds of cattle and horses.

With no cook in formal residence, mealtimes were haphazard affairs. Branch and I usually had breakfast and supper at the house while Ernesto did preparation and cleanup chores at the bunkhouse. Each morning I saddled Beau and rode off to explore the mountain's marvels, experiencing the sheer joy of riding through the early morning haze, inhaling the clean, fresh air. The days warmed, each one bringing with it additions to the vast display of indigenous flora. I watched the miracle of purple crocuses pushing through the last remnants of winter snow. Columbine, in various shades of blue dotted the landscape. I reveled in the feel of the horse under me as I rode up a steep trail through the pinion pine and sage, the only sound the muffled beat of the horse's hooves. We wandered far from the ranch, I confident in the knowledge that Beau could always find his way back.

Annie's Portion

By early May all hands were accounted for and a call went out to Claire who arrived soon thereafter, Howard and Star in tow.

Branch was all smiles as he lifted his surrogate mother off her feet. "Well you old reprobate, are you finally satisfied? I took your advice and now look what happened."

Claire was unrestrained in her approval as she hugged me fiercely. "First time ya did and best thing you ever did. Annie, ya wonderful, clever girl. Ya made him chase ya till ya caught him." She did not disappoint but let out her now familiar cackle.

Star nipped at my ankles, vying for attention, her rapidly moving tail raising small dust devils.

Activity at the ranch went into full swing as the wranglers prepared for the imminent roundup. It was time to gather the herds from winter habitats, horses first, then cattle. Branch agreed to let me tag along providing I rode one of the savvy cow ponies and left Beau at home.

"He will never be a cow pony, Annie. Smart as he is, he's still a wild stallion and can only be trouble on the trail," he cautioned. "There's no arguing on this issue. Beau stays home or you both do."

So it was on a pinto named Checkers I participated in my first roundup. I was surprised to learn how well the stock adapted to the cold winters on the open range. The horses grew long coats and stored layers of fat below their skin providing excellent insulation. As an additional safeguard a number of shelters were strategically located to protect the equines. Several wells, pumped by windmills insured a good supply of water for all the stock and an innovative method, suggested by Thad, kept the water in the troughs from freezing by use of solar powered heaters.

Old hands at tracking the herds, Pete and Fabian seemed to know just where to find the horses. Following a trail of trampled ground and ruptured brush the cowboys made their way to the top of a rise some distance from the ranch. From this vantage point they were able to see many miles in several directions. It didn't take long to spot one band of more than fifty horses grazing in a large meadow stretched between two hills, the conformation of which formed a natural bowl with an opening at one end.

"Kinda made it easy fer us," Pete said.

"Maybe, but they're not going to be anxious to go to work again." Branch had a tight rein on Jessie. Her flanks quivering, she was raring to go. "Annie, you stay here. You'll be able to watch the whole show and I won't be distracted by having to baby-sit you."

"You are a stinker. Didn't you put me on this seasoned animal so I could join the party?"

"This will not be a party. As soon as those horses get our scent they'll make a dash for the only exit and I don't want you in their way. You can rejoin us once we have them under control. I want your promise."

I was forced to agree, discretion the better part of valor, and tied Checkers securely to a pine tree. From my mandatory sanctum I was able to follow the men as they slowly snaked their way down the trail. The herd continued to graze contentedly on new green shoots. One of the horses lifted his head and turned toward the men now nearing the floor of the valley. With a shrill whinny he sped towards the opening immediately followed by the rest of the herd. The group of men separated in an attempt to head off the stampede. With ropes flying and a good deal of shouting the drovers moved the horses in the direction of the ranch. At every attempt by the leader to make an escape one of the hands would be there to cut him off. When it appeared the herd was under control, I re-joined the men for the drive back to the corral.

As it turned out, there were three separate bands requiring two tiring days of riding to get all the horses corralled. Branch allowed me to take part in rounding up the last and smallest group of mostly saddle-broken horses.

"No wonder you love this life," I said to Branch as we relaxed in front of the grand fireplace. "Watching that big stallion lead that herd and circling round it to get them all in line was the thrill of a lifetime...even better than sailing."

"Even better than me?" Branch quipped.

"Dahling, nothing is better than you."

"Tomorrow you're going to see why these animals are such a valuable asset to the cowman. They're easy to handle and quick to start and their mild temperament is very suitable for handling cattle under various conditions. They have a keen cow sense. You'll see some real horsemanship as each man chooses the ponies that will make up his remuda."

Branch explained the term "remuda," was used to describe either a band of saddle horses or the string of horses each of the cowhands would claim for his own use for the duration of the roundup.

"Rounding up cattle is a tiring job for the cowhand and especially for the cow ponies that do most of the work. So each man will need a fresh horse from time to time."

"How do they choose their horses?" I was getting a hands-on education in cattle ranching.

"Each man in turn picks one horse. Then he has to get in the corral, rope it, saddle it and ride it. The process goes on until each of the men has ten or so horses in his remuda. It's lots of fun watching the process. Sort of a mini-rodeo."

I was not disappointed in the show. The horses were smart. Having been out on the range all winter they were not about to capitulate without a fight. The more seasoned the horse the tougher to get a rope and saddle on. Those who managed to stay out of the lariat's loop or throw the rider were allowed to go out to the range once again. If additional horses were needed they would be returned to the corral where they had to be broken anew. Most of the cow ponies were the product of the union between the early Spanish horses, themselves bred from Arabian, Berber and Andalusian stock and the wild mustangs. They were smaller, faster and much more agile than the Quarter Horses. Each of the men had favorites and Branch was no different. He made his selections with care and apparent skill, riding each in turn. I watched with pride as my man went about the business of assembling his remuda. It was several days before all the vaqueros had selected their strings and the actual cattle roundup began.

The cowhands were saddled and ready to ride by sun-up, each with his string of cow ponies. Once more riding Checkers, I joined Branch on Jessie as we trotted our mounts ahead of the others. Sandy brought up the rear with the chuck wagon and Branch's remuda. We split into two groups and by mid morning much of the stock, which had had been sheltered in the many brush-filled canyons and draws were located. Finding the cattle was the easy part. Scouring them from the thickets and brush and driving them towards the corrals was something else. Each cowhand gathered his own bunch and kept it moving swiftly, driving it toward the main herd. This was less dangerous than driving the horses but much more tedious. As the cattle moved forward the riders were constantly obliged to leave the main body, which was strung out for almost a mile, to snare the strays. By four p.m. they'd rounded up about a hundred and fifty head and confined them in a box canyon with a narrow creek running through it. With water close by the herd was content to munch on mesquite beans, which when ripe were an excellent source of protein and sugars and a favorite of the cattle and horses.

"Get yerselves ready to chow down," Sandy called to the saddle weary drovers. The men removed the saddles from their equally tired ponies and by hobbling them, enabled them to graze and drink without straying too far.

Annie's Portion

I'd stayed with the chuck wagon throughout the day but was as sore as if I too had been driving steers.

"Still think this is such a glamorous lifestyle?" Branch asked as we sat eating beans, bacon and biscuits.

"Yes, I really do but I have sure gained a greater appreciation of how hard it really is. It's amazing how little verbal communication there is between the men. Yet they all seem to know exactly what has to be done."

"These guys are good. With the exception of a few new hands, they've all worked together for years. And the cattle are fairly predictable. They usually stay together in bunches with one leader, as long as things stay quiet and we don't get too much fuss from the new, or as we say, unbroke ones."

With cleanup completed, I enjoyed listening to the muted conversation of the tired men as the sun dropped behind the canyon wall. Two men were posted to take the first watch while satisfied with a job well done the cowboys undid their bedrolls, and using their saddles for pillows were soon dead asleep. I curled up next to Branch and despite the chorus of snoring men, lowing cattle and a howl or two from a lonesome coyote; with my scratchy, warm blanket wrapped tightly about me, dropped into a deep sleep.

Dawn broke all too soon, the heat generated by the rising sun producing an eerie mist along the creek bed. And with it came another ration of the three B's and hot, strong coffee. The early morning chill seemed to stimulate the steers who needed little prodding and took off at a run with cowhands in hot pursuit. Again, I remained with the chuck wagon listening to Sandy's endless but often entertaining tales of the west as the routine of the prior day was repeated. It was late afternoon when we reached the corrals and it was Claire's turn to ring the dinner bell and call us in for the best meal we'd eaten in days.

J. Fran Baird

Back in our own nest we newlyweds showered, sipped Irish coffee and fell asleep on the big, aromatic leather sofa.

I was angry with myself for having overslept the next morning. It was sure to be another exciting day, one in which the cattle were to be culled and branded. I hurried to join my husband at the cutting corral.

"You're just in time to see the exhibition. The cutting horses will do most of the work. The men just go along for the ride. Watch Pete and Baldy's performance."

Unlike the previous night, when the herd was untroubled and grazed easily in the canyon, the animals were now nervously crowded together in the corral. It was going to be up to the vaqueros to cut a selected animal from the assemblage of bulls, heifers and calves. I watched in awe as Pete edged his horse into the midst of the crowd. The animals began to circle in the pen as Baldy headed ever so slowly toward a white-faced calf. Trying to separate mother and baby was sure to be a hazardous event. With just the slightest movement of his hand Pete had somehow communicated to Baldy, the calf he wanted and Baldy went to work. The cow eyed the horse with obvious suspicion as he closed in on her. Before she had a chance to move her calf out of harm's way, Baldy had come between them. Every effort the cow made to move her calf back into the bunch was stymied by the horse. He seemed to anticipate her every move and with lightning agility headed her off. Pete had loosed the reins and seemed to become one with his pony. It was like watching a ballet. Suddenly, with one final thrust, Baldy bore down on the calf driving it toward the gate opened by one of the hands. Moments later Baldy had another calf in his sights and went at it with equal precision.

Each of the wranglers in turn tested his own and his favorite pony's skills in the corral and though all carried out

Annie's Portion

their tasks wonderfully well, none impressed me as much as Pete and Baldy. In the adjacent corral, Frank was adding mesquite to a heap of smoldering embers. The fire came to life and burned with an intense fury for several minutes until reduced to glowing coals when the branding irons were placed deep inside the pyre.

As each calf dashed into the second enclosure a cowboy threw a rope on it. The calf was wrested to the ground, held down and in a matter of seconds vaccinated, tagged and branded. If of the male gender it was also de-horned and castrated before allowing the calf to return to its frantic mother.

I viewed the scene with growing antipathy and thought, "It almost encourages one to become a vegetarian."

Branding process completed, the herd was further sorted by age, gender and apparent health. A meticulous record was maintained of each animal until the time of its final disposition. No longer productive, cows over the age of five, old bulls and lame animals would go off to the trader. Steers who had reached three to four-hundred pounds would be sent to the stockyards for further fattening before going to the slaughterhouse. Young animals were returned to the range.

Once they'd processed the first drove the cowhands departed to search for cattle that wandered further afield. They returned after four days of grueling effort, with an additional ninety head and the process of culling and branding was repeated.

I absented myself from the repeat performance, preferring instead long rides with Beau through the increasingly verdant countryside. By the end of May the roundup was over and preparations were begun to ready the cabins and otherwise provide for guests, the first of whom would arrive by the end of June. I decided the time was right to send for Sarah.

Chapter XXVI

Branch arranged for Dale Bennett to meet Sarah at Stapleton Airport and fly her to Meeker. Tall, charming and debonair, Dale was an irresistible scoundrel whose charms could convert a die-hard man-hater to a willing playmate.

"From what you've told me of Sarah's flirtatious ways, Dale is the perfect choice to escort her. She will love him instantly." Branch was in great good humor thinking of the meeting.

"I hope you're right. We need all the help we can get to soften her up," I agreed.

So another plot was hatched to win Sarah's seal of approval and Dale was at the gate to greet her with a dozen red roses. He was exceptionally groomed for the occasion in pilot's garb, with his cap perched rakishly on his head.

"I thought you must be Sarah," he said with a bright smile in a well-tanned face. "But I expected someone much older."

"And I suppose you're that Dale fella sent to soften me up." Sarah used her gruffest tone but was in reality, quite pleased with her escort.

They collected her luggage and Dale directed her to the small plane parked on the tarmac.

"You don't expect me to fly in that thing." Sarah was dismayed.

"Why Sarah, I heard you rode the tram to Mad Mountain. You certainly can't be afraid of this baby. Just wait till you see the world from here," Dale coaxed.

Although she had several moments of near panic, Sarah thoroughly enjoyed the flight. The azure sky, the color of which was intensified by an occasional puff of white cloud, was the perfect backdrop for the snowcapped Rockies. Once over the mountains, the Otter's lower altitude offered a detailed view of ski resorts, now devoid of snow and covered with a verdant carpet. Canyons, creeks and meadows were easily discernible in the clear, crisp air.

"This is absolutely beautiful, Dale. I'm so glad you came for me." Sarah was literally in seventh heaven.

We waited anxiously for the arrival of the small plane at the Meeker airstrip. As Sarah disembarked it became obvious to me that Branch's decision to send Dale was divinely inspired and executed with equal brilliance. Sarah, carrying her bouquet of roses, held her escort's arm tightly. She was all smiles and released Dale's arm with a certain amount of reluctance. There were hugs all around and an exchange of winks between the men. Sarah even called Branch by his name and gave him a peck on the cheek. It hadn't taken much coaxing to get the whole scoop from Dale. He was delighted with his performance.

"It's going to be okay," I thought. And to everyone's great relief, it was.

Life on the ranch assumed a comfortable rhythm. Claire and Sarah hit it off immediately and Sarah could often be found peeling potatoes, rolling out biscuit dough or slicing apples for Claire's famous pies. She had begun to feel useful once more and thought of the cowhands as her new family.

"This is terrific," she confided to Claire. "All these wonderful boys around and I don't have to do their laundry."

Summer came and the vaqueros moved the herds to the higher government range. On one occasion Branch returned from the high ground with a ranger who took supper with us at the house.

"Annie, Sarah...this is Will Harriman." Branch expanded on the introduction. "I want you to be real nice to him because he monitors our lease agreement with the Great White Father."

Will laughed and extended his hand first to Sarah and then to Anne. "Nice to meet you."

It was apparent he was shy and a little intimidated by the female company. I tried to put him at ease.

"I'm so glad Branch brought you back here. I'm very interested in this business and you must know how reluctant Branch is to talk about anything."

"Well, I've known Branch a long time and the one sure thing I've learned is that silence is not his specialty." Will seemed to relax.

Branch passed a platter of roast beef to his guest. "Right from the Bar L and you'll never find better. You just pay no mind to Annie and enjoy your dinner. We can chatter all we want over coffee."

We made small talk around the table, Sarah relating some stories of her early days in New York; me describing life in Hawaii and Will divulging his passion for preserving the environment. Once the table was cleared we carried our coffee mugs to the big room and took seats near the fireplace.

"This sure is a great place," Will sighed as he made himself comfortable in one of the leather chairs. "You and your dad must have worked like beavers for years to build the house. It's nice that you now have Annie and Sarah to share it with you."

"Oh, I don't know. Seems to me I used to be the boss but now I've got to take orders from two tough New Yorkers." Branch poured some brandy into his cup and offered a shot to Will. "No need to worry about driving home tonight."

"Annie," Will looked in my direction. "He sure is smooth. Doin' all he can to butter me up."

"Yes," I agreed. "I know exactly what you mean. But now you have to sing for your supper. Tell me about these grazing rights. I always thought National Forests were protected."

Annie's Portion

"Like most people, Annie, I think you confuse National Forests with National Parks. The parks are totally protected. No logging, no mining, no grazing or otherwise destroying the natural habitat. But the forests under government management are open to certain industry. Contracts are awarded to lumber companies or mining enterprises and large tracts of land are open to ranchers for grazing. I'm not real happy about the lumber companies; they pay too little, take too much, and it's the government who pays for construction of the roads they use. And the mines wreak havoc on the environment but grazing is a different story. While I believe the ranchers don't pay enough either ..."

There was a discernible "harrumph" from Branch which Will disregarded.

"But once ranchers began to put up fences, mostly to mark their territory and maybe prevent rustling, it was necessary to provide open ranges to guarantee the availability of forage and sources of water."

Branch interrupted, "It must have been something he ate, Annie. I never heard him do more than count."

A hint of red crept into Will's cheeks. "I'm sorry. I do seem to be talking too much."

"Ignore that old bear," Sarah added. "He's just used to being the center of attention. You go right on with your story."

"Sure," Branch goaded. "Don't let me stop you. Tell em how you shrunk our herds, fenced off the range, and make us pay to rent it back."

I was dismayed by my husband's attack on our guest but Will just grinned.

"Don't pay him no mind, Annie. He's just sore because I make him keep such detailed records."

"It's obvious you two share some secret so now let us in on it. What actually happens?" I insisted.

J. Fran Baird

"I'm sure you know that in addition to the parks and forests, the government set aside huge tracts of land for the public good. Well, the ranchers screamed their heads off." He bent towards me and whispered conspiratorially, "and rightly so." Assuming his relaxed position Will continued, "And used their political savvy...and dollars...to get Congress to enact a law establishing an agency under the direction of the Department of the Interior which would provide for the leasing of public lands for livestock grazing."

Unwilling to be overshadowed Branch interjected, "The Taylor Grazing Act of 1934, followed thereafter by more governmental incompetence that combined the Grazing Service with the General Land Office to form the Bureau of Land Management in 1946." Now on a roll, he asked Will, "And was that enough?"

Will knew he was not expected to reply and contentedly took a sip of his spiked coffee.

Branch went on, "Certainly not. In 1976, those bureaucratic bunglers enacted the Federal Land Policy and Management Act...and you know what to expect from anything that includes the words, 'Federal' and 'management.'"

The warmth of the fire and the healthy shot of brandy were having a visible effect on Will.

"Was that good or bad, Will?" I asked. Turning to Branch I dispatched a disapproving message but he just grinned back at me.

"It was very good, Annie. For the first time there was a comprehensive mandate to retain and manage public lands for the public good."

"So how did these lands end up in the control of people like Branch?" I realized that the two men were enjoying the repartee.

Annie's Portion

"It's really good to have the land put to use and the leases bring in a few dollars that help fund the Bureau. However, I restate my earlier remark that it is by no means enough."

"Not enough!" Branch leaned toward Will. "First you make me pay for a permit. Then I have to put up with your company for hours while you count my cows and tell me how much more I have to pony up."

"I've got to keep you honest," Will replied.

"Honest, the man says. He takes every last pound of flesh and greedily scrutinizes my records, silently analyzing the bottom line to see if there is some way to get the bones. Then to add insult to injury he critiques me about my operation and makes recommendations. As if I needed any advice from a greenhorn." Branch took a breath. "But does he share in the losses? Ha! Now that's a dumb question, isn't it?"

"Enough, you two. I think I get the picture. Thanks Will. I thought I could escape Branch's longwinded explanation but I see how unrealistic that is."

"Thank you for the wonderful dinner and the good company." Will stood and prepared to make an exit.

"C'mon, Will," Branch said placing his arm on Will's shoulder. "I'll get a flashlight," he smiled in my direction, "and see you to the bunkhouse."

Pete, Frank and Fabian now spent most of their days on the range and I only got to visit with them at supper time. I missed having my favorite cowboys around. The other hands were busy as well, with vacationers who kept the cabins full. But I could always count on Sandy for a story or two and often joined him taking trail rides with the guests. Beau learned to mind his manners around the saddle horses but as Branch had warned me, he never did become a cow pony. He was somewhat restrainable when herding cattle but could not be trusted to behave when allowed to join any of the range horses. If let loose he'd instinctively search out a harem and battle another stallion for dominance of the herd. I was the only one who had any real control over him and even I could not rein him in when he exhibited all the characteristics of the wild mustang. Most of the cowboys gave him plenty of room and the name "El Diablo" stuck.

The summer flew by. Samantha had a summer internship with the Fort Collins Journal, a publication that printed a weekend edition. Her days off were few and irregular but Thad, who was taking summer classes, somehow managed to arrive at the ranch on those same days. Samantha made one of the upstairs rooms of the ranch-house her own and luxuriated in the privacy of her domain. Thad preferred the camaraderie of the bunkhouse where he enjoyed the exchange between cowhands. He was an avid listener and had a captive audience when he expounded on the new techniques of animal husbandry.

Colorado State University prided itself on offering the most comprehensive equine program in the U.S., and while it had taken weeks of persuasion for Branch to get him there, Thad absorbed the curriculum with enthusiasm and sense of dedication that surprised both of them. Although some of his ideas were received with undisguised skepticism he found an advocate in the usually taciturn Pete. "Yep," Pete said in his slow, deliberate manner. "I think Thad's got the right idea. Things are changing and we gotta change with 'em or we'll be out of business. Us drovers are gettin' old and we're gonna go the way of them dinosaurs. Horses are gonna be bred in barns and cattle will ride in trucks to them big feed lots. As fer me, I'm glad Thad's gonna be part of the future of the Bar L."

Frank bellowed. "Well, doggone. That's the longest speech I ever heard Pete make. It's sure gonna be a sad day for all them bulls and stallions when we ruin their sex lives."

Annie's Portion

"Pete now, he don't know much about that. That's more like to be a subject for Thad," Sandy proposed.

In late summer the cattle that were not going to market were moved from the high meadows, where they'd been feasting on the fresh grasses, to the winter pastures which had been cultivated throughout the summer. Green and lush with tall grass, the pastures had been cut a second time and the grass spread for drying. The baled hay would supplement the animal's feed through the cold months.

Preparations were made for the fall roundup and a couple of extra hands were hired to help with the expanded cattle herds. The cabins had been fully occupied all summer and the added excitement of the roundup insured another full house. I was busy from early morning to late evening, taking out trail riders, helping tend saddle horses and acting every bit the gracious hostess. Suppers in the bunkhouse were lively affairs, with great victuals provided by Claire and entertaining, often embellished stories, recounted by the cowboys.

There were tales told by Chubby Blacket, a recent arrival who probably tipped the scales at one hundred and forty pounds. No newcomer to the saddle, Chubby could keep the dinner crowd spellbound with his tales of "the old days".

"Men was tough back then. Had ta be ta survive in them conditions. We didn't have no chuck wagon and had ta be sure we provided fer ourselves. Why we had ta be prepared fer anythin'. Carried what we needed on a mule or tied to the saddle. Why I been caught in turrible blizzards that come up so sudden ya couldn't make out a trail, never mind a cow. Had ta git a fire goin real fast and keep it goin or we was sure ta freeze ta death. I been throwed and kicked by horses so many times my backside looks like one of them trails ya greenhorns ride."

"Hey Chubby," one of the cowhands was sure to interject. "Yer supposed ta stay on the horse, not under him."

There were Saturday barn dances and chuck wagon picnics, and fishing which when successful provided a change from beef at the supper table. And finally, it was October.

Branch and I took a few days off and went back to Sandwash basin to look for the mustang herds but with the temperature dropping, disappointed by our unsuccessful search for the wild bands, we returned to the line shack where we'd spent a night the year before.

"Maybe your meztano warned them off," Branch teased. "Kind of gave them the signal to beat it."

"It would be more likely for him to seek them out and join them. I was really a bit nervous about that. I couldn't bear to lose him."

"Well you'd better worry about taking care of me or I'll be the one you'll lose." Branch pulled me close.

"It seems like such a long time since we were here and you took advantage of me."

"Shall we try to recapture the moment?" Branch tossed our bedrolls on the floor and pulled me down next to him.

Warmed by the wood stove and our lovemaking, which after nine months of marriage had lost none of its original ardor, we were oblivious to the storm that raged outside. Morning brought with it temperatures that had dropped into the teens and several inches of snow.

"Well Annie, my girl. I guess it's our turn to see what we're made of. When we get back we'll be able to tell our story of how we survived them 'turrible, blindin' blizzards'." Branch tried to make light of it but he was noticeably concerned about the worsening conditions.

We had a quick breakfast, cleaned up the cabin and brought our gear out to the yard where Beau and Jessie

Annie's Portion

huddled in the horse shed, their breath forming long white plumes as they stamped the ground.

"Let's get the horses packed and out of here before the wind picks up."

The sky was hidden behind ominous dark clouds and Branch feared that more snow, combined with a rising wind could create white-out conditions. We made for the trail now buried under the fresh white blanket, its existence evidenced by the occasional appearance of rangy mesquite and scrub growing beside the path. With Jessie leading the way we had been making slow, labored progress for more than three hours. The horses plodded through the drifts, navigating the slippery grade into the wash where the sides of the gully clearly defined the route. Eventually we would have to leave its protective confines and move up to the high ground. Branch struggled to locate familiar landmarks but it was Jessie who detected the pullout.

Reining in Jessie he said, "Let's give the horses a respite before climbing out of the wash." He handed me a cup of hot coffee."

Holding the welcome brew in my cold hands I asked, "Are we in trouble?"

"Not yet," Branch answered honestly. "But if we don't get out of here soon we very well may be."

As we made our way up to the plateau the snow began to fall anew, lightly at first then with intermittent large, wet flakes. Up until the moment we crested the incline, the only sounds had been the heavy breathing of the horses and the muffled ripples of the stream running below us. Suddenly the howling fury of the storm struck us with a vengeance. We were enveloped by sheets of white gossamer—frightening but eerily splendid. With increased velocity the southerly wind hurled the snow at us, blinding horses and riders. Branch tried to tie a lead rope on Beau to prevent being separated from me but Beau would have none of

"Not really. How about we just stay here and make love for the next three months?"

"Now that sounds like a plan I can live with."

December arrived with a storm that dropped four feet of snow in two days. The vaqueros were kept busy checking on the stock and preparing for the National Western Stock Show which would be held in January in Denver. Branch's father had experimented with crossbreeding back in the '40's. His first attempt, a cross between Angus and Brahmin produced the Brangus. It was difficult to breed, requiring a mix of three-eights Brahmin and five-eights Angus but did not possess the characteristics Emil was looking for. Much later, he and Branch tried crossbreeding Brahmans with Hereford and Shorthorns. The resultant Beef Master had been successfully bred in Texas to withstand the arid climate and the scant grasslands. After Emil's death Branch eliminated the Shorthorn from the mix, substituting the French Charolais which could adapt to harsh terrain and was able to go for long periods without water. He carefully selected the animals with an emphasis on their disposition, fertility levels, optimum weight, hardiness and flavor. This careful selection had earned Branch a reputation for developing good breeding stock and he was planning to auction off several prize bulls. A number of fine Quarter Horses were also going on the block.

In his junior year Thad designed, and with Sandy's help built an addition to the barn, fitting it out for use as a lab. Branch financed the project and Thad was able to equip his new lab with the best scientific tools for developing a successful breeding program. Substantial quantities of semen were obtained from the animals in July, when the highest number of spermatozoa was present. Some of this reserve would be sold to other breeders. Wanting added assurance that he too would be able to continue the lines of his prize animals, Branch had Thad collect, test and freeze semen from the bulls and stallions prior to their sale. Thad, who had never quite conquered his feelings of inadequacy where Branch was concerned, welcomed the opportunity to display his skills and prove his worth to his father.

With the collection process completed and the animals shipped out to the Denver stockyard Branch, Thad and I headed off to join them with the precious frozen cargo stowed safely in the truck. During the five hour drive to the city I bombarded Thad with questions about the breeding process. Thad in turn was only too eager to provide detailed explanations. Branch was given little chance to comment but seemed content to listen to the lively discussion. The traffic increased as we neared the city, which appeared to be enveloped in an amber cloud.

"What happened to the blue sky?" I was disheartened by the vista. "Is Denver really one of the most polluted cities in the nation?"

"The winter skies are generally smoggier but what you're seeing today is the dust raised by the thousands of animals at the show." Branch hoped to rekindle my somewhat diminished enthusiasm. "A good breeze or a little rain will help clear the air and once we get inside the buildings the smell will erase the last vestige of smog from your consciousness."

Many of the downtown streets were cordoned off to allow for a grand parade, newly revived following an extended period of absence. It took us nearly an hour to reach the Brown Palace Hotel, an historic red granite and sandstone building on the corner of 17th Street.

Following dinner at the opulent Victorian era restaurant our threesome retired to the lobby lounge where a tuxedo-garbed pianist sat fingering the keys of a resplendent baby grand piano. Seated on burgundy tinted, tufted velvet love seats we enjoyed after-dinner drinks before heading to our equally elegant rooms.

Branch pulled out a gift-wrapped box from his suitcase. "Just a belated anniversary present," he said tossing the package onto the goose down coverlet. "Open it now."

"You sneak. How did you manage to hide this from me?" I tore off the ribbons and lifted the box cover. Pulling the tissue paper aside I removed a black lace bustier, g-string, garter belt and fishnet stockings. "You are a wicked devil. Do you really need this stuff to turn you on?"

"After all, we are an old married couple and I'm growing a little bored with you. Anyway, you missed the other box."

I rummaged through the paper and retrieved a small silver box. Opening it deftly I lifted out a gold chain on the end of which hung a sparkling pendent; a diamond-encrusted heart holding my birthstone, a multi-faceted aquamarine. I drew in my breath. "Oh, Branch! This is absolutely the most beautiful thing I have ever seen."

He reached over, and taking it from my hands placed it around my neck and fastened it. I grasped him about the neck and pulled him down onto the bed.

"Oh no you don't. I'm waiting for my present." He pushed the undergarments in my direction.

I gathered them into a bundle and disappeared into the bathroom. When I re-appeared the lights had been dimmed and Branch was stripped and waiting for me.

On its 80th anniversary, the 1986 Stock Show drew record crowds. Nearly half a million people attended the auctions, exhibits and the two dozen Rodeo performances. There was to be a special dedication for Willard Simms who died that year following twenty-three years of service as General Manager of the National Western. The Denver Fire Department was forced to close access to the grounds for nearly an hour in order to regulate the pedestrian traffic.

The Longbranch's arrived long before the paying customers in order to check on the animals and the booth

Annie's Portion

Thad would man to promote the sale of the reproductive cache. Leaving the men to their respective chores, I made my way to the auction area and found a seat in the gallery. The animals were displayed, one at a time, like so many models on a fashion show runway; the stereotypical auctioneer making his pitch in the unfathomable, rapid-paced nomenclature of his trade.

"What am I bid for this delectable Duroc, this superb sow, this pig producing powerhouse?" And again, "Do I hear three hundred for this pulchritudinous porker? There's three hundred. Do I hear three fifty? Three fifty, goin' once, goin' twice, goin' three times. Sold to the big fella with the red mustache."

There were hogs of every breed, color and size, lazing in pens next to those housing wool producing Merino sheep and rams raised for sale to commercial breeders. Young members of the 4-H Club offered the end products of a year of dedication and hard work. And it would be the debut of an Andean import, the lovable llama. But for me the best part of the auction was the display of horses. An eclectic variety of equines was represented including spotted Appaloosas, silky brown Tennessee Walking Horses, well mannered Quarter Horses, frisky Pintos and the ever popular, powerful Percherons. I sat with rapt attention, viewing the procession and auction for several hours before rejoining my men.

Samantha joined me later in the day and she and I covered the short distance to the Coliseum via the overpass. There we mingled with the throng of spectators at the main arena where tough, hardened cowboys matched their skills against those of bulls, steers and bucking broncos in the world renowned Rodeo.

The auctions were held every day. In addition to animals he would sell directly from the stockyards, Branch entered eight horses and three impressive registered bulls to be auctioned off during the course of the show. Without exception his stock sold for top dollar. But a magnificent bull dubbed "Hercules" by the Bar L ranch hands, exceeded all expectations, selling for $280,000, close to a record price of $301,000 paid for a bull in a 1981 auction. The vast sum obtained for Hercules triggered a run on the limited frozen reserve of his reproductive promise, which was being steadfastly guarded and grudgingly allocated by Thad.

For Branch the stock show had been a financial success. For Thad it had been an unequivocal affirmation of his potential. He had redeemed himself and become the son Branch could respect. He had made his father proud of him.

Chapter XXVII

In mid-May Thad received his Bachelor of Science Degree from Colorado State at a ceremony held in Fort Collins. A sizable retinue of Thaddeus Longbranch fans was there to commemorate the momentous occasion. Looking out into the assembly as he accepted his sheepskin, Thad beamed when he spied father, stepmother, Sarah, Claire, Howard and Samantha.

Branch's eyes were moist as he grasped the son he had once denied, the son who for so many years had been deprived of kith and kin, the son who was now surrounded and embraced by an adoring family. Trying to hide the obvious, he cleared his throat. "So you finally got a BS degree. Just confirmation of what we have all known for a long time."

In June Thad joined the returning cadre at the Bar L. Samantha went off to New York where she'd managed to finagle a three-month internship at the Post and was sharing an apartment the size of a large closet with a former housemate.

The summer was cooler than usual but the weather had no effect on normal ranch operations. Branch divided his time between the range, the corral and hosting duties. Thad joined his father on inspection tours, identifying the most promising animals for propagation and spent a good deal of time in the stalls and lab pursuing his passion. In addition to my hosting chores I was now guiding trail riders and helping Thad. I managed to spend every free moment alone with my majestic mustang exploring the broad plateaus, deep canyons and sparsely forested slopes within the ranch's boundaries. If it was in any way possible, the bond between Beau and me deepened with time and it was rare either of us was seen without the other. Sometimes Star ran along side us but those times were becoming less frequent as she found it increasingly difficult to keep up. Beau resigned himself to his stays in the pasture with some of the saddle horses but persisted in his wild behavior whenever let out on the open range. Branch was sure that the mestano was the cause of an increase in expectant mares.

"Annie," he chided. "That dang horny horse of yours is riding roughshod over my mares. He's bound and determined to make the most of his free time and put his mark on every one of them."

Lying in bed beside him after a particularly satisfying sexual encounter of my own, I sighed. "Although the results will certainly not be the same, you seem pretty determined to leave your mark as well."

"Wench," he responded by pulling me closer to him. "I'm serious. We're going to have to restrict his activities or I'll be out of purebreds. And he could really injure a mare. Maybe we should geld him."

I was outraged. "What! Geld my Beau. Are you mad? He's one of a kind. There's absolutely no way in hell I'd let you do that. We'd run away first."

"I always knew it was the horse you came back for."

"Oh Branch. You're not really serious, are you?"

"I have done some thinking about it. Sometimes a good woman can change a man. What do you think of the idea of mating him with Jessie?" He added quickly, "under controlled conditions of course."

I could not contain my excitement. "Could we really do that? Do you think it would make a difference in his behavior?"

"I'm sure it would have no effect at all Annie, but I'd really like to have a foal that's the product of the best two animals we own."

My mind was racing ahead, at thoughts of a domestic scene starring Beau, Jessie and the foal. "He would be a family man."

"No, not in the sense you mean. But we could pen him close to home where we can restrict his contact with the range herd."

"Take away the little freedom he has left?"

"There are few choices. If he sires a colt, we could geld Beau and let him run with the herd in the winter months. We'd be assured of continuing his line."

"I'd rather see him with the wild herds." I began to cry.

"You know he can't do that now. And besides, there is always the risk of his capture again or worse."

"Can't we just file his shoes down or take them off altogether so he can't hurt the mares?" I knew I was acting like a fool but wanted desperately to keep Beau just as he was.

"Let's take it one step at a time. We'll talk to Thad and see what he thinks about the mating and take it from there."

"I do love you, you know." I moved into the crook of Branch's arm. "I came back for you."

"I'd hate for you to have to make a choice," he chuckled squeezing me so tightly I winced.

Thad was enthusiastic about the possibilities of breeding Jessie. "She's a wonderful animal, a perfect candidate. But we'll have to do a lot beforehand to increase the probability of success."

I remembered my conversation with Branch about the low reproductive success rates among horses. "When was that?" I thought. "It seems like that was years ago... it was years ago—when I first moved into Branch's bed." I laughed aloud.

"Did I say something funny?" Thad asked.

"No, just thinking about something that happened a long time ago. How do we begin?"

"We'll want to breed her sometime this summer, July or August. The vet will have to come out here to examine both animals to insure their breeding soundness. Jessie will have a vaginal-cervical exam to determine whether or not she is fit and ready for breeding. We'll start testing her to calculate her estrous cycle and keep detailed records in order to determine when she is most receptive."

"It doesn't sound very romantic to me," I volunteered.

Thad smiled. "I promise you it will get better."

"What about Beau? What wonderful things do you have in store for him?"

"He'll be examined to check on his general condition and then we'll do a semen evaluation." Thad was showing signs of discomfort and the discussion was bound to get more embarrassing for him. "Branch can fill you in on the details."

That night, I told Branch about my discussion with Thad. "I think he was a little embarrassed, discussing sex with me. He bugged out after he told me about the semen test."

Branch smiled. "Just think about him telling his stepmother we have to use masturbation to collect several samples of semen."

"Is that what he meant when he said better things were in store for Beau?"

"That and a little teasing of Jessie. Kind of what I do with you only we call it foreplay. Talking of which, I'm getting a little excited myself. See?"

I reached over and touched him. "Hmmm. So I do. Guess there's no need for sexy underwear tonight."

Matt was discharged from the Navy in July and arrived at the Bar L in time to witness the breeding process. Thad was happy to have Matt's company and Matt, who had always

Annie's Portion

been in love with the sea, made an attempt at becoming a horseman. Awkward at first, with lengthened stirrups and Thad's guidance, he made steady progress. During the lessons they discovered they'd been at the Naval Station at the same time. With much in common the two bonded almost immediately.

At dinner one night Matt declared he wanted to check out Florida State. "Hey, Thad. Why don't you take a break and come with me? We can visit my brother Josh while we're there."

Thad had earlier confessed he and Sam were romantically involved and solicited Matt's help in getting away from the ranch. Matt went on to Florida and Thad spent a week in New York sharing the closet with Sam. It wasn't until much later Branch and I got the whole scoop.

I viewed the young men's budding friendship with pleasure thinking, "Those two don't know how much they really share. Two stallions with questionable parentage." To Sarah I commented, "Look how handsome Matt is. And smart too."

"Yes," Sarah agreed. "You've always spoiled him but he seems to have turned out all right in spite of you."

I had to admit with a sense of guilt that Sarah was right. While the love for all my children was indisputable, Matt had always held a special place in my heart. It was with undisguised sadness I heard of his acceptance at FSU and impending departure.

Thad undertook the breeding project with more than his usual ardor, enlisting Matt as his temporary official record keeper. The mating of "El Diablo" was the subject of conversation at every meal. Even Sarah was caught up in the on-going proceedings. The results of the physical examinations were satisfactory. Beau proved himself to be exceptionally potent by producing motile sperm cells in the upper range of the established criteria. The results of

Jessie's exam were equally gratifying. It was determined that her estrus cycle, the period from one ovulation to the next lasted twenty one days. During the five days of Jessie's active estrus she displayed obvious signs of being receptive when teased.

Remembering his own, near calamitous experience with Beau, Pete shook his head. It was, in his considered opinion, "gonna be a catastrophe."

Fabian was in complete agreement. "That mestano is goin' to kill that poor mare. It will take ten men to handle them."

"You guys have no faith. Annie will make that boy behave, won't you Annie?" Frank directed the question to her.

"I certainly hope so. But I think Jessie can take care of herself."

For three months Thad monitored Jessie's cycles and added food supplements to her diet. With me replacing Matt as record keeper he continued to test Beau's reproductive capabilities and was satisfied of the pair's soundness and physical ability to mate. Branch and I took long rides together on our respective mounts to insure they were comfortable with one another. We would dismount and leaving our horses tied close to each other, monitored their behavior. I would often take Beau to visit Jessie in her stall, allowing the pair to greet one another through the stall window.

Thad made the announcement near the end of August. "On the 26th, Jessie will go into estrus. It should last four or five days. We'll do it then."

When Thad phoned Sam to announce the upcoming event, she wasted no time in handing in her resignation and headed for JFK.

On the morning of the 26th, having examined her one more time for estrus, Thad checked to be sure Jessie's shoes had been removed. He tightly wrapped her tail with a surgical bandage; making sure to include all the hair at the base of her tail. He washed her genitals well with surgical soap, then rinsed and dried them with paper towels. At the same time Branch and I were leading Beau past several paddock mares in estrus. Thad led the mare to the breeding area where he placed a breeding hobble on her. A leather strap was buckled around her neck in front of her shoulders. He attached a rope to the lower part of the neck strap and led it down between her front legs, beneath her abdomen. The rope was then attached to another set of straps that buckled around her rear hocks. With the rig in place Jessie was able to walk forward but would not be able to kick. Thad was taking no chances with the safety of either horse.

A small, silent group gathered near the breeding pen to watch the historic event. I brought Beau to the fence that divided the pen and tied him to it. Branch now handling Jessie, led her to a spot facing Beau and tied her so the horses were nose to nose. Jessie took a step toward Beau and spread her back legs. In a process called winking she displayed her genitalia, contracting and releasing the covering folds.

Branch washed Beau's now erect penis while I gentled him. He was then led by a short chain attached to his halter to the mare waiting to be courted and coaxed into a state of readiness. Branch steadied her as she urinated, splashing his boots. He smiled knowing she was ready, hoping the inexperienced stallion would do his part. Jessie stood quietly as Beau vocalized a tender greeting and nuzzled her shoulder. I'd been coached by Thad to lead Beau away after this first greeting then repeat the process one or two more times until Beau made his way to her flank. Jessie spread her hind legs in a breeding stance and flexed her pelvis. Beau mounted Jessie and with help from Thad, who moved her tail aside and guided Beau in, the deed was done. Beau signaled his completion by raising and lowering his tail, an action called "flagging". The actual breeding time lasted a total of one and a half minutes. Both horses were rinsed again and led to their respective pastures.

Branch and I retreated to our own paddock. The audience applauded and no one noticed when Sam and Thad slipped away.

Three weeks later Thad palpated Jessie and to everyone's delight announced that Jessie had conceived.

Autumn arrived spawning warm, sunny days; what I would describe as a "northeast Indian summer." The initial bustle associated with Jessie's and Beau's successful coupling had gradually abated and it was business as usual at the Bar-L. The guests departed, freeing all the cowhands to begin making preparations for the fall roundup.

Will Harriman's arrival signaled the official end of the season. Branch and I accompanied the ranger to high country where he took his annual count of the range herd. There was the familiar mock dispute between ranger and rancher as they tallied the numbers and dollars, each accusing the other of cheating. The day would not have been complete without dinner at the house where Sarah joined in the repartee. Missing Samantha who had gone back to Fort Collins and Thad who had decided to enroll in a post graduate course in animal breeding at Texas A & M, I welcomed Will's visit.

The shortening days and chill of October nights resulted in a subtle but perceptible transition in the landscape. Intermittent flashes of gold sent signals through the green of the woodlands, and scrub oak took on a hint of red. Once again I marveled at the changes as my palomino and I roamed the mesas, arroyos and pine forest surrounding the homestead. We observed the elk from atop Yellow Ridge and visited the beaver dam where Beau grazed and I munched a sandwich as I watched the ever-industrious

Annie's Portion

creatures. Over Branch's objection, we explored remote areas of awesome natural beauty; rainbow-striped canyons and mountain lakes that reflected the reds and golds of the changing season. Beau's good behavior on these excursions belied the fact that fatherhood had not mellowed the wild stallion one whit.

All too soon another hunting season arrived, putting an end to a welcome but brief period of tranquillity. A number of new faces appeared beside the familiar ones at the dinner table. They were younger, cruder, louder and drunker. It became quickly apparent that they were also inexperienced, careless sportsmen. Following a particularly unpleasant incident when a member of Fabian's hunting party fired prematurely, narrowly missing Tom Haggert, Branch insisted they leave. He arranged for Dale to fly in and haul them back to Denver. While Tom and his buddies remained for another week, enjoying the comradeship and great food, they were unsuccessful in bagging any animals. Following their departure Branch suggested he and I take advantage of the temperate conditions.

"How about we take a twofer?"

"What do you have in mind?" I asked skeptically

"We might visit the Little Bookcliffs range to scout some mestanos. If you're ready for some serious hiking we can drive to the Coal Canyon access just off Highway 70 and trek in from there."

With last year's near-disaster still in mind I replied, "I'm for it if you can promise there will be no blizzards. After all, we won't have Jessie or Beau to find our way home."

Branch laughed. "I've checked the park service meteorology reports and it looks like there's at least another week of fair skies to look forward to."

"What's the second part of the twofer?"

"I've wanted to take a ride down to Canyon to see if they've brought in any new mustangs. We can haul the trailer and make a stop at the corrals before heading home."

"Do you really expect to find another Beau?"

"No, Annie. He's one of a kind." Thinking of how I might object to the competition he added, "Besides, one of him is as much as we can handle."

We departed at dawn towing the horse trailer, its diesel engine intruding upon the perfect stillness. Headlights pierced the mist that clung, shroud-like, to the trees. The road was barely visible as we made our way down the mountain toward Rifle. After what seemed an eternity the sun broke through, lifting the fog and our spirits. A short drive west on Route 70 brought us to the Palisade exit and the entrance to Coal Canyon from whence we would proceed on foot.

Branch helped me slip into a backpack. "Here you go, Annie me girl. Everything your little heart can desire."

"You mean like woolies and army rations?"

"Grumble, grumble, grumble. They're not army rations...just freeze-dried delectables." He slid his arms into the shoulder straps of his own pack. "Here we go. The trail is easy and fairly level for the first half-mile."

"And then?"

"Then those great legs of yours will get a workout. This area is quite different from Sandwash. It is heavily wooded in places and harder to find the horses."

It was still cold and touches of frost glittered on the scrub oak and pinon pines. The reds and golds of early autumn had changed to muted shades of brown. As we made our way up the hillside, patches of dry brittle grasses crunched under the heavy tread of sturdy boots. The white peaks of the Rockies stood like sentries against a cloudless blue sky. We walked on in silence, awed by the shear magnitude of the environment in which we found ourselves. The trail

Annie's Portion

took us through stands of cedars and low-growing junipers, opening up suddenly as we worked our way down the rocky slope of a wide canyon. Progress become slow and tedious as the sandstone crumbled away beneath our feet. After twenty minutes of difficult scrambling we reached the safety of the chasm floor where we stopped for a breather.

"What do you think of this place?" Branch moved his arms in a wide circle. The striated walls of the canyon loomed above us, displaying bands of purple, red, yellow and blue.

"This is absolutely remarkable. I want to shout for the joy of it. But I'll just kiss you instead." I threw my arms about my husband's neck and kissed him hard and long.

"Wow!" he responded when I finally released my strangle hold. "What brought that on?"

"Sometimes I forget to tell you just how much I love you. I'm so happy."

"Me too. Remember the first time I tried to tell you what I felt?"

"Yes. I think you were interrupted by a wild herd."

"And I've said since, not even a wild herd of horses could take me away from you. But unless my nose is deceiving me I smell them again."

Rising dust at the far end of the canyon indicated the presence of animals. We waited until the dust settled but there were none to be seen.

"The canyon branches off up ahead. They probably turned in there. Shall we follow them?" Branch asked.

"You bet your sweet bippy," was my excited reply.

"We'll have to be extremely cautious and remain upwind of them. If they get the slightest hint of our presence they'll bolt."

Staying close to the wall we made our way to the spot where the chasm diverged. We were looking into a box canyon, the horses crowded around a cleft in the wall where

"If you heard it from Branch, it's probably all bad information."

"Not about you, Chuck. Just the system. Anything interesting?"

"Not this time. Most of these guys are pretty scrawny. Some will find homes but I don't think you'll find any to your liking. Look around and see me before you leave."

After looking over the bunch considered saleable, Branch had to agree with Chuck. "There's not a one worth a damn. They've been run into the ground. Just look at them. They're half starved."

"Don't they take good care of them here? What about this inmate, horse relationship they brag about?"

"That part's okay. But it will take months of care to return them to health and I don't think some of them will ever make it. Let's say goodbye to Chuck."

"Pretty bad this time," Chuck agreed. "But say Branch. I had another thought. Sometimes we get a fella here who just had some bad luck. Gets picked up for stealing a purse or maybe breakin' into a car...somethin' like that. They're in for a short time but can't get a job when they leave. There's always one who stands out for great ability to work with horses. If you ever find yourself shorthanded think about us, would you?"

"Sure thing, Chuck."

Goodbyes said all around, we headed home with the same empty trailer towed behind.

"Would you ever hire one of the inmates? It might make a real difference in someone's life."

"I don't think so, Annie. I'm not one to pick up strays like you do. Not worth the risk."

The November weather remained milder than normal inducing Sarah, Howard and Claire to stay for the Thanksgiving holiday. With a surprise visit from Samantha and Thad and the inclusion of Pete, Frank, Fabian and Star,

Annie's Portion

the Longbranch table was crowded with happy faces and the bountiful traditional dinner disappeared in short order. Branch and I retired soon after leaving the others to enjoy coffee and dessert in front of the blazing fire.

"Have you noticed anything suspicious?"

Branch played dumb. "Suspicious of what?"

"You know what, you faker. Thad seems to be spending much less time with Jessie." I gave him a gentle poke in the region of his distended belly.

"Ooh," he groaned. "Have pity."

"You know as well as I do what's happening. It's the kids, yours and mine."

"What about the kids? And no poking."

"Don't you find it the least bit strange they always turn up together? Or go on vacations at the same time, or disappear at the same time.

"We disappear at the same time."

"That, my dear husband, is exactly what I mean. Something here is not *kosher*."

"Well they are healthy, normal, interesting youngsters."

"They stopped being youngsters a long time ago. Do you think they are lovers?"

"Lovers? I really hadn't thought about it."

"Don't you notice how they look at each other? Would that be considered incest?"

"Annie, be serious. You know very well, it's no such thing. But if they like each other that's fine. I'd certainly approve of that more than his infatuation with Magdalena."

"Magdalena! When was that?"

"It was the time he left home. That was a big part of our falling out. They were screwin' around and I wanted it to stop. He told me to mind my own business and he was planning to marry her. I thought maybe she was pregnant but as it turned out she was not and Fabian took her back to

Mexico. Thad was furious and left. I suppose he tried to find her but gave up after a while and joined the Navy."

"Claire told me you had a fight about school."

"That was another part of it."

"What do you think about this new situation?"

"I won't make another mistake. I think we should let them work it out for themselves. They're not babies, as you just reminded me."

"Thad and Sam. Who woulda thought."

The snowbirds and students had been gone a week when winter arrived with a vengeance. Excepting for brief intervals, from the fourth through the eighth of December a blizzard raged, bringing with it more than four feet of snow. Branch and the few remaining wranglers struggled valiantly to keep paths open in order to tend the paddock inhabitants. Jessie was now entering her fourth month of the eleven-month gestation period. She enjoyed the company of several other expectant mares and a number of saddle broncs sheltered in the horse barn. In addition to feed and water the equines needed to be exercised regularly. No longer able to ride Jessie for long periods, Branch usually took her on several slow laps around the fenced pasture where Beau continued to hold sway. Beau always greeted her affectionately which was not to say he'd become an adherent of monogamy. Given the opportunity, he would not hesitate to mount a lady of his choice, even if it meant battling another stallion for her.

The temperatures remained below freezing for days, too cold to melt the snow. Branch was restless.

"Annie, how about we make that trip to Hawaii. We can spend our anniversary there."

"I don't need any convincing but how will we get there, dog sled?"

"Hey, this is Colorado. Tomorrow may bring us 80 degree weather. Have faith."

Annie's Portion

He was off by two days. The road that was choked by snow just days before was cleared by a warming trend enabling us to get to Meeker where Dale waited to carry the Hawaii bound couple to the Denver airport.

I planned the trip, starting on the big island of Hawaii, spending a day in Kailua-Kona before taking a course along the southern coast. It was my turn to play tour guide. Stopping in Captain Cook I explained it was so named because it was where the unlucky sailor was killed, barbecued and served for dinner. We continued down the coast to the "City of Refuge", a holy site where any criminal could seek sanctuary. The road wended southeast passing the cutoff that led to Ka Lae, South Point, the most southern part of the U.S. Mauna Loa, an active volcano, rose thirteen-thousand-six-hundred feet above a lava-strewn plain. As with all the islands, the windward or western slopes of Mauna Loa received most of the rain, producing lush tree fern forests and a profusion of tropical vegetation. The road began to ascend gradually, rising to four-thousand feet, skirting the boiling Kilauea crater.

"This is the largest active crater in the world. Called the 'House of Everlasting Fire', it's been erupting steadily for the past several years."

My husband was suitably impressed. The air was heavy with the smell of sulphur as we climbed higher into the Hawaii Volcanoes National Park. I insisted on doing the circle tour following the rim which overlooked several steaming craters. At last we pulled into the driveway of the world famous Volcano House, a lodge of impressive proportions overlooking Kilauea.

From the large windows of our room, we were able to peer into the gaping mouth of the percolating volcano.

"This is quite remarkable, Annie. Nothing would have prepared me for this sight." He had his arm around me and

"He's fine, just a little excited is all." I continued to hold him in tight rein. "He is a handful," I muttered under my breath.

"Hey, there's Pete and Fabian," Branch pointed to two dark spots on the horizon. He urged Rocky forward making for his wranglers.

Beau needed no urging and reached them first, dancing around them with his head thrown back and his mane flying in the wind.

"Ah, it is Miss Annie and El Diablo. Buenos tardes. Did you have a good trip?"

"Wonderful, Fabian. And it was a lot warmer than here."

"Si. It has been very cold. But now that you are back you bring the sunshine."

"Hi, Pete. I kind of wondered where you both had got to." Branch knew very well where he would find his top hand. "Thought you might have run off with some sweet young thing."

"Tain't a one that'd have me. Me and Fabian here, we been tryin' to find them ornery cows." Pete raised his hat and scratched his head.

"Have you been able to locate any of the herds?"

"Yep. The horses are doin' fine but we got a buncha dumb critters got themselves trapped in a canyon. No way out till the snow melts down some. By that time they're like as ta starve ta death."

Branch turned to me. "Annie, you'd better head back to the ranch. I'll ride out with the boys and see if we can figure out some way to rescue the stock."

"Be sure you boys all get home by dinner time. I'll help Ernesto rustle up some real good grub." I loved using the cowboy jargon, especially since it bugged my husband who responded just as I thought he would...with a frown. Beau was eager to head for the barn.

Annie's Portion

I was in for a pleasant surprise. Samantha was at the house, warming herself in front of the great fireplace.

"Hello there. We weren't expecting you." I gave my daughter a great big hug.

"Skipped out a couple of days early so I could help with holiday stuff. How was Hawaii?"

"Just as wonderful as ever. Don't you ever miss it?"

"Yes. Sometimes I get a terrible urge to go back but I realize there's nothing there for me. All my friends and family are on the mainland. I've made my life here now. Maybe I'll go back for a vacation."

"How much of a role did Thad play in her new life?" I wondered but did not ask.

"I'm going over to the bunkhouse to see if Ernesto needs help with dinner. Want to come?"

"No. I think I'll sit here for a while. Maybe go up and get some Christmas cards written. Give a holler when dinner is ready."

"Christmas cards," I thought. "If Sarah was here she would have something to say about that."

It was dark by the time the cowboys returned, cold and hungry. I banged out the call to dinner while Ernesto dished out the hot chili and biscuits. Samantha and Frank joined us in time to share the thick steaks smothered in onions.

"This is a fine meal, Ernesto," Pete said as he sipped hot coffee. "Only thing missin' is Claire's apple pie."

"Yes sir," Frank piped in. "Now all we got ta do is git ya a pink kerchief."

Later that evening I questioned Branch about the stock.

"If we don't get some feed to them they're goners."

"What will you do?"

"I think I'm gonna try an airlift."

"An airlift. How in the world will you do that?"

"I don't mean lift the cows out, Annie. I mean to drop the feed in."

On one occasion I confessed I was much less interested in talk about cattle than I was about horses. On another I brought up a subject that had long been on my mind.

"Say guys," I began. "It sounds to me like you've got us on the road to a bright, successful, financially rewarding future."

The men exchanged knowing looks.

"Do you suppose," I continued, "we could eliminate the hunting program from our curriculum?"

The same topic had been a subject of discussion several times. Branch had already made up his mind to end the practice which, while very profitable, he found extremely distasteful. Last year we'd been lucky to avoid a serious accident.

"Why, Annie," Thad responded. "Branch and I were just saying how we're looking forward to the hunt his year. Maybe get us a buck or two, maybe even an elk."

"Thad," I demanded. "You're not really going to participate in that barbaric practice. I'm disappointed in you."

Thad laughed. "No, Annie. I'm more interested in production than destruction."

Realizing I was being had, I confronted my husband. "Branch, you are a devil. It should be you the hands call 'El Diablo'."

It was with great satisfaction letters of farewell went out to our hunting guests. I would miss Tom Haggert and Murray Blackman who never failed to provide entertainment at meal times and Lincoln Gould, who I admired immensely. I told them so by way of personal messages to each. For the others it was just "so long Charlie."

June saw the return of Sarah, Claire, Howard and an obviously aging Star. Summer bounded in with an extravagant explosion of color. Lacy-leafed, pink and blue Rocky Mountain columbine and yellow dogtooth violets bordered the paths and spread across the hillsides. Pink honeysuckle and wild roses growing in red and white profusion were framed by the vivid green of the pines. The brilliantly colored bracts of Indian paintbrush spiked in sharp contrast with the young foliage. Trail rides became botany lessons as I demonstrated my new-found knowledge of the local flora.

Mares foaled and calves were born. Family and ranch hands alike eagerly awaited the birth of Jessie and Beau's offspring. Not wanting to miss the blessed event, Samantha returned to the Bar L at the end of July. Jessie had no lack of company. At any time there would be at least one member of the family visiting her. She'd been prepared for the event earlier. Her shoes had been removed once more and her nails shaved to prevent even the slightest possibility of her injuring the foal. She received, at the hands of an anxious Thad, a multiple vaccine shot. Her stall had been scrubbed clean and lined with fresh hay. When she seemed unusually restless an around-the-clock watch was set up. Thad was the first to notice Jessie was expelling milk from her teats, a sure sign the birth was imminent.

"It's time," he informed the family excitedly.

In order to insure the mare would not be disturbed, he gave instructions to Fabian to keep all comers at a good distance from the paddock. Branch paced like an expectant father while Sam and I sat on a bale of hay watching Thad as he tended Jessie. When she finally lay down Branch joined Thad in the stall. He talked to her quietly and stroked her neck. She groaned slightly with each barely discernible contraction. At last two small hooves appeared, covered by the amniotic sac. With each push, more of the foal could be seen.

"Look," Sam whispered. "There's the nose. It's dark, like Jessie."

ordered additional supplies of hay which were distributed across the lower range.

On the day of Samantha's departure, she and Thad announced their betrothal. It had come as no surprise. She returned to Fort Collins to complete her senior year, leaving Thad to take up permanent residence at the ranch. Will Harriman arrived later than usual to take his count. It was the first time Thad experienced the process.

"Get used to this, Thad. Will here, comes to collect his tribute. But this time he's going to have to give us a refund."

"Now what do you have up your denim sleeve?" Will asked.

"We lost a bunch of money trying to keep those dumb cows alive. Only reason we had anything left to sell is Thad figured out a way to feed them."

"Thad, what in the hell is your father talking about?"

All the joking aside, the Bar L did not show a profit for 1986. The bottom line in the journal was drawn in red.

When it was time for Claire and Howard to leave, Star refused to go with them. She laid herself across my feet with her head on the ground. "It looks like Star's determined to stay here, Claire." I reached down to give her a pat.

"Sure looks that way. She seems to have lost her bounce. Even her tail don't work like it used to."

"Why don't we just keep her with us this winter? She can stay with us in the house and enjoy the warm fire and lots of attention."

Branch tried to hide a frown. He was never in favor of animals in the house.

"Look at that sour puss," Claire pointed to her surrogate son. "He don't like that idea one bit."

"Don't mind him. He's just afraid I'll give Star more attention than I do him. He feels the same way about Beau."

Annie's Portion

"Okay ladies. You win. Star can move in with us. I didn't know how well off I was when I lived the bachelor life. This house is sure getting crowded."

Sarah made her annual sojourn to Florida soon after Claire's departure. The weatherman's prediction came to pass. Long before Thanksgiving Day, Jack Frost turned up to forewarn of things to come. The feast was held in the bunkhouse because of the increase in participants. As usual, Pete and Frank had stayed on, joined this year by Fabian and several new wranglers. Branch hired a young man from the Canyon mustang facility who had worked out well, to his surprise and satisfaction. Thad became Jorge's mentor and invited him to remain through the winter. Ernesto and I prepared an outstanding dinner, one that appealed to every taste. While Ernesto provided a number of Mexican specialties, I stuffed and roasted a twenty-five-pound turkey.

With Thanksgiving behind us and Thad minding the store, Branch and I left for an extended vacation in Mexico where we explored Mayan and Aztec ruins and lounged on the beach in Cancun. We celebrated another anniversary in the luxury of our hotel suite, drinking champagne and making love.

The 1988 National Western Stock Show was another big success with attendance reaching the half-million mark for the first time. Among the stockmen, the Bar L was fast becoming recognized as having a top Quarter Horse breeding program. Artificial insemination programs were gaining in popularity and Thad was only too happy to expound on the methods he was using to develop a herd that combined the best characteristics of the breed. In addition he promoted the use of the same techniques to improve the cattle quality. As a result of his efforts all the animals put up for auction brought in top dollar and his sperm bank was depleted.

In early spring Thor, now seven months old, began the weaning process. He was put in a corral with other weanlings, out of sight of the mares, for short periods of time. In addition, the youngsters were encouraged to start using special feeding stations placed in the pastures. These creep feed stations provided the nutritional balance needed by the foals once they were completely weaned.

"Our baby is growing up," I said sadly. "Will we breed Jessie again?"

"We sure will. But this time it will not be with Beau."

"What?" I was aghast. "Are you going to turn her into some hussy?"

"What I did was completely out of order. That little guy, wonderful as he is, is not considered a blooded Quarter Horse. Nor will any of his offspring be. And that my dear lady, is what I'm in the business to produce."

"Why is he not? Jessie is."

"There are very strict rules governing the process. Both the dam and the sire have to be registered with the American Quarter Horse Association and given an ID number. Unfortunately, Beau is just a half-breed or worse."

"If Thor is bred to a numbered dam will his offspring be considered a thoroughbred?"

"No. There is only one exception. There is an appendix registry for foals with one numbered American Quarter Horse parent and one thoroughbred parent registered with The Jockey Club. But Thor doesn't qualify."

"Wow! Talk about snobbery."

"Don't knock the hand that feeds you." Branch grinned.

"Now don't go mixing your maxims."

In April, we got word from Claire that Howard would not be returning with her. "Seems he found some boob enhanced bombshell to move in with. And that's fine with me. He was never much more than a bed warmer and a pain in the you know what." She exploded with her customary cackle. "But I sure do miss Star."

I assured her that Star was anxiously awaiting her return as they all were, but in fact, Star's health was declining. She spent little or no time outdoors but seemed content to lie on the rug in front of the fireplace. She ate little and had been spending her nights at my side of the bed. To Branch's dismay, Star soon had a place on the bed where she lay on a blanket at my feet. Believing it would not be for long, he said nothing.

Things at the ranch were in full swing in May when the family drove to Fort Collins to see Samantha graduate from Colorado State. We celebrated at a nearby steak house and Thad presented Sam with a beautiful diamond solitaire.

"Now it's official," he said kissing her cheek.

We returned to the Bar L, leaving Thad behind to help Sam pack and bring her home.

The summer of '88 brought good news and bad. Rose called to tell me about the death of our dear friend Tom.

"He died peacefully in his sleep. When he didn't show up for bible study, his friend Bruce went to check on him. He found Tom in the tiny apartment no one ever got to see, and no wonder. Bruce said it was like that old Collier brother's mansion in New York. There were hundreds of books and magazines, all about Israel. Stacks of Jerusalem Post newspapers, hand written journals and photo albums. And you remember all the pictures he took in Israel?"

I recalled the boxes of slides Tom had taken back to Hawaii. "Yes Rose. I sure do. He never could get enough of Israel."

"Well there were cartons filled with them...all neatly labeled. He must have made twenty trips to Israel."

"He talked about returning to stay after he retired."

"Yes he did, often. Too bad he never could afford to do it."

I envisioned standing with Tom at the Mount of Olives, overlooking the vast cemetery just outside the walls of Jerusalem. "He truly believed he'd be buried in the Holy Land."

"God works in His own way." Rose theorized.

Soon after Rose's call, I heard from Margie Rieder.

"Is it too late to get a reservation for August? We have something we want to show you."

"Oh Margie, it's so good to hear from you. We'll make room, even if I have to give you my bed. When are you coming?"

"The last week in August?"

"That will be great. You'll be here for Branch's birthday. What is it you're bringing to show me?"

"Our new daughter, Cathy."

I lay awake a long time that night. "Branch?" I called softly. "Are you awake?"

"Mmmm, sort of," he answered sleepily.

"God does work in mysterious ways," I reflected.

"Boy, that's certainly a profound statement. What brought this on?"

"Just think. We've only been together four years but it seems like I've never had any other life. Yet look at what's happened in such a short time. Danny's getting a divorce. Thad and Samantha have fallen in love. Margie and Bob have a daughter and dear Tom has died."

"I know this sounds trite but all these events are part of living." Branch drew me close to him. "Are you happy, Annie? Any regrets?"

"My only regret is I didn't meet you sooner. Until you I never knew what happiness was."

"I love you, Annie. I know I'm not very good at telling you that. I just figure you know. But I love you more than anything else in my life, more than life itself."

We made love that night with renewed ardor, Branch as unrestrained as he had been on a night that seemed so long ago—a night when he first admitted to himself how much he loved me.

August was exceptionally hot that year. The shallow lake had as many swimmers as it did trout. Claire threatened to put a few of the unruly "young frys" on the barby. Thor, with his remarkable lightning bolt remained the favorite attraction. He had his first birthday in July but would not be given the title of "yearling" until January. No one told him and he grew tall and sturdy as a yearling, with full black mane and tail that skimmed the ground. He was as feisty and full of fire as his sire but Jessie imparted some of her gentle traits to her foal, and he was always well behaved around children. Beau still preferred his own company, barely tolerating that of Samson and Ginger who was now past estrus. He let me know when he felt neglected by racing around the pasture and bellowing every so often to remind me he was waiting. I found excuses to take him on long jaunts while the guests were at supper. Branch still teased me about the uncanny relationship between us, referring to Beau as "my rival."

For the first time in years we were shorthanded. Sandy met and married one of his ski students whose daddy just happened to own a large sporting goods outfit in Denver. Daddy made his new son-in-law an offer he could not refuse. Thad's protégé Jorge decided to go back to school and with the Longbranch's help got into the equine program at Colorado State. When Pete suffered a broken leg he was relegated to stable duty and Branch went down to Canyon to see if he could get a line on some hands for the next season. As it turned out Chuck Wells had gone to do battle in Washington, D.C. The BLM was appealing a recent decision that put the onus on the Bureau to insure the adopted mustangs were not being sold to slaughterhouses.

J. Fran Baird

Chuck was one of a few managers that believed the current policies regarding roundups should be changed. Without his input Branch was reluctant to interview any prospects. He resolved to return after the next wild horse roundup, which would occur before the onset of winter.

Disregarding Branch's preference to let birthdays pass unnoticed, I used his absence to plan a private party at the house. "A sixtieth birthday is a milestone," I confided to Claire and Sarah. "And with Bob, Margie and little Cathy here to help celebrate it will be especially nice."

To Thad's delight Sam arrived from Grand Junction where she was interning at the Daily Gazette. It was an enjoyable evening, birthday cake and all. I'd been hiding a present I bought for Branch in Denver months earlier. I retrieved the package which had been difficult to disguise. He tore off the paper revealing an old rifle in mint condition.

"Where in the world did you find this beauty?" He was obviously pleased and held it up for all to see.

"Is that a Henry?" Thad exclaimed.

"It sure is. A Henry Repeating Rifle, circa 1866 – 1871." Branch examined it carefully. "Hey, Thad. It's got the original folding leaf sight still in place. Look here! There's some Chinese writing on the stock." He passed the rifle to Thad.

"I wonder if that was some kind of ownership brand. This is great."

I was pleased with the reception my present received. "It was the forerunner of the Winchester, you know. It has a twenty-four inch barrel and a brass frame where the sight is mounted."

"Anything else I should know," Branch asked with feigned ignorance.

"Oh yes, much more. It was engraved by the foremost firearms engraver of the day...a Mr. Nim...something or other. His initials are on the vang."

"His name is L.D. Nimschke, and the initials L.D.N. are engraved on the tang. I believe a vang is something used to hold a line on a sailboat," Branch interjected.

"Ooh…you're such a smarty pants. I know you've got lots of guns…and love them all. Besides, it's not a line it's a halyard. But kidding aside, the bullets were the hardest things to find. The bullet is a 216 grain with 26 to 28 grains of black powder...I think. The dealer made an extraordinary effort to get these four." I handed Branch a clear plastic box containing four shining shells.

Branch and Thad chortled to hear a lady who hated guns now expound on the extraordinary uniqueness of this one. Uncharacteristically, Branch gave me a public peck on the cheek.

"Annie, you are a wonder. It will have a place of honor over the fireplace, next to my flintlock."

There had been an article in the Gazette concerning a major mustang roundup. When Sam told us about it Branch and I drove down to Canyon for a look-see. There were more than two hundred horses packed into pens with barely enough room to move. They were in deplorable condition, haggard with eyes sunken in their drooping heads. Stallions were separated from their harems and nipped at each other in their distress. Mares looking starved and ill were penned with their equally malnourished foals.

"Branch," I was angry. "Where is Chuck? How can he let something like this go on?"

"I don't know the answer, Annie. This is the worst I've ever seen." Branch was sickened by the sight. "Let's see if we can find him." Just as he turned to walk away he spotted a stallion with an unusual marking on his head. "Annie, look over there."

I turned to follow his finger. "Is that the one we saw at Bookcliffs? The one you called a 'Medicine Man?'"

"I think it is. And it's 'Medicine Hat.'"

We located Chuck and Branch lit into him calling him every vile name he could think of.

"Hold on, hold on Branch. I just got back. I'm trying to find out what happened myself." Chuck had just returned from Washington. "It's been a bad time. We lost our case but there's been all hell to pay. I don't know how much longer I'll be here."

"I'm sorry, Chuck. You're a good man. I want you to do me a favor."

"If I can. What is it?"

"You have a stallion in one of the pens. I want him."

"You know I can't do that. He hasn't been gelded yet and you'll have to wait for the auction."

"He won't last till then. It'll be our little secret. There's worse done than that by the law- abiding Bureau."

Chuck sighed. "Let's go look."

The mustang was easily loaded into the trailer. There was little fight left in him. Thad made him a personal challenge. He was cleaned and medicated and given vaccinations. They named him Bonnet and nursed him slowly back to health.

Sam was doing research on the recent decision by the U.S. District Court in Reno to hold the BLM accountable for its handling of the mustang adoption program. She showed me an article she'd found in the Gazette's archives.

"I think you will find this really interesting. It was written by Hope Ryden and it's about the wild horses at Bookcliffs. She's written a number of very well researched books about the plight of the mustangs. Check it out."

That article and Hope Ryden's book, "America's Last Wild Horses," had a profound impact. After reading the heartbreaking story of the mistreatment of those remarkable animals and the failures of the government to protect them, I began a crusade of my own. I began to research the history of the wild horses and the eventual involvement of the Bureau

Annie's Portion

of Land Management in their protection, discovering that when it came to carrying out their mandate, the BLM did everything but protect the herds. I learned more about "Wild Horse Annie"; a woman whose real name was Velma Johnston, who almost single-handedly brought the plight of the mustangs to the public's attention. Her adversaries, in an attempt to discredit her, gave her the nick-name "Wild Horse Annie." The story of the slight, quiet spoken woman appeared in a children's book and made "Annie", the name she adopted, a national hero. In 1959 she was called to testify before Congress about the mistreatment of the mustang herds. She presented indisputable evidence of her charges; evidence, including photos she'd been gathering for ten years. Congress passed a bill providing protection from the use of aircraft or motorized vehicles in the capture of wild horses. Called the "Wild Horse Annie Bill," the law, while somewhat limited in scope, was hailed as a victory for horse lovers.

I began reading everything I could find about the plight of the wild herds. My enrollment in the American Horse Protection Association provided me with access to the most current information on pending legal action. I became a fierce advocate for the American mustang, bombarding State and Federal legislators with letters condemning the abuses and mismanagement of the wild horse programs. Sam continued to inform the public of the plight of the horses in the Gazette. We were determined to make an impact, accepting speaking engagements in towns throughout Colorado and its environs.

You know," I told Branch and Thad. "It's the fault of the ranchers. They don't want to share the public lands with the wild herds. It's ridiculous for the cowmen to have that kind of power."

"Whoa, there. You're talking to some of them thar ranchers." Branch responded.

"You're different. But don't you think you should take more of an active interest in the problem?"

"I tried, Annie. I joined one of the local stockmen's advisory boards. The members are supposed to make recommendations to the Bureau for the management of the herds. But most of the ranchers had no interest in protecting the horses. They were there to serve their own interests. Most meetings became shouting matches. I gave it up."

"Karol Longbranch! I'm ashamed of you."

I continued to amass a large collection of books, magazines and newspaper articles related to the survival of the mustangs. Books were piled on the bedroom floor and the dining room table was often covered with news articles waiting to be glued into an ever-growing scrapbook.

Sarah complained to Branch, "This is getting to be a mess. It's time you said something to that *meshuggeneh*."

Branch laughed. "If that means nut house case, you're right."

He asked Pete to have some shelves built in the bunkhouse. "Make sure there are enough shelves to hold Annie's growing collection. And put them in a place where the guests have access to them."

Pete made an addition of his own with a hand-crafted sign that read, "Annie's Library."

Chapter XXIX

Matt called to invite his family to visit him, insisting that we celebrate the holidays together in Florida. "I have someone I want you to meet."

"It will be hard for us to get away so close to the stock show," Branch had protested.

"It will be so nice to be there for the holiday and Sarah's birthday. If we spend just a few days in Florida, there will still be lots of time to get things ready for the show. Besides, you know the boys don't really need you anyway," I pleaded.

"Annie, you know how Thad is going to react. He's really irreplaceable."

But once I enlisted Sam's help the battle was lost.

It had been such a long time since I'd seen the Christmas tree and Chanukah lights in the same room. Josh and Wendy were wonderful hosts, surprising Sarah with a cake for her eighty- fourth birthday. Matt introduced us all to his friend Tracy Brenner, a beautiful, graceful, enchanting girl. He'd met her in a lab at FSU where they were both working towards their degrees in marine biology.

Sarah pulled me aside. "Is she a *yiddisha?*" she asked in a loud whisper.

"Yes Mom, she is."

"Ah, it's a *mitzvah.*"

The trip was all too short but it served its intended purpose; an opportunity to meet the girl who was destined to be the next member of our growing family.

As for my daughter and I, the 1989 stock show took a back seat to the wedding planning. There were numerous discussions about the time of year that would be best. Sam at first thought May or early June would be a good time, before guests arrived. Thad thought it would be too cold and maybe they should have the wedding in Denver. Branch and I both felt it would be nice to have the wedding at the ranch and maybe we could wait until early fall. In the end it was agreed to close the ranch to guests early and have the wedding in mid-September.

In March I had my fifty-fifth birthday. My health was good and all the exercise I got helped me maintain a younger appearance, but as was to be expected I was experiencing the onset of menopause. Branch woke in the middle of the night to see me standing buck naked in front of the open window, the snow blowing across my face.

"Annie," he called.

"Don't ask," I shouted back.

Claire arrived from Lake Havasu, alone and looking tired. Star greeted her with as much energy as she could muster even managing to deliver a few enthusiastic wags of her tail.

"We need to lessen Claire's chores," I suggested to Branch.

"I think you're right. She is not looking well. But she'll be a demon to deal with. She won't give up her kitchen without a fight."

"I know. We'll ease Ernesto into her domain. He's really pleasant and easy to like and would be a real help to her. He can learn a lot from Claire and eventually take over her chores altogether."

"I worry about her. She is really alone now. Howard may not have been a bargain but at least he was company. We have to find some solution, one she may not altogether agree with," Branch mused.

There never seemed to be enough hours in the day to accomplish our tasks. Although Pete was whole again and sat his horse with the best of them we were still shorthanded. Fabian recruited two "cousins" to help with the seeding and free up the wranglers for the work they did best. Thad

Annie's Portion

was busier than ever adding baby sitter and nursing to his other chores. He'd tended Bonnet with infinite care and the mustang had been restored to health and claimed by Thad for his personal use. With Thad's monitoring and Jessie's mothering, Thor had grown into a beautiful stallion, well-formed and high-spirited. Jessie was pregnant again and would foal in late summer but this time the sire was a purebred Quarter Horse.

In April we got a call from my former assistant, Karen. She had left her husband and accepted an offer to transfer to the Denver office of BGM. She would arrive in May and while I was sorry to hear of the failed marriage, I was delighted to have Karen close enough to visit. I offered to meet her in Denver and help her get settled. In May Matt phoned to announce his engagement to Tracy. No surprise.

I had several speaking engagements in Denver, using each trip as an excuse to spend time with Karen. There were Samantha's wedding invitations to choose, the perfect wedding dress to buy and fittings to see to. The library was growing and I added a number of children's books to the collection. Sometimes after dinner, I gathered some of the young guests and read to them. I told Branch, "These kids will grow up to be the next generation of mustang advocates." Spring and summer were busier than usual allowing me little time for my golden mestano. But there were occasions when I would sneak off to enjoy the splendor of the mountains and meadows, giving Beau a chance to release his stored energy and reaffirm his preeminent position in the equine world. His quasi-captivity had in no way diminished his free spirit or his ability to tear across an open field, feet barely touching the earth, wind-blown mane brushing my face. These all-too-few excursions left both horse and rider in a state of euphoria; in my case, lasting for days. In late August Jessie welcomed her pure-bred filly into the world.

Saturday, September 23rd, dawned crisp and clear. The Colorado sky did not disappoint and in a setting enhanced by white-crowned mountains and gilded aspens, Samantha became Mrs. Thaddeus Longbranch in front of an audience of friends and family, which included Matt and his fiancé, Tracy.

I marked each year by the advent of the National Western and again added an Official Badge to my growing collection. The 1990 show lasted two weeks with attendance again exceeding the half-million mark. There was talk of proposing a ballot initiative to fund the expansion of the buildings. It was a far cry from the first one that opened in 1906, which ran for six days with an estimated attendance of fifteen-thousand. In that year a Horse Division first became part of the activities. Streetcars and carriages carried the attendees to the site near the Denver stockyards and steers sold for twenty-three cents a pound. The show had since survived a cancellation in 1915 due to an epidemic of "hoof and mouth" disease, the Great Depression and two World Wars.

This year the Bar L, with the sale of two prize registered bulls, a fair number of Quarter Horses and all of Thad's carefully gleaned spermatozoa, would realize a healthy profit from its enterprise.

Samantha continued to work at the Gazette where she'd developed a popular human interest column. She provided me with up-to-date news regarding B.L.M activities or legislative changes regarding mustang management. The agency had submitted a budget request of thirteen and a half-million dollars to cover the cost of removing eighty-seven-hundred more horses from the public domain. Shortly after the budget was approved the General Accounting Office issued a report stating that there was no evidence to support the claim the lands were overcrowded. The G.A.O. found that removals were based on 1971 data which had been

Annie's Portion

provided by advisory groups, comprised largely of livestock owners holding open range permits. A spokesman for the Bureau responded to the report by saying that the problems cited occurred in the '80's and assured the agency that the new administration was committed to making the wild horse program more effective.

Thinking about Chuck and his futile efforts to make improvements, I said to Branch, "I hope this will really lead to a change for the better. There is so much misinformation put out for public consumption, it's hard to know what to believe."

Thad had been commuting between Grand Junction and the ranch since the wedding, spending four days a week in Junction. With the return of the seasonal wranglers he reversed his schedule, spending four days at the ranch. He was overjoyed when Jorge returned for the summer.

As usual, Claire arrived in May looking thinner and paler then when she left for Lake Havasu in November.

"Branch we must do something about Claire. She is obviously very ill." I said with concern. "I think she is hiding something from us. I'm going to insist on her seeing a doctor. You have to back me up."

"I'll try, but she's worse than an unbroken bronc." Branch was not looking forward to the confrontation.

We found Claire in the bunkhouse kitchen, seated at the small table with a cup of coffee in front of her. Her pink kerchief dangled from her apron pocket.

"Oh, hi, you two lovebirds." She attempted to stand but Branch laid his arm on her shoulder.

"Don't get up. We'll join you for coffee."

I poured two cups and we pulled chairs up to the table.

"What is this?" Claire asked suspiciously.

"Claire," I began. "I'm going to take you into Junction to see a doctor."

Claire started to protest but Branch interceded. "We will not take no for an answer. You are not well and we need to find out what's wrong." He looked lovingly at this eccentric woman who had mothered him most of his life.

"Ain't no argument and ain't no use." Claire pulled out her kerchief and dabbed at her eyes. "I been to a doctor already."

"And what?" I asked afraid of the answer.

"I got that damn killer disease." Claire could not bring herself to say the dreaded word.

Little by little, Branch and I coaxed the information from her. Claire had noticed a dark bruise on her leg but had ignored it thinking she had bumped it somehow. It did not seem to get any better and when it enlarged she finally went to see a doctor. He insisted on a biopsy the results of which indicated a melanoma. Further tests confirmed the diagnosis and she was referred to a surgeon.

"Why didn't you call us?" I was distraught. "I should have been there with you."

"You're a tough old hen," Branch said. "But even you need help once in a while. Did they get it all?"

Claire could no longer hold back the tears. "No, it was too late. The rotten thing had already spread. I got it in the lungs too."

"It metastasized?" I said in disbelief.

"I guess that's what you call it. Kind of spread around... glands and all."

I put my arms around Claire and pulled her close. "We'll get chemotherapy. There's a good medical center in Junction."

"No. I ain't doin' none of that. Besides the doc said it's too late."

"We'll get a second opinion, or a third," I argued.

"It's God's will. Besides, I got things ta do here."

Annie's Portion

"You've got nothing to do here but rest," Branch added.

"You ain't gonna make no invalid of me," Claire retorted. "I'm gonna be cookin' in this here kitchen till they carry me out."

"Well argue as you may you're going to have some help here." Branch was firm.

"Branch is right. Ernesto can be a great help. He cooks for the boys all winter." I added, "Not anywhere as good as you and no apple pies."

It was agreed that Ernesto would help in the kitchen but only under Claire's direct orders. Branch explained the situation to him and asked him to be tolerant and try to ignore Claire's temper tantrums. Ernesto, who was mild mannered and as agreeable as could be, made the adjustment well.

Sarah returned in June and fussed over Claire until Claire yelled for help. But by the end of July, it was clear she was losing the battle. I took her into Junction to see a specialist who told me there was nothing more to do for Claire but keep her comfortable. He suggested we move her to a nursing home or hospice care but I insisted on taking her home.

"We have lots of people there who will be able to take care of Claire."

"It's going to get very difficult. You'll need special medical equipment."

"Just tell us what we will need and we'll get it."

Claire's body was failing her but she tried to maintain some control of the kitchen. When she couldn't remain standing she gave Ernesto orders while sitting on a stool. He tolerated her brusqueness with good humor and compassion. When she was no longer able to deny the inevitable she was moved to the main house. Branch drove the truck into Junction to pick up a hospital bed, oxygen tanks, medicine and assorted apparatus that would be used to keep Claire comfortable. We tended her unceasingly; bathing, feeding, medicating and administering the morphine that eased the pain. Sarah was her constant companion, reading to her or telling her stories of the old days. When it became apparent she was nearing the end, Branch and I took turns sleeping in her room with Star lying on the floor at the foot of the bed. We were with Claire on the September morning when she breathed her last. She was buried in the little cemetery on the hill, next to Emil.

In November, the four Longbranch's flew to Florida to attend Matt's wedding. The ceremony was performed in beautiful Temple Beth Torah in West Palm Beach. Tracy was a vision to behold in demure white silk, her long, dark hair capped with a crown of miniature white roses that held a short tulle veil in place. Matt, tall and stately in his well-tailored tuxedo, stood at the foot of the altar waiting for Mr. Brenner to place the bride's hand in his. Matt and Tracy ascended the steps stopping under a white satin wedding canopy where the Rabbi waited to unite them. Sarah's joy was immeasurable. Matt was the first of her grandchildren to be married in the traditional way—in a synagogue, under a *chuppa*, by a Rabbi. The wedding was followed by a reception held at the Yacht Club. The event provided an opportunity for a family reunion. Danny arrived with his fiancée, Jeannie; a shy, pretty girl a dozen years his junior, weighing no more than a hundred-ten pounds. Sarah did not miss the opportunity to remark the *shiksa* needed some good Jewish cooking to fatten her up. Julie and her husband attended as well as Rose and other family members who had relocated from New York to "Brooklyn South".

Back in our hotel room, I sat brushing my hair in front of the dressing table mirror. I noticed the creases beginning to appear around my eyes. "You know," I said to Branch who was lying in bed watching me. "There is a song from

'Fiddler on the Roof'...that is so apropos. Do you remember it?"

"I think I know the one you mean...about children growing up."

"Yes. 'Sunrise, sunset...quickly fly the years. One season following another, laden with happiness and tears'."

Chapter XXX

The new Expo Hall and Stadium Hall were completed just in time for the opening of the 1991 Western Stock Show. While I still enjoyed the events, especially the auction and the rodeo, the initial novelty had worn off. I spent much of the time shopping in Denver or visiting the museums and galleries. I met Karen for lunch in Laramie Square and reminisced about the "old times" in Hawaii; sailing, old boyfriends and sucking up margaritas at Compadres.

Spring arrived with its usual explosive display of colorful flowers and budding trees. The vaqueros returned full of enthusiasm and expectations. Some of them had worked together for years, enjoying the fellowship of men who shared the love of cowboy life. The first days of their reunion were replete with many exaggerated stories of shared times; driving longhorns through untamed country or busting fierce wild horses, of rustlers and famous bronco busters. Each year the stories became more and more the stuff of legend. It was part of the cowboy mystique.

Sam surprised us one weekend with the announcement she, like the other mares in Thad's care, was with child.

Branch slapped his son on the back. "Good work, Thad. You're batting a thousand."

"Hey, what about me? Don't you think I had something to do with it," Sam said with pretended irritation.

There was much celebrating, especially by Sarah who was about to become a great- grandmother for the first time. After her second glass of champagne, she giddily plopped into an armchair and fell asleep, snoring loudly.

Privately, Branch and I discussed housing arrangements for the soon to be parents.

"It's a sure thing that they can't split the time the way they're doing now."

"We need Thad here so you've got to convince your daughter to give up her job and move to the ranch."

"What they really need is a place of their own. Why don't we suggest they build another house somewhere here on the ranch? Heaven knows there's enough room."

"Hey Annie. I always knew there was a reason I married you. You're so damn smart."

"Maybe Sam will be less reluctant to leave her job if she has a carrot offered her."

"We certainly know how effective those carrots are."

The kids were delighted with the idea of building their own home. They spent all their spare time searching for just the right location. Thad often saddled Bonnet and went off to scout on his own. Bonnet had regained his former vigor. His muscles once more rippled and his beautiful roan shield was prominently displayed on his well-muscled breast.

After a month of searching, he and Sam decided on a location two miles west of the main spread. They hired an architect who helped select the perfect building site. Partially protected by tall pines, the log house would be built on a rise overlooking a broad meadow. Plans were completed, permits approved and construction begun in late summer.

With the baby expected in November, and Thad still commuting, I wanted Samantha to leave her job and move up to the ranch. My daughter reveled in her pregnancy but stubbornly resisted giving up her job, insisting on remaining in Junction as long as possible.

"Besides, I don't want to take the chance of going into labor in a snowstorm up there."

"You can't keep making that awful ride up here every weekend. You'll shake that baby out prematurely," I persisted.

In the end we reached a compromise. Sam would move up to the ranch but would return to Junction to await the birth two weeks before her November due date.

Thad fussed over her like a mother hen. When Branch began treating her like an invalid she threatened to leave them both and return to Junction. As earlier agreed, Thad and Sam moved down to Junction on November 3rd. Jonathan Emil Longbranch, weighing in at eight-pounds six- ounces, arrived on the morning of November 9th, 1991 at three o'clock. A week later, the new family moved into the ranch house to await the completion of their own home.

Sarah had not gone to Florida as was her custom, in order to be there for the birth of her great-grandchild. Jonathan had no lack of love or attention, prompting me to chide my mother.

"And you said I spoiled Matt."

"Oh," was Sarah's response. "Infants can't be spoiled."

The house was ablaze with lights at holiday time. Branch and Thad cut down a seven-foot evergreen, which was trimmed with colored lights and ornaments, toy soldiers and tinsel. It was topped with a six-pointed star. A brass menorah graced the dining room table and candles were appropriately lit. The base of the tree was hidden under a heap of multicolored, ribboned packages. The staircase banister and the mantel were festooned with swags of fragrant pine.

On Christmas Eve the house was crowded with spiffed-up cowhands; hair slicked down, clean shaven, sweet smelling, boots shined. Dinner was buffet style and the seating arrangement casual, the men parking wherever they could. Chairs were brought in from the dining room and scads of large pillows decorated the floor. The fire blazed, the eggnog flowed and the music supplied by two guitarists, added to the holiday atmosphere. Little Jonathan was in

Annie's Portion

attendance, snug in his bassinet, oblivious to the noise. We welcomed 1992 with a much more subdued celebration. Branch and I were the only ones awake when the clock struck twelve.

For the first time I did not attend the National Western, preferring to remain at home with my new grandson. He was a very accommodating child, suckling well and sleeping for long stretches between feedings. He responded to visual and auditory stimulation with what I was sure was a smile.

"He's such a bright baby. He's doing things well ahead of time," I *kvelled* at what I considered Jonathan's extraordinary achievements.

"Oh Mom," Sam chided me. "You know it's only gas. Isn't that right grandma?"

"Sometimes. But this *boychick* is very special. Your mother is right."

"You two are impossible." Sam too, doted on her son.

After a two weeks absence, the men returned from the stock show in near blizzard conditions. They were disappointed by the smaller than usual turnout.

"The bad weather limited attendance this year. It was hard for folks to get here I guess. Kansas was especially hard hit by the blizzard and none of the Nebraska crowd showed up," Branch told me. "I think Thad was especially let down."

"Well, he'll just have to put those little fellas back in the freezer."

Branch laughed. "Don't let him hear you say that. You know how serious he is about that stuff."

Thad soon got over the setback, enjoying his son while complaining that Jonathan would learn to speak Yiddish before he spoke English.

"You two old ladies have to speak to him in English," he complained.

"Get used to it, Thad. It comes with the territory," Branch advised him.

March came in like a lamb, causing concern that it might go out like a lion. Each of the cowpokes made a forecast based on folklore and years of experience, none of which materialized. Samantha's boss asked her if she would like to continue her column with the Gazette. She was thrilled with the idea and arrangements were made for her to fax her articles to the paper twice a week.

In April, Star refused to leave the house. She ate little and only when I sat with her. Branch carried her outside twice a day to allow her to eliminate, most times to no avail. During the day she slept on the rug in front of the fireplace even though there was no longer a fire in the hearth. At night Branch lifted her onto the bed where she slept on my feet. It had been more than four years since he'd lifted Star to the bed for the first time.

"I didn't think it'd be for long," he reminded me.

"I guess bringing her in gave her these extra years. But I'm sure she doesn't have much time left."

Branch thought it would be more humane to put her out of her misery but did not have the heart to suggest that alternative. Sam found Star near the hearth one morning and realized that she had gone. She was buried on the knoll not far from Claire.

On May 9th Jonathan reached his six-month birthday. He sat in his chair and was presented with a cupcake after Sam blew out the single candle. He received a stuffed bear, another in the family of eight he already owned, and several other inconsequential gifts. He happily slopped the food on his tray, banging his small plastic spoon for effect.

The house on the hill was completed In July. Leaving Branch, Thad and Jonathan to fend for themselves, Sam, Sarah and I delighted in going into Denver to order furnishings. While enjoying the luxury for a day or three at

Annie's Portion

the Brown Palace, we shopped, lunched and shopped some more, ending the days with pleasant dinners at the hotel. An exhausted Sarah would head off to bed leaving daughter and granddaughter sipping after dinner drinks at the Palace Bar.

Thad and his family moved into their wonderful new, spacious log home in August. Sam had taken great care to furnish the place in western style, unpretentious but comfortable and warm. The large deck afforded a view of the meadow dotted with wild flowers. With Jonathan in his playpen Sam was able to enjoy the long, warm days outdoors while she prepared her articles for publication. I would often ride up to visit them, spending happy hours with Jonathan; pampering him with gifts and goodies, reading stories to him from books with colorful illustrations of horses. On one such day Jonathan was making an attempt to stand, trying to pull himself up on unsteady legs.

"Just like the foals," I remarked to Sam, suddenly aware that there were tears in my daughter's eyes. "What's wrong darling?"

"There's nothing wrong, Mom. Everything's so right. Sometimes I can't believe how lucky we are. It's almost like we lead a charmed life. I read and hear so many stories of other families who have experienced terrible tragedies; children born with horrible birth defects or incurable diseases...accidents resulting in death or paralysis. And I get so scared."

I clasped my daughter in my arms. "Darling, you only read or hear about the bad stuff. No one ever talks about what is usual or good. You should know it doesn't sell papers. Most people never experience the kind of tragedies you're talking about. Besides, we've had our share."

Jonathon had managed to get his footing and stood holding the side of the playpen for a few seconds. He let go of the rail and sat with a plop, looking startled, his eyes large as quarters. Both of us laughed and I lifted him from his kennel.

"This is what you need to be thinking of. This wonderful little boy."

The days grew shorter, the weather cooler and the first frost turned the aspen leaves to gold. September became November and Jon, the recently adopted, shortened version of his name, celebrated his first year with a full blown bash. His aunts and uncles arrived to join in the festivities, which lasted for days and included an early Thanksgiving dinner. Jon had just taken his first steps and was delighted with all the attention and hand clapping that greeted his jerky motions. Hands reached out to grab him when he appeared headed for a fall. Laughter accompanied his flops on a well-padded posterior.

All too soon the party was over and the crowd gone. Finding the winters too cold for her aging bones, Sarah went back to Florida with Josh and Wendy.

That year the holidays were observed quietly; a small tree decorated and a menorah lighted for Jon's sake. I had extracted a promise from Sam that she would provide Jon with a Jewish upbringing, teaching him about his history and heritage. Thad concurred, assuring me that he too would learn more about Judaism so they could share the culture as a family. I knew I could count on Thad to keep his word and was satisfied Jon would know from whence he came.

The earth made another journey around the sun. Jon accompanied his family on the trip to Denver for the 1993 Stock Show. Mother Nature cooperated this time and once again there were record crowds. The Rodeo featured "Mutton Bustin'" for the first time; an event in which kids roped and tied sheep, drawing more than a hundred and seventy-five-thousand attendees. Coors sponsored an extremely successful Western Art Exhibit and Sale for the benefit of the National Gallery Western Scholarship

Fund. I scoured the Exhibit Hall hoping to find some horse sculptures as good as the ones I'd first seen in the Laramie Square gallery. Nothing merited a second glance. Determined to find the artist whose work I'd seen earlier, I sneaked away and headed for the downtown art district. Half-an-hour of walking the streets yielded nothing but sore feet. I was discouraged.

"I should have paid more attention to the location," I berated myself. "No wonder I've never shaken my nickname."

About to give up, I stopped to rejuvenate myself with some strong coffee. Providing the waitress with a description of the object of my search, asking if she knew of any such place; she pointed to a shop just across the street. There it was—the gallery I'd been searching for. A number of browsing customers filled the small shop. Two men were engrossed in a lively discussion, one of whom I remembered speaking with before. The other, a rangy, long-haired man in his mid-thirties had the look of an artist.

"Excuse me, I hate to interrupt but you look like you might just be the person I'm looking for."

"I remember you," the proprietor responded. "You've been here before...asking about the sculptures. Well, this is your man."

"I thought it was. He looks the part." I introduced myself and pulled the pictures of Jessie, Beau and Thor from my purse.

"Would you accept a commission to create one bronze sculpture of all three animals using these photos?"

"They're beautiful horses. Is this a mustang?" He pointed to the picture of Beau.

"Yes he is. He was rounded up years ago and my husband rescued him from the BLM. Jessie is a registered Quarter Horse and this is their colt."

"They are quite a family. The coloration of the colt is spectacular. It would be difficult to capture the uniqueness in bronze."

"Is there something else you could suggest?"

"I might be able to work a sculpture in wood using different varieties for the blacks and blondes. I've never done anything like that before and it would be a kind of experiment."

"Will you try? I want the sculpture for my husband's birthday in August."

"That certainly gives me time to work on it. It would be a real challenge to create a piece that would capture the essence of these three. It might be possible but I can't promise anything."

"Please do try," I encouraged. "I love your work and Branch would too."

"Branch? Is your husband the Longbranch of the Bar L?"

"Yes. Do you know him?"

"Not really. But I know of him. You folks have done some great work in the field of cross- breeding."

"Yes. Our son Thad has developed methods to re-establish certain bloodlines through embryo transfer. His grandfather was a pioneer in the establishment of the American Quarter Horse Registry."

"Would it be possible for me to visit the ranch and see the horses?"

"We'd have to be sneaky about it. I want this to be a surprise. Can you come on short notice? It would have to be sometime when Branch is away. It's a five hour drive, the last hour of which is on a very rough road."

"He's at the show now, isn't he?"

"Yes he is. If you can get away now, I'll call my foreman and ask him to show you the three animals. Of course Thor is no longer a colt but you can see his color and the unusual marking on his nose. Beau is not too friendly...the hands call him 'El Diablo,' so you may have to view him from a distance or tempt him with an apple. Jessie is a lady and you'll love her."

"Why don't I plan on going up in my jeep tomorrow? I can leave about eight and get there by one or two. I'll bring my camera equipment and take some additional pictures."

I was elated. "This is so great. It was the hand of Providence that brought me here today."

"By the way, I'm Willard Robins." He extended his hand.

I reached to take it. "My pleasure, I'm sure. I'm Annie."

The arrangements were made for Pete to give Willard a tour and show him the intended subjects. I used the excuse he was a photographer who wanted to do an article on the Bar L. By the time the family returned to the ranch the deed was done.

Willard and I kept in touch as the work progressed. He had taken two dozen pictures of the animals and had been greatly impressed with them.

"They are more magnificent in person. Beau is one of the finest mustangs I have ever seen. And that young stallion is something else. You've also got another mustang there, a most unusual stallion."

"You must mean Bonnet. Branch thinks he's a 'Medicine Hat'."

"I took the liberty of photographing him too. Just in case you decide to give him another present."

I could feel Willard's smile. "No, that's Thad's bronc. But maybe next time."

Spring came and once again Branch found himself short-handed. Pete finally had to admit he could no longer sit a horse for long hours and was reassigned to less strenuous work closer to the homestead.

"It gets harder every year," Branch complained to Thad. "There aren't many real cowboys left."

"They're all in school," Thad agreed. "Learning about the industry rather than the animals. There's much more money to be made working for drug companies or blood stock organizations."

"Yes," Branch agreed. "And a lot less work. Well, grumbling about it won't get us any help. I think I'll call Chuck at the Canyon facility and see if he can recommend anyone. After all, we did get Jorge from there."

"It's too bad we sent him off to school," Thad complained. "He'll be one of those guys we just talked about."

Branch never seemed to get the time to go to the mustang facility so he gave Chuck a call. "Hey Chuck. Glad to see they haven't put you out to pasture yet."

"Don't kid about it. I'm sure it's about to happen. I guess I just make too many waves. What's up Branch? I have no other stallions fit enough for the likes of you."

"How about a couple of wranglers instead? We're gonna be awfully shorthanded this summer. Anybody you know who'd be good?"

"There is one young fella, Ricky Black. Got caught with some pot, probably trying to sell it. He's really a good kid and great with the horses. Father had a ranch over in Kansas somewhere. Did a bit of wranglin'. He'll be out in just a few days. There's another guy, older. He's in for breaking and entering...a vacation house. Took the TV and some electronic stuff. He's got a real knack with mustangs. One rebel to another, you might say. But I'm not awfully sure about him. I get the feelin' he just tells you what he thinks you want to hear. Real smooth...you know the kind."

"But he's good with horses?"

"That he is. But I sure wouldn't want him around my daughter."

Annie's Portion

Branch laughed. "What if I send Pete down to pick them both up. See what he thinks of them. When's this other fella getting out?"

"A week from Saturday. I can bring Ricky here for a few days...until they release Anson Perry. Then Pete can come for them both"

"I guess we'll give it a try. Right now it seems to be my only option. Thanks, Chuck."

"You got it. Now don't you go blaming me if they don't work out."

Pete returned from Canyon with the two ex-cons in tow. He told Branch, "This kid Ricky. He seems like a right good boy. Just made a bad choice. But I don't take much to that half-breed."

"Is he part Indian?" Branch asked in surprise. "Chuck didn't say anything about that. Not that it should matter," he added.

"I ain't sure, but he sure looks like one. With that long hair and them beads he wears." Pete spat.

"Chuck says he's a good horseman. Let's give him a chance, Pete. You can set him straight."

Spring was followed by a hot, windless summer. Horses and cattle were rounded up and sold. The two new cowhands worked hard and Pete somewhat modified his opinion of Anson.

"Ricky, now he tries to do the job of a man. Never complains even though things is tough on him. That Perry fella...he sure kin handle them horses. He kin break a bronc in no time flat. Talks ta them and they seem ta know jest what he says. But," he added ruefully. "I still don't like him. Quiet like, keeps ta himself. There's jest somethin' I can't put my finger on." He shook his head.

"Boy," Thad remarked to his father. "I sure wouldn't want to be on Pete's shit list. "

"Nor I. When he gets to disliking someone, he never gets off it. Maybe it's the hair thing."

"And the beads." Thad and Branch had a good laugh.

It was neither. His success with the horses often came at the animal's expense. He was rough on them and used the whip frequently. He made sure he was not being observed when he punched an uncooperative horse in the neck or jerked so hard on the bit that it caused bleeding. But Rick noticed the events and wasn't the least bit surprised by the same actions he had seen before. He wanted no trouble and figured it was better to keep it to himself.

Anson had been taken with Beau from the first time he laid eyes on the palomino. Early on Fabian cautioned him. "You don't wanna mess with El Diablo. He is mucho trouble. Only Miss Annie rides that hombre."

"There ain't no horse I can't master." Fabian's warning only served to whet Anson's appetite for the mustang. At first he tried to coax Beau with an apple or carrot. But the horse was wary of him. Anson was not the kind who discouraged easily and found any reason and every opportunity to be near the mustang. During one of my absences Anson rode into the pasture and tried to rope the stallion. He chased Beau for half an hour until his horse was spent. On another occasion Pete asked Anson to bring Samson in for shoeing. Samson was sharing a corral with Ginger and some young stallions and was not anxious to leave. Anson threw a rope on him and tied it to his saddle horn. He dismounted, leaving his cow pony to do what it was trained to do—hold the line taut. Moving to Samson's side he stunned the gelding with a powerful thrust to the throat. With the debilitated horse in tow Anson made for the gate. Beau had been sequestered in a smaller pen adjoining the corral, awaiting his turn with the blacksmith. Letting loose a roar of outrage he reared up, then lunged toward Anson who, had he not been behind the fence, would surely have received a damaging blow from the stallion's hooves. Anson struck out with his whip, delivering a glancing blow to Beau's lower jaw. Then he dug his heels into his mount and headed out the corral gate with Samson still struggling behind.

"One of these days I'm gonna get you, you son-of-a-bitch," he vowed.

Rick had been watching the scene from the sidelines. He'd seen Anson pull the same stunt with horses at the BLM facility. Anson was meaner than a skunk and Rick was scared to death of him so he kept quiet about the incident and Anson's obsession with the golden palomino.

Beau was jittery and more difficult to manage whenever Anson was nearby. Returning to the ranch from an exceptionally arduous ride, I discovered a raw spot on Beau's back when I removed the saddle. A further search revealed a burr stuck to the blanket.

"How in the world could this happen?" I queried as Thad treated the abrasion. The incident was puzzling though I suspected the barb might have been put there intentionally.

Sam had also been filling his ears with her premonitions and woman's intuition. To say that she disliked Anson would be a gross understatement. In her words, "The man is slimy. He's mean-spirited and vulgar...gives me the heebie-jeebies. The horses don't take to him. Maybe you should get rid of him."

Thad's response, "We're shorthanded as it is. We can't afford to let him go." But he was beginning to have some doubts of his own, especially regarding Beau's reaction to Anson. He promised he'd watch for further indicators, but with the busy days of summer he failed to keep an eye out.

Guests came and went. Sarah returned to spend time with her adored Jonathan who had quickly learned that running got you there faster than walking. Determined to adhere to the slogan "full speed ahead", he was difficult to keep up with. His vocabulary increased and was more intelligible. Words like "mama", "da" and "moo" were formed into sentences. Jon's hair had darkened and his blue eyes sparkled with deviltry. An engaging grin now displayed a number of teeth.

Branch's sixty-fifth birthday was near at hand and I sought help from the family in planning a surprise party to celebrate.

"You know he'll refuse to take part in any such thing," Sarah admonished.

"Sarah's right," Thad agreed. "There's no way he'll agree to it."

"That's why I need your help. We'll have to make it look like it's a regular end-of-summer barbecue for the guests. We'll send invitations to special friends...Dale and Chuck...and Will. They'll keep it secret. Maybe some of the kids will be able to come."

"Where will we hide all these people?" Sam asked. "It doesn't seem very doable to me."

"We'll have to think about that. Maybe wheedle some of our neighbors to help. I know we can do it." My persistence paid off and the plot was hatched.

Willard called the first week in August. "Annie, I'd like you to see the piece before I put the finishing touches on it. Maybe we can meet up at Vail. I'll buy you lunch."

Eagerly, I drove through the mountains to meet Willard and get a first look at the sculpture I'd commissioned. Willard was seated at a corner table in the Skier's Club, an art deco restaurant popular with the jet set. He had a large package on the table and wore a grin that covered his face.

"You look like the Cheshire Cat," I smiled back. "Let me see it now, before I burst."

Willard carefully unwrapped the bundle.

I drew in my breath. "Oh Willard, it is indescribably brilliant."

"Do you really like it, Annie?" Willard was beaming with satisfaction.

"Like it!" I exclaimed. "It's better than anything I could have imagined. How in the world did you get the colors so right?"

"I used several woods," he explained. "Mahogany, white ash and ebony."

"But it's seamless! It looks like it was carved from one piece of wood." I was astounded. "It looks just like Beau... golden with his white mane flowing. And the tail! How did you do it? He even has white boots on his forelegs."

"It's all in the technique," Willard answered. "Some bleaching, some staining and a bit of laminating. The little guy...now he was the problem. Getting the color just right... and the lightening bolt gave me sleepless nights and sore fingers. I finally used an inlay of ebony. But I don't want to give all my trade secrets away."

I glanced at his hands, stained and roughened by the tedious chiseling and sanding.

"It is Thor. It's just as I remember him as a colt. And look at Jessie. She actually has a look of pride as she bends her head to admire her colt. Oh Willard! You have outdone yourself."

"I guess you like it?"

Several patrons came over to admire the sculpture. He received two offers to buy it. I put my arms around my horses protectively. "This is not for sale," I said firmly.

Willard went back to Denver to put the finishing touches on his masterpiece and I returned to the Bar L with some excuse for my absence. By this time, plans for the party were well under way. Friends and family alike were glad for the excuse to come to Cutter Lake for the big event.

"Don't you think we're kind of going overboard with this barbecue thing?" Branch asked his wife.

J. Fran Baird

"Probably," I answered. "But with Julie and her new husband coming from New York and Rose making the long trip, I want it to be really special."

I was obliged to make one more trip to Denver to fetch Branch's present before I could consider my chores done. Looking forward to Sam's reaction at the sight of the carving, I asked her to accompany me. During the drive in the twelve-year-old Beemer, she confided she was expecting again.

"That's just the best news, Samantha. It will be an added present for Branch."

We met Willard at his studio, where he showed off with the finished product, now sanded and lacquered to a mirrored sheen

"Oh, Mom!" Sam viewed the artwork with as much or more enthusiasm I had.

"Have you ever seen anything more wonderful?" On the verge of tears I tried to make light of the situation. "I really shouldn't act so pleased. I just realized how much the price would go up."

Willard laughed. "I should be paying you for the pleasure this piece gives me. But have no fear. The price will be fair. Besides, I got a whole new clientele from those people we met up in Vail."

"Is it mine now?" I asked, taking the prize in my hands.

"It's all yours. You may take it home."

It had been a challenge to keep Branch's sixty-fifth birthday celebration a secret. Branch was the consummate overseer. Nothing escaped his keen-eyed curiosity or his probing inquiry. We'd had to arrange accommodations for family members and friends; plan and prepare a feast for forty and do so without raising any suspicions. While Sam and I were claiming the "objet d'art" in Denver, Julie, Josh and their respective spouses arrived in Grand Junction.

Annie's Portion

They linked up with Danny, Matt and their wives to enjoy a couple of days of sightseeing before driving to the ranch. Will Harriman turned up the night before the party and had been recruited to keep Branch occupied until mid-afternoon on the day of the big event. At an agreed upon time the horde, in wagons and on horseback converged at the "great meadow" where we were making final preparations. The long kept secret was out.

Branch was truly surprised when he and Will terminated their rounds at the picnic area. He pretended to be annoyed when greeted by the cheering crowd, but was in truth quite moved by the outpouring of good wishes. All the preparations and plans so painstakingly devised came to fruition. Food and beer were consumed in equal proportions. Guitar-playing meztanos provided lively music and a cake was presented, sporting sixty-five blue candles and a single white one for next year. Frank toasted Branch with a flowery speech. Usually reticent, Pete offered a simple heartfelt wish for Branch's long and happy life. Even Fabian added his good wishes.

When it was time to light the candles, Thad raised his glass, "To my father, Karol Longbranch—a man who has been a quiet inspiration to all of us—the most honest, most sincere man I have ever known. He's smart too, just look at the wife he chose for us. Happy birthday, Dad!"

Branch's embarrassment was evident. He looked for his wife who had been the architect of his present discomfort.

As Thad lifted his glass to toast his father, I realized I'd forgotten to bring Branch's present. "Oh, damn! How could I have been so stupid?" Taking Sam aside I said, "Sam, I've got to go back to the house. Cover for me." I whistled for Beau who was at my side in a second. "Let's go, my friend. We are on a special mission." I raised the reins ever so slightly and Beau responded with the lightning start he was famous for.

Reaching the house I purposefully dashed through the entry hall and headed directly for the bedroom where I'd stashed my beautifully wrapped surprise behind an assortment of boxes on the closet floor. With the object of my mission safely in hand I heaved a sigh of relief and made for the door.

In great haste I'd failed to notice Anson Perry's presence. I was stunned when I turned to find him blocking my only exit. "Anson, what are you doing here?" I tried to appear calm and in control but the rapid beating of my heart nearly drowned out my own voice.

"Just thought I'd maybe do an extra chore or two...pick up some extra pesos."

His feral grin sent shivers through me.

"Ya caught me off guard there for a minute. Kinda froze when I heard those hoof beats. Didn't have enough time to find my treasure."

At the mention of hoof beats I became aware of the sounds. Beau was restless—stomping the ground and making noises that could only be described as bear-like growls. He'd recognized Anson's voice.

"Do yourself a favor and leave now." My voice trembled just a little bit.

"Or what?"

"Or you'll find yourself in a hell of a lot of trouble." I was regaining my composure and getting angrier by the second.

"I ain't goin' till I get some cash."

"We don't keep any money in the house."

"Don't try that bullshit on me. You got lots of dough here...payroll stuff 'n all." His voice had grown heavier, darker, more menacing. "There must be a safe. Where is it?"

Trying to appease him, I pointed in the direction of the main room. "There's a safe in there but I don't know how to open it."

"Show me...now!"

I left the package on the bed and hesitatingly moved toward the door. He grabbed my arm twisting it behind my back, pulling me close to him, so close I could smell his foul breath. He placed his free hand inside my shirt and rubbed my breast, pinching hard enough to make me wince.

"Ya know. Fer an old broad ya ain't so bad. I hear tell, older women make real good lovers...them bein' so grateful and all." His evil laugh set my teeth on edge.

Summoning up an air of bravado I did not feel I said, "Someone must have missed me by now." I thought, "Oh, God please help me."

Anson gave my arm a painful wrench, the smile now gone. "Get the money now."

He ripped the gold chain from my neck and pushed me roughly through the door. I focused on the gun in his hand, realizing he must have gotten it from Branch's desk.

"Yeh, and I ain't afraid ta use it neither."

There was no doubt about what he was capable of and I hurried into the great room, filled with the golden glow of the afternoon sun. "I think it's on the wall," I said, playing for time, hoping as I made my way to the office area help would arrive. "It's behind the computer."

"It damn well better be." It was obvious Anson had been in the house for some time. Papers were strewn about and the battered drawer that held Branch's hand-gun was on the floor, a poker iron thrown near by. I saw it, lying on the desk next to a box of shells. "Oh my God," I thought. "He's got the Henry."

He saw me eyeing the rifle. He put the gun down and fondled the Henry.

That foul grimace returned as he said, "Damn nice piece ya got here." Slowly, with exaggerated care he slid a shell into the rifle.

"You can't possibly think you'll get..."

"Get the damn money." Anson bellowed as he loaded two more bullets into the Henry.

Just as I lunged for the fire-iron we were both startled by the stomping of boots. Anson's first shot, intended for me, came from the rifle. It hit Branch with such force it knocked him off his feet. He hit the floor without ever having uttered a sound, a dark stain spreading across his chest.

I grabbed the poker and lunged at Anson, screaming, "You dirty piece of shit."

"Ya fuckin' bitch," he yelled. "Now look what ya done." He turned at the sound behind him, a look of utter terror on his face.

There was a golden horse, in the golden light, rearing above him. All the demons of hell were screaming at him. He fired the Henry twice before he felt the full impact of the powerful hooves stomping out his last earthly breath.

Book Three

Sam

Chapter I

2005 – Cutter Lake

"Some memories are realities, and are better than anything that can ever happen to one again." So contends the noted author Willa Cather. While there is much truth in the remark; be they bitter or sweet, memories prompt us to relive, enjoy and learn from them. They enhance and influence our every-day existence. Memories shape us.

There are moments when some physical or sensory experience evokes a long-gone chapter in my life, but it's the sight of old cars that most stir my memories, transporting me on a road to the past. Sighting an old hard-top Ford LTD on a highway, I recall the white one John gave my mother in Rhode Island, the one Danny wrapped around a pole the night of his senior prom; replaced by an Olds "442" bought on the cheap from a sailor. Mom realized it had been a mistake when she pulled into the driveway and Danny raced to meet her shouting excitedly, "Oh boy! A 442." He bought it from her before we departed for Hawaii.

Then there's the Volkswagen bus; the 1973 yellow bus that had toted us from Atlantic to Pacific. Whenever I pass one on the road—there were several on the campus at Fort Collins—I am reminded of the trip. My mother estimated the trans-continental journey would cover about thirty-five-hundred miles, little realizing with "Wrong Way Corrigan" at the helm and Matt, Atlas in hand in the role of navigator, we would put more than seven thousand miles on the odometer.

The middle seat of the van was removed to make room for luggage; summer clothes, bedding, camping gear and fifteen cartoons of books Mom refused to leave behind. My grandmother carped about the books blocking the view. Our quartet departed Rhode Island in April, before school let out but after Matt made his Bar Mitzvah, a simple ceremony held in an anteroom of the Synagogue. Ten old-timers, the number needed for a *minion*, agreed to conduct the service privately because Matt refused to perform in front of the entire Saturday congregation fearing he would mess up his Torah portion.

The first stop had been in Brooklyn where a night was spent with Cousin Julie and good-byes said to my thrice-married father. From that point on it was camping out time. Days were cool but nights frigid. Matt, Mother and I slept in a pup-tent with two sleeping bags zipped together and a third covering us all. Matt griped constantly about Mom's cold feet. Gram slept on an air mattress in the van, with a *nacht teffel* near at hand to be used as a chamber pot.

A routine for setting up camp was developed, timed to see if the process could be improved. Mom and I pitched the tent; Matt got a fire going and prepared the less-than-gourmet meals while Gram sat on the sidelines enjoying the show. I remember eating burnt Spam and soggy spaghetti quite often. It seemed to be the dinner staple.

Matt chose the scenic routes, the reason for the excess mileage, but to his credit we did see the best of America; visiting D.C. and camping in the Great Smokies at a state park where we woke in the misty morning chill to see does and fawns munching dew-covered grass. Gram's tinkling in the pot scared the deer off. The first trial was faced in Tennessee when the van came to a dead stop just feet from a service station. Talk about serendipity—the owner was a German who not only replaced a part, but at the suggestion of his genial wife, housed and fed us for two days.

From there it was Nashville where we saw two headliners at "The Grand Ole Opry." Nelson and Cash were unfamiliar names at the time. The navigator then instructed the chauffeur to proceed to "Natchez Trace," a less traveled, forested road leading to a TVA dam and eventually Alabama. On several occasions Mom tried to interfere with map-reading, pointing to red lines and blue ones, bringing an outraged burst from Matt.

"Mother," he decried. "That red line is Route 57. The blue lines are rivers."

Crossing the great Mississippi Matt commented on the mud and poor fishing conditions. I defended the river by bringing up the exploits of Tom Sawyer and Huck Finn. Gram, as always, intervened and restored calm. Upon the approach to Arkansas a large sign declared, "Welcome to Arkansas Land of Opportunity." The opportunity for the mostly Negro populace was to work as sharecroppers in fields devoid of vegetation.

In Little Rock there'd been a frightening storm with hailstones so large they left dents in the roof of the van. In Oklahoma we easterners saw the first oil wells; although because of their small size it was thought they were irrigation pumps, only one resembling those of movie fame sighted on the capitol grounds. Another first, a taste of Mexican food in Oklahoma City; where a friendly diner who'd overheard our conversation concerning Passover preparations, guided Mom to a small Jewish Sanctuary. All that was needed to conduct a *Seder* dinner was procured. Paradoxically, the Seder was celebrated in a Texas desert at a place called "El Diablo Canyon." A blanket was spread on the sand; prayers recited candles lit, wine consumed with matzos, concluding as always with the phrase, "Next year in Jerusalem."

"This is just like Moses did at the first Seder," I declared. It was a vision that remains stored in my memory bank, retrieved every year at Passover.

We drove through Lubbock, encountering further hail storms and tornado warnings; sleeping for the first time in a motel, enjoying the comfort of real beds and warm showers. The next stop was Carlsbad where we toured the and riding the world famous cable cars decorated with the logo for Ronzoni Macaroni.

But timing couldn't have been worse; a transportation strike had begun on the morning of our planned departure. Mom deposited Gram and me on a park bench while she and Matt went to find a taxi. Seated beside two delightful elderly ladies, my grandmother struck up a conversation. When told of the predicament the family was in, the octogenarians offered a ride to the airport. Sighting the pilot and navigator, I waved frantically. Once introductions were made Gram enthusiastically explained the proposal made by Elizabeth and Gloria. Mom gratefully accepted the offer, but her misgivings were soon confirmed when we discovered the car was a mini two-seater convertible. Anticipating an adverse reaction, Gloria had devised a perfect solution.

"We can squeeze three in the space behind our seats, and Sam can sit in my lap. It's a good thing you don't have much luggage."

"I think we can make it," Elizabeth shouted while cutting in and out of the traffic on the clogged interstate. I shut my eyes for most of the ride and it was with great relief we reached the airport approach ramp.

"See, I told you we could do it," Elizabeth grinned as she screeched to a halt in front of the United Airlines terminal.

Gloria and I popped lithely off the front seat, followed by Matt, Gram and Mother—who peeled themselves off the floor and painfully stretched their legs. Hugs were given all 'round and promises made to stay in touch, which we kept for many years.

Chapter II

The VW joined us in Hawaii two weeks after our arrival.

With hindsight, I think the timing of our arrival on Oahu was just right for me. I'd missed the hungry years, or at least could not recall them and by the time I was old enough to understand or care, Mom was making lots of money and we were in clover.

During those formative years my grandmother played the most important role in my life. She was my indisputable hero. Not even my mother, whom I cherished and admired, had greater influence. Gram was the one who set the example for us all. Tough, fair, honest and fun-loving, Gram was ever there. We took her for granted, believing nothing would change.

Things were always easy for me. My mother would often tell people how unspoiled I was, even as the only girl, coming after three boys. But in all honesty, I'd always been overindulged. I cannot remember a time when I didn't have everything I wanted. It wasn't even necessary to ask. All my wants and needs were anticipated by either my mom or Grandma, both of whom absolutely doted on me.

It's true there wasn't much to need in Hawaii. We had a roof over our heads, food in our bellies, fair skies, sandy beaches and a lovely ocean at our doorstep. All I ever really needed were some bikinis and a few dancing dresses. When I turned sixteen, old enough to drive, Danny gave me his Toyota, the car that replaced his "442."

As graduation neared, Mom took me to the mainland to look at colleges and when I chose Colorado State there was no further discussion. When I barely passed my first year, racking up a C average, there were no recriminations. As a matter of fact, Mom took me to Europe for a month to get a taste of the world. We had a great time back-packing with no planned itinerary; riding the rails, biking in Holland along the North Sea, sailing up the Rhine and Rhone rivers, touring castles. At mom's insistence we detoured to make an unpleasant stop, Dachau.

"To be sure you never forget," she admonished.

In Austria we lucked out when we discover the Salzburg Music Festival in progress and were able to obtain seats. We sledded down a chute in a salt mine, rode the highest funicular in the Swiss Alps, ascended the Eiffel Tower, descended the Tower of London.

But by my sophomore year, the same year I became a stepchild, I'd managed to get my act together. Oh, I remember how angry I was when Mother told me about Branch. I reacted with a rare spate of off-color language, telling her she was nuts, asking why, when she had the world by the balls, she would want to give up everything she'd worked for? She had money, houses, boat, cars, boyfriends and best of all...freedom.

Her answer was simple. "I love him."

How could I have been so thoughtless? I guess I was jealous. And just a little more than afraid...afraid that I would lose her and the closeness we shared. It was stupid of me and it was my grandmother who made me realize how self-absorbed I'd been.

"You should be happy for your mother," she chided. "It's wonderful at this time of her life she has found someone to love and love her. She will have a friend and companion in her old age. All of you are off doing your own thing. Why shouldn't she have the same right?"

Of all the people who should have been apprehensive, one would think it would've been Gram. After all she would be losing the most. But her only concern was he was not Jewish and what a fuss she made about that. When

Mom went to the mainland and returned a married woman, Grandma would have none of it.

"As far as I'm concerned," she fumed, "they are not married. Your mother is living in sin."

It wasn't until Mom and Branch faked a Jewish wedding in Hawaii that she was finally appeased. The biggest surprise of all was that she agreed to move to Colorado.

There was no need for me to grow up. I was having a wonderful life. Now the new life would include a wonderful stepfather, a ranch with horses to ride, ski slopes a short drive away and my mom and Grandma near by.

But of course the story is incomplete. Thaddeus Longbranch entered the picture. It was strange to think of him as my stepbrother. We'd actually been school mates but it was only at Mom's wedding we discovered the fact and had the distinct pleasure of sharing our parent's honeymoon with them on Maui. It was a pleasant trip and even though I found Thad somewhat reserved, it was good to have someone closer to my own age along for the ride.

We did not return to Colorado together, and since we shared no classes had no opportunity to see each other. Occasionally we'd spot one another at one of the pubs on "three-point-five" beer nights. We traveled in different circles so just waved in greeting.

It wasn't until spring break when at Branch's suggestion; we arranged to make the trip together to the ranch. It was a long trek and by the time we arrived at the homestead we'd found out a good deal about each other. By the time we returned to school I discovered my feelings for Thad went far beyond those of a sister.

We began seeing each other frequently, on campus and of course at the ranch. It soon became difficult to keep our relationship secret. I was sure my mother had suspicions although Thad believed his father was too distracted by ranch business to notice anything out of the ordinary.

"He'd have to be hit on the head with a hammer before he'd notice," Thad opined.

But he was wrong and after months of hiding behind hay bales, doors and sheds, we confessed. The news was stale when delivered. No one seemed the least bit surprised.

We had a beautiful wedding at the ranch and suddenly I was a "Sadie"... a married lady. Life was good.

The joy of motherhood was accompanied by unreasonable anxiety. I'd read and written about so many tragedies I was beset by thoughts of a world filled with dire possibilities. What if something happened to Thad or Jon? I'd never known tragedy, was too lucky, worried constantly. Every sentence began with "what if."

Gram scolded me. "Be glad for this time now and the happiness you enjoy...and the family that surrounds you. Life is a journey and when you travel with loved ones you can meet the turns and twists of the road, no matter where they take you."

Little did we know.

Chapter III

Of all the cars we ever owned, and for all intents I guess the VW bus could be considered a car, the one that touches me most is the Beemer.

Mother insisted we refer to her car as "The Beemer"—a term, Matt informed her, was used by those in the know for a BMW. We later learned the term "Beemer" referred to the motorcycle not the car. But "Bimmer," the correct title did not slide off the tongue easily and so the label, "Beemer" stuck. She and Matt shared a love for that car, her first and only new auto, presented to her by Adam Rice in the courtyard of Gothic Center for a job well done. It was Matt's expectation, although from the start she would allow no others to drive it he would someday become its recipient.

Branch thought it was foolish to bring the car to Colorado from Hawaii. "Not very practical," he advised. "Sell it. That little car would not make it up the road to the ranch."

"Beemer," Mother corrected. "You'd be surprised at what that baby can do. Besides, there's no way I'd leave it behind. It's an extension of myself and I plan to be buried in it."

"Ridiculous," he'd said. "It's too small to be of any use and if it breaks down, there's no one here who can fix one of those foreign implants."

But he knew it was a battle he couldn't win and when it arrived in Denver after a trip by boat and semi-trailer, he and Frank went to the city to pick it up. He admitted, but never to Mother, that the Beemer was fun to drive.

No one drives it anymore. It was put away in one of the outbuildings. For a while it had been Mom's custom to visit the Beemer often; times when she would start the car just to be sure it was in running order but more often than not, times when she would sit in the driver's seat for hours, silent and brooding, just sitting with her hands on the wheel staring at a road that didn't exist. We allowed her grieving time and eventually those times diminished. The car had been locked away for years; hence my curiosity when I noticed the door to the shed was partially open. The car had been kept clean and polished, its beautiful metallic opal body as glossy as the day Mom first introduced her Beemer to the family. It looked so small and if an inanimate object could be described as forlorn, this car certainly was.

I was gazing at a memory and had suddenly been overcome by the desire to talk to my mother. I shut the door and walked with purpose up to the knoll. It had been a long while since I visited the modest cemetery, capped with too many head stones. I sat on the river-rock bench Pete built with great care, and thought about the last time I'd ridden in the Beemer.

*   *   *

It had been a couple of days before Branch's surprise birthday party, Mom asked me to join her on a trip to Denver to pick up a present she'd ordered for him. We left Jon with his ever-doting great-grandmother and made our departure in the Beemer. It was a lovely summer day, sunny and warm—a perfect day to open the sun roof and enjoy the breeze and the view. During the long drive I revealed I was pregnant again and Mom was really excited.

"That's wonderful, Samantha. Maybe we'll have a little girl this time. We need a break from all this testosterone."

Lost in our own thoughts for a few moments, we broke the silence at the same time. "This is just so great. Branch will have two surprises today. I'm anxious for you to meet Willard and see what magic he's wrought," Mom exclaimed

Annie's Portion

as I remarked that I could hardly wait to see the finished product.

Willard Robbins was as happy to see us as we were to see him. His studio, in the Larimer section of the city, was replete with tools of his trade. There were drawings, art paraphernalia of every size and description and bronze and wood sculptures in various stages of creation.

"Come in, come in, ladies. Welcome to the bedlam of the artist at work. You must be Sam. Your mother has told me about you and I've seen the unique horse your husband rides. I'm hoping to have some excuse for sculpting him as well."

"Willard, you know why we're here. I can't wait for you to show Sam the finished product. Where are you hiding the masterpiece?"

"Patience, Annie. I think I can find it."

With that statement he opened a box lined with tissue paper, then in dramatic fashion, slowly unwrapped the piece we had come for. It was truly remarkable. No doubt as to the identity of the horses; Beau with his beautiful white mane, Jessie with her shining chestnut coat and little Thor with his prominent lightning bolt.

Mother had tears in her eyes, but then tears were always spilling from the corners of her eyes. Sometimes they seemed glued to the new wrinkles she'd developed.

"I shouldn't act so pleased. I imagine you'll raise the price now."

"I loved making it. I should pay you." Then he whispered in Mom's ear.

She took out her checkbook and began to fill in the blanks. I tried to sneak a peak over her shoulder but she used her arm to hide the figure. She never did tell me what it cost.

Chapter IV

Branch had been truly surprised on the day of his birthday party. Will was assigned the task of keeping him busy until mid-afternoon, by which time the guests and ranch hands had assembled in the meadow. There was much cheering when the two men rode in and the festivities began in earnest. With its many candles waiting to be lit, the cake was revealed and many glasses raised in toasts. For the first time I heard Thad publicly refer to Branch as "my father."

It was at that moment Mother called me aside. "Sam," she said. "I can't believe how stupid I am. I forgot Branch's present. I'm going back to the house to get it. Cover for me."

Mom's hasty departure on Beau had been observed by several guests and an ever sharp-eyed Branch. "Where's she off to in such a hurry?" he asked me.

"I think she's headed for the house...something she forgot."

"More shenanigans, I suppose. Think I'll just see what she's up to now."

"You're the host. You can't leave your own party."

"You just watch me." He mounted Jessie and was off at a gallop.

Seeing no way to stop him, I signaled Pete and enlisted his help. "Pete, please go after that mule-headed man. Mother has a surprise she's trying to keep from him."

"Another surprise," he muttered. "I'll do my best but you know there's no stoppin' Branch once he sets his mind."

Mounted on Baldy, Pete was soon just a few lengths behind him. He later explained what had happened.

"Couldn't been more'n an eighth of a mile away when we spotted that agitated stallion at the front steps of the

Annie's Portion

house. Branch gave Jessie the spurs and sprung off'n that saddle before she even had time to come to a halt. The door was open and he took them steps two at a time. By the time I got there that devil horse had jest disappeared. Didn't have time to think about that."

Pete heard a shot followed by a piercing scream, loud and gut-wrenching. He described it as, "somethin' not of this world." There were two more shots in rapid succession. "It's like a nightmare. I keep prayin' I'll wake up...but it was all too real. That yeller light comin' from the skylight lit the whole thing up. There was Branch, jest lyin' there... with that spotlight on 'im." Pete stifled a sob.

Pete's nightmare had only begun. He trembled as he described the horrible scene. "Miss Annie was on her knees, cradling Branch in her arms. She jest sat there, rockin' and rockin.' And there was Beau, on the floor with his head right close to her...heavin' and wheezin'. That horse, he had two bullets in 'im, one in the head and t'other in the neck. I had ta do somethin'. I knew Branch had a gun in the desk and when I turned to git it, there he was...Anson, or what was left of 'im."

Perry lay in a crushed and bloody heap, Annie's heart shaped diamond pendent in his outstretched hand. Beneath one of his mangled legs, the Henry rifle glinted in the last rays of sunlight.

Wild with grief, Pete picked up the rifle and loaded it with the last cartridge. He pointed it at Anson with clear intention. Remembering Beau and Annie, he turned away. Nearly blinded by tears, he knelt and rubbed Beau's neck. Mother didn't hear the shot that ended the life of her valiant stallion.

In a brief funeral service conducted by a Rabbi, who at Sarah's insistence had been brought in from Denver, my beloved stepfather Karol Longbranch was laid to rest on the knoll beside Emil and Claire. The interment was attended by family and friends who had assembled to help Branch celebrate his sixty-fifth birthday. My mother did not attend.

Beau was buried nearby, next to Star. Pete erected a short picket fence to mark their graves and carved a marker for each of the animals.

Retreating into her own private hell, my mother was inconsolable, spending her days with Jessie, allowing the mare to go where she would—stopping randomly to view through eyes clouded by tears, the places she had seen through Branch's. Mother talked to no one, didn't eat and had not been to bed since the tragic event. At night she sat in the dark in one of the leather armchairs, staring at the cold fireplace, dozing for brief periods. She paid no mind to appeals from Thad and me and we began to fear for her sanity. Not even Jonathan was able to break through her silence.

In the end it was my grandmother, bending but not breaking, ever-staunch Sarah, who in her own grief was able to reach my mother. Unbounded love for husband and son—for she'd always regarded Branch as a son—forged an immutable bond. It was my grandmother who got my mom to eat and bathe and at last go into the bedroom she'd been avoiding. It was then Mother spied the gift-wrapped package placed on the bed. Untying the ribbon she slowly removed the colorful wrapping and lifted the lid from the box. The sculptured piece had been swathed in white batting and tissue. As if seeing it for the first time, she beheld the magnificent work of a gifted artist and wept.

Locked in the unrelenting grip of a bitter cold winter, the inhabitants of the Bar L mourned.

Chapter V

Grief is not constant. It reveals itself in fits and starts, taking many forms; denial, withdrawal, anger, self-pity, resignation, acceptance, re-birth. Mother had little time to make the transitions. Her mourning was interrupted by necessity. Abruptly removed from self-imposed isolation, she was thrown before the madding crowd.

There had been an inquest and as a matter of course the news made headlines. It didn't take long for the media hounds to latch on to the story of a well-known rancher, killed by a wrangler who had served time. No one showed up to claim the killer's body, or what was left of it, nor did the media have more than a passing interest in his malevolent history. But the rehabilitated convict who had been brutally crushed by a horse became a cause celebre.

Branch was described as a rich but compassionate cowboy who gave a murderer a break and was rewarded for his kindness by a bullet in the chest, and with his very own antique rifle to boot. The public clamored for news and the media tried to be accommodating. Cable and network stations bombarded us with requests for interviews. The insatiable appetites of talk show hosts needed to be sated. All were rebuffed.

The media thirst for titillating information could not be quenched. The calls and letters they dispatched to the Bar L went unanswered so for a while the news-hounds tried a different tack, going after the BLM in Canyon. Now, there was a really big story; coddling hardened criminals, promoting expansion of the wild herds and limiting the use of government lands. Chuck Wells was prominently but unfavorably mentioned several times, depicted as the real villain of the saga.

Just when the media furor seemed to be waning there was Branch's last will and testament to be read and submitted for probate. There were no surprises. My mom was appointed executrix. She and Thad were bequeathed equal partnership in the ranch, stock and all else "appurtenant thereto." A trust fund had been established for Jonathan. Fabian and Pete received bequests as well. Pete's included a twenty-acre parcel of unimproved but arable land.

Back at the ranch we were encircled by trucks loaded with reporters and camera crews. We tried barring the road from Rifle but a few of the hounds managed to bypass our hastily constructed roadblock. An even more resourceful pack uncovered the route from Meeker. We prayed for an early snowstorm and at last our prayers were answered when one blew through, dropping a foot of wet snow on our besiegers.

The reprieve was short-lived. The mail began to pile up. There were condolences from friends, solicitations from charitable organizations and offers; offers to purchase the ranch, the horses, the cattle and the bank of spermatozoa.

Mother seemed oblivious to the happenings around her. I hesitated before asking her if she would allow me to write a brief article for the Gazette. "It would help," I explained, "to set the record straight about Chuck Wells and the mustangs."

"What about Chuck and the mustangs?" Mom's downcast eyes were suddenly raised. She glared at me and for the first time in months I saw the spark.

"Fan it," I thought. "Fan it."

"You haven't answered me. What about Chuck? Is he in trouble?"

"It will be easier to show you than tell you." I ran to get the latest newspaper and dropped it in her lap. The front page had a picture of Chuck standing at one of the corrals in the Canyon facility. The horses milling about behind him were some of the worst we'd ever seen. The bold headline read, "Who's The Real Culprit".

"The real culprit? What do they mean by that? He's a hero. He should be thanked for all he does on behalf of those horses...the men and boys he rescues too."

In a rage, she continued to read the article. "We've got to do something about this. He's being made a scapegoat. We've got to help him. Where in the world is Thad?

Thankfully I thought, "Annie's back."

Chapter VI

Sarah had been our mainstay during those first terrible weeks but the strain exacted a heavy toll. Mom's recovery soon lifted the pall that had hung over the homestead and life regained some semblance of normalcy.

"Samantha, we need to have a powwow."

When Mother called me Samantha, I knew we were about to do some serious talking. "What's on your mind, Mom?"

"There are many decisions to be made and I think we should convene a meeting of the clan."

"By 'clan' do you mean brothers and all?"

"No, I guess that's an overstatement. What I mean is the four of us, initially. Then we will counsel with our trusty thralls."

"By 'thralls,' are you referring to Pete and Fabian?"

"Yes."

"This sounds ominous."

"Not ominous...more like essential."

"When would you like to do this?"

"As soon as we can. Have dinner here tonight and we'll discuss it over dessert."

When I relayed Mom's request to Thad he nodded. "It's time."

Sarah and Mother had been thick as thieves. They took their meals at the ranch house and were awake long into the night. We could see the glow of the house lights from our deck, our curiosity aroused.

"What do you think those two find to talk about," I asked Thad, not really expecting a satisfactory answer.

"You ought to know better than me. What do women always talk about?"

Annie's Portion

We were about to find out. Mom had prepared a simple dinner but Ernesto provided us with a wonderful chocolate-cream pie, my favorite. When the dishes were cleared we moved to the great-room. The fire crackled and I remarked to myself, not for the first time, "What a wonderful house this is."

"Okay, Annie. Let's have it," Thad said with his usual aplomb.

"We're all partners in this so we need everyone's input. I've made a list of questions that need to be answered. The answers can only come from us as a family."

Smiles all around but Sarah was the one to voice our thoughts. "Was there ever a one as organized as your mother? Questions she has."

"Yes, lots of them so let's not waste time," Mother said as she handed out paper and pens. "First and all-encompassing...how are we going to run the ranch? Do we want to maintain the herds? Who will manage the operation if we do?"

"Whoa, Nellie." Thad lifted his hand. "That's more than one 'first'."

"Thad, since you asked, you may go first. You've got the most to gain or lose."

"Well...actually I've been giving it a good deal of thought. Yes, I want to keep the ranch as it is...at least for the time being. The herds are a good source of income."

"I agree with you, Thad. What about you, Sam? Any thoughts?"

We were back to "Sam." "I'm concerned about question number three. Who will manage that part? Thad can't do it. He's busy enough as it is. And besides, he's not the cowboy his father was." The moment those words were out of my mouth I regretted them. I glanced at Thad and stammered as I groped for something to say in an attempt to lessen the damage. "I mean 'cowboy' in a riding, roping, branding kind of way."

Mother dispatched a disapproving glare in my direction.

"Oh, you know what I mean."

"Yes dear, we all understand." As usual, Sarah consoled. Thad smiled.

"We'll pull Pete out of retirement, if he's willing. He hasn't started collecting his Social Security yet."

"Yeah. He'd do anything you ask, Annie but is he really up to the task?" Thad was concerned about Pete's bum leg.

Mom had an answer. "He's very capable of overseeing the wranglers and managing day-to-day operations. The men respect him and that's very important. We'll just exempt him from roundups or any of the more strenuous jobs. Fabian greatly admires Pete so I'm sure he'd be more than willing to fill the spot of second-in-command."

"Will you be able to handle the accounting chores?" Thad asked.

Before Mother could reply Sarah piped in, "More importantly will she be able to handle Will Harriman?"

"Mom will have no trouble with the books, and Gram, you can take care of Will."

"Then we're agreed. Pete will oversee, I'll account and Thad will do what he does best... make babies." Mom waited for the laughter to subside. "Thad, I have another idea."

There were mock groans. The fire snapped and sparks scattered up the flue. Thad added another log and poked around a bit. "What's next?"

"Do you suppose Jorge would like to return to the ranch to work in the lab with you?"

"Oh, Mom, what a great idea. I bet he'd be thrilled to work on the breeding program."

"Seems as though you've got this all figured out. You and Sarah been staying up nights to plot and plan?"

"That reminds me. What about the summer dudes?"

"Gram, you are a corker. Dudes?"

"Yes, dudes. Isn't this a working dude ranch?"

Hearing no arguments Sarah continued, "Annie wants to stick with it. I just think it's way too much work for her. Any opinions?"

"I think we should too. I can certainly help her with the guests, though I refuse to go on any trail rides."

"Have you forgotten our Jonathan, Sam? What about the baby when it arrives?"

"We can get another of Fabian's 'cousins' to help care for the children and Gram can supervise."

"Can we do it, Annie?" Thad asked. But he already knew the answer.

"We can and we will. Your father would be so proud of you, Thad."

"He would be *kvelling*," Sarah said.

"That means bursting with pride," I translated.

"All right then. It's a done deal. Now git! Tomorrow will be a busy day. I've got a ranch to run, ranger to save, wranglers to round up and the wonder-child of Jessie and Beau to train."

The April sun warmed the earth and hibernation was over. I gave birth to another boy, one with red hair and blue eyes. We named him Karol.

Chapter VII

Our world was forever changed with Branch's death. We'd come to terms with the fact that he was gone but he was never out of mind, not ours or the ranch hands. Reference was made to Branch whenever there was a dispute over practices and procedures; tactics and technique; strategy and system. It was, "Branch would do this or that." Invariably, Pete would settle the argument and in time the allusions diminished.

Mother never spoke of him but I knew there were many nights when she cried herself to sleep. She was determined; to succeed, to carry on the Longbranch family traditions, to keep the name alive—determined to make a new life for herself. She may not have been a thoroughbred but she was bred of tough stock and it showed.

In addition to the ranch chores, she'd taken up Chuck's cause, enlisting the help of several legislators and a few ranchers to clear his name and increase funding for his facility. She spent every morning working with Thor who'd become a beautiful stallion.

"He's prettier than his father," Mom commented. "But nowhere near as smart."

"At least he doesn't have his father's temperament." Thad was quick to respond.

"You're right on that one. He definitely has his mother's disposition. Maybe we won't have to geld him."

"Mother," I exclaimed. "You wouldn't do that to him… would you?"

"Samela, they're just teasing you."

"Gram, have I told you lately how much I love you?" I gave Sarah a big hug.

By late spring most of the wranglers had arrived and the place was active as an ant hill. Mother's days were crammed-

Annie's Portion

full. Fabian's numerous relatives needed instruction in kitchen duties and housekeeping procedures. There were supplies to be ordered, reservations to be handled, accounts to be reconciled. Outwardly genial, Mom performed these tasks with her usual fortitude while she silently mourned.

. Ranch operations were going well. Pete proved capable and efficient, exceeding expectations. Frank's return following a brief hiatus was greeted with cheers from Pete and Fabian.

"Well, fellas," Pete remarked. "Looks like we're just stuck with each other."

"It's a damn sight better'n havin' a wife."

Fabian agreed with Frank. "Si, but does not come with some of the benefits."

The three caballeros made a formidable team and the ranch profited.

Jorge had been a providential addition. With his up-to-date knowledge he expanded research far beyond what Thad had been able to do alone. The two spent hours in the lab doing whatever it was they did and were seen only when they went to select the animals to use in the next round of propagating.

I hadn't gotten involved in the activities yet but knew I had better take advantage of the situation for as long as it lasted. Often I brought Jon and Karol to the homestead to visit with Sarah. It became evident she was losing some of her spunk. She no longer made the trip to Florida and spent the winter dozing in front of the fire.

"You know, Mom. Gram is showing signs of diminished cognition."

"Sam, if you're trying to tell me she's losing her gray cells, I'm well aware of it. She forgets what year it is and often talks about past events as though they are happening now. We're going to have to keep an eye on her. When we get busy, there will have to be someone with her all the time."

"Oh Mom, I want to cry. I'm not ready to lose her."

"There you go with your 'what ifs.' We have her with us now and we will for a long while, even if we must travel back in time to have a conversation."

"I know I'm just a worrywart. If Gram was able she would surely remind us this was her 'portion.'"

Summer arrived early and beautiful that year. The herds were fat and happy and so were the guests. Every cabin was filled, and when the last guest left we heaved a collective sigh of relief.

The seasons changed, horses foaled, children grew taller. Looking back, those years just seem to run together. But 1998 was a memorable one. That was the year Jorge and Thad were honored at the Stock Show for developing a means of extending the life expectancy of collected sperm. They had also perfected the insemination process.

Ninety-nine was another banner year, when Sarah celebrated her ninety-fifth birthday. Our annual Christmas-Chanukah party was expanded to include my brothers and a cake large enough to hold all the candles. Thad remarked he hoped we didn't set off the smoke detectors.

The family had greatly increased in the five years since Branch's passing. There were five little ones for Sarah and Mother to *kvell* over. The party had to be moved to the bunkhouse.

January and February were especially mild and my mother took advantage of the spare time and weather to take Thor on a jaunt. She complained that he misbehaved like a child. I knew she was disappointed in the colt.

Thad tried to console her. "Annie, you know he's still an adolescent...and a stallion as well. Look at the time and effort it took to get Beau to cooperate. And then he was only good with you. Remember Thor has a lot of wild mustang in his genes."

"You're right, Thad. I guess I'm just getting too old and impatient."

"Mom, please don't get discouraged. You'll do it yet," I encouraged.

"You know I don't give up easily. Have no fear."

Sarah seemed to wake from a daze. "Is Beau giving you trouble again?"

"Yes, Mom. But we'll get him straightened out."

"Good, good."

I wondered if she even heard my mom. Her hearing was almost gone and she no longer wore her aid. I looked at Mother. She shook her head.

March came in like a lamb, the proverbial lion conspicuously absent.

"This weather is so glorious. I'm going to enjoy my ride today. To ensure that will be the result I'll take Jessie and leave her offspring in the corral."

"Now Mom," I countered. "You're too hard on him. But you're right. Go with Jessie and have a wonderful ride...but do be careful."

"Samantha, do you realize how much like your grandmother you've become?"

Mom returned from her ride looking a bit disheveled. "What happened to you?"

"Oh, I was negligent. We were having a delightful canter. Jessie has the most wonderful gait. I was admiring the scenery...the shoots are coming up early because of the unusually warm weather."

"And...You're becoming as spacey as Grandma."

"Oh yes. I forgot to duck and ran smack into a low-hanging branch. Knocked me out of the saddle."

"Were you hurt? Are you okay? You have a bruise on your forehead."

"I'm fine, as you can plainly see. Just a little headache."

Mother's headache worsened and I went for Thad. On returning we found her, unconscious on the floor in the bathroom. Thad called for a medi-vac plane but by the time we got to the Junction hospital, my mother was in a deep coma.

A CT-scan revealed the presence of an epidural hematoma. "Epidural bleeding is effusive because it is usually from arteries. We'll try to relieve the pressure within the brain cavity. She's being prepared for surgery now but the prognosis is not good. It's unfortunate that we were unable to treat her more quickly. A considerable amount of time has elapsed since the injury occurred." The doctor didn't hold out much hope.

Mother never regained consciousness. She left us before the surgery could be completed. Arrangements were made and Annie Longbranch made her final trip back to the Bar L, where Pete and Fabian had prepared a place for her on the knoll next to Branch.

Chapter VIII

I shivered as a dark cloud passed overhead; shrouding the gravestones, concealing the names so painstakingly etched years before.

"Well Mom, I think we'll have an early winter. Last week's dusting of snow turned our golden aspens to brown overnight. Even now there's a trace of it in shaded places and the slightest breeze sends a cloud of leaves swirling to the ground. You'd love it.

"Thad has gone to Junction with Karol. He's a wonderful father you know. As usual, little Annie is with her brother Jon – taking her riding lesson. She's so like you, a natural around horses. I never did inherit your abilities with those critters, even though I like them well enough and enjoy an occasional ride. With my men out of the way and Annie taken care of I've time to visit. I seem to have less and less free time these days – what with chores, home schooling and my writing. I can't believe Jon will be making his bar-mitzvah this year. Then he'll be off to prep school.

"Did I tell you my first book, 'The Golden Stallion', won the Children's Book Award? And since the second book has also been well received, my publisher has grudgingly agreed to consider using my illustrations for the new one. They have this thing about using their own artists. Maybe there's more money in it. I still write some articles for the Junction paper but they're getting fewer and further between. Last month I went into town to add some books to your library and kind of check on things. It's very popular in town, especially with the many retirees who've moved into Junction. You wouldn't believe how that burg has changed; boutique shops, outdoor cafes and even a couple of Starbucks. Where did all the cowpokes and rednecks go?

"I wish Grandma hadn't insisted on being buried in consecrated ground at Golden Hills. It would be so nice to have you both here to talk to. I miss you both so. Even though the children don't realize it, they miss you too. They'll always miss out on having you and Gram here to share stories, wisdom, advice and fun times. Me too. We are her progeny, Mom, her legacy – you and I, Jonathan and Karol too – and now there's Annie, the little girl we waited for."

The sky cleared and a fresh breeze carried the acrid scent of damp soil and decaying leaves. I inhaled deeply and was compelled to look toward the white-capped Rockies, to another time, to Golden Hills Cemetery when those same matchless mountains, starkly etched beneath a vaulted ceiling of cerulean blue, formed a painted backdrop suggestive of a stage setting.

How vivid that picture was. Just as today, a billowing cloud passed briefly between sun and earth, casting shapeless shadows across the stage. As though from a fan hidden somewhere in the wings, an impromptu zephyr rustled through the cottonwoods brushing my skirt, creating dark undulating folds in the soft linen fabric. I can see Danny and Matt, tall and steadfast—standing with shoulders barely touching, eyes downcast and red-rimmed. In their dark suits they formed a curtain above a gaping hole, obscuring my view of the extras. At my side, Josh seemed transfixed, disconnected, staring blankly—unaware of the other players, as if viewing the surreal scene from a great distance, waiting for the play to begin. His tall frame bent slightly, the lines of his tanned face pulled taut, he was lost in thought trying to remember the notes he'd scratched out the night before. My light tap on his shoulder roused him from his trance and for a flickering moment he lifted his eyes as though searching for someone, Mother. The thought evaporated quickly. He looked past me, and seeing Thad standing awkwardly, hat in hand, just the hint of a smile softened his countenance. I was sure he was remembering the title Grandma had given Thad, "the cowboy." It was a title she'd initially laid on Branch but passed on to his son because Thad was never seen without his Stetson, a title they both pretended to dislike immensely.

Wanting to ensure Josh had gotten the cue I'd pressed his arm, feeling the firmness of it, unwilling to remove my hand as though by that touch I could absorb some of his strength. He straightened his shoulders preparing to speak, but his first words were indistinct and muted. He cleared his throat and the mourners turned toward him expectantly.

"I remember his words as though he'd spoken them yesterday. He was so eloquent. You'd have been proud of him, Mom. 'I've been asked by my wonderful family,' he said, sweeping his arm in a half-circle, 'to give the eulogy, a speech of praise, for a woman who would have wanted none. I guess as the eldest the sad duty naturally falls to me. I'm not very good at speeches but I'm glad for the opportunity to pay homage to Sarah, my grandmother who embraced us unconditionally and whom we dearly love. So now I need only do the impossible – condense a lifetime that spanned ninety-five years into a few lines of tribute. Sarah was a wonderful woman who lived life to its fullest, a woman whose remarkable life epitomizes the American experience.'"

A sudden gust of wind rustled the trees and I was reminded of the breeze that had lifted some strands of Josh's thinning gray hair. He'd reached up to brush them aside, momentarily distracted by my futile attempts to keep my skirt from ballooning. Hoping to delay the inevitable he'd said more than he intended. Josh had wanted to impart some of the history Grandma shared with us but realizing he'd been over-long concluded, "A pioneer in every sense of the word, tough and uncomplaining, Sarah never bemoaned her lot but took whatever the fates handed her with grit and good humor. We have all benefited from knowing her."

The simple truth of his words caused stifled sobs but obviously near the breaking point he seemed not to notice. Josh looked directly at me. I can see and hear him now as he added, "All of us but most especially we, her four grandchildren, are here today as testimony of the love, devotion and friendship she bestowed so freely." Turning back to the assembly he'd concluded, "Sarah was loved by many and will be sorely missed. Good-bye dear, dear Sarah."

"We buried Grandma in Orthodox tradition, just as she instructed, Mom – wrapped in a white linen shroud and placed in a simple pine box."

There had been no viewing of the body, no flowers, no organ music and no pre-burial wake. The funeral service concluded with the final, dismal Jewish graveside ritual. The Rabbi wearing his *tallit* and *yarmulka*, recited the *Kaddish*, and stood back from the breach. It was the signal for the pine box to be eased into its final resting place.

Dreading what was to come, Josh had shuddered as it was lowered, reaching bottom with a thud. With slow, deliberate movements he bent down and clenched a handful of the newly dug earth. Murmuring the Hebrew prayer he tossed the soil into the grave. Danny and Matt emulated his actions. I'd hesitated a moment before adding my handful of damp earth to the scattering on the pine box.

"You know Mom, how much Josh hated public displays of emotion. When the ritual was finished he turned quickly and strode to the car – your car, the Beemer you never let him drive – the Beemer he'd resurrected for the service."

With tears running down his cheeks, he'd remained in the Beemer for some time, reflecting on what he thought was the inadequacy of the eulogy. He was the last to leave Golden Hills.

"I can see the ranch-house from here, Mom. It seems strange not to see smoke rising from the chimney but it's used mostly for special events these days. It's often filled with uncles, aunts, cousins and friends. We hold most of our holiday celebrations there. It's such a wonderful house – so many happy memories. Maybe one of the kids, more than likely Annie, will make it her home one day. Occasionally my boys will 'camp out' there, leaving Annie and me to have a girl's night, just like we used to

"Well, the chill of the stone bench has crept through my layers of clothing and I can feel its icy fingers creeping up my spine so I guess I'll get on home. I love you, Mom."

LaVergne, TN USA
07 March 2010

175123LV00001B/1/P